Other books by Susan Isaacs

COMPROMISING POSITIONS

CLOSE RELATIONS

SUSAN ISAACS

Almost PARADISE

1817

HARPER & ROW, PUBLISHERS, New York
Cambridge, Philadelphia, San Francisco, London
Mexico City, São Paulo, Sydney

FIRST EDITION

Designer: C. Linda Dingler

Library of Congress Cataloging in Publication Data

Isaacs, Susan, date
  Almost paradise.

  I. Title.
PS3559.S15A79   1984   813'.54   83-48357
ISBN 0-06-015236-2

84 85 86 87 88 10 9 8 7 6 5 4 3 2 1

To my children
Andrew and Betsy Abramowitz
with all my love

PROLOGUE

Jane Cobleigh was on a British Airways Concorde, flying faster than sound to try and reclaim her husband. At the end of the flight she managed to look out of her window. Gray London was opalescent under the haze of a summer heat wave.

She got to her hotel about the time Nicholas returned to his townhouse from the studio. "Good evening." A desk clerk in formal dress greeted her. He must be so hot; his neck swelled red over his tight wing collar.

Jane swallowed her instinctive Ohio hi. "Good evening," she said.

"So good to have you with us, Mrs. Cobleigh." He clearly relished pronouncing the celebrated name. His voice was fruity and so consummately English that she half expected him to pour forth with a sonnet: *When forty winters shall besiege thy brow,/And dig deep trenches in thy beauty's field* . . .

Instead of reciting Shakespeare, the clerk said, "Will you be paying by check or credit card?"

"Credit card," she said.

"Excellent," he replied.

What if she'd said check instead?

His entire face was flushed, as if trying to keep up with his cherry of a nose. The lobby of the hotel was too much in the grand style to be degraded by anything as crassly mechanical as air conditioning. The clerk, appropriately dressed for all the marble and gilt, wore a starched shirt, heavy waistcoat, and wool cutaway. Soon he might swoon from the heat. She probably would. But no, he merely moved slowly, presenting her key to the bellman as if it were part of some ceremony as old as the Magna Carta.

At last in her cool room, she must have overtipped the bellman, because he bowed as if she had come to England to establish her rightful claim to the throne. She couldn't remember what five pounds was worth; she was too tired to think.

After her bath, she admitted it wasn't only fatigue. It was nerves. The estranged wife of the world's most famous actor should not be popping up in London. Hi! My affair is over. It never really meant anything. How about yours? Ready to ditch her? What does a forty-year-old man need a twenty-four-year-old for anyway—someone people describe as having shining, cascading red hair and a figure like a very expensive, extremely delicate porcelain doll?

Jane, he'd begin. He'd be so sorry for her.

But all your phone calls. You sounded as if—I was positive—

Jane, I'm sorry. I thought it would make it easier for the girls if you and I had a more cordial relationship. I was just trying to be—well, friendly. I'm truly sorry you misinterpreted the calls. You see, I love Pamela. I told you that two years ago—

Nerves. Not nerves. Terror. Humiliation. Here she was, ready to make a complete transatlantic ass of herself. What could she say? Oh, hi. Just hopped a plane to London even though I've never flown before in my whole life and thought I'd drop in and see how you were doing.

What if Pamela was with him? Everyone who saw them together said she was always holding on to him. Clutching his hand. Resting her head against his chest. She must be a midget, Jane thought. No. Petite, adorable. I'll look like King Kong next to her.

What would she say? She had nothing rehearsed. Nick, we have to talk. Nick, I still love you. I love you so much, you have no idea—

He had loved her too. After their marriage, his parents had cut off the flow of money Nicholas had always assumed was unstoppable; the elder Cobleighs were stunned and hurt that he was giving up law school to be an actor. Suddenly, and for the first time in his life, Nicholas was no longer floating in the warm sea of upper-class security.

Jane had caught him one morning, mesmerized by the crazed skittering of the cockroaches across the drainboard of the sink in the kitchen of their cold-water flat on West Forty-sixth Street. His disgust, his humiliation even, tore at her. Everything had always been so nice for Nicholas until she had seduced him into acting, conned him into poverty.

She'd come up to him and said, Nick, listen. I'm sorry. I'm sorry it's crummy and we're so broke and—

She'd stopped short. Where he came from, self-pity was probably viewed as a lower-class indulgence, and if she kept on he'd realize what a mistake he'd made. Whoops! he'd say and fly out the door, run east as fast as he could, back to Park Avenue. But he'd put his arm around her and said, Take it easy. We'll survive. Just look at us. We could be a play in summer stock—a young couple, madly in love, poor as church mice. Have you ever heard a romance like that which doesn't have a happy ending? Come on, smile. Come on, before I get a cockroach bite standing here in bare feet and we end up with a lousy melodrama—me dying from bubonic plague and you huddling in your shawl. She'd smiled. Good, he'd said. Now say you love me. I love you, Nick.

I love you, Nick. That's what she'd say. Then it would all be up to him.

No matter what happens between them, a man cannot be married to a woman for nineteen years and not care about her. A man cannot be married to a woman for all that time and not remember they were once in love.

So it was not surprising that about the time Jane finally fell asleep in her London hotel, Nicholas Cobleigh, less than a mile away, dreamed about her. He wakened just before dawn in a too-elegant canopied bed in a too-chichi rented townhouse with Jane on his mind. The old Jane. He couldn't recall most of the dream, only a moment that was actually a sliver of memory: Jane having dinner with his family for the first time.

It was right after commencement exercises at Brown, and there was Jane—dark-skinned, with that heavy black braid hanging to her waist—in the Falstaff Room of the Sheraton-Biltmore in Providence. In the midst of eight fair-skinned, bright-haired, well-tailored Cobleighs, she looked like an immigrant. Her green shirtwaist dress—a little too tight across the bust—glared like a go light among the beige silks and tan tweeds. Jane was gazing down at the artichoke his father had ordered for her. She looked miserable, so intimidated by the strangeness of it she could not lift her fork.

Nicholas turned over his pillow to the cool side. It wasn't part of the dream, but he recalled how Jane had kept her head down and then finally let her eyes rove around the Cobleighs, searching for clues on how to approach the thing on her plate. She pulled at a leaf. The artichoke slid up in its oily vinaigrette and would have flown into her lap had she not managed to grab it with her left hand.

Nicholas remembered how he'd waited then for her to make one of her funny, self-effacing remarks, but she kept silent, and he'd realized how cowed she was by what she saw as eight sophisticated New Yorkers. She was sitting between his father and his brother Tom, so he couldn't reach for her hand and squeeze it, let her know just how fine she was doing.

Too bad her eyes had been lowered. They were beautiful. He'd wanted his family to admire them. Deep blue and velvet, like pansies. Much nicer than his eyes, despite all the fuss.

That day, his makeup man had said, "Oh, dear, Mr. Cobleigh, slightly bloodshot." Nicholas sighed, but he understood. *William the Conqueror* was a thirty-five-million-dollar film riding on certain assets, among them Nicholas Cobleigh's world-renowned blue-green eyes.

His eyes would be bloodshot again. He hadn't been sleeping well. Jane kept intruding. If he didn't dream of her, he awakened in the middle of the night and there she was anyway, stretching out in his mind—big, long-limbed—taking over.

Turning the pillow to its cool side did not banish her. Nor could deep, deliberate breathing. Not even moving toward the center of the bed helped. He tried it anyway, pressing up against Pamela's back, reaching his arm around her and cupping her tiny breast.

Nicholas eased away, out of the bed, tiptoed downstairs to the library, and lifted the telephone receiver.

He had no idea why he kept phoning Jane or what he would say this time. It embarrassed him, calling her three or four nights a week, making up excuses about the girls. Could you send me a copy of Vicky's final grades? Did you speak to the camp doctor about Liz's ear infection? Jane would know it was almost dawn in London.

One night he'd decided to say something, to see how she would react. He'd thought he'd say, I think it's about time we spoke to the lawyers. I can't keep Pamela waiting forever. He'd see. If Jane sounded indifferent, he might just go through with it. But then when he'd heard her familiar hello—still a trace of that drawn-out, funny-sounding Cincinnati *o*—his throat had tightened and all he could say was, The accountant said you *still* didn't send him your W-2. We only have an extension until the middle of this month. She'd said, Okay, I'll look for it. Hey, by the way, how is *William* going? He'd told her for nearly an hour.

He dialed the apartment in New York and the house in Connecticut, waking the housekeepers in both places. Mrs. Cobleigh wasn't expected in. Mrs. Cobleigh had gone on vacation. A message, sir? No, he'd told both housekeepers, no message. I'll speak to her some other time.

He hung up the phone and went upstairs, back to bed. Pamela curled up against him, tendrils of her hair invading his mouth and nose. Nicholas brushed them away, then closed his eyes.

He wondered where Jane had gone. He thought about the dream, about the bright green dress that pulled too tight. Then he began to imagine what it would be like to see her again.

Their meeting didn't happen the way either of them planned it. What happened was, sometime around noon the next day, an unspeakably hot July day in 1980, a day when three extras fainted inside their armor, when the makeup department ran out of Alabaster #6 body makeup because the actors were sweating it off every ten minutes, a day when—it being England—the commissary used its last ice cube at ten thirty, Jane Heissenhuber Cobleigh, dressed in cool cream linen, stepped out of a gray Daimler limousine across from Blackheath Studios calling *Nick! Nick!* to the occupant of another limousine leaving the studio, ran into oncoming traffic, and was hit by a blue MG driven by a drummer for an obscure rock group who—for the first time in three weeks—was clean, straight, and sober.

What happened might have occurred by cosmic design or by chance. Neither Nicholas nor Jane was the sort to have spent much time debating which it was. Things happened. So much had happened in their own lives they had little faith that the future would be predictable and neat.

But they would never have expected anything like this. Who would?

BOOK ONE

JANE

We've just received a dispatch from Reuters saying Jane Cobleigh was hit by a car while crossing a street just outside London. Her husband, famed actor Nicholas Cobleigh, has refused to talk with reporters and is . . .
— Excerpt from NBC News Update

Jane Cobleigh's mother would have loved the chance to talk to reporters. She would have opened her blouse an extra two buttons' worth, slid a wet tongue over her lips, and ambled out and murmured "Hi, boys." Of course, that would have been during her show business days, before she became a house-wife, mother, churchgoer, canner of vegetables. Before she became Mrs. Richard Heissenhuber.

In her show business days she was Sally Tompkins, chorus girl. She was an actress, too. In 1926, in the comedy skit *Belle of Broadway*, she had six lines that ended with "Well, Mr. Prescott, you can take *that* and *that*," with each *that* swinging her chest from one side to the other. Then she would stomp off, stage left, and there would always be whistles and applause. The director, Mr. Norton, observed she had great comic talent, although he'd be the first to recognize her range was probably broader. But, he whispered later, if you got a pair of jugs like this, no one's gonna let you play Lady Macbeth. And a few nights after that he told her that Sally Tompkins wasn't a good name for her type. It was too girl-next-door and she was definitely an exotic. Since she was half Spanish—right?—why didn't she use something like Lola Torrez or—let's see, one of those one-name names, Bonita or Caramba. But she told him, what could she do? Sally Tompkins was her real name.

It wasn't. Her real name was Sarah Taubman, and she was born a bastard in 1906 on the Lower East Side of New York.

Her mother, Jane's grandmother, Rivka Taubman, was a fat, dreamy girl of fourteen, so nearsighted she could neither baste nor finish the women's shirtwaists her parents worked on; she was only able to sew buttons. She would hold the fabric close to her eyes and stitch on button after button. What looked like freckles on her nose were tiny scabs where the needle pricked.

One April night when the wet winter chill finally left the air and it was too dark to sew, Rivka left the two-room apartment and clomped down five flights of stairs. She sat on the stoop, breathing clean spring air that was free of the indoor smell of boiled onions, smiling a gentle smile. Her pale round face was haloed by curly black hair. And who should come along and sit next to her but a boy from around the corner, a snappy dresser, Yussel—Joseph—Weinberg. He was sixteen years old and tall like a regular American, a baseball player or policeman. He put his face up to hers, and she could see he was darkly handsome.

"Hello, there, good-looking," he said. His English was perfect. So they talked a little and she saw him a couple of days after that and then a few times more. One evening he said "Come with me" and she did. They went into the hall of the building next door. He led her behind the stairs. She said "I can't see," and he told her to shush. Then he kissed her, and before she could say no he was touching her all over. She knew it wasn't such a good idea, but he got angry when she pushed his hand away. So she let him. When she got back upstairs her mother yelled because she'd forgotten to bring the piecework to Mr. Marcus. "Stupid!" her mother screamed. "Blind and stupid!" At thirty-four, her mother had no teeth.

So she would meet Yussel in the dank shadows behind the stairs where sometimes people threw their garbage, and she prayed the rats wouldn't climb up her skirt. They didn't; Yussel did. He lifted her skirt and pulled down her drawers and stuck it into her every single night. Of course, she became pregnant.

Her mother knew it before she did. Her father beat her and almost choked her and her mother dragged her to a lady on Rivington Street with four long hairs growing out of her chin who made her drink something that was warm and smelled like urine. Still, the baby would not go away. Then they beat her with a hem marker until she told them Yussel's name. But by that time she hadn't shown up behind the stairs for two nights and Yussel—no stupnagel—must have known the jig was up. He ran away from home and got a job taking tickets at the Belzer movie house on Twenty-eighth Street, but then he had to skip town because within three months he had impregnated Pearl Belzer, the boss's daughter.

Two weeks before her fifteenth birthday, Rivka Taubman gave birth on her mother's kitchen table. The baby wasn't born dead the way its grandparents had prayed. It was a beautiful, sturdy girl, and Rivka named her Sarah.

But her parents wouldn't let Rivka keep the baby. Her mother had heard about the Rose Stern Hoffman Home where they took Jewish babies and gave them away for adoption, so when the little girl was a week old, Rivka's father wrapped Sarah in a fabric remnant, smacked Rivka across the jaw to stop her screaming, and went all the way to the Upper West Side. A sign nailed to the door explained the Rose Stern Hoffman Home was closed until February fifteenth for refurbishment, but he couldn't read English so he brought the baby back with him.

4

Unlike her mother, Sarah grew up with keen vision and a quick mind. Although the child couldn't put it into words, by age six she recognized that there were two types of people who dwell in the slums: those with hope and those, like her family, without. She visited other girls' apartments and saw parents cuddling children, pinching cheeks, stuffing little mouths with too many sweets, thrusting books into pudgy little hands. These parents knew their children's lives would be better than their own. Her family had no such ambition. Sarah was their shame. All hope had died at her conception.

She shared a bed with her mother, but Rivka never cuddled her, although now and then she smiled and every day plaited Sarah's shiny black hair into a long braid and tied it with a piece of bias tape. But that was the only tenderness Sarah was ever shown.

By age nine, Sarah realized she wasn't doomed. She was a leader of the neighborhood children, who admired her ability to whistle and play potsy. Her teachers were fond of her. Impressed by her intelligence, they encouraged her reading and corrected her pronunciation. "The word is 'song,' Sarah, not 'sonk.'" Mrs. Pierce took her to the library and told her she might be a credit to her people some day. Miss McNulty kept her after school and allowed her to grade the other students' papers and erase the blackboard. She told Sarah about high school and even mentioned college. Before they left for the afternoon, Miss McNulty would go to wash her hands. Sarah would pitter-pat across the empty classroom, open the door to the closet where Miss McNulty hung her fur-collared coat, and steal a few pennies or a nickel from her teacher's handbag. At first she spent the money on licorice or sour pickles, but soon she discovered vaudeville.

Sarah saved Miss McNulty's pennies for admission to the Goldfarb-Buckingham. For ten cents she sat through a one-reel slapstick comedy in which she had little interest; if someone had said, "Sarah, believe it or not, you will have a daughter, and she will marry a man who will be a world-famous movie star," she would have said "Big deal." Her world was the stage. After the movie, the Goldfarb-Buckingham presented the newest—or the shakiest—acts in vaudeville; Sarah leaned forward in her wooden chair. Ludwig and Schuller did their dumb-Dutch routine. "Hey, shtupid, vot's dot boil on your neck?" "Dot's not a boil. Dot's mein head!" Sarah howled out loud, enormous *hoo-hoo-hoos*, something she never did at home. And her feet copied the movements of Brian O'Brien, the world's thinnest dancer, as he soft-shoed across the stage. She knew she could dance. She could be up there in a red flounce dress and black shoes with bows and slide and shuffle her way to fame.

But her favorites were the singers, Doris LaFlor and Mary Heckman and Leona Welles. Leona Welles was her favorite; Sarah could sing "My Heart Is a Rose" as well as Leona. "Like the pink bud kissed with dew," she would warble. Her soprano was even thinner and less distinguished than Leona's,

5

but Sarah didn't know it. She throbbed with unsung melodies and believed that when she opened her mouth, magic occurred. When she was ten, the ticket seller heard her sing a few measures of "My Son, My Son" and said "Very nice, girlie." Sarah took this as an omen; she would be a star.

She confided in no one. Her teacher, Miss Driscoll, suggested she consider teaching as a career. Sarah said, "Oh, there is nothing I would love more," and Miss Driscoll allowed Sarah to help the slower children with their reading. At the end of the day Sarah would smile and say, "Thank you so much for letting me assist you, Miss Driscoll," and her teacher would reply, "You are certainly welcome," and then correct Sarah's dentalized *t*'s.

The coaching helped. By 1920, when she was fourteen, Sarah left the Lower East Side and its accents behind. The year had begun poorly. Years of close work had strained Rivka's already limited sight, and Sarah was forced to leave school and take over her mother's role as family button-sewer. The greasy tenement air was charged; at this age, her own mother had gotten pregnant, and Sarah's family peered over their sewing and watched her with fatalism and grim hostility. She had grown quite lovely, with lustrous hair and sparkling black eyes and—her only inheritance from Yussel—smooth dark skin, soft brown tinged with the gold of the Orient.

Although quite short, she was no longer a girl. Her breasts grew so fast and so large that her middy blouse strained at the seams. Her hips flared from a dainty waist, and her stick legs softened at the calves and thighs. Her grandfather averted his eyes as this lush child walked about the apartment. Her grandmother must have seen this because she became harsher with Sarah, criticizing her button-sewing, mimicking her soft singing by shrieking *la-la-la*, and saying "Oh, pardon me, Miss Lillian Russell," when Sarah cried. One night in bed Rivka began to weep but shook off the child's attempt to console her. "Leave me be," she said to Sarah.

So two days later, in an August heat wave so intense that fruit on the pushcarts rotted by midday, Sarah trudged four miles uptown to Abramowitz's Rooming House and, before she fainted in his arms, told Nat Fields she would marry him.

She had met Nat four months before as she waited outside the stage door of the Heritage Theater, praying for a glimpse of her latest idol, the chanteuse Marie Minette. Instead, Nat Fields, a young blackface singer, sauntered out—without makeup. "Hiya, toots," he said, and winked.

"Excuse me," Sarah said and turned her back. "You must have the wrong party."

Nat must have preferred the front view because he scampered around, got down on his knee, and crooned, "'An' tho' the sweet magnolia die, I gwine to see my mammy by an' by.'"

6

"You're—" Words deserted Sarah.

"Nat Fields, in person." He leaped off his knee to his full five feet six inches. "And who do I have the honor of addressing?"

"Me?"

"No one but you, lovely lady."

"Oh," said Sarah Taubman, "I'm Sally Tompkins."

She managed to see Nat a few times each week. Eventually he introduced her to Paulie, the stage manager, as "my girl" and she was allowed into the theater for free. She watched all the new acts rehearse—all of them, even the trained snakes. Sometimes Nat would sit beside her and grab a handful of the glorious fourteen-year-old body he thought was eighteen. But he didn't get it all. "Please, Nat," Sally would say, her dark eyes flooded with sadness at having to deny him herself. Naturally, Nat fell in love.

They were married by a clerk in City Hall. Sally said her birth certificate had been lost, so she borrowed one from an acrobatic dancer; a marriage license was issued to Nathan Finkelstein (Nat's real name) and Hannah May Essmuller. On their wedding night, Sally proved to Nat that her virginity was no act. He was blissfully satisfied.

Sally was his lucky charm. Two months after their wedding, Nat auditioned for Messrs. Bixby and Putzel of the Bixby Lyric Circuit. Two weeks after that they went to Stroudsburg, Pennsylvania. For the first time in her life, Sally left Manhattan Island.

The marriage lasted three years. In that time, Sally visited fifty-three cities in nineteen states, had one abortion, and made her theatrical debut. That happened in Wilmington, in classic show business fashion. In the ten-girl chorus surrounding romantic song stylist Mina Hawthorne, two girls were felled by influenza (one would die) and another ran off with a cad who claimed he was a du Pont. The theater manager, dramatically, was tearing his hair and wailing when Sally piped up. "I know the routines, Mr. Prosnitz." Nat and Louis Prosnitz stared at her in disbelief, but she dashed up on stage, tucked her dress into her garters to show off her dark, curvaceous legs, and danced and sang, a cappella, the chorus of "(Don't Tease Me) I'm Just a Co-ed."

"You can't do it!" Nat shouted. Sally sat on the bed in their room holding a kelly green satin costume. She was letting out darts under the bust. She mumbled a response that Nat couldn't hear because her mouth was full of pins. "What? What? Talk, for chrissake."

She jumped up and spat the pins near his feet. "I said, I'm sick and tired of sitting on my ass and watching you do five shows a day and me doing a big fat zero. This is my big chance."

"You crazy? Since when do you have talent? Now listen, Sally, we're leaving for Baltimore tomorrow night."

Nat went to Baltimore alone. Sally swore she'd meet him in Trenton two weeks later, but she never showed.

They ran into each other ten years later in Chicago, and by then their marriage was a hazy memory for them both. Nat was out of blackface and into tuxedos, singing romantic duets with his wife, Edna Jones. They called themselves Giovanni and Flora, and they were strictly small time.

So was Sally. The year before, in 1932, she had arrived in St. Louis, part of the troupe called Louisa Whyte and her Golden Girls, and found the theater in which they were to have appeared had collapsed the night before. Louisa and the three other Girls had enough money to move on to Wichita; Sally did not. She had fourteen dollars and a suitcase full of lavender dresses and two blond wigs.

Sally was alone and broke in a strange city in the middle of the Great Depression. She lay in her lumpy bed in the Red Bud Rooming House, swaddled in an itchy wool blanket, but she shivered and her toes were so cold they hurt. Frigid, damp air blew off the Mississippi and crept beneath the covers. Her last meal had been the day before: an orange and a glass of water. For the first time, Sally had regrets.

At twenty-six she was an experienced enough trouper to realize she would never return to Ludlow Street in a chauffeur-driven Packard. She had dreamed it so often: the big black car gliding almost noiselessly through the Lower East Side, the children following it screeching "Sally Tompkins! Sally Tompkins!" and her grandparents sticking their heads out the window—no, then they couldn't see her—walking home from buying herring, peering in the car and seeing this star, and realizing who it was. And she'd take handfuls of hundred-dollar bills and toss them in their faces and then, gracefully, with everybody watching, walk up the five flights of stairs and take her mother away and set her up real nice in a beautiful apartment somewhere.

But Sally was a realist. In a profession where the highest-paid chorus girls were Amazonian, she was four feet eleven inches tall. Her voice lacked luster. She danced well, kicking high and strutting boldly, but at least five thousand women in America danced better. Her assets were three: a quick mind and two beautiful breasts.

Sally left her bed. No one in St. Louis needed a chorus girl. But Mrs. Barrows, the owner of the Red Bud, said, "Honey-pie, you got two choices. No, three. One, find some chucklehead and marry 'im. Two, get on your back—but not here at the Red Bud; I don't have none of that. And three. What's three again? Oh, try Mr. Reeves at the Gayety. Sure, it's burlesque, but I don't see no one busting down your door. Don't take that personal, sweetie. Lots of other girls in the same boat these days. It's bad times."

So like hundreds of marginal entertainers, Sally made the painful decline from vaudeville to burlesque. She was no longer family entertainment, but at least she made a living. And at last she got her own act.

"Ladies and gents, the Gayety Theater"—or the Republic or the Royale or the Mayfair—"proudly presents, all the way from sunny Spain, Señorita Rosita Carita!"

The band—at some theaters just a piano—would play pulsating flamenco music and Sally would march to center stage, head held proud, dressed in high-heeled shoes, a flouncy flamenco skirt, and a red and black sequined brassiere. *Da-da-DA, da-da-DA*, the music went, and Sally would shake her shoulders to its passionate rhythm. *DA-DA-DA*—and she shimmied so fervently the combs fell from her hair and her black tresses cascaded over her shoulders. The tempo grew faster. Sally shook and writhed, a slave to the music, wild, abandoned. And just as her ecstasy reached its peak, her breasts shook out of the sequined modesty of her brassiere and half the audience went crazy.

That was the trouble. Sally was so short that from the loge and balcony she appeared a little odd, almost deformed. "Tits on legs," as one theater manager tried to explain. She would never appeal to a full house, so she never became a featured act. But she kept at it, following Miss Lydia and her Dainties or Irene LaPointe in stock burlesque houses around the country.

She missed the camaraderie of vaudeville days, when after the last show the performers and their families would crowd into someone's room and drink beer and gossip and wander off for side talks, private confidences. People there cared about Captain Tompkins, her father, lost at sea; about her mother, the beautiful doomed Dolores, a Spanish ballerina. Sally had created an autobiography so poignant that the men she went with often asked for more details before taking her to bed.

But the men around the burlesque circuit weren't interested in her history. They didn't care how Sally Inez Alicia Tompkins had, in spite of her marvelously exotic background, grown up to be the all-American girl, how she had been offered a full scholarship to Vassar College, how her brilliant mother taught her to pirouette. These men just wanted to squeeze her boobs and bang her.

In 1936, when she was thirty, she thought she had finally found happiness. A fan dancer, one of the elite of burlesque, a tall broad-shouldered redhead named Katy Swift, invited Sally up to her room in their Port Huron, Michigan, boardinghouse to make fudge. While the hot plate was heating up she kissed Sally on the lips. Sally was shocked but didn't want to make a fuss and allowed Katy to put her tongue in her mouth. After a minute or two she realized she wanted more. They became lovers. But even though Katy would hold her tight every night and stroke her thighs and whisper she'd never let

9

Sally go, their love did not last forever. Eight months later, in Bristol, Tennessee, Sally opened the door to their hotel room and found Katy in bed with Rimba the Jungle Girl, a shrill, hairy woman she and Katy had often laughed about.

By 1939, Sally felt tired and old. She was thirty-three, and although her dark skin was smooth and her body beautiful and supple from six shows' worth of shimmying a day, she knew she couldn't last much longer in the business. Her arms and shoulders were sore most of the time, and her head ached from shaking it to loosen the combs in her hair.

The headaches were knives slicing through her brain, and they were coming two or three times a week. So when she got to Cincinnati she asked the drummer for the name of a doctor, and it was there, sitting in Dr. Neumann's waiting room, fanning herself with an old issue of *Life*, that she looked up and stared right into the eyes of her future husband, Richard Heissenhuber.

2

MALE VOICE: We are trying to get some comment from Mr. Richard Heissenhuber as to the condition of his daughter, Cincinnati's own Jane Cobleigh. Is she in serious or even critical condition, as has been reported? So far, Mr. Heissenhuber, from his home in Edgemont, has not been available for comment. Meanwhile, we have reporter Sandra Saperstein in the studio. Sandra, you went to Woodward High School with the girl who was then Jane Heissenhuber. Tell us a little about her.
FEMALE VOICE: Thank you, Ken. Jane Heissenhuber. Woodward, Class of '57. Perhaps even then she knew show business would beckon. . . .
—WCKY All-News Radio, Cincinnati

Richard thought the woman sitting across from him was the most beautiful woman he'd ever seen. Beautiful wasn't even the right word, because since college he had been going with Patsy Dickens and everyone—including him—said Patsy was just beautiful. And she was. Patsy had huge blue eyes and soft blond hair and a tinkly laugh everyone said was infectious or contagious. Patsy was everything a man could want: good-natured, sharp as a tack, and beautiful.

But this woman was something more—gorgeous. Her jet black hair and dark eyes seemed to suck up all the light in the waiting room, so that everything except her own exotic loveliness seemed dim. Her skin, he thought, was the rich color of honey, and he began to imagine kissing her on her neck, the sweetness of honey filling his senses. He could see her skin was smooth, not grainy like most dark-skinned people. And he imagined more about honey, about its sticky wetness, and that made him remember a book he'd read that a fraternity brother at UC had passed around, where it described what a woman was like down below, and one of the expressions in the book for it was "honey pot."

Richard lowered his head to hide the flush that was creeping across his face. It was wrong for him to think of the woman like this. She was obviously a serious person. Her hair was pulled back tight, off her face, and knotted into a bun like a schoolteacher. He raised his eyes for an instant; he couldn't help it, he was so drawn to her. And she was looking right at him, and then she smiled. He was nervous but he smiled back and prayed Dr. Neumann's nurse wouldn't call him into the office until—he felt so embarrassed. Like a fifteen-year-old kid who couldn't control himself. He didn't know what to do next, so he peered at his watch. It was nearly eleven.

The pale skin of his wrist reminded him of her honey color. She was showing a lot of skin. Her dress was cut low in the front, and you could see the beginning of what he knew must be two beautiful—he shifted in his chair—bosoms and the shadowy valley between them. But she wasn't fast, he was sure, because her hairdo was serious and her smile was friendly, not a come-on smile, like from a cheap girl.

"Mr. Heissenhuber." The nurse called him into the office. Richard rose and, more because he didn't want this woman to notice what was happening with him, he smiled at her again. But he almost didn't make it into the examining room. From his height he'd been able to see even farther down her dress, and though he knew she must be wearing a bra, he couldn't see any. All he could see were two luscious, magnificent, firm . . . In the last six months, once they'd set a wedding date, he had gone below the neck with Patsy. But Patsy's ended where hers were just beginning. He sat on the examining table, waiting for Dr. Neumann to find the acid to burn the warts off his hand, and wondered if she was wearing one of those little bras that just covered the tips, like in the French postcards. When he glanced down to his lap, he saw his hands were cupped, as though he were already feeling them. He was so embarrassed. But he had never wanted to touch anything so much.

Sally smiled. The kid had a hard-on the size of a baseball bat. Although he wasn't such a kid. Even though it was Saturday, early in June, he was wearing a suit and tie and looked like a real solid citizen, not one of the creeps who hung around the burlesque house waiting to grab a handful and have a party. This kid—this guy—must be in his late twenties. He was really good-looking, with light brown hair so neat you could see the comb marks and a manly, square-jawed face and a terrific mouth, kind of wide and full, but not slobber-lips. Sally figured if she played it right, he'd buy her a full-course dinner first.

He couldn't believe what he was doing. He went back to the waiting room, smiled at her, and said then and there, "I know you must think I'm very forward, but would you have lunch with me?" As he was saying it, he had a flash of dread that she was a foreigner and that she'd laugh at him or blurt out something loud in some garlicky language, but instead she said, in a breathy but genteel voice, "I'm sure I'd like that very much."

Then the nurse called "Miss Tompkins," and she stood. "You'll wait for me?" she asked, and all Richard could manage was a nod because he was so taken with her. She was tiny, a little bit of a thing. But a phrase he had read somewhere returned: "She's all woman." After she'd brushed past him to go into the doctor's office, he all but fell back into his seat. He knew it wasn't right, but he kept thinking about touching those big . . . he bet they were warm . . . he wished he could think of something else. But Richard Heissenhuber needed something to hold on to. He was a lonely man with no friends and few pleasures. In fact, he had not had a really good time since he was a child.

Certainly his parents' house, where he still lived, did not rock with mirth. Anna and Carl Heissenhuber were two humorless people who did not so much fall in love as discover a mutuality of interests. They both hated what they were. Coming from large Lutheran families, from homes where German was spoken, where May Day and Whitsuntide were celebrated with hearty revelry and heavy platters of wurst and pitchers of creamy beer, they shunned the easy *Gemütlichkeit* of their boisterous, embarrassing relatives. They detested accordion music, hated wine. Their only passion was for blandness. They wanted to be completely American.

So they married in a Presbyterian ceremony and moved from the German "Over the Rhine" section of Cincinnati to Walnut Hills, a neighborhood of graceful trees, Victorian houses, and inhabitants named Smith and Johnson and Turner. Their house was small, cleaner than most hospitals of the day, and utterly fitting for a family of their station in life; it was as if there were an invisible sign on the front gate: Residence of Bank Teller. It was painted a gray so dull it was almost invisible. The Heissenhubers made certain not to drink or smoke or appear to enjoy anything to excess. (Naturally, they never knew Margaret Smith told Bessie Johnson that Anna was duller than dishwater or that Tom Turner named them the Booberdoobers.)

When America joined to fight the Great War, Carl was the first man in Walnut Hills to try to enlist and, although he was rejected because of severe myopia, the Heissenhubers felt the pleasure of knowing they had earned their neighbors' respect. Only once during the entire war did they feel uncomfortable, and that was brought on by a thoughtless "Heinie" uttered by old, crazy Mr. Phillips.

Richard was the only child of these two relentless Americans and a model one; he learned early and well that any act that called attention to himself was ill-considered: raucous laughter, bravado on the ball field, flashy friends were not for him. Life should be like the bank Carl worked in: muted and a little chilly.

He was happier at his grandparents'. Carl's thickly accented parents had mercifully died before Richard was born, but Anna's parents, the Reinhardts, welcomed the boy with "Achs" and "Liebe Kinds" and powerful hugs. He visited them each Saturday, helping his grandfather whitewash the front stoop of the red brick house, sitting on a chair beside the enamel kitchen table and taking the eyes out of potatoes for his grandmother, listening while she recounted her week's battles with Herr Bauer, the conniving butcher, and with Frau Meyer, her next-door neighbor whose slothful ways were the cause of the infestation of cutworms that were probably attacking the cabbage patch at that very second.

But Christmas was the happiest time. From early morning, the kitchen was filled with odors so tempting Richard giggled with excitement. He would sit beside his grandmother and roll the dough for *Pfeffernuss* into balls between his floured palms, sneaking little bites of the dough when his grandmother ostentatiously looked away. Everything frowned on by his austere parents was encouraged here: huge meals and loud music and booming conversations in the forbidden language.

Later that night, stuffed with goose, heavy with *Honigkuchen*, he and his cousins would follow his grandfather up the stairs, singing "O Tannenbaum" and "Stille Nacht" in high, clear voices. The sounds they made thrilled Richard; he believed he could hear an angel singing in the background. At the top of the stairs, his grandfather would slowly open the door to the *Weihnachtstube*, the Christmas room, which always seemed dark and empty at first, but then his grandfather switched on the lights and Richard beheld what seemed to him a miracle: a room full of dazzlingly wrapped presents, gifts in gold and silver and red, as rich as any brought by the Magi.

But after his eighth year, Carl and Anna decided to celebrate Christmas at home. Holidays at the Reinhardts' were too much. They glanced at each other over Richard's head as they said this. Too much. Too much noise, food. Didn't Richard always have diarrhea the next day?

They had a real American Christmas at home. They had a tree with a simple star on top, Anna served turkey instead of greasy goose, and everyone's stomach was fine the morning after.

Richard recognized he was not one of the guys. He knew his contemporaries found him too serious. But for a time he had hopes that he would be accepted and make his parents proud. In his first year at the University of Cincinnati, he had been tapped for the best fraternity on campus, a fraternity of rich young men. But after his pledge class's initiation, few bothered with him. They discovered his father was a teller, not the banker they had assumed. He was treated with hurtful courtesy. Still, he hung on the fringes of fraternity life, realizing he needed some brightness and fun.

At first, he believed Patsy Dickens was the answer. She had been pinned to the president of his fraternity and everyone acknowledged she was one of the most popular girls on the UC campus. Definitely one of the prettiest. And she had fallen head over heels for Richard. After just two meetings—a conversation at a beer bash about whether home ec was a good major and a chance meeting in the library—she actually gave back the fraternity pin. Richard was stunned and embarrassed, but his fraternity brother had been most gracious, shaking his hand and saying, "Guess the best man won."

So Patsy was his. He gave her his pin. Her adoration amazed him. "Richard," she said, "you are absolutely the handsomest boy I have ever in my whole life seen. I mean it. Like a collegiate Cary Grant. Really and truly. Except you're not a boy. That's what really attracted me to you, you know. You're a man. So serious, so mature. And respectful. I can't tell you how important that is to me. Oh, Richard, I'm the luckiest girl in Ohio."

At first, his parents told him he had made a wise choice. Patsy's father, after all, was an executive with Procter and Gamble and belonged to one of the finest country clubs in the city. Her mother, from whom Patsy had inherited her fluffy appeal, was a Daughter of the American Revolution.

When they became engaged, the Dickenses invited the Heissenhubers to dinner to celebrate. They had never been in such a big house before. A maid in a black uniform and white apron served dinner. But something was out of joint: the Dickenses were so gushing, so absolutely, completely, and totally thrilled with Richard, that Carl and Anna began to have their doubts. Ken Dickens could buy and sell Carl Heissenhuber. Something wasn't right. Couldn't Richard feel it?

"Are you sure she has a good reputation?" they asked him. "Are you positive her father is *head* of Household Abrasives?" Of course there was nothing really wrong with Patsy, they said. She was the bubbly sort, the type who might make a fine wife for a corporate executive. But Richard's future world, banking, demanded, perhaps, a less outgoing personality.

Carl Heissenhuber, although a key employee at Queen City Trust, was still a teller. Richard, however, an honor graduate of UC, had that piece of paper that would allow him to go all the way to the top. But it would be a treacherous climb, filled with peril, and one thoughtless remark from a flighty wife could drag him down before he was halfway there. He did not want his son's potential compromised. Nor did Anna, who noticed that Patsy did not hold her liquor as well as she might and, though she never acted drunk, tended to chew noisily after two Rob Roys.

"But she's a wonderful girl," Richard insisted. "From a fine family."

"If you're satisfied," Anna said, "then so are we."

But now Richard had his doubts, and to his astonishment he found himself sitting beside Sally Tompkins and confiding them to her. "It's not that I don't love Patsy," he explained. "It's just that she's so willing to go along with anything I want—" Without even wanting to, his voice had stressed "anything," so he quickly explained, "Please don't think I mean *anything*." He could feel his face glowing red and was glad the restaurant was dimly lit. "I would never ask her to do *that*."

"Of course not," said Sally. She lifted her water goblet, pursed her lips, and took a tiny sip of water. "You have too much respect for yourself."

Richard nodded. Sally was so amazingly sensitive. They had been together for no more than twenty minutes, and already she comprehended him as nobody else ever had. She was an enigma: a one-hundred-percent woman who had a complete grasp of a man's mind. "You must think I'm terrible, talking about personal things like this."

"You know I don't, Richard." And he did know. He knew Sally somehow, some way, looked within him and saw his best nature. She rested her hand on his arm. "You're a fine person. I can tell."

He shrugged and gazed at the breast-shaped mound of potato salad on his plate. The heat from her hand was so powerful it radiated through his jacket and shirt. And then he felt her leg, not actually pressing against his but dangerously close. He knew the proprietor of Kautz's Restaurant thought he was doing him a favor, seating them beside each other in one of those tight little booths, but it was almost too much. He swore he could feel the outline of her thigh through her dress.

Sally shifted so she could face him, and the tip of her breast grazed his arm. "Maybe it's because I'm an actress that I'm—well, sensitive to other people." She gave him a small, understanding smile, and he became so confused and dizzy with desire that he nearly keeled over. "But a man of your type wouldn't be worrying about Patsy unless there was something to worry about. There's something wrong and I think you know it, but you're too much the gentleman to admit it to yourself." She shifted back and took a small bite from her club sandwich. A crumb of bacon dropped from it and landed halfway down her cleavage. He didn't dare say anything.

Sally couldn't believe this guy. Here he was, a big, tall, good-looking he-man with class up the ass like the Duke of Windsor, and he was talking like a kindergarten baby. That Patsy sounded like a prize jerk. And his mother and father must be a couple of nut-cracking Krauts. Who could believe that such a guy, a college grad, a big cheese in a bank who even wore a suit on Saturday, would be acting this way with her? Not just hot for her in the pants department but lapping up every single word like she was Miss Fountain of Wisdom, 1939. Something stunk in Denmark. He wasn't one hundred percent. It was like he was from another world, almost the same but not quite, and was wandering around, a little lost. She really felt for him.

Going to the doctor and having lunch with Richard, she missed three shows. When she got back to the Royale, the manager grabbed her shoulder. She looked down at his hand, at the lines of green dirt under his long nails. She said, "Listen, Mr. Boyd, you keep your paws off me," and he replied, "You listen, Madame Tits. You skip any more shows and you can take your crummy act across the river and start selling your stuff in the hoo-ah houses."

Anna had told Richard that women—nice women—under thirty did not

16

wear black, but here was Sally, walking up Race Street in a tight black dress. Not so tight as to be cheap, but as she came closer he could see the slight swell of her stomach and the shape of her hips. It wasn't low-cut like her dress earlier in the day, but in a way this was worse because each breast seemed to be wrapped separately, but too tightly, fighting the severe black fabric of the dress. He could almost imagine the material, stretched beyond its tolerance, ripping apart, and her two huge breasts bursting free into the warm spring air.

He had called Patsy and told her he couldn't go to the Five Oaks Country Club's Merrie Month of May dance. He was very sorry but he had a terrible sore throat.

All he really had wanted was to spend a little more time sitting beside Sally Tompkins, but now, seeing her, her gleaming hair caught up in two Spanish-looking combs, he wanted to dance. He wanted to go someplace where they played a lot of fox trots and pull Sally up to him, press her against him real hard.

Sally knew culture when she saw it. So she tossed the old sea captain overboard and spoke tolerantly of her father, Reginald Tompkins, the Oxford-educated Shakespearean actor who never quite made it. "He wound up doing a lot of character roles," she explained.

"How come?" Richard asked. They sat on a blanket in a park on one of Cincinnati's highest hills. Beneath them, the city gleamed in pure Sunday sunshine.

"Well, he was so in love with my mother. I mean, he was always dashing from London to Madrid and back again. And even though my mother was a ballerina her parents were typical Spanish parents, *very* strict. So he spent years wooing her instead of playing in the provinces. You know, acting Hamlet in some two-bit English town somewhere. That's how you get into the Old Vic Theater. But Father just took odd roles here and there so he could be free to travel to Spain."

"How did they finally marry?"

"They eloped to New York." Sally eased off her pumps and ran the soles of her feet over the cool, damp grass. "I guess I don't have a—well, normal background like you're used to here in Ohio."

"Not at all," Richard said.

"I know you're just being polite. But really, we're not your average family. We act on feelings. I mean, that's what makes us actors to begin with." She let a soft sigh escape.

"Sally," Richard said, leaning toward her. "What's wrong?"

"Nothing. Nothing, really."

"Please. Tell me. I've told you so much about myself. Don't you think you can trust me?"

17

"Oh, Richard," she whispered, the tears nearly drowning her voice. "I'm so weary of the stage. I know—" She groped in her handbag until she found a handkerchief. "I know I'm a good actress, but I'll never be a great one. Please, it's true. And I'm twenty-six years old and I've been on the road since I was eighteen, when my parents died. I'm so very, very tired."

"Sally." He sighed, circling his arms around her. "Oh, Sally." She was so warm, so firm, and her perfume seemed to come from some rich jungle flower, sweet and hot as she was. "Sally, I love you."

She left her sequined bras and flamenco skirts at the Royale. She moved out of Montgomery's Rooming House—a notorious burlesque hangout—and checked into Knauer's Hostelry for Young Ladies. She had sixty-seven dollars, a small wardrobe of dresses unfit for decent Cincinnati, and a fourteen-carat gold bracelet an elderly admirer in Schenectady had given her after a long weekend. She severed all ties to her livelihood. She was taking a gamble. But she was playing poker with a raw amateur and she knew it.

He broke his engagement to Patsy. Sally had pleaded with him to wait, to see if their love could stand the test of time, but he had merely smiled and shaken his head. He was ready. He felt he had been afflicted with a horrible numbing disease all his life, and now he was cured. For the first time he was truly alive. He looked at the roses climbing the trellis on the side of his parents' house and for the first time gazed into their dark red hearts, stroked the silky petals with a fingertip. At the bank he inhaled the heady, important odor of ink rising from the trust indentures on his desk. He was alive. He stopped buying the *Cincinnati Enquirer* each morning and began surveying the ankles and arms, the breasts and backsides that bobbled about as the bus bumped toward downtown. He looked at women and women looked back at him, and for the first time he comprehended that he was truly handsome. And desirable. Women smiled at him or brushed against him as they got off the bus. Nice women. Pretty. But none of them like Sally.

To tell the truth, she wouldn't have minded having him. Who wouldn't, with his big blue eyes and those long, straight eyelashes and a pair of shoulders like a bull? And he was dying for her, just dying, and she could feel whenever he held her that he had a set of family jewels that would make other guys green with jealousy. She liked to keep him that way, all fired up and ready. She'd stand behind him in a store or someplace and rub her boobies against his back until a soft groan would break from him.

Sometimes she could see tears in his eyes, he wanted her so much. And it would have been easy. Instead of pushing his hand away and saying "Please, Richard," she could let him get a fast feel, diddle the nipple she knew was his goal. After all this time, it wouldn't feel so bad, that rough pressure. But the more he pleaded with her to say yes, the easier it was to say no. Because that's what Richard really wanted. He wanted a woman who wasn't easy, a woman who would be a self-possessed, respectable wife. And Sally was no Patsy.

"No, Richard."

"Please. Just on top. I swear, Sally—"

"I can't. Don't you understand? If I lower my standards, I might as well do everything."

"Sally, just for one minute."

"No!"

Two nights later, after knowing her for three weeks, Richard Heissenhuber asked Sally Tompkins to marry him.

It was agonizing but courteous. "More tea, Sally?" Anna Heissenhuber asked, leaning forward toward her flowered teapot, which would impress anyone who knew anything about china because it was Wedgwood, but this— this creature wouldn't know about that. She wouldn't know about anything fine or decent or even polite. She'd plopped three cubes of sugar into her tea and stirred like she was mixing cement and then left the spoon right there in the cup while she drank. Anna glanced at Carl, nearly frantic, but all he could do was stare as Sally narrowly missed gouging out her eye with the handle of the spoon.

"No more tea, thank you, Mother Heissenhuber."

And Richard. Richard sat there, all big eyes and little smiles, as if this trollop were a Vanderbilt. With her dark, oily skin and red lipstick that smeared on her teeth and that dress—a milkmaid's costume, ridiculous except it was so tight she was bursting out of it. And Richard looking at her like she was Little Mary Sunshine and not what she was, a strumpet, a Jezebel who would drag him into her own filth.

Anna lifted the plate of shortbread and offered it to her husband. His lips were as pale as his skin. "Carl?" He shook his head. He looked as bad as she felt. Anna moved the plate to the side, toward the tramp, but kept her eyes on Carl. She mumbled to him in the German she had not used since she escaped her parents' house. Her husband hung his head in agreement.

It hadn't been the best time in her life, so Sally tried hard not to think about it, but she had spent the first fourteen years of her life on Ludlow Street. And if you lived on Ludlow Street you spoke Yiddish, and if you knew Yiddish you could figure out German and you knew what this Nazi bitch was saying: that she was a bum. But naturally she couldn't show she understood. Well, fuck her and the horse she rode in on. Sally leaned forward to put down her cup, giving the old man an eyeful of the best titties he'd ever seen—his eyes nearly bugged out of his head—and turned to her future mother-in-law, smiling. "May I see the house, Mother Heissenhuber? I'd just love to see the home Richard grew up in."

"Why him?" Carl demanded. Outside the light was turning pearly and soft, a prelude to dusk, but inside it was dark, harsh, like hell. "Why Richard? We're not wealthy. She must have seen that."

"But his potential," Anna said. "He could rise in the bank. Be a vice-president." She sighed. "But tramps don't care about potential."

"Maybe he's right," Carl said. "Maybe she's just a little flamboyant. An actress."

"Actress, my eye. A slut is what she is. You saw that as well as I did. 'Where are your parents?' Dead. 'Any other family?' Yes, in England. 'Oh, where in England?' And then you saw her, you saw what she did. Looked up at the ceiling, like an answer was written there, but it wasn't and she obviously couldn't think of anything, so she looks back and blinks and says London. Smiles that smile and says, Oh, Mother Heissenhuber, there are Tompkinses all over London. Of course, now with the war coming they won't be able to come over for the wedding. I'll miss them so. Especially Aunt Mary." Anna gazed at her husband. "But why Richard? Why our son? It makes no sense."

They sat on the glider on the front porch of Knauer's Hostelry for Young Ladies. Sally took Richard's hand and covered it with small kisses. Then she ran her tongue over it and licked between his fingers. "I'm going to buy my trousseau tomorrow," she said. "Nightgowns. Very, very sheer."

"Do you take this man to be your lawful wedded husband, to love, honor, and cherish until death do you part?" Sally said she did and raised her head, crowned with a white hat with a three-foot-long ostrich plume—she knew it was stunning—to gaze into Richard's shining eyes. She only had eyes for Richard, although she realized the City Hall clerk thought she was a real peach, all dolled up in that expensive chapeau and a white linenette sheath. It was really the perfect wedding dress for her because it was pure white but cut tight enough to display exactly what Richard was going to get. Without looking cheap. And Richard had said the contrast between the white dress and her dark skin was the stuff that poetry was made of. He was always saying romantic things like that.

And doing romantic things, like handing her a pink carnation one night and wrapped around it was a fifty-dollar bill, and when her mouth dropped open he said, "I know you don't have parents to buy you a wedding dress, so please let me. I want to be your family, Sally."

20

He'd been grateful she'd been willing to have a civil ceremony. When his mother, between nearly clenched teeth and pulled-tight lips, had asked if she would like to meet their minister, Dr. Babcock, Sally had said, "I'm sorry, Mother Heissenhuber. I just can't get married in a Presbyterian ceremony. I was raised as an Episcopalian and I just wouldn't be comfortable." Sally must have seen his mother's eyes ice over even more because she added, "I do so hope I'm not offending you."

His parents refused to see Sally's depth and goodness and instead focused on her clothes or her makeup or the way she crossed her legs. They could not accept the fact that she was an *artiste*. He had never seen them like that, so narrow and unfair. And each time he defended her, their rage billowed, until the entire house seemed to emit an acrid smell.

But he had fought them, for the first time in his life, and he was relieved not to have a church wedding because then he would have had to ask his father to be his best man.

He had no friend to fill the role. He had considered his boss at the bank, Mr. Forsyth, or a fraternity brother from college, Bill Beidemaier, whom he sometimes saw on the bus in the morning, and then thought of their response: "Yes, glad to, Richard" or "Sure. Be honored." But he knew they would then realize his friendless status and would stand for him with resignation and contempt. He had never been the outgoing type, and it dismayed him when Sally demanded, "When am I going to get a chance to meet the guys and gals in your social circle, sweetheart?" She seemed to think he was the toast of Cincinnati; he didn't know how to tell her that after his first week at the bank, no one had asked him to go out for lunch.

But as he bent down to kiss his bride, he knew his luck had changed. Life would be better.

From the moment Sally Heissenhuber emerged from the bathroom of the honeymoon suite of Hoosier House in French Lick, Indiana, her complexion aglow from shyness or rouge, it was a magnificent wedding night. Her hair, blue-black in the dim lamplight, spilled over her shoulders. Through the translucence of her white silk nightgown, Richard could see the exuberant rose-tipped breasts and the dark flower of hair between her thighs.

He was out of his blue and white striped pajamas as fast as his trembling hands would allow. Sally uttered a barely audible "Oh, boy." After all those years of floppy-fleshed comedians and unwashed trumpet players and pallid patrons of burlesque, she was embraced by a tall, strong young man who cried out not "Fuck me, baby" but "I love you" and "You're so beautiful" as he stroked her over and over, as if memorizing her shape.

"Oh, Richard."

"Oh, Sally."

For her, it was better than she thought it would be. Although he touched her with too much awe, like he was feeling up the Statue of Liberty, he appreciated her. He let out deep, throaty cries of pleasure. His body was warm and smelled clean. Her only fear, that she couldn't pull off the virgin act, was allayed when he tried to enter and she winced. "Ooh," she moaned, "ooooh," and he cried "I'm sorry, Sally" but didn't stop because he was too far gone. If she hadn't had to keep alert, pretending to writhe with pain, she might have smiled with pleasure at this big, handsome guy grinding deeper inside her. Here she was, with her own husband on top of her who was groaning "Sally, Sally" and he was a real he-man; you could actually see muscles in his shoulders. And a college grad. A junior bank officer.

For him, it was as blissful as he'd dreamed. Finally, finally, he could touch any part of her and he did. She was like a goddess, perfectly formed, and when he caressed her, she was perfection. And from the intuitive way she moved with him he sensed that if he were careful, gentle, understanding, she would learn to like it. Love it, he prayed, love it, as he finally succeeded in deflowering her. For the first time in his life, he was on top of the world.

Wedded bliss lasted four days, happiness three weeks, and contentment another month and a half. Their illusions dissolved slowly enough that they felt no loss. By the sixth day of their honeymoon Sally began to see that Richard's endearing shyness was less the mask of a sensitive soul than a cover-up for a personality some might call drippy.

While still on their honeymoon, Richard watched the other new husbands staring at Sally's body. For the first few days of marriage, he accepted the stares as Sally's due and as an endorsement of his taste. It was almost as if these men were tipping their hats to him and saying, Richard, you lucky so-and-so. You must be quite a man to land this lady. But a few of the stares became leers, and a couple of sneers.

"Maybe you should cover up a little. A shawl or something." He suggested that before dinner on their seventh and last honeymoon night. She was wearing a breath-stealing purple dress with a big pin shaped like a daisy at the bottom of a deep-cut vee neckline.

"Oh, Richard, you're so cute."

"Seriously, Sally, the other women aren't wearing such low-cut dresses, and it's a very conservative crowd." She reached for his hand and guided it toward her damp cleavage and they were a half hour late to dinner.

They returned on Saturday to Cincinnati, to a three-room apartment on the second floor of a sprawling white frame house twenty minutes from downtown. On Sunday, just as they were leaving to visit Carl and Anna, Richard suggested Sally take off her nail polish. It was maroon, a color suitable for automobiles but startling for fingertips, and he wanted their reunion with his parents to be as placid as possible. Sally's index finger inched forward and traced the outline of his penis, the maroon point making larger and larger arcs. They were fifty minutes late, and Anna's ham had brown striations where it had dried out.

After two months of marriage, Sally knew Richard was a social flop. Her fondest daydream of married life had been about entertaining; she had imagined herself holding a silver tray dotted with cheese-stuffed olives and offering it around the room to a host of bright young couples. "An olive, Biff?" "Why thanks, Sally. Don't mind if I do." But Richard couldn't think of any young couples to ask over, and the only invitation they received was from his clearly unassimilated cousins for a nearly silent dinner of *Zwiebelfleisch* and *Salzkartoffeln* and a piano recital by the cousins' nine-year-old son, an obese child with cropped blond hair whose buttocks hung over the edge of the piano stool.

Richard was disappointed too. He slowly realized Sally's love of heavy makeup, sleazy dresses, and potent perfume had nothing to do with her being an actress; it had a great deal to do with her having bad taste and a powerful desire to excite men. His favorite daydream—taking Sally on his arm and parading to their seats at the Zoo Opera and receiving admiring nods from upper-crust Cincinnati in recognition of his fine taste in women and his obvious devotion to the arts—dissolved. He hadn't the strength to admit to himself that he'd been conned. But his two semesters of English literature at college were sufficient to make him realize that Sally's knowledge of serious theater was limited to knowing the titles of three Shakespearean plays, and he began to feel there was either more or less to Sally than met the eye; he wasn't sure which.

They never spoke of their disillusionment. Indeed, for a long time they considered themselves to be in love, for they made love often. Each night after dinner—usually a Chopped Meat Surprise culled from a women's magazine—Sally would wash and dry the dishes while Richard read the sports page to garner conversational tidbits for work the next day. Then, wordlessly, she would walk to the bedroom, massaging lotion into her hands, and he would follow. With neither smiles nor words they would undress, climb into bed, and squeeze and fondle each other for a half hour; for another quarter hour, they'd have vigorous intercourse, with Sally in whatever position Richard arranged her. He secretly referred to a marriage manual he kept in a shoebox high on a closet shelf. At last they offered each other a courteous "Good night" and fell asleep.

Sally tired easily. She was pregnant. Conception had occurred on the fifth day of their honeymoon—she had not thought it would happen so fast—and each day she grew imperceptibly heavier and wearier.

She had, after all, slept with over fifty men and, besides the one aborted pregnancy she had had while married to Nat, she had never again conceived—and she hadn't always been careful. She had feared she had contracted one of those diseases that decompose a woman's insides and could never have a baby. But she hoped she could. She was thirty-three—although Richard thought she was his age, twenty-six—and, as she admitted to herself, she wasn't getting any younger. A big belly was the best marriage insurance a girl could own. And it might be fun to have a cute little thing around all day. Something to do. She was bored.

No one wanted to be her friend. The young married women in the neighborhood were a clannish lot of native Cincinnatians, and they coldly rejected her offer to drop by for coffee and a sweet roll any old time. She tried to win them over by admiring their cocker spaniels or their infants, seeking their wisdom about morning sickness. But they were laughing at her and Sally knew it. She knew they were whispering when she lounged on a blanket on the front lawn sunning herself, wearing her pink shorts and aqua halter. And they snickered when she went to the grocery to buy candy for the trick-or-treaters wearing Halloween colors: a black skirt and a cute orange fuzzy sweater. They were eating their scrawny hearts out with jealousy.

Sally knew she could be accepted into the society of coffee sippers if she became one of them—scrubbed off her makeup and wore low-heeled creep shoes. But she wouldn't make that compromise. Rather, she kept to herself, knowing that after the baby was born she and Richard would probably be moving to a fancier neighborhood and she would meet a livelier, classier type of woman.

But meanwhile it was so dull. After years of six ass-busting shows a day, she had little to do but wash a few dishes, shove around a dustcloth and a carpet sweeper, and play with herself. She began reading for the first time in almost twenty years and enjoyed it, but books were only good for twenty minutes, a half hour a day, tops. She listened to the radio, but all the announcers sounded like her father-in-law, with their brisk Cincinnati accents and deep voices—"Ged merning, ladies. At the chime, WCPO time will be—" and she'd switch the radio off rather than hear that mirthless midwestern voice.

After her sixth month, when her stomach finally outdistanced her breasts, Richard stopped wanting her. The only time she could get him was if she awoke first—a rare occurrence—and dipped her hand below the waistband of his pajamas. By the time he was alert enough to make an excuse, he was too far gone to stop. Other times he said no, it might hurt the baby. But she knew the real reason was that he thought her pregnancy repulsive, that in his eyes she had gone from being a hot number to a fat, boring lump.

By the start of her ninth month, she no longer cared. Her back ached. Her nipples turned from pink to ugly brown. She was so fagged out that she went back to bed when Richard left for the bank and set the alarm for four thirty, an hour before his return. In that last month of pregnancy, Richard found himself almost unable to talk to her. He had married a glittering, charming, effusive *artiste* and barely nine months later was living with a cow. "Oh, my back," she would complain. "Oh, my feet. Oh, I couldn't make dinner; I can hardly stand up." And her endless "Oh, Richard, can't you invite someone over? Someone from the bank? It's so boring."

He returned every night with dread, afraid that in bed she'd dangle a mammoth swollen breast over his mouth and say, "How about some lovin', lover?" Or that she'd grab him in the morning and say, "I know a nice little pot for this cucumber." Even when he realized she no longer desired sex, the evenings were difficult because they could think of nothing to talk about. She could barely make it through the dishes without yawning or moaning. And he would sit in the quiet embrace of a wing chair reading *Ohio Accountant* or *Modern Estate Practices* until ten, when he was too sleepy to ponder how ashamed he was for the way he was treating Sally. And how ashamed he was that he had married her, married a laughingstock.

Sally broke her waters on Anna Heissenhuber's blue couch on a snowy Sunday in March. "Uh-oh," was all she said as she felt the hot trickle of amniotic fluid dripping through her underpants. She sat long enough to leave a permanent stain, then reached out a hand for Richard and chirped, "Curtain going up."

"Please?" he inquired.

"Let's go to the hospital," she said.

Fourteen hours later, the same Dr. Neumann in whose office they'd met delivered her of a six-pound five-ounce baby girl.

"It's a girl," the obstetrical nurse said to Richard. He nodded and thanked her. When she returned ten minutes later to show him the baby he was already a quarter mile away, in a drugstore, buying cigars to pass out at the bank. Then he went to his parents' house to bathe and shave before going to work.

"It's a girl," the nurse said to Sally as she drifted down from an anesthetic cloud.

"Me see," Sally mumbled. Her mouth was dry and her tongue felt as big and heavy as a banana.

The nurse held the pink-wrapped bundle and lowered it to bed level. The child was not pretty, but Sally had not seen enough babies to realize this and thought her beautiful. The baby's skin was as dark gold as Sally's, her eyes a deep blue like Richard's, her tiny fingers delicately shaped. And Sally's worst fear, that the child would inherit the telltale Taubman nose, was not realized. Her nose was small, although pushed to the left from the delivery.

"Isn't she something?" Sally said. "Absolutely gorgeous."

"What's her name?" the nurse asked.

Sally knew Richard wanted to name the baby for his parents. She looked at her baby, its mouth busy making sucking motions, its cheeks soft and round and kissable, and said "Jane."

She was baptized Jane Anna Heissenhuber in a small Presbyterian church three blocks from her parents' apartment. The minister, Dr. Plum, said she was one of the sweetest, prettiest babies he'd ever seen, although he may have just been being kind to his newest congregant, the baby's mother, who had been raised as an Episcopalian—at St. John the Divine in New York City, in fact—and who everyone noticed seemed a little nervous taking communion at Easter, as if she expected some primitive ritual from Presbyterians. Dr. Plum smiled. By the following Christmas, young Mrs. Heissenhuber was a pillar of the church.

Sally hulled three hundred pints of berries for the Strawberry Festival. She accepted the chairmanship of the Gently Used Books subcommittee of the Mission Society—a serious responsibility—and her suggestion to the Tree Trimmers about decorating the big blue spruce outside the church with hundreds and hundreds of red velvet bows was inspired. (It became a church tradition until 1968, when the tree was struck by lightning and died.)

What she wouldn't do for her husband she did for her child: Sally removed the maroon polish and trimmed her nails because Jane loved to grasp Sally's index finger and draw it into her mouth. Jane sat up in the carriage, glanced around, and looked lonely, so Sally abandoned her thick red lipstick and Cuban heels and soon was invited on long strolls with the other neighborhood pram-pushers. Jane had the companionship of her gooing, drooling contemporaries.

Despite Dr. Plum's kind remarks, Jane was an ordinary baby, pleasant but a little funny-looking, with a shiny bald head and a single tooth slanting rightward from her upper gum. However, her mother persisted in thinking her gorgeous and gifted; every liquid gurgle was irresistible music.

"Here comes the choo-choo with the yummies for the tummy." Every spoonful of mashed banana and soft-boiled egg nourished the talent of the child who would become the world's greatest star.

That's how Sally saw Jane. At twelve months, Jane walked. At fourteen she danced, imitating her mother's "step-kick, step-turn" as agilely as her high-laced brown baby shoes would permit. At fifteen months she said "mama," "dadada," and "mook" for milk. At a year and a half, Jane could sing "Mary Had a Little Lamb," "ABC," and "I Don't Care That My Man's Gone Blues."

"Janie, honey, you're gonna be a headliner," Sally confided. Jane, at two, with, at last, a full complement of teeth, smiled. She thrived on mother love. If her own idea of heaven was digging up dirt with an old spoon and mixing it

26

with spit to form mud cookies, she was sweet-natured and smart enough to realize that paradise for her mother was her singing "Little Baby Booboo" and wiggling her fanny; so she sang and wiggled a great deal and dug in the flower beds less often than she might have wished. "You're gonna be a big star," Sally said, and kissed the toddler on her little pot belly. "But listen, Janie, you're gonna have to change your name. Know what I mean, jelly-bean?"

Her father was more distant. What thrilled Sally unnerved Richard. He did not like Jane to sing and dance. She had tried once, flinging out her pudgy arms and belting out "Love Me Again," but he seemed more shocked than appreciative. After that, when she tapped her tiny toe to a radio tune or adjusted the ribbons in her pigtails, her mother would cut short her warm-up techniques, yank her away, and offer her a lollipop—management's recompense for a canceled performance. Jane was bright. She caught on fast.

Richard was fond of his daughter, but he was stiff. He simply did not know what he was supposed to do with a very small female child who did not wish to be read to. He would return from the bank and call out "How are my girls?" and Jane and Sally would run and welcome him with a kiss, Jane's somewhat more enthusiastic than her mother's. Then they would sit down to dinner. Jane would move the tiny dices of pork chop around her plate and listen to her parents' forced, effusive recountings of their day. She did not understand the words, but she could see Sally lean forward, waiting until Richard put the last spoonful of custard into his mouth, then leap up to clear the table. And she watched Richard sighing, patting his lips with his napkin, then plodding toward his wing chair and the evening's reading.

She was not to disturb him until, bathed and brushed and powdered, she climbed into his lap and received his good-night kiss. Then Sally escorted her to her crib, where she received more lavish bedtime embraces. The only time she spent alone with her father was the half hour on Saturday afternoons when he took her for a strawberry ice-cream cone. However, if Richard couldn't give Jane warmth and tenderness, at least he wished her well. Many little girls have had to do with less.

And big girls too. Sally knew Richard's inquiries into her day were strictly for show, so the baby wouldn't have to sit through a silent supper. He didn't want anything to do with her except in the hay. His interest had bloomed again after Jane's birth, not with the ardor of early marriage but with real three-times-a-week, humping, pumping sincerity. Except she wasn't interested. His rejection of her during her last huge trimester of pregnancy had hurt and she just couldn't kiss and make up, especially since there had been no apology. And he only wanted her Tuesdays, Thursdays, and Saturdays and always the same way. No more twisting her up into all sorts of funny positions or stroking or probing one part of her. Now it was kiss-kiss, squeeze-squeeze, boom-boom-boom. He spent more time on his crossword puzzle. Or listening to his records, those Wagner operas that sounded like funeral music for a dead cat.

Richard needed solace. He was not doing well at the bank. A man two years younger than he had been made a junior vice-president. Mr. Forsyth, the head of the Trust Department, who was reputed to have independent wealth, had invited each young executive out for lunch at his private club. Richard was the last one asked. He could not understand why.

He had expected better. Much better. Soon after Pearl Harbor, when he learned a relatively innocuous quirk in his kidneys had rendered him 4-F, he had expected to rise high and fast. He had confided to his father that since his competitors—Buzzy Long and Matt MacDougal—were about to be delivered into Uncle Sam's good hands, his path to the top was clear. "No place to go but up," Carl had agreed. "You'll have your name on a door by next December. March at the latest." But nothing happened. And he still had to share the secretaries' pencil sharpener.

So when he came home from work and Sally waved the invitation in front of his nose—*Mr. and Mrs. Ralph Forsyth cordially invite you to attend their New Year's Day Open House*—Richard experienced a flash of hope he had not felt since his wedding day.

"Can I get a new dress?" was, naturally, the first thing Sally demanded.

"Nothing too dressy," Richard said. "The Forsyths are old money." At least he didn't have to torture himself any more about what new plunge-necked atrocity Sally would be wearing. Since Jane's birth nearly three years before, Sally's wild Spanish nature had been conquered by her better British half.

"Very tony," Sally said to Richard.

"Shhh."

"You'd think with all their money they could afford wall-to-wall carpet."

The Forsyths' house, with its Chinese rugs, matching Chippendale dressers, and Sheraton secretary, was in that part of Cincinnati that reflected the antebellum mint-julep gentility of the South that lay across the Ohio River. The Forsyths' house might have served as a set in *Gone With the Wind* if it had been a low-budget movie; it was a white-columned demi-mansion on three acres of bluegrass.

Sally ran her fingers over the chintz on a club chair. "I suppose you're going to tell me this ratty old flower print is old money too."

"Shhh."

"I bet they haven't reupholstered in twenty-five years. No wonder they have all that old money lying around."

"Sally, someone will hear you."

There were probably fifty people in the Forsyth living room and an additional fifty hanging around the mammoth silver punch bowl in the dining room, but none of them seemed keen on eavesdropping on the Heissenhubers' conversation. In fact, nobody seemed keen on them at all. Mrs. Forsyth had greeted them at the door, exuding charm. "Happy New Year. So very, very pleased to meet you, Sally and Richard," she had said. "Just walk right in, grab a drink, and I'll see you later." But she didn't. Richard glanced toward the door; DeLayne Forsyth was still greeting her guests.

Richard turned back to Sally and in a soft voice began identifying Queen City Trust employees. He didn't really care if Sally was interested; he merely wanted to seem absorbed in a social encounter. In their three trips to the punch bowl and their two to admire Mrs. Forsyth's collection of porcelain cats, they could find no one willing to stand and chat with them. "And that's John Crane, in Foreign Correspondence. No, not the fat one. The one next to him in the plaid jacket."

"Oh," said Sally. Her new dress was white wool with a white lace collar.

"The fat one is Tiny Brody. He's with—"

"Hello, Richard." A deep, soft voice slid between them. "Now don't tell me. This must be Sally." Ralph Forsyth, who had begun drinking at six the evening before and had not stopped since, lifted his bourbon in a toast. "To Sally Heissenhuber! A beautiful—" He listed to the left and grabbed Sally's shoulder for support. "Um, a beautiful snowflake!" His puffy face had the purple luminosity of the binge drinker. His body was severe and lean. "Richard, can I steal her away for a minute?" He didn't wait for Richard's nod. "Come on, Snowflake Sal. Let's get you a drink." He slid his arm around Sally's waist. "Love to be around the pretty ladies," he said to Richard, who looked stupefied. He had believed Mr. Forsyth was interested only in wills, horses, and dogs; he kept a picture of his golden retrievers on his desk in the bank.

"Well, Mr. Forsyth," Sally began as they headed toward the dining room.

"Ralph."

"Well, Ralph—" He had led her to a window and, pointing out his property with his glass of bourbon, showed her the stables and the paddock. "Lovely paddock," she murmured. "One of the nicest I've ever seen."

"Know what else is nice, Sally? You. Sweet little you."

"Thank you." The hand that had been around Sally's waist inched up and girdled her midriff. Up and up. By the time Mr. Forsyth was speaking about his favorite mare, Lady Linda, he was kneading Sally's breast. "Please, Mr. Forsyth."

"Ralph, Snowflake. Listen, you are one cute little package. I mean, here's old Richard, coming in day after day, year after year, and no one knows what a sweet little Snowflake he's keeping at home. I mean, keeping such a doll locked up in the house." He moved his hand from her left breast to her right. "What a shame, keeping so much all to himself." He sipped the last of his drink. "Like the view, Sal?" he whispered.

"Yes, Ralph." He was drunk and getting sloppy, but Sally couldn't figure out what to do. He was her husband's boss, so she couldn't offend him. She couldn't tell him to get his clammy claw off her and that he was an old fart with nose veins who was stewed to the ass. Besides, what he had said about Richard keeping her locked up really made sense. Here she was, thirty-six years old with so much to offer, and her biggest thrill in life was Dr. Plum's asking her to make her lima bean and green onion salad for the Elders' annual dinner.

"Really great view, Sal." Mr. Forsyth was wheezing. She hoped he was getting excited, not sick.

Actually, it was exciting to be admired by a top bank officer, not a junior exec. And looking out the window, innocent as can be from the back and getting the world's biggest feel in the front. She peered outside at the still-green lawn, the split rail fence, and, on the edge of her consciousness, began imagining herself in a pink gown with a pink feather fan, greeting guests at the front door. "I really should be getting back to Richard," she said.

"Oh, come on, you sweet little flake." Mr. Forsyth tightened his grip on her breast. "It's Happy New Year. Happy. Happy time. Come on, I'll show you another view."

Obediently—in fact, obligingly—she followed him through the kitchen, through the mud room, down the stairs, and there, in the octopus shadow of the boiler, Sally Heissenhuber and Ralph Forsyth welcomed 1943 with a bang.

The big boys throw curves; in the world of commerce, action is subtle and oblique. Thus, it was not until mid-March, a week after Jane's third birthday, instead of January 3, that J. Rufus Curry, bank president and Ralph Forsyth's boss, called Richard into his office late one afternoon and told him he would never be an officer at Queen City. Richard managed to ask why. Mr. Curry said it was that indefinable something Richard lacked to fit in with Queen City's top echelon. But he might fit in elsewhere, at another bank. Mr. Curry offered to help Richard find a more comfortable slot. Naturally, if he was happy at Queen City, if he felt he was fulfilling his potential, he was welcome to stay on. Richard said thank you, he would think about it. He was not one of the big boys. He did not understand that he was dead and that Ralph Forsyth had killed him.

"What does it mean?" Sally demanded.

"Nothing. I don't know. They think I'd be happier someplace else."

"What do you mean, 'happy'? Bankers aren't happy. I don't get it." She pulled her voice into tight control so she would not wake Jane. "Did Mr. Forsyth say anything to you?" It was the first time since New Year's Day that she'd mentioned him. Down by the boiler he had sworn to call her the next day. She waited for four days, cooking one-pot dinners from canned foods so she would not have to market, doling out sweets to Jane, hush money so the child would not protest her imprisonment. For two weeks after that, she left the house for only an hour at a time. Then she knew.

Richard, of course, never knew anything. In fact, he believed Sally and Ralph Forsyth had gone for a long, companionable walk. When they returned to him in the living room, their faces were still flushed and Mr. Forsyth said, "Richard, sorry I kept Sally so long. But she's an admirable woman. Admirable." Sally had smiled sweetly, although later that night she admitted that holding up her end of the conversation had been a bit of a strain.

"What are you going to do now?" Sally asked.

"I have to weigh all the possibilities." Richard wished someone would tell him the right thing to do.

"Does this mean we can't buy a house?"

By July, Richard had still not weighed the possibilities sufficiently. He still received the same courteous "good morning" from all the bank officers, still was handed his biweekly pay check every other Friday at eleven, but his desk grew to be an island of tranquillity in a turbulent sea of trusts and estates. Queen City clients continued to die, wills were probated, and everyone in the department seemed to vibrate with activity. Except Richard.

On an oppressive July afternoon, they sat on the clammy wrought-iron benches in the elder Heissenhubers' back yard. For the sixteenth Sunday in a row since Mr. Curry had summoned him, the family discussed Richard's future.

"It's a solid institution," said Anna. She wanted Richard to stay, put his nose to the grindstone, and show Mr. Forsyth and Mr. Curry that he really had the stuff.

Carl, a teller at the Mt. Airy branch of Queen City, thought Richard should move on. "They're getting a little stodgy, Richard. A little too cautious." He hefted a cloudy pitcher of lemonade and poured himself another drink. "You ought to be someplace where they're open to young, fresh ideas. Maybe not a bank. Maybe a brokerage house. Maybe—"

"Do you have any idea where?" Richard asked. He leaned forward so eagerly he stepped on Sally's foot.

"Well," said Carl, "I can't think of anything right off the cuff. Anywhere they'll appreciate a solid man with a good education."

Sally sighed. She had started wearing makeup again, and her mother-in-law was giving her the fish eye. Big deal. She'd had it with looking dead from the ass both ways, with people not even seeing her, much less admiring her, when she walked down the street. She had done it for Janie, but it was really funny; when she bought the mascara and the pancake makeup and the rouge and the new kiss-proof lipstick and put them on, Janie had said, "Mommy, you're beauty-ful!" The kid had been born with taste. The old lady was giving her dress the once-over, which was t.t.—tough titty—because she wasn't buying any more ugly, baggy frump dresses.

She'd had it. Just the other night she'd begun thinking how she'd love to pack Janie up and sneak away, take her somewhere nice, like California. He'd be too dumb to figure out where she went. Maybe she'd go to Hollywood and try and get some bit parts in movies. Not be a star or anything. She wouldn't kid herself. She was a little too old for that. She'd thought about it a lot since. "I think I hear Janie," she said, rising slowly from the bench.

"She's perfectly quiet," Anna said. "She's only been napping a half hour."

"Sometimes that's all she needs." In her high patent-leather heels, Sally left a trail of small holes in the ground as she tottered on the grass back to the house.

"I wish you'd take your shoes off when you walk on the lawn," Anna called after her. "It's not just reseeding, it's—"

"What?" Sally stopped and turned back toward her mother-in-law. "I didn't hear you."

"I said—" Anna began.

"Ow!" Sally yelled. She slapped her hand over her heart, as though saying a fast Pledge of Allegiance, hitting herself with enough force to kill the wasp that had stung her. But it was small vengeance. "Shit!" Her whole chest burned. It was terrible. Sally stared at the Heissenhubers with frightened eyes and then flopped forward.

"Something's wrong," said Carl.

Richard ran to her. "Sally, what is it? Sally?" He turned her over. She was slippery with sweat. The spot where the wasp had struck was so swollen it looked like a small third breast. Sally's eyes rolled in her head. Her breath came in hoarse gasps. "Call an ambulance," he cried. "Sally, what happened?"

Of course, she'd never tell. Sally had been a city girl, an indoor girl most of her life, or it might have happened sooner. She was fatally allergic to wasp stings. Richard held her head up, but her breathing became more labored. And finally it stopped. Just stopped. The woman who had been Sarah Taubman and Sally Tompkins and Señorita Rosita Carita and Mrs. Richard Heissenhuber died in her husband's arms a full five minutes before the ambulance came screaming up the street.

After that, all was quiet until Jane awoke from her nap and called, "Mommy?"

3

. . . according to Jane Cobleigh's British neurosurgeon, Sir Anthony
Bradley, who met with reporters last night. However, the standard American work on the subject, *Stupor and Coma*, is somewhat more specific. It
says . . .

—*Detroit News*

Richard Heissenhuber wasn't a merry widower. Not that he moaned, wept,
and mooned over Sally. On the contrary. For three days and nights he sat
erect—stiff-legged, dry-eyed—between his parents on a brown horsehair sofa
in the Norris J. Vernon Funeral Parlor. A floor fan whooshed air over them,
and he continually brushed back the lock of brown hair that blew across his
forehead. "I just can't believe she's gone," announced Miss Compton, secretary to the president of Queen City Trust. It sounded like a challenge.

Richard tried to rise to meet it, but the viscous July heat sapped him. He
sat poaching beneath his banker-white rayon shirt and his navy winter suit—
the only one his mother said was dark enough for mourning. Every few
minutes a new trickle of sweat would begin and run down his chest or behind
his ear. "Hello, Miss C," he said. "Sorry to bring you out in such hot
weather." Pimples of perspiration gleamed on her upper lip. Richard saw
everyone else was hot too. People paid their respects and left as fast as they
could.

He observed neighbors, relatives, and Queen City Trust executives
sneaking glance after glance at Sally. He didn't like it at all. She did not look
like a young wife and mother who had come to a tragic, untimely end. Somehow, someone downstairs, some warped Vernon employee, had known precisely what Sally was and had given her the star treatment.

She was laid out peach-cheeked and carmine-lipped, her lids ultra-
marine, her lashes so thickly coated with mascara they looked like a pair of
upside-down eyebrows. Either the navy white-cuffed dress she had worn to
Jane's baptism had shrunk or they had pinned it tight in back, because instead
of making her look respectable, like any decent dead woman, it made her look
absolutely voluptuous. And though he knew it couldn't be true, for a minute
he thought he heard one of the Queen City officers mutter that she was a real
hot number. Then Richard realized that she would be cold forever and that in
a few days she'd begin to— He clapped his hands over his eyes and squeezed
his fingers into his forehead.

"Richard? Son? Is anything wrong?"

Richard's knees began to shake and his feet jerked as if he were starting a minstrel number. "The heat," he managed to whisper. He swooned and would have fallen sideways into his mother's lap if Ralph Forsyth from the bank had not been standing right near him and grabbed for him and set him straight.

"Thank you, Mr. Forsyth," he managed to say. A drop of sweat dribbled from his hairline, across his forehead and onto Mr. Forsyth's sleeve. "Thank you very much."

"Glad to help, Richard."

It was not until the next day, with the patter of pebbles and clods of earth raining onto the coffin lid, that he felt safe. It was finally over.

As the weeks passed, Richard realized he missed neither Sally's company nor her moist heat three nights a week. But he did not enjoy the role of widower. He sensed that no one, not even his parents, to whose house he had returned to live, really pitied him, so what was the point? Everything was the same. No one from the bank had come up to him at the cemetery and patted his shoulder and said, "We've changed our mind, Richard, old man. Stay at Queen City. We want you on our team." All anyone had said was "Sorry" and "Bad luck." His luck wasn't bad, it was rotten. What was he supposed to do? And what in the world was he supposed to do with a three-and-a-half-year-old girl? Especially one like Jane, who would not admit her mother was dead.

The Heissenhubers' dining room was small, and Anna had compensated for its size by papering the walls in a green and pale-yellow stripe, which in fact did make the ceiling appear quite high. She chose a cherrywood dinette set—table, chairs, breakfront—that was a scaled-down version of regular dining-room furniture and took up relatively little space. But the effect was wrong. The Heissenhubers were a big-boned family, and they looked grotesque when they sat down to dinner, like teddy bears at a dollhouse table.

"Eat your meat," Anna pleaded. A cube of stewed beef cut into thick strings lay cold on Jane's plate beside three circles of carrot and several peas in a puddle of congealed tan gravy.

"No."

"Do you know how many coupons that meat is worth?" Carl demanded, referring to the war-rationed beef. "Do you?"

"My mommy says I don't have to."

"Jane," Anna said in the soothing tone the minister had advised, "Mommy's in heaven with Jesus. Remember we talked about that? Mommy is very happy in heaven and she misses you but she can't come back."

"She says I don't have to eat my meat."

Carl folded his napkin and put it beside his plate. "Don't you lie to us, young lady. There's no one talking to you."

"Mommy says it's—"

"Eat that meat!" Carl bellowed.

"It's dog food and I shouldn't eat it."

"Eat it!"

Richard, who had been sitting across the oval dinette table from Jane, said his first words of the evening. "I'll handle it, Dad." His parents and his child looked to him, their curiosity blended, perhaps, with incredulity. "Jane," he began. Then he stopped, because he couldn't think of anything to say.

"Yes, Daddy?" She was trying to help him along.

"Jane, you have to eat your meat. It's good for you."

"Mommy says it's smelly."

"No, she doesn't."

"Yes, she does."

"Jane, it's Grandma's beef stew."

"It's doody soup, and Mommy—"

"Stop it, stop it! She's dead."

"Daddy, Mommy says she loves me and she loves you and you shouldn't yell at me and you shouldn't make me eat the meat."

"Jane—"

"You know what Mommy says? She says—"

Richard stood so quickly his chair crashed backward. He raced around the oval table to Jane's seat. She lowered her head. Her black braids grazed the tablecloth. Richard seized her fork and stabbed a shred of the meat. With his thumb and index finger, he squeezed Jane's cheeks, forcing her mouth open. He thrust the fork inside and then withdrew it, clamping her lips together with his fingers. "Chew it. I'm not letting go until you chew it and swallow it." With a gag no one heard because of her closed mouth, she managed to swallow.

"She swallowed, Richard," Anna said. "I saw her."

"No, she didn't."

"She did. Really. Didn't she, Carl?"

"I couldn't tell for sure."

"She didn't," Richard said.

"Just look in her mouth, Richard," his mother suggested.

"Open your mouth. Lift up your tongue. All right. Now eat the rest of your meat." She picked up her fork. "That's better." Richard started back to his place. Jane murmured something. He was rounding the table behind Carl, walking back to his seat. "What did you say?"

"Mommy says I can eat now. It was too hot. That's why she didn't want me to put it in my mouth. But now it's just right. Mommy says—"

"Don't, Richard," Anna called out, as he charged back to Jane's place. "See? She's eating."

The gray December light in the playground was diffused by the thick web of bare branches that hung, like a canopy, over the row of swings. Anna clutched her tweed coat against her neck and turned to Jane, who appeared dwarfed in the big swing, a swarthy Goldilocks in Papa Bear's seat.

"Swing," Anna ordered. "That's why I brought you here."

The swing didn't move. "Grandma, I'm hungry."

"Dinner's in an hour."

"But I'm hungry now."

"You'll ruin your appetite."

"Couldn't we go home and get just one little thing? Like a doll would eat."

"No. You have another fifteen minutes in the playground."

"A bite of apple when we get home? One bite?"

"No."

"A baby drink of milk?"

"Stop it."

"My mommy—"

Anna stamped her foot on the ground. "Do you want me to tell your father you're making up stories again? Do you?" She stomped over to her granddaughter, grabbed the chains that held the swing, and drew Jane up toward her. "Do you?" she demanded.

"No."

"Then you had better mend your ways, Jane. Do you know what God does to little girls who lie?"

"What?"

"They go straight to you-know-where."

"Where?"

Anna released the swing abruptly, causing it to arc back farther than it usually did. Jane's green-mittened hands tightened on the chains. "Your father wants you to be a good girl. Don't you want to be a good girl? Don't you want everyone to love you?"

"Yes."

"Then behave. And for heaven's sake stop being such a nervous nelly. You won't fall off the swing."

Jane was too emotional for Anna's taste. Nightmares. Fears. Five months after her mother's death she still dashed to the front of the house each time the bell rang, still was grieved when she realized the caller was not Sally.

But as Anna was well aware, she was a clever child, able, at almost four, to read with a fluency that would have put a first grader to shame. Anna had taught her in just four months, sitting with a pad of paper and writing J-A-N-E in big letters and saying, "That's you. Jane. See?" The child caught on quickly, although she had asked with irritating frequency to see the word "Mommy."

Jane had all the intelligence Anna had observed years before in Richard, as well as a strength of will—Anna was the first to admit—her thirty-one-year-old son lacked. But it wasn't easy, wiping clean the slate the girl's mother had written on, ordering Jane to control herself when she started jitterbugging on street corners as they walked to church, spanking her for spilling out epithets—she had called Carl a dum-dum—when her way was thwarted.

But the child had her good points. She was affectionate, climbing onto Anna's lap late afternoons with a storybook and putting her head on Anna's bosom and her thumb in her mouth after saying "Read to me, Grandma." And she was surprisingly neat for a young child. They had put her in a small finished room in the attic, but her nightmares about a monster chewing off her arms and legs were so vivid and her screams so shrill they had finally put her cot in a corner of Anna and Carl's bedroom; Richard was in his old room and it wasn't right for her to share it with him. Carl went to the grocery store and brought her a cardboard box to keep her toys and books in. She kept the box scrupulously tidy and even insisted on making her own bed, as if to demonstrate that bringing her down from the attic had been a wise idea. And she was actually eager to stick by Anna's side, to help in any household chore.

Anna glanced over at Jane, who, in her usual cautious fashion, was slowly sliding off the swing, lowering her feet inch by safe inch. "Just get off, Jane. Don't make a production out of it." Anna watched her granddaughter's agonizingly slow descent from the swing. "Jane!" The child's head was lowered; her dark bangs hung over her eyes like a fringed shade.

Anna's mouth twisted. The child had her mother's coloring. Suspiciously dark skin—sallow, really—and that black hair. Like the Italians in the shoe repair store. But at least the child had inherited Carl's and Richard's eyes, a beautiful blue. Unfortunately she had also inherited their strong, square chin, their long limbs and broad shoulders. She was simply not beautiful. But not repulsive in the greasy way her mother had been. And she had brains. That might help. Anna only hoped her prayers had been answered, that the child's willfulness and shocking language were only residues of the tramp's waning influence. And that morals were not inherited. She reached for Jane's hand. "Let's go home. I have to finish supper."

Grandma was cooking salmon croquettes again and the kitchen smelled. Mindlessly, Jane ran the coloring capsule over and over the white brick of oleomargarine, streaking it bright orange. Her mother had made wonderful things to eat, like Pineapple Star: a famous singer resting after her act on a bed of ice cream. Pineapple had a marshmallow head and chocolate syrup hair and pineapple spear body and, finally, two bright red cherry boobies that she and her mother had laughed and laughed about. Grandma Anna said there was a war on and there was absolutely no excuse for waste and nonsense.

"Jane, put the margarine back in the Frigidaire and then go and get four napkins. And fold them properly. No triangles. Do you hear me?"

"Yes, Grandma."

Her mother had loved her so much.

Richard would be out of work as of January 1, 1944. He announced, with an understanding smile, "Mr. Forsyth says they need my desk, and besides, they think the incentive of really needing a job will have a bracing effect on me."

"What?" The funny pages dropped from Carl's hands.

"I thought you said they'd let you stay if you wanted to," Anna said.

"Well, you know how things are," Richard replied. "Anyway, I'm not so sure they're wrong. Things work out for the best."

Anna flushed and turned away. Richard wasn't the son she'd expected. It was as if the tramp, Sally, had sucked the juices out of him. What remained was a tall, handsome, educated . . . Anna swallowed. What remained was something less than a man.

Anna could hear every word the woman said. "Not *that* red," she intoned. "I told you last week I didn't care for it. Don't you remember, Betty?"

"Sorry, Miss Rhodes." The manicurist slipped the offending color back into its hole in the palette of nail polish bottles on the table between them. It was actually shaped like an artist's palette; in the middle, black letters said, *Fingernail Artistry by Lolette Charnay*.

"I want the soft red, two bottles to the left. Not that way, the other way. Left. That's right."

She was obviously a career girl, that much Anna could tell. The average Cincinnati housewife would not come to the local beauty parlor first thing on a Saturday morning in a beige wool sheath and brown bolero jacket and brown kid pumps. She wasn't one of those fast married women out for a good time with a man while her husband risked his life in Italy or the Solomons. No, indeed.

Her clothes were very smart, but her face was somber. Although well into her thirties, she wore no makeup. Her lips had lost most of their color, but they were firmly set and you could tell she meant business. Even as she sat under the dryer with the manicurist massaging lotion into her hand, she tapped her foot, as if measuring out the seconds until she could leave for something important.

She was not wearing a wedding ring. Anna, who was seated across from the woman and who had been studying her in the mirror, found the view blocked by her beautician, who was twirling a row of pin curls on the top of her head. Although the woman wasn't married, she still could afford to come to the beauty parlor, not only for her hair but for a manicure. Anna herself went every five or six weeks for a cut and set, and once every six months for a permanent, and each time, a Saturday morning, the woman was there. Anna had asked Mr. Charles who she was, and although he was not sure—Mr. Wayne did her—he believed she worked downtown in one of the department stores and lived in the area, in Walnut Hills, with her parents. He thought her mother had gray hair in a feather cut.

Somehow, Anna felt Mr. Charles was wrong about her job. She could not imagine this woman—with her obedient short hairdo with its upswirled bangs, her thrust-back shoulders, her rather heavy arms held close to her body—standing patiently behind a department store counter and smiling while a customer chose between capeskin or leather gloves. No. Not her.

Anna examined her own yellowed nails and recalled a line from a movie she had seen years before, a line she had tried to apply to herself but which never really fit: "An admirable woman, that Lady Veronica." Admirable. Anna had to admire this woman. A lady. You could tell by the way she paid her bill, extracting dollars from her purse with delicacy and a little distaste—with just the tips of her thumb and middle finger. A real lady. Unlike most career girls, she neither smoked nor chewed gum. She had a way about her that made everybody, but everybody, fall all over themselves, trying to please her. But she was never loud or pushy. She just said exactly what she wanted: "No spit curls" or "Don't cut the cuticles today, just push them back." And people nodded and smiled and bent over her, trying to accommodate her, because she had that way about her.

Of course, Anna didn't think she was perfect. The woman only said "please" and "thank you" to Mr. Wayne, as if assuming the rest of the people in the beauty shop were servants. Also, unlike Lady Veronica in that movie, the woman was no great beauty. In fact, she was utterly average, with an ordinary figure—except for her arms and legs, which were a little thick and unshapely. But she had a way about her. Yes, indeed.

Mr. Charles slid the final bobby pin across the last pin curl, placed the cotton over Anna's ears, and tied the net in the middle of her forehead. As she stood to go to the dryer, Anna again glanced into the mirror. The woman was looking straight at her. Anna felt her cheeks burn and was about to turn away so the woman wouldn't think she was staring, when, right there in the mirror, the woman gave her a warm, welcoming smile.

Dorothy Rhodes was not free with her smiles, for, as she well knew, a person in her position could not afford to be. Just a simple "good morning" and they'd expect a full refund. A smile and they'd probably insist on double their money back. She was the most competent Assistant Adjustments Manager in the history of McAlpin's department store, and she was certain that if Mr. Pugh hadn't recovered from his heart attack, she would be sitting at his big desk in the rear of the office, conversing with head buyers, attending Tuesday afternoon meetings, making only the most arduous adjustments.

Not that she didn't have enough responsibility. Her desk stood between Mr. Pugh and chaos, where she could supervise the work of three other employees and handle the daily onslaught of difficult customers, the men and women—mainly women—trying to put something over on McAlpin's.

The simple cases—the dresses with tags still on, the still-cellophaned fruitcake returned January 2—went to Miss DeBord or Mrs. Wigglesworth or Mr. Uhl, and all they really had to do, unless they suspected foul play with the sales slip, was say, "Shall we credit your account or would you prefer scrip?" Dorothy's work required real skill.

"The toaster isn't working," one of them would whine. Without a word, Dorothy would turn on her high-wattage desk lamp and examine the toaster, looking to see if the cord had been chewed by animals or if the interior was coated with black grease, a sure sign that someone had tried to toast buttered bread or a sweet roll. Ninety seconds after her examination had begun, most of them were squirming, trying to small-talk her to distraction. "Durned thing burnt up the last slice of my raisin loaf." They gave themselves away.

"Did you touch the element with a knife?" she'd demand suddenly, her first words to them.

"Please?" But she didn't repeat the question. "Well, I had to put a knife in there because the toast was burning. The thing wasn't working right in the first place. But I—"

"I'm sorry. You can't expect a refund, not if you yourself damaged the element."

"But I didn't—"

"If you would care to speak with Mr. Pugh, the Adjustments Manager, you may take a chair out in the hallway and you will be called as soon as he's free." Nine out of ten took their toasters and slunk away. And if they tried again, if they came back with slippers with scuffed soles which they swore they hadn't walked in or with blouses with stains they said they never saw in the store—well, they'd take one look at Dorothy and give up. Just with her card file on chronic returners, she saved McAlpin's thousands each year.

She was intelligent, so even though she did her best to be pleasant she knew many people thought her heartless. But, as she told her parents, they didn't go through what she went through: having to listen to a Roman Catholic priest lie to her, telling her he hadn't even tried on the undershirt when in fact it had perspiration odor under the arms; looking at a pillow alive with lice that a woman swore came from McAlpin's; listening to bluffers and cheaters call her Sourpuss or Old Maid and worse. It's not that she didn't recognize there were legitimate returns, she explained; of course there were. But somehow you could always tell a real lady who was disconcerted over a pulled thread in a linen handkerchief, just as you could spot a sly, coarse housewife who got grease stains on a tablecloth and blamed them on the Napery Department. It was Dorothy's job, and she was good at it. She worked from ten until six, Mondays through Saturdays, taking only a half hour for lunch—which she ate with her father—alternating liverwurst, American cheese, and ham sandwiches that her mother prepared each morning. She was entitled to a forty-five-minute lunch hour but never took it. She was too dedicated.

McAlpin's was a family tradition. Her father, Fred, started as a stock boy and eventually found his niche in haberdashery. "I've got an eye for the tie," he was fond of saying. He became the senior salesman in Better Suits.

Six days a week Dorothy waited for the bus beside Fred in high heels, a hat, a leather handbag, and, always, a pair of pristine gloves, dressed exactly, if less expensively, like the ladies she admired. On the seventh she went to a movie.

The Rhodeses were each other's best friends. "Everybody else is gravy," Dorothy's mother, Wanda, often remarked. They would have been content with the rhythm of their lives—the Sunday pancakes and sausage, the annual two-week car trip to visit relatives in Kentucky and Tennessee—but the day before Thanksgiving, 1942, Wanda was told she had tuberculosis. The doctor said to rest and Wanda did. Suddenly Dorothy was spreading mayonnaise on the ham sandwiches, sometimes ripping the bread with the knife, and Fred was dropping into Curtsinger's Delicatessen after work to buy head cheese and potato salad for the dinner Wanda was too weary to prepare. The rhythm had changed.

Dorothy sensed it. For her birthday the following August, she bought herself a tube of lipstick and a bottle of Jasmine Nights. She could not stay in the ocher brick house in Walnut Hills forever. At thirty-six, with thick legs, thin hair, pale lips, but a nice McAlpin's wardrobe, Dorothy Rhodes was ready to take on a man.

She tried several that fall: Mr. Hardee in Notions returned her smile once but not the second, third, or fourth time; Mr. Kingham in Accounts Payable was polite but kept adjusting a photograph on his desk—it was of a glamorous young woman, and Dorothy, who at first assumed the picture had come with the frame, discovered it was his wife; Mr. Klein in Personnel, who hummed arias in the elevator, gave a curt "no thanks" when she offered him the extra opera ticket she happened to have; and the bus driver, with whom she tried to chat, asked her to move toward the rear. Naturally, she did not tell her parents she was seeking a way out of their house. Nor did she recite her litany of failures.

It was Wanda who first heard about the Heissenhubers. Her physician, Dr. Neumann, said Inhale, exhale, and then told her about Sally's death, a day after it happened. "My, my, my," Wanda had said to him. To Dorothy and Fred she'd said, "Dead as a doornail in less than five minutes. She wasn't a Cincinnati girl, you know."

On the bus the next morning, Fred recalled actually meeting Richard. "The girl that died from the bee bite? Heissenhuber. The name just won't leave my mind. You know something? I sold her husband his wedding suit. How do you like that. I remember he gave the address and I said, 'You live in Walnut Hills? Well, I'll be! Small world.' It was a gray worsted, thirty-eight long, if I recall correc-a-tickly. Handsome fella too. Long legs."

And then Saturday, at Milady's, Mr. Wayne had murmured, "That big woman, just getting up from the shampoo sink? The bee lady's mother-in-law. You heard about it, Miss Rhodes? Just buzz, buzz, buzz, and like they say, the rest is silence."

It was armed with this knowledge that, several months later, Dorothy finally caught Anna in the mirror and overcame her with a smile.

Richard was frightened. Dorothy expected him to marry her, and he couldn't think of a way to say no. But he barely knew her. They were introduced when Anna had phoned him at home, ordering him with uncharacteristic imperiousness to come and escort her home from the beauty parlor. "Miss Rhodes, this is my son, Richard."

"Hello." He had replied automatically, not really noticing her. She looked like a strict teacher. But then he felt his mother's foot pressing against his, the way she had when, as a boy, she reminded him to say please and thank you. "How are you?" he asked the woman. She looked older than he, but he couldn't tell how much.

"Fine, thank you. How thoughtful of you to ask. And you?"

That evening, Anna thrust a slip of paper into his hand as he was sitting feet up, eyes closed, in a chair, listening to the war news. "She's a very high-grade person," Anna said as he opened his eyes. "You'll be doing yourself a favor."

A week later, the first week in December, he took her to a movie about a Nazi spy posing as a milkman in New York City who is exposed by a clever young war widow, and then out for ice cream. She'd let her strawberry ice cream melt into pink mush while she listened to his résumé and had him relate, twice, the details behind his dismissal at the bank.

"Don't you like your ice cream?" he had asked, running his spoon in a spiral path down his mound of chocolate, like a mountain road. He was afraid to look at her. Her eyes were plain brown, but each time he looked into them he gave something away.

"It's fine," Dorothy said, although her spoon remained on her napkin. "Now, let's go over this one more time. Do you mind? I'm interested. Your college grades were good. Your work at the bank was satisfactory."

"Well, I thought so, but—"

"It wasn't?"

"It was. And the clients seemed to like me. I mean—"

"Excuse me for just a second, Richard. I hate to interrupt, but it seems to me your real problems began after your wife's first introduction to your associates at that New Year's party. Now, was there anything she said or did—"

"Really," said Richard. "I don't think we should discuss this. I mean, it happened . . . I mean, she only passed on in July."

"Fine," said Dorothy. Her hands remained in her lap. The forest green sleeves of her knit dress fit like stockings over her heavy arms. The bright lights of the ice-cream parlor reflected off the tile floor and white walls and lit up her face. Her skin was smooth except for tiny lines perpendicular to her lips, like the eighth-inch marks of a ruler; her color was pale and on her left cheek there was an oblong of red, where she had not blended her rouge properly.

"Uh," Richard stammered, "would you like another flavor? The chocolate's good."

"No. Thank you, though."

"I just think—well, some things are very personal. Anyway, I don't think my wife had anything to do with—with whatever."

"Then it must be something you did. Or didn't do."

"No, really."

"Well, I may not have gone to college, but it seems simple enough. You were asked to leave. Now, there's a war on and I know at McAlpin's we treasure the men we have, even if they're half-baked. So why, when Queen City Trust is so fortunate to have a B-plus UC graduate who is 4-F with some minor kidney problem, why would they up and fire him when there's really no one to fill his shoes?"

"But they said they have someone. That's why—"

"Now, Richard. You're just too kindhearted. You can't believe anyone wouldn't be as nice as you. But something went wrong. Don't you think so? Don't you feel it? You're a college graduate. You should be on top of the world."

Richard swallowed his last dab of ice cream and looked up into her eyes. "My wife," he began.

"Well?"

"She had been in show business." Dorothy's lips pursed and she leaned forward, nodding a little. "You see," Richard continued, now eagerly, "there was something about her that she always had to be in the limelight. I mean, that day she met all the execs, she was wearing this tight white dress. A very bright white. And, you know, all the other wives were wearing—well, not white."

"You're so nice. You don't have the heart to say she was—well, flashy. That's how show business people are. I don't mean to take away from her personally. I'm sure she was very nice. But try to remember the details. Did your wife actually talk about being in show business in front of all those people?"

"I don't remember," Richard said softly. "She may have."

"I hate to say this, Richard, but she probably did. Not that there is anything wrong with that, but bankers are a conservative group. Not that I have to tell you that."

"I guess so. . . ."

He asked her out to dinner a couple of times. "You like her!" Anna said one night, helping him on with his overcoat. Actually he didn't like her. But he didn't not like her. Mainly he found her fascination with him intriguing. She was like a devoted, uncritical maiden aunt. But she wasn't his aunt.

She would say, "Now, Richard, tell me all about college. From your first day." Or, "You actually did the accounting work on Mr. Paul Buchhorst's estate? Did you meet Mrs. Buchhorst? She's a very famous equestrienne. What did she look like?" Or, "When did you first begin to sense your wife wasn't up to the demands your position imposed? Hmmm. But you never considered divorce? Oh, no. I agree with you totally."

The fifth time he saw Dorothy was at her parents' house. She had called and said, "I know you must be deluged with invitations, but my mother and father—well, we'd all be pleased if you could join us for Christmas dinner." Anna had insisted he go, saying he'd have all day with Jane and by dinner she would be cranky anyway. So he had shown up in a suit and tie, with a Whitman's sampler for her mother.

"Gee, Richard, it sure is good having you here!" Fred boomed, as smoothly as if he'd been meeting his daughter's boyfriends each week. Fred wore a red and green plaid bow tie and a red handkerchief in his breast pocket. His cheeks were red too, as if recognizing the importance of color coordination. When Dorothy told him about her invitation he had gaped. "A man for dinner?" Wanda had been so flustered she began to wheeze; Dorothy had helped her up to bed. "A little more cornbread dressing?" Fred urged. "Wanda's famous for her dressing." Wanda smiled and coughed. "How about the other drumstick? Come on. A big fella like you needs to keep up his strength. Dorothy, pass the turkey to Richard. Don't want him saying he didn't get a proper Christmas dinner at the Rhodeses. No siree bob."

After dinner, Fred and Wanda shut the kitchen door behind them, and nothing more was heard from them except the clatter of dishes. Richard sat beside Dorothy on the sofa, which was covered in dark red velvet; its feet were wood lion's paws.

"Nice dinner," he said. "Very nice."

"Have you done anything about a new job?"

"Well—"

"You said you were going to start applying right away."

"I am. But what with last-minute Christmas shopping and all—I promised my little girl a sled."

"How long does it take to buy a sled?"

Richard shrugged and ran his hand back and forth over the velvet.

"All right," Dorothy said. "You probably need a little push in the right direction. I can tell. You need— You're an accountant. You can go all the way to the top if you want to. You just need a little help. Do you want me to help you? Do you?"

"Yes," Richard said. "Please."

Dorothy went to a small table and extracted a pad and pencil from a drawer. She returned and sat closer to Richard than she had before. "All right. Let's make a list of possible jobs. Wait. Before you start talking, listen to me. Not just with banks. You're an accountant; think of other places. Stockbrokers. Is that a possibility, Richard?" He nodded. "Let's see. The Internal Revenue? A tax examiner?"

"Well, I think I would rather be in private enterprise. You see, there's only so far a person can go with—"

"Of course. That's a dead-end job. Let's cross it off. How about the big companies? They must need accountants. Procter and Gamble. Cincinnati Gas and Electric. All right?"

"Yes. Oh, I heard—"

"Well?"

"There's an employment agency that specializes in young executives."

"Good. You can go there first thing Monday morning."

"They'll probably be closed. I mean, between Christmas and New Year's nothing much is happening."

"Richard, if you don't want me to help, all you have to do is say so."

Of course he told her he wanted her help, and by their sixth date, four days after the Christmas dinner, she had a typed list of businesses with their addresses, telephone numbers, and, in most cases, the names of their personnel managers. She handed it to him across the checkered tablecloth. They were in a restaurant called Gino's, which had candles burning on the table and a mural of Venice but, except for spaghetti, served no dish even remotely Italian. "Careful," she said. "You're holding the list too close to the candle."

"Sorry." The list had about twenty different banks and businesses on it. "Thank you. Thank you very much, Dorothy."

"I'm just glad I can help, Richard." They picked at the vegetable plates they had ordered. Richard reported on his visit to Collegiate Employment; the man had been very encouraging. "What will their fee be?" Dorothy asked.

"I'm not sure."

"You didn't ask?"

"I'm sure it's standard."

"Richard, make sure before you go on any interviews that you know what their fee will be. Besides, they expect that sort of question from an accountant."

"Do you think I'll have to pay it all right away, I mean, before—?"

"You'll pay it when you have to pay it. Don't worry. I have some money put away." Dorothy's eyes held his as she said this; she knew he understood that she expected him to marry her. It wasn't something he could fudge, sit back for days and think about one way or another. He seemed to have no control. It was predestined. "I have several thousand dollars," she declared, then put down her fork and offered him her beautifully manicured hand to hold. He sat still for a second, his head and throat vibrating with a tingling numbness. For a second, he remembered Sally alive, her tongue inching across her upper lip, her eyes two coals, heating him up. But that was for just a second; the next, still held by Dorothy's watery brown and slightly protruding eyes, he took her hand in his, brought it up to his lips, and kissed it.

"I haven't met your daughter or your father" were her next words.

"Tonight. We can go—"

"New Year's Day would be better."

"Fine. Good. I think you'll really like Jane. She's a nice little girl. Very bright. Not even four, and my mother taught her to read."

"Richard."

"Yes, Dorothy?"

"If you find a job quickly, we'll have enough for a down payment on a house. And a living room suite."

As children often do, Jane misheard the name and thought the lady beside her on the sofa that New Year's Day was "Miss Rose." Jane thought, Rose? She sniffed deeply and conspicuously, and her grandmother gave her a warning look. Her father had told her if she didn't behave they would take back all her Christmas presents, so she clasped her hands in her lap like the good girl on the cover of *Poems for Christian Children* and lifted her eyes to the yellow-haired angel on top of the tree. The pointy top of the tree went up the angel's skirt and that's how come she didn't fall off. Jane inhaled again, cautiously this time. The lady didn't really have a bad smell, like the bathroom after her grandfather had been there, but it wasn't good either—a little like how it smells between your toes after you take off your socks.

The lady had patted the couch and said, "Come sit beside me, Jane," and her father and grandparents had smiled hard when they heard that, the kind of smile where all your bottom teeth show so it wasn't a real smile. But they acted like it was the best thing in the world, this lady in the blue dress paying attention to her. They were making a big fuss for her, all right. Her grandmother had taken off her hair net, and her grandfather had put on his new Christmas sweater and a tie. And her father kept passing the lady the chocolate cherries, trying so hard to get her to eat one, but at least she didn't do that, which was good, because if the grown-ups were talking a lot during dinner, Jane could ask to be excused to go to the bathroom and they'd let her and she could pass through the living room and grab two candies and run upstairs and eat them in the bathroom and flush the little brown papers down the toilet and then rinse her mouth so there wouldn't be any chocolate on her teeth and nobody would ever notice they were gone because there were still so many in the candy dish.

"Where did you get those pretty black braids?" the lady asked.

"Jane, answer Miss Rhodes," her father commanded.

"What?"

"Never mind, Richard," the lady said. "Jane will warm up to me soon enough. Won't you, dear?" The lady put her hand on Jane's head, but she didn't pat it or caress her hair. She just left it there, a big fat hand-hat. Her hand was so heavy. Its dead weight made Jane recall the different touch of her mother's hand on her head, how Sally had stroked smooth the bangs, how she'd take a braid and tickle Jane's nose with it. At night, after Sally brushed out Jane's hair, she'd twirl it around her hand and say, "This is an upsweep, only for *real* fancy occasions" or "See? A French knot. *Very* chick."

Jane tried to shake her head so the lady's hand would fall off, but it didn't move. In fact, the pressure increased, as if the lady knew what Jane wanted but wasn't going to give in. "I want my mommy," Jane said softly, directing her words away from the lady, toward her grandmother. But no one heard her. "I want my mommy!" She tried to shout it, but she had begun crying. "Where's my mommy? I want her. I—" The lady pulled her hand off her head. Her father came, grabbed Jane by the arms, and dragged her up from the couch.

"Stop it, you!" he barked and then, to the lady, said, "She hasn't done this in a couple of months."

Carl chimed in. "It must be the excitement."

"Too many sweets," Anna said.

The lady said nothing. Her father let go of Jane's arms.

She stood alone, motionless, her head lowered, fat tears plopping one after another onto the rug. Suddenly she felt a hard tap on her shoulder, like one of the big kids in the playground trying to punch her. It was the lady. "We'll be gooood friends," she said to Jane, but she was looking over Jane's head, to Richard. "I just know it."

Jane looked right into the pale brown eyes. "You don't want to be my friend."

"Oh, I do, Jane."

"No, you don't. You're just making believe, you big—"

She was sent to bed without supper, so it was not until the next day, the second day of 1944, that Jane learned Dorothy Rhodes would be her new mother.

On Tuesday, February 15, the day before her wedding, the last day she was entitled to her McAlpin's employees' discount, Dorothy Rhodes prepared for her transition from career woman to housewife by buying five house-dresses and an eggbeater.

On February 16, Richard and Dorothy were married by Dr. Clyde Babcock of the Walnut Hills Presbyterian Church, the minister who had baptized Richard. (The Rhodes family had been solid Kentucky Baptists, but since their migration to Ohio in 1902, they had settled into a dilute, secular Christianity whose only sacraments were the playing of a record by the Bagshot Sisters, *"Sleigh Ride in Bethlehem" and Other Yuletime Favorites,* throughout December and the serving of hard-boiled eggs in pink and yellow and blue shells on Easter morning.) After the wedding ceremony, the new Heissenhubers and their guests repaired from Dr. Babcock's study to the Rhodeses' house for sparkling burgundy and Wanda's renowned liver paste finger sandwiches. Naturally, no one mentioned that seven months before there was another Mrs. Richard Heissenhuber.

On February 17, Dorothy Heissenhuber, no longer a virgin, served her husband a breakfast of orange juice, Wheatena, and coffee in the small green and white kitchen of their new house in Edgemont. Dorothy had heard the area touted by the real estate agent as an enclave of dynamic junior executives and wives on the rise, but the rising had settled elsewhere. It actually was what it appeared to be: a community of factory foremen and retail clerks so dreary it could have been assumed bodily from Gary, Indiana, and dropped, splat, onto the edge of Cincinnati. Richard, who had not met the real estate agent, suggested there were nicer neighborhoods, but Dorothy had said no, this was a good location, and his parents backed her up, saying it was important for his new employer to know that he wasn't living too high, and besides, as he worked his way up the ladder of success they could always move. Richard ate slowly. He did not like hot cereal.

"Is the cereal all right?" she asked.

"Oh, yes. Delicious. Thank you very much."

Dorothy wore a canary yellow housedress with black and white checked collar and pockets and large round black buttons. Richard stared down into a minuscule puddle of milk that floated on the brown gritty surface of the cereal. The night before, their wedding night, Dorothy had asked him to change in the bathroom, and when she said to come out she was ready for bed in a batwing-sleeved white rayon nightgown.

For weeks he had been terrified about having to make love to her, afraid he would fail. He, who had never had much of an imagination, could picture Dorothy's face when she realized he couldn't get an erection. It wouldn't be an angry face, but her nostrils would dilate. She'd sit up in bed and want to talk to him about it. He could imagine the conversation: "Is there something *I* should be doing that I'm not? Don't be afraid to hurt my feelings." But that first night she had simply flipped off the lights, so he couldn't see her at all. When he found her bed and slipped under the quilt he discovered that, on her own initiative, she'd pulled her nightgown all the way up, into a ruffle of fabric above her bust. He said "Oh." The first thing he touched was her bare stomach. Compared to her arms and legs, her torso was slender, but her stomach, which looked flat, felt loose, as if the skin was not attached to the muscles. He moved his hand in soft circles. She said nothing. He could not hear her breathe. He eased his hand up to her breasts. Although somewhat flat, they were spread out and covered a large area of her chest. Her nipples were inverted. They felt like toothless mouths. He ran the tips of his fingers over and over them, in a mindless, metronomic rhythm, until finally, to his surprise, he felt an erection. Not only an erection but, an instant later, a frenzied need for release. He drew his legs up. He gasped for air. Then he began to whimper and thrash about, like a baby. His wife had lain still and silent, flat on her back. And then, at last, she had given permission. "All right, Richard."

Dorothy's hair was combed that morning as neatly as if she were at her desk at McAlpin's. "A half spoon of sugar in your coffee?"

"Yes, please."

"Milk?"

"Yes. I don't mind doing it myself, Dorothy."

"No. I'll do it."

"Thank you very much."

The following day, Friday, on his way home from the job the employment agency had found for him, Richard stopped by his parents', picked up his daughter, and brought her to her new home. "This is your new mommy," Richard said to her. They stood in the small alcove beyond the front door. "Say 'Hello, Mommy.' *Say* it, Jane."

"No."

"Jane, you better say it!"

"Richard, don't push her. It will take time." Dorothy put a hand on Jane's shoulder and hoisted the child's chin with the other. "Jane, dear, I know this is hard for you, but won't you just try to call me Mommy? You know I love you and want to take care of you. Come, dear. Say Mommy."

"No."

Richard tried to yank Jane from Dorothy's grasp. "Say Mommy!"

"Richard," Dorothy said softly, "please." She gazed down at Jane. "Now, dear, you see you are getting your father angry. In a minute he'll take you upstairs and spank you. Do you want that, Jane? Do you? A hard spanking and then to bed without supper your first night in your brand new house? Is that what you want? Please, Jane, just call me Mommy. That's all you have to do. Don't make your father angry."

Jane's mouth tightened. She looked up at her father. Richard looked to his wife. Dorothy looked at Jane. "All right," Dorothy said. "I'm sorry. I really wish it didn't have to be this way."

"And *then*," Jane breathed to her friend, "the wicked stepmother locked Princess Cindy up in a tower." Her friend, Charlene Moffett, who was six and lived next door, paled at this latest atrocity and gripped Jane's forearm with the passion of the perfect audience. "It was a teeny room," Jane continued, "*very* dark, with spiders and—"

"No ghosts," Charlene whispered. "You promised."

"I know." The two girls lay beside each other under an elm, their heads resting on the yellow belly of the Moffetts' cocker spaniel. It was a hot July afternoon with a humid wind that assaulted them like a blast of bad breath. It was the first anniversary of Sally's death, but Jane did not know that. All she knew was that Dorothy had one of her stomachaches and, as usual, had suggested Jane spend the afternoon next door. "Anyway, Princess Cindy is in this dark room and the only thing in it is an old stool to sit on."

"No bread and water?"

"No. And so she's sitting on this stool and crying." Jane slapped her palms over her eyes and made noisy sobbing sounds. Then she put her hands back on the dog's comforting fur. "See, it's pitch black and there are spiderwebs in her long golden locks."

"But if Prince Charming sees spiderwebs in her hair—"

"Charlene, you stop or I won't finish. Anyway, all of a sudden she hears magic music. You know, tinkle, tinkle. And then . . ."

"What? What?"

"The room gets all lit up and right there, in front of Princess Cindy, is a beautiful, lovely, magic fairy godmother. And she says, 'Don't you worry, Cindy. No more spiderwebs.' And she waves her magic wand—it's a red stick with a gold star on top—and all the spiderwebs and spiders disappear *and* Princess Cindy is all dressed up in a pink evening gown and a diamond crown. And so she looks at herself and says, 'Oh, thank you, Fairy Godmother.' But then do you know what happens? The fairy godmother disappears. Just like that. Poof! No more beautiful fairy godmother."

"Did the light go out again?"

"No. It stayed on, but Cindy kept crying and crying, because she wanted her fairy godmother back. But then she heard the fairy godmother's voice, coming down from heaven. And she said, 'Don't cry, sweet Cindy. I'll always take care of you.' And sure enough."

"Sure enough *what?*"

"Sure enough, she waved her magic wand in heaven because the light got even brighter, and there, before her eyes, was—"

"Prince Charming."

"Charlene, will you please? Anyway, Prince Charming gave her a kiss"— Jane lifted her cheek slightly, as if to receive it—"and the tower door opened up and he took her away to his castle, but first he killed the wicked step-mother. He took his sword and stuck the point all the way into her eyes, and then he cut her belly open and all her green, slimy guts—"

"You crossed your heart you wouldn't say that part."

"Well, anyway, he took Cindy on his white horse and they lived happily ever after."

"That's it?"

"Of course that's it, Charlene."

Richard worked for one of the richest men in Ohio. John Hart had sold the heavy machinery manufacturing company founded by his grandfather. He added that fortune to the wealth he'd inherited from his father, who had invested early and heavily in several chemical companies, and formed his own company, to serve his own ends. Then he married a Cincinnati debutante, Rebecca Corey; the papers called her Beauteous Becky. All these arrange-ments were complete by the time he was twenty-five.

At the time Richard was hired, however, John Hart was a lieutenant commander in the navy, a master of the M1 rifle, fighting the Japanese in the Marshall Islands. Thus engaged, he was unable for some time to meet his new employee, Richard Heissenhuber.

Not that it would have been much of a meeting. Richard was hired as the Hart Company's comptroller. "Comptroller," Dorothy breathed.

"Some firms call it 'controller,'" Richard said.

"And to work personally for John Hart."

"Well, he's in the navy now."

"Yes. Of course. But when he gets back. To be his comptroller." Richard nodded. "It's like being his right-hand man."

However, on Richard's first day of work old Mr. Tisman, who had worked for three generations of Harts, declared, "You have a problem, you come to me. Not to Mr. Grooms. Not to Mr. Weiskittle. And for chrissake not to Mr. Corbett." The last was Hart's commodities expert, a fat, volatile man whose moods fluctuated with the movements of pork bellies. Once, in a bad moment, he had slammed his fist onto his desktop, shattering the wood. "And for the love of Pete, when Mr. Hart comes home, you say Good morning and Good night and *that is all!* No How are yous. No Isn't it a nice day?"

The Hart Company's sole function was to invest and enlarge John Hart's personal fortune. It had fourteen employees. Richard was its internal auditor. He checked the bookkeepers' ledgers and records, monitored Hart's financial transactions to make certain that brokers, bankers, and businessmen who dealt with the company were on the up-and-up, and examined the expense accounts of Hart employees.

"My comptroller," Dorothy said expansively some months later. She and Richard were alone in the living room, her favorite part of the house. She had picked out the suite of furniture in one minute after she had entered the store—a couch, two chairs, and an ottoman, all covered in dark green rayon damask. The assistant furniture buyer at McAlpin's, whom Dorothy had admired for her fine breeding and beautifully arched eyebrows, had once mentioned blue was for the newly rich; secure people chose dark green or gold.

"Your own secretary, Richard. I'll just bet you're the heart of the Hart Company." She smiled across the room at him. Richard shrugged. He did not have the heart to tell her that the secretary had been hired to replace one who had quit a month before he was hired. And he couldn't tell her how the strategy she had urged he use had failed, how brusquely Mr. Tisman had refused his request for a private office, telling him he belonged with the bookkeepers, not the financial analysts. "And once the war is over and Mr. Hart comes home . . . Richard, there's just no limit. Didn't I tell you that the first time I met you?"

"Well, I'm sure there's a limit."

"No, there isn't, and you know it. I just know by the time the baby is born you'll be on top of the world." She referred to her pregnancy so rarely that Richard sometimes forgot about it. But now he glanced at Dorothy's stomach, a heavy mound resting on her broad lap.

"Dorothy," he said, then licked his lips nervously. "I'm just an accountant. There's a limit."

"You're *comptroller,* Richard. The sky's the limit. You and I and the baby. We'll be on top of Cincinnati. The Harts and the Heissenhubers. You'll see."

*   *   *

Whenever a momentous event occurred in the life of a key Hart employee—birth, marriage, death—Rebecca Hart sent flowers from Cincinnati's most elegant florist. Following the first two events, a gift from Tiffany's in New York would arrive: a silver porringer for newborns, a pair of handblown glass candlesticks for newlyweds. (Young mothers and brides would make themselves ill for weeks drafting thank-you notes to equal the simplicity of Rebecca's *Our best—The Harts.*)

After Rhodes Heissenhuber's birth, Dorothy remained in the hospital the requisite week. No flowers arrived. The porringer inventory at Tiffany's remained stable. Eleven days after she and her son were home, she received a note on Rebecca's stationery—ivory paper monogrammed in dark gray.

Dear Mr. and Mrs. Heissenhuber,

Please accept my congratulations on the birth of your son, Rhodes. I know if my husband were here he would join me in wishing you the best.

> Sincerely,
> Rebecca Hart

Thus Dorothy reached the same conclusion her predecessor had: Richard was a loser. He never gave her any reason to change her mind.

Only their eyes showed they were brother and sister—big and deep velvet blue. His would gleam as they met hers, as she crawled along the floor, sneaking up to his crib. "Shhh," she whispered.

But his delight was too vast for silence, and he welcomed Jane with an aria of monosyllables, love notes sliding up and down the scale. "Nin, nin, nin, nin," he sang, "baa, baa, baa," and he wiggled his tongue at her between his toothless gums.

"Shhh, Rhodesie."

It was dangerous, meeting like that, sneaking into her parents' bedroom while Dorothy was taking her afternoon nap, creeping across the floor to the crib, praying the inevitable squeak of the floorboards would not waken her stepmother.

But it was the only way she could play with Rhodes, tickle his little belly, run her finger against his incredibly tender cheek. "Shhh." She hooked her index fingers onto the sides of her mouth and stretched it into a monster face, crossing her eyes at the same time. Rhodes smiled and said "Nu." Jane grinned and slipped her finger between the slats of the crib. The baby grabbed it. "Rhodesie Poadsie, puddin' and pie. I love you," she whispered. Dorothy's snoring changed tone, to a growl. Jane froze. Dorothy turned from her back to her side. Her breathing grew soft and regular. The baby drew Jane's finger into his mouth and gnawed it with his hard gums. Then, as usual, he rejected it, peering at Jane with a disappointed expression, as if to say, I expected better from you. Jane pulled back the finger he was still grasping and kissed his knuckles, and he said "Mee" and held her finger even tighter.

Late afternoon was the only time Dorothy let Rhodes out of her sight. Almost always, he was close to her. She cradled him in her left arm and carried him from kitchen to living room to bedroom, dusting and vacuuming and waxing with her right arm. When she cooked she put him in his high chair, but that was only two feet away, so she could stir the beans, put down the spoon, and, in two steps, bestow a kiss on the top of his head.

She never expressly forbade Jane to touch Rhodes, but every time the girl went near, Dorothy would murmur her concern about polio germs or explain that Rhodes was tired and if Jane bothered him he would be cranky and cry. Dorothy was distraught by his crying. She'd stop whatever she was doing and rock him back and forth with a frightened look in her eyes until he was finally soothed. And she watched Jane watch Rhodes. "Do you love your brother?" she had asked.

"Yes."

"You're not jealous?"

"What?"

"You don't wish you were as beautiful as he is?"

"He's not beautiful. He's a boy."

"Jane, you know we still love you. No matter how handsome—is that better?—Rhodes is, or how much attention he gets, you're still part of the family. I know sometimes you may not think so, but we do love you. Even when—"

"Why can't I hold him?"

"I want you to answer that question, Jane."

"What?"

"Answer your own question. Why won't I allow you to hold Rhodes?"

"I don't know."

"Say 'I don't know, Mommy.'"

"I don't know, *Mommy*."

"Well, I want you to think about it. Think about the kind of girl you've been. All right? Will you? And then we'll talk some more."

Cautiously, Jane withdrew her finger from Rhodes's hand; she did not want him to cry at his loss. "Shhh." In a way, she could understand Dorothy's proscription. Rhodes was probably the most beautiful baby in the world. Everyone thought so. Neighbors said "Oh, my word!" and "My heavens!" each time they saw him. Passersby, glancing into the carriage, stared at him and, after a moment, at Dorothy and then quickly back to him. The pediatrician's nurse swore to Dorothy he was the most magnificent child she'd ever seen in all her fourteen years as a nurse and said she bet when he grew up he'd be discovered by a Hollywood talent scout. When Dorothy had told Richard and her parents that at Sunday dinner, they'd beamed, until they saw her sneer; she had better things in mind.

Dorothy grunted in her sleep. Jane's arms and legs went rigid. The dizzy feeling came, where she couldn't tell the floor from the ceiling, where up and down kept getting mixed up. If she was discovered, nothing would happen. Not right away. Dorothy never hit her. She would wait for Richard to get home and then, standing in the hall and taking Richard's coat, deftly hanging it up with one hand while holding Rhodes with the other, she'd relate Jane's trespasses in a sad, almost defeated voice.

Richard would march Jane upstairs, sit on his bed, pull her across his lap, draw up her skirt and take down her pants, and spank her until her shrieks were so loud that Dorothy would come upstairs, hugging Rhodes's face tight to her chest so he would not have to see. "Enough, Richard," Dorothy would plead then. "Please. They'll hear next door."

Holding her breath, Jane wormed her way toward the bedroom door. Just as she slithered past Dorothy's bed, Rhodes screeched, shrilly protesting his abandonment. Dorothy jerked up, her face white with terror. "Rhodes?" she called, and rushed from her bed. She tripped over Jane. "Oh, my lord!" Dorothy wailed. "What did you do to him? What did you do?"

4

... whether Mrs. Jane Cobleigh, aged 40, might ever regain consciousness . . .

—*The Guardian*

The Heissenhubers' house, 7510 Ross Avenue, had a lawn but no garden. The contractor had thrown in the lawn, as well as the swan decal on the glass shower door in Dorothy and Richard's bathroom and the front door three-note chime, which had been meant as a refined touch, but which rang out *Yan-kee doo*— leaving callers unsatisfied, waiting for the *dle*. The Moffetts and the Donners on either side of the Heissenhubers put in tulip bulbs, but Dorothy had seen no point in it, since she was waiting to move up and away the moment Richard found his place in the Hart Company, by the right hand of John Hart.

But Richard remained an internal auditor. The secretaries never called him "Mister," he ate his bologna sandwich at his desk, and the closest he got to John Hart's right hand was when the multimillionaire investor offered it each year before Christmas, to hand Richard his bonus check. When Dorothy realized that Ross Avenue was as high as she would step with Richard, her interest turned to her son, Rhodes, and she never planted so much as a sunflower seed.

The best and the worst to be said for the house was that it was modest. Set on a forty-five-by-ninety-foot plot, it was a 1940s adaptation of a Cape Cod and a free Cincinnati interpretation at that, white clapboard with a sort of mansard roof and a side-entry front porch. It was not a house to love at first sight, but the average American family who would buy such a house would have made it at least slightly lovable—painted the trim forest green or plunked a weather vane on the roof. The Moffetts' house had nearly as much ivy as a college, and the Donners had enclosed their property with a white picket fence. The Heissenhubers' lawn was mowed and the clapboard repainted every five years, but there were no touches to show that a particular family—Richard, Dorothy, Jane, and Rhodes—lived in that particular house.

The inside of 7510 was nearly as undistinguished as the outside. The furniture, purchased in suites in department stores, was designed neither for comfort nor for beauty but to fill rooms. Everything matched; chairs, ottoman, and sofa were covered in the same dark green rayon damask; dresser, chest, nightstands, and headboards were all maple, with brass drawer pulls like buck teeth. That was it. No afghans drooped over sofa arms, not a single ashtray or vase marred the tabletops. All the walls were bare.

If the house had the ambience of a motel room, it did not really bother Jane, whose status was that of an undesired guest who'd checked in. The house was Dorothy's, and Jane could no more suggest a watercolor over the couch than offer ideas of what to serve for Sunday dinner. But sometimes, coming home from her friend Lynn's house with its coffee table full of family photograph albums—giant leather books with *The Friedman's* tooled in gold—she'd imagine a picture of Sally in a heart-shaped frame, right where her fingers touched her bedroom wall.

There were no photographs of Sally. Jane had only fragments of memory: the dry crinkle of a taffeta slip as she climbed into her mother's lap; picking fat gold raisins, one by one, from Sally's cupped hand, sucking the wrinkles out of them, thinking how much more satisfying they were than the black ones. She could recall two complete sentences: "Honey-bunny, you remember where I put the clothespins?" and "Red is definitely your color." She remembered the soft skin on the underside of Sally's arm.

Richard never explained why all traces of Sally were lost. He'd once shrugged and muttered that the two or three photos he'd taken must have been thrown out with the old *National Geographics*.

When Jane was eleven, her grandmother died of a stroke. Jane, assigned to clear out Anna's closet, found a photograph in the bottom of a hatbox under layers of yellowed tissue paper. (Along with it she unearthed a pornographic postcard—a picture of a Gay Nineties woman wearing only high-button shoes sitting open-legged on a footstool, fingering her vulva.)

The photo in the hatbox was of Richard, who looked astoundingly hand-some; his hairline had not yet crept back, leaving a huge, shiny forehead, like an alien from a brainier world, nor had his strong jaw melted into a fleshy chin. He was holding an infant Jane in the crook of his arm. A hand with long polished nails rested on his sleeve; it was a black-and-white picture, so the nails appeared black. When Jane examined it, she saw the white edging missing from that side of the photograph. Grandma Anna had cut Sally off.

But it was source material for Jane. She added the graceful hand and dark nails to the maternal portrait she'd created from the fragments of her memory. The pieces couldn't form the real Sally, but they served. They were a living portrait, an internal mother who soothed "Sweetie, he didn't mean it" each time she received another spanking from her father. Jane would lie face-down on her bed, her backside throbbing like a sore heart, and embrace the cool comfort of her pillow. Sally's voice—not heard so much as felt—murmured, "Janie, baby, don't cry. Shhh, now. Shhh. She made him do it." The soft manicured hand with its black-lacquered nails sleeked back her hair. "He didn't want to."

Richard told her little. He remembered Sally was short, and Jane filled in the rest. She was indeed short, but delicate, with a neck a swan would covet and regal posture. Sally could sit motionless and straight for hours, her back never seeking the support of her chair. Her hair was black, like Jane's. Jet black, Jane always thought of it. Since Richard could not recall her eyes, Jane made them crayon colors: blue, green, occasionally violet. And since Sally had been an actress, her voice was rich and full, yet gentle. But not soppy. Sally was no mushy madonna memory. She remained in death what she had been in life—Jane's center of gravity.

Jane needed a mother. From the time she was four, Jane antagonized Dorothy several times a day, angered her into colitis attacks at least weekly. As Dorothy confided to Rhodes, it was Jane's *manner*.

"I know you don't mean to be, but you seem surly," Dorothy explained in one of the frequent heart-to-heart discussions she'd demanded since Jane was small. "Please look at me when I'm speaking to you."

"I am."

"No, you're not." Dorothy hunched forward in her chair, her hands clasped on the Formica kitchen table: the judge. Jane, now twelve years old but oversized for her age, with her father's long limbs and the beginnings of her mother's large breasts, occupied the position that had been assigned to her since she was four, on the ten-inch square of green floor tile beside the pot cabinet, slightly more than an arm's length from her stepmother. Round-shouldered to compensate for her height (she had already reached five feet six of her eventual five feet ten inches), with straight black hair cut in long bangs that hid her eyes, head hanging down, she looked guilty as charged. Her feet shuffled on the green square.

"You don't say a word around the house, Jane, except when you pick on Rhodes or steal his colored pencils, and that's jealousy, I'm afraid to say, jealousy pure and simple. And your appearance just shows your contempt. You walk around with those blue jeans and that shirt hanging out like the Wreck of the Hesperus. Look at me, please, not at the floor. You let your hair get—well, greasy, to be perfectly honest, and then you wonder why Charlene Moffett gets calls from boys and you don't. I'm sensitive to these things, even though you think I'm not. I know it bothers you, so don't bother denying it."

"I don't want boys to call. No one has boys call yet, until you're fourteen or fifteen, and the only reason Charlene—"

"Dark hair and dark skin can be *very* attractive, but you have to scrub. If you look clean you'll feel clean, inside and out. Clean and *cheerful*. Please stop that pouting. And no mumbling under your breath, Jane. I am trying so hard, even though you've set me up as your enemy. I'm trying to work *with* you. I bought you that expensive shampoo for oily hair. . . . All right, have it your way. Make all the faces you want. Don't think I didn't notice. I obviously can't get through to you. You'd rather have your father handle it, is that it? *Is it?* All right, don't answer me. Just get up to your room *this minute*."

Jane would comply. Upstairs she'd crawl beneath her bedspread, nauseated from the encounter, slick with sweat, anticipating her father's reaction. But then she'd soothe herself with Sally's words until, even if it was midmorning, she'd ease into a deep sleep.

But Sally's maternal spirit wasn't potent enough to bank the rising outrage in Jane. Between her thirteenth and fourteenth birthdays, she tried to fight back.

"Daddy, can I talk to you? Daddy, just one second. I just want to know one thing. Can't you put down your newspaper for just one minute?"

Richard leaned forward in his club chair. The wash-and-wear fabric of his cord suit pants made a scratching sound against the rayon damask. "Is that a fresh tone of voice?"

"Daddy, could you just explain one thing to me? I just want to know why Rhodes gets everything and I don't."

"You know, Mother warned me you've been acting very jealous, and she says she's at her wit's end—"

"I swear I'm not jealous. It's just that he goes to Country Day even though you're always saying we have to cut back and there's no money for this and no money for—"

"Mother and I think he'd be better off in a private school. You're doing fine at Woodward. Now go outside and play."

"Daddy, I'm thirteen and a half. And I also want to know why you never ever lay a hand on Rhodes, and—"

"Dorothy? Dorothy? Could you come in here, please?"

"Daddy, please just listen to me."

"Anything you can say to me you can say to your mother. Oh, Dorothy. Would you explain to Jane why Rhodes is going to Country Day?"

"Explain?"

"Well, you see, Jane asked why—"

"Jane," Dorothy said, "if your father was a wealthy man don't you think we'd send you to private school too? But he's not."

"You wouldn't send me anywhere and neither would he!"

"Jane—"

"The only one you care about is Rhodes."

"Stop it!"

"You don't even care about my father. You don't! It's just Rhodes, Rhodes—"

"Enough! Richard, did you hear that tone of voice? Did you? I want you to make her get control of herself."

"Jane, get a grip on yourself."

59

"Daddy, *please* listen to me. She makes it sound like I'm bad, but I'm *not*. It's not fair. Every time, she makes you—"

"Richard! Listen to her tone of voice. Just listen to it!"

"All right, all right. Come on, you. Upstairs."

Punishment for her crimes was severe, and nothing—not even the sweetest words she could conjure up for Sally's spirit to utter—could ease the mortification of Dorothy's inevitable triumph and the pain of Richard's punishment.

The spankings grew harsher as she matured. They usually began with an after-school affront to Dorothy, and by evening at five thirty, when Richard was walking up the street on his way home from work, Dorothy would push open the door of Jane's room, snap on the light, take a step in, her shoes sounding sticky on the linoleum, and say, "Your father's coming." Jane would get out of bed, stiff, slit-eyed from the brightness, and follow her stepmother downstairs. Together they'd wait for Richard in the frame made by the open front door, backlit by the sickly orange light of the colored glass hall fixture. "I'm sorry, Richard," Dorothy would say as he climbed the first of five steps to the front porch. "I know you're tired, but she called me . . . I can't say it . . . a witch with a 'b' today. I can't deal with her. You *know* how I've tried."

While Dorothy laid his dinner on the table, Richard would say "Upstairs" and march behind Jane, pushing her forward with his index and middle fingers when she slowed or tripped, until they were in his and Dorothy's bedroom. He'd shut the door behind them, pulling at the knob a few times to make sure it was properly latched, and then remove his jacket, loosen his tie, and open his collar button. Slowly, he'd lower himself onto the edge of his bed, so the springs contracted without a squeak. "Let's get this over with," he'd say. Jane would lie across his lap, awkward, the tips of her shoes and her fingers touching the floor, for she was nearly as tall as he.

He would pull down her pants so her backside was bare and hit her. At the first smack, she'd let out a noise between a gasp and a shriek, a cry of horrible surprise, although she never had reason to doubt what would happen. Her eyes would dart frantically, searching for something to focus on: a castor on the leg of Dorothy's bed, a bit of fluff under the dresser. She'd stare, trying to transcend the pain of the smacks the way she'd read an Indian swami can a bed of nails. But Richard's hand cracking down—its speed and power increasing with each slap—soon overcame her concentration. Each smack made her jaw snap shut. Her teeth crashed together, sometimes biting deep into the spongy flesh of her tongue.

Then, finally, pain took over; Jane began to scream. Her mind darkened and took in nothing more until her father stopped, apparently exhausted—slumped over, red-faced, perspiring.

When her pain diminished there was further pain: going down and seeing

Rhodes's face, a sick-white oval, staring up at her from the bottom of the stairs, his eyes growing wider and wider to accommodate the tears he could not shed; hearing Dorothy's "Jane, I need some help" from the kitchen, the voice buttery with generosity, allowing Jane another chance, but strained with the knowledge that such compassion was futile; looking at the juice glass filled with whiskey Dorothy placed beside her father's plate, watching Richard—who did not otherwise drink—take small, fast sips as if it were a hot liquid he had to get down; watching Dorothy dish out the slaw or Jell-O, tapping the spoon on Rhodes's plate to get the last morsel off, determinedly ignoring the explosions of coughing when the whiskey seared Richard's throat.

It was too much. Jane might have borne the spankings—many children do—but she could not tolerate the unspoken family knowledge that what went on upstairs was more than discipline and that, whatever it was, it was she who made it happen, again and again and again.

By the time she was fifteen, she learned to take great pains to keep out of everyone's way. She rarely came downstairs except for meals, to do her chores, or to leave the house. She stayed and studied behind her closed door. Better isolated in her own bedroom than risk having to go with her father to his.

Jane's bed—a mattress on a low wood platform—stood under a bulletin board. The board overflowed onto the wall. Childhood favorites—a picture of a kitten and a puppy, retouched so they appeared to be smiling—had been covered by fifth and sixth grade class pictures, which in turn were obscured by a newspaper photograph of Elvis Presley on which she'd penned ELVIS! and a *Seventeen* magazine article, "Flower Your Bower!" on making chrysanthemums and zinnias from crepe paper. All this, even her yearly certificates from the Junior and Senior Honor Societies, were finally hidden by theatrical memorabilia: Drama Club programs, ticket stubs, the ABC listings clipped from a Sunday *New York Times*, her membership card in the National Thespian Society, quotations from Shakespeare—"The play, I remember, pleased not the million; 'twas caviare to the general"—on index cards. She had told her friend Lynn, "The theater's in my blood." The legacy of the mother she could hardly remember filled her room.

But by Jane's last year in high school, her mother's presence had faded. It had to, for there was no place in Dorothy Rhodes Heissenhuber's house for even the ghost of a loving mother. Sally dwindled to a shadowy comfort, a vague presence who visited her daughter only in the dim, troubled moments before sleep.

"O-u-t," Jane said.

"It's okay. She went to the store," Rhodes said. "Uh-oh, what did you do, stupid, steal that doily?"

"I didn't steal it, moron."

"You *know* your ass is grass if Mom finds out."

"Your ass is grass if you open your big mouth." Jane sat on the blue fringed oval scatter rug, the one warm spot on the linoleum floor. Her back rested against her bed and its spread of dotted Swiss, its white dots nearly invisible against the background of faded blue. She glanced from her sewing over to her half-brother, who was lounging against her chest of drawers. "And anyway, Mr. Sophisticated, it happens it's not a doily, it's an antimacassar and she won't know it's gone because it's been in the back of the linen closet for the last nine hundred years and anyway it was Grandma Anna's and Mom never used it because antimacassars are lower class, for people who don't know enough to keep their greasy heads off the backs of chairs."

"That's why I didn't know what it was called, because it's lower class and I'm not. Of course, that's why *you* recognized it right away."

"Then how come your mother knew it was lower class? Hmmm?"

"Would you stop calling her 'your mother'? You know and I know that she brought you up since—"

"My mother's name happened to have been Sally Tompkins Heissenhuber, and she was an actress and a beauty. *Your* mother—"

"How do you know your mother was a beauty? You never even saw a picture of her."

"Because Dad said she told him she played Juliet, and you can't not be beautiful for that role."

"If she was so beautiful, what happened to you?"

"Nothing happened to me, stupid."

"Ever look in a mirror? Six more legs and you'd make the perfect octopus."

"Four, you jerk. You didn't count my arms."

"I was trying not to remind you." Rhodes lifted his chin and adjusted the knot in the tie he was required to wear each day to the Cincinnati Country Day School. Although only thirteen, he was even handsomer than his infant beauty had intimated. He had a square jaw, lips just full enough to make his mouth alluring without cheapening the strength of his strong bones, and dark blue eyes like his father's and sister's: large and velvety. His beard had not come in and his skin was light with an underlying glow, like porcelain. He was tall for his age (although not the six feet he would reach) and looked like the star guard of the lower school's basketball team that he was: graceful, strong, controlled. Girls his age telephoned the house several times a day, giggling or asking for him in silly, disguised voices. Older girls, sixteen-year-olds in tight skirts, offered him rides in their convertibles. So what might have seemed an affected gesture in any other boy—tightening his tie in the manner of a 1920s playboy—appeared suavely correct.

Jane returned to her sewing, tacking the piece of lace she'd cut onto the neckline of a plain black blouse. "You think just because you go to Country Day you're h-o-t s-t-u-f-f, but you know and I know that all the boys in your class know you live in Edgemont."

"It just happens, tall, dark, and ugly, that they know exactly where I live and couldn't care less. They like me for what I am."

"Then they obviously have no taste."

"They have enough taste to know you're ugly. Beaky."

"Do me a favor, Rhodes. O-u-t. I have to finish my costume."

"That's why you're in such a bad mood. Because you're playing Clementine and you really wanted the other part."

"I did not."

"You did too." Rhodes crossed the room, which took three steps, and in a fast, fluid movement crossed his feet and lowered himself onto the rug. His knee touched Jane's.

"Get out of here."

"No. Anyway, you wanted the lead and—"

"I have the lead."

"You know what I mean. The good juicy part. Whatever her name is."

"Deirdre Brooks-Elliott."

"Sure. That was the one you tried out for."

"Read for."

"Why didn't you get it?"

"Because. Come on, Rhodes. Leave me alone."

"Because why?"

"Because Mr. Gluck said I wasn't the ingenue type. But it's not really an ingenue role, and anyway I *could* play it. I'm an actress. By definition versatile."

"What did he say to that?"

"Nothing."

"What do you mean, nothing?"

"Nothing. *Rien. Nada.* I couldn't exactly have a screaming argument with Mr. Gluck, could I?"

"You wouldn't have to scream. Just say, 'Hey, look, Mr. Gluck, I really deserve—'"

"It wasn't worth it."

"It was *too*. I don't get you. Why don't you ever try?"

"Mr. Gluck had his reasons, and there was no point in making things unpleasant."

"You're so full of shit your eyes are brown."

"Rhodes, the only reason he wouldn't let me have Deirdre is that Bucky Richards is Aubrey Weston and he's five-five, five-six if he's lucky."

63

"Well, he is lucky. He got the part he wanted."

"I know, and he's a junior. This is my last year. But instead Gluck gives the part to Vicki Luttrell just because she's short. Oh, well, water under the bridge and all that rot."

"Listen, you'll be okay as Clementine. You'll probably wind up outshining them because they're even worse than you."

"I don't want to outshine them. This is my last Senior Drama Club production and I wanted it to be special. And here I am, playing an eighty-year-old British dowager in a production that absolutely screams Cincinnati. Bucky Richards thinks all you have to do to put on a British accent is stick out your front teeth, so all he sounds like is a stupid talking rabbit. And that Vicki! Do you know how many gestures she has in her repertoire? One." Jane rested her sewing on her lap and looked up at her brother. "I have to finish this. Would you please leave me a-l-o-n-e?"

"You think it's chic to spell."

"Rhodes, go play in traffic."

"You better sew nice little stitches. Otherwise Bobby Spurgeon won't like your costume."

"What does Bobby Spurgeon have to do with anything?"

"Are you kidding? 'Oh, Lynn, I can't quit *Noble Hearts* because I couldn't bear not seeing Bobby Spurgeon every day at rehearsals. It's my only contact with him, with his darling little nose and his big strong hands and—'"

Jane reached out to grab Rhodes's upper arm, but he sprang up. "You absolute creep. You were listening in on my phone call."

Rhodes backed toward the door, holding an imaginary receiver to his ear. "'Lynn? Jane. Hi. Listen, Bobby Spurgeon actually looked at me in Latin today. I mean, with both eyes. Just for a second, but—'"

As he backed out the door, Jane clutched her sewing in her fist. "I'll never speak to you ever again."

"Ta-ta, Lady Clementine. Break a leg."

Lynn Friedman gazed up at Jane. The student director of *Noble Hearts* was just five feet tall and appeared fragile, with delicate bird bones protruding under her pale skin. Her hair, a pixie cap of dark brown, and her huge eyes, black and bright, only made her seem more the waif. But a well-dressed waif. Her aqua cashmere sweater coordinated with an aqua and cream plaid skirt and thick aqua wool socks her mother had sent for to Bergdorf Goodman's in New York.

Jane stood on the Woodward High School stage in costume and full makeup, her long hair pinned up and gray with talcum powder. Lynn looked like her granddaughter.

"Jane, move about four inches right. Stop. God, this lighting is terrible."

64

Lynn made a megaphone with her hands and shouted to a boy in the control room in the back of the auditorium. "Bobby! I didn't ask for high noon." The spotlight on Jane turned from brilliant white to blue. "Is this unbelievable? Bobby, this is a dress rehearsal!" She turned to Jane and in a hushed voice said, "I honestly can't understand your crush on him. Except that he's tall. Is that it?"

"Lynn, quiet."

"He can't hear me unless I scream at the top of my lungs."

"But Vicki's standing right there. Would you look at her, staring at us? I bet she heard every single word. God, I'm going to die."

"You can't. We open tomorrow night. Now listen, you'll come home with me after and my mother will force-feed us, but then we can talk and then I'll drive you home by ten so Dorothy the Hun doesn't kill you. It cannot go on like this, Jane. You're a senior and you're really neat-looking if you'd ever do anything with yourself, and there's no reason why you can't have a boyfriend and a date to the prom, especially since there are literally dozens of boys who aren't going with anybody."

"I don't want to be fixed up with anybody."

"Then *do* something about Bobby Spurgeon."

"Do what? I've been saying hi. I let him copy all my Virgil notes and I was wearing bright red lipstick, just like you said, and if it brightened me up totally he sure didn't notice. Anyway, I think he likes Gail Renner."

"Well, I don't think he does, unless he just loves retard cheerleaders, and I also think he would definitely like you if you just—I don't know, played up to him."

"I don't know how."

"Oh, God, Jane. You're seventeen."

"Sweet seventeen and never been kissed."

"When I'm finished with you you'll be kissed so much you won't be able to stand it."

It was five minutes before Jane's ten o'clock curfew and they were parked on Section Road, just a block and a half from the Heissenhubers', so Lynn said, "Let's go through it one more time."

The front seat of the car was pulled up as far as it could go, and even so, Lynn sat on a cushion to see over the wheel. It was a convertible, a two-tone blue and white—Woodward High School's colors—with a tiny brass plate with LMF, Lynn Marlene Friedman, on the driver's door. Although it was March, the top was down, the heater warming the lower halves of the two girls.

"It's tomorrow night. You're at the cast party, and Bobby Spurgeon is standing in a corner drinking a Coke and looking lonely. What do you do?"

Jane shifted, but the car seat was so near the dashboard she had little room to maneuver, and all she could do was move her knees, which were nearly at chin level. "I say, 'Hi, Bobby. Whew, am I glad it's over!' and sort of collapse into his arms."

"Not collapse. He'll think you're some kind of spaz. Just lean against him for a minute. So he gets the idea you're a girl. Now okay, what happens if he doesn't say anything?"

"I ask him if there were any problems in the control room."

"No! That calls for a yes or no answer. You ask him what was the absolutely worst moment in the control room all night. Then he has to talk."

"I'm cold."

"No, you're not. You're absolutely paralyzed that you'll be two seconds late and the Blob will go 'Naughty, naughty.' God, you're a senior! What can she do to you? You don't have to be perfect, you know."

"Come on, Lynn."

"I mean it. You're so busy being wonderful you can't relax. Smile, smile, smile. Work, work, work. Oh, Jane. I didn't mean to hurt your feelings. But just—I don't know. You get so panicked if you get less than a ninety-five on a test or if you forget one thing on a shopping list out of fifty million things the Wicked Stepmother asked you to buy. No one's going to think any the less of you if you're not perfect. You're a super-neat kid, and if you'd just take it a little teensy bit slow you'd make things much easier for yourself. You'd probably get a billion boyfriends if you didn't seem so—you know. Imposing."

"Just like that. One, two, three."

"I'm not saying it will be easy. If it was easy you would have been pinned junior year, for God's sake. It's hard because you're always being Best Person of 1957 and that takes work, and also your self-confidence quotient with boys is minus one million, for some weird reason that's absolutely beyond me, and you give off waves of insecurity. I mean, you can be the most charming person in the world. But the minute, the absolute second a boy gets close, you freeze. Rigor mortis of the personality."

"Maybe I'm frigid or something."

"That's dumb. You've never even had a boy kiss you, so how can you tell? Maybe deep down you're a real nympho and that's why you've been avoiding it all these years."

"Lynn, please listen to me. First of all I did not have the good luck to be born cute like you. Really. You're cute and dainty and everyone in the world wants to buy you an ice-cream cone. I'm big and gawky and have an awful nose—"

"You don't. You have a wonderful nose. Perfectly straight and in proportion. What would you do with a little teeny baby one? Look, I know about noses. Didn't half my sorority get nose jobs?"

66

"Rhodes calls me Beaky."

"Rhodes is a younger brother. What do you expect?"

"And my clothes aren't nice."

"You're crazy. They're fine."

"I only have orlon sweaters."

"Do you think any boy who's interested in your personality and wants to—um, get really friendly is going to care whether there's orlon down there or cashmere? Not that you would do anything like that, except maybe if you were pinned. I can't believe you. You're absolutely statuesque, plus you don't have to wear falsies, and you're worrying about orlon. Boys don't know about these things, so stop it. You're number three in the class. You're a terrific actress, and you're the only girl who got over seven hundred on the math boards. And you're my best friend."

"But I'm scared. What if Bobby—?"

"What if he what?"

"Tries something."

"Tell him no."

"How?"

"Just push his hand away and shake your finger at him and say 'Uh-uh, Bobby Spurgeon. No way.'"

"I can't say that. That's what you would say. It's cute. I stopped being cute seven inches ago." She sighed and rubbed her palms together under the heat that poured from beneath the dashboard. Within seconds she was wringing her hands.

"Stop it! You always anticipate the worst. How many boys have you had crushes on? Come on! You keep liking this one and that one, but you're always afraid to even smile. Live it up. Take a chance. It's going to be fine, and by midnight tomorrow Bobby Spurgeon will be madly in love with you."

One night, the week before *Noble Hearts* had been cast, she'd slept over at Lynn's and had tried to tell her. She'd begun with a question across the darkened bedroom. "Did your father—I know he's not strict, but—did he ever hit you or anything?"

"Oh, my God, did he ever! One night, after some big dance. I forget which one—maybe the Presidential Ball. Anyway, that's when I was going with Chuckie Nudelman and we went to Frisch's after and then Chuckie and I parked but I swear to God we were just talking and all of a sudden it was four thirty and—"

"But he doesn't—"

"Does your father hit you? I can't imagine him. Dorothy, yes, with a cat-o'-nine-tails, but your father is such a nice—"

"Oh, he is. It was just a couple of times when I was a kid."

67

"Anyway, let me tell you what happened. I was absolutely terror-stricken and so was Chuckie, but he walked me to the door and . . ."

Jane shut her eyes. The spankings had stopped two years earlier, but Richard recently had made two ominous midnight visits to her room. There was no one she could tell about them.

"Jane," Miss Bell breathed. "Why won't you?"

"Because I want to go to University of Cincinnati."

"But you can go to any college in the *country*. The world is yours for the taking."

"UC's a good school." White pages of applications and bright-colored college catalogs splattered all over the shelves and spilled onto the floor of the guidance counselor's office. The black filing cabinets were so crammed with transcripts their drawers hung open, defeated. Jane sat on the edge of the wooden chair, smiling at Miss Bell, her heart racing so fast her chest hurt from the pounding.

"Of course it's a good school. But is it the school for Jane Heissenhuber?"

Jane kept smiling and shrugged. "I think so." She was dizzy. She hooked her feet around the front legs of the chair and grabbed the sides of the seat as if the chair were trying to buck her off. Her breathing was deep and conscious, but she could not get enough air. "I like it here," she whispered. A trickle of sweat ran from behind her ear down her neck.

"Jane, are you *afraid* to go out of town?"

"No."

"Some students are—well, intimidated by the very colleges they belong in. 'Oh, not Vassar, or not Smith. Not *me* at those schools.' Is that a factor, Jane?"

"No, Miss Bell. Really." She knew her lungs were expanding, but something was clogging them and they didn't seem to be able to absorb the oxygen in the air. Miss Bell had a wen on the end of her nose, and for a second Jane had a terrifying compulsion to reach over, squeeze it, and see if it exploded.

"I wish you would give yourself a chance, Jane. You deserve it."

"Please, Miss Bell." She could not stand feeling this way, and she knew if she went east, to one of the colleges with all the New York and New England girls in their camel-haired perfection, the girls in *Glamour*'s college issue, she would never feel right. She couldn't go. Having to sit in a classroom and not understand the witticisms of the professor who had all the other girls choking with laughter and being the only girl left in the dorm on Saturday nights— there was one every year, and that year even the fat girl would be pinned to a senior. Or the humiliation when the boys from Harvard and Princeton sneaked out the back door of the dormitory when they saw she was their blind date. Eating her meals alone, or carrying her tray to a tableful of girls in flawless pageboys and saying "Mind if I join you?" and having them give each other funny looks before saying "Oh, do."

"Jane, take the risk."

"Please?" She'd been concentrating on breathing, deep in, deep out, deep in.

"Don't withdraw your applications. All right? All right, Jane?" Jane lowered her head. Miss Bell took it for a nod. "Good!" she said. "I'm very pleased with your decision, Jane. Very pleased."

The cast and crew of *Noble Hearts*, as well as forty additional members of Woodward's Senior Drama Club, crowded into the Friedmans' finished basement. Not precisely crowded, because the huge room extended nearly the full length and width of the house and easily contained the seventy-five high school students. But most of them pressed against the bar, a long affair of dark polished wood, hoisting steins of cola, tossing peanuts into each other's open mouths, analyzing the great, unexpected laugh at the end of act one, and, in general, behaving as if they were at Sardi's waiting for the first reviews and not in a finished basement in the Cincinnati suburb of Amberley Village.

Unlike Vicki Luttrell, who was still flitting about in her ingenue costume, a tea gown and trailing hair ribbons, Jane had creamed off her makeup and changed from her lace-collared dowager dress into black slacks and a red sweater, an outfit chosen after a half-hour wardrobe analysis with Lynn at lunch that afternoon. There was no time between play and party to wash, set, and dry her hair, so she'd brushed out as much of the talcum powder as she could backstage, let her bangs flop back over her forehead, and tied her ponytail, which hung halfway down her back, with a red rubber band.

"Why don't you go right up to him?" Lynn demanded. "I don't understand you. You look fabulous. Everything is absolutely perfect, including your lipstick which you usually smear, so just do it."

"I can't."

"You can. Now where is he? Oh, at the end of the bar, talking to Teddy Collier and Mike Braun. See?"

"Oh, God, I can't go up to three boys." Jane was blushing so hard her scalp felt tight. Bobby's back was to her. His foot rested on the brass rail that ran along the bottom of the bar; his long legs were in tight jeans. He wore a plaid shirt with rolled-up sleeves and stood with the casual slouch of a rancher. His hair, worn longer than the conventional crew cut or flat top, was pale and straight, and he ran the fingers of his right hand through it from time to time, in comblike strokes. Jane chewed her thumbnail and watched the smoke from the cigarette he held in his left hand curl up and merge with the haze about the bar. "Lynn, look how he holds his cigarette. So masculine."

"Jane, you cannot stay in a corner all night. Now come on. You have to start sometime."

"Lynn, I really think I should wait till college. Please—"

"Hey," Bobby said later, "you are some dancer." The lights were out and most of the people left at the party were slow-dancing. "You really know how to follow."

Jane had difficulty swallowing. Bobby had pulled her so near and was holding her so tight she could barely breathe. Her ear pressed against his cheek, which was slightly damp from the heat of the room and the moment, and she was afraid if she pulled back her head to talk the ear would lose suction and make an embarrassing *thwack*. The elbow of the arm he encircled her with inscribed a small, slow arc on the top of her backside and she could not think of how to stop him because, technically, he wasn't doing anything wrong.

The hand of the arm with the arcing elbow began to move, squeezing at the hooks of her bra, but it did not slip under her sweater, and she couldn't think of a way to protest. The singer on the record had a satiny voice, and when he sang "'You're my angel girl in whi-ite/Your love lights up my heart,'" Bobby lifted her hand to his mouth and bit her palm.

"Bobby, please."

"It's all right."

"No. Really."

"Shhh. Don't pull away."

"Bobby, please." He began bending his knees and then standing straight, so his penis rubbed between her legs. She tried to arch her hips away and said, "Why don't we go upstairs and get some air?" She'd imagined slow-dancing with him so many times, but then there'd been a soft light, not blackness, and he'd lifted her chin with his index finger and, gently, warmly, kissed first her lower and then her upper lip. And he'd stroked her hair in these imaginings and confessed how he'd had a crush on her since the beginning of junior year. "Bobby!"

"Shhh!" He unhooked her bra and loosened his grip just enough to snake his other hand up the front of her sweater.

"No! Stop it."

"Come on." He grabbed her breast as if it had a will of its own and might roll away to escape him. "Oooh, wow."

"Stop it!" It was the closest a whisper can come to a scream. "I don't want to!"

"Yes, you do." He squeezed harder. "You started. Rubbing them up against me. Come on, you don't want everyone to hear you, do you? Just let me. *Relax*." He began to twirl her nipple between his thumb and forefinger.

70

The record, a long-playing one, ended after two more love songs. She just managed to slip her breasts into the cups of her bra before the lights flashed on. "O-kay," he said, "let's get out of here. We'll go for a ride or something. Hey! You don't just walk off on me."

"Let go of my hand."

"Come on. Get back here."

"No. Stop it. Leave me alone."

"What do you mean?" His grip crushed her fingers. "You're the one who came over to me. Come on. I'll get some three-two beer and we'll have a real blast. Did you hear me? Come *on*." He started to pull her.

Jane did not think; she reacted. She stabbed her nails into the damp flesh of his hand. "Ow!" he yelled. "For chrissake!" A few of the students turned.

"I'm sorry if I hurt you," Jane whispered. "I just don't want—"

Bobby Spurgeon lowered his voice to a muted snarl. "Who the hell do you think you are? You're the one who's been begging me for it all night."

"I wasn't. I'm sorry if you misinterpreted what I—"

"Misinterpreted? You know what you are? A loser. A prick-teasing loser."

As he stalked across the room, Jane put her hand to her mouth. Her lips were dry. She still had not been kissed.

"Do you *know* what time it is?" Dorothy demanded, fifteen minutes later. She clutched the front of her bathrobe, a heavy quilted Christmas present of years before, with both hands, even though it was tied tight at the waist. The shiny yellow of the robe's nylon reflected up into Dorothy's color-less face, and with the cords of her neck standing out in anger, she looked dead. Jane turned away, for the bottoms of Dorothy's eyes seemed pulled down by invisible hooks, displaying liquid redness. "You look at me! What time is it?"

"I don't know. One."

"It's one *thirty!*"

"Okay." Dorothy glared at her. "You didn't have to wait up, Mom."

"Is that all you have to say? Dear God in heaven, just look at you!"

Jane's answer was almost in a child's voice. "You said I should be home at a reasonable hour."

Dorothy moved in close to Jane, her leather slippers flopping against the backs of her heels, until the tips of her toes touched Jane's saddle shoes. "You don't even know, do you?" Her breath was damp and sour.

Jane leaned back her head. "Know what? I told you we were having the cast party after the play and the play wasn't over till ten thirty. Daddy or Rhodes could have told you that, Mom."

"'Mom,'" Dorothy repeated. "Well, *Daddy* and Rhodes went straight to bed when they got home. Now what were you doing for the"—she paused and clutched the bathrobe even tighter, as if Jane might rip it off—"for the three hours since ten thirty? Look at me when I'm talking to you."

Jane lowered her head and looked at Dorothy. The odor of rancid breath remained in the air. "I was at the party at Lynn's."

"And you expect me to believe that? I thought you were supposed to be such an accomplished actress."

"Oh, for God's sake. Call the Friedmans. They were there."

"I'll bet."

"What's wrong? I told you—"

"Did the *Friedmans* see you half undressed like that? Did they? *Hanging*."

Her coat was wide open. Jane inhaled and felt the dangerous freedom of an unhooked bra. "I just opened it up in the car going home. With Sissy Davies. I swear, Mom, it was cutting into me and—"

"Don't even bother. Do you honestly believe I don't know what goes on with teenagers? Don't you think that just by looking at you I can tell what kind of a party you were at? Go. Take a look at yourself. Your hair is a rat's nest. Your lipstick is completely worn off."

"I was eating. They had wieners and hamburgers."

"Don't you have any respect for my intelligence after all these years?"

"I swear I wasn't doing anything."

"You can't even look me straight in the eye, can you? Can you, Jane? And you know why? Because you know what you are."

"I've never stayed out this late before."

"Staying out's the least of it, and you know it. But it's starting now, isn't it?" Jane averted her head but Dorothy, who rarely touched her, grabbed her chin and held it inches from her face. "You sweet-talk your father into letting you stay out past your curfew, and then you strut in here—"

"I didn't strut, damn it!"

"Go ahead, curse some more. It'll all come out in the wash, the way I always knew it would. All that sweetness was as phony as a two-dollar bill. Don't you think I knew it? You're your mother's daughter, all right."

"What do you mean by that?"

Dorothy shrugged, as though she were repeating the most tired cliché. "A tramp."

"No! That's the biggest lie in the world, and I'm not going to listen to you."

"A tramp."

"You didn't even know her!"

"No, I never had the pleasure, but everyone who did knew what she was, and it was only a matter of time before it showed up. I saw it coming. You think I didn't see you parading around in front of Rhodes in your underwear

72

last August? Do you think I'm blind to what's going on? Do you? Well, let me tell you something. You're going to toe the mark for the rest of this year and then you're on your own. No UC for you, driving around with that spoiled-rotten Friedman girl and her crowd in their convertibles. If you want college, you'll get yourself a scholarship and go out of town and *out of this house*, where you can't ruin Rhodes's chances of a decent life. Do you think you're going to parade around in front of the Country Day boys in your slip, tramp? In your brassiere and underpants? Not so long as I have breath in me you won't."

After she heard Jane's bedroom door slam shut, Dorothy counted slowly to one hundred and then walked over to Richard's bed. He slept on his side, his knees drawn up to his chest. One hand was under the blanket; the other, next to his face, was curled into a limp fist, the knuckle of the thumb resting near his lower lip. His mouth hung open, and while he did not snore, he exhaled and sighed simultaneously. "Richard."

He did not drift up from sleep, but popped open his eyes and looked wakeful and frightened, as if he had been caught doing something nasty. "What is it?" Dorothy sat on the edge of his bed. He tried to raise himself, but she was sitting on the bulk of the blanket, so he only managed to turn on his back. He lay there, swaddled and immobile, staring up at his wife's heavy arm, her face unreadable in the nearly dark room. "Dorothy?" She clasped her hands in her lap. He could not understand what she wanted, but it was surely not him. She had allowed him into her bed a few times after their son's birth, but they had not had sexual relations for more than ten years. "Did someone die?"

"No. No one *died*. Listen to me. Do you know what time it is?" He could not tell if she saw him shake his head no. "It's the middle of the night," she continued, "and your daughter just strutted in a minute or two ago. Richard, listen to me, it was horrible. Her *bra* was open. Richard, I think she's done it."

"Done what?"

"Do I have to spell it out for you? She couldn't look me in the face."

"Did she say anything?"

"For pity's sake, Richard, do you think she'd admit it?"

"No, but—"

"I never told you this, but I caught her lounging against a wall, talking to Rhodes last summer, and she was half naked, with nothing on but her underwear, and you know what she looks like and Rhodes may have only been just a boy, but dear Lord, a boy is a boy and he was *staring* at her and I will not have that in my house. Not that and not with her staying out until practically daybreak and coming in that way, like a—a streetwalker." Again Richard tried

73

to sit, but the blanket held him. "You know what she's going to do, don't you?"

"What?"

"It's like cigarettes. One is never enough. It will be more and more and soon she'll be bringing boys to the back yard, the way Charlene Moffett did, and then they'll all be driving up and down past the house, honking the horn, sniffing the air for her. Calling on the phone till all hours. Look how the Moffetts can't hold their heads up since Charlene was caught with that gang of boys. And let me tell you something: you're not a factory foreman like Bill Moffett. If Mr. Hart gets wind of this, you'll be *finished*. Do you think he can afford an employee with a black cloud over his head, with a you-know-what for a daughter?"

"What should we do?"

"I told her. I told her she'd better watch her step every single minute of the day and night and that this was it."

"All right."

"No, listen to me. This is her last year here. She's out. On her own. If she doesn't get a full scholarship we'll have to help her along, but no living here, no University of Cincinnati for her, hanging around with that Lynn Friedman who has no restrictions whatsoever. Whatever *her* little heart desires she gets. Her parents indulge her every whim. What they say about them is true: they know the price of everything and the value of nothing and that's what's influencing your daughter, but since she can't get a convertible and she can't go to Florida she wants something more. Why not? Everything's up for grabs, so she's grabbing the boys any which way she can because they've never given her a second look. But she's not going to do it in Cincinnati, I can tell you that. Oh, no. Not her. Not where she could undermine everything we've ever worked for. She's going and that's final."

"Dorothy."

"What?"

"We can't afford out-of-town college *and* Country Day."

"We'll have to. Anyway, you're due for a raise. Overdue. You can speak to Mr. Tisman about it first thing Monday. Ask him to go right to Mr. Hart. Don't take no from *him* for an answer. Do you hear me, Richard?"

"Maybe Jane just stayed out late, you know, talking."

"Do you believe that?"

"I'll go speak to her."

"Now? No, it's too late. I know you've gone to talk to her late at night and I never minded, because she obviously needed more than I could give her and I hoped you could talk some sense into her. But let her stew in her own juices for a while. Let her know that what she is will not be tolerated in this house."

"All right. But, Dorothy, maybe if I—"

"Richard, listen to me. She's an actress, just like her mother was. She can be very, very convincing, but don't let her trick you. Promise me. You've always been soft where she's concerned, and it's brought us nothing but anguish. I want her out of the house for *all* our sakes. Promise me." She reached out and stroked his forehead. "Promise me, Richard."

Her father had not come to her room since before the night with Bobby Spurgeon, and nearly two weeks had gone by since then, so the past few nights she'd allowed herself to fall asleep before midnight instead of keeping vigil. Thus, it was not until he lifted her blanket that she knew he was back. "It's only me," he whispered. She twisted her arms in front of her in the manner of a child imitating an elephant's trunk, to hide as much of herself as she could. "I thought you could use some company." As he had before, he climbed into her bed and lay beside her under the covers. His pajamas smelled of Clorox. "It's all right. Don't get upset. I don't believe you were a bad girl. Do you want to tell me your side of the story?"

She managed to whisper back, "I didn't do anything."

"All right. Don't get yourself all upset now. If that's what you say, I'll believe you. No, don't turn over. Stay like that. Now let's have our talk. I know you really don't want to go east. It's true, so don't shake your head. Your guidance counselor called Mom. Didn't know that, did you? She said we should work on you, that you belong at one of those high-power colleges. Now don't be upset. Come on, let me see a big smile. That's my girl. Don't think I don't understand. No big fancy schools for you."

"Please. I think I want to go, Daddy. Smith or Pembroke, whichever gives more money."

"Oh, come on. I could talk to Mom. Wouldn't it be nice staying here, where you have so many nice friends? Have your own nice, comfortable room?"

"No, Daddy, really, I—" Suddenly her whole body began to shake.

"You're cold."

"No."

"So cold, my little Jane." He had never touched her before. He'd only lain beside her, talking for the first time about Sally, about her beautiful black eyes, her smile, her bewitching ways. But now, as Jane's legs convulsed in spasms, he hooked his leg over hers. "Poor Jane," he said, and he rubbed against her, much more slowly than Bobby Spurgeon had, but with the same intent. "Let me warm you up. Isn't this nice? Such a sweet girl you are. So pretty. I know you're not a bad girl." His hand ran back and forth along the curve from waist to hip. "Like your mother. Do you know that? You remind me so much of your mother. Just like Sally. Just like pretty little Sally." His

hand grazed her stomach and her breasts, then slid under the elastic waistband of her pajamas and rubbed her pubic hair.

"Oh, no."

"Shhh."

"Daddy, don't."

"I'll talk to Mom. You can stay here, go to UC. Wouldn't that be nice?
Hmmm? Isn't this nice? Loosen up a little bit. Come on. Feeling better?
Warmer?"

"I want to go east."

"No, you don't. No. Easy. Take it easy."

"I do. I really do."

"My girl. Doesn't this feel nice?"

"I'm going east. I am. Now stop. Please, stop—"

"Quiet."

"Daddy, don't. Please, I don't want you to—"

"Shhh. You'll wake the whole house."

"Don't!"

"Quiet, I said!"

"No!" She began to scream. "No! No! No!"

BOOK TWO

5

. . . we have our movie critic, Patricia Hynes. Pat?

Thank you, George. I'm standing here on Fifth Avenue in front of Nicholas and Jane Cobleigh's exclusive co-op apartment. But I could be standing in Connecticut, in front of the Cobleigh country home, or on the sunswept California coast in front of the Cobleighs' Santa Barbara estate. Where did it all begin? Well, for Jane Cobleigh, now fighting for her life in a London hospital, it began with a typical midwestern family. But her husband, superstar Nicholas Cobleigh, is used to the trappings of wealth. He was born into a family rich in privilege and tradition, an aristocratic . . .

—Excerpt from WABC Eyewitness News, New York

Despite his genteel name, Nicholas Cobleigh's grandfather, Henry Underwood Cobleigh, was of exceedingly humble extraction. Henry's father, Johnny, had sailed to America from England in 1868, ten years before Henry's birth, with twenty pounds of another man's money in his breeches. A warrant for his arrest on charges of robbery and manslaughter had been issued in Liverpool, and he obviously thought it politic to skip town. Johnny jumped ship at the first port in America—Newport, Rhode Island. But Newport was a real jog-trot city and Johnny wanted action. So he wandered north a bit until he found a spot congenial to his temperament.

Pawtucket, Rhode Island, was industrial, ugly, and brutal, its air yellow-gray from its own waste. Johnny felt at home. And soon, with the gold in his pocket combined with his entrepreneurial spirit and ham-size fists, he was owner of a thriving tavern in his adopted city.

The tavern was in the toughest part of Pawtucket, and with all the beatings, knifings, and shootings, most tavern owners in the area were, within a few months of opening for business, either disfigured or dead. But Johnny Cobleigh had no trouble with homicidal millworkers or schizophrenic whores. He was six feet tall, weighed three hundred and forty pounds, and had a veiny, triple-chinned face. He resembled a side of beef.

Henry's mother, born Henrietta Underwood, was the daughter of a millworker whose leg had been irreparably crushed by a falling bolt of ice-blue taffeta. Thus, her marriage to a man of commerce like Johnny Cobleigh was considered a big step up. Henrietta was vaguely pretty—with blue-black eyes like Concord grapes—and dull-witted. She was completely unremarkable except for her thinness. She was average height but weighed only eighty-three pounds. As a child she had been taunted with "Henrietta Underfed" and "Henri ett a stick and that's why she looks like one. Har, har."

But a happy marriage made up for a bleak girlhood. Unfortunately, her happiness was short-lived. On May 3, 1878, Henrietta bled to death giving birth to a strapping eight-pound son.

Johnny named the baby for his wife and gave him away to the Catholics, a decision not as unfeeling as it sounds, for Johnny could not raise an infant in Pawtucket, where its lullabies would be the wails of syphilitics and the retchings of drunks. Although he had been christened in the Church of England thirty-one years before, Johnny gave Henry to the Roman Catholic Sisters of Saint Helene in nearby Providence because, having visited four orphanages, he found that theirs was the only one that did not smell of feces.

Johnny probably did the right thing. Henry Underwood Cobleigh had garnered a couple of recessive genes from his parents and, as a result, was quite handsome and intelligent. The nuns doted on him as he grew, on his little-boy lisp when he breathed "Yeth, Thithter" to their commands, on his glittering blue-black eyes, on his quick mind, his modest mien, his cleanliness, his decorum. So when Johnny's Sunday visits ceased, when Henry was four (he was preoccupied with his second wife, another pretty, dim-witted girl, his growing business success—he now owned three taverns—and his new avocation, local Democratic politics), his boy scarcely seemed to miss him, surrounded as he was by twelve good, nurturing sisters.

Not that they were putty in Henry's hands. The nuns were demanding and strict, and by the time he was seventeen they had taught him Latin and history and geography and mathematics. He could recite *Macbeth* by heart. He was a budding Aquinist, having already read and reread all seven *quaestiones disputatae* and *Summa theologica*.

And his manners. He no longer lisped, but he still offered a courteous "Yes, Sister" to any request. The sisters were mostly from well-off Catholic families, and they reached back into their girlhoods for standards of excellence in male conduct. Henry, tall and slender and fair, grew into manhood with the bearing and courtliness of an upper-class Catholic gentleman.

What a charmer he was! His mind and his manners were nearly flawless. Unfortunately, his soul was another matter. Perhaps his father's rejection really did hurt; Henry may even have heard that Johnny and his second wife had had twin daughters. Or possibly twelve mothers are eleven too many. Love gushing from so many sources can seem a flood; the boy may have been so busy stemming it that he never comprehended that it was meant to flow back.

More than anything else he wanted to be a man of substance. He loved to imagine himself all decked out, looking natty. His light hair would be parted stylishly on the side and kept perfect with sweet bay rum hair tonic, the kind

Mr. O'Keefe, railroad man and trustee of the orphanage, wore. He'd own fifty pairs of silk hose and a homburg. And naturally he'd have a fine lady in a pink brocade gown with leg-of-mutton sleeves clinging to his arm, and she'd murmur, "Oh, Henry, you're the finest figure of a man in all of Rhode Island."

Henry never mentioned his reveries in the confessional. Nor did he allude to his liaison with Minnie Halloran, a middle-aged spinster who came to the orphanage to help with the laundry. For more than four years, he had relations with Minnie at least once a week, but his Saturday afternoon confessions were so bland that the priest, on hearing Henry's voice, slouched in his seat, believing he was about to hear the small sins of an amiable soul. "I cursed five times this week, Father," or "I committed the sin of avarice. I wanted the jackknife Billy Thomas's uncle from Maryland sent him, and . . ."

So it was just as well that the day Henry turned eighteen, he laughed off the sisters' prayers that he become a Jesuit. He simply said goodbye to twelve stunned nuns with as much warmth as if he were taking leave of a shopkeeper and strolled out of the orphanage, never, of course, to return. Then he paid a surprise visit to his father's tavern, where Johnny, now a Democratic ward leader, held court. Two hours later he emerged with enough money to pay for his college education—and then some. Naturally, he never saw his father again.

Henry Underwood Cobleigh became an Ivy League man. He entered Brown University in Providence as a member of the Class of '99 and emerged four years later with a bachelor of arts degree, a letter of acceptance from Harvard Law School, a mastery of poker and polo, and a passion for young high-born women which he managed to satisfy surprisingly often.

Louise Kendall was a beauty, the third of six gorgeous daughters of Roderick Kendall, a Baptist minister and descendant of one of Providence's oldest, most distinguished, and, alas, impoverished families. It mattered not a whit, however, that the Kendall girls had no dowry, for all were extraordinary-looking, with thick, wavy, strawberry-blond hair and the fine, angled bones of aristocrats. Gentlemen from as far away as Boston were so eager to call that Mary Kendall, Roderick's wife, actually had to allot parlor time to each of her daughters.

Louise was eighteen when one of her sister Abigail's beaux brought Henry Cobleigh to the Kendall house. As she confessed to Abby that night, it was simply love at first sight. He was handsome and regally straight-backed and so—Louise giggled with pleasure—and so elegantly dressed, with matching gray spats and gloves and a gray frock coat with a black velvet collar. "And did you hear him, with that deep, deep lawyer's voice, the way he said 'Good afternoon, Louise' to me?"

"Hush, Louise. You'll wake Mother."

"Do you think he finds me attractive, Abby? Do you think he'll be back tomorrow?"

He came back. Henry, worldly at twenty-five, was both a connoisseur and a realist. He was impressed with Louise's face and form, her flawless breeding. Such a woman would be an asset as a wife. And she was the best he could do; he had sought the hands of two wealthy young women, both wildly enamored of him, and their fathers had rejected his suit out of hand. "Who *are* you, young man? Who *are* you?" one had demanded. Despite his lofty social position, the Reverend Kendall could not afford to turn away a fine-looking, brilliantly educated, well-spoken man of substance, a man who was on his way to becoming a pillar of the bar of the city of Providence.

If Louise Kendall's marriage was not as advantageous as her sisters', it was certainly the most exciting. She adored her handsome husband, adored their jewel of a Georgian house on Benefit Street, adored birthdays, anniversaries, even the Fourth of July, for each holiday eve Henry would come home from his office and call from the entrance hall, "Where is my angel girl? Where is my lovely Louise?"

"Henry, is that you?" Louise would descend the stairs one graceful step at a time, lifting her skirts so she wouldn't trip and allowing her husband a peek at her shapely ankles. "How was your day?" she'd ask, standing on tiptoes to kiss his cheek, trying so hard to act demure and suppress her rising giggles of anticipation—she knew what the hand hidden behind his back was holding. But her eagerness was so great she couldn't stay still. She fussed with the curls on her forehead, patted the dainty embroidered bodice of her blouse. "Oh, Henry," she would finally blurt out. "Show me. Please show me. Pretty please."

"Show you what?" he'd demand in mock ignorance. But then he'd relent, perhaps wanting to see the glee that was hiding behind her dazzling blue eyes. "Oh, all right. Take it. It's for you." He'd move his hand from behind his back and hold a gift box high in the air. Louise would jump for it.

"Oh, pooh!" she'd exclaim after a few unsuccessful jumps. "You're too tall for me." Her soft mouth would form a sweet pout, and Henry would lower his hand and allow her to grab it. Ripping off the ribbon and the wrapping, squealing with delight, she'd find her holiday present, what her husband called "a little trinket"—a rope of pearls or a brooch, hair clip or ring, often set with sapphires to match her eyes.

There were those in Providence who wondered at the Cobleighs' elegance: For a man from nowhere and a girl with nothing, they lived, perhaps, too well. But most people didn't speculate because watching the Cobleighs was such fun. Henry (far handsomer than his movie star grandson would ever be), strolling along Waterman Street in a blazer and white trousers, doffing his boater to passersby, had the grace of nobility, and indeed the younger members of the bar referred to him as Prince Henry. But with affection.

And Louise, chin high, looked as majestic as a Gibson girl. Her already slender form was held in further check by a tight corset with long metal straps in front and hook fastenings in the back, and it molded her figure into a graceful S curve, her breasts thrust forward, her posterior pushed back. At church, at a lawn party, at a banquet, her costume was always the height of Edwardian fashion: elegant, chaste, and rich. Her body was a dressmaker's delight, a man's dream.

However, such indulgence is costly. Henry could not sustain such high style on his lawyer's income, and he had seen the last of his father's money disappear across a card table in his last month at law school. But Henry found a way.

He began his legal career in the offices of Broadhurst & Fenn, probably the most distinguished law firm in Providence—certainly the oldest. At such a venerable institution, life moves slowly. Papers are passed from attorney to attorney with languid courtesy. Old partners never die, but shuffle to high-backed chairs and dictate memoranda in the shaky voices of nonagenarians. Young men of twenty-four are given a small desk, a low salary, a modest amount of encouragement, and a fair degree of prestige. It was not sufficient for Henry Cobleigh.

After his first two weeks at Broadhurst & Fenn, Henry recognized that he would not be rich for another thirty years. And then not really rich. Lawyers might belong to the best clubs, smoke the best cigars, and run the country, but they didn't own yachts.

He brought some papers to Spencer Howell to sign. Mr. Howell was one of the firm's most important clients, fabulously rich, the owner of the second-biggest textile mill in New England, T. L. Howell & Sons.

"What's your name, son?" Mr. Howell was a decent man, one of the rocks upon which the First Baptist Church of Providence rested so securely. He always took time out for the little fellow.

"Henry Cobleigh, sir."

"Cobleigh. Cobleigh. Any relation to that—that Democrat in Pawtucket, Johnny Cobleigh?"

"No, sir." Mr. Howell nodded and picked up his pen to sign the contracts spread before him. "I've no family, Mr. Howell. I grew up in an orphanage." Mr. Howell, his eyes glistening with sympathy, put down his pen.

In November of 1902, a month after meeting Spencer Howell, Henry Cobleigh left Broadhurst & Fenn and became house counsel to T. L. Howell & Sons for three times the salary he had earned at the law firm. By the following year, he had so won the heart and mind of childless Mr. Howell that he was told that someday he would own a share of the company. Someday he would be truly rich.

It was not enough. The fabric alone for Louise's gowns, flawless copies of Worths and Paquins, cost hundreds of dollars. And there were the house, servants, a stock of good port, trips to Newport, Boston, Saratoga, the coast of Maine. Not only that: within half a year of his marriage, Henry realized he would occasionally need more sophisticated companionship than Louise could offer. But this sort of discreet, knowledgeable companion was too expensive for even a well-off young attorney to enjoy more than once every few weeks— unless he could augment his income.

Henry found a way. He was a superb lawyer, but certain matters were beyond his competence: patents on machinery developed for the Howell mills; lawsuits in other states in which T. L. Howell & Sons was a litigant; negotiating esoteric international contracts. But he had the responsibility of finding the right man to do the job. Thus, within weeks of joining the company, Henry had to refer a problem arising from the strictures of the Sherman Act to a law firm. He chose Hamden & Hamden because they were acknowledged as experts in the field, but also because Hamden & Hamden had offered to say thank-you for its two-thousand-dollar fee: Elias Hamden, Jr., the littlest Hamden, slipped Henry two crinkly hundred-dollar bills in an envelope over the table at the League Club.

That became Henry's standard; ten percent of the action was his. Other law firms were not as forthcoming as Hamden & Hamden. Broadhurst & Fenn needed prodding; Henry reminded old Mr. Pratt, a senior partner, that he had just been married, that keeping a wife was a costly business, that he often worried about keeping Louise happy. The next day, he received a wedding gift that came to slightly more than ten percent of Broadhurst & Fenn's fee. After a while, he grew more direct. "I'm not interested in negotiating, Willard. Ten percent. Take it or leave it. There are other lawyers in Providence, you know." Willard took it.

For nine years Henry Cobleigh flourished, fed by the avarice of the leaders of the bar of Providence. He was tapped for membership in the city's best club. He was too finicky now for prostitutes; his mistresses—the young widow of his father-in-law's assistant pastor and the alto soloist of the Rhode Island Negro Spiritual Chorus—were as beautiful and cultured as his wife. They too received trinkets. And Spencer Howell, increasingly dependent on Henry's canny judgment, sent him, first class, to New York and Charleston and finally to London as his personal representative; he returned with five Savile Row–tailored morning suits and a silver Queen Anne tea service, gifts from a grateful tool and dye maker who had received a Howell contract.

But it was not enough. As Louise pointed out with increasing frequency, she was the only Kendall girl whose husband did not own a summer house in Newport. "Truly, Henry," Louise said, "I'm not even thinking of one of those dreadful gaudy places. Just a sweet, modest cottage so we can summer near Abby and Irene. And Margaret. And Violet and Catherine. I know, I understand you don't *own* a business like their husbands do, and I don't want anything nearly so elaborate as they have. But something small and nice so I could be with my sisters. You would be so happy there too. Oh, you are my darling, darling man."

So Henry said to Reggie Blount, "I'm thinking about some real estate, Reggie."

"Oh?" Blount said. He was a partner in a firm that specialized in patent law, and he feared Henry was considering demanding more than his customary ten percent. "Any place in mind?"

"My wife likes Newport."

"That's rather dear, isn't it?"

"Yes. Now, Reggie, I've been thinking about our arrangement. My taking ten percent doesn't seem fair. Why don't you simply add an extra, say, three—no, four thousand to your regular bill—I approve all the bills—and turn the difference over to me after you get the company check."

"Really, Henry, we have already gone further than we care to."

"There are other patent attorneys in Providence, you know. Take it or leave it, Reggie."

That evening, Reggie Blount paid a call on Spencer Howell. Mr. Howell refused to believe what he heard, but Blount stood firm and stayed for more than an hour. As he left, Spencer Howell lowered his head into his hands and wept.

"But Mama, I don't *know* what happened." Louise Cobleigh's eyes were swollen and pink, but her final tear had trickled away the week before. Still, she rarely put aside her handkerchief. She twisted it until its fine lace edging hung in threads. "He came home that morning and slammed the door—I had just that moment come from the dressmaker's." She paused and patted her dry eyes. "I was having that pale yellow dimity shortened a little more. You know the one, Mother, with the flowered ribbon edging and those tiny—"

"Louise." The Reverend Kendall's voice rose from deep in his convex chest. It was a brilliant instrument, mellifluous and authoritative. "My dear child, we are in, alas, a most unfortunate position. Few of our connections are willing to, shall we say, disturb us with—well, evil tidings. Especially if the news concerns a member of the family. Therefore—"

"Would you like some tea, Louise?" her mother asked. "Or perhaps—"

"Mary, I was speaking."

"Oh, Roderick, forgive me. It was simply that she looks so terribly

85

peaked." Mary Kendall pressed her handkerchief hard against her eyes; she still had tears to shed for her daughter.

"Father, please. All I know is that he came home that morning and told me he was finished working for Mr. Howell. And he just stays at home, in the morning room with the door locked. He's gone out only a few times. And when I asked him what had happened, he told me it wasn't my concern. Then—" Louise lowered her golden head in shame. "Father, he went to my jewelry box. He took nearly everything he's ever given me, except for that pair of opal earrings I never really liked."

"Perhaps he has to sell them, Louise."

"Of course he has to sell them," she snapped.

"Louise!"

"I'm sorry. But he gave the cook her notice. And the tea service is gone and so are the candelabra. And when I mentioned—truly, it was barely more than a little whisper—that they were missing he told me—he said, 'Shut up, Louise.'"

"Dear Lord!"

"Mary!" The Reverend Kendall turned to his daughter. "Child, something serious is afoot. We must get to the bottom of it. From the little I've been allowed to know, it seems a most serious situation. Fraught with peril. But we will endure. We're Kendalls, aren't we?" The women nodded. "Don't you worry, my dear. Let me take charge." Roderick Kendall had a great Christian voice, strong and soft.

Louise loosened her grip on her handkerchief and leaned back in the divan. "Oh, thank you, Father. I feel better already."

"I must think." The Reverend Kendall pressed his index finger against his forehead, as if to accelerate the process. His voice, combined with pale, aristocratic features and eloquent gestures, made him a compelling figure. Few of his congregants recognized how profoundly superficial Roderick Kendall was. "It *might* be well, Louise, if you suggested to Henry that you—well, that you come home for a time. Stay with us until he—until his affairs—"

"Oh, Father, really? Could I?"

"Roderick. How would that look?"

"Hmmm."

Louise wiped her damp palms on the tissuey muslin of her dress. "Father, Mother. It's been so very difficult. I've tried to speak with him, to be a proper helpmate to him, but he just reviles me." Her mother reached across the divan and patted her arm. "I can't tell you how hard I've tried to comfort him. But he pushes me aside. He says it's all my fault. That all I ever think of is dresses and jewels, and you *know* that's not true. I'm not selfish. I never once asked for anything. Never once. He just loved to shower me with gifts. And now he says I'm greedy."

"My dear," Mary Kendall murmured.

"And Father. I was cut by Mrs. Welles."

"I know, dear. Your mother told me. I'm certain it won't happen again. Perhaps you'd be more comfortable here with us. But of course—"

"Oh, no, Father. I feel I'm only a burden right now. And the house is so big, and the maids are complaining they haven't been paid. It would be more economical. A help to Henry." Her mother gave her another pat. "Just one small thing."

"What is that?" Roderick Kendall asked. Even in the dusky light of the parlor, he could see his daughter's face redden. "Well, Louise?"

"It seems I am in the family way." She forced a small laugh which did not hide her mother's gasp.

"Oh, my!" Mary Kendall breathed. "Are you quite certain?"

"Yes. I was planning on telling Henry the news three weeks ago. I mean, we've waited all these years and never . . . But then he came home that morning and—well, you know the rest."

"When is the day?" her father asked delicately. Louise muttered an answer. "Speak up, Louise!"

"In about four months."

"You can't mean you're five—" Mary Kendall began.

"Mother, please. I just wanted it to be a big surprise to Henry, and I didn't want to tell you until Violet and Catherine had their babies because I knew you were worrying about them, and—and I didn't want to wear those ugly clothes and since I didn't get very—well, very large, I just thought wouldn't it be a grand surprise for everybody and remember I had asked you and father to dinner for that Saturday and—"

"'For better or worse,'" the Reverend Kendall began to intone.

"Father, no!"

"'For richer or poorer.' How often I've spoken those words and yet how tragically simple it is to put them aside when they do not suit our whims. On reflection, Louise dear, perhaps your mother and I were overzealous in our desire to spare you some of the harsh—well, harsh may be too strong a word—some of the unpleasant realities a wife must endure and transcend in the course of married life. Yes, it would be wrong for you to leave Henry at a time like this."

"But Father, he's so mean to me. He hates me. He blames me."

"Perhaps this—um, wonderful news will improve his spirits. Give him the faith and confidence he needs to—"

"No! Please, Father, he hit me. He did. I swear it's true. He slapped my face and called me a—"

"Louise, Louise. Hush. It must have been a moment of great anguish. I know Henry. I'm certain it will not happen again. All will be well."

James Kendall Cobleigh was born on a cold, clear April night in 1912 to parents who did not want him. It was a pity. He was a beautiful baby.

His mother looked upon him as the glue that stuck her forever in a repellent marriage. So she could not marvel at his eyes, more sparkling a blue than her own, or exclaim over the perfection of his tiny toenails, or wonder at the delightful chicken music of the peeps he emitted. She merely found his bowel movements unspeakably loathsome and the inch-square brown birthmark under his left ear a deformity. Most of the time she left him behind a closed door in the cradle her sister Abby had charitably handed down to her and only picked him up when his shrieks from hunger or pain from the festering rash from unchanged diapers were so loud as to break through her fog of silent fury.

Now and then she tried to be a good mother. Several times she began to crochet a little hat, but she could never get the brim right and finally laid aside the wool when it became matted from the perspiration on her hands. Twice she pulled a chair up to the cradle and began a lullaby, but it ended the same way both times: James, frightened by the noise in his dark, silent bedroom, let out whoops of fright, and Louise, terrified by the monster she'd created, fled.

His father seemed unable to love, and what little interest he had vanished when he realized the child was useless as a pawn in regaining money and status; Kendall hearts softened but did not melt at the sight of James. But however venal Henry was, he was not vicious. Now and then, hearing his boy's cries, Henry would lift the baby from the cradle, sponge him clean, and carry him outside into the blinding sunshine and cool, rosy spring air. He'd sit in a splintery wooden lawn chair with James on his lap, humming an unrecognizable melody, his finger mindlessly tracing the child's upturned nose and pink, pouty lips. (The melody was actually "Donny O," an Irish lullaby Sister Concordia had sung to him when he was an infant.) But these backyard outings were the exception. As a rule, baby James was left pretty much alone.

His parents had a lot to think about. On the day he fired Henry, Spencer Howell paid a call on the District Attorney, where he was told that commercial bribery was not a criminal offense in Rhode Island. He then visited Isaiah Bingham, president of the Bar Association, who, as luck would have it, was Mary Kendall's first cousin. Bingham soothed Mr. Howell. "Dastardly! But Spencer, if you file a complaint, if this is bruited about, you'll be—"

"Be what? Be what, dammit?"

"Laughed at, Spencer."

So Henry Cobleigh got off easy, although he left T. L. Howell & Sons at a bad time: he owed over ten thousand dollars to various jewelers, furriers, and antique dealers in Providence, and another twenty thousand to a stockbroker in Boston. He sold his wife's jewelry and the family silver to pay some of his debts.

At nine on a Saturday morning, a month before she was due to give birth, he locked Louise in a closet to muffle her hysterics and showed the house to prospective buyers. By noon he let her out because the house had been sold— for twenty percent less than he'd anticipated he would get.

But he needed the money. After two days of seeking employment, Henry Cobleigh recognized that he was a pariah. Not one lawyer he called on would receive him. At the League Club, the butler cold-shouldered him, and Winthrop Craig, a trustee of Brown University with whom he had gone whoring, sneezed directly into his face, about-faced, and marched off.

After he repaid the mortgage on the big brick house on Benefit Street, Henry had enough capital left to make two investments: a frame house with a termite-riddled front porch and a modest law office. Both were in Cranston, Rhode Island, a working-class town not far from Providence. Not that proximity was an issue; Louise's agonizing embarrassment over her slide down the social ladder made everyone feel uncomfortable; instead of keeping her head high and her upper lip stiff, she would visit her sisters and weep, or stroke the velvet skirts of their new dresses and say, "I will never have anything as pretty as this ever again." A year after she gave birth to James, she visited her father's church for Easter service and wept in humiliation that she hadn't even known about the change in hemlines. In the middle of her father's sermon, when Roderick's great, silky voice demanded, "If the son of God walked among us here in Providence, tell me, how would we greet him?" Louise's huge sob was his only response.

Nothing gave her pleasure. After James's birth, seeking solace or thrills or maybe revenge, she gave herself to any tradesman who happened into the house, but their wet kisses and the red blotches they left on her throat and breasts neither excited nor disgusted her, so she stopped after fifteen men in three months. But by that time word had buzzed through the neighborhood, and she had to put up not only with the snubs of the Cranston wives she herself had planned to snub but with the redundant propositions of the iceman and the palm tickles of the pharmacist returning her change as well.

Although the Kendalls had always been teetotalers, Louise began to drink a cordial or two before bedtime, to ease into sleep. She was an alcoholic. Within six months, she was rarely sober and usually sloppy; her once-glorious golden hair hung in greasy strings. She forgot about time and, indeed, her own presence. Often she did not remember to bathe for weeks, and her stench remained in a room after she left it. She hardly ever saw her family in Providence.

And Henry, booted out of the League Club for nonpayment of dues, too bloated from his own drinking and eating binges to fit into his Savile Row suits, broke and nearly broken, had long since left city life behind. Each morning, he would shuffle to his office; the soles of his handmade shoes quickly wore thin from his dragging feet. There, he'd smoke penny cigars and eat candy and occasionally handle the legal affairs of Cranston millhands and madams. Fat, pasty, and dispirited, he tried nevertheless to remain a lady's man, but only the loneliest ladies accepted his mechanical advances and the only one who behaved tenderly toward him was a severely retarded sixteen-year-old who had been manhandled and mistreated by many of the local merchants into whose shops she'd wander. He had no men friends, for he trusted no one. The only thing that drew him was a Catholic church he passed each day, a boxy brick building pitted by the acid air. Occasionally the doors would be open and Henry would gaze at a statue of the Blessed Mother shining ivory in candlelight. But the church itself was dark except for the small red light signaling the presence of the Eucharist, and Henry could never make himself walk inside.

So his son, James Kendall Cobleigh, grew up among the Italian-Americans of Cranston, a pale Protestant in a sea of Mediterranean Catholics. A good thing, too. They treated him with more love than his own parents did.

It was as if God said, *Do it over and this time get it right.* James seemed destined to follow in Henry's footsteps, but his path to the summit was cleaner and surer and straighter. As soon as the boy could walk, he toddled down the rotted front porch steps and into the kitchens of his neighbors, looking for attention. Dazzled by his blond light and filled with pity—the Cobleighs' neglect of their child was a Cranston scandal—the mothers pulled him up onto their laps and insinuated bits of meat and pasta between his lips. The fathers tousled his silky curls. As he grew, the boys taught him how to hold a bat and how to roast a potato over a trash fire in a vacant lot. Although he lacked the coordination to be a good athlete, his cheerful willingness to play any position and risk his limbs to win assured his being sought by team captains. When he turned twelve, the boys taught him how to look a girl up and down without ever lifting his eyelids. The girls took care of the rest.

Like his father, James lost his virginity at fourteen. But his partner was not a deranged middle-aged laundress; she was an eighteen-year-old Venus named Laura DiMarcantonio who followed him home from school and showed him what was what in the back of Mr. Paglia's milk wagon. "You know something, Jimmy honey? You look an awful lot like Conrad Nagel. I mean it. That's how handsome you are. And—ooh, you want to do it again so soon?" James met Laura every day after school for three months until the afternoon when Mrs. Delvecchia waylaid him and asked if he would mind helping her carry her rugs out to the back yard. Although not as beautiful as Laura, Mrs. Delvecchia was pretty enough, and she gave him wine and played her Caruso records for him after they made love. When James told Laura he couldn't meet her any more, she sobbed and grabbed his shirt and pleaded with him.

90

"Please, Jimmy. I need you. I love you. Listen, I don't have to see you every day. Just once in a while. Please. You're my sweetie, Jimmy."

"Laura," he said, smoothing back his pale hair which Mrs. Delvecchia had mussed, "you can't get blood from a stone." A month later, Laura married a cousin newly arrived from Calabria. Seven months later, she gave birth to a baby girl.

And about that time, he uttered those same words to a weeping Mrs. Delvecchia. Her role had been filled by his French teacher and, after her, by a succession of sweet, ripe neighborhood women and girls eager to succor the aloof but charming and beautiful son of the crazy Cobleighs.

But James was no run-of-the-mill Cranston Lothario. Even at fourteen, he never doubted that he could always get a girl. But he wanted more than sex and, unlike most high school students, he loved to work and he worked to his capacity—which was extraordinary.

When James was seventeen, Henry pointed to a chair opposite his in the living room, the stuffing peeking out through a hole worn in the seat. "Sit. Listen to me. I hear you're a smart kid."

"I'm doing fairly well."

"Don't use that phony crap talk with me. Now listen. You want to do something with your life? Get the hell out of stinkpot Cranston? Then you have to go to college. Don't look at me like that; I don't have any money. You speak to your grandfather. Don't wait till Christmas, because your mother will be there then and probably be falling face down into the cranberry sauce and he'll be upset. And have your hair cut before you see him."

James was accepted at Brown University after his grandmother, Mary Kendall, pleaded with three of her five illustrious sons-in-law to write letters of recommendation for him. His grandfather interceded on his behalf and arranged for a scholarship, one given to the families of Baptist clergymen. Perhaps the Kendalls felt they owed their daughter something. The Christmas before, she had lurched to the table, drunk, knocking a platter of sweet potato balls onto her sister Violet's lap. She looked shriveled and yellow and weak, and her family's disgust at her degradation was mingled with fear for her health. They were perceptive. Although she would not die for quite a time, her insides had gone bad; she would never be right again.

Although a member of the Ivy League, Brown, in the late twenties, was not known for its intellectual ferment. It had a reputation as a playboy school, and a good many of its students were the sons of movers and shakers who were not up to Harvard and Yale's standards—where students felt obliged to attend classes prepared and sober. Brown, even more than Princeton, was the fun school. But while his classmates were roaring "Here's to good old Brown, drink 'er down!," hanging out dormitory windows and vomiting the hooch they'd been drinking, or engaging in tapioca pudding fights in the dining halls, James was studying.

His professors, impressed with his intellect and engaged by his manner, welcomed James into their offices and homes. He learned to sip sherry and be seduced by faculty wives. He was gifted enough to receive straight A's in his field, American history; indeed, his perfect transcript was marred only with one B minus, which he received in English composition, where his instructor noted, *Writing graceless/content gd*.

Of course his education continued after class. From the moment he stepped into Hegeman Hall, James watched the well-born eating breakfast, mailing letters, showering, and shaving. He added these observations to those he had picked up at the occasional Christmas or Thanksgiving dinner at the Kendalls'—the use of fingerbowls, the correct method of buttering a roll— and before long seemed just another well-brought-up son of the upper class. Despite his lack of even an extra quarter to buy an ice-cream soda, his smooth ways, keen mind, and exceptional looks made him one of the most sought-after men on campus. In 1931, any Pembroke girl who could say "I've got a study date with Jimmy Cobleigh" was the envy of her dormitory. "Jimmy" generally got what he wanted, and, unlike Henry, he never had to hand out a single trinket. Most of the girls he dated were keen to get married, and many of them had wealthy fathers who would have been pleased to have a smart, handsome son-in-law join the family business. But James was not ready to marry and, with all his considerable courtesy, told Nan and Missy and April and Gwendolyn that the time wasn't quite right. Perhaps James sensed he could do better if he waited. Possibly he was waiting to fall in love.

Meanwhile, he followed in his father's path. He would be a lawyer. In September 1932, in his first year of Harvard Law School (where, unlike Henry's, his grades would be high enough to make *Law Review*), he sat on the yellow, sun-scorched grass on the banks of the Charles River, gazed into the water, and sighed.

"What is it, Jim?" his cousin asked. Three days before, on his first day at Harvard, James Kendall Cobleigh had met Bryan Kendall Devereaux, the son of his Aunt Catherine, when Bryan slipped on a pencil and fell in the aisle of the Constitutional Law lecture hall. James had helped him up and, after a courteous thank-you and a polite you're-welcome, the two young men had suddenly gaped with recognition. "Out with it, Cousin Jim. What's wrong?"

"Nothing much, Bryan."

"You can't be worried about your scholarship, can you?"

"No. I think I'll manage."

"Probably get a ninety-nine. I'll flunk, naturally. Don't know why I couldn't inherit the brains you have."

"Don't know why I couldn't inherit the money you have."

"Oh, Jim, not broke, are you?"

"Flat out."

"Can't I lend you—"

"Thanks, Bryan, no. I have a job this weekend. Tending bar at Wally's after the Princeton game."

"You need some fun in your life, Jim. All work and no play and all that rot."

"I play a little."

"Damned little. And it's not play, hitting the sheets with that cross-eyed Cliffie math major. It's work. You need some excitement, some glamour. Don't worry. Cousin Bryan will come up with something."

And that's how James met Winifred Tuttle, who would be his wife.

. . . Murray King, Nicholas Cobleigh's agent, said the actor did not wish to speak with the journalists who have gathered at the hospital, as he considers his wife's medical condition "a private matter." However, Mr. King did acknowledge that Mr. Cobleigh had consulted with Sir Anthony Bradley, the British neurosurgeon who . . .

—*Philadelphia Inquirer*

The Tuttles were not as rich as the Rockefellers or the Mellons, but they were rich enough. The first American Tuttle, Josiah, landed in Manhattan in 1701. He was a warmhearted seventeen-year-old illiterate who bore features that would recur in generations of Tuttles: a bush of carrot hair and a broad nose so coated with freckles it looked brown. Unlike so many young immigrants, Josiah was neither an indentured servant nor a ne'er-do-well. He had a job. He was a bootblack, a member of the household of Lord Cornbury, the British governor of New York.

However, the governor did not like boots. Like so many New Yorkers after him, the governor loved to dress up. He was particularly fond of low-cut gowns, so Josiah soon learned to be an expert corset-lacer and wig-dresser.

"Think I'm odd, Jo, fancying petticoats?"

"No, m'lord."

"Rot! I don't like liars, Jo. I am odd. Damned odd. But pretty too."

"Lovely, m'lord. Especially in blue."

When his lordship was kicked out of New York several years later, he did not forget his bootblack, the only member of his entourage who had seemed sincere in his compliments; before his ship sailed, he gave Josiah a single ruby earring.

Josiah, whose taste ran toward basic linsey-woolsey, sold the earring and with the proceeds bought five acres in what is now Greenwich Village. A year later he sold off two acres and with his profit purchased ten acres farther uptown. He continued in this fashion and, by 1740, owned a sizable chunk of Manhattan, dined with the Jays and the Van Cortlandts and the Livingstons, and had his own bootblack. When he succumbed to influenza in 1764, Josiah Tuttle was patriarch of one of New York's first families.

In 1792, Hosea Tuttle, Josiah's pale, frail, orange-haired great-grandson, liquidated about a fiftieth of the family's real estate holdings and founded the American Bank, thereby reinforcing the Tuttles' grip on the city and the nation's economic life for generations to come. He also made one other wise move: he married beneath him.

Hester Smithers was the daughter of the Tuttles' carriage driver and the family was aghast at Hosea's choice, but he would have none of the female Stuyvesants or Philipses or Marstons they paraded before him. Big, earthy Hester, who could take a full-grown financier, throw him to the floor of the carriage house, and ravish him, was the only woman Hosea Tuttle wanted.

So while other founding families intermarried into idiocy or lost fortunes through the machinations of incompetent heirs, the Tuttle line was invigorated by the three dynamic sons and four daughters Hester bore Hosea.

Like financial genius, exogamy became a recurring family trait. Every two or three generations, the eldest male Tuttle would discover the daughter of a stevedore or a blacksmith, drop to his knee, and propose. The family, whose memory of its plebeian heritage was faulty, would clutch its chest in horror or weep into its collective handkerchief each time a scion rejected the hands of eligible aristocratic ladies. But the process worked well and the family thrived. Throughout the eighteenth and nineteenth centuries, there were Tuttles not only in the marketplace but in universities and on pulpits. They wrote poetry and fought slavery. They were lawyers, surgeons, horse-breeders, suffragists. And while there was a compulsive gambler or two, an opium addict, and a pederast, by and large the Tuttles entered the twentieth century with a distinction nearly equal to their great wealth.

On March 24, 1900, thirty-year-old Samuel Tuttle, rushing home late for tea, knocked a young woman into the gutter right outside his parents' house on Washington Square. "Oh, my," he said. "I'm sorry. Terribly sorry. Really, you have no idea. Here, let me help you."

"Fine gentleman you are!" She sniffed, eyeing his well-cut Chesterfield, and struggled to rise, but her long skirts, logged with the filthy water from the gutter, held her down.

"Please, allow me." Samuel offered his hand, but she reached for it as though he were presenting her with a rotting fish. Because he was a homely, awkward man, he read her vexation as disgust. "Sorry," he murmured, letting his long, thin arm drop to his side.

"You're going to have me sit here in this puddle and catch my death of cold, mister? Fine fellow indeed. Don't just stand there turning red, help me up. It's not hand-holding I want from your sort anyway, you skinny boiled-out carrot." Samuel's skin flushed, clashing with the orange of his hair, but he offered his hand again and pulled her up. "Sorry," she said. "I mean, about going on. My father calls me Flap-jaw. Mister, I didn't mean to hurt your feelings, really I— Oh, my, look at my dress!"

She was tall, nearly as tall as he. Samuel bent over to inspect the side of

95

the thin wool skirt. "Oh, dear," he murmured. Besides the fetid water in the gutter, there had obviously been a mound of horse manure, for there was an unpleasant blotch of dark brown on the pale gray fabric. When he found his voice, Samuel said, "You must let me buy you a new dress." He delved into his trouser pocket and came up with a handful of coins. Like many rich men, he did not find it necessary to handle cash. "Really, I have money in my house. I would like to make amends."

"You couldn't make a cow moo, you big faker. Buy me a new dress, my Aunt Tilly." Collecting her sodden, stinking skirt, she took a step away, but only a step. The hem of her petticoat had drooped onto the ground, and she caught her foot in it and would have fallen if Samuel had not caught her around the waist. "All right, you can let me go now."

He was blushing so hard the tip of his nose and his ears tingled. The irises of her eyes were as black as her pupils and her hair was a color Samuel had never seen before, an auburn tinged with bronze. Her skin was soft ivory except for a spot of pink on each cheek. Until he felt her hands against his chest, pushing him away, he didn't realize he was still holding her. "Sorry." Then he noticed tears in her eyes. "I'm so terribly sorry. It was a good dress, wasn't it?"

"Oh, leave me alone." This time she managed to walk and he followed her across the street, into Washington Square Park. It was nearly sunset and the great stone arch glowed yellow. The grass was a green so dark it seemed blue and the air above it was gray mist, enveloping the park in a magic cloud that made the city beyond its borders seem sketchy and lifeless. Her skin was flawless in the enchanted light. "Stop looking at me like that! Go away. Away! What are you, a masher too? I'll call a policeman."

"If you'll just come back across the street with me. I live in that house over there. I could get money for a new dress and one of the maids could help you—um, brush yourself off."

"One of the maids!"

"But—" Samuel could not stop gaping at her. More beautiful women had been thrust into his arms once he came of age, the most delectable, dazzling temptations American society could offer its Crown Prince Tuttle. But, as all the smitten swear, this one was different. Her face was riveting; her bronze-brushed dark red hair demanded emerald eyes, yet her black eyes were right for her, as if she had insisted on them just to be contrary—or because she was too strong to assent to others' ideas of beauty. And she was strong. Samuel was not a particularly sexual man, but—behind his proper facade—he was an emotional one, and his soul swelled at her vigor. Unlike the pretties, whose voices were wispy because their corsets prevented their inhaling properly, whose personalities fell into two categories, languid or giggly, she was forth-right and vital. Vital enough to break through his upbringing and his inhibitions and, for the first time in his life, to turn Samuel Warren Van Dusen Tuttle into a passionate man.

"Do you think I'm batty enough to go with a stranger into a strange house?" But her tone was more gentle, as if she finally recognized he was not deranged.

"I have an idea!" Samuel found his voice shaking, and this shocked him. He was always in control. But now his palms were moist, and when he rubbed his hands together he realized they were as shaky as his voice. He swallowed and felt his large Adam's apple throb in his throat. "Just wait here one moment. I'll dash across the street and bring back my mother or one of my sisters. They'll vouch for me. And a maid. With a damp cloth. Or—" He charged across Washington Square North and barely missed being trampled to death by an onrushing carriage horse. But Samuel didn't notice because he had fallen in love.

It was not until a half hour later, as he sat across from the young woman in the front parlor of his parents' townhouse, gazing at her, at her gorgeous hair, at her flowerlike complexion blooming in the mauve dress borrowed from his sister Dora, that he learned, in answer to his mother's polite interrogation, that her father worked in a grocery store on Sixth Avenue and her mother was dead and she had an older brother who was a fireman and a younger brother in the merchant marine and no sisters and she was twenty-one years old and her name was Mary Sue Stanley and all her friends called her Maisie.

During the third week of their honeymoon, Samuel reached across the tiny table of a Parisian café and stroked Maisie's hand. "Do you still think I look like a carrot?" he asked.

"Yes. But a splendid carrot, Samuel." Already she was gleaning adjectives from his vocabulary and planting them in hers: "splendid" and "solid" and "nice." Sacre Coeur was "a splendid church, really splendid, don't you think, Maisie?" and she had replied, "Quite splendid, Samuel dear."

Maisie was not merely mimicking her husband's upper-class vocabulary; she was absorbing it, becoming an aristocrat herself, and very quickly. Maisie Stanley Tuttle had class. She was perceptive, assertive, humorous, and kind, and although she had been born in a railroad flat in lower Manhattan, her beauty and high spirits were patrician. Had she not been knocked into a pile of manure by Samuel Tuttle and raised up, she would have made her own way in the world.

By the fourth year of their marriage, the Tuttles had three sons, a house on Fifth Avenue, a farm in Fairfield County, Connecticut (which their grandson, Nicholas Cobleigh, would inherit), a hundred-acre camp on Taylor Lake in the Adirondacks, and a flat in Mayfair.

They were as happy as they deserved to be. Samuel was as dedicated to the Oratorio Society and Washington Heights Home for Cripples as he was to his own financial interests. In 1906, Maisie founded and funded the Greene Street Settlement House, built two blocks from the railroad flat where she was born. Unlike the new oil and copper and sugar kings, the Tuttles were confident enough to put their money where it wouldn't be noticed.

In 1915, fifteen years after they were married, Maisie, even more startlingly beautiful than she had been as a young woman, with the grace and bearing of the New York society leader she had become, knocked on her husband's bedroom door. "May I come in, Samuel?"

"Of course, my dear." As he closed the door, she put her soft, slender arms around his neck and kissed him on the mouth. "Oh, Maisie."

And that night their fourth child, Winifred Lucinda Theodosia Tuttle, was conceived.

7

. . . But the editor, Elizabeth Rose, said "no matter what," *Harper's Ba-zaar* planned to run the three-page weekend wear spread Jane Cobleigh posed for two weeks ago.

—*Women's Wear Daily*

Tall like her father, with kinky orange-red Tuttle hair and a sinewy body, seventeen-year-old Winifred was most comfortable being sloppy and active and eccentric, wearing her brothers' sweaters and riding their big Arabian stallions at the farm, announcing her admiration for the New Deal to a shocked Thanksgiving table.

Her mother's world—first nights and dress fittings—did not merely bore Win, it frightened her. On a tennis court she was all fluid grace, but on a dance floor, oafish, and she knew it. At seven or eight, she sweated through Miss Adeline King Robinson's Wednesdays at the Plaza until her pink crepe de chine hung like a mildewed curtain. The little boys in their blue serge suits would bow, put their hand on her back, and make a face: *ick*. In her early teens, as a pre-subdeb at Middle Holidays, she observed even the least desirable boys, the ones afflicted with juicy speech defects and the rosy pustules of perpetual acne, tighten their mouths with resignation when it was their turn to be her partner. Sipping punch, she heard herself called "Old Horse Face" and overheard chaperones: "Look at that red hair! At least she's living proof that Maisie didn't have a lover." "But my dear, even Samuel is better looking. Her hair is positively Nee-gro in texture."

"I won't!" said Win.

"You will!" said Maisie.

"Perhaps something less elaborate than Newport," Samuel interposed. "My sisters came out at home."

"At home." Maisie sniffed. "Three violins behind a potted palm and white wine punch. Is that what you want for your only daughter's debut, Samuel?"

"It's perfectly nice, Maisie, really. Perfectly acceptable. Winifred isn't the sort of girl who would enjoy five hundred people and a twenty-piece orchestra."

"Perhaps I should hold my tongue. You must know best. After all, you're a Tuttle born and bred and I'm just some girl you picked up from the gutter."

"Oh, stop that, Maisie. You know you're as fine as they come."

"Then please trust my judgment. Frankly, Samuel, Winifred's idea of a grand party is three horses and a clean pair of boots."

"Mama, you make me sound so terrible. I'm not being unreasonable. I'd be willing—"

"This matter is not open to negotiation, Winifred. You must be presented, and since your brother and Polly have so graciously offered Breezy Point, one of the architectural triumphs of Rhode Island—"

"Mama, no one will want to go. Please, it will be awful! All the boys hate me, and the only reason they'll be decent is because of—you know what I mean, of who we are, and they'll laugh behind my back and say the only reason we're in Newport is that no one in New York will have me—"

"Winifred! Stop that!"

"It's true, Papa. And that you had to pay for a big husband hunt, and—"

"Win, baby." Maisie reached over and smoothed the curly red hair of her daughter's eyebrows. "You are a lovely girl. Marvelous looking. Tall and athletic and fine and elegant."

"I'm not elegant."

"You will be, Winifred. You'll see."

The Great Depression put a crimp in the coming-out business, but as Win's brother Jeremiah observed, "Gets rid of the marginals, you know. All those Ford dealers from West Orange sneaking their daughters into Foxcroft. Down, up, down in one generation, and good riddance." Actually, Jeremiah was the stupidest Tuttle in five generations and his wife, the former Penelope (Polly) Czeki, was the daughter of such a marginal man; her father had made a fortune in his native Pittsburgh manufacturing industrial septic tanks and, in 1930, had bought Breezy Point, a Newport mansion owned by a Boston banker who had gone bankrupt. Mr. Czeki added tennis courts, stables, and a swimming pool overlooking Rhode Island Sound and bought a yacht, *La Reine de Pittsburgh*. Then he turned purple and died of coronary insufficiency, leaving his entire estate to Polly. Jeremiah, who loved tennis and riding and swimming and yachting and hated working, married her a year later despite Maisie and Samuel's disapproval.

But Polly was at least twice as smart as her husband and hadn't married a Tuttle for nothing. She wanted to be valued by the people who were merely polite to her. So, recognizing the social leverage of a first-class debut, she cultivated her in-laws until, exhausted by her sweet, relentless devotion, they accepted her—and her offer of an unforgettable evening at Breezy Point for Win.

Bryan Kendall Devereaux two-stepped into his cousin's room at Harvard

Law School cradling an imaginary girl in his arms. "'I'm puttin' on m' white tie,'" he sang. "Jim, old pip, old poop, put on your dancing shoes. I've got you on the Boston list and we're going to a fab party. Totally top drawer."

"Hmm?" James Kendall Cobleigh was sprawled on his narrow dormitory bed, naked in the heat of Indian summer. A casebook lay open, face down, covering his genitals; he rested the constitutional law text he had been reading on his chest. "Hello, Bry. How are you?"

"How am I? Ecstatic. Mad with joy at my brilliance. My God, J.C., you are fortunate to have gotten yourself related to me. At this late date I have pulled the strings of some of the toughest, stringiest matrons in Boston and gotten you on the list. *The* list, Jim, for Christ's sake. That which will get you invited to the best parties of the season, and already we've been asked to the best. Only the upper-upper of the Boston and New York lists, which is too bad because the girl is strictly lower-lower in the face and figure and personality categories, but at least we'll get to see Breezy Point in Newport and she may have a friend or two or fifty who isn't completely creepy and—for God's sake, cover yourself up better, Cousin Jim. Just because I have to put up with your company doesn't mean I have to go eyeball to—whatever—with your pecker every time I walk in the room. Now listen, it's a major bash for Somebody Tuttle—I hear there are prettier prunes—so you will report to my suite at eight on the nose on Saturday, full dress."

"Don't these people ever worry what the rest of the country thinks of them? I mean, people are standing on bread lines. They can't get jobs."

"J.C., don't be tedious. All the proles pick up the newspaper and positively devour the society pages. You know that. They want debutantes in unspeakably expensive gowns and French champagne. The bread lines are for bread and we provide the circuses. Really, it's to everyone's advantage. So get out your good duds and—"

"I don't have tails, Bryan. I don't even have black tie. I could manage a navy and red stripe, but—"

"Well, go out and buy tails. Oh, damn. I forgot you're the poor relation. And you won't fit into anything I have, with your flat ass. Can you rent one? Look, I can lend you—"

"Maybe I'd better not go, Bry. I've never been to one of these things, and I'd probably just stand in the corner looking like a waiter from the caterer."

"Of course you're going. The Tuttles are crème de la crème of New York society, and Breezy Point is supposed to be totally sublime even though Pushy Polly—the sister-in-law of the debbie, the one who really owns the joint—is très, très nouveau. And there will probably be hundreds of gorgeous, rich, curvaceous girls just dying to surrender their virtue to an older man from Harvard Law School. Jim, with your looks you'll get so many offers you won't have to put on your pants for the next five years. I won't take

101

no for an answer. White tie, eight o'clock, and we'll have a few thousand drinks and then off to Newport. There's no reason *not* to go. You've got the bluest blood in Rhode Island swimming around your veins. Well, a little diluted, but blue enough. Come on, J.C. Let yourself live."

At ten at night, six footmen dressed in the blue and gray livery of Breezy Point stood before its Ionic facade and began welcoming the first of five hundred guests to the "small dance" Polly Tuttle had arranged. From inside the ballroom, strains of "What's a Girl to Do?" and "Boom-Diddy-Boom," played by Cappy Caplin and his twenty-two-piece orchestra, spilled out and flowed over the drive and across the ten-acre lawn.

A warm, humid breeze blew in off the Sound and into the house, and as she stood receiving beside Maisie, before a trellis heavy with pink flowers and white ribbons, in the massive pink marble foyer, Win felt her hair—which the maid, supervised by her mother, had ironed straight a half hour before—kinking up, rising from where it had lain softly on her shoulders into a red arc around her face, like a cartoon character who's received a violent electric shock.

There was something about Newport, something in the air that made everyone else glow, that was poison for her, Win thought. She had never looked so putrid before. Her freckles probably looked like disfiguring blotches; the boys would titter that her shoulder, bare in her Grecian-cut gown, looked like a leopard's skin. Her hair, always a problem, had never been this hideous; she had gone riding in the rain, played tennis on the muggiest August mornings, fished in mountain streams so obscured by dawn fog that she couldn't see where her line entered the water, and her hair had been uncontrollable but bright, right for her. And her skin had felt as soft as a butterfly's wing.

"Stop fussing with your hair," Maisie finally whispered when the relentless waves of guests subsided for an instant.

"But, Mama, it's—"

"Winifred, darling," Maisie crooned, "you remember Mrs. Peterson, don't you?"

The room felt hellishly hot. Win could not understand why all the guests were not red-faced and dripping. She extended her arm, steaming inside its long white glove, and shook hands. "Of course. How do you do, Mrs. Peterson."

"And Mr. Peterson!" Maisie, welcoming the three hundred and fiftieth guest, was as cool and gracious as she had been two hours before, when the first arrived. An instant later, still smiling, she turned to Winifred and murmured, "Stop behaving like a neurasthenic, darling. You look absolutely lovely." And then louder, "How do you do."

"Bryan Devereaux, Mrs. Tuttle. From Providence. And my cousin, James Cobleigh."

Cappy Caplin crooned "'Conchita, give back my heart'" and James peered down at Ginny's mahogany hair. Or maybe it was Valerie. He had danced with six or seven girls who were—according to Bryan—the pick of the year's crop of debutantes, and though each was supposed to be a beauty in her own right, he could not tell them apart. "'Conchita, with your wicked eyes,'" Cappy sang, and Ginny or Valerie rubbed against him, trying to locate his erection with her pelvis. "'With your breathless sighs.'" But despite the permeating, seductive scent of hundreds of thousands of flowers, the sexual wail of the brass, the moan of the reeds, the high exhalation of the strings that filled Breezy Point, these eighteen-year-olds did not arouse James; good bones and knowing how to eat snails were no longer enough to interest him. He had been through several post-pubescent socialites during his first two years of college and found they had an annoying tendency to chat during lovemaking. And these debutantes, with their white gowns and white shoes and gleaming hair, seemed as frivolous and asexual as the others he had known. They looked like nurses on the evening shift of some terribly formal hospital.

"Were you at Harvard as an undergrad?" asked Ginny/Valerie.

"No. Brown."

"Oh, a Brown man. You must be sublimely wicked."

He remembered now. Her name was Philippa. "That's me. Evil personified."

She giggled and tossed back her head the way all the debutantes seemed to be tossing heads, with a fast uplift of the chin so her glossy hair flipped and reflected the ballroom light. So did her platinum and diamond bracelet. It could bring enough money to feed a family of four for a year or to put him through law school. Slowly and suggestively, she ran her tongue over her lower lip. James sighed. "Do you do terrible things to poor innocent girls?" She rubbed her breasts against his chest, and his starched shirtfront made a scratchy retort.

Fortunately, Cappy and the trumpets joined for a mighty "'Conchita, I'm yours!'" and James stepped back and bowed in the slightly graceful, slightly mocking way he had observed the other young men bowing.

"Excuse me for just a minute, Philippa."

"Philippa? I'm Priscilla."

"Having a time of it, J.C.?" Bryan Devereaux demanded. His moon face was flushed and glazed with perspiration. "Whew! That little sugarpuss, that Rosemary, loves to be whirled around, makes her lose her center of gravity or

103

her virtue or some such thing. I'll let you know. She has cousins in Boston and what d'you know, next weekend she just happens to be visiting them, so I'll whirl her around a few more times and see what develops. And what was developing with you and Prissy McGuiness? Hmmm? I hear little Prissy's not so prissy. In fact, I hear Daddy McGuiness may have to endow the McGuiness Home for Embarrassingly Wayward Girls—and fast. Little Pris has worked her way up Park and Fifth and there's nothing left but Central Park West. I mean, the girl's a human welcome mat. But r-i-c-h, J.C. Daddy's daddy's daddy got a little nibble of Standard Oil, and the rest is history. Oh, sweet bloody Christ, will you look at that!"

"What?"

"There. Just past the French doors, Titless Tuttle's getting twirled to death by that gorilla from Dartmouth, what's his name—Paget Trent. He's really giving her the business."

Paget Trent had buck teeth, a prominent jaw, tiny eyes, and an unusually low hairline, and actually looked more like a Neanderthal than a gorilla. He had known Win since dancing class days—where he had once dipped his hand into the punch bowl, withdrawn a few floating strawberries, and given Win a friendly slap on the back, rubbing the cold, mushy berries into her dress. Now, perhaps egged on by his friends, he was twirling her around faster and faster and faster. He spun her into smaller and smaller circles until they were whirling in one fixed spot.

"Paget, please," Win breathed.

"Giving up?" he demanded and spun her even faster.

Win did not believe he would be deliberately cruel. He was just being silly. She smiled at him and fixed her eyes on the flat bridge of his nose. He spun faster still, and she prayed that focusing would steady her, like staring at the horizon on a rough sea.

"Paget." They were whirling like a top gone wild and she was dizzy. And then sick. Oh, Lord, if the music stopped and he didn't wind down slowly she would fall on her face and—it was inevitable—throw up. At her own ball.

Bryan twisted his mouth into a sneer. "Jesus Benevolent Christ, would you just look at her? Smiling with those big teeth. All she needs is a bit and a harness. You know what she's saying to Paget Trent right now? 'Neigh.' I mean really, she—"

"She's not so bad," James said. She was tall, and while her broad shoulders bulged beyond the chiffon drape of her white gown, and her bright red hair seemed too garish for this sleek crowd, he found her the classiest person in the room. She was not meant for elegant evenings, but he bet she glowed in sunlight: horsey and homely, long-limbed, wide-striding, upper class. James Kendall Cobleigh knew what Winifred Tuttle was. Top drawer.

"Not bad? Are you kidding? J.C., I've ridden prettier mares. Really."

104

James said nothing, but he heard the music slow a little, and he edged away from his cousin. "Pinch her ass, J.C.," Bryan continued, louder. "She'll whinny."

She didn't belong in this expanse of marble and gilt and crystal. It may have been the best American money could buy, but around her it looked merely gaudy. James rubbed his hand over his clean-shaven cheek. He felt silly, intrigued by the girl the stag line was laughing about—a plain, awkward girl who looked ready to bawl on the happiest night of her life, a girl who, with luck and her father's money, would wind up marrying someone socially acceptable, a timid academic or a drunken yachtsman who would never make love to her properly. Paget Trent spun her even faster and bent over her, so her back arched and her head hung backward.

Clean. She looked so clean and healthy and strong. James stared at her. He thought if he smoothed back that crazy red hair and sniffed the dark little pocket under her earlobe, there wouldn't be the dank, suspicious odor so many girls had. And no misleading perfume, no jasmine or musk. And the rest of her would be clean too. And strong. He ran a practiced check of her body. Her legs were long, her breasts small but high and firm. And a wonderful tight backside. He began to smile.

From where he had been left, Bryan called to him. "J.C.?" James moved on.

A clarinet moaned, but it was quickly countered with a happy *Ta-da!* The song ended. Paget Trent yanked his drippy right hand out of its clasp with hers; a second later, he dropped his left and grinned. Winifred felt herself swaying, first to one foot, then the other. Falling. She was falling and everyone was watching and she was going to go flat on her face and break her nose and the blood would gush all over her gown and her parents would rush across the ballroom floor to her—and now she was really falling. Backward. There was nothing she could do, and—

And James Cobleigh caught her in his arms and said, "Gotcha!"

It was as if the night were a wonderful movie, a sparkling romantic comedy, and, by magic, she had been given the starring role. And what made the magic even more wondrous was that her leading man was the handsomest man in the world and so nice and so—he was taken with her. And he wasn't putting on. Everyone around them could see that. All her friends from her earliest days at Miss Chapin's were giving them the Look; they knew something important was taking place.

James Cobleigh had magnificent eyes and they were probing her as though she were the most desirable woman in the world. But the most desirable woman in the world wouldn't blush bright red when she gazed back into glorious blue eyes. Win swallowed and lowered her head.

At one in the morning the footmen had opened the doors to the dining room and Win and James, followed by five hundred formally clad guests, trooped in for the traditional scrambled eggs and champagne supper. "My sister-in-law did all this," Win mumbled, as she pushed away the long-stemmed white rose that dipped into her eggs. She was trying to sound casual, but she could feel James's breath on her bare shoulder. "The flowers, I mean. She insisted, so my mother let her."

For reasons known best to herself, Polly had decided the theme for the ball would be "A Springtime Country Garden" and had—in September—managed to unearth enough apple blossoms and Canterbury bells and roses and candytuft to make Breezy Point a vernal paradise. Her centerpieces were so lavish, however, that a guest could barely lift a knife to butter a roll without knocking a freesia blossom or snapdragon leaf onto the plate. "She wanted me to wear a wreath of sweetheart roses—like a tiara. But my mother said that would be gilding the lily. Or gilding the petunia, or some such thing." Win felt the warmth of James's leg beside hers. It wasn't pressing hers in any sort of obvious way, but his easy masculinity made her simultaneously tense and limpid. Her mouth went dry. Again, she tried to make conversation. She glanced toward the man-sized Chinese urns, overflowing with ostrich fern and rose and white larkspur, that stood before the tapestried walls of the dining room. "I didn't think there would be quite so many flowers. I've been worried all evening that someone who's got bad hay fever would start choking, and no one would notice because the orchestra was playing away. Dear, that sounds dreadful, as though I'm not grateful to my brother and sister-in-law and Mama and Papa for—" James took the fork from Win's hand and placed it on her plate. Then he brought her hand to his lips and kissed the tips of her fingers and licked her thumb. "Oh, Lord," she whispered.

They found out about him fast. Maisie said he hadn't a sou and Polly said his mother was a rotten apple from a good tree—a drunk—and Samuel said his father was a lawyer with a filthy reputation. And Jeremiah said James was ambitious. Win said James had told her all that the second time he saw her, the morning after her debut, and so what?

And furthermore, she wasn't going to spend the rest of the season going to balls in New York and then sail off to France and England for months and months. She wanted to enroll immediately at Wheelock or whatever college in Boston would accept her, and she was going to see James whenever she could and that was that.

Maisie said she was behaving like a lunatic and Samuel said he was shocked—shocked—at her willful behavior, and Polly said James was a Svengali, and Jeremiah said men like James Cobleigh were interested in one thing only. Win wasn't sure if he meant her money or her virginity, and it made her cry. But it did not make her relent.

"Please, James."
"No, Win."
"Oh, God. Please."
"No."

A year after they met, they lay hidden in the unmown grass a hundred feet behind Court Six of the Boston Racquet Club, where she had just beaten him in two out of three sets. "James, I love you so much and it will be all right, really it will, and we'll be married a year from August and no one will ever know and I want to so much." James trailed a long blade of grass along Win's thighs and over her stomach. "Please." Her shorts and underpants had been thrown aside. A sneaker, laces open, tongue askew, lay on top of her racquet. James pushed her blouse and brassiere up until they formed a tangled rope around her throat. He caressed her breasts with the blade of grass. His other hand clamped over her mouth to muffle her groans.

"Soon, Win," he murmured. "Just as soon as we're married."

Samuel Tuttle's study was the only plain room in the house. He had resisted all Maisie's attempts to panel it in mahogany or drape it in brocade or stuff it with leather. She had sniffed that his need for a monastery was so strong it was a shame he hadn't been born a Roman, and far be it from her to interfere with his monkish tastes, and added that if he insisted upon a crucifix for the bare wall she'd be happy to find one for him. But after that discussion, she had never entered the room, claiming its lingering odor of cigars gave her a headache. Perhaps she took her husband's insistence on simplicity as a rebuke: he, a Tuttle by birth, needed no external ornamentation to remind him of his status.

James, too, seated in a chair opposite the desk, felt uneasy in the study. Its white-painted walls and unembellished oak desk and straight-backed chairs would please only austere spirits. That Samuel Tuttle came to this room to relax was intimidating. "Well, Mr. Tuttle," James began. Samuel laid his cigar on a glass ashtray, met James's glance, and held it. Suddenly, James realized Samuel knew precisely the effect this spare, drafty room would have. He had chosen it over the opulent library, the warm, inviting music room. He had chosen it to put James at a disadvantage. James sat as far back as he could in the stiff chair, crossed his legs, and smiled. "Mr. Tuttle, you know why I am here. I want to marry Winifred. I would like your blessing." He peered into Samuel's pale, watery eyes. "Or at least your consent."

"You have that."

"Thank you, sir."

"Thank Winifred. Her protests exhausted her mother last Christmas. It took several months longer, but finally I had to admit that I was too weary to fight. If I live long enough I shall doubtless regret my weakness. You will not be a good husband to her."

"I will be, Mr. Tuttle. I am not an opportunist. I love Winifred very much. And I'll be able to take care of her without . . . I neither expect nor seek your help."

"That is fortunate, Mr. Cobleigh, because you will not get it. Winifred has some money from her grandparents and an aunt—as I expect you know—and I have no control over that. But she will get no more from me. Nor will you." James had observed Winifred long enough to recognize the Tuttle flush, the scarlet blush of passionate feeling.

"I don't expect anything, Mr. Tuttle."

"No gifts, Mr. Cobleigh. No assistance. No letters of introduction to New York law firms."

"That won't be necessary. I have a position already."

"Oh." The "May I ask with whom?" remained unspoken, but James heard it.

"I will be an associate with Ivers and Hood."

"Ivers and Hood."

"Yes."

Samuel lifted his cigar, then put it down again. "When were you offered this position, if I may ask?"

"In February. Two of their partners had been interviewing third-year students up at Harvard in January. A few weeks later they asked me to come down and speak with some of the others."

"In February. I see. Four months ago. Winifred must have forgotten to mention it to me. Perhaps she has been preoccupied. By the way, did Ivers and Hood happen to know of your connection with my daughter? Did they, Mr. Cobleigh?"

"No. They did not, Mr. Tuttle."

"I see." He lifted his cigar and relit it. "Ivers and Hood represents some of my interests. Did you know that?"

"No, sir."

"They're a very respectable law firm, Mr. Cobleigh."

"I'm a respectable lawyer, Mr. Tuttle. I think I have a chance of doing well there. However, if you would feel more comfortable, I suppose—well, I've had other offers."

"Here in New York?"

"Here in New York. And also in Boston."

"Winifred's mother would like her to live in New York."

"Then we shall, Mr. Tuttle."

"You may as well stay with Ivers and Hood. They're solid."

"Yes, sir."

Samuel exhaled a small cloud of smoke. "Do you prefer brandy or port, Mr. Cobleigh?"

In September 1938, Winifred Tuttle answered truly "I will" when asked, "Wilt thou obey him and serve him, love, honor, and keep him, in sickness and in health?" A few moments later, as Mrs. James Cobleigh, floating in a sweet cloud of white tulle, lilies of the valley, and orchids, she walked up the aisle of the Park Avenue Congregational Church on her husband's arm, gazing into his soft blue eyes, not even seeing the three hundred beaming faces in the pews.

Outside the white stone church, the society reporter from the *Times*, glimpsing Win's dazzled face emerging into the gray late afternoon light, murmured "Love match" to the society reporter from the *Herald Tribune*, who replied, "You're half correct." The *Times* reporter shook her head. "No. He looks genuinely happy." And the man from the *Trib* said, "Wouldn't you be if you were marrying a Tuttle?" and she said, "I suppose, but I'd be happier if I were marrying *him*. He's divine. Those shoulders and those eyes and"— she glanced at her notes—"magna cum laude from Brown and *Law Review* at Harvard, so at least he might have a thing or two to say at breakfast."

Her colleague clicked closed the cover of his fountain pen and said, "You are originally from Detroit, are you not?" She nodded. "Love matches may still occur in Michigan, and I am sure they are charming to behold. This, however, is New York. What Mr.—hmm—Cobleigh says or does not say at breakfast does not matter. His devastating shoulders do not matter. *He* does not matter. Only she, or should I say her Tuttlehood, is of consequence. That is what caught him and that is what may keep him." The *Times* reporter said, "You're awfully cynical." The *Tribune* reporter responded, "My good girl, she looks like a hockey coach at a bad boarding school. She should lower those pale, skimpy lashes and give thanks for her manifold blessings."

The reporters watched the couple standing on the steps of the church, surrounded by bridesmaids in claret-colored gowns and leghorn hats with velvet ribbons, ushers in cutaways, striped trousers, and gray waistcoats. James lifted Win's chin with his index finger and gave her a light but long kiss on the mouth. "Wow," said the woman from the *Times*. "If your editor heard you say 'wow,'" said her colleague, "he would beat you and chain you to a desk and force you to write about small, nasty weddings in Brooklyn where the bride's name is never less than five syllables." James ran a finger over and over Win's lips, as though massaging in the kiss. The *Times* reporter closed her notebook.

109

*   *   *

Occasionally they would go to the opera and sometimes James would work late, but usually he would arrive home from Ivers and Hood by eight, put his hat on the tiny Chinese table Win's uncle had given them, toss his topcoat and jacket over a Queen Anne armchair Win's godmother had given them, loosen his rep tie, grab Win, and carry her into the bedroom, where he'd throw her on the bed and make love to her for the remainder of the evening. The Victorian brass headboard, which James's Aunt Violet had given them, would bang against the wall, sometimes laconically, sometimes with extraordinary force and speed. (Their neighbors in the apartment next door, a Mr. and Mrs. Bingham Van Pelt, hearing the banging and the love cries, first found them amusing, then awesome, and finally disgusting. "Really, Bingy, can't you say something to him in the elevator? I mean, really!")

In their first year of marriage, Win lost seven pounds and James five because they so often skipped dinner—which was probably just as well, because in all her life Win had never even cooked a piece of toast and the only dish she seemed to be able to make was creamed chicken with peas, and it tasted tough and gelatinous at the same time. But they glowed with newlywed happiness. Even Samuel saw it, and by Christmas he had softened enough to allow Maisie to buy Win a seal coat and James a pair of gold oval cufflinks with his initials engraved in rich, flowing script. On their first anniversary, Samuel offered to pay for a maid so Win could have her days free for her friends and charity work, and when James said no, Samuel insisted and even threw in the use of the Tuttle cook on nights when the young Cobleighs were entertaining lawyers from Ivers and Hood.

"Tell me everything that happened to you today," Win said. They had been married a little more than a year. She ran her fingers over the dark gold hair on James's stomach.

"Let's do it again."

"Not now. Come on, take your hand from there. Really, we ought to start behaving like a mature married couple. I ought to tell you things so you'll find me interesting. For instance, do you know what I did today?"

"You had lunch with Jill McGrew and Prissy Ross."

"Yes. But that was after a dreadful, screamy morning with Lollie Kuhn, where she swore that if we insisted on Mr. Cropper catering the Infants' Infirmary Ball, she would quit the committee or kill herself. And in the afternoon I found a lovely bit of old fabric for the footstool Aunt Bessie gave us."

"What color?"

"See? Aren't we being marvelously adult? It's beigey-brown, but has a raised—sort of an embossed leaf pattern on it. I called Mr. Calussi and he swore he'd have it finished before the twenty-sixth, when we're having the

110

Blacks and the Ripleys to dinner. He's such a sweet little man. I love Italians. They're so full of life. It must have been such fun growing up in Cranston, with all of them running about. Did you ever have an Italian girl friend?"

"What do you think?"

"Mmmm. I'll bet you did. Was she pretty? Was she?"

James kissed her. He had a way of doing it, of pressing so hard her teeth hurt her lips, that inevitably brought tears to Win's eyes. It moved her so deeply that for the duration of the kiss she was incapable of motion or thought. And by the time he moved and took his tongue on a leisurely journey down her body, he owned her. When she cried out, it seemed he had willed it, and when her tears began again and she pleaded for relief it was as if it were all part of some plan he had devised.

"Now, James. Now."

On that night, the Cobleighs conceived their first child.

Ivers and Hood stood close by the New York Stock Exchange, Trinity Church, and Federal Hall, and without making too much of the juxtaposition of commerce, God, and country, it may be said that most members of the firm believed it was their calling to serve all three. Obviously it was they—and not the men in beards and black coats a mile away on the Lower East Side—who were the Chosen People. The sense of specialness extended down to the firm's associates. Gifted men in their twenties and early thirties, they realized that if fate was just and their genius recognized they would one day be made partners and, from there, ascend to heaven: they might rise to become Secretary of State, governor of the Federal Reserve Board, chairman of the Council of International Affairs. Presidents would seek their advice and their company at dinner. Charities would honor them. Beautiful women, trained from birth to sniff out the scent of power, would pursue them.

Every other Thursday, the associates of Ivers and Hood reserved a table at an undistinguished seafood restaurant and, from twelve thirty to two, debated European military strategy, planned a Republican presidential victory, and got the economy moving again.

"Mr. Gloom has spoken." Matthew Whitley sighed out the smoke of his cigarette, flicked his ash, and shook his head. "Jim, you are a doomsayer. A Cassandra."

"Cassandra spoke the truth," Dick Halloran interjected.

"Obviously we can't say the same for Brother Cobleigh. Any man who believes that Adolf Hitler is about to gobble up France and England in one bite and then come marching across the ocean, still hungry, and devour us—"

"I didn't say that," James said quietly. "I merely said that the Maginot Line will not protect France."

"Well, I say nuts to that," George Grunwald said.

111

"George, how the hell are ground fortifications going to fend off the Luftwaffe? Answer me. Come on. I'm waiting."

"France isn't England. And I don't appreciate that condescending look in your eye, Cobleigh. You don't have a monopoly on brains, you know. I mean, the best military minds agree that you can't win a war from the air, so the Luftwaffe really isn't a factor. The Germans would have to move troops, supplies across land. Ergo, my friend, the Maginot Line will afford just the sort of protection France needs."

"Look at the Great Wall of China, damn it." James slammed the table with his hand for emphasis.

"Our world geography lesson continues," Peter Wooster remarked, his cool interruption a signal that the atmosphere was becoming too hot for an associates' lunch. "Must we look at the Great Wall of China, Jim?"

"Yes. Did it protect China from invasion after invasion from the north? Did it?"

"I don't know," Peter said. "I suppose if you're using it as an analogy, it must have been some half-assed excuse for a wall. But George isn't talking about a bunch of half-baked Chinamen, Jim. He's talking about the French. They'll send the wicked Hun reeling back to where he belongs."

"Are you serious?" James demanded. "Good God, look what the Germans did to Poland four, five months ago. They crushed it. And if you think that can't happen—"

"For Christ's sake," George Grunwald cut in. "Poland! Poland was born to be invaded. To compare it with France is to . . . is to be taken in by the Anglo lobby. I hate to say it, Jim, but you are the perfect dupe for the Democratic-British-Jewish propaganda machine. You're just the sort of stooge they're looking for, the gullible American willing to sell short his own country so that—"

"Ram it, Grunwald."

"You ram it."

"Do you honestly believe we're not in jeopardy?"

"I *know* we're not. The only thing we have to fear—to paraphrase that man—is our own stupidity."

"Then you're a bigger ass than I suspected."

"If that's your attitude, Cobleigh—"

"What's wrong with Jim? Why is he so damned emotional?" Peter Wooster whispered.

Dick Halloran shrugged. "Can't understand what's bothering him. For God's sake, we all know there's a war and that it's serious, but it's pointless to take it personally."

"Tell me what happened today at the office," Win said. She sat curled up

112

in a big club chair, her hands resting on her flat but pregnant belly. Once in a while she'd stroke it, as though it were a kitten resting on her lap.

"Nothing terribly exciting. René Thibaut from the French-America Steamship Line is in town, and I've been assigned to calm him down, but that's nearly impossible. Well, at least he's crazy for a reason."

"What's his reason?"

"He's afraid Germany may invade France."

"Oh, of course. James, you don't have to squeeze your eyes together and glare at me. There could be another reason why a man becomes upset. His wife could be sick or his children doing poorly in school or maybe his business is in trouble."

"That's true. Sorry. We had that associates' lunch today, and I almost bit off George Grunwald's head. He's such a fool. And the rest of them. I just don't understand them. Why am I the only one who feels this way?"

"What way?"

"Well, we were discussing the Maginot Line—"

"Oh, I read about it the other day, although I must say it's all very depressing. If you weren't so terribly wrapped up in it, I'd skip the front page entirely. It doesn't seem real, all those tiny countries falling. I wake up and turn on the radio and it's goodbye Latvia or Bohemia or Budapest or some such place. I know it's a dreadful situation, but the real reason it upsets me is that I know it upsets you. You're taking it so to heart, James. I mean, we're all on the same side, aren't we? No one really likes the Germans. They're so—I don't know—so lumpy. Mama's friend Nellie Weldon married a German count or baron, and Mama says he looks like a troll and has the ugliest castle and he's so tightfisted he won't allow Nellie to fix it up and she wouldn't be surprised if Nellie leaves him and comes home. It *is* a third marriage, you know. Oh well, this Maginot Line will keep them out of France. Did Monsieur Thibaut talk about it?"

"No."

"James, why are you so abrupt?"

"I am not abrupt."

"You are so. Just because I don't want to spend the evening poring over maps of Europe doesn't mean I'm worthless."

"I did not say you were worthless, Win."

"But you get so—so piqued with me whenever I don't want to spend an entire evening discussing Winston Churchill. It's war, war, war all the time, and then you expect—"

"Expect what?"

"I don't know. I forget what I was going to say."

"You were saying all I do is talk about war and then I expect—something. What do I expect?"

113

"You expect me to get into bed and laugh and be gay after an entire evening analyzing the war. I know I'm not as clever as you are, James, but I never felt it mattered until now."

"Win, please. You're very clever."

"No, I'm not. I can't even find the Netherlands on the map. But you never cared about that, and all of a sudden you are so angry with me for not being smart about troop movements and Maginot Lines."

James walked to Win's chair, pulled her out of it, sat, and then drew her onto his lap. His arms went around her and he rubbed the back of her neck and her back. "You're very smart, Win. Really you are. Now tell me, what do you want to talk about? Anything you want."

"I just want to know about you. Tell me about your day with Monsieur Thibaut." Her eyes closed as he massaged her back. She nestled her head on his shoulder. "That feels so soothing. Tell me things. How is your French coming along? I think your accent sounds perfectly splendid, although languages were never my strong suit. Can you actually carry on an entire business conversation with Monsieur Thibaut?"

"I manage."

"Hmm? Sorry, I didn't hear you."

"I said, I'm doing fairly well, although Thibaut insists I sound like a Provençal fisherman who studied diction with a Parisian shopgirl—not the sort of accent one expects from an American. He did say that for someone who had never been to France and who had only studied French in college, I speak passably well. What he actually said was that I didn't befoul the language, but he intended it as a compliment."

"That's marvelous. I can barely read a menu, and if I say anything it has to be in the present tense. Oh, well, maybe when all this nastiness is over we can spend some time abroad. You know, Mama was telling me she ordered all my baby things from France. All those dear little dresses with the tucking. It's too bad things are so awful there. Well, we still have my christening gown to use. I saw it the other day when I had lunch with Mama. It's a bit yellowed, but it really looks fine. Such beautiful detail on it. Oh, James, I don't think I can bear waiting six months more for Baby to be born. It's just the most exciting thing in the world." A sudden flush spilled across Win's face. "Except for you."

"Come," James said. "Let's go inside."

"You don't want to talk any more?" she asked.

"No. We've talked enough."

"Jesus, Jesus, help me. Oh, it's so bad. Oh, please."

"Shhh," said the labor room nurse.

114

"No. I can't any more. I can't take— Give me something. Please. Some medicine for the pain."

"Come on now, Winnie. That's your name, isn't it, Winnie? Be a big, brave girl and Dr. Ward will be here in just a minute. Come on now. Screaming doesn't help. It just makes things worse."

The only other man in the fathers' waiting room at Lying-In Hospital had rushed out two hours earlier after learning his wife had a baby girl. "Good luck to you, bud," he called to James as he went through the door, although the two had not exchanged a word in the three hours they had spent together.

James picked up the *Times* the man had left. July 2, 1940. The paper was soft from folding and unfolding, the ink smeared by the man's sweaty hands. The headline was about the invasion of Rumania. The sub-headline read: *Reich Prestige Up*. He closed his eyes, then opened them to an adjacent article:

Striking with increasing boldness, German bombers yesterday carried out their first daylight raids over Britain since the western offensive began. . . .

"Mr. Cobleigh. Mr. Cobleigh," a nurse called from a doorway. She came up to James's chair and stood before him. "No. Not yet. Dr. Ward just said to say that Mrs. Cobleigh's headed for the delivery room now. Something should happen in—oh, the next half hour or so. I'll let you know."

"Thank you."

"It's quite a day, isn't it? By this time tomorrow, you'll have some sweet little thing to call you Daddy. Can you believe it? Quite a day."

Another headline, lower on the page, read: *Nazi Forces Take the Channel Isles*. The article reported that Jersey, Guernsey, Alderney, and Sark were lost and that, by taking them, the Germans had established a position on British soil.

"Give her a little more," the obstetrician said to the anesthesiologist. "Be over in a minute. No problem. She's got the pelvis of an elephant."

He read that former French premier Paul Reynaud was not the victim of an auto accident, as had been reported, but had been "'taken for a ride' by the Gestapo to prevent his flight to Morocco to form an anti-Nazi government."

"Here it comes," Dr. Ward announced.

Reich Sees Alarm in Britain Growing, he read. He covered his face with his hands. Later, when the nurse tapped his shoulder, he removed them. Gray smudges from the newsprint dotted his forehead and cheeks.

"Congratulations," she cooed.

"What?"

"It's a boy!"

"Nicholas," she said. "It's so manly, isn't it? I mean, we've gone through hundreds of names and always come back to Nicholas. I've always been mad for the name. Unless you want to name him for your father."

"No, Win. Nicholas is fine."

"No James Junior?"

"No. One is enough."

"Isn't he beautiful, James? With that teeny button nose?"

"He's very beautiful." He took her hand to his lips and kissed it. In the bright light of the hospital room, her freckles had a yellow cast. "Like you."

"Oh, James, no. He's handsome. He has your looks. And your brains. Look at his sweet forehead. All those important thoughts going on behind it, just like his father. Oh, James, isn't this the happiest time ever?"

On the third weekend in October, 1940, they left Nicholas and his nanny with the Tuttles and drove through the autumn blaze of color to a small cabin on a two-hundred-acre preserve in the Berkshires they had bought with Win's inheritance from a great-aunt. "Are you sure you won't join me?" Win asked. She stuffed her corduroy trousers into her high-topped shoes and double-knotted the laces.

"No. I have some reading."

"Oh, James. This was to be a second honeymoon. You promised. Long walks in the forest and stargazing and chopping wood and drinking gallons of cider. And you haven't even looked out the window."

"Stop it, Win."

"Well, you haven't." She threw a thick wool vest over her flannel shirt. "Tell me. What color are the leaves on the tree right outside the front door?"

"I don't know. Red."

"They happen to be yellow."

"Enough, Win."

"You're so wrapped up in newspapers and magazines and all those dreary reports from your war lobbyist friends."

"Leave me alone."

"It's true."

"You don't know what you're talking about."

"I do. This is the most beautiful time of the year and here we are alone in this darling cabin and you don't even know the color—"

"I saw five million goddamn trees driving up here. They were beautiful. I *said* they were beautiful. What more do you want, Win?"

116

"I just want to have fun. I don't want to hear about Nazis all the time. I don't want to hear that Western civilization is doomed unless we go to war. This—this thing has nothing to do with us. We're thousands of miles away. Why can't you stop thinking about it every minute?"

"I don't think about it every minute."

"You do. And every time I want to do something exciting—buy a horse or visit Prissy and Glenn in St. Croix—you look down your nose at me."

"All I'm saying is that there is more to life than inspecting the stables in Central Park to see if they're luxurious enough for some damned horse."

"If you rode you'd understand."

"If I rode I'd still find the time to take a look at the world I'm living in. And I'd still realize that if something doesn't happen fast, all that will be left of England is that stupid Hepplewhite chest you had to run out and buy."

"We can afford it, James."

"That's not the point, damn it!"

"You think I'm frivolous. Go ahead. Say it. Say, 'Win, you only think of silly things while I think deep and important thoughts.'"

"Leave me alone."

"The only time you take me seriously is in the bedroom. It's true. Whenever you come home from the office and I dare start to tell you about buying a rug or Nicholas's tooth starting to come in, you can barely stifle a yawn. You can't wait to get to your study and plow through that briefcase full of boring papers until midnight, and then you expect me—"

"Go take your walk, Winifred."

"James—"

"Do me a favor. Get the hell out of here."

Nicholas began walking a week before his first birthday and by the day of his party, dressed in navy shorts and a sailor's middy blouse, was tottering about the living room, now and then stepping on his own foot or tripping over a toy truck and flopping to the floor. But he got up immediately and, gnawing away simultaneously on his red tie and his thumb, went from grandparent to grandparent, from chair to piano to table.

"Good lord," breathed Samuel. "When does he stop?"

"When we're so exhausted we don't care any more," Maisie said. "Now come here, Nicholas. That's my big boy. Good. Climb right up here and destroy Grandma's stockings. That's my sweet boy. Oh, Win, he's so precious. Tiny nosey-nosey. And that hair!"

"Just like James's."

"Well, not exactly. I mean, there's a definite red Tuttle tinge to it. I'm sure James will allow us that. Now, Nicholas, let Grandma help you down. That's my boy. When is James coming?"

"He said he'd take the noon train from Washington. But he said to go ahead with the cake without him."

"He's certainly busy these days," Maisie observed.

"Yes," Win said. "No, no, no, Nicholas. Don't put the ashtray in your mouth. No. Dirty. Good boy."

"Winifred, you really must find a decent nanny. This Miss Horrible with the walleyes isn't teaching him a thing."

"It's difficult, with the war in England. The man at the agency told me he's at his wits' end. Can't bring anyone over here."

"You'd think they'd be grateful to get away from the bombs."

"Maisie," Samuel interjected. "There are higher priorities than nannies. Win and Nanny Whatever are doing admirably. Now, Win, what business does James have in Washington?"

"I'm not sure, Papa. But he was supposed to meet Mr. Donovan yesterday. He's very—um, concerned about the world situation. He wants to do something."

"Do what, Winifred?" her father asked gently.

"I'm not certain, Papa. He really hasn't told me. But he's taking all this— all the world problems—very much to heart."

"Well, the problems are serious, Win."

"I know. But serious enough to miss his son's first birthday?"

On July 11, 1941, nine days after Nicholas Cobleigh's first birthday, President Roosevelt appointed a Wall Street lawyer, William Donovan, director of an agency called the Coordinator of Information. The agency was to "collect and analyze all information and data which may bear upon national security." Donovan sought recruits. Although America was not at war, he knew war was coming and he had some odd jobs he wanted done. He wanted young men of intellect, honor, valor, and ingenuity, men of his own kind. So with the help of his friends, he sought them in the one place he was convinced he would find them, his own turf: the largely white Anglo-Saxon enclaves of eastern law firms, universities, and banks. In other words, the COI (which evolved into the OSS, which evolved into the CIA) began as a nest of Ivy League spies. And James Cobleigh was one of them.

"Of course I'm not a spy," James said.

"But James, Papa said that Colonel Donovan—"

"Win, all I'm doing— Nicky, no. Stop that. Don't let the dog kiss your mouth. All I am doing is managing a few things for Bill Donovan. My French isn't bad, and I'm speaking to one or two fellows who know what the situation is in France."

"You're not getting involved with secret agents?"

"Secret agents? Win, I'm an ordinary Wall Street lawyer. I toil in the fields of Ivers and Hood and— Come on, Nicky, don't let Buster lick you like that. That's my big fella."

"Then why can't you tell me where you're going? You never want to talk to me any more."

"I can't tell you where I'm going because it's secret. Believe me, it will be a quick trip, but it's important. If there were a choice, do you think I'd willingly leave you and Nick?"

"I just don't understand why you have to go."

"Do we have to go through this again? I'm going because it's important— vital—that I gather certain information."

"You don't have to. Someone else could go who doesn't have a wife and—"

"I want to go. Now, don't start crying. It's not fair to me. I'll be back before you know it. Before you have a chance to realize how much fun it is having me out of your hair."

"James, you know I can't enjoy myself if you're away."

He took a deep, long breath before he spoke. "I know, Win."

They sent him to England. From there, along with a member of de Gaulle's secret-service-in-exile, the BCRA, James—whose only time at sea had been afternoon jaunts on Long Island Sound with an Ivers and Hood colleague—crossed the English Channel. He traveled in an X23, a British submarine only fifty-seven feet long. He was barely aboard when a crew member put a waxed bag into his hand. "For vomit," the man said cheerfully.

James and his escort were dropped at a fishing village in the department of Pas-de-Calais. They spent two weeks with three of the leaders of the French Resistance movement. The youngest of them had been an assistant professor of classical languages before the German invasion. Her name was Denise Levesque and she was slightly overweight, with lank, mouse-brown hair and large-pored skin. Frenchwomen have a reputation for chic, and even the plainest of them is supposed to carry herself with the élan of a favored courtesan. But Denise proved stereotypes were nonsense. She was simply plain. However, she was very smart.

She lectured James about why Ovid was such an abominable poet and demanded an immediate explanation of each amendment to the U.S. Constitution and showed him how to disarm a grenade and convinced him that, with sufficient arms, the underground could rout the Nazis.

That was their first day together. On the second, she made him dinner: stewed rabbit, followed by glasses of home-brewed Calvados. "You never studied Greek?" Denise demanded. James was just sober enough to realize she was not drunk at all.

"No. Just French." He pronounced each word separately and slowly, examining each to make certain it was the right choice.

"No Latin?"

"No."

"And you are considered an educated man in the United States?"

"Yes. Be fair. What do you know about common law?"

"A respectable amount, I assure you. Enough so I can realize your system of advocacy is very strange. Presumption of innocence is such an eccentric doctrine. So typically Anglo-Saxon. No. Do not close your eyes. You will fall asleep and I will be lonely. Understand, James? Now, tell me all about New York. I want to hear all about the restaurants." She stretched her thick legs out on the floor and sighed. "I can't remember the last time I had a decent piece of bread. And then you must tell me about the theater. Do Americans like Aeschylus? Are his plays performed often? God, I haven't spoken like this in months. Well, enough of me. Tell me about your life in New York, James. Tell me everything. Are you happy?"

The following night, she told him she knew she would be dead before the war was over. He put his hand over her mouth. "Don't say that."

"Oh, James. Don't be so serious. Wartime lovers are supposed to be doomed. If you thought I'd be waiting for you after the war in a dear little house in Cherbourg with a chocolate soufflé in the oven you'd be swimming back to England before I could put my dress back on. Your life has gone too well, my love. You need a little terror, the shiver of impending doom, to make you happy."

"That's not true, Denise. You know it's not."

"Come, James. Don't pout. You are very, very courageous and sincere. I know that. And so handsome—but I shouldn't tell you that because it must be very boring for you and I don't want you to be bored. Now, you must do something for me. Give me your big American Douglas Fairbanks smile. Ah, there it is."

He held her and kissed her, and before he pulled her on top of him again, he confided that he had special American magic. "You see, I just pass my hands over you like this and, presto, nothing in the world can harm you. Do you believe me?" She laughed and shook her head no. "Denise," he said, pulling her tight against him, "it's never been like this before. Oh, God, I swear it. I never thought I could feel like this about anyone."

He went home three weeks later to a pregnant wife and a law practice he no longer cared about and a son who saw his father so infrequently that he didn't even cry the next month when he saw James's suitcase standing by the front door. "Say bye-bye to Daddy," Win said. Her face was a frozen white circle animated only by the red halo of her hair. Nicholas did not look up at his father. He lowered his head so his chin rested on the child-sized football he was hugging. It was not regulation red-brown football color, but a baby blue with uniformed and helmeted teddy-bear quarterbacks and receivers printed on the spongy fabric. "Please, Nicholas. Daddy's going away again. Be a good boy. Say bye-bye."

"Bye," Nicholas said. Then he turned away from his mother, who had begun to sob, and from his father, who was glaring at her. He stood motionless for an instant, a tiny towheaded figure in yellow pajamas. Then he kicked his football down the dark corridor toward his room.

8

Is Nicholas Cobleigh for real? Or is his vigil at Jane's London bedside a carefully staged media event? There's whispering here and in L.A. that the Golden Couple haven't been kissy-kissy for some time (at least not with each other) and in fact . . .

—*New York Post*

"All right, damn it." And then, with a sigh so begrudging it came over the telephone as a groan, James Cobleigh promised Winifred he would be home from Washington on Sunday to interview the newest nanny. But that particular Sunday was December 7, 1941, Pearl Harbor Day, so by the time James got back to New York to pack his valise, Nanny Williams and her cod liver oil had been settled in the back bedroom for more than three weeks.

James packed very little. He was commissioned a captain in the army but was attached to the OSS and knew exactly where he was going: on New Year's Day 1942 he sailed for England, and several weeks later—for the third time—slipped into Nazi-occupied France and into the arms of Denise Levesque.

Nicholas didn't remember his father's departure, even though James had spent that final morning in New York on the floor of the nursery with his son, building awesome skyscrapers of wooden blocks and then encouraging Nicholas, flushed and damp with delight, to kick them down. In the entire year and a half of his life, Nicholas had never spent so much concentrated time with his father alone, and it made him giddy.

All during the war his mother would say, "Remember Daddy? Remember the blocks? You kicked over the big pile of blocks and then you said 'Bye-bye, Daddy'"—Win fluttered her fingers—"and you gave him a kiss. Remember?"

The first time he had words enough to answer her, when he was a little more than two, he said "No." But his mother had looked so sad, and Nanny Benson—Nanny Williams had been sent away—standing behind Winifred, had nodded her head so violently that he had smiled and said, "I remember."

James's photograph stood in a wooden frame on a shelf in the nursery, between a giant glass jar of cotton balls and a music box shaped like a grand piano that played a torpid "Minute Waltz." The picture had been taken a few days before James left. He was in full uniform and at the height of his handsomeness: his cap angled perfectly over his thick, straight fair hair, his eyes wide, his smile warm, although not obscuring the determination of his jaw; he appeared so blondly virile that with a change of uniform his photo could have been used on an S.S. recruiting poster.

Nicholas passed the picture each day. Sometimes when he noticed it, the man—he knew to call him Daddy—looked familiar and reassuring. The smile was that of a nice man who knew him well, like Pete, the afternoon doorman, or his grandpa, and who wished him only happiness. Sometimes, usually when he was preoccupied, tying his shoes while the new one, Nanny Keyes, timed him on her big watch or playing soldiers with a friend, the picture looked neutral and impersonal, like a magazine advertisement; it could have *Gillette razor* stuck in a corner. Now and then it seemed malevolent. Nicholas would race through his room on a dark winter afternoon and catch a cold smile that fooled everyone else in the house, the mask of a man who hated him, who wanted to break out of his picture world and do something bad. But by the time he was three, Nicholas forced himself to stare down the sinister smiler, and the demon who had taken over the picture's spirit was defeated and never returned.

Nicholas's brother Thomas, who was born soon after James went overseas, had a far less complicated reaction. "Daddy," Nicholas would prompt, each time Thomas waddled to that corner of the room. "That's *Daddy*, Tom." Nanny Coe would pass it and give the frame a kindly pat. "That's your daddy, Thomas. A brave officer." And Win, visiting the nursery, sitting on the old brown rocking chair with Thomas on her lap, clutching the photograph in her hand, would say, "Let's give Daddy a great big kiss!" She, then Nicholas, would kiss the picture, leaving lip marks on the glass. "Daddy!" Thomas would say. He'd seize the picture from Win and give it a wet, chirping kiss. However, he also shouted "Daddy!" to each soldier, sailor, marine, and policeman he passed on the way to the playground in Central Park.

The photograph, in a monogrammed silver frame, also stood on Win's night table. The photographer had air-brushed out the crinkles at the edges of James's eyes, so he looked as he had the night of Win's debut, handsome and youthful, with that small I-have-a-secret smile. For the four war years, the last thing Win saw each night was James's smile; he was a male Mona Lisa, mysterious and desirable. The smile teased Win—I know something you don't know—as she pulled the chain to turn out her lamp. Without realizing it, she'd often smile back, the shaky, innocent smile of a homely debutante flustered by the attentions of the sophisticated law student.

But on a few nights, when the bedroom was thick in ink darkness, a hole in space created by a closed door and drawn blackout shades, Win would waken with a shudder, the covers in angry knots, her silk nightgown clinging to her wet body, and she knew exactly what was making him smile. It wasn't the girl he'd left behind.

123

James Cobleigh's papers identified him as Giles Lemonnier, born in Boulogne (parents deceased), a baker's assistant. Thus the two times he was picked up by German patrols as he rode his bicycle on back roads at three or four in the morning, he was able to explain that oh, my, oh, yes, he was on his way to bake the loaves that Colonel Oskar Baron von Finkhenhausen would find on his tray that morning. They waved him on.

He no longer looked like the man in the photograph in the apartment on Park Avenue. His hair was chopped short and ragged, the sort of crazily uneven haircut the dull-witted give themselves. The slow speech and slight lisp he affected to camouflage whatever was left of his accent, and the lope he learned to cover his American stride added to the image he cultivated—a man not worth thinking about. Even so, he did not seek to test his acting ability but kept out of the way of Germans and ordinary Frenchmen as much as he could. His business was with the Resistance.

James (and the other OSS men in northern France) had two jobs: to report by wireless to the OSS in London the complexion and effectiveness of the various Resistance groups in the department of Pas-de-Calais and, later, to help mount operations that would seduce the Germans into thinking the inevitable Allied invasion would come at Pas-de-Calais instead of the less likely Normandy. His first job was difficult because of the diversity of the Resistance groups; there were Catholics, Communists, Loyalists, Protestants, Gaullists, Jews, Socialists, saints, patriots, psychopaths, and collaborators. His second was painful and dangerous because, for it to succeed, the Germans had to suspect major Resistance activity in Pas-de-Calais, and this could only be accomplished by sacrificing some *résistants* to the Nazis.

And it was all complicated by Denise Levesque, who had gone from teaching Greek and Latin literature to organizing and leading attacks on German emplacements. James loved her. She was completely different from his wife, neither tenderhearted nor well bred, but she had two qualities Win lacked: a fine mind and self-esteem. For the first time, James had a friend who loved what he loved. Worldly affairs that mystified Win delighted Denise. She argued with his politics, mocked his pretensions, belittled his abilities, and still loved him. And when she made love to him it was not with the closed-eyes abandon of Win, waiting for him to pull her over the edge, but with leisurely sensuality, occasionally following but usually leading him where she wanted to go. He wanted to marry her.

Dear Win. It was April 1944, two months before D-Day. He wrote leaning on a wood chopping block in the cellar of Denise's small house. (His monthly letters were taken to London by the planes that flew in and out by night, bringing ammunition and supplies. After being routinely read and censored, the letters were routed to New York.) *There is no decent way to say what I must say. Certainly no kind way. Therefore—* He put the stub of a pencil in his mouth and ran his tongue over its chewed end. Denise frequently gnawed on pencils and pens and occasionally book bindings, as if to regain the taste of her lost academic career. *I will be direct and cruel. I am—*

"You are writing to Winifred?" Denise asked. James jerked his head up, startled. His face went white. Denise was an experienced enough guerrilla to descend the twelve rickety steps to the cellar unheard.

"Yes."

"What are you writing?"

"Just that I'm well and—"

"You are lying! Look at you, rubbing your palms together like a nervous schoolgirl. Do you know how long you would last under interrogation? Now tell me, what are you writing to her?"

"What you told me not to write."

"Oh, James! You must not. You promised."

"Denise—" She snatched the thin sheet of paper from the wood block and ripped it in half, then in half again. "Denise, I'll just write the same thing over and over."

"Enough!" She stuffed the papers into the bodice of her dress and then stood before James, fists on her hips, her heavy legs planted a foot apart on the packed dirt floor. If Win was a tall cypress, Denise was short, tough scrub. "This is stupid melodrama. What will it serve? Tell me. Go ahead, tell me. I'll tell you what it will serve. It will serve your need for cheap romance. You will be the heel, the rotter, but all for love. Enough, James. You cannot get a divorce now. You cannot marry me now. So why torture her?"

"Because I want nothing, no one, between us."

"Listen to me. The war is not over. What if I die?"

"You won't die."

"And what if you die, James? Have you thought of that? You get caught and some German pig puts a gun to your head and shoots and then what? What do Winifred and your boys have to remember you? A letter saying you love someone else?"

"Denise—"

"When it's all over we will talk."

"Don't you love me?"

"Yes. Oh, yes. You know how much."

"Then why—"

"Because I want you when life is real."

"This is real. We've been together for more than two years, and it's still as wonderful and—"

"When there is peace, whom will you want, James? Your good, sweet, rich wife? Your two handsome boys? Your law office? Or a fat teacher of Greek who—"

"I'll want you. I don't love Winifred. You know that."

"Then you have time to tell her that when the war is over."

So instead James wrote:

Dear Win,

I think you are absolutely right to start Nicky on his riding lessons this spring. As you know from my own humiliating experience, if you wait too long to get on a horse . . . . . . and kiss Nicky and Tommy for me and tell them their dad loves them very much.

All my love,
James

"But if you were the sort of woman who *had* to work," Win said to her mother, "wouldn't you much, much rather spend your time in a lovely apartment caring for children instead of on some assembly line, packing parachutes or riveting whatever it is they rivet?"

Maisie Tuttle plucked a bright pink crab-apple blossom from a branch overhead and tucked it behind her ear as if it were a hibiscus. They stood in a meadow that rolled from the edge of a pond and spread across several acres of the Tuttles' Connecticut farm. The trees were in May flower, and beneath the clean blue sky the meadow air was hazy with a pink and lilac mist. "Don't I look like an island maiden?" Maisie demanded. "Perhaps an island maiden of a certain age, but nevertheless—what is that word?—ah, nubile. I've never been quite certain what it means, but I'm sure it's the sort of thing one ought to be if one can." She withdrew a tortoise-shell comb from her chignon and tucked in a stray strand of white hair. Her hair and the ropy veins on her hands were the only signs that Maisie was in her middle sixties. She was firm-figured and silky skinned, and her dark eyes were still bright.

"Mama—" Win said.

"Well, you really don't expect an answer to your question," Maisie said sharply. Win hung her head. Beside her mother she felt thin and brittle, like an unused piece of leather. She had not been loved or petted since James went off to war, and the lack of pleasure seemed to drain her of her femininity, reducing her to the gawky girlishness of her debutante days. Her kneecaps and elbows seemed to have swelled into bony knobs while her breasts deflated. Despite the moist, sweet spring air, her cheeks felt parched, her neck rough like chicken skin. "If I were a servant in your house, Winifred, I would dash for the nearest factory gate as fast as my little feet could get me there. Or I'd lie on a chaise longue swilling scotch, deciding whether to steal the silver this Tuesday or next. My dear, your life is topsy-turvy. You run out the door and assume everything will be taken care of, that chandeliers will get polished and children will get winter coats. How? Will a host of heavenly angels trumpet your desires to the servants while you're having lunch with that silly Prissy Ross? No wonder maids come and go and come and go. And nannies! Ninnies. You hire the silliest of them and then worry why Tommy hasn't made ka-ka for six weeks or why Nicky keeps trying to touch himself down there. Honestly, Winifred, I don't see how— Now, please. Stop quivering your chin."

"Mama, I try very hard. Really. But I'm not like you. I can't tell a maid, 'Oh, Minnie, the tablecloth is creased' or tell Nanny the children's ears aren't clean."

"And why can't you?"

"Because I'm not like you. I'm not sure of myself the way you are."

"Winifred, the children's ears are either clean or dirty, and I can't see why it would take a great surge of self-confidence to say 'Nanny So-and-so, Thomas's ears are so loaded with wax we could put wicks in them and set him on the table beside the centerpiece.'"

"But see, Mama, I could never think of something like that. You're quick and clever, and I always feel at a loss. I sit with all the girls I grew up with and everyone's saying such smart things and I know they think I'm all right, but only because I've been around for ages and because—"

"Winifred, you are a married woman with two children, and you have obligations. If you choose, you can feel as ill at ease and as doltish as you like. No one can stop you. But it still doesn't take away your obligations. Period. You are an adult, Winifred."

"But, Mama, don't you understand? I don't *feel* like one."

"Then you must pretend, mustn't you?"

"'Yippee ti yo / I'm a lone cowpoke / Ridin' the range / On m' pal'mino.'" Five-year-old Nicholas sang the theme song of his favorite radio program, the *Texas Pete Show*. His voice was deep for a child's, and husky. "'Yippee ti yay / Yippee ti yee.'" He squashed a clod of wet black Connecticut earth with the toe of his boot. The air was rich with Yankee smells, manure and mown grass and spruce, but he was able to imagine his grandparents' farm a Panhandle ranch. He hooked his thumbs over the waistband of his hated jodhpurs, transmogrifying them into leather chaps. "'I'm the loneliest cowpoke / You ever did see.'" The collie, barking at the station wagon making a delivery from the local liquor store, became one of the beasts of the west—a coyote or a buffalo. "'Where the land is gold / And the sky's so bluuuue / I'm Texas Pete / Big and brave and truuuue.'"

"What'd you say, kid?" Mr. Sullivan, his grandfather's groom, came around the side of the stable leading the only horse Nicholas was allowed to ride, a small rheumy filly named Lady Red.

"Nothing, Mr. Sullivan."

"Ready to take on Lady Red?"

"Yes."

"Okay. Come on over. I'll give you a boost up."

"Is Lady Red a wild stallion?"

"Well, not exactly. But close, kid. You gotta control her. Know what I mean? Stay with her every minute. Don't let her get away with nothing. Can you manage?"

"I think so."

Nicholas was happiest at the farm. Despite his rarefied Manhattan-Tuttle lineage and his respectable Providence-Kendall blood, he was—ultimately— a descendant of English peasants. The country air stirred something primeval in Nicholas, and when out of doors often he wore the same goofy smile of contentment a Saxon sheepherder might have on a fine May morning.

He had to keep moving. Like his mother, Nicholas was a natural athlete, and he was incomparably more content racing the dogs down to the orchard than sitting imprisoned in a velvet suit watching *The Nutcracker*. His energy needed a place to go.

He was born in Manhattan but he really wasn't of it. On the days he couldn't chase his ball down the path to the playground in Central Park or hang by his legs from a jungle gym, he would often be sent to his room for some misdemeanor: crunching one of Thomas's toy tanks under his shoe or tracing the outline of his hand in aquamarine crayon on the hand-painted silk wall coverings in the dining room.

He was not a natural urban child. Instead of lugging a well-groomed teddy bear about as Thomas did, snuggling with it in an overstuffed chair, or begging for one more elevator ride, Nicholas hopped and jumped and bopped on the balls of his feet. He was rarely without a ball appropriate for the season and would toss it, rhythmically and mindlessly, toward the ceiling or from hand to hand.

On the farm he was free from the endless parade of ladies in hats who squeaked and tried to pinch some part of him. Nicholas was warmhearted, but, unlike Thomas, he did not curl into a ball of anticipatory pleasure whenever he was hauled onto a lap. Thomas behaved as if the adult world were created to delight in him. Nicholas was too careful an observer; he recognized that the matters which really intrigued his mother and her lady friends and his grandparents had nothing to do with children. Their world of soft voices and abrupt laughter, cocktail shakers and newspapers, was different from his and exceedingly complicated. Weekends at the farm he could keep his distance.

"Hey, kid," called the stableman, "you're doing good. You're doing some good posting there." Nicholas smiled and blushed and then peered at the horizon with Texas Pete eyes, a gaze of confidence and dignity. "You're doing real good."

However, as much as the women of his childhood, women of the 1940s, may have admired strong, silent men, they preferred the perky politeness of a Thomas. Nicholas was by far the more handsome of the brothers, but in his early years he put people off with his vague hellos and dreamy expression. Five-year-old Nicholas's temperament was not the sort New York society matrons and proper English nannies found engaging. They quickly turned to Thomas, with his broad smile and crinkly freckled nose, for amusement. Nicholas exhaled relief when they moved away from him and on to chuck Thomas under his chubby chin. Left alone, Nicholas could relax. He could stick his thumb into his mouth, hook his index finger over his nose for maximum comfort, turn his ear to the undemanding universe of Texas Pete and Ned Wickham, Private Eye, and stay out of the proper English nannies' world as best he could.

Not that there were many proper English nannies in Nicholas's earliest years. Nanny Budd was dismissed for swilling Jamaican rum, Nanny Williams for locking Nicholas in the bathroom for an entire morning—supposedly to encourage his toilet training—Nanny Benson for stealing half of Thomas's layette to send to a pregnant niece in Dorset. Nanny Keyes left in a huff because Win persisted in making disruptive visits to the nursery, and Nanny Coe, sloe-eyed and pigeon-toed, aborted herself on her day off and was found, by Nicholas, lying in the linen closet barely conscious in a puddle of blood. "Get Mummy" were the last words she uttered in the Cobleigh household.

From 1940 to 1945, the sea lanes between Southampton and New York were not swelling with waves of nannies seeking employment. Many upper-class American women looked at the help that was available, sighed, and raised their children themselves. Win could not do this. She felt no more competent to change a diaper or nurse a croupy child than she could tap-dance.

Also, she was beset by obligations. Because of her social position, she was on the boards of three charities. Because of her altruistic nature, she served on committees for another four. She planned house tours for the Manhattan Chorale, dinners for the Interfaith Council of Greater New York, dansants for the Soldiers and Sailors League, and raffles for the Iron Lung Association. She rolled bandages, knitted hats, packed medicines, and presided over teas. She had about two hours a day to spend with her children, and while the hours were happy, it never occurred to Win to seek more.

She was too tired. The rest of her schedule was so wearying. Unlike the friends with whom she'd grown up, she found that the social side of the numerous good works she performed gave her no joy. It was an onerous burden. She was not naturally sedentary, and the long luncheons and longer teas where she sat, stock still, straight-backed with crossed ankles, drained her. Gossip and ridicule, as much a staple on these occasions as watercress sandwiches, unsettled her because she sensed she was a perfect target. But Winifred could not break out of this world because it was the only one offered her. She lacked not only the initiative to create another life for herself but also the imagination. She accepted the package that had been handed to her and tried to behave the way a woman of her station was expected to behave: appreciative and gracious.

"There aren't enough hours in a day," she complained along with her friends as they sipped Manhattans and drew up guest lists for the next theater benefit or rode each morning in Central Park. "If only I were a twin," they'd murmur to each other as they left the hospital where they'd spent the early afternoon reading to young soldiers who had been blinded in battle. "I need an extra set of hands *desperately*," they'd moan as they led their children and nannies and maids to Grand Central Terminal for the weekend trek to their parents' country estates or their own more modest cottages.

Win rubbed her throbbing shoulder. Weary from her week in the city, she had still felt obliged to spend an hour leading Nicholas's horse through the woods that edged her parents' property. The hour before that she'd picked six baskets of blueberries and, before that, had planted sunflower seeds with Thomas. Her neck felt as if there were a clenched fist inside it. Her hair was a million dry wires. "Hurry, now," Maisie said to her. "You have exactly ten minutes to get ready." Some neighbors were coming to the house for drinks. "And make sure you pay attention to Nora Vickers. The one whose front teeth make an X. She lost her son on Iwo Jima. Winifred, perk up. Only eight more hours in the day."

"I'm nearly done in."

"Who isn't? Come, Winifred. I wouldn't want to think you're feeling sorry for yourself. You're only going at half speed now. What will you do when James comes home, hm? You'll have a whole new set of wifely obligations. Now get into the shower and don't forget poor Mrs. Vickers."

Pallid, freckled, seventy-six-year-old Samuel Tuttle sat before an electric heater in his study, frail after a nasty cold that had worked its way up to bronchitis and finally to a month-long siege of pneumonia. His doctor (who held one of the four professorships at Columbia University's medical school that Samuel had endowed) had forbidden him to work. Maisie had confiscated all his cigars, and none of the servants would accept his five-dollar bribe to sneak out and buy more. He had reread his Whartons and Jameses and Conan Doyles. Although cranky after weeks and weeks of coddled eggs and poached chicken, he could imagine no morsel that would tempt him. "Well, Nicholas," he said to his grandson, "what do you have to say for yourself?"

"Nothing, Grandpa."

"I see. Did your mother send you in to cheer me?"

"No. Grandma did."

"Oh. What did she say? It's all right. You can tell me."

"She said 'Grandpa Samuel is in a blue funk' and I should come in and you would give me paper and pencils and I should draw pictures to make you happy."

"Well, if I had a blue pencil you might draw my blue funk and show it to your grandmother, but I have only a black pencil. Here. And paper is in that cabinet there. Open the little doors. Now, what are you going to draw for me?"

"My daddy?"

"Oh. That would be very nice, Nicholas."

"He's in Europe in the war."

"I know."

"Do you know him?"

"Of course I know him. He married my daughter. Your mummy is my daughter."

"I know that. And Uncle Jesse and Uncle Caleb are your boys, but now they're grown-ups."

"Yes. And Uncle Jeremiah in Rhode Island."

"Grandpa, can I ask you something?" Samuel nodded. "You aren't my daddy's daddy?"

"No."

"Does my daddy have a daddy?"

"Yes. He has a mother and father. And do you want to know something? They live in Rhode Island too, just like Uncle Jeremiah and Aunt Polly."

"Do they know each other in Rhode Island? I mean—"

"I don't believe so, Nicholas. Your grandparents live in another city, and your grandmother is very sick."

"They're my grandma and grandpa too?"

"Yes."

"My daddy's mummy and daddy?"

"Yes."

"Don't they want to see me and give me Christmas presents?"

"I'm quite sure they do, Nicholas. But they are very old and sick, and they can't make the trip to New York."

"Can I go see them in Rhode Island?"

"Well, perhaps one day you will. Perhaps when your father comes home from Europe."

"Could they send me a birthday card?"

"Maybe they're too sick to go to the store."

"Couldn't they send the maid?"

"Nicholas, many people—most people—don't have maids. Shall I tell you why? You have to pay maids to work, and most people don't have extra money to do that. So they do all the work themselves."

"Texas Pete grooms his own horse. Bravo. That's the horse's name."

"That's right. And there they are in Rhode Island, old and sick, and they have to do many, many things for themselves."

"And that makes them tireder and sicker."

"That's right."

"Why don't we give them some money for a maid?"

"Well. That's a difficult question. People have to do things for themselves, even though it's hard. It's the way of the world. But your grandparents must think about you and Thomas often, though they may not have the strength to do all the things they'd like to do, like buying Christmas presents and traveling. Do you understand?"

"I think so. Does my daddy know his mummy and daddy are old and tired and sick and poor in Rhode Island?"

"I would think not."

"Should Mummy write to Daddy and tell him, and he could come home from the war right away and—"

"No more questions, Nicholas. I am waiting for one of your fine pictures, something to cheer me."

"I'll be four weeks at the most," James said.

"Four weeks?" Denise asked.

"Well, maybe five or six. If I get stuck in London for a few days— meetings and so forth—and if I miss the *New Orleans* I'll have to wait for the next troopship and that may take—"

"I am not planning a Mediterranean cruise. If you return, you will find me here."

"Stop it, Denise! Just stop it! I said I'll be back. I just need time to explain to Winifred and sign a few papers, and I'll be on the next ship back to France. You know that. You have my word."

9

And to fill us in on some of the technical details, we have Dr. Andrew Herbert, Chief of Emergency Medicine at Bellevue Hospital and author of . . .

—*The MacNeil-Lehrer Report,* PBS

Five-year-old Nicholas sat beside three-year-old Thomas in a wing chair so big it nearly hid them in its brown shadows. He pulled his brother's knee socks straight. "Just sit still," he whispered. "If you keep moving, your socks will fall down again and your shirt will get mussed."

"Do I say 'How do you do, sir. I'm Thomas Josiah Cobleigh'?"

"No. He knows who you are. He's your daddy."

"And your daddy?"

"Yes. I told you that a million times, Tommy. Just like Mummy is both our mummies. You just go up to him and kiss him."

"Are you going to kiss him too?"

"Of course. First Mummy kisses him at the door. That's why she's waiting there now, because she saw him get out of the taxi. And we sit here and don't do a thing until she brings him into the room, and then we get up and say 'Hello, Daddy' and kiss him."

"Who goes first?"

"Me. I'm bigger."

"That's not fair."

"It is too. You never even met him yet."

"It is *not* fair, Nicky."

"I said it is and I'm boss."

"You aren't either. You're a dummy stupid-head."

"You shut up or I'll punch your fat nose, you baby."

"You shut up, Icky."

"Shhh."

"You poopy poopface. You—"

"Shhh. He's here." Nicholas took his brother's hand and held it between his. "Don't worry, Tommy. It'll be okay."

He knew he would have to kiss her, but then, at the earliest moment, he would pull back and say, "Winifred, we have to talk." But James had not anticipated what a shock his own apartment could give him, how after more

133

than three years of mildewed cellars and outdoor privies he would be stunned by a richness he'd forgotten was his. Just in the foyer, the red glint of the dark wood floors, the perfume of the dried petals of potpourri in a celadon bowl seemed almost too pleasurable; it made him want to cry.

Neither had he anticipated that the woman in his arms, his lanky, electric-haired wife, would feel so warm and smell so clean and look so inviting, her freckled arms reaching out from the neat cap sleeves of her crisp blue linen dress, her tears staining her pale lashes dark. He closed his eyes, held her close, and rubbed the soft skin and vertebral bump on the back of her neck.

And while all along he knew he would see his sons, he had certainly not anticipated how shattered he would feel when his shy older boy finally lifted his head to say hello and he saw his father's face on his five-year-old son; Nicholas was a miniature Henry Cobleigh, but with Winifred's sweet seriousness shining from behind the wide turquoise eyes. And he could not have planned on Thomas—all fat-faced, freckled Tuttle—screeching "Daddy" and flinging his pudgy arms around James's leg. "Daddy, Daddy, Daddy!"

Nor had he considered roast beef and champagne by candlelight, served by a maid in a black uniform and white apron, nor the brief visit paid by the Tuttles where Samuel actually grasped his shoulder and said, "Glad you're home, James," nor, finally, the silky economy of Winifred's lean body.

By the end of his first week home, he realized that, after all, Denise Levesque had been right. Theirs had been a wartime romance, intense, unreal. He belonged in New York. Several times in the weeks that followed he tried to write Denise, admitting that she had been the more perceptive; he could not return to France. But all his letters sounded clipped and analytical. Denise would mock them: lawyer's letters. So finally he did not write at all, knowing that Denise, who had so wisely predicted what would happen, would understand.

Everything at the Broad Street Club in downtown Manhattan was larger than necessary. Easy chairs could accommodate gorillas. Chowder bowls might double as foot baths, and a swordfish steak would supply the average American family of four with its requisite protein for three and a half days. It was as though the Club's fourteen-foot-high ceilings and mahogany-paneled walls afforded enough protection for the upper-class white Protestant male to feel secure enough to abandon his habitual understated tastes and self-control and to shriek—silently, of course—*Gimme! Gimme!*

Samuel Tuttle lifted a giant shrimp from its bed of crushed ice. "I think I do understand," he commented, and ripped off a third of it between his teeth. "You want to leave Ivers and Hood, abandon the practice of law, drag

Winifred and the children to Washington, and work for an intelligence agency that has not yet been formed."

James took a double gulp of his double scotch. His father-in-law's club was so exclusive that only two members of his own exclusive law firm had been admitted as members. "You make it sound so frivolous. It's not."

"It is. You have no business being a spy. You have a family."

"I'd be working in Washington. There would be relatively little traveling. Please, just hear me out, Mr. Tuttle. I think the need for an overseas network of—"

"Mrs. Tuttle does not wish her only daughter to move to another city and live the life of the wife of a civil servant."

"For Christ's sake!"

"And I think there is a time in each man's life when he must abandon his urge to slay the next dragon and seek the Holy Grail. In short, he must grow up. His quest must lead him to the world of commerce."

"Please—"

"And I might add it would seem unwise, most unwise of you, to leave Ivers and Hood now that a partnership may be just around the corner."

"Just around the corner and five years away. I have no patience—"

"That is eminently clear. You have no patience for normality. You are an adventurer. Alas, although you are very clever, you married a Tuttle, and we are a placid lot and do not like our lives disturbed. Your adventures ended on V-E Day. Your spying days are over. You will be an attorney for the rest of your life. It's time for you to realize that. As I've indicated, it might not be so painful. I believe a partnership is imminent."

"Mr. Tuttle, I don't want to be tapped for a partnership way before the other lawyers in my class. I don't want to be treated differently because I'm your son-in-law and you're a major client of the firm."

"You don't believe you deserve to be a partner?" Samuel hefted his goblet of water and took a deep drink.

James upended his scotch and finished it in one great gulp. "I deserve it, yes, but—"

"Then perhaps it is a case of virtue being rewarded a bit prematurely."

"I won't accept it, Mr. Tuttle. I'm going to Washington. Win agrees—"

"Winifred would agree to immolation if you lit the match. It's unfortunate but true. However, I don't think Washington is in the picture for you."

"I've been offered a job as—"

"Have you? I heard the offer was rescinded, James."

"What do you mean? What did you do, damn it? Whom did you speak to?"

"Everyone concerned seems to think you'd be far more content practic-

135

ing law in New York. Naturally, there may come a time when you would be called on to serve your country again, but that time would not seem to be now. Another scotch?"

James lay on a towel in the short grass just beyond the sandy edge of the lake near the Cobleighs' Berkshire cabin. He covered his eyes with the crook of his arm. His pearly skin, which had not felt such heat since the summer before Pearl Harbor, began to roast in the sun.

Nicholas sat beside him cross-legged. Slowly, holding his breath, he lowered his hand until his palm grazed the tiny circles of hair on his father's chest. The hair went from the bottom of his throat all the way down his chest and stomach into his bathing trunks and reappeared on his legs, curly and gold in the sunlight. Nicholas withdrew his hand and stroked his own smooth chest.

"Daddy," he whispered. James grunted. "Daddy, are you sleeping?"
"Yes."
"Can we go fishing again?"
"Later."
"Can I have hot dogs and cookies for lunch?"
"Come on, Nick. Let me have a few more minutes."
"Will I get hair like you?"
"What?"
"All over my belly?"
"I don't know. Probably."
"On my legs?"
"Look, I had a rough week, Nick. I need some rest."
"What happened?"
"Nothing. Just let's be quiet for a while. Okay?"
"Okay." Nicholas watched his father maneuver into deeper ease on the towel and slide his hands beneath his head as a pillow. The hair under James's arms was straight and so pale it was almost white. Nicholas wished he could snuggle his head under his father's arm, throw his arm over James's chest, and enjoy the heated skin and the pungent, up-close smell of a man.

Nicholas's ideal father would have been a combination Yankee third baseman and U.S. marshal, an athlete-moralist; James preferred deep chairs and oblique behavior. But living as Nicholas had in such a haphazard, manless household, he was a flexible child, and within a day of James's return from the war, Nicholas was pitching his voice so low it hurt and sneaking into his parents' bathroom to rub his face with the wet fur of James's shaving brush.

Nicholas studied his father and then copied him, arranging his small, strong body on the grass, but the damp, pebbly ground as well as his own

136

unliberated energy made him uncomfortable. He sat up and rocked back and forth, observing his father, trying to will him awake and athletic.

But no matter how inactive his father was, Nicholas wanted to be with him. He would have preferred sitting motionless on a Chinese rug watching James examine a contract than going rock climbing with his mother. Life with father was uneventful, but Nicholas needed calm. Weary from six years of domestic chaos, of nannies swooping in and out of his life, of his mother's unpredictable daily visits—bestowing a chocolate bar at eleven in the morning or a midnight kiss after the opera—of the social demands of family friends, of the continual refurbishment of the apartment, and of the pressure he felt to spare Thomas from this pressure, Nicholas wanted to be with his father.

"Daddy, how come you only brought me up here and not Tommy?"

"Nick, let me be."

"Because he's too little?"

"Yes. He's better off at the farm with Nanny . . ."

"Nanny Stewart."

"Yes, Nanny Stewart and Grandma and Grandpa."

"And Mummy needs to stay home and take naps before the baby gets born."

"Yes."

"Why?"

"Why don't you take a little walk? Okay, Nicky? Come back in fifteen minutes."

"Daddy."

"What?"

"I don't have a watch."

"Nick—"

"And I can't tell time anyway. Should I go over there and dig some worms for fishing?"

"Yes. Good idea."

"What should I put them in?"

"Nick, figure it out yourself. All right? Just let me relax."

"You had a rough week."

"Right. I had a rough week."

A month later, it was still rough. On Monday, James had stayed at his desk from eight in the morning until ten at night, reviewing a draft of a securities registration statement for one of Ivers and Hood's biggest clients, Republic Petroleum. Although he'd been made a partner three months earlier, his interest in his law firm was minimal. Nor, as he rubbed his hand over the soft evening stubble on his cheeks, did he care about the regulations of the

Securities and Exchange Commission or the prospects of Republic Petroleum as it gouged deeper into the bowels of Texas and Arabia. He who had helped save Western civilization now found it boring.

On Tuesday, he and Winifred dined at Le Nuit Bleu as guests of Dwayne Petrie, the president of Republic, and Mrs. Petrie, a big woman whose thick lips were so smeared with dark red lipstick they looked like raw hamburger hanging beneath her nose. Mr. Petrie wore a tie pin with the initial D in large diamonds and Mrs. Petrie a diamond necklace with a ruby, diamond, and sapphire D suspended over her abyss of a cleavage. "Deedee," Mr. Petrie said to his wife, "Jim here spent the war in France. In the OSS. The Oh So Social. All Ivy League boys playing foreign agent. Sitting in cafés and passing secret messages."

"Mr. Petrie," Win said softly. James, sitting opposite her, clamped his mouth shut so his sigh was filtered through his nose. In her ivory maternity dress, a double strand of Maisie's pearls, and her brown freckles, Win faded into the beige velvet banquette until she seemed almost invisible to James. As usual she wore no makeup. Her carrot hair might have redeemed her, but she must have spent that afternoon flattening and taming it into a flat knot at the nape of her neck in order to look, James assumed, sophisticated, a fitting wife for a worldly husband. As a result, before she spoke the only attention she'd received were the polite hellos due the wife of a young partner and the much warmer how-are-yous due the daughter of Samuel Tuttle. James sighed once again, a more attention-getting sigh, but Win's attention was locked on Mr. Petrie. "You see . . . about the OSS . . ."

"It's all right, Win," James murmured.

"Oh, James, please." She put down her fork and clasped her hands on top of her balloon of a pregnant belly. "I think—well, perhaps some people have the wrong idea about the OSS. James risked his life—"

"Win—"

"Jim, big fella," Mr. Petrie said. "You got one loyal wife there. I like to see that in a woman. Shows character." His wink to Win was so broad it would have been noted in the last row of the last balcony of a large theater. "I like your spirit, honey. I really do. Now come on. Finish up your lamb."

Joining them that evening was the senior corporate partner of Ivers and Hood, Hamilton Cummings, and his wife, Ginger. Ham Cummings wore thick wire-rimmed glasses and had no lips at all. His straight line of a mouth smiled only for Republic Petroleum. Ginger, a woman in her middle forties, had a delectable blond beauty not unlike that which James's mother, Louise, had possessed before James was born. She even had Louise's thin nose with flaring nostrils. Unfortunately, she was afflicted with the same disease, alcoholism, and after dessert her embarrassing slurred overtures to James—pressing her spoon full of mousse to his lips: "Would you like to taste mine, Jim?"—

had diminished into silence. She stared into the flame of the candle in the middle of the table, regal in pinned-up pale hair and black silk; still, like a duchess in mourning.

That had been Tuesday. On Wednesday he sat down for dinner and discovered a small Impressionist painting hanging over the sideboard. He couldn't recall the painter's name, but the triumph of lemon daylilies over ground and moss, lit by an afternoon haze, was unmistakably the work of genius.

"Well, James?" Win breathed. Flushed with heat and pregnancy and eagerness, she glanced from the painting to her husband and back again. "James? Isn't it something? I mean, there I was in the Wasserman Gallery with Westy Redding—she was having her Boullet watercolor appraised—and I nearly gasped, but then I said to myself, I said, 'Win, you mustn't,' but it was so marvelous and it hypnotized me, pulled me into it. I mean, there I was, in that garden, what Eden must have been like, and—what's wrong? Oh. Don't you like it, James?"

"'Don't you like it, James?'"

"James—"

"Ring the bell, please. She forgot my iced tea."

"James, I simply assumed you'd think it was beautiful. It never occurred to me you wouldn't like it. Please, please don't look through me like that."

"I'd like my iced tea."

"I'm sorry. I never thought—"

"That's a habit, isn't it."

"James . . ."

"Winifred, how many times do I have to say it? I'm drowning in your money. We live in an apartment I can't afford with furniture I can't afford and servants I can't afford and you wear a pair of goddamn earrings that would cost me a year's draw and—"

"But Mama gave them to me."

"And Mama gave you the nice watch too. And the nice pearls and the nice clothes. And Papa gave you the nice car and the nice check and the nice—"

"James, he gave the money to *us*."

"My ass he did."

"You're just talking like that because you think it will upset me."

"I'm talking like that because I'm sick of it. What's wrong with you? That check was made out to you. Every time I turn around someone is slipping you another few thousand and you're running out and buying something to improve my life. I tell you I have enough clothes, and two days later I find three shirts and a silk evening scarf—"

"But you *needed* one, James."

139

"*You* needed it. All I needed was to be left alone. How about that, Win? Could you manage that?"

"I do leave you alone. When you go into your study and close the door I never even *think* of knocking. But what does that have to do with a scarf?"

"A scarf and trusts for both boys and now a new painting I couldn't buy if I—"

"I used the money Uncle Joseph left me. And it's beautiful. You have to admit it, James. It really is. And everyone says it's a good investment. All I want is a beautiful house for you to come home to and for us to be happy, the way we were before the war. And everything I have belongs to you, James. You know that."

"Good. Then you won't mind if I sell the painting."

"James, stop it."

"Then it's not *ours*, is it? Is it, Win?"

"James, I hate to say it, but you don't seem to mind having Ogilvy's make your suits and going on trips and having your dinners cooked and served and your shirts pressed and the boys all fresh and shiny when you come home from work. You know I can't do any of that."

"You can. You won't."

"But it's silly."

"It's not silly, Win. It's just unpleasant."

"Well, why should things be unpleasant if they don't have to be? Do you really want me on my knees, scrubbing floors?"

"Winifred, I'm not a coal miner. I'm a partner in a Wall Street law firm, and you know damn well you wouldn't have to get on your knees."

"But why should we live like all the other young partners in those teeny two-bedroom apartments or those suburban Tudor things? There's no need for it, James. All I'm doing is making it nicer for us."

"You don't want a husband, Win. You want to do exactly what your family wants you to do, and then have a man around because that's just another Tuttle requirement. What you really want is a whore, and you're trying to turn me into one."

Winifred rose, walked to James's chair, and went down on her haunches, so she could look up to him. "James, please. James, don't talk like that. You know how much I respect you. I know it's been difficult since you've been home, making adjustments to civilian life and all, but everyone's going through it. Really they are. It must seem terribly dull, but you'll get used to it again. And you know all my sympathies are with you. If I can do anything—"

"Come on, Winifred, go back to your seat. I mean it. Just leave me alone, damn it."

"Oh, James, I know you don't like me to go on about it, but I love you so much, and it—"

"Win."

"Yes?"

"Let me be."

On Thursday morning, his secretary slunk into his office and closed the door behind her. She hid her mouth with her hand and mumbled through her fingers like a convict in a prison movie. "Mr. Cobleigh, the reason I didn't buzz is there's a lady on the phone who wants you but she refuses to give her name and I've asked her three times."

"Hmm. Oh, I know. It must be Mrs. Snoud. Hudson Container's widow. Her daughter is trying to have her declared incompetent."

"Oh. Gee, sorry to have come in here like this, Mr. Cobleigh, but I didn't know—"

"That's all right, Gert."

A moment later, James lifted the telephone to take the call he had not exactly expected but was not surprised to receive.

At noon on Friday, the interior windowless area of the law office where the secretaries sat was so hot that an hour earlier one of the women had collapsed, pitching forward and concussing her head on the keyboard of her typewriter. James glanced at his secretary. Her round face looked dangerously pink, and her white blouse was glued to her ample wet back. She managed a weak "Fine, Mr. Cobleigh" when he told her he'd be having lunch at his club.

Instead, James entered the tropical rain forest atmosphere of an uptown Lexington Avenue IRT station. A quarter hour later, only four blocks from his own apartment, his tie in a tight knot, his jacket properly buttoned, not a single hair out of place, he strode one block west on pavement that had softened in the heat.

A half hour later he was sipping his second iced gin and tonic and having his thighs stroked by the cool hands of the wife of the senior corporate partner of Ivers and Hood, Ginger Cummings.

Late on the night of September 1, 1947, when Win lay stirruped and exposed on the delivery room table in Lying-In Hospital, sweating and grunting, giving birth to Olivia Rebecca Cobleigh, James was in Southampton, Long Island, in the sea-scented white wicker bedroom of the Hamilton Cummingses' summer house, making love to Ginger Cummings for the third time that day, even though Ginger was so drunk she did not seem to comprehend she was having sexual intercourse and kept announcing it was late and time to say good night. (Ham Cummings, in Chicago for a five-million-dollar real estate closing, was at that moment lying back in his bed at the Ambassador, having a fifty-dollar prostitute do to him what Ginger had done to James two hours earlier.)

That same night, Nanny Stewart, a thick-jointed, six-foot-tall Scots-woman with dark brown eyes and a light brown mustache, allowed Thomas, who was crying, and Nicholas, who was not, to get into bed with her. "Now, Thomas. Do not fret. Be my big man." Her voice was so deep it made her body vibrate in a comforting hum. "Now, boys. Now, now. Your mother will soon be home with a new brother or sister, and your father will come home from his business trip just as soon as he hears about your mother, and all will be fine."

Thomas slept in the crook of her arm, his thumb a respectable half-inch from his mouth. Nicholas lay flat against her stomach, under her giant bosom, which shielded him the way a canopy might shelter him from the rain.

"There now. Such good boys. Oh, yes. Very good. Nicholas, are your eyes closed? You're a big, brave boy, aren't you? Too old for a nanny, of course, but stay here with Thomas. Shhh. Such a big boy. Don't fret any more. All mothers and fathers have words. Everyone will be home soon. You'll see, Nicholas. Shhh now. Sleep."

James's cousin Bryan was the outgoing sort who led the conga line at country club dances and hoisted his friends' undershorts up the flagpole at the yacht club, but he became a partner in the Providence law firm of Broadhurst & Fenn anyway because his father's costume jewelry company was the firm's third largest client. "The law is so effing boring, J.C.," Bryan said. The two men saw each other twice a year, when Bryan came to New York on business. "Is it boring in New York, too?"

"I don't know. I guess so."

"Law school was boring, but I said what the hell, it's Harvard and it's supposed to be boring. But this is even worse because it's still effing boring but there aren't any girls around. I mean, it's one thing to sit through Evidence if you know five minutes after it's over you can go out and squeeze titty. But here. Jeee-sus, J.C., I'm working my dick to the bone and then going over to old man Potter's desk to get his okay for every diddly-shit paper I draw up."

"Well, you have Jeannie and the kids."

"J.C., Jeannie's idea of a hot night is eating cheese toast in bed. And the kids are okay, nice kids, but not at ten at night."

"Jeannie's not . . ."

"Definitely not. Three kids and closed up shop. 'I caaan't, Bryan. I've got my little visitor and it would be all icky for you.' And on the two days a month she's not on the rag she's . . . forget it. Ever see those ice cubes with the holes in the middle? That's what it's like wonking Jeannie. Even practicing law is better."

"Um, do you have anyone else?"

"Sure. I don't have a choice, do I? I've got one of the secretaries, sweet, kind of dumb, takes care of her mother in a wheelchair and can only sneak out for a fast poke Wednesday nights. And the golf pro's daughter, built like an Amazon, get smacked by one of her tits and you can get knocked from here to Newport, but she's giving it to half the club so I don't get to see her that much. And then . . . you know, some sweet numbers who need a couple of twenties to lubricate their little cylinders. What the hell. It beats bar association meetings."

"I suppose."

"Hey, J.C., don't look so glum. It's not so bad."

"I suppose not."

"Stop supposing, for Christ's sake. What's wrong? Hmm? Having trouble with Winnie the Pooh?"

"No."

"No, I guess not. She must really crave it, popping out kids like it was more fun than a clambake. How many now?"

"Five. Nick, Tom, O—that's Olivia—and the twins, Michael and Abby. But that's it. Win knows it."

"She wants more?"

"I think so. It makes her feel important. Look, Bryan, she just has them and then there's the nanny and the maids and she doesn't have to actually fuss with them, but it gives her something else to do, another body to take for dancing lessons or buy skates for or talk about with her friends. She runs around with all those girls she went to school with—they're all wealthy and social and she's related to half of them—and they gossip about their lovers and she talks about her children and they give her a little pat on the head and say, 'Aren't you too, too marvelous, Win, managing the way you do.' She needs something to make her stand out so she forgets to put in that thing, and what do you know, eight months later she's guest of honor at another baby shower and she and her mother are planning the christening breakfast and then— one, two, three—the baby goes to Nanny Stewart and Win's off riding and shopping and lunching. You know Win. Perpetual motion. Busy with fifteen charities. Making dinner parties for some crippled harpist or spending a week looking for a new brush for her horse."

"Ah. So she doesn't have time for you?"

"No. She'll give me all the time I want. So would a couple of those friends of hers. What a crew they are."

"The question is, how much time do you want from her, J.C.? Come on. Talk to me. I'm your cousin. Your oldest buddy. Your best man, for Christ's sake. Didn't I get you into this in the first place?"

"I'm seeing someone."

"Jesus, I knew it. I just knew it."

"It's not—I'm not in love with her. I like her. She's great to look at.

143

Blond, everything nice and tight, with a kind of thin, cold bitch face, but . . . well, she really likes to be persuaded not to be such a cold bitch. Really likes it a lot."

"Christ, J.C. You are something. I mean, everything you touch turns to gold. Jesus, she sounds . . . Jesus, you are one lucky effing bastard. No kidding. I get Jeannie with her fat-mouth father and his chain of three lousy drugstores and some dumb little secretary with a flabby ass and you get a Tuttle and—"

"And a drunk. She knocks down more than a fifth of brandy a day. It takes her all day to work on it, but by nine, ten at night she's completely gone."

"Oh. When do you see her?"

"At lunch, usually. That's when she's best. Or when her husband is out of town I spend nights with her, dole it out so she doesn't turn into a rag doll before I'm ready to go to sleep. It works pretty well. Win thinks I have important business in Boston. My—um—lady plays long-distance operator."

"Sweet Christ, J.C., you've got some pair of brass balls. No kidding. What does the lady's husband do?"

"A lawyer."

"In a big firm?"

"Yes."

"Which one? Come on, J.C."

"Mine."

"Yours? You're kidding. Oh, shit."

"He's the senior corporate partner."

"Oh, shit! Are you *crazy?*"

"Why?"

"Dicking it to some drunk whose husband's over you? Are you kidding? What happens if she ties one on and starts blabbing about what you've been doing?"

"She has. At a party one night, about six months ago. We all laughed at her. Win said she thinks the lady has delusions about me. Delusions."

"You're out of your mind. Don't you realize what you're risking? You could screw up your whole life. Your job. Your family. Why pick *her?* You're not in love with her."

"No. But she's fun."

"Fun? She's poison. She could kill you. Jesus, didn't you get your fill of danger during the war? Why don't you just find someone and have a good time? This one is walking trouble. What if her husband finds out?"

"I think he knows. He's not as naive as Win, that's for sure."

"Oh, Christ. What's he going to do?"

"Nothing, probably."

"But what if he does?"

144

"Then I'll have a problem."

"J.C., don't you understand? You could piss everything away. Everything. If old man Tuttle—"

"So far, so good. I'm still on top."

"You could fall flat on your ass, J.C."

"Haven't yet, Bryan, have I?"

Gray stone window boxes, like miniature sarcophagi, rested on the window ledges outside the Cobleigh nursery eighteen floors above the street, and
Win had planted them so lavishly with trailing blue lobelia and upright pink
phlox that if Nanny Stewart had not shepherded the children downstairs each
day, they might think Manhattan was a pink and blue paradise, a vast alfresco
nursery.

That was the beginning. As if to deny the pressures of Manhattan, Win
tried to bring the clean country life of her parents' farm to Park Avenue. In
January of 1949, eight months pregnant with Abigail and Michael, she had
begun ordering large quantities of seed from catalogs and sowing them in
hundreds of tiny pots until Nicholas and Thomas could no longer use their
bathroom. African daisy sprouts filled the tub, and the sink and toilet seat
cover were obscured by a future salad of lettuce and parsley and tomato.
When spring came, she divided her bounty between the Cobleigh cottage in
the Berkshires and the Tuttle kitchen garden and bestowed homeless seed-
lings on friends, neighbors, and servants.

She could not be fruitful enough. In the autumn of 1949 a small white
truck with a discreet *Les Fleurs* painted on the driver's door began pulling up
to the delivery entrance, and a white-jacketed Mr. Plotsky and his green-
jacketed assistant would spend nearly an hour arranging the week's cut flowers in twenty freshly washed vases and bowls.

On Christmas morning, the children opened their presents under a
gleaming blue spruce. Mr. Plotsky had decked the halls with holly and ivy,
and the bill for the red and white poinsettias encircling the living room was
nearly five hundred dollars, although Win gave them away that afternoon
when she learned they were poisonous and might inadvertently be chewed by
Olivia or the twins or one of the two new Doberman puppies she had bought
for Nicholas and Thomas.

When the noise of five children watching a puppy urinate on the rug
compounded by six visiting Tuttles and Tuttles-in-law offering to clean it up
and calling for rags and club soda and paper toweling reached such a cre-
scendo that it blasted James out from his fog of scotch and cognac, his eyes
opened on masses of red and white roses scattered on chests and tables
throughout the bedroom. He lifted the crystal bud vase from his night table

and slammed it, along with its single perfect red rose, across the room, where it shattered against a silver pitcher of white roses that rested on Win's dresser.

Beyond the bedroom there was sudden silence. Within seconds, Winifred entered the room. "What was that noise?" she whispered.

"Who asked you to open the goddamn door?"

Winifred closed the door behind her and leaned against it, as if afraid of the consequences of getting too close to her husband. "It's eleven o'clock."

"Win, can't you leave me alone?"

"It's Christmas. James, you were gone all last night, and—"

"Get out."

"Nick *knows* something is wrong, James. And Tom—"

"I told you, get rid of that thing."

"I can't."

"You can."

"Oh, God. Oh, please, James, please. It won't be any bother to you. I swear it. I can't. I can't."

"I told you once and I'll tell you again. Either you go to Puerto Rico and get an abortion or I'll never touch you again. I mean it. I told you I'd had enough. I'm not going to be some goddamn stud to keep up the Tuttle line."

"It was an accident."

"They were all accidents."

"No they weren't, James. Please, if you'll just—"

"Get out of here."

"Dinner's at three. Tom and O made place cards. They're so cute, James—"

"I have other plans."

"Please. You can't."

"Can't I?"

The sky hung leaden, the air damp and heavy. It was one of those gray days that persist in Manhattan, chill, seasonless weather which underscores how far from unambiguous nature—from clear sun, cleansing storms, silent snow—the city has shifted. But the boys who ran through the thick air of the playing field, boys with red cheeks and shiny hair and brilliant school colors, seemed alien to the dullness, as if they'd been bred in a healthier place, an English meadow, a Danish seaport, and were immune to New York.

Nicholas shone. His arms stretched skyward, his fingers spread wide, and he sprang at precisely the right moment to grab the soccer ball as it hurtled toward the St. Stephen's goal he was tending. His coordination was equaled by his grace, and he would have drifted to the ground, a prepubescent demigod descending to earth to present a black and white orb to mankind, if the Cunningham center forward, an ox of a ten-year-old in green and gold, hadn't

146

tried to head the ball toward the goal and, in doing so, butted his thick skull into Nicholas's chin.

The pain started narrow as a dagger, but as it moved up through his jaw and the roof of his mouth into his head, it burgeoned until it felt like a shovel digging into his brain. Nicholas screamed, but the noise was muted as his cracked jaw locked onto his tongue, filling his mouth with blood. He came down on his right side, trying to open his mouth to spit out the blood and the broken teeth, afraid he would choke. But his jaw wouldn't work and the best he could do was blow a little blood out between his lips.

"You okay, Nick?" Coach Jensen demanded. "Nick? Nick, say something. What hurts, son?"

The pain that was tearing apart his head spread down his neck into his shoulder. Nicholas tried to take a deep relaxing breath, but his mouth was closed and his nose filled with mucus from involuntary tears, and the only way he could get air was in short, panicky sniffs. He lifted his hand to gesture the hovering coach away and then realized part of his agony was coming from the hand. He had fallen on it and his wrist was broken; his hand hung before him swollen, deformed, a fat flipper. When he saw it, and the red-purple streaks where the skin of his arm had come off in strips, he moaned, but his own voice sounded like an animal's, and it frightened him.

It frightened the Cunningham and St. Stephen's teams too, for he saw pairs and pairs of cleated shoes stepping back from him. "Nick!" Coach Jensen demanded. He sounded angry. "Nick! Say something."

"Jesus. Shit." The Cunningham coach sounded hoarse and angrier. "You better get an ambulance fast, Jake. His arm looks like a piece of raw meat. And the mouth."

He either fainted or slept on the way to New York Hospital, but that was a short respite. They swabbed his cuts with burning cold liquid and said "Hey! Hey!" when he tried to twist his way out of their grasp. They let his head droop as they lifted him from the bed on wheels to the X-ray table and said "Okay!" when he shrieked from the pain in his jaw. The doctor who wired his jaw held a huge needle up in the air and said, "You're what, ten years old? Come on, be a big boy! It's just a broken jaw and a broken wrist. We'll put you back together in no time. Easy as pie. You'll just be out a couple of back teeth. Who needs back teeth, huh? Now come on. Stop the crying. Be brave." When he tried to scramble out of the restraining straps that held him, the nurse demanded, "How can we help you if you're acting like this?" And when he wept when they pulled straight his curled fingers as they applied the cast, they said, "All right, now. It's been a little rough but it's almost over."

They would not release him because there was no one to claim him. Nicholas lay on a spare bed facing a white tiled wall in a corner of the emergency room, plastered and bandaged and very cold. The coach had told him to grab some sleep and then had excused himself to find a pay phone. "I'll keep trying your house and your dad's office, Nick." He also called the school's lawyer.

He kept his eyes closed and tried to think happy thoughts, but the pain would swell until it broke through in tears or a loud moan. Now that there was nothing more to be done to him, the interns and nurses behaved as if his bed were empty. They leaned against it and gossiped and drank coffee and whispered about him, that he was a spoiled rich kid from a private school. One said, "Yeah? What ever happened to the stiff upper lip they're supposed to have? Noisy little stinker. No, he's out like a light." But a minute later they forgot Nicholas and circled around their newest patients, the victims of a fire in a dry cleaning store.

Nicholas shut his eyes but it was too late; he had seen them, three people, one perhaps a woman, and he could smell them. He prayed, "Dear God. Please save these people. Don't let them die. Let their skin grow back. Please. Help them so it doesn't hurt and they stop screaming. Oh, God, let my mummy come. Please. Or my daddy. Just make my throat stop hurting, and my head and ear, and I'll never be fresh again, and God, please fix these people or let the doctors give them some better medicine so they stop the screams. Please, where is everyone?"

It was one of the few times he asked. Nicholas was the eldest, the strongest, the bravest, the quietest. He did well in school and in sports, and had a sweet smile, so his mother tousled his hair or kissed him as she passed on the way to soothe Thomas, Olivia, Michael, Abigail, or Edward, and the utter gentleness of her touch, the sweet odor of her perfume, softened the moment she was beside him and was so precious he would have felt greedy demanding more. His father worked late nearly every night and when he was home seemed perpetually stunned by the assault of the younger children and the dogs and the cat and the parrot. Nicholas could almost feel his father's temples throbbing and couldn't bear to burden him further with a demand for a game of checkers. And of course he never sought his brothers and sisters, for they were always there, on his lap, in his toy chest, yanking his sleeve, screeching in his ear, drooling on his shirt. *Nicky! Nicky! Nicky!* Hug me, read to me, take off my Band-Aid, tell Nanny I don't have to eat tapioca, fix my barrette, show me how to hold the ball for a sinker.

But now he needed someone. "Dear God, please let Mummy or Daddy know I'm here. Please let Nanny Stewart or Grandma or Grandpa. Anyone. Please find them. Thank you."

Win was five blocks from New York Hospital, at her friend Prissy's, where she was sipping a second martini and helping divide three hundred charitable New Yorkers into thirty congenial tables for the annual Cranberry Ball. James was two miles away, in the steam room of the New York Athletic

148

Club, getting ready for cocktails with his latest mistress. (Her name was Germaine Bonnier. She was the French teacher at St. Stephen's. James had met her two days after Ginger Cummings was admitted to a small institution in New Jersey to dry out. James had spied Mlle. Bonnier at Thomas's class's Fête Française and had propositioned her moments later—in French—while Win stood at his side smiling and nodding and trying to catch a word here and there.) Nanny Stewart was a mile away in Central Park, supervising Michael and Abigail as they wheeled the big pram with the baby, Edward, along the path to the zoo.

"Dear God, please have someone stop and come over here and ask me if I want some water. And let them give me a blanket. I'm sorry I hit O. I'll never do it again. Please make that man stop screaming like that. Please, the pain is going up behind my eye."

The headmaster of St. Stephen's tracked Win down nearly two hours later, and when she arrived at the emergency room what made her shudder was not so much Nicholas's ballooned purple face as his silence. He gazed at her from his one open eye and neither wept nor moaned nor tried to say "Mummy."

He was home by 6:00. At 6:02, Nanny held a straw to his lips and he managed a few swallows of vanilla milk, but all Nanny got for her trouble was a slight incline of the head. At 6:15, Thomas stroked Nicholas's good left hand. At 6:30, Olivia screamed and sobbed and wiped her nose on Nicholas's blanket and laid four of her dolls on Nicholas's bed. Olivia and Thomas got a flutter of his left eye. At 7:00, the Tuttles arrived with their chauffeur, who lugged a complete set of Hardy Boys books into the room. Nicholas offered a single tear. At 7:15, they all decided he wanted to sleep and left his room.

"The doctor says he'll be fine," Win explained to her parents. She rested her elbow on the high marble fireplace mantel in the living room and let her hand support her cheek. "I mean, he looks dreadful and of course he's in pain, but he'll be just fine."

"Of course he will," Samuel said.

"He'll have to take the pain pills for the next few days. They said they might make him a bit woozy."

"They do," Samuel said.

"But he'll mend."

"Of course."

Maisie, who had been sitting on a couch beside Samuel, stood suddenly and marched over to Win. She grabbed her daughter's arm from the mantel and shook it. "Where is your husband?" she demanded.

"Mama—"

"Where is he? His son has been injured and he was called at the office and they said he was at his club and he was not . . . naturally."

149

"Mama, he must be with a client."

"A most demanding client."

"Maisie."

"Really, Samuel, I do think I can speak to my own daughter. Winifred, how many times will you endure—"

"Mama, please."

"He is so unspeakably public! Christmas Eve. Your brother's fiftieth birthday. It is as if he takes pleasure in— Winifred, stop sniveling!"

"Maisie, now is hardly the time."

"Samuel, the time was never more opportune. Nicholas looks as if he'd been trampled by a horse and she bears up admirably, nobly, shoulders back, chin firm, hup-two, take charge. But look at her now. One *word,* one single criticism of that husband, and tears enough to bathe in. It is insufferable! My grandson is battered, unable to utter a single word, and is Winifred weeping for him? Oh, no. She is weeping because I dared suggest—"

"Mama, Mama, it's not that."

"Then what is it, you foolish, foolish girl?"

They sat in a silence broken only by the clatter of coffee cups until eleven thirty. Then a key turned in the door and James entered the apartment and walked to the lighted living room. "What is it?" he asked. His speech was thickened, and while he was not drunk, neither was he sober.

"Your son has been hurt," Maisie said.

"Hours ago," Samuel added.

"Which son?"

"Nicholas. James, please, he's fine; I mean he'll be all right, really, but he—"

James shouldered aside his in-laws and ran down the long corridor to Nicholas's bedroom. They pursued him.

"He's sleeping."

"He's been sedated."

"Do you think you can just—?"

James threw open Nicholas's door and flipped on the light.

"Christ almighty!" he gasped and rushed to the edge of the bed. "Nicky. Nicky, honey," he breathed.

"James, please don't—"

"Look at that. He woke him."

"His jaw is broken. Careful, for pity's sake."

"James, it was during the soccer game. One of the boys—"

James kneeled at the side of the bed. "Nicky, it's Daddy."

Nicholas peered out at James through his clear blue eye and the red, watery slit of the swollen one. He groaned, but managed to turn over onto his side. So slowly it seemed not to be happening at all, he raised his arm in its

150

plaster cast and put it around his father's neck. It hung there, white, heavy, motionless for a moment, and then began hugging James, drawing him closer.

James kissed his forehead. Through Nicholas's wired jaw came high-pitched whimpers. Win and the Tuttles edged nearer to the bed. They lowered their heads to try to discern if there was meaning behind the small, pathetic sounds. What they heard was Nicholas saying, "Daddy, Daddy, Daddy."

10

With thirty-five million dollars and, some say, its corporate head resting
on the shoulders of *William the Conqueror*, the studio has decided to
continue production of the Anglo-American epic. The film's star and executive producer, Nicholas Cobleigh, has notified them that he will not be
available as long as his wife's medical condition remains critical.
—*Wall Street Journal*

In the years after his smashup in soccer, Nicholas broke his leg (football), his
arm (riding), separated his shoulder (lacrosse), and sustained contusions, abra-
sions, cuts, and gouges so often he was never without a raw, unhealed patch.
He was an athlete without reservation, barreling past hulking opponents,
oblivious to fists, knees, and cleats. After his first year away at school,
Winifred no longer cringed at his swollen fingers or purple-yellow shins.

The girls at the nearby prep schools were not at all repelled. They
seemed fascinated by his bruises, reached with trembling fingers to touch the
spongy flesh of his blackened eye. Other Trowbridge boys were as bloodied
and broken as Nicholas, but none of them got such sweet probing.

It wasn't that he was the handsomest boy in school, although he was,
indeed, good-looking. His baby blond hair had darkened to straw color, shot
with strands of copper. It was silky straight. His eyes were a brilliant blue
washed with green, the color of a tropical sea, but they were his only exotic
feature. His appearance was conventionally Anglo-Saxon, with clear pale skin,
a longish face, and a nose so high-bridged it began between his eyebrows.

In repose his face appeared a little cold, and the young girls romanticized
him. Strong, silent. Still waters run deep. A cruel, sensuous mouth. Sadness
behind the eyes. The truth was that Nicholas was a fairly conventional boy,
and the passionate crushes he aroused confused him. A girl he barely knew
would kiss his palm or caress his legs and when he drew back—embarrassed,
stimulated, a little frightened—the girl would sigh "Oh, Nicky" or "You won't
let anyone get through to you, will you?" Of course, reports of his icy control
drew more girls, most of whom found in him an irresistible something that, in
fact, wasn't there.

Their desire for him was magnified when they saw Nicky at the beach,
Nicky in shorts, Nicky with his shirt knotted around his neck on the ball field.
He had a beautiful body, more slender than massive, with hard risings of
muscle. Even the least sensuous of girls felt their fingers flexing, aching to
trace the veins running up his arms. The others wanted to rub his shoulders,

or press themselves against his back, or ruffle and smooth the pale hair on his calves.

Heather Smith was the first girl who got the chance. There was nothing outstanding about her, although Nicholas was attracted to her cheerfulness and her simpleness. She smiled at him a great deal and didn't seem to expect something mysterious, the thing the other girls kept seeking and he could not find. At the mixer where they met, Heather told Nicholas he was too cute for words and demanded he make a muscle for her. He did, even though he felt silly at the request, holding his forearm tight against his waist and squeezing his bicep until it trembled. Heather felt through his blazer sleeve and said "Oooh." By the end of the evening he was enchanted by her friendly dopiness, by her indifference to proving she was capable of an intellectual discussion. She wasn't capable and Nicholas, a good enough student, was relieved. He didn't like intellectual discussions with girls. They never seemed satisfied with his answers and would say "Oh, you mean . . ." as they fox-trotted past the chaperones. Heather liked him just the way he was. And Nicholas fell for nice, dumb, sexy Heather Smith.

As a young boy, Nicholas had heard his Grandpa Samuel refer to a pretty grandniece as an absolute peach, but it wasn't until he was sixteen years old that the phrase lived. Heather was truly a peach.

Winter vacations in Hobe Sound and summers in Martha's Vineyard had warmed Heather's fair skin to a golden pink and bleached the fuzz on her arms and legs and upper lip. Prep school athletics solidified her natural pudginess into muscle, and she looked firm and round and juicy. Her bare thighs spread slightly on the seat of her wooden lawn chair; the insides were paler and more tender looking than the burnished tops.

Nicholas realized Heather had seen him staring because she was moving again. She wriggled her bottom in the chair and then raised her knee so her heel rested perpendicular to the crotch of her loose gray camp shorts. When he looked her straight in the eye to break her magic, she lowered her heavy eyelids and sucked the soft pad of flesh on her thumb. He didn't know if she was teasing him by doing sexy calendar-girl things to get him hot or if she was an innocent who had no idea of what a peach she was. He wanted to take her big ripe thigh and bite it. Instead, he crossed his legs so her father couldn't see the evidence of his bewitchment and accepted a vanilla wafer from her mother.

"I hear you're captain of the lacrosse team," Colonel Smith said. He had retired to his sprawling family home in East Hill, Massachusetts, two years earlier, but his hair was still more regulation army than patrician Yankee. Stiff bristles of gray poked out all over his scalp, like a two days' growth of beard. The skin beneath was badly sunburned, although the colonel did not seem to be discomforted by anything more than Nicholas's presence on a Sunday afternoon. Heather, a student at the girls' school East Hill, lived at home. Though it was the custom for girls in her position—townies—to invite their beaux to meet their parents, the colonel did not seem pleased; he sat at the edge of his chair, as if planning an attack with his aides. "I said, I hear you're captain of the lacrosse team."

"Oh. Yes, sir." Nicholas nearly stammered. It was the first week of June, but the sun was as blinding and relentless as late July. The sugar on Mrs. Smith's frosted grapes had melted, and they lay on a glass plate, a syrupy mess, on a small white wrought-iron table that stood like a hub between them. Across from Nicholas, Heather held a grape between her thumb and index finger and was licking the melted sugar that had dripped down her forearm.

"What position do you play?" Nicholas was staring at Heather's flicking tongue. "For Christ's sake, Heather, get a napkin," the colonel ordered. He turned back to Nicholas. "Did you hear my question?"

"No. Sorry, sir."

"You have a hearing problem?"

"No, sir."

"I said, what position do you play? Position! Lacrosse!"

"Oh. Midfield, sir." The colonel's face was growing brighter. Nicholas hoped it was from the heat. He knew he was making a poor impression. The colonel wanted snappy answers, not vagueness. Vagueness was fine for Heather, who had let her face drift up toward the sun. It was probably warming the peachy fuzz that ran between her cheeks and her ears down to her jaw. Nicholas whipped his head back to the colonel. "We have a pretty good team, sir." His voice sounded reedy. He didn't want the colonel to think the lacrosse team was the dog of Trowbridge's athletic program. "We have an eleven–four record, sir." He hated saying sir all the time, like an army recruit, but he wasn't sure whether the title Colonel was correct for someone who had retired, and he didn't want to say Mister for fear of eliciting even more contempt.

"Bad losses?"

"No, sir."

"What were the scores?"

"I really can't recall now, sir." He wanted to turn and look across to Heather. She was probably doing something new, maybe running her hand over her hair or massaging the back of her neck, her arm raised so the half-moon of sweat on her blouse showed.

"Lose to Middlesex?"

"Sorry. I didn't hear you. Sir."

"Mid-dle-sex."

"Oh. No, we didn't play Middlesex."

154

"I'm Middlesex."

"I didn't know that, sir. I have a friend there. It's a good school."

"I know it's a good school."

"Did you go to West Point after Middlesex, sir?"

"Who told you I went to West Point?" The gash that was the colonel's mouth grew tighter.

"Oh, well. I mean, you were in the army."

"Do you think every officer is a West Point graduate?"

"No, sir. Of course not."

"I went to Dartmouth. Are you thinking of Dartmouth?"

"Well, I thought I'd think about colleges this summer because I don't have to apply until next fall and—"

"Where did your father go?"

"Brown." The colonel did not react, as though he had received no new information. "I said, my father went to Brown, sir."

"I heard you. Any other sports?"

"I beg your pardon, sir?"

"You should have your hearing checked," the colonel boomed. "I said, Any other sports? *Do you play any—*"

"Oh, yes."

"*—other sports?*"

"Sorry. I mean, yes, I play football."

"Varsity?"

"Yes, sir."

"Position?"

"Back."

"Record?"

"Seven–nine, sir."

"All right." The colonel turned away. "Heather," he snapped. "Stop fiddling with your toes, for Christ's sake. It's four thirty. Walk back with him to the depot."

Nicholas stood. His muscles were cramped after the afternoon in the low lawn chair, and he swayed on his unsteady legs and from the cumulative effect of too much sun and too little food. Heather had invited him for Sunday lunch, but Mrs. Smith had brought out only the grapes, vanilla wafers, and a pitcher of uniced lemonade. The colonel squinted at him and Nicholas knew he suspected he had been drinking. He wanted to reassure the colonel, but he couldn't say he was just a little dizzy because he hadn't been given any lunch. Heather walked over to him, pressed her side against his, and took his hand. The colonel's squint narrowed. "Thank you, Mrs. Smith," Nicholas said. Heather's mother had said nothing more than "How do you do?" to him, and most of the time he had forgotten she was there. If Heather was a peach, her mother was a banana: skinny, bent a little, yellow. She looked ill. He would have thought she had cancer, but Heather had told him she was a terrific athlete and had won the club's women's cup in both golf and tennis.

"Y' welcome," Mrs. Smith said.

"Thank you, sir," he said to the colonel. The man was a good deal over six feet tall, with the solidity of a wrestler. "I'll think about Dartmouth."

"You don't have to," the colonel said.

"I had a very nice time," Nicholas said to both Smiths. "I appreciate your asking me." They were silent. "Well, have a nice summer." Heather pulled his hand, and he followed her around the side of the house. "Nice meeting you," he called, but the colonel had disappeared and Mrs. Smith, bent over her sticky grapes, did not seem to hear him.

"They *loved* you," Heather said.

"God, Heather." She lay on top of him. She had unbuttoned his shirt and was running her hand over his chest and nipples. Nicholas wavered between frenzy and fear. They were right in the middle of East Hill, inside the village commons, but were hidden by a bank of junipers. The earth under him was cold and gritty. Scratchy branchlets of juniper reached out and tickled his shoulders. "I can't take it, Heather." She had opened her blouse and lifted up her bra. Her breasts were like two hard auxiliary peaches. She tried to squash them against his chest. "Oh, God, no. I'll miss the bus."

"There's another at six. Come on. Put your tongue in my mouth."

"I have to be at dining hall at six."

"My Nicky is so cute."

"Heather, this isn't a good idea." She was rocking back and forth. Actually humping him. He thought about the condom in his wallet that his roommate bought for him a year and a half before. The red foil wrapper was worn and cracked. It probably wasn't any good. "Don't do that, Heather." She bent forward and stuck her tongue in his ear. "Jesus, Heather." He'd remembered the condom when his bus pulled into East Hill, but she'd been at the depot, jumping up and waving at him, so he couldn't exactly stop at the drugstore and ask for a couple of rubbers when the druggist probably knew her since she was a little girl and might even be a deacon at her church. He opened the button of his khaki slacks, but as he reached for the tab of the zipper Heather's hand closed over his and pulled his away.

"Nicky, no. You'll be too tempted."

"Please. I swear I won't get carried away."

"No. Stop." He waited for her to slide off, but instead she licked her lips and humped him harder than she had before.

"Heather, I'm not kidding. I can't take any more of this."

"Oh, Nicky." She sat tall, as if riding a skittish horse in a show. Her

156

breasts and pageboy flopped to her rhythm. He had never seen anything like it.

If she didn't stop, he'd come and would go back to Trowbridge with the telltale dark splotch on his slacks and would have to hear, for weeks and weeks, "Cobleigh didn't get it." He groaned. Heather clamped her hand over his mouth and pointed with her chin under the junipers. He could make out two pairs of adult legs dangling from a park bench not more than fifteen feet away. A new wave of passion washed over him and he said "Heather" louder than he had before, as if daring them to come and stop them. Heather sat still. "Oh, Heather," he murmured, much softer. He didn't know which was worse, the terrible torture she was inflicting or its cessation. "Please, Heather."

"Love me, Nicky?" It was not the time to admit he wasn't sure. "Nicky?"

"Yes. Yes."

She squeezed her legs tight against his hips, but instead of thrusting her pelvis back and forth again, she ground herself into him. "How much?" The village commons ceased to exist and so did the junipers and the chill earth under him. Even Heather didn't matter. There was only sensitivity now, centered in one swollen spot, expanding until the pressure became so unendurable he began to whimper. "How much do you love me? Come on, tell me, Nicky."

"More than anything," he choked. "Everything." He was almost there. He knotted his arms around her waist and pulled her in so close she could no longer move. He pressed into her as hard as he could.

"You'll give me your varsity sweater?"

"Yes." The pressure became pain.

"And we'll see each other every—"

"Yes!" An instant after he made the commitment he came, clutching Heather as the spurt of hot semen splashed forth. "Oh, boy."

At the depot minutes later, she kissed her index finger and placed it on his lips tenderly, like a wife. "'Bye, Heather." His madras shirt hung over his slacks. Its loose, flapping tails might have been an arrow pointing out to every passerby exactly what had happened.

"Nicky, try to come up to the Vineyard. It's so much more fun than boring Connecticut or the boring Berkshires. Really, Mummy and Daddy would adore having you, and I know a bunch of really great kids."

"We're probably going to England. One of my mother's friends—"

"Nicky, England looks just like all the pictures and you can't get hamburgers. Come on. Promise me you'll try."

"Okay."

"Okay what?"

"Okay, Heather."

"No! I mean, 'Okay, I'll try to get up to the Vineyard this summer.' Nicky, you are just so-o-o cute."

The bus approached along the main street of East Hill, its rumble muffled by the dark green canopy of elms, and stopped. Heather held him back until the two other East Hill passengers—another Trowbridge boy and a wrinkled man in carpenter's overalls—climbed on, and then, as the driver and passengers watched, she threw her arms around his neck and kissed him a goodbye that was longer on suction than on passion. He boarded then, his muted, obligatory echo of Heather's "I love you" making him blush. As the bus pulled away he dropped his head into his hands. His temples throbbed as if they'd been punched. His forehead felt feverish. But he lifted his head again because he heard "Nicky! Nicky!" Heather was running alongside the bus. He waved. Smiled. She was shouting something to him. He managed to drag open the window and stick his head out. "Think about Dartmouth!" she was yelling as the bus left East Hill, Massachusetts, and drove north.

Trowbridge School (the "The" had been dropped in 1884) lay on the east bank of the Connecticut River, just outside Beale, Massachusetts, a town so New England pure and Christmas-card quaint it might have had the heart of America beating inside its old clock tower. It was a cold heart, for outsiders weren't welcome and antique dealers and amateur photographers soon learned to drive south to Felsham, where they could dine at the Powder Horn Inn and watch candles being dipped at Early Light. But the frostiness of Beale suited the Trowbridge boys, for the school was accepted as an adjunct to the town and as such the boys became honorary old-line Yankees. The boys, in turn, embraced the spirit of the town so intensely that upon graduation most felt bereft at leaving, as if they'd been kicked out of Pilgrim heaven.

Trowbridge lay in a deep green valley just by the river. From Beale, the buildings looked like thick white brushstrokes. The pristine steeple of the school's chapel rose gracefully and modestly and gleamed against the sky. In the winter the buildings and the snow seemed to compete to be the standard of perfect whiteness.

For all its physical perfection, the school's reputation was a little blotchy. Other prep schools consistently graduated boys who knew one end of a receiving line from another and could return a serve or parse a sentence with at least minimum competence, but people never knew what to expect from a Trowbridge boy; he might be a psychopath or a pig or the most honorable gentleman.

The school had a flexible admissions policy. Historically, many of its students came from New York families of Dutch or English stock, families who had settled in Manhattan and the Hudson Valley in the seventeenth and eighteenth centuries. Thus, if a boy was sufficiently Tuttle or Sprague or Van

Essendelft, whether he had a genius for mathematics or a talent for torturing cats, he would be assured a Trowbridge education.

Likewise, a man might have made his reputation and fortune as a whoremaster, but if his pocketbook was open wide enough, his boy could room with a blueblood. There were other sorts too: a few brilliant scholarship students; boys of distinguished lineage who had been rejected by or thrown out of other prep schools; rich little princes from washed-up countries.

The Tuttles were loyal, sentimental, and lazy Trowbridge alumni. It never occurred to them that their children might get a better education elsewhere. And since James Cobleigh's attendance at a public school had disqualified him from offering an opinion in the matter, it was Samuel Tuttle who made the decision. Samuel called the headmaster—bypassing the director of admissions entirely—and announced Trowbridge's newest Tuttle, whose name happened to be Cobleigh. The headmaster declared he anticipated Nicholas's arrival with pleasure. So Nicholas (and later his brothers Thomas, Michael, and Edward) followed his uncles Jeremiah, Caleb, and Jesse, his Grandpa Samuel, and Tuttles of earlier generations to Trowbridge. There he roomed with Charlie Harrison, the son of a fifth-grade dropout who had founded a chain of supermarkets that speckled a map of the East from Bangor to Baltimore.

Charlie was everything Nicholas wished he was: six feet tall, hairy, worldly, a whiz at math. From his mother, a willowy Boston Irish-Catholic girl, Charlie had gotten his height, his fine looks—dark hair, sparkly black eyes, a button of a nose—and his charm. Mrs. Harrison had worked as a bookkeeper for a cheese processor and had met Mr. Harrison when she was seventeen and he was forty, an overweight, fat-mouthed bachelor who had transformed his family's corner grocery into (then) twenty-six Corner Groceries. Of course he won her, but not before he agreed that the house and children would be her business. They both flourished, for Mrs. Harrison was bright and ambitious but never so eager for advancement that she seemed embarrassed by her husband's lack of polish. He continued to chew cigars, spitting bits of the ends into ashtrays, and sit on her Federalist wing chair spouting off about the Red Sox to her Preservation Society friends, his undershirt gaping where the buttons of his shirt had popped. Mrs. Harrison merely explained that her husband was a character, and he was, and no one had to be told he was a very rich character as well.

The Harrison children, Charlie and a younger sister who unfortunately resembled their father, were molded with capital care. While the six Cobleigh children had that series of English nannies, the two Harrisons had nannies and a French governess. They had piano, violin, elocution, drawing, dancing, and riding instructors. While Nicholas spent most of his summers at his family's cabin in the Berkshires or at his grandparents' farm in Connecticut—

with an occasional awed weekend at his Uncle Jeremiah and Aunt Polly Tuttle's mansion in Newport—Charlie spent his summers in Europe, grandly touring with his mother, her maid, his sister, and the annual Harvard student who had been hired as Charlie's tutor, instructing him ostensibly in art history or German but really in social graces. Nicholas, who had not inherited James's facility for languages, was awed by Charlie's mastery of French, Italian, and German and wowed by Charlie's experiences with the prostitutes of Nice, Rome, and Munich. Not that Charlie was a braggart; one of his charms was his willingness to tell elaborate, humiliating tales of being an arriviste, of paying top price for ballet tickets to impress an international socialite and discovering the seats were behind a pillar at the Paris Opera House, of being at a dinner in the Midlands, seated next to an earl's daughter, and having the first course, woodcock—a game bird that resembled a roasted parakeet—go flying as he stabbed it, soaring from his plate into her lap.

From his father, Charlie got his sense of reality as well as his most dominant trait: ambition. He was not as fine a natural athlete as Nicholas, but he trained with a dedication incomprehensible to Nicholas, slogging across a swampy football field until it was dark, long after Nicholas was back in their room, long after the coach, huddled in a blanket and sick with cold and fatigue, ordered him to stop. He became Trowbridge's finest athlete. Nicholas had never met anyone who tried so hard.

Charlie drove himself in schoolwork too. Nicholas was bright, his work was solid, but when he finished an assignment he'd lay down his pen and smile. Charlie would write an essay over and over, whittling it down to perfection until the moment it had to be handed in. Nicholas tried to emulate him once, but, by his third trip to the library to glean still more information on Woodrow Wilson's relationship with Congress, he grew irritable and resentful of Charlie's unbroken string of perfect grades. But his resentment did not last long. Nicholas was too good-natured to be covetous, and realistic enough to understand that he already was where Charlie was trying to go.

Their friendship was a warm one, closer than most of that era, because both boys had ascended to the mountaintop of 1950s manliness and stayed there without a struggle. They excelled in sports, were adored by girls, and so they were relaxed, exchanging views and confidences fairly freely, for it did not occur to them to feel embarrassed about being intelligent or even occasionally emotional.

By October of their last year at Trowbridge, Nicholas and Charlie were the most admired sixth-formers in the school. Nicholas was viewed as cool, able, and stylish. His quietness was held to be the epitome of self-containment, his faithfulness to Heather Smith clear proof he must be getting it.

Charlie was considered godlike. He had it all: a chest full of curly hair, a drawer full of love letters from twin sisters in Boston—two exquisite blond

160

china-doll girls—and offers from every Ivy League college to come and play on their football team.

Charlie sat at his desk in his gym shorts, rubbing the hair on his chest as if it were a beloved pet, occasionally making notations for a solution to a problem for his calculus tutorial. He banged his heels together in no discernible meter. The soles of his feet were dark gray from walking across the unwashed dormitory floor.

As sixth-formers, they were deemed young men, not boys, and so were not required to open their door for room inspection or even the twice-weekly swish of the janitorial mop. Most of the class responded to this expression of confidence in their maturity by allowing their rooms to degenerate into microcosmic slums, wallowing in their own filth like gleeful baby pigs. As in everything else, Nicholas and Charlie excelled; their room was the piggiest.

Nicholas sprawled in yellowed undershorts on a bare mattress. He'd spilled an illicit beer on his sheet the week before and had not bothered to remake the stripped bed. A book lay beside him on the stained rose and tan mattress ticking. Every few minutes he'd lethargically underline a phrase in red pen for his Shakespeare seminar paper, "Meteorological Imagery in *King Lear*." His pillow was a pair of gray flannel slacks he'd worn to church the second week of school and then crumpled into a scratchy but adequate ball. Although he was not as dirty as Charlie—whose weekly bath was a plunge into the swimming pool before a mixer and who never changed his wool socks, allowing the perspiration to evaporate overnight—Nicholas's half of the room looked more degenerate. Class notes, candy wrappers, T-shirts littered the floor, and he shared his bed with his lacrosse stick and his applications to Brown, Williams, and Amherst. Nicholas yawned and scratched his scrotum.

A moment later Charlie scratched his armpit, then lifted his arm and sniffed under it. "Mmm. Smells great. Sweets for the sweet." He covered his math notes with his textbook and glanced over to Nicholas. "Now?" he asked softly. "It's late enough."

"Now." Nicholas slithered down his mattress and flicked off the light switch with his foot. The room went black. Charlie's desk drawer creaked open and closed. "You have it?" Nicholas demanded.

"Yes," Charlie said. "Here. You first."

Nicholas swished his hand in the dark until it touched the vodka bottle. "Cheers," he whispered, then hoisted it and took two long swigs. "Holy shit," he croaked.

"Good stuff?" Charlie grabbed for the bottle. Nicholas heard a glugging like water going down a clogged drain. "Jee-sus! High octane."

The bottle was passed many times. Within minutes Nicholas had trouble holding up his head, but he ascribed that to being disoriented in the dark.

Certainly he did not know he was drunk, and when Charlie announced "All gone!" in a baby voice, Nicholas was surprised. The bottle rolled on the floor, making what Nicholas thought was a catastrophic racket for glass on wood. "Wowie," Charlie said. "It goes straight to your dick."

"Shut up, Charlie. You're talking too loud."

"No, I'm not. Wow. Hey, Nick, wouldn't it be great if Babs was here right now? I mean right now, this minute. Oooch, bad Babs. I'd stick it in so far it'd come out the back."

"What about Betty?" Betty and Babs were Charlie's identical twins. "If you're doing it to Babs, what would you do about Betty?"

"Do her later. Or give her to you. Hey, how about that? Betty's nice, Nick. Just like Babs. You'd really like her."

Nicholas let his feet drop to the floor. He tried to remember where the door was, but he kept confusing the room with the one he had had the year before. He could not recall in which direction Charlie was either. "Oh, shit."

"You sick?"

"No."

"Listen, Nick. You can have Betty or Babs. Which one do you want?"

"I don't know. How can you tell them apart?"

"I'm not really sure. Anyway, what's the difference? They're both good."

"Charlie, I don't know. What about Heather?"

"Jesus, you're nuts. I mean, she's an Epsilon semi-moron. Fat, and all that dumb fuzz on her face, like a goddamn tennis ball. No one gets her, Nick. You could have any girl in the world—you know how they all get crushes on you—and you stick with that toad-load Heather. She's so dumb! Don't you want to have a girl you can talk to? Now listen, Babs is crazy about you. So is Betty. Great girls. They're what girls should be. You know. Gorgeous. Smart. Fun. And they're nice too. You can have either one. Come on, let's call them."

"No."

"No? You don't want one?"

"Well, I don't know, but we can't go out of the room. Remember? Not even to go to the john. If we have to piss, we piss out the window. Open the door, trouble."

"We can go, Nick. Come on. Betty or Babs? We'll be quiet. Just take your pick."

"It's too late."

"It's never too late."

"You sure?"

"Sure I'm sure." Charlie rose. His desk chair crashed to the floor. Nicholas covered his ears. Seconds later, Charlie opened the door. Hall light

162

streamed in. Nicholas shut his eyes. "Come on. Move ass, Cobleigh. We're going to the phone."

"What about Heather, Charlie?"

"Forget her. She's bad news." Charlie dragged a limp Nicholas out of the room and into the hall. It was filled with the silence of the sleepers behind their doors. "We're gonna get it!" Charlie called so loudly that the first of the wakened boys began murmuring almost immediately.

"Gonna get it?"

"I'm gonna call Babs and Betty and say come over right now and give it to us." Nicholas tried to walk faster along the narrow hall to get to the telephone at the end, but he stepped on his own instep and crashed against a wall, slamming his shoulder and the side of his head. He reached toward his head to rub it but then sank to the floor laughing, quietly at first, then with huge whoops. "Up, Nick," Charlie said. Doors opened, but just a crack. Charlie grabbed Nicholas's wrists to yank him up, but Nicholas crashed back, pulling Charlie face down on the floor with a monstrous thud.

"How're we gonna call if we can't get up?" Nicholas asked. He assumed his voice was modulated. In fact, he was shouting. "How're we gonna get it if we can't get up?"

Charlie lifted his head. "We can get up. Hey, wait. Get it up! Get it up! Get it, Nick?"

"Hello, Babs," Nicholas yelled. "Hi, Babs. You really like me, Babs? You wanna get it? I'm gonna give it to you!" He began laughing again, holding his sides to keep control. He made a fist and banged the wall beside him. "Babsie, open up. Knock, knock. Gonna knock you, Babsie."

"Bang, asshole," Charlie shrieked. "Bang, bang, bang."

"Mr. Harrison! Mr. Cobleigh!" The housemaster, Mr. Keil, loomed above them, his bony shins shining white behind the spidery hairs on his legs. He yanked the belt of his bathrobe. "What have you done?"

"Bang," Nicholas said to him, in a very small voice.

Martin Wigglesworth looked more like an Indiana funeral director than headmaster of a New England preparatory school. His skin appeared thick and waxy, as if over the years he'd sniffed too much embalming fluid. His chin came to such a sharp point that from a distance it looked like a goatee, and his pursed mouth and eagle-beak nose added to his air of a professional non-smiler. He eschewed reassuring tweeds, preferring instead solid black broadcloth suits and somber, skinny ties. When he greeted visitors with "Good morning" or "Good evening," his tone implied the "good" was mere convention.

The scores of silly nicknames his last name inspired died on the tongues of new boys. The students of Trowbridge spoke of him as Dr.Wigglesworth, as did their parents, nearly all of whom were just as afraid of him as their sons were.

Winifred Cobleigh, for example, answered Dr. Wigglesworth's "I assume you know what Nicholas has done?" with a "No" so high and quavering she might have been a three-year-old accused of soiling her bloomers. She wrapped the straps of her alligator handbag round and round her index finger. She was seated before the headmaster's desk, her back toward Nicholas. He was standing beside Charlie, leaning against the closed office door. He wished he could see her face and give her a little smile, just so she'd stop fidgeting, anticipating the crime of the century.

His father wouldn't have fidgeted. James would have sat straight and perfect, his wing tips polished to a cold gleam, his hair so flawlessly cut it didn't move, his handsome hauteur daunting Dr. Wigglesworth. But when they were summoned by Mr. Keil, the housemaster said to Charlie, "Your father is with Dr. Wigglesworth." He turned to Nicholas. "Yours was apparently at some legal function and could not be reached. Instead, your mother is here."

Winifred squirmed in her chair as if trying to locate the softest spot with her backside. She had tied her hair in a bun at the back of her neck—a proper visit-the-headmaster style—but it had reasserted itself, and frizzy wisps of red stuck out all over her head. It was the hair of an overwrought person.

Nicholas looked at Charlie. Although it was four in the afternoon, sixteen hours after their first taste of vodka, Charlie still looked drunk. His eyes were open unnaturally wide, and he was staring at his father with a doltish expression, his mouth agape, his tongue resting on his bottom lip. Nicholas still was queasy. His eyeballs felt swollen. He had a terrible taste in his mouth, as if he had bit into something mushy with decay.

"And you, Mr. Harrison?" Dr. Wigglesworth asked Charlie's father. "Do you have any idea why I asked you to repair to Trowbridge immediately?"

Louis Harrison (known as Big Lou to his colleagues in the supermarket industry and to the FBI, who was investigating his sweetheart contracts with truckers, butchers, and warehousemen) grunted. "What?"

"I asked, merely, if perhaps Mr. Keil or Charles happened to mention to you just why it was necessary to make this trip, no doubt at great inconvenience to yourself."

Mr. Harrison sat beside Winifred facing Dr. Wigglesworth's desk, but his chair was angled so that Nicholas could see his quarter profile. He was of average height, his torso long in comparison to his stumpy legs, but his two hundred fifty pounds of hard, authoritative fat made him look imposing. And he was impressive in his disregard for the ambience of Trowbridge. Most nonalumni fathers tried to look like the sort of man their sons were becoming, but Mr. Harrison wore a sky-blue suit with an open-necked red sports shirt with tiny dog faces printed in black all over the fabric. Nicholas shifted his weight from one foot to the other. Mr. Harrison was taking more time to respond to the headmaster than anyone ever had. He looked, and his mother had pulled her handbag strap tighter, choking off the circulation to her finger, and Dr. Wigglesworth had lifted one of the glass paperweights on his desk and hefted it in his hand. It dropped with a hideous clunk when Mr. Harrison finally spoke. "We got a problem, Doc. Let's talk."

"Well, naturally, it is my hope we can do just that."

"Okay. Now listen. I get a call at six this morning." Mr. Harrison's Boston accent was much more pronounced than Charlie's, and Nicholas had difficulty hearing where one word ended and the next began. "I drove over from Boston. Mrs. Cobleigh here came—what did you do, drive up?" Winifred shook her head. "Fly?" She nodded, turning from Dr. Wigglesworth to Mr. Harrison. Nicholas noted she seemed more fascinated than appalled by him, staring at his chins and his dog-print shirt. "She flew up from New York, Doc. You can see she's white as a ghost, all upset, so why don't you just tell us what the boys did."

Dr. Wigglesworth's entire face seemed to narrow, as if forming itself into the cutting edge of a cleaver. He bent sideways, opened a low desk drawer and lifted the empty vodka bottle to his desk. "They have admitted drinking the entire contents of this very bottle."

"They smash up anything?"

"Fortunately, no."

"Fight?"

"I beg your pardon, Mr. Harrison. Perhaps you don't realize the import—"

"Did they hurt anyone?"

"No."

"So what happened?"

"They were drunk, sir. Drunk and making a horrible spectacle of themselves, coming out of their pigsty of a room and shrieking the most obscene, the most—"

"That's it?"

"Perhaps you don't understand our ways, Mr. Harrison. Alcoholic beverages are strictly—"

"You called me six in the morning because two kids tied one on?"

"We restrained ourselves, actually. We didn't want you driving through the night."

"Doc, tell me. What's the big deal?"

Winifred reached out and gently touched Louis Harrison's cuff. "Mr.

Harrison," she said, so low Nicholas could hardly hear her, "they're really quite unbending about this sort of thing."

"Well, let's see about that, Mrs. Cobleigh." He gave her hand a reassuring pat, the way a trainer does his boxer between rounds. "All right? Let me handle it." Winifred nodded. "Now listen, Doc, you're a minister, right? So why don't you just have a little—what do you call it?—a little compassion. These kids made a mistake. It happens. Turn the other cheek and forgive and forget."

"Mr. Harrison, both as a minister and as headmaster of Trowbridge, I am obliged to uphold certain standards of behavior. I am afraid we cannot tolerate this flagrant violation of our rules. Even from—or, perhaps, most especially from—two of our finest students, two young men for whom I personally held the most exalted hopes, two boys who might have reached the heights of excellence, who I prayed might bring honor to—" He stopped because Win had suddenly dropped her head and hidden her face in her hands. Nicholas looked away, wishing he were alone so he could cry, wishing for the hundredth time that day that his father could have been found. Dr. Wigglesworth was too much for his mother; she could not even correct a surly maid. "Mrs. Cobleigh, your family's history has been interwoven with Trowbridge's and it pains me more than I can say to have to—"

"Cut the crap!" Mr. Harrison's voice was so powerful that Nicholas and Charlie started, banging into each other, and the headmaster gripped the edges of his desk. "You got her all upset! Now what is it? In or out? Your two best boys, one of them from a family who's been coming here since before the flood, and my Charlie, who's bringing along you-know-how-much for that new field house you say you have to have. So just get it over with. In, out. Yes, no. Don't upset her any more. You don't treat women that way."

"Perhaps if we might discuss the matter alone, Mr. Harrison."

"Doc, I don't have time to stay for tea. Know what I mean? The Teamsters are trying to organize my cashiers."

"Mr. Harrison—"

"Look, Mrs. Cobleigh's a New York society lady, and her Nick can write his own ticket and she'll pull the little kid out for good measure—what's his name?"

"Thomas," Winifred whispered.

"So she'll pull Nick and Thomas. And she has a couple more boys— right?—who'll go someplace else, that St. Somebody's, and who knows, half their New York friends could go with them. And for me, Doc, do you think I give a flying—a hoot about Trowbridge? My wife says Charlie should go to private school; I say fine. She says Trowbridge; I say fine. You say no Trowbridge; I tell my wife we buy another school a field house. You think I give a—"

"A student's academic record is always a mitigating factor," Dr. Wigglesworth said quietly.

"That's what I thought."

"Although I am profoundly disappointed in both these boys, I would certainly not wish to have them leave Trowbridge. Of course, we will have to invoke certain disciplinary measures."

"That sounds okay to me. Okay with you, Mrs. Cobleigh?" Winifred nodded.

"I believe I am a balanced man, Mr. Harrison."

"Good. Me too." Louis Harrison stood and, for a man of his astounding girth, strode toward the door with terrifying speed. Nicholas tried to move aside, but Mr. Harrison grabbed his shirtfront with his left hand and grabbed Charlie's with his right. He dragged both boys toward him until their faces were so close to his Nicholas could feel the heat from his skin. "Charlie," he said so low only the boys could hear him, "you little stinkpot. You do this again and I'll break your legs." His small puffy eyes turned to Nicholas. "We're all gonna go out for dinner in Beale before this discipline shit begins, and you're gonna bust your butt telling your mother how sorry you are, how you'll never do anything like this again. You hear me, pretty boy?" Nicholas nodded. "She can't take this kind of thing. Look at her. She's stretched as far as she can go."

Nicholas looked. His mother's hands, now folded in her lap, were trembling. She was staring out the window, away from Dr. Wigglesworth, the Harrisons, even him.

It was two days before Thanksgiving, 1956, and Samuel Tuttle knew he was dying. He lay in a cranked-up bed in a suite in a wing of New York Hospital his father had endowed. He was eighty-seven years old and his heart was failing. His lungs were so filled with fluid that each breath came with a horrible gurgle, the sound of a drowning man trying to drag oxygen from the water. The sound disturbed him more than the pain in his chest, for each time he inhaled he saw Maisie stiffen, bracing herself so she would not wince or show that she knew he was dying and that his dying terrified her. Her chair was pulled to his bedside. Her posture was unnaturally erect, as if invisible hands were lifting and holding her under her chin. "I'm comfortable, my dear," he managed to whisper. She nodded but could not look into his eyes. Instead, she watched her own finger trace a stripe along the length of his pajama sleeve.

He didn't want to die because he knew it would end Maisie's happiness. She would go on, of course, but it would end her shine just as surely as her silver candle snuffer killed the light, leaving nothing but smoky darkness. It was such a shame, he thought, for at seventy-five she was still lovely. Her complexion seemed as flawless in the merciless hospital fluorescence as it had that first day on Washington Square; the only lines on her face were the spiky shadows cast by her long dark lashes. She was too good to leave, and although he believed absolutely in a heaven, he did not know what it would be, whether heaven meant all souls sitting by the hand of God or if each soul created his own heaven and he could sit by Maisie for all time.

He could leave his sons, for they would mourn him but not really miss him. He hated to leave Winifred, though, because her life was incomplete. Or perhaps it was complete. Perhaps for the rest of her life she would sit waiting for that husband, pinching her pale, freckled cheeks to give them color to lure the unlurable, a box of shirts or ties or cufflinks or a watch beside her, as though he were a gigolo whose favor she had to purchase each night, even though he invariably came home late and often drunk, stinking of liquor and some other woman's perfume. Plain, simple Winifred, still trying to entice the handsome, cunning, cold man she'd married, after eighteen years and six children still unable to keep her eyes from him, still grabbing onto his hand or reaching to stroke his hair, pleased to humiliate herself, like a peasant crawling on his belly to kiss the hem of the king's robe. And such a disdainful king.

Samuel knew that James Cobleigh could keep him out of heaven. He hated his son-in-law; how he played Winifred and the children in his game against Samuel. Using his hold on Winifred to get Samuel—a major client of his law firm—to plead his case after he'd disgraced himself in a flagrant affair with the wife of the senior corporate partner.

On the family occasions when Samuel had to see his son-in-law, James had wrapped his children around himself, listening to loquacious Olivia's half-hour recounting of her exhausting internal debate over whether to have her hair cut, marveling at Thomas's biographies of the twelve apostles, reading *Treasure Island* to the twins, even helping Edward assemble a model ship— all to insulate himself from Samuel. And he used Nicholas most of all, because he was astute enough to realize the boy was Samuel's favorite. Just two months earlier, the weekend before Nicholas left for his final year at Trowbridge, James was in the Tuttles' library, sitting beside the boy and studying the world atlas for hours while Samuel, the outsider, watched the two fair heads bent over a map of France, James following the coastline with his fingers, stopping here and there to recount one of his adventures in the OSS. Samuel had hoped that at his age Nicholas would be past hero-worship, but the boy was unable to resist James's cool recollections of extraordinary danger, and while his father sat back, legs stretched out and crossed casually at the ankle, Nicholas flushed, paled, clenched fists, and flexed muscles as the narrative progressed, fighting Nazis beside his father on a camelback sofa.

Samuel loved Nicholas the most because the boy was most like him: serious, truehearted, a little sad, with a deep hidden pocket of passion most other Tuttles and Cobleighs seemed to lack, the same sort of passion that had allowed Samuel's love for Maisie. He could see it behind the boy's eyes when, home from school, Nicholas opened his arms to receive his brothers and sisters; when—even while being whipped by his mother on the tennis court—he watched Winifred's great strides and awesome backhand with pride and delight; and when, alas, he saw James merely walk into a room and smile at him. Samuel considered this weakness for James the only flaw in the boy's character; he would not allow himself to think Nicholas might have inherited anything besides his father's admittedly good looks. And he was an admirable-looking boy, not with the cheap appeal of his father, but with a face that reflected his fineness. As usual, Maisie had said it best: "The marvelous thing about Nicholas," she'd remarked, "is that if you told him what an absolutely splendid boy he is, he'd believe you'd confused him with Thomas."

So at the moment he died, Samuel Tuttle was thinking of the two people he loved most, his wife and his grandson. Fittingly, his final thought was a quiet little prayer that Nicholas find someone as good and beautiful and, yes, as grand as Maisie. He might have asked for more, but he had no more time.

The cuffs, collar, and shirtfront of Nicholas's evening shirt were so stiffly starched that when he touched them they emitted a tapping sound, but his father didn't hear. James rested his arms on the ledge of the box at the Metropolitan Opera House and strained forward, trying to position himself directly in the path of the music as it soared upward from the stage. Nicholas ran his index finger under his collar, but while it relieved one side of his neck, it pulled the starched fabric tighter on the other, and the itching and the rawness were nearly unbearable. He tried to concentrate on the opera—Mimi was in bad shape, lying in bed and singing "Rodolfo! Rodolfo!"—but she was such a skinny little thing, and besides, he had seen *La Bohème* twice before and knew it was hopeless. The other soprano, however, looked strong and healthy, with broad shoulders and big feet like Heather's best friend Patty Bollinger's. It was too bad she couldn't give Mimi a transfusion. He fidgeted with his cufflinks, trying to take them off in the dark box so he could roll up his sleeves and at least relieve the terrible itch on his wrists, but the movement disturbed his father, who turned and shot him an irritated look.

Nicholas sat still. He did not dare annoy his father, because James had been in a tense mood all during Christmas vacation. When Nicholas had come down from Trowbridge with Thomas, who was a fourth-former, and Charlie Harrison, they had walked in on a mood that had not lifted, although much was done to cover it over. His mother had come out of her bedroom to greet them nearly two hours after they'd arrived. The underneath part of her eyes were red, but they were not swollen, as though she'd been crying frequently, but not recently. She was dressed for dinner in a long, dark green velvet skirt and a white frilly blouse, but her hair was uncombed. Not just messy the way it usually got after a long day, but untended to. She'd kissed the two boys, and even Charlie, but in a strange, slow-motion manner, as if someone were behind the scenes whispering, All right. Now kiss Thomas. Put your hands on his cheeks and bring his face up to yours. That's right.

None of them remarked about it, of course, even though at dinner she didn't say a word except "No, thank you" when she was offered something. She looked drawn, and the skin beneath her freckles, always pale, was a sickly yellow white. James, who rarely ate dinner with his children, presided over the table that first night as if his wife were absent, eliciting amusing tales of Trowbridge from the three oldest boys, admonishing Edward not to clang his knife against the bread plate, and ringing a small crystal bell for the maid, as though there were no electric buzzer under the rug right by Winifred's foot. After dessert was served, James had peered across the table to his wife. She had her hands in her lap and was staring down at her fruitcake. He said quietly, neutral and cold, "Why don't you go and rest, Win." She left the table without a word, an obedient, slow-motion child with tangled hair. James glanced at Charlie and explained, "Her father died last month. She's a bit down about it," and Charlie nodded.

But Olivia, who was nine, slipped into Nicholas's room after that dinner and at great length explained that Winifred had been acting strange even before Samuel had gone into the hospital. "Do you think," Nicholas began, "I mean, you know she had to come up to school for me. Do you think—"

"No, Nicky. God. It's been going on since school started, and it's really awful. She doesn't go out any more. I swear. She's not going anywhere and she doesn't want to take phone calls and she cries a lot."

"She wasn't that bad when she came up to school."

"It's getting worse and worse," Olivia said. Of all the children, she looked most like Winifred, with the same horsey face and large teeth. Her hair, red and wild, was trapped into a ponytail and tied with a red and green plaid grosgrain ribbon. "I mean, you know Mummy, Nicky. The day after Thanksgiving she starts Christmas shopping. Well, she couldn't because that was Grandpa's funeral—I'm not trying to make sick jokes, really—but she didn't even make up a list; and you know December first she takes out the tree ornaments to make sure nothing's been broken, but she kept putting it off even though I reminded her a million times and so did Abby, and it turned out we had to make Daddy go and buy the tree yesterday even though he's very tired because he's working late all the time, and then Abby and Michael and I decorated it by ourselves and when we called Mummy to come look she didn't want to but when we finally got her to see the tree all lit up she started to cry."

"What does Daddy say?" Nicholas asked.

170

"I can't ask him. You ask him. Please, Nicky. We've all been waiting for you to come home."

Nicholas had, just as they were taking their seats in the box. It was his first time alone with his father that year. James had offered Charlie his ticket, but Charlie had declined for a party given by a girl who had been pursuing him with letters and phone calls since they'd met at a mixer two years earlier. Nicholas finally had simply blurted out, "What's wrong with Mummy?"

"Nothing. I told you, she hasn't gotten over your grandfather's death."

"But she wasn't right before that, and Olivia says—"

"Nick, your sister dramatizes things. You know that."

"But I can see Mummy isn't right. Is she sick? Does she have a—any kind of disease?"

"No."

"She doesn't eat and she—"

"She'll snap out of it. It just takes time. Now sit back. This is a very special performance."

But it hadn't seemed special, and yet when Rodolfo realized Mimi was dead, Nicholas glanced at his father and tears were streaming down James's cheeks. He had never seen his father cry, and it frightened him, because he thought it must be horrible for him seeing a woman lying there so pale and motionless, in a terrible way just like his wife. The curtain fell and the ovation began. Nicholas reached out for James and touched his sleeve. James turned. His face was so filled with emotion Nicholas could barely recognize him. He waited for James to find his voice. When it came, it wasn't what Nicholas expected. "Isn't she magnificent!" James exclaimed.

"Who?"

"Who? The soprano."

Nicholas almost asked which soprano, for he couldn't see that either of them was all that great but instead he nodded, for he sensed his father would not like his question. "Magnificent," he echoed.

James rose as the tiny soprano, the one who sang Mimi, came out. He clapped wildly and called "Brava! Brava!" Nicholas stared at him. His mother had always been the opera lover; his father had attended infrequently and unwillingly. "Brava!" She bowed, clutching the brown shawl that was part of her costume, then stood as she was pelted with roses hurled from the audience. "Bravissima!" James shouted. He turned to Nicholas a moment later. "Wasn't she something?" he demanded.

"Yes, Dad." Nicholas thought his father was about to say more, but then he lowered his head. "What is it?" Nicholas asked.

His father looked up, hesitated, then inquired softly, "Would you like to meet her?"

*   *   *

171

They waited backstage until her regular visitors, her fans and friends, had left the dressing room. Then James knocked and was summoned. "C'mon in." Before Nicholas even noticed her, he spotted her maid in the far corner of the dressing room, brushing out the thick dark curls of her wig. It was only then that he looked and saw her sitting on a stool before a huge lighted mirror. "Two secs," she said, and continued pulling off her false eyelashes with a tweezer.

She seemed even smaller than she had onstage. Her costume, a beige dress with brown trim, was thrown over a chair and she was wearing a pink satin robe trimmed with feathers, a prima donna robe if ever there was one, but Nicholas thought she looked as if she should be playing roles like— whatever—Peter Pan or Huck Finn instead of Mimi. She didn't look like an opera singer.

Lucy Bogard looked like what she was, the daughter of migrant laborers. She was short and scrawny. Her own hair was thin and sand-colored and her right eye, without the frame of the lashes, was a bland, watery hazel. Her nose was so pug it looked like a pair of nostrils on display. "Just another little minute and I'll be with y'." She removed the final row of lashes, then dipped her hand into a jar of cream, slapped it around her face, then wiped it away. Her bright complexion came off on the tissue. "All right now," she said, and spun around on her stool. "What have we got here, Jimmy?"

"We've got my son Nicholas," James said.

"Have we now?" she said, and stood. With one hand on Nicholas's arm and the other on his chest, she guided him to her stool and pushed him down. "Let me look at you. My, you are one fine-lookin' boy, aren't you. A little like your daddy, but not too much. Now tell me, did your daddy tell you he knew me? I didn't think so. He just dragged you down here, and I bet you think your daddy's some crazy old fan, just trying to get my autograph on his program. But you know, I do know your daddy real well. You know how?"

"No, I—" She was standing right next to him, fluffing his hair, and he could see inside her robe. He didn't know where to look. If he looked down he could see the very top of her leg and if he looked straight ahead from his stool he could see her breast where the pink satin gaped open. It was a little breast, but she was still a grown woman.

"Come on, Lucy. Stop it." James spoke harshly but a little nervously, as if he knew she was in control of what was going on in the room.

"You come on, Jimmy. You brought him here." Her voice thawed as she turned her attention back to Nicholas. "Where were we? Oh, yes. I was telling you how I know your daddy. Well, here I was at this awful, silly charity thing—" She took Nicholas's face between her hands, forcing him to look into her face. "Well, an old friend came over to me and said, 'I have someone you simply must meet. The answer to your prayers.' And there was your daddy.

172

And was he ever!" She paused, and it was as if every person in the entire Metropolitan Opera were holding his breath. Then, at the perfect dramatic second, she added, "The best lawyer in all of New York City." He couldn't see anyone else, but he could feel the relief that swept through the room, across his father and Lucy Bogard's maid. "You know that, don't you, Nick? Your father is a real legal genius."

"Lucy—" James began.

She cut him off. Her hands were still on Nicholas's face, her thumbs tracing the outline of his jaw. "He just came and took over and solved every single last one of my problems. Now isn't that somethin'?"

That same night, Charlie Harrison fell for a girl he had met at a party, a Hollins freshman, and the next morning he sprawled on his stomach on the thick brown rug in Nicholas's bedroom, searching through a Lovejoy catalog for a college in Virginia equal to Harvard, so he could convince his parents it would not destroy his life if he followed his new beloved and became a southern, rather than a New England, gentleman. "William and Mary!" he announced. "Jesus, Nick, you look like hell. You hung over?"

"No." Nicholas lay on the lower level of his bunk bed, his right arm and leg hanging listlessly over the edge of the mattress. He was pale except for his neck and wrists, which were red from his overstarched shirt of the previous night. "You know your parents won't let you go to Virginia. Your mother will faint dead away if you don't go to Harvard, and your father would beat you to a pulp for getting her upset. Anyhow, it's stupid because you'll be over her before we have to go back to school. I guarantee it. You're just intrigued because she's an older woman."

"No. I swear, I've never met anyone like her. She's flawless, Nick. Perfect. A titian-tressed Scarlett O'Hara."

"Come on, Charlie. I went to St. Stephen's with her brother. I've met her. She's lived on Sixty-fifth Street all her life. Don't fall for that southern belle bullshit."

"What's wrong with you? She's not pretending to be a southern belle. I just mean she has that, you know, that tiny waist and that soft way about her. But she's really got it upstairs too. Do you know what she does before she goes to bed every night?"

"She stands in front of the mirror and feels herself up."

"You know, there's a time to be serious, Nick. It so happens she reads a poem by John Donne every single night. She says it's the crowning glory of her day. Not the light stuff. The deep, religious ones. 'O Saviour, as Thou hang'st upon the tree.' She quoted the entire thing by heart."

"I can't believe you're falling for that crap. She probably spent six years memorizing one poem so she can catch divinity students, because no one except a creep—"

"Hey, what the hell is wrong with you, Nick?"

"Nothing."

"Is something bothering you?"

"No."

"Maybe with your mother not feeling so great."

"My father says she's fine. She'll snap out of it, okay?"

"Was your father leaning on you last night?"

"No. He was fine. He says just because he went to Brown doesn't mean I have to, but if I want to he'd be happy, but whatever I decide to do is fine with him and he doesn't care that I didn't have the grades for Yale."

"How was the opera?"

"Okay. Nice."

"It's my favorite. I mean, I know it's not cool and I should be more sophisticated and love *Götterdämmerung*, but there's something so perfect about *Bohème*."

"Then how come you didn't take the ticket?"

"I don't know. I thought you'd want to be alone with your father, and anyway, I really was hot to trot for a big night."

"Charlie, I'm sorry it's been lousy here for you."

"Are you nuts? It hasn't been lousy. I'm having a great time. And I met Libby, so I'll thank you for the rest of my life. Do you know what? You'd be a hundred percent better off if you just loosened up a little. Don't worry so much about your brothers and sisters. They'll be okay. Your mother isn't going to stay like this. She'll be fine. Maybe she'll go someplace and relax."

"I guess so."

Winifred made few forays from her bedroom. Nicholas had tried to visit her, but she lay in gloom. The brocade drapes were no longer pulled back but hung over the window, filtering out all light except for a dull amber fog. She seemed to sleep most of the time, and when she was awake she could barely answer his questions. She'd murmur she was fine, but her voice was tired, as though she hadn't been sleeping at all but spending her days in exhausting labor. She didn't even have the energy to try to appear cheerful. She didn't seem to care whether Nicholas was frightened or worried or even that he was in the room with her. She had no other real diversion. The maid tiptoed in once a day, but James now slept in his study. Winifred stayed on her side of the bed, leaving James's half tightly made, his two pillows plump against the headboard.

"Come on. You shouldn't be so—I don't know—so glum. You're only young once, and that's when you have to have a good time. Now listen to me. I know I promised not to criticize Heather and I won't, but can't you cut loose a little here in New York? It's Christmas vacation, Nick. Have a little fun with some nice girl."

"I bet you'd rather be with some cute little thing your own age," Lucy said.

"No," Nicholas lied. "Not at all."

She had called before noon, just as he and Charlie were leaving the apartment, and asked if it would be too much trouble to help her out of an awful fix; she'd forgotten to send her nephew his Christmas present and he was just Nick's size and would Nick come up to her apartment and the chauffeur could drive them over to Brooks Brothers and Nick could try on jackets. It wouldn't take more than—well, a half hour or so. He'd said yes only because he couldn't think of a way to say no. And Charlie agreed it was the right thing to do because she was his father's client and because how could you say no to a world-famous diva? Charlie had heard her sing Violetta the year before and seemed awed and thrilled with Nicholas's good luck. He instructed Nicholas to call her Madame Bogard and, if she offered her fingertips, to brush his lips across them, not really kiss them.

But she hadn't offered her fingertips. Instead, she had answered the door of her penthouse apartment wearing skin-tight shiny black slacks and a black sweater with a deep vee and had greeted him by kissing him on the lips. It was a light kiss, the sort of kiss a prima donna might give to anyone, but it surprised him so much he licked his lips right afterward and she had laughed. She led him into a living room filled with ultramodern furniture—long low couches and tables and high-arching lamps—of the sort he'd only seen in magazines. She offered him a drink and he'd asked for a beer, because he couldn't think of anything else he could drink before lunch, and then she'd sat right beside him on the couch, sipping something with a cherry from a pink frosted martini glass. Her legs were crossed and her shoe, a very high-heeled shoe, rubbed against his pants leg. She seemed to know all about his family, about Abigail's chicken pox and Thomas's good grades and about his mother's not feeling well, although she probed him on this until he changed the subject by asking for another beer.

"Are you havin' a high ol' time with your friend visiting?" Lucy asked him.

"Yes. Very nice." Her toenails were polished bright red, and they were long and oval-shaped, like large fingernails. She wore a gold chain hardly thicker than a hair around her ankle. He tried to make conversation, even though his tongue felt thick from the beer. "Are you going to be here in New York for the rest of the winter? Singing, I mean."

"Oh, a little singin', a little dancin', a little whatever."

"How old is your nephew? The one who's my size."

175

"Nick," she said, and set her glass down on top of the kidney-shaped coffee table before them. "You know you didn't believe a word of that old Brooks Brothers story." His heart lurched. He tried to stand, but the low couch seemed to slant back so he found himself sliding even farther back. As if to ensure his imprisonment, Lucy put her hands against his chest and kissed him hard. "My God, what a gorgeous, delicious mouth. Do you know that? You have a beautiful, sensuous mouth, lambie. Let Lucy have some more of it. Come on."

He found himself kissing her back, opening his mouth to let her tongue capture his even though she tasted unpleasantly of whiskey. He found himself reaching into the vee of her sweater, even though he didn't really want to touch her bony chest. Her breasts had a strange texture, as if there were goosebumps under the skin, but soon he didn't want to stop playing with them, even though he was afraid at any moment she'd jerk back and give him an outraged, grown-up crack across the face.

He had thought her scrawny, homely, a little piggy-looking with her awful pug nose, but he discovered he desired her so much that even though his hands were trembling with fright, he kept trying to pull her slacks down over her narrow hips.

She did it for him, undressing in the narrow space between the couch and coffee table in the bright light of early afternoon, her fleshless body turning red and green as her Christmas tree lights blinked on and off. She was a woman—even though she had the body of a starved child—and he had never seen a woman completely naked before. He'd never even seen Heather. Whenever Heather pulled off her bra she kept on her skirt, and whenever she allowed him to touch her below the waist her blouse remained closed to the collar.

But here was this naked woman pulling him up from the couch, rubbing herself against him. "We're goin' to the bedroom now," she said. She held his arm and pulled him along. "Come on, honey. Follow Lucy."

In the bedroom, her talk became adult. Her explicitness was so startling—"I'm gonna take your balls in my mouth, Nick, and first I'm gonna suck on them"—that when she shoved him onto the bed he was ready to do precisely what she told him. She took over completely. "Turn over on your stomach now," she ordered, or "Stick your tongue all the way in, as far as it can go. Come on. More. More."

He stayed in the bedroom for three hours and did everything she told him to do. At the end he felt she had taken everything from him and he had nothing left.

When she went in to shower he began to sob, clutching the sweaty pillow to his face. She came out with a towel draped decorously around her. "Come on, sweetie. Stop carryin' on. It's what you wanted, so stop cryin'. Come *on*.

You were a real man. Don't mess it up." She sat on the bed and pulled the pillow from him. "Don't hide from Lucy. Do you want some more, honey? I bet that's it. I bet one little suck and I could get it goin' again. Oh, look at it, startin' to stand up. There you are, still cryin' and actin' like a baby, but it knows what it wants. It sure does. I knew it would be this way, I just knew it. What do they say, honey? Like father, like son."

BOOK THREE

JANE & NICHOLAS

11

CHILDREN FOLLOW STAR TO LONDON
from PETER HEPWHITE in New York
The teenage daughters of cinema star Nicholas Cobleigh were rushed past
journalists at John F. Kennedy Airport and escorted onto a British Airways
Concorde by an official of the airline. The girls, Victoria, 18, and Elizabeth, 16, on their way to their mother's hospital bedside, lowered their
heads to avoid the photographers who were . . .
—*Daily Mail*

Jane Heissenhuber and Nicholas Cobleigh first noticed each other in their
sophomore year of college when they sat one row and three seats away from
each other in Social and Intellectual History of the United States. For the few
seconds he focused on her, he thought she behaved like a typical Pembroke
girl: intellectually aggressive and too intense. She did not look like a typical
Pembroke girl, however. She was very tall and exotic, with dark skin and a
thick black braid hanging to her waist, a figure out of Gauguin incongruously
dressed in a pleated skirt and sweater. She did not interest him at all.

He interested her, though. His looks were clean, classic American. He
was smooth, most likely the product of a prep school, but his voice was deep
and pleasant, with an intriguing catch in his throat—not the nasal sound many
of them made, as if their adenoids were bigger than their brains. Everything
about him seemed right; even his oxford shirts looked better pressed than
anyone else's. But he didn't seem arrogant. He sat straight in his chair,
avoiding the contemptuous classroom slouch—legs stretched out, head
thrown back as if the discussion were too boring to be borne. Although he
never volunteered an answer, when called upon he was prepared, and his
responses were well considered if not brilliant. She did not have a crush on
him because she was too practical to pine for the unattainable. But three or
four times that semester she glanced at the back of his head and shoulders
and, just for an instant, wondered what it would be like.

They noticed each other once the following semester. They picked up
their laundry at the same time and were about to leave the store when it
began to rain, the cold, comfortless rain that takes the joy from the early
weeks of Rhode Island's spring. They reached the door at the same time.
Jane's laundry bag was cradled in her arms, Nicholas's slung over his shoulder. They glanced at each other. It was a moment that might have led to coffee
if either had said, "Isn't this weather awful?" but instead he pulled back so she

could pass by first, and they both rushed through the rain, Jane to her dormitory at Pembroke, the women's college of Brown University, Nicholas to his room in the Alpha Delta Phi house.

One night the following year when they were juniors they worked at the same table in the library. They noticed each other at different moments and kept their heads down so they would not have to waste time deciding whether to acknowledge the other and then whether to simply nod or to say hello.

Several times they just missed each other. In their sophomore year, Jane went to a party at the A.D. Phi house with a senior she was dating and danced within inches of Nicholas, who was dipping a Connecticut College freshman, a girl he'd seen on and off since they'd met the year before at a coming-out party, but they didn't notice each other. They didn't see each other the last week of their junior year either, when they actually sat beside each other in the theater watching the cartoons that were run late afternoons the week of final examinations. And the first week of their senior year, they both ate chicken chow mein at Toy Sun's restaurant at the same time, but Jane was gossiping with her colleagues from Sock and Buskin, Brown and Pembroke's oddly named drama group, and Nicholas was holding hands with Diana Howard, the girl he was pinned to, so they never knew the other was near.

It might not have mattered. Probably each of them had been that close that often to a large percentage of students of the opposite sex. Jane and Nicholas were merely following the law of averages, which says that X, a certain Pembroke girl, will be in the same room with Y, a certain Brown boy, 28.92 times during their four years in Providence. Of course, it might have been Fate trying to set something up, but, if so, Fate took a while to get it going.

Nicholas saw Jane once when she did not see him. In November of his junior year he was watching a Sock and Buskin production of *The Nights of Jason Weekes*, a play set in Mississippi with conventionally decadent characters. Along with the alcoholic father, satyric brother, sapphist sister, and schizophrenic mother there was a sharecropper's daughter, a slut named Delia. Delia wore an appropriately sluttish costume, a tight slit skirt and a revealing blouse loosely laced up the bodice, and behaved like the archetypical lust-driven slattern, so it wasn't until the curtain call that Nicholas realized the whorish girl with the black hair spilling over her bare shoulders was the tight Pembroke grind who'd sat behind him sophomore year.

Jane was rehearsing Gertrude in the Sock and Buskin production of *Hamlet,* and since she'd drunk poison moments earlier and was slumped back, dead, in a chair, she did not see Nicholas walk out onto the balcony above the rear of the stage, lean over, and look down the seven feet to the floor. What she heard was the director, Professor Ritter, call out from the first row, "Do you think you can do it?"

"Just jump?" The voice came from above and behind her. She opened her eyes and twisted her head in time to see the flash of a figure hurtle itself off the balcony and land with a horrible thud in a half crouch two feet behind her. For an instant the figure stood as he had landed, head lowered, hands resting just above his knees, and Jane rushed to him, thinking he'd injured his spine and was paralyzed in that hunched-over position. But just as she reached him he straightened up, so they met almost nose to nose. "Hi," he said.

He was so close his breath felt warm on her mouth, an impending kiss. Recognizing him as the cool, handsome boy who'd been in her Social and Intellectual History class, Jane flushed and drew back. "Are you all right?" she asked.

"Sure," he said, and stood straight and bounced on the balls of his feet. His eyes were an extraordinary blue tinged with green, and when he offered her a polite smile and turned his eyes to Professor Ritter, she felt as if she'd lost something precious. "Was that what you wanted?" he called to the director.

Professor Ritter was a giant blob of a man with the low forehead and buck teeth of a village idiot, so his dainty gestures and high-pitched voice seemed false, as if he were constantly giving a corny impersonation of effeminacy. He held his hands together prayer-fashion and rested his chins on top of his fingers. "Perfection. Absolute perfection. Except for one small thing. You forgot to shout, 'Where is this sight?' before you jumped. You're Fortinbras! You've only just come upon this dreadful—what have you—carnage in the Danish court and so, in essence, you gasp, What's happening? and leap down, flinging yourself directly into the center of a world gone mad and, in effect, by your sheer physicalness, provide a hub, a new center of sanity, of wholeness." The director's nose was squashed into his face, and his right nostril was much larger than his left.

"Professor Ritter, really, I'm no actor. I just came here because one of my fraternity brothers hauled me in and said you needed someone to jump and I thought it would be fun—"

"I need that life-embracing leap into the abyss. Don't you see that? The man of action, the man of muscle, you—Fortinbras." Professor Ritter rose. His slacks stretched so tight across his massive thighs the blue flannel seemed the outer layer of his skin. "Don't you see . . . ? Tell me your name once again."

"Nicholas Cobleigh."

"Listen to me, Nicholas. Hamlet, who lived the life of the mind, lies dead, and you—you leap in, stripped to the waist, brandishing a sword. You

183

are the embodiment of the life force itself"—the director's voice climbed to a squeak—"fighting to reassert itself in the midst of this terrible negation."

"I'd really like to help," Nicholas said, "but I'm not good at memorizing." He put his hands in the back pockets of his khakis; his palms must be sweating. Jane thought the jump had frightened him—none of the company regulars had been willing to try it—but then she realized he was unnerved by being onstage. His eyes darted from Professor Ritter up to the lights, then flickered down to her and then to Hamlet and Laertes, still lying on their backs. "Sorry." His voice, which she suddenly remembered from class, had had a tantalizing trace of hoarseness. Now it sounded raspy, and it didn't carry. It seemed only she had heard his apology.

"You'll be grand. Alive, muscular, powerful. Take off your shirt. I want to see if you'll seem credible bare-chested."

Nicholas backed away a few steps. One hand moved flat over the top buttons of his yellow cotton shirt. "Isn't it a little cold in Denmark to go around without a shirt? Anyway, I really don't think I'm your man. I wouldn't be able to remember a word, and I'd just clam up. I appreciate—"

"Jane!" the director barked. "Raise your hand! Do you see that girl? She'll help you with your lines. You'll be splendid. The quintessential warrior king. Now take off your shirt."

"How can I feel horror?" Nicholas asked. "I know you're not dead."

"Of course I'm not dead," Jane said. "Not that Ritter wouldn't love it. He's a fiend for authenticity. He wanted us to throw up onstage after we drink the poison, but we finally talked him out of that. I mean, how can I say 'The drink, the drink, I am poison'd' if I have a mouthful of oatmeal? He's still trying to get us to make disgusting retching noises, but that's neither here nor there. We'll probably end up compromising by holding our throats and gagging a few times. That's show business. Anyway, what was your question?"

She was not what Nicholas had expected. At the director's insistence, he'd made an appointment to meet her the following morning, on the Faunce House porch, and although she didn't seem the black stockings–white lipstick–beatnik type, her tallness and powerful features—the long nose, large mouth, and square jaw—made him think she'd have an overbearing personality. He imagined her booming voice. Most likely she'd be hyperintellectual and condescending. Or she'd be pretentious, calling him "my dear" or waving a cigarette in a holder beneath his nose. He'd regretted arranging to meet her at so public a place, because she probably had a brash laugh and would make sweeping, theatrical gestures that would attract attention.

Instead, she was reassuring and friendly, telling him his cooperation had saved Professor Ritter from his monthly psychotic episode and how everyone

184

appreciated what a good sport he was. She had a wide smile that showed most of her teeth, and its openness went well with her midwestern accent.

Her friendliness was tempered with awkwardness or shyness. They walked from Faunce House to the campus and sat under an oak whose leaves had just begun their autumn fade from green to brown, and she avoided looking at him, gazing instead through the branches or over at a touch football game under way across campus. She fiddled with the pages of her worn paperback *Hamlet*. She crossed and uncrossed her legs, which were far too long for the Bermuda shorts she was wearing, and played with her long braid, bringing it over her shoulder and brushing it against her cheek. Between bursts of chatter, her fingers floated up to cover her mouth.

"My question was, how do I act shocked that all of you are lying around dead when you're not dead?"

"Think dead."

"Come on."

"I mean it. You look down from the balcony. . . . Don't you get scared looking down from that height?"

"It's really not that high."

"Anything over three inches is high. Anyway, you look down and what do you see?"

"I don't know. A bunch of students pretending to be dead."

"No! You see the king and queen—that's me, so it's really profoundly tragic—and Laertes and Hamlet all lying dead. Think about it. Denmark's political, moral, intellectual, and social leaders are wiped out. The cream of the cream is gone, and now you have to take over the throne."

"Good," Nicholas said.

"No, it's not good. That's the wrong attitude. You're supposed to be noble, and it's very déclassé to gloat when the entire royal family of Denmark bites the dust."

"Aren't I supposed to be ambivalent?"

"Are you kidding?" When she smiled she tilted her head to the side, like a child trying to get another angle on absurd behavior. It was a gesture at odds with her mature appearance. She was big, as tall as Nicholas, and had probably looked like an adult when she was twelve. No youthful bloom could penetrate the darkness of her sallow skin. Even though her sweater was loose, he could see she had heavy, womanly breasts, and then he remembered the play he'd seen her in, where she was half hanging out of her blouse. He stared at her, searching for the wanton character she had played, but all he could see was a big, plain-looking Pembroke girl in a dark green sweater. Although she was studying the ribbing on her knee socks, she must have sensed his staring because her smile flickered. "Do you think Fortinbras feels ambivalent?" she asked.

"I guess not. The girl I'm pinned to is an English major, and in English literature everybody's ambivalent. At least according to Diana."

"Is she at Pembroke?"

"No. Wheaton."

"Oh." Jane recuffed the sleeves of her sweater. "Well, anyway, on with the show. Do you see this root here?" She patted a large gnarl on the twisted root beside her. Nicholas nodded. "All right. Pretend it's Hamlet and he's dead."

"I can't do that."

"Yes, you can. Come on. No one's going to notice."

"They'll notice if they see me talking to a tree."

"Don't be so self-conscious. Just tuck yourself away in a corner and become Fortinbras. Come on. You've read *Hamlet*. What's Fortinbras like?"

"He's not a major character."

"You can play Hamlet next time. Meantime you're Fortinbras. What's he like? Come on. Three adjectives."

"I feel . . . all right. Strong, brave, and—I don't know. Uncomplicated."

"What do you mean, uncomplicated?"

"Do you do this all the time?"

"Sure."

"Isn't it like playing games?"

"Sort of." A triangle of sunlight beamed down between the leaves and shone on Jane's cheek, brightening her skin to bronze. "It's a game in that it's not real. And it's playing the way children do, when they pretend to be lions or pussycats or fairy princesses. Whatever. But it's playing for a purpose. It satisfies our need—well, my need, anyway—to be someone else. But it's more, because I'm not just a child playing games alone. I'm being someone else before other people and they accept me not as Jane Heissenhuber—and Lord knows with my name that's a blessing—but as another person, a person who inhabits another universe: the play. And the play isn't just a dream, or a game, something that has no substance. It's real. It adds something to the audience's life that wasn't there before. And I'm an intrinsic part of that process." She pulled her head back and her face was again shaded, but she smiled. "You don't get it, do you?"

"Not really. I mean, I can understand a little why someone else might like to do it, but it's not for me." He paused, then added, "Sorry."

"That's okay. How about this? How about doing it just because it's fun? You know, jumping from balconies and waving a sword and having everyone in the company in your debt forever because you stood between Professor Ritter and existential darkness or whatever he thinks is after him. All right?"

186

Her smile was so genuinely nice. He couldn't think of a way to say no that would save her smile. "All right."

"Good. Now talk to the tree. Come on. You're Fortinbras. Brave and strong and uncomplicated. Shoulders back. Head up. Look down at Hamlet. He's dead. No more Hamlet. Stare at him. That's it. Feel the loss and then begin with 'This quarry.'"

Nicholas licked his lips. He stared at the bulging root of the oak. "'This quarry cries on havoc.' I feel really dumb."

"Come on. You're doing fine."

"Where was I? Oh, 'cries on havoc.'" The root did not change into a Danish prince, but Nicholas became absorbed in the swirls and black speckles on the bark, its thick, jagged texture. The voice that spoke the lines did not feel completely his. "O proud death! / What feast is toward in thine eternal cell, / That thou so many princes at a shot / So bloodily hast struck?'" He lifted his eyes to Jane. He felt embarrassed.

"You're a natural," she said.

Jane's roommate and closest friend, Amelia Thring, was the only other Pembroke student as tall as she. But while Jane appeared strong and substantial, Amelia was so elegantly thin Jane felt she belonged to a different species, the product of the mating of man and swan. (Her father was a Bar Harbor, Maine, policeman; her mother a cashier in a lobster pound.) Amelia, supine on her bed, lit her cigarette with the distinction of a priestess burning incense to her god and dropped the match into the ashtray resting on her stomach as if it were part of the ceremony. "I won't even bother to say I've never seen you like this before," she said to Jane. Then she added, "I've never seen you like this before. You're a wreck."

"I know." Jane sat cross-legged on her bed, resting her head against the wall. "I've never felt like this before. It's like being dead with none of the advantages."

"Jane, stop it."

"This is the stupidest thing that ever happened to me."

"Oh, dear. You're crying!" Jane wiped her eyes with the back of her hand. Amelia flowed upward from her bed. The cigarette and ashtray seemed to disappear and instead she held a tissue. "Here." She put it into Jane's hand and sat beside her on the bed, drawing up her knees so her chin rested on them.

"It would be one thing if it were just some crush, Amelia. You know, if I just saw him on campus and mooned over him. Or if I had dated him and he broke it off because he wasn't interested. At least those things have an end. Eventually you stop mooning. Eventually you realize you've had all of him you're going to get and that's that, and you go on with your life."

187

"Jane, let's be rational."

"Please don't play psych major now."

"Listen to me. There *is* an end to this. The end is you stop crying and realize he's pinned. By June he'll probably be engaged and the following June he'll be married. He introduced you to her, for heaven's sake."

"If she was beautiful I could have stood it, but she's just okay. I swear, Amelia, I'd imagined this beauty and there she was, this ordinary nice-looking girl."

"Let me get another tissue."

"She didn't let go of his hand the whole time. Just held it in this calm way. I mean, she wasn't being possessive. Why should she? She didn't consider me a threat. 'Diana, this is Jane.' 'Jane! I'm so glad to meet you. Nick's told me you've been just marvelous, helping him with his part. I can't wait to watch him tonight. Oh, and you too. He told me what a fine actress you are.' And all the time holding his hand."

"Jane, listen to me. I'm a logical person."

"And it's not logical for me to feel this way."

"No, it's not. He likes you. You're a friend to him. No more. You've told me so yourself, over and over and over. You simply have to accept him as a friend or, if it's too painful, cut it off. Stop seeing him now that *Hamlet*'s over."

"I can't. Oh, God, I can't."

"Stop it. You can."

"No, I can't. You have Matt. You know what it's like to have someone who's the center of your life."

Jane's hair was loose, and Amelia stroked it as if she were soothing a distraught animal. "Easy, easy. Now I'm going to tell you something you don't want to hear, but I'm going to tell you anyway. Matt is my fiancé. But this boy isn't the center of your life."

"He is."

"He is not. You don't have a center, Jane. Don't you understand? You haven't been home to see your family in—what, three years? You spend vacations with me or Peg or Debby, and then you work every summer. And now it's senior year and things are changing. All your friends are about to get engaged and married or go to graduate school, and you're scared. Things didn't work out with Peter last summer, so you don't have a boyfriend, and—"

"He spent all July trying to get me to go to bed with him like it was some sort of military campaign, and then—"

"And then he hooked up with that girl from BU. Well, I wouldn't have expected more from him and you shouldn't have either. But that's another story. Meantime, you're twenty years old, rapidly approaching twenty-one, and you're suddenly realizing that whether you go to Yale Drama or New York, you're going to go alone. It's frightening, I'm not saying it isn't. But face

188

it. Don't get all wrapped up in some dream world." Amelia hugged Jane. "This boy is smooth and good-looking and nice as hell. And I'm telling you, if you let him know how you feel about him, all that decency you keep raving about is going to disappear and he'll look at you like you just made poo-poo on his shoes. Believe me. He wants some girl just as nice and rich and cool as he is, and they're going to have nice, rich, cool babies and send them to private schools that are so snooty they wouldn't even let us work in the kitchen. You know what they're like."

"Amelia, he's not like anyone else. I swear."

"Jane, don't do this to yourself. He's not worth it."

"Oh, Amelia, you're wrong. He is."

At the end of his junior year, soon after Nicholas and Diana Howard were pinned, they laughingly decided something was wrong. They were so well-matched they should hate each other.

They were both from Manhattan families—their mothers had actually gone to school together—and they felt the same conflict: they loved what the city had to offer but really preferred country life. Diana claimed an ideal world would be one where three days a week she could spend afternoons going to museums and matinees, evenings at great French restaurants, nights at the ballet. "And the other four days, to be magically transported to some tiny little house in the woods, reading, working in my garden, going for walks. And you're going to tell me that's impossible."

"Well," Nicholas had said, "how about highly unlikely? Magical transport is a little beyond the average Wall Street lawyer."

"No, it's not, Nick," she'd whispered, and then she'd kissed him.

Both preferred theater to opera, tennis to golf, England to France and Italy—neither had a flair for languages—pancakes to waffles and intercourse to foreplay. Rather than being bored, they found pleasure in sharing their thoughts with someone as receptive and congenial as the other. And because they were so exquisitely attuned, their first serious disagreement upset them.

"You're acting as if I told you I was going to commit murder." Nicholas stood and drew on his undershorts. He did not want to lie next to Diana, and he could not talk naked. Diana's back rested against the headboard of the hotel bed. Her lower lip was thrust forward, more a sign of despondence than a pout. She clenched the sheet that covered her. "All I'm going to do is try out for a part in another play."

"It's the *lead* in the play."

"So what?"

"Oh, Nick, come on. Once it's fun. Twice is something else."

"It's not. Look, this is my last year of college, my last year to let loose before—Christ!—before a whole life of responsibilities, and I don't see why you're so—so emotional."

"Me, emotional? Nicholas Cobleigh, listen to your voice."

It was an October Saturday. He'd met Diana at the train and taken her to the football game, where they'd sat with a group of his fraternity brothers and the girls they were pinned to, drinking beer, laughing, not caring very much when Brown lost badly to Harvard. After the game the couples drifted off, the boys with girl friends from out-of-town schools escorting them to the Biltmore in downtown Providence, where the girls could change into dresses for the night's fraternity dance and, in many cases, draw their boyfriends onto the high single beds for a few hours of luxurious private sex.

Diana's short brown hair had been mussed by their grappling, and it curled into a cap of ringlets. Her face was round, her features dainty, her skin white and pink. She looked like one of his sisters' dolls. To her right, on the nightstand, something caught his eye: his used condom. Its wrinkled, white, translucent skin made it look like a big dead worm. He took it into the bathroom, flushed it down the toilet, then came back and sat on the edge of the bed. Diana lowered her eyes. Nicholas put his forefinger under her small chin and lifted it until she was forced to look at him. He knew the gesture was false and cinematic, but he also knew it would work. "Don't be angry," he said.

"I'm not angry. But this semester counts for law school. You know that. It could mean the difference between Columbia and someplace else. And it seems so frivolous to me to risk your future just to act in some silly college play, a bedroom farce. Not even something serious."

"I'm not risking my future."

"You are. You know how much time the *Hamlet* took."

"Would you feel better if I promised you it won't affect my grades?"

"Nick!"

"It won't. Come on, Diana. I probably won't make it anyway. Ninety-nine percent chance I'll get thrown out on my rear at the first audition."

"I don't see what attracts you about it."

"It's fun. It's a diversion."

"Do you like the people?"

"Yes. They're nice."

"They seemed artsy to me."

"Not really. A couple of them are—well, theatrical, and they tend to be a little clannish at first, but once you get past that, they're a really good group. And they've been very friendly to me."

"Because you had a sponsor."

"What do you mean?"

"That girl."

"Jane? She's not my sponsor. She just helped me with my lines."

"And I'm sure she'll be more than happy to help you with your lines again." Diana had blue eyes with long, curly brown lashes—baby-doll eyes—and when she blinked Nicholas realized she was a moment away from tears.

"Diana, are you serious? Do you really think it's Jane who's keeping me involved with Sock and Buskin? I can't believe it. You've met her, for God's sake. Does she look like a threat to you? Does she?" Diana shrugged. "Jane Heissenhuber. *Femme fatale.*" He reached out and smoothed the skin on her throat and chest. "Is that how you see her, the kind of girl who drives men mad?"

Diana smiled. "Oh, Nick."

"Did you notice my heart pound when we ran into her? Did you see my knees start to shake?" Diana pressed her cheek against his chest. "She's a nice, good-natured girl," Nicholas said, as he tousled Diana's curls. "And that," he added, bending to kiss her forehead, "is that."

Although she had never gotten a rush, Jane had dated a fair number of boys from the time she arrived at Pembroke, although only three of them had really meant anything to her. In her sophomore year she'd dated Bob Curtis, a senior who was a fraternity brother of Nicholas's. He was a tall, suave boy from New Jersey with thin hair who dressed a little too well and drank a little too much, but for a while he wowed Jane by sending flowers to her dorm and tracing the outline of her lips with the tip of his finger. He did little more than that, and by June, when he graduated, she knew him no better than she had in November. She saw him once after the summer. He was working as a junior account executive for an advertising agency in New York, and he came up to Providence for Homecoming weekend, but it had gone badly—he'd gotten drunk, thrown up in the restaurant, then fallen asleep on a couch in the Alpha Delta Phi house, and Jane had walked back to Pembroke alone. He never called again, and she was neither surprised nor really sorry.

She met her second boyfriend a few weeks after that. His name was Steve Breslau and he was a lab partner of Amelia's boyfriend, Matt. She had never met a boy as sweet as he. If a day came that he had too much work to see her, he would call to find out how she was. He came to rehearsals and embarrassed and delighted her by applauding her performance. He bought her the Sunday papers each week, saying they were part of the Saturday night date. Although he obviously wanted more, he accepted her drawing the line at her waist and for four months contented himself with kissing her and caressing her breasts. He was attractive in a pale, long-faced, absentminded way, and although he himself was a little somber, he appreciated humor in others. They might have gone on to pinning, engagement, and marriage, but he was Jewish and his parents objected to his dating a Protestant girl and made him break it off.

Steve cried when he told her his parents' edict. Jane did not, and told him she understood, which she did not.

She'd known Peter Mackie from her first month at college, although she did not date him until April of her junior year. He was a year older than she, and one of the luminaries of Sock and Buskin. She played Amanda to his Elyot in *Private Lives* and they carried their bantering, bickering, and teasing straight through the performance into real life. Jane said "I adore you" to his "Aren't you marvelous?" and she did. She followed him to Williamstown that summer and, although she could not afford a job with the theater—she needed to earn enough for the books, clothing, and pocket money her scholarship did not cover—she saw him daily. He was assistant stage manager for *A Streetcar Named Desire*. Within days he turned from sophisticate to animal. Each night, he strode into her room behind the motel where she was working as a chambermaid, pushed her onto the bed, and tore at her blouse and brassiere, grabbing and sucking hard on her breasts as if it were the way to draw all resistance out of her. She allowed that, and allowed him to take off his clothes and come on her, but she fought him each night as he tried to take off her slacks, even though he warned her that her teasing would drive him away. After more than a month, she decided to give in and told him so, but he yanked at the recalcitrant zipper of her slacks so hard it frightened her. Shuddering, she told him no. He left her and, that same night, found himself another girl.

Jane was thoughtful but not analytical. She had teasingly told Steve Breslau that she was frigid and he had smiled, but his disbelief did not reassure her. She knew she had never been left breathless. She knew that saying no took everything some girls had, but it was easy for her. In truth, she was not tempted. But she never allowed herself to ask why. She certainly never permitted herself to connect the horror and titillation of her father's touches to her surfeit of control. In fact, she rarely thought of her father at all; she had not seen him since Christmas of her freshman year. And she never considered that the years spent under Dorothy's censorious eye had turned her into her own harshest critic, the keen observer who knew precisely how unattractive her broad shoulders and long nose were, how unappealing her heavy thighs, how cheap-looking her big breasts—and how Bob, Steve, and Peter were all somewhat unmanned in her eyes for being blind to or tolerant of these and all her flaws.

But another force had shaped her also. She hardly ever thought of Sally any more, but in their three years together her mother had given her the best she had. There was enough Sally in Jane to soften her, to make her affectionate and kind and tolerant. There was enough of Sally's skepticism and optimism to give Jane her honesty and her humor. And there was enough of Sally's hot stuff aglow in the deepest part of Jane that she could yearn for

Nicholas. She'd lie beside him on a chaise longue during rehearsals and, while he planted tiny kisses on her hand and called her "My dear, my darling Miss Whittleby," she'd half imagine the lights were out, his kisses were on her mouth, his shirt was off—as in *Hamlet*—and her hands were stroking his beautiful, muscular back.

It was not until the day before technical rehearsal for *The Other Sister* that Nicholas bothered to consider that Jane had a life outside Sock and Buskin. A few days after they met, he'd spotted her at the counter in the Brown Jug eating a hamburger, hunched over class notes, a pencil stuck through the top plait of her braid. He'd nearly gone over, but she was studying so intently he was afraid to disturb her; also, he'd just come from Walgreen's, where he'd bought athlete's foot ointment and a foam vaginal contraceptive Diana was too self-conscious to buy for herself, and he did not want to speak to anyone while his private life dangled before him in a paper bag. His times with Jane were fun, but they were theater business: at formal rehearsals, or when they'd meet in one of the small rooms backstage or in the makeout room of his fraternity house, the only places she could help him with his lines and they could go over their scenes together without interruption.

But the day before the technical rehearsal he'd been walking across campus on the way to lacrosse practice, wrapped in a fog of self-absorption, imagining the hoots from his friends when he walked out on stage in complete hunting regalia, including scarlet frock coat and tight white breeches, for his first scene. From there, it was easy to imagine forgetting his lines, standing dumbstruck while Diana squirmed for him. "'Mathilda Whittleby has fallen from her horse onto her nose,'" he proclaimed softly, to reassure himself, and just then Jane walked by, hand in hand with the handsomest boy he'd ever seen.

She was laughing hard, her head thrown back, her forehead and cheeks flushed, having such a good time and so absorbed in the boy she didn't even notice him. Nicholas stared. The boy obviously didn't go to Brown; he could never be overlooked. He was taller than Jane, probably six feet or so, and carried himself like a magazine model—his trenchcoat thrown over his shoulder, his strong chin a quarter inch higher than was natural, so the rest of his awesome features could be seen to perfection. But he didn't look phony because he was obviously what magazine models aspire to be: physically flawless and completely self-assured. Nicholas turned as they passed. The boy had begun laughing and gave Jane a playful punch in the shoulder, never letting go of her hand. Jane reached in front of the boy, grabbed the hand that had punched her, and aimed the boy's fist at himself, as if helping him punch himself in the face.

Nicholas discovered he was squeezing the hard rubber lacrosse ball he was carrying. He loosened his grip. He wasn't sure what he felt, but if he had to put a name to it he would have said annoyed. He'd seen Jane nearly every afternoon since he'd agreed to play Fortinbras. He'd felt easy with her and thought they were on the way to being friends. He liked the idea, because he'd really never been friends with a girl and looked forward to it, because Jane was just the sort of person he admired, a sort of female Charlie Harrison; she was smart—smarter than he—good-natured, and fun. Sassy, teasing him that he trained his hair to flop over his forehead so he'd look boyish (not true), that he used his eyes as a weapon to stun girls into submission (he wasn't sure), that part of the reason he wanted to act was that it shocked people close to him who expected him to do only what was conventional (true). "It's as if you joined a bowling league instead of playing whatever that game is you play—the one with the stick that looks like a petrified butterfly net."

"Lacrosse."

"Acting isn't for people like you. It's a public admission that you're not a responsible citizen."

"I am a responsible citizen."

"No, you're not. First you say you're for Kennedy—"

"Nixon wears his tie in a Windsor knot."

"You really aren't responsible."

"Yes, I am. A Windsor knot is a symbol. He's sleazy."

"But to tell them you wouldn't vote Republican, even though you know that supporting a Democrat—that's practically admitting to treason. And on top of that you say you want to act in a play. You're leaving yourself wide open. They'll kick you out of the Power Elite. Go ahead and laugh, but it's true. If you had any brains, you'd act under an assumed name. When they check your background for the Supreme Court, do you think they'll believe this was just a youthful indiscretion?"

But despite her intelligence, she'd seemed completely guileless. Yet she never mentioned to him that she was going with someone, even though he'd told her more than he'd planned to about Diana, that although he wanted to marry Diana he didn't think he'd be ready by summer, which was the time Diana seemed to have in mind. They were on their way back to Jane's dorm after a particularly late rehearsal, and when he told her that she'd stumbled over a small rise in the pavement. "Sorry," she muttered.

"What's the matter?" he asked. "Don't you think I should get at least a year or two of law school under my belt?"

"Oh, Nicholas," she'd said, her voice high with emotion. "Diana loves you."

He'd laughed at her romanticism and told her he pitied her, because when she finally fell for someone, she'd end up wearing her heart on her sleeve—and pointing it out to the boy if he failed to see it.

194

He thought he had a good sense of her, but watching her cavort he never would have guessed she could be so uninhibited. Silly, even. She pulled her hand from the boy's, brought it around back, whacked his backside, and then—although Nicholas couldn't be sure because her back was turned—doubled over with laughter.

Nicholas watched them until they rounded a corner. He realized he was angry. It was as if Jane had been false to him. The good-humored, kind, vulnerable facade she'd presented to him was just another role. At the technical rehearsal the following evening, he chose to be cold to her.

Nicholas lounged against a wall backstage a few feet away, in animated conversation with another actor, a junior who was playing his valet. Beside Nicholas in his third-act bright yellow breeches and white ruffled shirt, the gray-clad junior looked like a five-foot seven-inch rodent. A perturbed rodent: he kept shaking his head in disbelief as Nicholas, player by player, analyzed the New York Giant defense and found it wanting.

Jane approached and said, "Nick?"

He brushed his hand, a gesture between just-a-minute and leave-me-alone.

"I wanted to talk to you for a second," she said. "If you're busy . . . ?" The junior broke away, to go for coffee. "I didn't mean to interrupt," she said.

"What is it?" he demanded. He'd done little more than nod hello to her at the beginning of the rehearsal. Now he would not meet her eyes. He glanced past her, as if searching for someone better to talk to. His manner matched his frilly shirt and his sleek, slicked-back hair: disdainful.

"Could we sit for just a minute?" Jane asked. She walked to a chaise longue that had been used in the first act and sat. Grudgingly, eyes still searching for someone better, he sat beside her.

"Getting the jitters?" Jane asked softly.

"No. I'm fine."

He moved farther from her, to the edge of the chaise. His forearms rested on his thighs, the posture of a player waiting to be called into the game. She touched his shoulder and as he pulled away, he widened the rift between them. One of the axioms of their friendship was that they did not touch the other, and his flinching made her fear that she repelled him or, worse, he had somehow found out how she felt about him and found her feelings repugnant. She knew she should not pursue the matter, but with his withdrawal she felt a swelling of emptiness more profound than even she could have predicted. She'd known she would lose him, but not so abruptly and so soon, and she suddenly realized that the love she'd described to Amelia was not even the half of it. She stared at his hands. The fingers were long, the knuckles big and red; his wrists, dangling from the cuffs of his shirt, were thick, with a knot of a wristbone. She reached out and touched the top of his hand, even though she knew it was the worst thing she could do.

"Nick, what's wrong?"

"Nothing."

"Please, I know something is. You've been ignoring me all night."

"I haven't been ignoring you. I've been talking to a few other people. Is that all right? Or do I need your permission?"

"Nick—"

"Look, I didn't want to be here in the first place. I was stupid to have taken this part. It's taking too much time and for what? It's a waste. I'm sorry I let you talk me into it."

"Nick—"

"Two papers overdue and I'm three hundred pages behind in History. I can't believe I'm jeopardizing my chance for Columbia for this dopey play."

"But you said—"

"Forget it, Jane."

"You said how much you loved it, what a kick it was playing someone totally unlike you, some fop, and having everyone believe in your character."

"All right," he snapped.

"And you liked all the Sock and Buskin people so much."

"Terrific bunch."

His sarcasm was almost physical, knocking the wind out of her.

"Were you angry that I couldn't rehearse with you last night?" she whispered.

"Come on, Jane. Would you just lay off?"

"I was tied up."

"Forget it." He folded his arms, almost hiding his hands.

"My brother was here, and my roommate and I drove him back to Boston, and by the time we got back we just made curfew, and I didn't want to call you that late."

Nicholas turned and, at last, looked at her. "You never told me you had a brother."

"Well, I do. He's visiting colleges." Nicholas nodded and unfolded his arms. She felt as though some lenient judge had given her a reprieve. "He's a high school senior. He's with our—his mother, my stepmother, actually— you can see there's a little problem in that area. But anyway, she stayed at the hotel in Boston because she had a stomachache, so he took a bus. I haven't seen him in three years. He's gotten so tall—" She sensed she was babbling. She breathed in and said in a cooler voice, "He had an interview at Brown, but I don't know—"

"Reginald! Mathilda!" Professor Ritter screeched onstage.

196

Nicholas stood, grabbed her hand, and pulled her from the chaise. "We're being summoned," he said.

"Nick, I just want to say—"

"Listen, I'm sorry I snapped. I was being moody." He grinned at her. "If I wasn't temperamental, what kind of actor would I be?"

Nicholas was uncomfortable with Professor Ritter. The director was so unredeemedly ugly that when Nicholas looked squarely at him he was afraid to be thought disgusted or mocking or pitying. "I suppose you must know why I asked you to stop by," Professor Ritter said. Nicholas made himself gaze right into his eyes, except the lids and surrounding area were so fleshy the eyes themselves were only glints behind puffy slits. The nose could have been a rubber one made for *The Hunchback of Notre Dame*.

Nicholas sat as far back as he could in his chair. The director spat as he spoke, and Nicholas had been sprayed before. It was one of the few social occasions he was unprepared for. He did not know whether to remain still, leaving the man's spittle on his face, or wipe it off and thereby underscore the awkwardness of the situation. In the end, he'd decided to ignore it.

"Well, Nicholas?"

"I'm not sure, Professor Ritter."

"But you can guess. However, I shan't make you say it. I shall say it. You were fine as Fortinbras, although—how best to put it?—the role is not exactly the supreme test of the actor's craft." Nicholas nodded and waited. Professor Ritter was unpredictable. He might emote for hours or, because he could be wildly effusive and dramatic, he might at any moment hurl his bulk around the desk and grab Nicholas in a hug of enthusiasm. He did neither. Instead, he pounded his fist against the wall behind him and yelled "However!" Then he cleared his throat and moderated his voice. "However, Reginald *was* a test of the actor, albeit only in the high comic range, and you not only passed, you excelled." Nicholas looked up. "Really, you were quite, quite brilliant."

"Thank you. Coming from you takes that out of the category of a compliment and into—well, high praise, I guess."

"It is high praise. In all my years at Brown, I've never seen a student with as much presence as you. Note, Nicholas, that I've said presence. There are others who are better technically, who do not lose their British accents half-way through sentences—"

"I know. It was gone before I even missed it."

"Please. And there are those who, when they forget to move from table to fireplace mantel, do not attempt to remedy their lapse by sidling upstage in a movement more appropriate to the tennis court than a turn-of-the-century drawing room. However, all that can be learned, even by you. But you have something else—presence—and that is a gift. You strode onto that stage and the audience adored you. You were sly, calculating, but they forgave you, for they could see into your heart, and they knew in the end it would eschew Mathilda and beat only for Eloise. Not only are you believable, you are magnetic. You drew the audience into that play last week and kept them there."

"Thanks, Professor, but Jane and Penny were—"

"They were fine. It was an altogether admirable cast. But we are talking about you: Nicholas Cobleigh. A good name. You won't have to change it."

"Professor Ritter—"

"And now, onward and downward. Downward in the sense of plumbing deeper. We are doing *The Choephori*, and you must try out for Orestes."

"I can't. I wish there were some way, but I'm way behind in all my courses, and even though I know I shouldn't be thinking about grades, I need at least a three-five this semester for law school, and at the rate I'm going I won't even get a three-oh."

"Law school?"

"Yes. I thought I'd mentioned it at some point."

"I'd assumed you'd gotten over it. Why law school, may I ask?"

"I've always wanted it."

"Wanted to be a lawyer? Even as a little tot in the sandbox?"

"My father's a lawyer."

"It's an admirable profession. But are you willing to squander your gift?"

"I can still—"

"How? Amateur theatricals where some pretentious little director whispers 'Break a leg' before your entrance? You're too big for that, Nicholas." The director sprayed each time he said "Nicholas." Saliva dotted the papers on his desk. "You'd overwhelm any such production. They wouldn't even want you."

"I'll be busy for a while. Law school, a job. I appreciate your interest, Professor Ritter, but acting isn't for me."

"Tell me, how did you feel on the stage?"

"Okay. Nervous at the beginning."

"And then?"

"Then I liked it."

"It was wonderful, wasn't it, Nicholas?"

"It was. But I still have other obligations that—"

"Just try out for Orestes. Listen to me. Allow yourself to open up before you close yourself forever. It's only until early December and you'll have your friend Jane there. She's the only one with the stature for Clytemnestra; Pembroke has become a college of midgets. And then you have my word: no more pressure. If you choose law school, I'll dance at your graduation. I'll buy you a briefcase. I'll have you draw up my will. Good. I'm glad that's settled. Now, have you read *Agamemnon*?"

198

"Yes."
"Read it again."

Jane said she was overwhelmed with work and thus broke her two-year tradition of going with Amelia to Bar Harbor for Christmas. She also refused invitations to Brooklyn and Philadelphia, apologizing that if she had a few free days, she'd go to Cincinnati. She couldn't, of course. She knew Dorothy didn't want her and, in the back of her mind, dreaded that her father still might.

The truth was she hadn't the heart to go. More and more, she realized how profoundly lonely she was. She was a pleasant addition to other people's Christmas dinners; she would never be missed. She belonged nowhere and recognized with a pain approaching terror that all the people she'd bound to herself would disperse in June; every one of her ties would be severed. She tried to calm herself by thinking how lucky she was: she'd have a degree with honors from one of the best women's colleges in the country, and she was free and independent. It did not comfort her. She had no money, no job, no place to go, no one anywhere to send her off or greet her. And other than her brother (who she rightly guessed thought about her once or twice a month), she knew no one really loved her.

A merry Christmas would have made her ache. She stayed in Providence, alone in the dormitory, rehearsing her isolation. For more than a week she could barely leave her room. The tall brown rectangle of her wooden door was a reassuring seal until she had to open it to go down the hall to the toilet. Then it became an ominous barrier. She could not face the outside. The corridor vibrated with vacation silence. The stairs in the middle of the hall dropped down into blackness. She raced past the edge of the top step on her way to the bathroom because the dark stairwell seemed sinister, a malignant vacuum waiting to suck her down. Each time she returned to her room she was amused and mortified by her childishness but was only able to open the door again when her full bladder made her frenzied with discomfort. Direct confrontation with the stairs was worse. Because she could not force herself to edge close enough to them even to touch the railing, she made her meals from a box of crackers and from a tin of chocolate mint patties Amelia had left behind. She drank powdered instant coffee mixed with hot tap water.

On Christmas morning, in her old red pajamas, she opened her presents. Dorothy and Richard's was a yellow sweater set, so large it might have been knitted for a female grizzly. Their card said:

> Ho, ho, ho, ha, ha, ha
> Santa's on his way
> Bringing sacks of Yuletide cheer
> And laughter in his sleigh.

It was signed *Mother and Dad* in Dorothy's back-slanting script. Rhodes sent her a book, *Sixteen Famous American Plays,* and a note:

Dear Jane,

Hope you find the perfect vehicle in the enclosed. Miss you infinitely. Sorry you couldn't make it home. Have the happiest and merriest!!! Love and all my other bad habits, R.

From Amelia she got a glass paperweight and from another friend, Peg O'Shea, a leatherette-bound diary with *1961* tooled on the front cover. She got into bed, cried for a few minutes, then fell asleep. For the entire week she read all her own books and Amelia's psychology texts as well, but she could not concentrate enough to write the three papers she'd planned to.

When the church bells started to ring on the stroke of twelve New Year's Eve, she was running her tongue over her gums. Her whole mouth felt dry and fuzzy, but she was so tightly swaddled in her blanket she did not want to get up to brush her teeth. Then she thought about not being kissed and then she thought about Nicholas. He'd told her about the party he and Diana were going to that night. Good band, he'd said. Midnight supper. Jane put her hand on her shoulder and ran it down her arm, feeling the thin, pilled flannel. Nicholas had mentioned Diana spent a Saturday in New York in early December buying a new gown for the party. He had no problem, he'd said; he'd be wearing the same old tuxedo he'd been wearing forever. She closed her eyes and imagined Nicholas twirling Diana, the black and white glare of his evening clothes softened by the luminous chiffon of her dress as he held her tight and danced.

"Mother," Nicholas said softly from the foot of the hospital bed. The nurse had cranked it up so far that Winifred's back was at right angle to her legs. She looked flaccid enough to flop forward and fold in half, or sideways, crashing her head down on the lunch tray that rested on top of the metal nightstand. She had not eaten her lunch. The sandwich, crustless, cut into four triangles, looked dried out, and the bits of tuna or chicken salad sticking out of the white bread had turned brown. In a bowl, a cube of green gelatin lay limp in a little puddle of green juice, as if losing vital fluids. "Mother," he said again. She looked at him but neither recognized him nor responded to the presence of another person. He might have been a photograph of a young man pinned to the wall. He walked around to the side of her bed and sat beside her, taking her hand between his. It was cold and so soft it did not seem the hand of an adult. "Mummy," he said. "It's Nicholas. I'm home from college for the holidays." Her gray eyes had deepened to the color of shadow. Her skin had darkened too. He did not know whether the changes were caused by the electroshock treatments or if the high-ceilinged room in the psychiatric hospital was poorly lit. "I thought I'd come and say hello. Everything's fine."

"Nicholas," Winifred said.

"Yes. How are you?" Someone had tied a wide green ribbon around Winifred's unruly red and gray hair, placing the bow slightly off center in the front, so her head looked like a messy gift. "Mummy?"

"I suppose I'm fine. I'm tired. I could go to sleep now."

"Would you like me to leave and come back later?"

"No. No. I haven't seen you for a while, have I?"

"Not since September. It's December now."

"Nicholas, I know that. I'm not crazy."

"I know. I'm sorry." The last time he had held her hand he was a boy, and looking down he was startled to see his hand so much larger than hers. He gave her hand a small squeeze. When he let go, he noticed that her nails, always clear and oval-tipped, were yellow and ridged. Someone had clipped them straight across.

"How is college? Are you happy there?"

"Yes. It's a very nice place."

"I forget its name."

"Brown."

"Brown. The shock treatments make me forget things. Some things. All day I've been trying to remember the name of the beagle up at the farm. The one who limps."

"Flippy."

"That's right. I'm glad you can remember things like that. I worry so that I'll lose things I like, things I want to remember, and I won't ever know I've lost them. Every night I say all your names and all your birthdays, but what would happen if I came downstairs after a treatment and couldn't remember you at all? What if I forgot Abby or Edward? They could visit and I could look right into their eyes and not know who they were, and even if they said 'I'm your son' or 'I'm your daughter' they'd be lost to me forever. Of course, I'd know who they were supposed to be and I might be able to pretend to love them, but it wouldn't be the same. I wouldn't really know them, would I?"

"I think you're only supposed to forget the bad things, the things that made you so down in the dumps."

"It's called depression. Not the dumps. I have my own depression. Do you know about the other one? The real one?"

"Yes. Do you remember it? The soup kitchens—"

"Nicholas, I won't be home for Christmas."

"I know. But you'll be home soon after, and you'll feel much better."

"I don't think so."

"You will. The doctor is very optimistic that you'll be better."

"He said that the last time. Maybe there were two times. I don't know. Were there?" Nicholas nodded. "It's all right for a while. I go home, and your

201

grandmother has me to lunch with all the girls I went to school with, and for a day or two your father— I'm so tired."

"I know." Her shoulders had once been so broad. Now they sloped and the straps of her nightgown had slipped off. She let them hang. Nicholas wanted to lift them for her. When he was younger, she was always fidgeting, aligning the fingers of her gloves, centering the clasp of her pearls. Now, obviously fatigued by the conversation, she was utterly apathetic. If breathing hadn't been an involuntary act, she would not have had the strength to inhale again. "I'll come back tomorrow. Tom and the girls will be home by then. Michael and Edward are coming the day after. Is there anything you need?" She did not answer. Nicholas lifted one of the straps and placed it on her shoulder. It slipped back off, but Winifred did not seem to notice, nor did she realize that, after Nicholas kissed her cheek, stood, and walked to the door, his shoulders had the same defeated sag as her own.

For the next few days he let the whirl of activity exhaust him until he was too weary to think. Thomas arrived from college in Connecticut, Michael and Edward from Trowbridge, and his sisters, Olivia and Abigail, from their school in New Hampshire. He shepherded them all. All six went to a nursing home in New Jersey where their old nurse, Nanny Stewart, was living. All six were invited to dinner at their grandmother's. Maisie, in her early eighties, looked so regal with white upswept hair and a cameo at her throat she might have been a caricature of a grande dame. All six went ice skating in Central Park. Nicholas took his sisters, along with Diana, to a matinee. He drove Michael, who had a term paper in botany, to the greenhouses of the Bronx Botanical Garden and spent an afternoon helping Edward catch up on his trigonometry assignment. He called an aunt, the wife of one of Winifred's brothers, and got the name of a hairdresser for Olivia. Despite her hysterics, he refused to allow Abigail to go on a date with a boy she had met at the Museum of Modern Art. He and Diana took Tom to a Dixieland nightclub to celebrate Tom's nineteenth birthday.

In other words, Nicholas behaved more like a father than an older brother, but that was just as well, because James did not appear to relish his role. At breakfast, he seemed stunned to find six adult-sized children. Most of the time he was silent, staring into a space between the salt and pepper shakers, allowing Nicholas to organize the day's activities and pass on specific requests. When he did speak, he sounded like a lawyer making small talk with clients. He preceded the names of the younger four with an "um," allowing himself another second to attach the right name on the right child. "Um, Michael, are you still on the—the team?"

"Soccer. Yes."

"Good."

"Um, Edward?"

"I tried out for basketball, but I didn't make it."

"Well, next year."

"No. I stink at sports."

James appeared to divide his children as he did his life: into pre- and postwar periods. Children of hope and children of disaffection. He behaved as though the last four had developed parthenogenetically from Winifred and he had been named guardian. To Thomas, who had been conceived before the war and born when he was in the OSS in France, he was somewhat warmer, but he would have had to be catatonic not to respond to Tom's moon-shaped, smiling, freckled face and easy, gregarious nature.

But Nicholas knew his father loved him best, although it no longer gave him the deep secret pleasure it had when he was a boy. And so, on Christmas morning, when James put his hand on Nicholas's shoulder (a gesture he never made to the other children) and said, "Let's go into my study for a few minutes and shoot the breeze," Nicholas glanced about the living room at his brothers and sisters and saw how they each stared at the hand, imagining it on their own shoulders. Nicholas wanted to shove it off. Instead, reluctantly, he followed James out of the room, knowing five pairs of eyes were following them.

"Well," his father said. "How are things? Want a cigar?"

"No, thanks."

"Ever smoke them?"

"Once in a while."

"You don't smoke a pipe, do you? Or cigarettes?"

"No."

"How do things stand with law school?" James reached into a humidor, extracted a cigar, lit it with a gold and malachite table lighter Winifred had given him, then let the smoke drift out of his mouth. He rotated the cigar between his thumb and index finger. Every movement he made was easy and elegant. Diana was always coming up with the name of another movie star to compare James to. A stronger-featured Cary Grant, she'd say, or a blond, older Rock Hudson, or an intelligent Troy Donahue's father. None of the comparisons were right. Nicholas gazed at James's face, filmy behind a second drift of smoke.

It was too compelling and clever a face to have set its eyes on plain Winifred Tuttle without an ulterior motive. His father moved deeper into his tan leather armchair. His face was still handsome, Nicholas conceded, but with deep vertical creases in the cheeks and forehead lines that mimicked the arch of his eyebrows. The high color had faded after years of hard drinking. Nicholas remembered his father coming to kiss him good night when he was six or seven; James had seemed so bright in the dimness of the nightlight Nicholas half believed he glowed in the dark.

"Well?" James said.

"I've applied to Columbia and NYU."

"And?"

"That's all."

"Not Harvard? After all my years of contributing to their damned alumni appeals?"

"You have five other children."

"I'm not talking to them, am I? I'm talking to you."

"I don't have the grades."

"Did you bother to apply?"

"No. I want to stay in the city."

"What's the attraction?" This time, James drew hard on the cigar and blew out a jet of smoke between pursed lips.

"Everyone's here."

"They're all away at school."

"They come back. You and Mother are here. And Diana's family is here." Nicholas watched his father arrange his face into a neutral mask. He'd observed James respond to women often enough to realize his father did not find Diana appealing, and if a woman did not appeal to James, he had no use for her. Nicholas did not know why, but this indifference angered him.

"Are you planning to marry her?" James inquired.

"I think so. She has one more year of school, but that will give me time to get settled in law school."

"Columbia's not bad."

"I doubt if I'll get in."

"What do you mean?"

"I have a three-oh. They want about a three-two, and my boards weren't all that good. Not all that bad, either. I'll get into NYU. It's one of the top ten."

"You can do better."

"No I can't."

"I don't like your tone. What's wrong with you?"

"Nothing."

"You were so busy with that damn playacting you pissed away your shot at Columbia. Just pissed it away on that nonsense."

"I didn't piss anything away."

"What do you call it, then, a little foray into the arts?"

"Let's just forget it, all right? I enjoyed it. You might have too, if you'd come up."

"I had my hands full."

"I'll bet you did," Nicholas blurted. Suddenly he felt so flushed with anger the top of his head throbbed. Across from him, his father swallowed hard.

"What do you mean by that?"

"What do you think I mean?" Nicholas rose.

"Sit down," James commanded. "Who the hell do you think you are?"

Nicholas sat, but his anger expanded, pressing against his chest and throat. He had to push out his words. "You're so busy with your outside activities you haven't visited Mother. You haven't been to see her once."

"There are some things you don't understand."

"Don't I? Don't you think she knows why you haven't been to the hospital? Don't you know how it must hurt her?"

"She thinks I'm out of town."

"Don't you care about her at all?" he shouted, but his throat was so tight his voice came out hoarse. "She's your wife. Can't you even care enough to come up with a new excuse, something she won't see through?"

"You'd better watch yourself. You're way out of line."

"She's in the hospital, goddammit, getting shock treatments. She's as down and out as a person can be, and you give her a slap across the face with your lousy transparent excuses."

"Shut up, Nick. I'm warning you."

"What the hell did she ever do to you that was so bad you treat her this way?" He stood. It took the little control he had left to stay away from his father. His fingers contracted, ready to grab the lapels of James's bathrobe. Nicholas pressed his calves hard against his chair so as not to rush forward. His legs trembled. He unclenched his hands and rubbed them hard up and down his thighs. "Tell me," he yelled, "what did she do to deserve your nonsense excuses everyone can see through? Your whores you don't have the decency to hide? You come home stinking drunk or you don't come home at all."

"Shut up!" James shouted back, stabbing his finger in the air toward Nicholas. "Shut your fucking mouth!"

Nicholas had never heard his father use language like that. It sobered him like a hard slap. Then he spoke quietly. "She needs you."

"To hell with both of you!"

"Dad."

"I'm getting out of here." James threw his cigar in the ashtray and stood.

"It's Christmas."

"I have to go to the office."

"Jesus Christ, how can you do it? Who is so important that you walk out on us on Christmas? We need you. You're our father. Don't you care?" James did not look at Nicholas. He strode toward the door and, as he passed, almost as an afterthought, slammed his elbow into Nicholas's chest. Nicholas doubled over. The pain radiated through his breastbone. A spasm of nausea followed, so violent he dropped to his knees.

"Merry Christmas, you little bastard," James said.

Nicholas tried to lift his head. He could not catch his breath. As James opened the door, he managed to whisper, "You have five kids out there."

"Fuck them," his father said. "Fuck all of you."

"How was your vacation?" Nicholas asked.

"Wonderful," Jane said. "How was yours?"

"Great."

"Good." She paused. "Actually, mine was pretty awful."

"It was?"

"Yes."

"So was mine."

"Oh. Do you feel like talking about it?"

"No. I don't know," Nicholas said. "Do you?"

"I guess so. It's really nothing. I mean, it's going to sound somewhere between boring and pathetic. Closer to boring. You'll probably doze off before I get to Christmas Eve."

"Come on, Jane."

"You go first."

"Ladies first."

"What if I tell you everything and then you decide you don't want to tell me anything?"

"Then I'll have something on you and I'll spread it around. I'll tell all my fraternity brothers your deepest secrets, and if you're still able to show your face on campus after that I'll publish them in the *Daily Herald*."

"Nick—"

"What happened?"

The two letters had come the day before: one from New York University Law School saying that Nicholas had been accepted; the other from Columbia, that his name had been put on their waiting list. They both were in his back pocket, a little soggy from the damp ground. He lay on his back stretched out on a patch of new grass, his eyes half closed, the sweet, moist smells of early spring mingling with the manlier odor of the Seekonk River that flowed a few feet away. From far away, he heard crew practice, the coach calling "Stroke, stroke," with rhythmic monotony.

He turned his head to look at Jane. She sat on her raincoat in her favorite position, Indian style, trying to whistle through a blade of grass between her thumbs. Her head was bent and her hair, pulled tight into a ponytail, was so black in the sunlight it reflected glints of blue. The ponytail had fallen over her shoulder and spilled down the front of her green sweater, rising high with her breast, then falling in a loose wave below her waist. She was intent on her grass whistle, peering down at her thumbs slightly cross-eyed, but he knew any minute she'd drop the blade of grass and begin toying absentmindedly with her hair. He pictured her holding her ponytail in her right hand and combing it with the fingers of her left. He sighed and closed his eyes.

The stirrings of an erection made him open them. Embarrassed, he turned over onto his stomach. Nothing of that sort had ever happened to him with Jane. It was inappropriate and discomforting. He lay pressed to the ground and rested his head on his arm, concentrating on the weave of his pale blue cotton shirt, noting that some of the threads seemed inky blue, a few white. He examined the sparse, pale grass near his arm and then, closing his eyes, listened for river sounds. He heard "Stroke," but it was fainter than before. Closer by, a car's horn sounded three long impatient honks. The stirrings passed. He glanced at Jane. She'd wrapped her hair around her hand as if it were a bandage. "Well?" he asked. "What do you think?"

"I think you're probably crazy," she said.

"Why?"

"Hey, you have grass stains all over your behind."

"Jane."

"Well, you are crazy. Any sane person would weigh his chances of success and realize that the odds were pretty darn good in law school—"

"You really have a midwest accent. I can't believe you think you've lost it. 'Durn' for 'darn.'"

"I don't say 'durn.'"

"You just said it."

"I did not. What I just said was that you are crazy, and that's why you changed the subject."

Nicholas turned over and sat, pulling up both knees and resting his arms on them. "I thought you of all people would say to take the chance."

"But I am saying that. I think you're brilliant. I mean it, Nick. You have enormous talent, and you know I wouldn't tell you that if I didn't mean it. It's a terrible, rough life, and anyone with even a touch of mediocrity shouldn't try to be an actor. If I had any doubts I'd say don't do it. It would be cruel to encourage you to face all the awful things you're going to have to face."

"Then why do you say I'm crazy?"

"Because you'll be giving up a sure, safe career. You'll be trading prestige and money and maybe even interesting work—for what? A three-week run in an Off Broadway play or a chance to play Mr. Halitosis in a toothpaste commercial. You're crazy because you have a choice between security and insecurity, and you choose insecurity. You have a choice of having your rich family pay for law school—"

"We're not rich."

"What are you then?"

"I don't know."

207

"You sound pretty rich to me. Well, whatever you are—were—it won't be yours. Your family is going to cut you off, so you won't have any money. What are you going to do without money? You've never worked."

"I worked as a counselor at a camp three summers ago. I coached lacrosse."

"Good. I'm sure there are lots of part-time job opportunities for lacrosse coaches in Manhattan. You can make more than enough to cover your rent and food and clothes and acting lessons—"

"You're going to try to do it."

"But I've worked before. I've spent summers scrubbing toilets and making beds. I've worked in the library and as a waitress. I'm not the one who's going to miss the ballet and the French restaurants, Nick. I won't feel deprived not being able to go to Europe because I've never been to Europe. And I'm not doing anything that will upset anyone. No one really cares whether I become an actress or an English teacher or a chambermaid. I'm totally free and clear. I'm not pinned to someone who thinks the only place to be in a theater is center orchestra."

"That's not fair," Nicholas snapped. Jane pulled in her lower lip and gnawed on it. She looked so miserable he wanted to comfort her. Her remorse was too excessive for the crime. "Jane, stop it. You didn't say anything that terrible. Anyway, she'll come around."

"She will?"

"Well, she's very upset. Not because of—I don't know. I think she sees me as a very straightforward, well-adjusted person."

"You are."

"But actors aren't. Not in Diana's view, anyhow. Besides, you just said I was crazy."

"But you're crazy with cause. You're gifted."

"Well, talented anyway. I hope. If I didn't think I had a shot I wouldn't have the guts."

"You're more than talented. You'll see."

"Really?"

"Really."

"Well, maybe." He looked at Jane and grinned. "When I'm world-famous I want you to feel free to come backstage to my dressing room. I'll have my valet let you in to see me in my Mr. Halitosis costume and—don't worry, I won't forget poor little Jane Heissenhuber—I'll give you my autograph. And a free tube of toothpaste."

"You're a classy guy."

"Thanks."

"Even if you're not rich."

"Jane—"

208

"Nick, listen to me. Seriously. If there's any justice in this world, you're going to make it."

"What if there is no justice?"

Jane tilted her head to the side and shrugged. "Then you'll become the world's oldest living law school student."

She knew it would be their last time alone. The following night was the final play and then the cast party, but Diana would be coming down from Wheaton for that, and then there would be finals and graduation. In the past, Jane had imagined the different ways Nicholas would finally declare his love. At first she pictured herself helping out in the dressing room, smoothing on Nicholas's pancake makeup with the tips of her fingers, when suddenly he'd grab her wrist, say "Come here," pull her onto his lap, and kiss her passionately and expertly. But her imagination would not compensate for her height and weight, and she did not want to consider his pulling her onto his lap and saying "Wow, you're a big one" as one boy had. So she imagined them in Nicholas's car, ostensibly on the way to the Newport Creamery for ice-cream cones but never getting there; instead, Nicholas would park the car on some dark street and turn off the engine. "What's the matter?" she'd ask innocently, and, in answer, he'd put his hand behind her neck, pull her toward him, and kiss her, applying just enough pressure so her lips would begin to part.

But in the weeks before this last night together, Jane had finally surrendered her fantasies after repeated bruising attacks of reality. Nicholas had told her he and Diana had finally decided to wait two years to marry: one year for Diana to finish college and another, once they were formally engaged, for her to find a job and prepare for the wedding. If he wasn't earning at least a subsistence living by that time, he'd promised to give up acting and go to law school. There was not a single comforting dream left for Jane to cling to, because he'd let it slip that he and Diana had contrived to spend several days of intersession alone at her parents' beach house on Long Island, and so Jane's auxiliary fantasy—that Nicholas, while not loving her, would grab her from sheer sexual desperation and then realize how much he cared—was pointless. He and Diana had obviously been going all the way for a long time. His eyes would never grow shadowy with desire for Jane while they were alone rehearsing, nor would he pull her to the floor and tear at her clothes. He had no need.

Still, she wanted their last night together to be memorable. Nicholas would not oblige her. He'd cut off her reminiscences of the plays they'd been in together by asking her to cue him for his second-act lines. He was playing a British soldier in an all-male production, a play whose entire content was the conversation of three soldiers at Tobruk in North Africa waiting for Rommel's final attack and their own deaths.

209

"'. . . and what is the whole bloody point anyway? Is the point that there is no point?'" she read.

"'The point is,'" Nicholas said in a British accent far more convincing than his first attempt, "'that we were born and that we are about to die, and between those points—but what is between *is* the point after all, Alfred.'"

"Good job," Jane said.

"But you still don't like the play?"

"No. It's a bad combination of Samuel Beckett and those dumb, noble 1941 There'll Always Be an England movies. Pretentious, sentimental. And C minus to a D plus as far as substance goes."

"Well, anyway, thanks for helping. I just wanted to go over it one more time. I'll walk you back to your dorm."

"Do you want to go for coffee or anything?"

"Would you mind if we skipped it? I have that paper for my Roosevelt seminar I have to retype. I'll see you tomorrow night at the cast party."

She'd planned on saying, Nick, this is the last time we'll be alone and I just want to tell you how much your friendship has meant to me. If he said something encouraging back, she'd add, Maybe we'll run into each other in New York, and he'd look stunned that she could possibly think otherwise and say of course they would and they'd make arrangements to meet in Times Square or the Empire State Building right after Labor Day, as soon as their summer jobs were over.

He opened the door of the small backstage room where they'd been and held it until she passed through. His aftershave smelled lemony. He was wearing the rich boy's uniform—plaid shirt, khaki slacks, and loafers—and when Jane glanced at him, he was wearing the rich boy's cool, bland look. She was losing him. Tears dammed up until her cheeks ached. Each time she glanced at him he seemed less like Nicholas and more like any cool, bland Alpha Delta Phi brother, well-groomed, smooth, and distant. As they went into the warm night, he walked briskly, farther away from her than usual, with his hands stuffed into his pockets, not bothering to talk, as if he were taking home a dog of a blind date.

"Nervous about tomorrow night?" she asked, as they came in sight of her dorm.

"A little, I guess."

"You'll be fine." It was nearly curfew, and near the door to her dorm a couple was kissing good night. The girl was short, and even though she stood on her toes, her boyfriend had to hunch over her; her back was arched and he supported her head in the palm of his hand. Jane looked away from them and from Nicholas as well.

"See you tomorrow night," Nicholas said.

She turned to him. He was staring at the same kissing couple. The boy had his other hand on the small of the girl's back, massaging the area with small circular motions. "Nick," Jane began. He whipped his head around quickly, as if startled to see she was still beside him. "Nick, I just wanted to say—"

His hands burrowed deeper into his pockets and he shifted from one leg to another. She knew he was uncomfortable at the thought of her little speech, but she could not stop.

"This is the last time I'll really get a chance to speak to you and I just wanted to tell you how much—"

"It's okay," he said. "See you tomorrow night." Before she could speak again, he bolted. Jane watched as he hurried down the street, picking up speed until he was nearly running.

Nicholas ran for three blocks. He was stopped by his own confusion. He leaned against a parked car. He didn't know why he was running or where he was running to. For a second he believed it was to get back to his room to call Diana and arrange where to meet after the play, but he threw that thought aside. When it was gone, no other took its place.

The night, lit by a yellow-white moon, was balmy, but suddenly Nicholas was freezing. His teeth clacked. He folded his arms and stuck his hands under his armpits. His armpits were soaked with cold sweat. Still, he kept them there, hugging himself, shivering, not caring when a group of students passed and, seeing him, laughed, thinking he was drunk.

He felt sick with despair. His whole body was weak, as if joylessness were a condition that shriveled the cells. He might have been frightened of the way he was feeling, but his desolation was so profound he was almost insensate.

For long, terrible minutes no single thought could penetrate the void he felt. When at last one thought did, it was of Jane, of the final words she'd spoken: "This is the last time . . ." The words reverberated until, silently, he was saying them with her: *This is the last time*. Then he knew. He stood absolutely still. Then he ran back, faster than he'd ever run before.

As she entered the area on the first floor of her dormitory where boys waited for their dates, he saw she'd been crying. Her lashes stuck together in wet feathery fringes. "Jane," he said.

"It's five minutes till curfew," she said. Her voice sounded normal, but was so muted he could hardly hear her.

"Let's go outside."

"Nick, it's late." Her eyes, still moist, were a deep, dark blue, with a fine circumference of black around the iris he'd never noticed before. He wanted to laugh and tell her it was funny, she kept kidding about how he went around batting his big blue eyes, but hers were so much more special. Really beautiful eyes, especially with her dark skin. "I'll see you tomorrow night," she said. "All right? It's late and I have a hundred and fifty pages—"

"Marry me," he said.

"What?"

"Marry me."

"That's not funny."

"I mean it."

"Stop it, Nick."

"I'm serious."

"This is a very cruel thing you're doing." She blinked but could not hold back the tears. Her voice grew even softer. "I can't believe you'd do something like this to me."

"Jane—"

"I thought you were my good friend." He reached for her and pulled her to him and she yielded even as she was whispering, "This is terrible."

"No. No, it's not," he said into her ear. He kissed the lobe of her ear and then kissed her mouth. He'd never held such a tall girl, and the pleasure of being mouth to mouth, chest to breast, thigh to thigh made him euphoric. He put his hand on the nape of her neck, under her braid, and when he felt her quivering he realized she was still crying. He lowered his arms. "Jane," he breathed. "Do you think I would do this . . ." He paused and then plunged. "Do you think I would come here like this if I didn't love you? Look at me." She shook her head no. "Listen to me. I left you tonight and then I thought what it would be like never to see you again." A gulping sob escaped from Jane, and she clapped her hand over her mouth. "And then I realized—Jane, for Christ's sake, say something."

She took her hand away, but it took a minute before she could speak. "If you're kidding me, I'll never speak to you again. I swear, I'll hate you for the rest of my life."

"Marry me, Jane."

"You are kidding me. I know you are."

"You know I'm not."

"What if I don't want to?" She was overwrought, breathing hard. Her face was damp. "What if I don't love you? You never thought of that, did you? It never occurred to you that I might not—"

"I know you do." It was only as he said it that he knew it was true. He took her wrists and pulled her close again. . . .

"Did you know the whole time?" she finally asked.

"I don't know. Has it been a long time?"

"Yes."

"Since when?"

"Since the beginning."

"Why didn't you say anything?" She did not answer. "Well, what are you going to do about it?" She lifted her hand and gingerly, as though afraid he would slap it down, she touched his face. "Are you going to marry me?"

"I'll marry you," she said.

"Oh, Jane."

Before he could kiss her, she added, "But you're crazy, Nick. You're making a big mistake."

"No, I'm not."

"It's all right. It's the end of college. You're very emotional. I won't hold you to it or anything. You can change your mind."

"I won't."

"I'll understand."

"Jane," he said. He gave her a light kiss. She had a lovely, wide, passionate mouth.

"What?"

"This is no joke. This is real. Forever. Okay? Now say it to me."

"Say what?"

"What I said to you. Come on."

"Oh, Nick," she said. "I love you more than you'll ever know."

12

. . . also a marriage of opposites. Handsome Nicholas, the quintessential clean-cut preppy, is silent and mysterious as a Buddhist monk while the darkly exotic Jane is as straightforward as apple pie.

—*Los Angeles Times*

"Look, I can see where you'd want to—" James's voice broke off. He swung one of Nicholas's suitcases into the back of the station wagon, then sat on the tailgate. The car was parked not far from Nicholas's fraternity house.

"Want to what?" Nicholas asked. He hoisted another case, a heavier one loaded with shoes.

"Put that down for a minute," his father said. "Listen, I don't want you to get all hot under the collar, but—"

"There's nothing to discuss," Nicholas said.

"Don't give me that crap. Listen, let's not go at each other. I want to have an intelligent discussion with a mature college graduate. Okay?"

"Stop patronizing me."

"Nick, she's a nice girl. I'm the first to admit it. Smart as a whip. Much more on the ball than the other one. And I'm not blind. She has something. I can see where you'd want to sleep with her—"

"Dad, cut it out."

"—but that *doesn't* mean you have to marry her. She's crazy about you. She'll do anything you want her to do, and she won't need a wedding ring to make her do it."

Nicholas tossed the suitcase into the back of the wagon, then lifted his record player and jammed it between the suitcase and the side of the car. "It happens I love her. It happens I want to marry her."

"Marry her a couple of years from now, then, if you still feel the same way."

"No."

"You're a kid. You don't know what you're doing."

"You just said I was a mature college graduate."

James let out an exasperated sigh. "Christ, stop acting like a kid. You don't marry the first piece of ass you come across."

"You have no right to talk about her like that!" Nicholas barked.

James lowered his head. "Okay. I'm sorry. I'm just upset. First you throw

214

away law school, then you come up with some nobody whose parents don't have a pot to piss in—"

"How big was your parents' pot?"

"What?"

"Who were you when you met Mother? You were on scholarship. You've told me next to nothing about your parents, but it's pretty obvious they weren't the cream of Rhode Island society."

"It so happens my mother—"

"You said your mother was an alcoholic who never gave a damn about you. And your father was a shyster lawyer. . . . I'm sorry. Dad, listen, I don't want to fight."

"Neither do I," James said. His eyes remained cast down and he ran his finger over the latch of the tailgate. "But you're young. You'll change. In a couple of years, you'll realize you need something more in a wife: a girl from a decent family, a good background. . . ."

"Dad, don't you think Grandpa Samuel and Grandma Maisie made the same argument to Mother?"

"It was different."

"How?"

James's face lit up with the beginnings of an angry flush, but all he said was, "Nick, you can do better."

"No I can't."

"You can. Come on. You've had all the advantages. Who the hell is she?"

"Who the hell is she? She's the best there is."

The guest room Jane slept in in the old Tuttle farmhouse had a four-poster bed. The faded primary colors of a braided rag rug glowed against the gold of the pegged oak floor. Across the room, a blue club chair with fat round arms half faced the brick fireplace. The walls were the warm white of heavy cream. It was the loveliest room she had ever been in. She turned from her back onto her side, drew up her legs, and closed her eyes, just so she'd have the pleasure of opening them and seeing the early morning sky sparkling through the undulating old glass; the windows were framed with tieback eyelet curtains.

When the door opened she was in such a fog of contentment she could hardly lift her head, but when she saw it was Nicholas the fog was blown away by a blast of clear joy. She sat up and tried to mask her overwhelming pleasure with a yawn. "Oh, hi. I thought it was Abby or Olivia." She held the blanket tight against her. "You shouldn't be in here," she added.

"Everyone's asleep." Nicholas padded into the room in bare feet, wearing an old pair of khakis and a T-shirt which—judging from its snug fit and the

215

way it refused to remain tucked into his slacks—belonged to one of his younger brothers. He sat on the edge of the bed, smelling of soap and toothpaste. Jane slipped her arms around him, nuzzling her cheek against his. His face was sleek enough to show that he'd just shaved, rough enough to be manly. She kissed his ear and eased her hands up his back to knead the muscles in his shoulders.

Her own audacity—reaching out for him, taking his hand, often asking for a kiss—amazed her. She still could not completely believe she was really engaged. Several times before graduation she felt a shiver of horror as she lay in her dormitory bed, imagining Nicholas telling her his proposal had all been a huge joke planned by him and Diana Howard, to see if Jane was pathetic enough to believe he could possibly want to marry her. Nicholas put his arms around her and pulled her even closer. "Have a good sleep, sweetheart?"

"Fine." She edged back so she could see his face. "Don't get too close. I haven't brushed my teeth yet. Anyway, it was fine but short. I was up with the girls until after two. Olivia seems to like to talk."

"She never stops."

"And Abby told me I looked like an Indian princess."

"American Indian or India Indian?"

"I don't care. At least she thinks I'm nifty. Apparently that's the big word at their school, nifty. I'm nifty and my hair is the niftiest hair she's ever seen. And . . ."

"And what?"

"I'm much niftier than Diana. I'm only quoting now."

"Abby said that?"

"Yes, and she said—I'm sorry, who is her twin?"

"Mike."

"She said Mike thinks I'm nifty too. That only leaves Ed and Tom. Olivia was sitting right there and she didn't say I wasn't nifty, so I guess she thinks I'm okay."

"Well," Nicholas said, bringing his legs up on the bed, "you're in with Tom. He thinks you're great. And Ed's in that adolescent stage where anything with big boobs is nifty, so—"

"So all we need now is for your parents to think I'm nifty."

"Stop it. They like you."

"No they don't. They're just polite."

"Jane, it's not you."

"Yes it is."

"They just think I'm too young."

"You are. Why don't we forget the whole thing for now? Call me when you're thirty."

216

Nicholas twisted toward her, then suddenly grabbed her wrists and pinned her down in a wrestling hold. "Take it back."

She tried, not terribly hard, to break his hold. "Is this how you bully your brothers and sisters?" she demanded.

"Yes. Take it back."

"What's in it for me?" she asked.

"Me."

"Oh. Okay, I take it back."

Nicholas released her wrists and she put her arms around his neck. "Just wait," he said.

"For what?" She smiled knowingly.

"For your family to meet me."

She dropped her arms. "You had to remind me, didn't you?"

"Well, we have another two days here."

"Nick, please, there's no point in going."

"We have to go. We'll be working all summer, and you said they probably won't come to the wedding."

"Rhodes will."

"But you said they'll find some excuse not to come."

"Isn't that enough for you? Doesn't that indicate something about them?"

"Yes, but that still doesn't mean I don't have to meet your parents."

"Father and stepmother."

"Richard and Dorothy. Whoever. It's the right thing to do."

"We have a crummy, tiny house. You'll hate it. You'll feel suffocated. Rhodes never brought any of his friends home. I'll bet she still hasn't fixed the rip in the window shade in the bathroom, and I haven't been home in more than three years. And she buys the cheapest paper napkins and terrible toilet paper."

"Wait until you see the kind of place we'll be able to afford. Last night— when I went downstairs to see if the raccoons were at the trash cans—I ran into my father. Are you ready for his first and only words of the entire day to me? 'Not one thin dime, Mr. Barrymore.'"

"Was your mother with him?"

"No. She was asleep by then. Not that she would have stopped him." As he often did when preoccupied, Nicholas rubbed the flat of his hand up and down his thigh. "How does she seem to you?" he asked.

"She seems—not so bad."

"The truth."

"Well, I don't know. If I didn't know she'd been in and out of psychiatric hospitals, I wouldn't guess it. But there's something wrong. I don't know how to say it."

"Say it."

"She seems like she's reading for the role of a well-bred lady. Her carriage is just right, her accent's perfect, but it's as if she'd just been handed the script a few minutes before. There's no conviction."

"You should have known her. She was always dashing around, but she had such spirit. Even if I only saw her for five minutes, it was—you've heard this all before. Ad nauseam."

"No, Nick."

"Forget it. The point is, we're going to be totally broke."

"Now, come on. That's nothing new. We're going to live in a slum, period. But it will be a slum in New York."

"But guess what comes before New York?"

"Nick, listen to me."

"Let me under the covers. I want to be close to you."

"No. Please listen."

"You really think you can hold out until we're married?"

"Yes. It's only three months and most of the time we'll be working two hundred miles apart."

"I can't believe I was so dumb it took me until May to realize how I felt about you. Two months earlier, and we could have had jobs with the same summer stock company."

"And now you want to waste our last few days together."

"Come on, Jane, don't get yourself all worked up over Cincinnati. You're not a kid any more, dependent on them. You're Phi Beta Kappa hot stuff."

"I'm not hot stuff. And you'll see, it'll be so awful for you. You'll get one look at them and you'll say, 'Uh-oh, big mistake. Bad genes, bad environment, bad breeding—'"

"Just stop it."

"'Altogether bad news.' Better have your gas tank filled so you can put Ohio behind you before sunset. You think I'm kidding, don't you?"

"Jane, we're not moving in with them, are we? We're spending between forty-eight and seventy-two hours with them, and that will probably be it until whenever—probably at little Bubblehead's christening five years from now. Don't worry, I can take what they can dish out."

"You'll see, you'll wind up running or you'll feel so sorry for me you'll go through with it even though you don't want to." She'd tried to keep up the irony, but midway through her sentence she felt her voice break and expose her fear.

He took her hands between his and pressed them against his chest. The depth of his gentleness always took her by surprise. "Jane, I'll be there to take care of you."

*   *   *

218

"A little something to eat?" It was so terrible Nicholas wanted to laugh. Dorothy was offering him a slice of cucumber on a small square of white bread. Five minutes before, Dorothy had announced, "It's tea time!" and Jane had looked as if she wanted to die of embarrassment; she sat on the far side of the couch staring into her cup as though she wished she could drown herself in it. Dorothy had put paper doilies over every flat surface, including the saucers. On the table before them was the sugar, wedges of lemon, and a dinner plate with what had obviously been a frozen chocolate layer cake cut into finger-sized pieces.

"Thank you," Nicholas said. Not even his grandmother had ever offered him a formal tea, although he supposed she might have had them years before. The girls he'd gone out with at prep schools and some of the women's colleges had been taught to serve tea and he'd had to endure those a few times, but he'd never known anyone who did in her own house. Tea was for England or for the flu. He took one of the canapés. The cucumber, instead of a translucent wheel held by butter, was a thick circle squashed into the bread.

"You're very welcome." Dorothy smiled at him.

He had been surprised by Dorothy's plainness. He supposed he'd expected a witch or someone with a bright red mouth and long fingernails like the stepmother in *Snow White*, but she was ordinary. Her hair had the tight hardness of pin curls and hairspray. Her dress was navy or black with a white collar and looked more maid's uniform than stylish. Her arms and legs were heavy. She had the ugliest ankles he'd ever seen. But still, her meanness wasn't evident; she looked ordinary, like a member of the audience of a TV quiz show.

"Jane?" Jane shook her head. When they'd arrived the night before, Nicholas had observed Richard and Dorothy closely. Jane's father had acted in a removed manner. He couldn't seem to make up his mind whether or not to kiss her hello and ultimately was saved when Jane saw Rhodes and rushed to fling her arms around him. Richard alternated awkward attempts at conversation with exaggerated concern: was her room cool enough? would she like to read his *Time?* Mostly, though, he was silent. What Nicholas could not gauge was whether Richard loved, or even liked, his daughter. For the entire evening not a single discernible emotion passed across Richard's bland face. But Nicholas had no difficulty gauging what Richard was: a man of little consequence.

Dorothy sidestepped with the plate from Jane to her son. It was only after more than an hour the night before that Nicholas realized that she did, indeed, detest her stepdaughter. He'd tried to deny it, saying to himself that Jane's feelings had prejudiced him, but the more he watched Dorothy, the more certain he became of her hate. She seemed unable to look at Jane directly, yet when she did speak to her, her eyes narrowed and she pulled her arms close to her body, as if tensing for an attack by an evil and sly enemy. Her words were cordial—"Don't you trouble yourself, dear" when Jane rose to help clear the table—but after he listened for a while Nicholas could hear violence behind them. When Jane made an irreverent comment that made Rhodes laugh, Dorothy's face tightened horribly. Nicholas didn't know how he knew, but he knew Dorothy would like it if Jane were dead. It shocked him at first and then upset him so much it had taken him hours to fall asleep. He felt sick for Jane's sake. "Rhodes, you must have one. These are your favorites." It was obviously news to Rhodes, but he took two of the canapés and thanked his mother. She did not smile so much as glow back at him. Nicholas could not blame her for that.

Rhodes was so handsome it embarrassed Nicholas to look at him. His appearance was so extraordinary that it seemed wrong for him to be sitting on a lumpy couch in a drab house in Cincinnati. But, Nicholas conceded, he really wouldn't belong anywhere because his beauty would always diminish his surroundings; Rhodes would make Versailles seem shabby. Yet even though Nicholas didn't like to stare, he was drawn to Rhodes. The boy was too handsome not to look at. There was not a single feature that was less than beautiful. Even his forehead was magnificent. For the first time the phrase "noble brow" had meaning. All his life people had told Nicholas how good-looking he was, and he knew his appearance was an asset, attracting girls, smoothing his social path. But Jane's brother—they had the same deep blue eyes—was in a whole other league. Perhaps another world. It was obvious that Rhodes was used to people admiring him, even staring at him. Once or twice he'd caught Nicholas at it and simply smiled, as if to reassure him it was all right, that it was inevitable and certainly no breach of etiquette.

Rhodes sat between Nicholas and Jane. As he brought the canapé to his mouth, Nicholas saw Jane lowering her head—the tension she'd been under finally lifting—battling an urge to laugh. That instant, as Dorothy bent to put the plate on the table, Rhodes poked Jane with his elbow to stop her, but he too seemed ready to laugh. It was then Nicholas realized how important Rhodes had been for Jane; throughout her childhood, he'd been the antidote to the poison his mother exuded.

A moment later, when Dorothy left the room to get the milk for the tea he requested, Rhodes turned to his sister and said, "Creepette, don't you have the brains not to crack up in front of her?"

"I can't stand it," Jane said. "It's too terrible. Tea!"

"She's just trying to impress Nick. You should be thankful. You need all the help you can get." Rhodes turned to him. "Nick, aren't you impressed? The lovely teapot with the chipped spout and the Kroger labels dangling from the teabags? Isn't that how they do it in New York?"

"I'm very impressed," Nicholas said.

"I can tell," Rhodes said. Nicholas liked Rhodes. He liked him because even though he was not a relaxed, regular guy—Rhodes was too aware of the impact of his beauty for that—he was intelligent and amusing. But most of all Nicholas liked Rhodes because it was obvious Rhodes loved Jane, even though a good deal of their time was spent on mutual abuse. Rhodes turned to Jane. "Listen, Stretch, you can't afford to be so picky. I mean, tea is tea; be thankful you got anything. We're all numb, absolutely reeling from shock. You've snagged a winner—which is almost impossible to comprehend—and Mom's trying to make a decent impression before he comes to his senses and runs." Rhodes's face shone with the pleasure of having his sister home. He seemed to relish his New York audience too, for after each dig at Jane he'd glance at Nicholas, looking for his smile of acceptance. It was clear he thought Nicholas sophisticated. Rhodes readjusted his spoon, placing it on his saucer at the exact angle Nicholas placed his. The day before, Nicholas had spotted Rhodes opening the buttons on the collar of his shirt, which Nicholas had simply forgotten to do up. Rhodes turned back to Jane. "You must have gotten him *very* drunk. Or did you get yourself preggy so he'd have to marry you? Hmmm? A little backstage dalliance with the pride of the Ivy League?"

"If you weren't so emotionally crippled I'd be angry, but all I can really do is pity you."

"Nick," Rhodes said, leaning across Jane. "I don't have to remind you you're marrying beneath you, but—"

Dorothy returned from the kitchen with a pitcher of milk. She poured a little into Rhodes's cup, put it beside the teapot, and sat in Richard's chair across from the couch. She smoothed her dress over her lap and smiled at Nicholas. Suddenly her back went rigid, as if she had just remembered that the mark of a lady is good carriage. Nicholas knew he intimidated her and was glad. "Well," she said, "isn't this nice?" He nodded and took his first sip of tea. It was lukewarm. He set the cup down. "We're so pleased you and Jane were able to stop by." She paused and added momentously, "And isn't it something that you have a cousin in Cincinnati, a cousin like Clarissa Gray." Dorothy turned to Rhodes. "The Grays are often in the *Enquirer* society pages. Quite often. They're one of Cincinnati's finest families. And very close friends of the Harts."

Clarissa Tuttle Robinson had been New York's most touted debutante in 1939. In 1940, she had married one of the wealthiest, most dashing bachelors east of the Mississippi, Philip Gray. Clarissa's family was substantial on both sides. Her father's family owned a shipping company. Her mother was a Tuttle, Samuel's sister. However, there was nothing about Clarissa to indicate she was Winifred Cobleigh's first cousin. She had gone from a fresh-scrubbed beauty to being glamorous nearly to the point of hardness. Beneath prominent

221

slashes of cheekbone were hollows so deep it seemed she had no back teeth. Her makeup was not the two tender pats of peachy rouge common to Cincinnati society matrons; it was vivid and heavy. Her dark eyes had been outlined with a thick black pencil or crayon and the line was extended almost a half inch, Cleopatra-fashion. Deep pink rouge stained her cheeks nearly up to her eyeliner. Her lips were outlined too, in a red that contrasted with the dark pink of her lipstick. Streaks of gold and silver shot through her short brown hair, making it look very expensive.

"You must fill me in on all the family gossip," she said to Nicholas. Her voice, like Nicholas's and his brother Edward's, was slightly husky, but her pronunciation was a little stilted, as though she had a slight speech impediment or that English was not her first language, which was of course not the case. Her speech simply may have been a reflection of her frequent extended clothes-buying and vacation trips to Europe, where she spoke other languages, or her desire to disassociate herself from Ohio. Clarissa sat on a lawn chair covered in blue and white awning stripes on a terrace that overlooked a few of the twenty-five acres of the Gray property. Opposite her, behind Nicholas and Jane, the lawn rolled on and on until it stopped at a mass of oak, pine, and sugar maples; a rock garden nestled at one edge with the exquisite, studied randomness of the artificial.

"I guess you know about Aunt Polly and Uncle Jeremiah," Nicholas said.

Clarissa nodded. "Yes. But that he'd leave her! And at his age!" She crossed her leg. Her foot, nearly bare in the jeweled thong, moved in little circles. She wore an ankle-length white silk skirt printed with ribbons of raspberry, green, and yellow. Her raspberry shirt, also silk, was opened one button's worth too much for Cincinnati, exposing a great deal of deeply tanned skin. Around her neck was a thick choker that looked as though it were made of white Rice Krispies but was actually composed of twisted strands of small baroque pearls. Her earrings were the same sort of pearls resting in a cradle of diamonds. "I know he's your uncle, Nicky, but he's my cousin, and really, Jerry's never even voted in his entire life and suddenly he's off with Kennedy's—what is she?"

"I think she's a deputy assistant appointments secretary or assistant deputy. My mother and my grandmother haven't said a word about it and it happened the week before finals, so I haven't had a chance to hear the details from any of the cousins."

"How is your mother?" She put her hand on Nicholas's sleeve. She wore a knuckle-to-knuckle gold wedding band.

"Much better," Nicholas said. "Really. She came to my graduation and we went from there to the farm in Connecticut, all of us. I knew the only way to get Jane used to the family was to throw her right in. She survived." Nicholas turned to Jane, who was seated beside him on the low flagstone wall that surrounded the terrace, and smiled. She was wearing the same green cotton shirtwaist she'd worn under her commencement gown. She smiled back, still awed by Nicholas's relationship to the renowned Clarissa Gray— Rebecca Hart's dearest friend—and she had said little beyond hello. Fortunately, it was not necessary, for Clarissa had such a gift for charming chatter she could have had a fulfilling social life entertaining mutes.

"Jane," Clarissa said, "you'll have to forgive me for monopolizing your fiancé, but I haven't seen Nicky since—well, since he was a boy, actually. He was darling, of course, but he had a broken something—arm, I think. And here he is, handsomer than ever and engaged. In Cincinnati, no less, and to the daughter of one of John Hart's"—she paused for a fraction of a second— "key people."

Richard Heissenhuber did not look like a key person. He and Dorothy stood on the other side of the flagstone terrace, holding drinks a maid had brought them, looking more like a couple applying for positions as cook and driver than guests.

At his mother's insistence, Nicholas had called his cousin Clarissa, who demanded that all the Heissenhubers join them for dinner.

Richard had tried to demur, saying he didn't want to put Mr. Gray in the uncomfortable position of having to entertain an ordinary working stiff, but Dorothy had seized on the opportunity and—out of Nicholas's hearing—told Richard it would be wrong *not* to go, that an invitation from people like the Grays was like an invitation from the White House.

Now they both looked miserable. Dorothy, learning it was to be an informal evening, had worn a white dress with larger-than-life red and blue roses printed all over it and a new pair of navy patent leather shoes. The dress kept riding up in back despite continual surreptitious tugs on the skirt. The shoes were tight, and every few minutes she lifted her left heel, trying to relieve the pain where the shoe was slicing into her foot.

She sipped her ginger ale and Richard his screwdriver, and the two of them—now at the sort of house they had long ago given up hope of being asked to—chatted with the sweaty eagerness of people who know they do not belong. Richard was trying to appear comfortable and casual in his only sports jacket, a brown wool with elbow patches he hadn't worn for years. It was itchy around the neck, and the minute he got to the Grays' he realized the sleeves were too short. His shirt was short-sleeved, so his wrists and an inch of forearms dangled out of the jacket. He tried to keep his arms bent so no one would notice.

Although pained by her foot and, no doubt, by the knowledge that entrée to an Indian Hill estate had come through Jane, Dorothy was working hard, trying to memorize the Grays' life without seeming too obvious. She observed everything closely: the way Clarissa had held Nicholas's face between her hands before kissing him lightly on each cheek; the placement in terra-cotta pots of the bushes and small flowering trees that dotted the terrace; how the liquor and champagne glasses were not from one set. She noticed Philip Gray's posture was one she'd discouraged Rhodes from assuming; he sat with his long legs stretched out, his feet crossed at the ankles. Perhaps he had to sit that way. He walked with a bad limp; his thigh had been shattered by German bullets during World War II, in the battle at Anzio.

She saw that Rhodes, seated across from Mr. Gray, was at least not lounging as if he were a man of position. However, Rhodes was behaving too expansively for Dorothy's comfort. He was talking too freely—from his lopsided grin, perhaps talking in the snide, quipping manner he fell into whenever he was around Jane, although Dorothy couldn't hear what he was saying. But he was all too casual, sitting back in his chair with his legs spread apart and his hands clasped behind his head, as if Mr. Gray were a Country Day senior and not one of the biggest investors in the United States—bigger, some said, than John Hart—a man so powerful he received phone calls from Vice-President Johnson. An article Dorothy had read in the *Times-Star* said he'd inherited a controlling interest in a copper mining company, but it implied that that was the least of Philip Gray's holdings. Nervous, Dorothy chewed her bottom lip. A great deal was riding on this evening; her son was precisely where she wanted him to be. His whole future could hinge on how he behaved with such a powerful man.

Philip Gray threw back his head and laughed at Rhodes's remark. Then he took another sip of his gin and tonic. His daughter, Amanda, perched on the arm of his chair, laughed too, but she was painfully self-conscious and laughed with her head lowered and her lips together, as if she had ugly teeth. She did not. Amanda, who was conceived just before Philip Gray went off to war, had inherited her father's face and gray eyes. She had sleek dark-brown hair, which she wore in a pageboy, and a graceful figure. She was not beautiful but pretty enough, the sort of girl who'd be picked as runner-up for homecoming queen.

Amanda wore a long red skirt and a white blouse with huge belled sleeves and a deep scoop neck far too dramatic for her; it looked like an outfit her mother had chosen. Amanda did not speak. Instead, she listened to the conversation between her father and Rhodes, making her presence known by her laugh or a nervous staccato cough. She seemed so hypnotized by Rhodes she could do no more. She watched him speak. She watched him listen to her father, drink his Coke, twirl a thin pretzel stick between his fingers. Rhodes did not seem to notice her at all. All his attention was focused on his host.

If he hadn't been bald, Philip Gray, at forty-three, would have looked like an actor sent in from central casting to play a financier. What hair he had on the sides and back of his head was gray and cropped short. His eyebrows, black and straight, gave him a serious appearance but were not heavy enough to make him seem glowering. His features were small and perfectly symmetrical, but what gave his face distinction was his skin: absolutely smooth, deeply tanned like his wife's and daughter's, but pulled so taut over his face his bones seemed to be trying to slice through it.

He was tall and slim; his body appeared as tight as his face. Though he wore a blue blazer, white shirt, and rep tie just as Nicholas did, his clothes were far more elegant. His blazer was fitted rather than boxy, and instead of Nicholas's khaki slacks, he wore white flannels. His white Italian loafers were worn without socks. He was fashionable enough to look well-matched with Clarissa, although he lacked her theatricality and self-conscious chic. He was properly dressed for drinks on the Riviera with French socialites or Swiss bankers, yet he looked right for Cincinnati. In fact, Philip Gray appeared supremely content sitting on his terrace carefully nursing a single gin and tonic, giving his complete attention to an eighteen-year-old boy whose father he clearly considered a zero and whose mother was beneath consideration.

At dinner too, Rhodes was the center of attention, as if the evening were in his honor, a small gathering to celebrate his debut. He had never drunk wine before, but Mr. Gray kept refilling everyone's glass, so he had four glasses. On the last, Rhodes got up, swayed a little, braced himself by grabbing the back of his chair with one hand, and offered a toast: "To Nicholas and Jane, who are going to be like Lunt and Fontanne." He lowered his glass but did not see his mother's signal to sit down. Dorothy bowed her head in humiliation, but raised it quickly when she heard Clarissa Gray's soft applause and throaty "He's adorable, Philip." Amanda, seated beside Rhodes, was staring up at him with an intensity compounded of veneration and desire. Dorothy sighed with pleasure.

After dinner was obviously anticlimactic for her, because Clarissa brought several boxes of family photographs into the living room and she, Amanda, Nicholas, and Jane sat on the rug, passing them back and forth, Jane's shoulder pressing against Nicholas's, as if she were already one of them. After a few minutes, Philip Gray, obviously bored with pictures of several generations of Tuttles, offered to teach Rhodes billiards.

Dorothy and Richard sat stiffly and quietly on a gold velvet couch, Richard eating all the chocolate mints from a silver dish that sat on the lacquered Chinese table in front of them. Dorothy fingered the throw pillows of brocaded French silk, wondering what the fabric was called, and peered through the archway into the hall where Rhodes and Mr. Gray had walked on their way to the billiard room.

It was only when Clarissa said, "Down the hall, turn right, the first door on the right," that Dorothy seemed to realize she'd lost track of time and that the evening had ended. As she stood and hurried after Jane and Nicholas as they went to fetch Rhodes, she barely missed tripping over Amanda. Her apology sounded shrill. She got to the billiard room just as Nicholas was opening the door, so she saw precisely what he and Jane saw.

The light was low. A cue stick lay on the green plaid carpet beside Rhodes's madras jacket. Farther into the room, an ashtray had toppled onto the floor and cigarette butts were scattered around it. Two empty brandy snifters rested on the edge of the billiard table. The perfume of cognac and cigarette smoke permeated the room, although the doors at the far end of the room were open.

Rhodes and Philip Gray stood face to face in near darkness on the terrace beyond the doors. Mr. Gray appeared to be speaking to Rhodes, but they were so close to each other it was hard to say from whom the murmur rose. Their bodies were close too, just touching; they could have been dancing. Mr. Gray's hand reached up to Rhodes's cheek.

"Hello there!" Dorothy called.

Rhodes stiffened. Philip Gray dropped his hand, stepped back from Rhodes, and nodded to them. Then he came through the doors. He walked slowly, seemingly unaware of his limp. With each step, he dragged his left leg up to meet the right. "Hello," he said. "Rhodes poked himself in the eye with a cue stick. I was just checking it." Dorothy nodded. "He's fine now."

"Good," Dorothy said. "Good. I hope you've been having a nice time."

"Very nice," Mr. Gray said. If not for his bad limp, he might have been the hero in an urbane drama. His clothes, his bearing, his enunciation were flawless, but in the low light of the billiard room, any expression on his tanned, tight face was unreadable.

Jane looked beyond him, to her brother. Rhodes stood on the terrace just as Philip Gray had left him, his face still slightly upturned.

"Rhodes," Mr. Gray called. "Come inside." Rhodes began to walk inside, as if all he had been waiting for was the command, and came up beside the financier. "How is your eye?" Mr. Gray asked. "Better now? Is it better, Rhodes?"

"Yes, thank you."

"Good."

Jane stared at her brother. Both his eyes were huge, clear, wide open, and fixed on Philip Gray's face. His tie hung unknotted, the top three buttons of his shirt open. His chest and neck glistened with sweat. She glanced back to Philip Gray, but his face remained masklike, and she turned again to Rhodes. His face was so bright he looked illuminated from within, more dazzling than ever before. Jane inhaled so suddenly it was almost a gasp. Nicholas reached for her hand. He squeezed it so hard it became a clear signal to keep silent.

"Thank you for the lovely evening, Mr. Gray," her stepmother said.

"You're welcome." Philip Gray knelt down, picked up Rhodes's jacket, and handed it to him. "Here, Rhodes."

"What do you say to Mr. Gray, Rhodes?" Dorothy demanded.

"Thank you for the lovely evening, Mr. Gray," Rhodes said, his eyes even wider than before.

Jane watched Nicholas sprint down the stairs. He was wearing tennis whites and looked out of place, as if he'd made the wrong turn; he should have found himself on a grassy, sunlight-dappled court at Forest Hills, not on a dark, shabby carpet in a midwestern living room. "Hi," he said. He stood beside her chair and bent and kissed the top of her head. Next to him was a lamp she'd never really noticed, although it had probably been in the house all her life. But now she saw how ugly it was, with its base—a black cylinder with odd bits of colored glass embedded in it—and yellowed, fringed shade. She wanted to apologize. Instead, Nicholas did. "I'm sorry. Maybe I shouldn't butt in. But you could be wrong."

"Nick, you heard him. He said Mr. Gray wants to give him a summer job and he's taking him out to dinner to discuss it. Sending his chauffeur to pick him up."

"Maybe that's what it is."

"Rhodes is eighteen years old. Do you think a big tycoon like Philip Gray wines and dines a teenager before he offers him a summer job?" Nicholas shrugged. "Nick, I saw the expression on my brother's face. I know him better than I know anyone, and I've never seen him look like that, as if he suddenly came alive. And you saw them out on the patio."

"I don't know."

"Did it look right to you?"

"No," Nicholas said.

"And now he's on the phone with him again. How many phone calls does it take to arrange a business dinner? And the way he's talking, with his hand covering the mouthpiece. Nick, he's getting himself involved with something he doesn't begin to understand."

"Quiet. Here he comes."

For the first few minutes on the way to the tennis courts, Rhodes was silent, although he responded to Nicholas's questions about going to Lafayette College in the fall. But soon his natural exuberance, combined with what was obviously his desire to avoid being asked about Philip Gray, took hold and he began to distract them with his usual gusto.

Once out of his silence, Rhodes could neither be quiet nor sit still. He sprawled on the back seat of Nicholas's car and whistled, while his feet tap-danced on the door. He insulted Jane with greater-than-usual enthusiasm.

"You'll be sorry you ever thought of tennis," he said to Nicholas. "She's a human slug."

Jane could not rise to Rhodes's baiting. Whenever she turned around, she could only look beyond his white pullover and clear eyes to the scene of the night before, when his shirt had clung to him, damp and crumpled, and his eyes were huge, as if he'd just beheld a miracle.

Rhodes sat straight, edged forward, and suddenly grabbed Jane in a stranglehold. He pulled her back until her ear was close enough to hear his whisper. "How could you let him see you in shorts *before* you're married?" Jane tugged at his forearm. "Maybe he has a blanket in the trunk you can wrap around those thighs. Pretend you have a sudden chill. It's your only hope." She dug in her fingers and he let go with a whoop of laughter, sprawled back on the seat, then jerked himself up, this time to tell Nicholas about the time he was a little absentminded and wound up with three dates to his junior prom.

Nicholas pulled into a parking lot on the side of Rhodes's school and he and Rhodes climbed out, bouncing on sneakered feet, whooshing their rackets back and forth as if to blow dust off the strings. Jane sat in the car until Rhodes came around, opened her door, and made a deep bow.

She walked behind them to the courts, squeezing the grip of the old racket Rhodes had given her. It was wrapped with black electrical tape that had dried, and the edges scratched and made a dusty powder on her palms. She sat on a patch of grass just beyond the clay. It was a warm day, but dry. The few puffs of clouds were so crisp against the bright sky they looked as though they had drifted in from New England. "Get up," Nicholas urged. "We can play Canadian doubles. Me against you and Rhodes."

She shook her head. "I'll watch."

"Smooth move, Ex-Lax," Rhodes said. He opened the can of balls and popped them to Nicholas's side of the court. "You serve," he called.

They played two sets, although from the first it was obvious that Nicholas was a stronger, smarter player. His serves smashed up from the ground so close to Rhodes that he reflexively leaped back, or they soared, catching him hunched down. Nicholas was far more aggressive. The muscles in his thighs contracted like thick springs. Jane turned as the ball hurtled straight toward Rhodes, who jumped aside. "You may be my future brother-in-law, but you're definitely not worth dying for, Nick." When they finished the sets—Nicholas won both—Rhodes's forehead and upper lip were hardly more damp than Jane's. Nicholas's face was bright red. His hair lay against his scalp in wet strands.

Rhodes grabbed Jane's hand and pulled her to her feet. "He's our guest," he said, "so I let him win."

She held on to his hand. "Rhodes, I want to talk to you."

"Leave me alone." Rhodes pushed past her and started walking to the car.

"Rhodes," she called and pulled away as Nicholas tried to hold her back. She ran up the incline that led to the parking lot. "Please listen to me. You know I don't want to embarrass you and the last thing I want to do is hurt you, but you have to understand. What Mr. Gray may want from you isn't—"

"He wants me to work for him. He thinks I'm very bright. We're going to discuss it tonight. That's all. Really."

"Then why did he call you last night after we got home? It *was* him, and don't tell me it wasn't. And why did you spend almost an hour on the phone with him this morning? Please, Rhodes, I know you think you're sophisticated, but—"

"There's nothing to talk about. Okay?"

"Oh, Rhodes." He looked past her, toward Nicholas, who was coming up behind her. She brushed Rhodes's cheek with her hand. His skin felt cool. He was so beautiful she ached for him. "Rhodes, you don't understand what kind of a man he is."

"I *do* understand."

"No, Rhodes. You don't."

His skin was unnaturally pale, and for the first time she saw the faint blue shadows under his eyes that underscored his loss of the night's sleep. She ran her finger across one of the shadows, and at last he looked into her face. "Jane," he said softly, "if you think I don't understand what he is, then you have no idea what I am."

"You are beneath contempt." Dorothy's back was toward Jane.

"You were there! You saw what happened!"

"You heard what Mr. Gray said." Dorothy stood at the kitchen counter rubbing a carrot against the metal lips of a grater so fast her hand was a blur. "Rhodes poked himself in the eye." She turned and shook an orange stub of carrot at Jane. "And don't you *dare*—do you hear me?—don't you dare tell me my son would get mixed up in anything like that!"

"But you saw them. They were so close they were practically—"

"You shut up!"

"Can't you listen? He's your own son! He's eighteen years old and you're letting him go with this man. . . . What is it, the chauffeur? He's sending his chauffeur for Rhodes, so that makes it all right. You *saw*—"

"I saw nothing!"

"You saw his face. Listen to me. He's getting involved in something that can be so ugly, so awful, it can ruin him for life. Don't you understand that? Don't you understand that if you let him go off in that car Mr. Gray is sending for him he's lost?"

229

"All these years I thought you were just troubled. A poor, sick, sneaky girl who was too twisted to care about anything good and decent. All these years your jealousy has been eating you up alive, and you come back here trying to destroy my son's life with your filth."

"Please. Tell him not to go with Mr. Gray."

"Mr. Gray is taking him to supper at the Maisonette, which happens to be the most expensive restaurant in the entire city, to talk about a summer job."

"Why is he taking a beautiful young boy to the Maisonette? Don't you know what he wants Rhodes for? Don't you know what they do?"

Dorothy threw the carrot at Jane's face, but it flew by her head and fell in the middle of the kitchen. "He's going to groom him!" she screeched at Jane. "He's going to groom him for a position. A big job right by his side. And maybe an alliance with his daughter. He saw the way she looked at Rhodes, her eyes as big as her head."

"No! Listen to me! You saw him, the way he touched Rhodes's face. Caressed it. You know what he is; he's a homosexual. He *wants* Rhodes."

Dorothy stepped forward and, with the force of her entire body behind her hand, smacked Jane on the side of her head. "You're not going to ruin my son's chances, you pervert. You whore. You ugly whore. You think I don't know what you did with your father back in high school?"

"No! I swear! I didn't do anything!"

"No? You think I don't know how you lured him into your bedroom late at night? He couldn't help himself. He's a weak man. But you! You're so brazen and disgusting. And so stupid to underestimate me. Don't you think I heard him get up and tiptoe down the hall? And do you think I can forget how you tried with Rhodes too, whore? Strutting back and forth in front of his room in your brassiere and underpants, everything so tight you were gushing out of it, just waiting for him to see you half naked. You listen to me. You are leaving Cincinnati today and you're never darkening this doorstep again. And if you dare try and make trouble, just see if I don't tell your fine Mr. Cobleigh just what kind of a whore you are."

Jane cried so hard that, in Chillicothe, Nicholas pulled over to a drugstore and bought another pocket-size packet of tissues to replace the one she'd wept through. For the next hundred and forty miles, until they drove into Clarksburg, West Virginia, she clutched a tissue but never used it. She faced the opened car window, letting the onrushing stream of humid air lull her with its ceaseless hum, watching, in small town after small town, women in pink plastic hair rollers and short sleeveless dresses windowshop before hardware stores and shoe emporiums. She did not talk at all.

In Clarksburg, Nicholas registered in a motel, the Dew Drop Inn, and left Jane alone in their room, a small one decorated in such insistently cheery reds and yellows and shiny plastic furniture it first startled and then depressed him. He walked through the town to stretch his legs from the long drive until the tranquilizing smells of trees and earth and the sudden darkness made him realize he was four or five miles into the country.

He returned to the motel after ten. Jane was as he had left her, awake and dressed, but so listless she did not lift her head to see who was coming through the door. He switched off the lamp on the dresser, draining the room of its garish colors. Blue light from the motel's sign spilled through the uncurtained bathroom window into their room.

Nicholas slipped off his shoes and lay beside her in the hammock made by the sagging mattress. "I took a long walk," he said. When she did not respond he asked, "How are you?" She shrugged. "And you told me Ohio would be boring."

"Please, Nick. I don't feel like kidding around."

"I want you to snap out of it."

"I can't."

"Yes you can."

"No. Nick, I've been thinking. I have to tell you something. I'll understand—really I will—if you want to call things off. Just listen to me. I know you got much more than you bargained for. You deserve better. You deserve something normal."

"You listen to me. Every family has something."

"Not like mine."

"Jane, my mother's in and out of mental hospitals. My father's either pie-eyed or having a go at my mother's nurses or both, and all of us were shoved off on nannies and then sent away to school the minute we were old enough to pack our own suitcases. You're not complaining. Why should I?"

"This is different. They're sick. I come from them."

"Stop it. My mother's sick. I come from her."

"Nick, I'm tainted."

"Then so am I. Two tainted people. We'll probably have children who are tainted too. Big damn deal. I want you out of this mood. I don't like it. There's nothing you can do about your brother. Come to grips with that, and you won't feel so bad. No one's holding a knife to his throat. You saw how he was when we went to play tennis this morning, joking around, trying to hide that he was like a kid with a crush on a movie star. Come on now. Don't start crying again."

"It's more than Rhodes. It's my father, it's her, it's the whole thing."

"What did your father say?"

"Nothing. He wouldn't even listen to me. I tried to speak to him before we left, and he literally—literally—covered his ears."

"Well, she got to him first. But what did you expect? That all of a sudden he'd become strong and decisive?"

Jane twisted onto her side so her back was to him. "No," she said.

Nicholas moved closer and turned her so she was flat on her back again. "Your father's never going to change. I don't see why you let him get to you so hard. Look at me. That's better. I want you to tell me what she said to you."

"Nothing."

"Jane, tell me."

"Just something. That my mind was in the gutter. And then—"

"Calm down."

"Nick, she actually took Rhodes out to get him a new shirt! Can you believe that? So he'll look nice and neat when Mr. Gray does whatever he does to him. Rhodes hears the word 'Paris,' and he's such a big baby he actually thinks he'll be taken there, and he doesn't begin to comprehend what's going to happen to him. That she's so greedy, so full of lust for money or power or I don't know what that she'd sell her own son—"

"Jane, whatever happens, you can't stop it. Maybe he's a lamb being led to slaughter—"

"Oh, God."

"—and maybe it's his nature."

"It's not! Don't say that! You don't know him."

"All right. Quiet, now. Quiet. I want you to sleep."

In the middle of the night she wakened, her body stiffening so fast against his it felt like a convulsion. He held her close for nearly a half hour. Then, almost reflexively, he unbuttoned her blouse. He hadn't sex in mind. He just wanted the freedom to soothe her by stroking her throat and shoulders. But Jane, who had always responded a little timidly, reacted to his first caresses with an aggressiveness that astounded him.

She tore off her blouse and bra and seized his hands, crushing them so hard over her breasts that at first he interpreted the small noises she made as pain. Just as her nipples grew long and hard with arousal, she—who had never in the past made any noise—began to moan and beg. "Do it, do it, Nick. Do it." Moments later she untied her wraparound skirt and clamped her legs around his thigh. "Please. I want you to." She rocked up and down on him. Through his slacks he could feel the burning wetness under the crotch of her nylon underpants. "Do it." He pulled down her pants and slid his finger inside her until it reached the unimpeachable fact of her virginity. When he withdrew his finger he massaged her with the palm of his hand. Her cries became so loud he covered her mouth with his other hand, but she pulled it away. "Take off your clothes," she pleaded. "I want to tonight, Nick. Please."

She looked magnificent. Her dark hair had come loose from her ponytail, fanning out over the pillow, and as she tossed about, long, black, silky strands

232

fell across her face and arms. Everything about her seemed awesome. Her breasts were so big they swelled out of his hand, her nipples so elongated they seemed to point at him, demanding more. Her wide hips flowered out from her waist, and her thighs were so large and powerful they belonged on a Greek statue.

But the best part was her skin. It was warm velvet. He couldn't get enough of her, yet he knew he couldn't have her.

Every few minutes she'd reach to open his shirt or unzip his pants, but he pushed her hands aside and finally held them down on either side of her. "No." His face was resting on hers and he felt her tears. "Not tonight."

"Please. I swear it's all right. I don't want to wait any more."

"I don't have protection."

"I don't care."

"No. We can't." She twisted under him, and he realized he was nearly out of control. He let her hands go free and began running his over the velvet skin of her shoulders until he was almost clawing it. He encircled her with his arms and started making the thrusts of intercourse against her stomach. "Jane, I can't help it," he cried out. "I can't." At last, with a roar of relief, he came. He lay with her beneath him for a long time, and finally, as he rolled off onto the bed, he whispered, "I'm sorry."

"It's okay."

He ran his hand over her chest and between her breasts. "Tomorrow," he said. "I promise. I'll make it good for you."

They were married at four the following afternoon by a justice of the peace who charged them ten dollars above his usual fee, explaining that this was a courtroom of the state of Maryland, not a church, and while he'd be glad to perform a real old-fashioned ceremony straight from an old Book of Common Prayer a nice young couple had left behind years and years ago, it would be extra. He'd stretched his turtle head toward Nicholas and observed, "It's all for a good cause, now, isn't it? If it wasn't for Maryland, you'd be up a crick without a paddle, bub, you being just twenty and every other state around here requiring you, the man, to be twenty-one without consent, *and* a blood test, *and* a two-to-four-day waiting period. Some call it the cooling-off period, but since the folks in Annapolis say you don't have to wait, that is certainly good enough for yours truly. Now, you got the ring? Rings. Fine. You got them at Sherwoods, I see. That's a real smart move, if you'll pardon my saying so, because with jewelry from Sherwoods your pretty lady here can rest assured they're of genuine real gold. I won't tell you how some places around here sell you rings that go green before the honeymoon's over. You ready? You want the whole ball of wax, is that right, with the 'Dearly beloved' and 'forsaking all others'? Okay, then. Let's tie the knot, and you folks can be on your merry way."

13

Garlic from the hot dogs wafted through the air to join forces with the sweet
reek of orange soda in the Howard Johnson's on the New Jersey Turnpike.
The assault effectively depressed their appetites. Still, they had ordered,
mainly to get rid of the waitress. She was a tiny, pallid woman who looked too
frail to be balancing trays, much less to have the sexual energy she'd suggested by asking Nicholas in a sultry starlet's voice if he wanted his coffee
creamed. She seemed to take Jane's order only because she had to. Then she
stuck her pencil between her teeth and walked off, her narrow hips swinging
with slow ostentation.

"Do you want to follow her? Try one of her twenty-eight flavors?"

"Well, I hate to pass up anything like that, but I'm a married man."

"Do you want to know the best thing about it? About being married, I
mean?"

"Yes, since you have so much experience at it," Nicholas said. He peered
at his watch. "Twenty-six hours' worth. That makes you an expert."

"That's right, so you know I won't give you just a superficial analysis. It
will be well-reasoned and very, very profound, just like I am. Not to mention
insightful and sensitive and in the great humanistic tradition of—"

"Didn't you ever hear that wives are supposed to be seen and not heard?"

"That's children."

"Oh. Too bad."

"The best thing about being married is that I can be Jane Cobleigh for the
rest of my life. No matter what happens. You can join the Foreign Legion or
run off with a chorus cutie, but I'll never have to be Jane Heissenhuber
again."

"And that's why you married me? For my name?"

"Yes."

"Not for my personality?"

"Are you kidding?"

"Not for my looks?" She shook her head. "Not for my body?"

"No. It's so perfect it's boring."

"Tell me more. Come on. I know it's not true, but I love to hear it. What do you like best? Stop blushing. Look at you. Beet red. You're supposed to be a sophisticated married woman—"

"Your fried clams, sir," their waitress purred to Nicholas. "Tuna," she said to Jane and sashayed away.

They gazed at each other across the table. All conversation ceased. Neither could eat. Nicholas picked up a french fry, put it down, then moved a few clams around his plate. Jane left her sandwich untouched. She wiped the tops of the salt and pepper shakers with her napkin and sipped her ice water.

It was the last night they would spend together for two and a half months. In the morning, Nicholas would drop Jane at her summer job at the Westport Country Playhouse in Connecticut and then drive northwest to his, at the Guilderland Summer Theater, just outside Albany.

"Jane," Nicholas said finally, "I don't want to go without you."

"You have to."

"No. I've thought it through. I'll go with you and get a job in Connecticut. It makes sense. My grandmother's farm is only thirty miles from Westport, so if we have any free time we can drive over there and—"

"But there are no jobs for you at Westport."

"Not in the Playhouse, but I can find something."

"Nick, you need theater experience. You've had two semesters of college theater."

"But when we were friends you said—"

"We're not enemies now."

"I mean, before we fell in love. While you were still rational and objective. You said Guilderland was third-rate, that they put on the worst of Broadway and brought in has-beens to play the leads."

"But I also said that since you applied so late you were lucky to get it and that any experience was valuable and you should grab it. Remember?"

"I don't want to be away from you."

"Do you think I do? It's only a month since you first kissed me."

"Five weeks."

"Nick, I love you."

"I won't go."

"We were stupid to get married. We should have waited. You only did it because you wanted to comfort me because of my family, and now it's going to be so much harder than it would have been. But you have to go. You can't just walk into New York and say, 'Well, I've been in four college productions and I drove a truck in Westport.'"

Nicholas stood, walked around the booth, and sat beside Jane. He took her left hand and twisted her wedding ring around and around. "I can't do it without you. Listen to me. You coached me for every part I played. Ritter got the credit, but you know if my performances were any good it was because of you."

"No. It was because of you. You're the actor. No one in all my four years of Sock and Buskin ever got up on that stage and made people forget they were in a theater. You were *real*, Nick. You're gifted. You're beyond gifted."

"But I need your judgment. I can't go there alone. I'm new to all this. Really, it would be much better if I held off until the fall. Then we can get an apartment and I can start lessons and begin to make the rounds, and we can talk about things every night. I need your experience."

"You need this summer's work."

"I won't leave you."

Jane looked at Nicholas. It was one of the moments when she saw him fresh, as if he'd just leaped down from the balcony onto the stage during the *Hamlet* rehearsal. At that moment, she saw in him what so many other women—from the girls in Sock and Buskin to the waitress—saw and were drawn to: the refined, almost icy good looks that did little to cool the conviction of his virility. It was a moment when she could still feel surprise that he was bothering to talk to her; that he had married her and needed her was unreal, disturbing, and funny enough to seem a cruel practical joke. "I'll go with you," she said.

"What? You can't. You have a plum job. It's what every actor out of college would give his eyeteeth for."

"I want to be with you."

"Absolutely not. You can't throw Westport away."

"Nick, I'm the one who can wait until the fall. Really, I've had four years of solid college experience. It will count for something."

"No. That's final."

"Listen to me. You do need me. Just this summer. Just to show you that you can do it yourself. I'm not going to help you at all. I'm just going to be there so you can see I'm not necessary."

"I won't let you sacrifice Westport. It could be the beginning of important things for you."

"But important things will come later, to both of us, when we're together. Please, Nick, this is really and truly what I want. You were right. We can't be apart."

From a distance, Andre Shaw's Guilderland Summer Theater appeared

236

to be the perfect home for a summer stock company. It was a large barn, its dark red a beautiful, bucolic complement to the green foothills and blue sky. It looked innocent and honorable at the same time, a triumph of rural architecture, just the sort of place to draw vacationers and city dwellers hungry for authentic Americana: real true theater in a real true barn.

But, as the publicist pointed out to Jane, Guilderland had been built in 1957 not as a barn but as a theater. The red planks were aluminum siding; the curly-edged poster for the 1913 production of *The Poor Little Rich Girl* had been purchased in the same West Forty-eighth Street theatrical memorabilia shop as was the gown—displayed in a locked glass case—worn by Helen Mencken in 1933 in *Mary of Scotland*.

As for real theater, Carla Brandon, the publicist, confided to Jane, "Andre Shaw wouldn't know a good actor if they shoved one up his ass . . . and they probably have. All he knows is money. That's why the little grub hired you. He knew you were desperate and he could get you cheap, that no-good, ugly, oily piece of pig shit. My mouth isn't too much for you, is it?"

"Oh, no," Jane said. In her first ten-hour day working for Carla, she'd heard more bad language than in her entire life before, and if it hadn't been for the slight headache she'd gotten from tensing her shoulders and neck for the next barrage, she would have been numb. After the fourth day, Nicholas would routinely have her sit in the one chair in their boardinghouse room. He'd rub her stiff neck while she analyzed Carla's daily output, dividing her language into the categories of sexual, scatological, and other assorted bodily secretions. After the sixth day, Nicholas began to demand the Curse of the Day on their way home from the theater. "I can't say it," she'd objected the first time.

"Yes, you can. You're just reporting it."

"She said Randy Dale—you know, that pixie-looking little tap dancer who was in all those movie musicals—she said he has a . . . I just can't say it."

"Just spit it out. Come on."

"She said he may be short but has a wang that goes from here to Cleveland. You should hear her, though." Jane spoke in Carla's rough, wise-guy voice. "'What a wang!' I never even heard the word before. At first I thought she said 'wank,' until she repeated it fifteen times."

"Want to feel my wang?" Nicholas asked.

"No."

"That's not what you're supposed to say."

"How about your wank?"

"My wank's even better than—"

"Shhh! This is a public street."

"I want to do it with you everyplace."

*　　*　　*

237

"Who put these apples here?" the star was screaming. "What kind of stupidity is this?"

Nicholas's stomach contracted into such a hard knot he wanted to sink to the floor to catch his breath. He had not felt so awful since he'd been caught drunk in prep school. He'd screwed up his first professional assignment. Not a big screw-up, he knew. It was only a rehearsal. Another actor might have ignored it. But not Ron Lipscomb.

"What am I supposed to do?" Lipscomb's fury swelled. "Stop at the height of dramatic tension and move apples?"

Lipscomb could not memorize his lines. Some of the pages of the script were fastened to side flats and the backs of chairs for quick reference during the play; others were glued into the books he leafed through—he played a college professor. The ones in question were spread under the glass top of a coffee table in front of the couch where Lipscomb was seated. Nicholas, who'd been in charge of setting out props, had been called backstage and, without thinking, had placed a bowl of fruit in the middle of the table, not on its mark at the table's edge, thus depriving Lipscomb of access to his character's words.

Lipscomb rose, marched upstage, and lifted his head like Lear defying the storm. "What is expected of me, I want to know? Am I to memorize every single line?" He tossed his head, allowing his dark, wavy hair to bounce to good advantage. "This is beyond endurance!" he cried.

Nicholas looked up. Lipscomb's hysterics were so out of proportion to the oversight which had motivated them that he thought everyone must—by now—be smiling. He almost felt better. Lipscomb was obviously staging a scene. His foot-stamping couldn't be natural. His pronunciation was laughably theatrical; endurance was "endyoo-rance," the second syllable drawn out far more than customary usage required. But when Nicholas saw the expressions of the other Guilderland apprentices and the *No Body's Home* stage manager, the painful weight of apprehension pushed him down again. The apprentices appeared frightened by Lipscomb's tirade and glanced at each other for comfort. But when their eyes met Nicholas's, they looked away. The stage manager, who had been with the production since its inception, allowed a range of emotions to flash across his face: concern, disgust, weariness, and, finally, wariness. Not a single person was smiling.

People took Lipscomb seriously. As host of the hit prime-time quiz show *Climb to the Top,* he had garnered a reputation as an intellectual, tossing off questions about Xenophanes or the Fauvists with a grace that implied that, naturally, he knew the answers. He spoke as though it had been a toss-up whether to be a Cambridge don or a television personality.

"Is this a theater?" he shouted. "Is it? Is it?" Looming above the collar of his white turtleneck, his large oval face was so flushed it resembled a lollipop. His fans would not have recognized him, for he was famous for his cool; even

238

as a contestant reached Mount Seven, the seventy-thousand-dollar question, the most Ron Lipscomb would do was take off his glasses and wait for the answer a bit more intently than usual. "I want to see the idiot responsible for this debacle!"

Nicholas did not move forward, not because of fear—although he was afraid—but because he was stunned. No one in his life had ever spoken like that. Certainly not to him. Grown men didn't become hysterical because a bowl of fruit was a few inches from where it should be. Grown men said "Damn," at worst, or moved the bowl. And grown men, married men like Nicholas, didn't put up with that sort of nonsense. They went directly to whoever was out of control and said "Get a grip on yourself" and that was that. And just as he was about to stride out onto the stage and face Lipscomb, the stage manager whispered out of the corner of his mouth, "Apologize." Nicholas shook his head almost imperceptibly. The man inched closer. "Apologize," he insisted. "Come *on*. This is Ron Lipscomb, not some cruddy little New York actor. Who the hell do you think you are?" There were only the two of them now in the wings; the other apprentices had edged away, abandoning Nicholas.

Nicholas took such a deep breath that the exhalation propelled him out onto the stage. "Sorry, Mr. Lipscomb," he said.

"You!" the star said. "It had to be you, didn't it, Blondie? It wasn't bad enough yesterday when you scratched half my luggage unloading it, was it? Was it? Do you have a voice? Do you hear me or are you deaf?"

"I'm very sorry," Nicholas managed to say. The apology was so difficult to get out his jaw ached with the effort.

"I can't hear you!"

The worst part was that he knew it would all get back to Jane. Humiliation flooded him because he knew he had a choice, and he was choosing to be a coward. He almost wanted to cry, but he'd have no tears for someone like himself. Nicholas forced himself to lift his bowed head. He projected his voice the way he knew Ron Lipscomb expected him to, so everyone in the theater could hear him: "I'm sorry, Mr. Lipscomb."

"Did your mother ever tell you you were an idiot? Did she ever tell you you were a complete incompetent? Well? I can't hear you."

"No."

"'No, Mr. Lipscomb.' Well, let me be the first to tell it to you, you stupid little fairy. You can't do anything right. You couldn't carry a suitcase up a flight of stairs. You probably couldn't walk across the stage without falling flat on your face, and you're just the kind who'll try and sabotage anyone who can. I'm telling you you're not going to do it with me. And I'm telling someone— Milo!" The stage manager raced out from the wings. "If I see this imbecile anywhere, Milo, onstage, offstage, or even strolling on the grounds, you're understood? I am not going to begin a summer's tour with an ulcer caused by some idiot faggot. Get him away. Now! And get me some tea with honey for my throat."

"Where are you going?" Carla Brandon grabbed Nicholas by the shoulder of his shirt and dragged him into the publicity office. "To Andre's office? You bat-shit? He'll heave you over without twitching an eyelash, that stupid fart-face. Forget him. He doesn't count. He only thinks he counts. Now let's talk before Jane gets back. She's out looking to comfort you. Of course she heard. Everybody heard. El Stupido Lipscomb needs an audience for *everything* he does, if you get me. He's total dreck on toast. Sit down. There's no time to talk, and anyway I'm not interested in your side of it. You think I have time to hear another actor tell me his life story? Stop looking at me like that. I'm going to help you. I like your wife and she worships the ground you walk on, and if you go she goes and then I'm stuck with this crapola for the rest of the summer. Forget Andre. He wouldn't know a pile of shit from a hot rock. I know what goes on here. I know Lipscomb's crazy. You know Lipscomb's crazy. They're all crazy. You're probably crazy too, and if not now I give you two years. But he's famous crazy and he's going to be here a week, so you just make yourself scarce. Do you hear me? Nod. Say yes. Show me you have an IQ in the plus column. That's better. You want to take a week off? You need the money? All right. Go find Dizzy. Ask anybody. He's the janitor. You stick with him and don't show your face around here after six o'clock. Dizzy will put you on something. Probably toilets. He hates doing toilets. You could vomit from the ladies' room. And he hates floors too, but he's good under the seats. Gets the gum off, which is more than you can say for most of them. Listen, don't thank me. It's for her, not you. Anyway, it's not Shakespeare I'm getting for you, it's toilets. But what the hell. Twenty years from now maybe you'll thank me."

After the summer, their first home was a forty-five-dollar-a-month cold-water flat on West Forty-sixth Street in Hell's Kitchen, an immigrant neigh-borhood that by 1961 had lost its roiling, murderous energy and had fallen past squalor into decay. Their apartment consisted of a kitchen, a three-foot-square toilet, and a back room. (Except for the toilet, it was remarkably similar to the apartment Jane's grandmother, Rivka Taubman, had lived in on the Lower East Side.)

Jane made their double bed, a mattress on a metal frame, with pale blue sheets and pillow cases monogrammed JCN, a gift that had arrived with six monogrammed sets of towels when Maisie learned from Win that Jane's family had not provided her with a trousseau. The other monogrammed gift, a glass punch bowl set with *jcn* etched on its rim and ladle, sent by James's cousin

Bryan, was packed in the carton it had come in and pushed under the shelves that lined a portion of the longest wall in the room.

Nearly all the rest of the gifts, a thousand dollars' worth of salad bowls, sugars and creamers, bud vases, teapots, and demitasse spoons from Cobleigh friends and relatives, had been returned. With some of that money, they'd bought their bed, a kitchen table, and four chairs and equipped the kitchen; what remained they'd agreed to put in the bank. They had seventy-eight dollars left in cash. Jane thought, we're broke.

She'd known they would be, and so had Nicholas, but the actual fact of their poverty had been more of a shock to him. He suddenly realized the only way he'd be riding in a taxi was in the driver's seat. He'd taken Jane to Yankee Stadium on the subway, and they'd sat in the bleachers and shared the one beer and hot dog they could afford. She'd thought it was fun until she caught him staring at the box seats.

He was not greedy, his demands certainly were not grandiose, but he had never before been without anything he wanted. Just a look at the shelves and the clothing rods on the wall opposite the bed—the toilet took up the apartment's only closet—declared their differences.

Her side was dotted with books and the few clothes she'd accumulated during her years at Pembroke. Her clothes came in twos: two summer skirts, two blouses, two sweaters, two pairs of shoes. The only evidence that she'd had a life before college was Rhodes's still-unframed graduation picture propped up against her *Source Book in Theatrical History*.

But Nicholas had clothes for every location, occasion, and climate. His possessions delineated his upbringing. His clothes filled all the extra space she'd had on her shelves. He had rainbows of shirts and sweaters, including three identical yellow crew necks he couldn't explain, suits, a tuxedo, and jackets and blazers in such wonderful textures she'd rub a sleeve between her fingers each time she passed by. He owned three bathrobes, one of which, a thick white terrycloth, she'd appropriated. If all his shoes had been filled, there would have been a crowd. He owned seven pairs of sports shoes alone, four of them with cleats.

When she walked into the kitchen, Nicholas was standing in front of the sink naked, just finishing shaving before the retractable mirror he had nailed to the wall. He dropped his razor onto the drainboard with an unnecessarily loud clank. Two large pots sat on high flames on the stove with water for the kitchen tub. He tapped his bare foot, waiting for them to boil.

He'd been out of sorts for the week and a half they'd been in New York, although the most he'd admit to was being on edge. But on their second night in the apartment, for the first time since their marriage, and again on their fourth and fifth, he hadn't reached out for her. He'd wakened her several times during those nights, wrestling the blanket away from her, and in the times during those nights, wrestling the blanket away from her, and in the mornings he was sullen, although later he'd explained he hadn't slept well; he wasn't used to the neighborhood noises and the new bed.

Nicholas's moodiness clouded her delight in the apartment. She'd wanted the cold-water flat, thought it was romantic and sophisticated and eccentric enough to confer special status, making her feel more a true New Yorker, an identity Nicholas naturally never needed to question. She was secretly overjoyed when the only other apartment they could afford, a conventional third-floor walk-up on lower Eighth Avenue, was rented to another couple.

But although he tried to hide it, Jane knew Nicholas found nearly everything about the place appalling: its chipped, stained porcelain fixtures with splotches of blue and rust around the drains, its walls that peeled the minute the paint they'd applied was dry, its unkillable roaches and endless chain of ants. He hated taking a bath in the old, worn tub. She could see the way his toes curled with disgust before he climbed in. Unlike her, he could never ease down, hang his feet over the edge, close his eyes, and savor the noise of Manhattan.

She poured herself some orange juice. "Is the water hot enough?" she asked.

"Fine." He offered a pleasant, manufactured smile.

"Nervous?"

"No." She saw he felt he owed her more. He smiled again. "Maybe this sounds crazy," he offered, "but I'm more nervous about driving a cab than about my first audition. I keep worrying that I'll crack it up or forget where Coney Island is. Or that someone I went to school with will get in. And they'll ignore me, but then they'll see my name on the Taxi Commission license. I can just hear them saying 'Nick? Is that you?'" He made his voice tremulous for the role. She could see he was relishing escaping the reality of the gritty tub for the illusion of being humbled in a cab. "'What happened, Nick? I mean—' Or one of my mother's friends or one of my father's clients. 'Um—er, I noticed your name and was wondering, are you any relation to an attorney named Jim Cobleigh? Though there must be Cobleighs all over the place. Oh, you're his eldest son. How interesting.' Could you hand me the towel? I left it on the chair."

Like the sheets, the towels were light blue with a navy monogram. "Come out," Jane said. "I'll be your geisha." She dried his legs first, before he could drip a puddle onto the kitchen floor. When she reached his back and shoulders she asked, "Do you think they'd give you an extra-big tip if they knew who you were?"

"I don't know." He took the towel from her and rubbed his face. "I wouldn't take it if they did."

242

"You wouldn't take what?"

"A tip from someone I knew."

"You've got to be kidding."

"No I'm not."

"But you're driving a cab to make money."

"I don't make money from my friends."

"It's a job, for heaven's sake. Work. Employment. Something you do to earn money to pay for things you need, like acting lessons. To say nothing about food, rent—"

"Just cut out the sarcasm, Jane." He marched into the bedroom, leaving a path of damp footprints on the speckled linoleum.

She tried sipping her juice and staying cool, but a moment later followed him inside. He stood before his shelves in undershorts, pondering which shirt to wear to the audition he was going to for an Off Broadway play. "Nick, I'm not being sarcastic. I'm being realistic. We have money in the bank that we can't touch in case we need it for an emergency. Fine! Okay! But you keep telling me you don't want me to work. I just want to know, how are we going to afford everything?"

"You don't have to screech."

"I am not screeching! You won't sit down and go over a budget with me. If you would, you'd see we won't be able to cover living expenses and acting lessons unless I get a full-time job, and it makes no sense pretending things are different. Nick, darn it, listen to me! You've never had to think about money, and I have. Listen! I know how to apportion—"

"This is a real help, Jane. Just keep yelling so I can be in a terrific mood when I audition. Come on. Do you want to go on about how I'm just waiting for my family to see how poor we are so they'll bail us out? Hmm?" He yanked a dark green cotton sweater from a pile, pulled it over his head, pushed up the sleeves, and adjusted the neckline before the small mirror that hung between the two sets of shelves. "Come on, Jane. Look me in the eye. How about telling me what you're really thinking, that I'm afraid to test myself by acting professionally and I'm just setting things up so I'll be forced to quit and go to law school? How about a little of that song-and-dance? You've got it down pat. It's a good thing your roommate was a psych major."

She sat on the foot of the bed. "I'm just saying we should plan—" She stopped because she felt herself filling up with tears and knew she could not speak. She tried to compose herself, but also found herself waiting for the warmth of Nicholas's arms around her.

"Go ahead. Start sobbing now. Then you can make me feel really crummy. Good. That's very well done. Louder. Louder! You can do it. Deep sobs. Use the old stomach muscles. That's right. Let your diaphragm push up the air." She was crying too hard to look up, but she reached out her hand to another. He'd gone back to the shelves and was punching her books, knocking them off the shelves. "You're full of it!" he shouted. "Miss Maturity, let's-plan-our-lives, and the minute I don't go along with what you say you pull the crying act. Let them pour out. Go ahead. It's a real talent, crying on cue."

"Nick—"

"Come on. You're the genius at understanding what makes everybody else tick. Analyze me some more. Tell me the real reason I want the whole thing to fall apart is that I'm soft. You said it last night. Everything's come so easy for me."

She was able to whisper, "I didn't mean . . ." and then lost her voice.

Nicholas ripped a pair of pants off the hanger. "You're the only one who ever suffered. You're the only one who knows about money. You're the only one who knows about acting. My mother is some flighty society woman, but your mother—well, your mother made Sarah Bernhardt look like an amateur. And since you're positive you inherited your gift from the great Sally Tompkins—whom you can't even remember—then who am I to get in the way of the plans you're making for me? You're the one with the theater in your blood. Go ahead, Jane, spit it out. The truth. You don't think I can do it, do you? You keep saying how my looks are going to make it easy for me, and what you really mean is that's all I have going for me."

"Nick, no!"

"A-minus looks. I'm no Rhodes Heissenhuber, after all. And C-plus talent. Say what you're thinking. My whole family thinks actors are weirdos and sickies, and deep down that's what I believe too. So I'm trying to sabotage everything. Right? Is that right? But at least, at *least* you thought you could take me over, make up for all my weaknesses, turn me into just what you wanted me to be. You thought I'd be pliable, but I turned out to have a mind of my own."

"Nick, I swear I never—"

"This is tough for a great planner like you to swallow, isn't it? I won't try out for that stupid medieval morality play downtown with the rest of those creeps. I won't study with that half-assed acting teacher you and Ritter think I should go to—'Make believe you're a candle and melt': what bull! I won't let you go to work and be the noble, sacrificing woman. I won't do a damn thing you want me to do. Too bad, isn't it? You didn't get what you wanted. Do you know what you want? You want to run the show. You want to be the man. And I won't let you. Isn't that too goddamn bad."

The director and the playwright were feuding, so the audition did not begin until two, and since that first week he was to drive on the four-to-midnight shift, he'd had to leave at three thirty, without having a chance to try out. His last fare took him to central Queens, and since his only knowledge of that borough came from trips to the tennis matches and the airports he did not find his way back to the garage until well after midnight. Then he had to wait twenty minutes for a subway.

He hadn't been able to call Jane because they hadn't gotten their telephone.

But he'd thought about her all day.

At the audition, he couldn't study his lines. He didn't want to think about playing an aspiring middleweight contender. He could only think of what a terrible first home she'd come from, and now, less than two weeks into her second one, he'd undermined all the faith she'd had in him. He knew how little confidence she had, yet he'd attacked her. And since she didn't have the confidence to fight back, the way his brothers and sisters routinely had, the way Diana had, his anger had gone unchecked and unsatisfied and he'd attacked her even harder. He knew he was all she had. She had no family to back her up, no money; everything she owned fit into a large suitcase. She was alone in a slum in a strange city. He was the only person she knew in New York.

At the garage, the drivers told him to encourage chatty passengers; they would often give larger tips. But his first day driving a taxi was a silent one. He could only think that since he'd met her, he was happier than he had ever thought possible. She'd brought him to life. Only she knew what was in him. Only she could evoke it. He'd been loved before, but only Jane did it so well. She never wanted pieces of him: his looks or pedigree to parade around, his fraternity pin, his body, his friends, his self-assurance. She didn't want anything. She simply loved him.

On the subway, he thought how much he desired her, even though he had never been with anyone less accomplished with men. She made love like an awkward girl, pulling back every few minutes for reassurance that she was doing it right. She was so prudish she would only undress in the dark, and he knew that even though she had moments of great passion, she could never let herself go completely. Yet he thought her the most desirable woman in the world. He was enamored of her body, her hair, her velvet skin. He was enamored of her.

He ran the five blocks from the subway to their apartment and up the five flights of steps. By the time he reached the door he knew that if he hadn't met Jane, his life would have continued as it had, full of attractive people and congenial events; it would have been so pleasant a life he never could have comprehended his own sadness. He knew he needed her as much as she needed him.

She'd heard him coming. She opened the door and said "Nick, I'm sorry," but her face was so grieved it did not appear that she thought she would be forgiven. He led her into the apartment and closed the door. He would be forgiven. He led her into the apartment and closed the door. He wrapped himself around her. "I'm so sorry," she murmured. "Please, Nick. Forgive me."

"Jane, there's nothing—"

"*Please*, Nick."

"I forgive you."

The following week, he finally conceded he could not drive a cab five days and take acting lessons, audition, and perform in a play—if that ever happened, he added. He agreed to let Jane take a job for six months to a year, until he was earning enough to support them both.

After three weeks, she found a job in the reader mail department of *Deb*, which proclaimed itself "The Magazine for Today's Top Teen," answering letters that demanded *Dear Deb, I need help. I maybe pregnate. How do you know?* or *Dear Deb, Why don't you ever write about the Numero Uno Rock Group in all the U.S. of A.? Anthony Monte and the Starshines!!! Tony, Tony he's my man. If he can't do it, no one can!!!!*

The head of the reader mail department, a woman named Dina, was a Radcliffe graduate in her late twenties who, on Jane's first day at work, asked if Jane's husband had any single friends from any of the Ivy League schools or Amherst. Dina's features were so stretched out her face seemed contorted, like a mannerist portrait. The other woman in the department, Marge, a University of Chicago graduate, was under five feet and one hundred pounds, and her preoccupation with her own diminutiveness dominated her conversation. On Jane's first day, Marge told her that whenever she went home to her parents' in Lake Forest, Illinois, she slept in the same youth bed she'd been sleeping in since she'd given up her crib at two and a half. She confided that her father's thigh was thicker than her waist.

It occurred to Jane that the three of them, as well as the twenty or so other young women who worked at *Deb*, were embarrassingly overqualified for their jobs, that a degree from a prestigious college was not necessary for responding to letters requesting reprints of the article: "Mastering the Finest Art: How to Write a Letter to a Boy."

Still, the job was more enjoyable than not. *Deb* was the Pembroke dormitory in high heels and dark dresses. If most of her co-workers were subsidized by their wealthy families, she found that no different from college; she was used to being the scholarship student. In fact, much as her college friends had found her summer employment as a chambermaid noble and exotic, her co-workers listened to her tales of poverty—the lack of heat during a ten-degree night, the endless tuna-noodle casseroles Nicholas endured—as compelling as the stories of Scheherazade.

Their interest in her burgeoned after the evening Nicholas picked her up at work. Dina said virtually nothing while Nicholas was there, but the next day she told Jane, "You'd better watch out, Mrs. Nicholas Cobleigh. All the girls are going to start sticking pins into little dolls with long black hair." Marge said, "I'll bet if he held my hand very tight he would crush it."

"You were a hit," she told him. "Even the beauty editor, Charlotte, was impressed. She told me you were some hunk of man. Normally she only speaks to other senior editors. And the managing editor heard about you and said next time you come to pick me up, I should bring you down to her office. Maybe I'll wait another few months and bring you in, and while she's dazzled I'll ask her for a raise. I'll say, 'You see this hunk of man? Well, Hunk and I are getting a little tired of sneaking in after intermission and only seeing the second and third acts of plays. We want to buy tickets. Hunk loves first acts.' How about that? Does that sound good, Hunk?"

"Pretty good. Do you want to know what else sounds good? Look on the table, at what I circled in *Backstage*."

"Oh, wow! 'Young lawyer, good looks, Ivy League type.' Oh, when's the audition? Oh, God, tomorrow. I hope, I hope . . . Never mind. I don't want to say it."

"Say it. I won't take off points if you're wrong."

"This sounds right, Nick. I don't know why, but I have a feeling this may be it."

The letter Jane had been waiting for arrived the next day, just after Nicholas left for his audition.

Dear Jane,

Have you and Nick taken the Great White Way by storm yet? If not, why not?

I'm glad you tracked me down. The two letters I sent to the Westport Playhouse came back, and I couldn't figure out why I hadn't heard from you. I really didn't worry too much because no one your size could ever get lost.

However, your friend Lynn was not exactly subtle in the way she contacted me. Yesterday, the second I walked out of the house, there's this screaming-red MG with a lady at the wheel who looked at least fourteen months pregnant. [Jane's high school friend, Lynn Friedman, had, at nineteen, married a forty-year-old widower, a surgeon.] I mean, so pregnant they probably have to grease her to get her into the car. Anyhow, she was all dressed up for a secret mission, with a chiffon scarf tied around her head with flowing ends à la Isadora Duncan and *huge* sunglasses even though it was cloudy and about to snow. But she's still the same old Lynn, can't act for beans, and she kept beeping her horn until all Hamilton County, to say nothing of Mom, noticed her, and calling "Rhodes! Rhodes!" She said she was "heartbroken" to have missed you in June, but she and the eminent doctor were in Europe with a bunch of ear, nose, and throaters. . . . More about Europe and me later. She wanted to know if Nick was good enough for you, and I said much better than you deserved.

Anyway, she said you wrote her that you sent me a thousand letters and since I hadn't answered you thought (a) I was dead or (b) Mom burned them, and she handed me a piece of paper with your address. Then she told me the news!!!!! Wow!!!!! I can't believe he actually married you. Oops. Did I say the wrong thing? Did he come to his senses and leave you for someone worthy of him? Anyway, if he's still around, give him my regards and my pity.

Now, on to the Big E, i.e., Europe. I was there! I left the second week of July with the Grays—Mr. & Mrs. plus Amanda. Amanda was her usual scintillating self. She said two words per country.

We spent a week in London, five days in Paris, then on to the south of France, where we drove around visiting people in little villages that are so chic *you* couldn't have heard about them. Then Mr. G and I drove off north and spent another week and a half looking at vineyards, which are his latest investment craze. We stayed in an old château!

Now, promise me you won't have a shit fit. I'm not going to Lafayette. Okay, stop screaming. The reason I'm not going is that I have a great job that I love and I'm learning all about high finance. Don't worry, I'll be going to UC. They have great business administration courses, and naturally I'll take a load of liberal arts too. If I change my mind, I can always transfer.

Also, if I stay in Cincinnati, Mr. Gray will pay for college since I'm an employee, which is a *much* better deal than Lafayette, because unlike some smart people, I did not get a scholarship.

Please write to me c/o Philip Gray at the box number above. He'll make sure I get your letters. I *may*, since I'm earning some $$$, get my own place, but he thinks it might upset Mom and Dad because I'm only eighteen. But it would be nice not to have to come home and get grilled on everything I did all day and where I had lunch and what kind of sauce they served on the vegetables.

Have a Merry Christmas and a Happy New Year and give Nick my best. Don't worry, Lady Covetous, I'm sending your present separately. By the way, we'll probably be coming to N.Y. soon. I'll let you know when so you can wine me and dine me.

Please don't be mad at me. I know you may not think what I'm doing is the right thing for me, but I've really never been happier in all my life. *Really*.

Of course, the letter was signed *Love, Rhodes*.

"Nick, you smell like baby powder."

"I'm not Nick. I'm Harding Claybourne, Yale Law School, and I'm totally evil and corrupting."

"Harding, I just love evil lawyers."

"Jane, stop. I can't stay in character if you put your freezing cold feet on my legs. Wrap the blanket around them. Don't move away. I want everything but your feet. Where was I?"

"You were being totally corrupt."

"That's right. I'm having simultaneous affairs with a widow and her heiress daughter. The play is really about them, about the breakdown of love and trust. I'm just the snake."

"Just the snake? That's like saying 'Just Iago.'"

"Jane, it's a relatively minor character. And it's not a major production. It's as Off Broadway as you can get."

"Nick, come on. They *loved* you at the audition."

"I couldn't believe it. One of them, I couldn't tell if it was the author or one of the others, said 'That's my Harding!' after I had read two sentences. The director said he wants an upper-class accent and an icy sensuality. I'm— take your feet away; that's not the kind of ice they want—I'm supposed to speak like this: 'I cahn't dispense with the canon of ethics entirely, Lorraine dahling,' while I'm sneaking my hand up her skirt—the mother's skirt. I've just finished planking the daughter and getting her to contest her father's bequest to her mother. Then the daughter comes in and while the mother is making a sneaky phone call to demand the entire will be contested, I stand behind the daughter and start kissing her neck."

"Can't you just shake hands with them?"

"Jane, I'm the personification of capitalist decadence."

"I know, Harding."

"I'm lust poisoning love. I'm avarice. I may be Satan himself. The director says he'll decide by Monday."

"That would be nice: to have a little hell-fire here whenever the boiler breaks down."

"Can you believe this? A real part in a real play. For a huge forty dollars a week."

"Nick—"

"Harding."

"Harding, I love you. Oh."

"Relax. I'm rehearsing putting my hand up a skirt. Like this. Slowly. Tell me if I'm convincing. Does it seem like I'm acting? Hmm? Or does it seem authentic?"

14

I'd like to quote her. She once said, "If my husband sneezes, it's reported in the press as double pneumonia. The *Times* instantly updates its obituary, the *Village Voice* has a debate on whether sneezing is a political or an artistic statement and the scandal sheets offer bribes for his Kleenex so they can analyze it for cocaine." I can't but wonder what the very forthright Jane Cobleigh would say about the press coverage she herself is now receiving.

—Professor Edmond Coller, Columbia School of Journalism,
interviewed on National Public Radio

The only chairs in their apartment were the four ladderback kitchen chairs, so they spent most of their time on the blue field of their bed. Their serious discussions were held seated beside each other at the foot. Whenever they gossiped or unraveled the day's events for each other, they reclined, their heads just far enough apart to watch the other's expression.

When Nicholas told Jane about his father's philandering, their bodies formed a T; he used her stomach as a pillow and closed his eyes, like someone hypnotized, as he recounted his seduction by James's mistress Lucy Bogard, the opera singer.

Jane could speak about her childhood only when she curled close to Nicholas, her head in the niche between his chin and shoulder.

Their casual conversational posture was more improvisational, although Jane tended to sit on her side of the mattress Indian style. Nicholas, always confined by the small space of their apartment, preferred to lie spread-eagled but in motion, stretching and flexing his legs as he spoke.

But he caught Jane's attention when he lay flat and still, his hands on his chest.

"Do you want a lily and your navy blue suit?" she demanded.

"I'm thinking about Harding Claybourne. Why is he so rotten?"

"I give up."

"No, I'm asking you. I can't get a handle on his character." Nicholas sat up and faced Jane. When he was perplexed, he sucked in his upper lip and thrust out his lower. She thought it made him look like a little boy trying to look serious. "Every time I speak to the director, Dave says to play him unfeeling and play him upper class, but he can't tell me why Harding is such a bastard. He just says everything's been bred out of Harding except the will to power. He has to dominate."

"Harding Claybourne?"

"Yes. Dave couldn't dominate anything. Every time I ask him what he wants, he says 'What do *you* want?'"

Jane's impulse was to hug and comfort him. She held back only because she knew she could not. He was in the midst of a problem he couldn't solve. Still, it was hard not to try to succor him; there was something about Nicholas that made people want to make him happy. She was not sure whether it was charisma, something in his manner drawing people to him, or if it was his appearance.

Nicholas sighed again. She decided it was charisma. Her brother, who was far more handsome than Nicholas, attracted attention, evoked desire, but unlike Nicholas, if Rhodes decided to run for office, he'd get few votes. The other handsome man she knew, her father-in-law, was so cold he might be encased in a block of ice. Only the bravest or the neediest would dare approach James without an invitation.

But Jane realized that besides good looks, Nicholas had an air of power and confidence. Even a trace of discomfort crossing his features seemed terribly wrong. People didn't like to see him upset, and they'd cater to him, trying to alleviate his discomfort. They wanted him strong. They wanted to acknowledge his power and receive his approval. She recognized that she felt that way about him and had observed that so did his brothers and sisters. But it was the same with strangers, too. Once, in the supermarket, she'd wheeled the cart into the aisle where Nicholas had been waiting for the clerk to help him select and weigh tomatoes; he looked annoyed at waiting, confounded by the piles of vegetables. But by the time she'd covered the thirty feet to join him, two middle-aged women and an elderly man were helping him, the man holding a bag, the women squeezing and rejecting tomatoes for him, all three shyly returning his smile.

"Tell me what the problem is," Jane said.

"I hate to say it."

"Say it anyway. We're discussing Harding Claybourne, not Nicholas Cobleigh. You can say the most evil, awful thing in the world and then say, 'That's not what *I* think. It's the character I'm playing.'"

"The problem goes beyond the character. The problem is the play itself. I really thought it was good. I mean, there's this big, juicy scene at the end where Harding sits back and watches the mother and daughter destroy each other. Remember? You read it. At the end they have no money, no love, no self-respect, no man. The mother grabs the tails of his jacket as he's leaving and begs him 'Can you give me a reason to live?' and he looks at her—through her, really—and just says: 'No.' Just 'No,' and then he exits. I thought that was great at the beginning. A great bastard role. But I didn't read it right. The play says nothing about him. *Why* does he want to destroy them? Who is he? I have no idea where he was born, what his life was like. All I know is his name and that he went to Yale Law School. Oh, and that he plays squash. In the first act he says 'I'm off to play squash.' That's what the author thinks is an upperclass thing to say."

"It's not?"

"Jane, be serious. I can't walk out on stage pretending to be the personification of some economic class. That's pathetic."

"That's boring."

"Then help me. Come on. Play the sweet, sympathetic wife."

"I'm off to play squash."

"The day you play squash . . ."

"Are you insinuating I'm not a magnificent athlete?"

"Jane, come on. Help me."

"Okay." Without realizing it, they both edged down to the end of the bed and sat with their feet on the floor, their serious-business posture. "I'm assuming you're the only one who finds Harding a cipher."

"Well, Gina, the actress who plays the mother, says she can't figure him out, but I don't think she's staying up nights worrying about it. And all anyone else will say is to play it like I went to all the right schools and am rotten as hell."

"Typecasting. Oh, come on, Nick, don't look so gloopy. Let's work on it. Let's psych out Harding Claybourne. Now, he's old shoe or white shoe or whatever you call it. Top drawer. Where was he born?"

"Obviously not in Cincinnati."

Two hours later, when they'd finished constructing a biography of the character he was to play, Nicholas began making love to Jane. He turned her onto her stomach and slowly ran his tongue over the backs of her legs, up her spine, and under her arms, moving with a lazy sensuousness foreign to him. When he finally entered her, he was lying on her back, licking her ear and cheek. He had never done anything remotely like it before, but then she wasn't quite sure who was doing it: Nicholas Cobleigh or Harding Claybourne.

Jane's cooking was so bad it would have been funny, except Nicholas had to eat it. Trying to obscure the inexpensive origins of the meat they bought, she'd veil it in a sauce made from undiluted Campbell's Cream of Celery soup. It left a white coating on his tongue and mouth that even her extrasweet gelatin molds—she used a half cup less water than the directions suggested to make the molds firmer—could not penetrate. He'd been used to terrible food at Trowbridge and Brown, but at least that had been terrible and plain: scrambled eggs made from dehydrated powder, green ham, half-dead carrots.

But Jane could not leave food alone. A hot dog had to be stuffed with cheese and rolled in bacon. Canned fruit cocktail was mixed with cream cheese and sugar, broiled, and served hot and cloyingly sweet. Nothing remained unembellished.

But he loved how she looked when she cooked. Home from *Deb*, she'd take off her clothes and put on a bathrobe, claiming she was saving thousands on dry cleaning and that, by six, her bra straps were slicing into her shoulders. To keep her hair out of the food, she tucked her long ponytail into the back of the bathrobe so, for a change, the swinging shine of dark hair did not distract him from her strong features and her incredible eyes. Sometimes he'd set the table, and as he took the dishes from the cabinet he'd glance at the V made by the lapels of the bathrobe, hoping for a glimpse of breast. He was never completely unrewarded; at the least he'd see the dark gold skin of her chest glowing against the white of the robe.

He probed Jane for details of her day, because he loved to hear her talk. She interested him thoroughly. Her observations about the women at *Deb*, their alternatingly hilarious and tragic search for husbands, her recapitulations of what she'd read in the paper or seen on her walk to the office were so fresh and insightful he felt privileged to be her audience. She made him feel more intelligent than he'd thought he was. She'd even awakened a sense of humor he'd never known he'd possessed. Compared to Jane, all the girls he'd gone with were, at best, nice. Nice, but he would have been so bored. He wondered if he would have known he was bored or if he would not have thought about it, believing that that was what life felt like. He could not imagine wanting to watch Diana dice celery.

"Do you realize," she said, "that a week from tonight theater history will be made? I'm serious. When they list your credits, *Last Will and Testament* will be first and people will pay hundreds for the program. I'm going to save a lot of them. Make a killing." Her midwestern accent comforted him; it made whatever she said as accessible as the Miracle Whip she was mixing into her tuna and chopped pickle salad. If she had possessed the cold champagne voice of the New York girls he'd known, she would have been too much for him.

Still, her cooking was so awful it made him dread dinner. He'd made a few casual suggestions, that she stop using miniature marshmallows in salad, that he preferred a simple baked potato to the thing she stuffed with cheese and sliced olives, but he didn't have the heart to tell her that the only thing she made decently was chocolate pudding.

When the phone rang he was watching her shell hard-boiled eggs. "Could you get it?" Jane asked. "It's probably Hollywood." When he got off the phone, he sat at the table. He stared down at a plate in the middle of the table. The eggs were deviled, the yolks polka-dotted with pimiento. "Nick? Who was it?"

"My father."

"Is everything okay?"

"He asked us out for dinner a week from tonight."

"You're kidding."

"He wants to take us out to an early Christmas dinner."

"A week from tonight is only—"

"He's going to spend Christmas in Paris."

"He wouldn't! How could he?"

"He said . . ."

"What? Nick, tell me."

"My mother threw him out."

James Cobleigh told the wine steward what type of champagne he wanted to go with the oysters, and during the few minutes before he lifted his first glass, Jane realized he was already drunk. His eyes seemed floating in a bloodshot red pool, and they did not stay on her but swam off in his son's direction.

"A toast!" he blasted, hoisting his glass, as if toasting a noisy party of three hundred. "To your loving mother." People at the other tables in L'Huître glanced toward their table and quickly glanced away, for the expression on his face was not at all jolly. In repose, Nicholas appeared aloof; his father, hard. But animated, holding up his glass and addressing his son, James looked mean. Every feature was transformed: eyes narrowed, nostrils dilated, mouth tightened.

"Merry Christmas, Dad," Nicholas said.

"Merry Christmas," Jane added. Unlike his wife, who had asked to be called Winifred, James had never made it clear how he wanted to be addressed, so she never called him anything. If she called him "Mr. Cobleigh," she sensed he wouldn't say "Call me Jim," and then she'd be stuck with that formality, forever underscoring her position as an outsider.

But if she felt like an outsider with Nicholas's big-toothed, redheaded family, so must he, marrying into the Tuttle clan with their old money and their old schools and their old furniture. Nicholas had said his father came from a poor family, was estranged from them, refused to discuss them. Nicholas didn't even know whether his father's parents were alive.

James lifted a shell to his mouth and sucked an oyster out of it with the loud slurp of a suddenly unclogged drain. She guessed that must be the way it was done and tentatively touched one of the shells before her, trying to ignore the slimy sheen of the raw seafood, but then she noticed Nicholas eating his with the tiny pitchfork the waiter had put down. Her father-in-law finished six oysters in less than a minute and then stared perplexed at the insides of the shells as though someone had sneaked off with his food. She bet that, like her, he had never seen an oyster until he got married.

"Um," she said to James, "how are you . . . how have you been?"

"How the hell do you think I've been?" he exploded. This time, the other diners did not look toward their table. Like Jane, they just flinched. "One night she says she's had enough, and the next night I come home and there are five suitcases in the front hall and her mother's goddamn nigger driver is standing there. 'You wants de Plaza, Mr. C?' She wasn't even home. She was at her mother's. Had the maid pack my bags."

"Dad, please," Nicholas said softly. "Stop it."

"Shut up!" The headwaiter started toward the table but then changed his mind and hurried toward the front of the restaurant. "You feel sorry for *her*, don't you? Don't you? She gets whatever she wants. All these years. Six kids? Who the hell wants six kids. New apartment? New apartment. You think *I* bought all that jewelry? You think *I* give a damn about Chinese screens? You think I even know what she has? All the brokerage statements went right to her father's office and then, when he died, right to her brother's. Dragging me out every goddamn night to some new black-tie bullshit."

"Are you still using your client's apartment in the Waldorf Towers?" Nicholas asked softly.

Jane peered about and saw the waiter. As unobtrusively as she could, she pointed to her plate, indicating that she was ready to have it taken away. He began a slow walk to the table, but James's voice stopped him.

"I'd be on top of the CIA today, but her father queered it for me," James said. "You know that, don't you? That old bastard pulled every string to ruin my life. He hated my guts. He thought the only reason I married her was for her money, and right after the war, when I could have—"

"Dad," Nicholas said. "You really ought to tell Jane about some of your experiences in the OSS." Nicholas turned to her. She moved her head slightly, signaling the front of the restaurant—escape—but Nicholas just continued. "Dad was undercover, posing as a French baker, in Pas-de-Calais. His accent is so perfect that—"

"It's the psychiatrist. He's the one pushing her, taking a weak woman and making her a hundred times worse. She doesn't need a psychiatrist."

"From what Nick said—" Jane was cut off by Nicholas's kick, which landed sharply on her ankle. Nicholas had his elbow on the table and was gazing squarely at his father. She could not believe he was pretending they were having a normal family dinner. She could not believe he was allowing his father to rant on as if it were a conventional conversation. The entire restaurant was under James's control. The door of the kitchen was opened a crack and an eye observed the siege.

255

"The psychiatrist and the old lady. Both of them. They work her over until she's so confused she doesn't know if she's coming or going. And before that her father. They all jumped on her from the day we met. 'He's no good. Not good enough for you.' And in the back of her mind, she was never a hundred percent sure they weren't wrong." Suddenly he stopped talking. He sat back, an abstracted look on his face, as if he were adding up a long column of figures. The waiter approached the table cautiously, paused for an instant, then rapidly took the three oyster plates and hurried away. James did not seem to see him. Nor did he see Jane's lips form *Let's go*. Nicholas saw her but gave no sign. He broke off a piece of his roll and buttered it with exquisite slowness.

The waiter returned with their dinners, muttered "Hot plates," and rushed off. James remained in his silence. Nicholas picked up his knife and fork, began to eat, and signaled Jane to do the same. She knew she was eating something with veal that James had ordered for her, but she couldn't taste it. The stillness, with its implicit violence, oppressed the entire restaurant. At other tables, men raised their fingers or made scribbling motions in the air, demanding their checks.

"Well," she said, as if talking, contact, might soothe James's anger. But her voice sounded strident. "Well," she said again, nearly whispering, "this is a big month. Christmas and your son's first professional appearance. You know, the play was mentioned in an article in—" Nicholas shook his head, warning her to be silent. It was too late. Her father-in-law moved forward. She sank back. Nicholas looked away from them both.

James leaned over the table. His tie billowed, suspended less than an inch away from the reddish sauce that blanketed his meat. "This one's an actor. The other one's going to be a minister. The only two with brains. Two sons with brains but no guts!" He slammed his fist onto the table. His tea-spoon jumped and fell to the floor. "Real men wouldn't take those jobs."

"Dad," Nicholas said. His voice was so calm and hushed he might have been talking in church. "You know what I was thinking about the other day? The time the two of us went up to the cabin and—"

"Olivia can't get into a decent four-year college. And the others . . ." He sat back, but the abstracted look Jane expected did not return. She sighed, then turned her attention to her meal, eating as much as she could, although she was beginning to feel sick. When she glanced up, she saw that Nicholas had hardly touched his food. He was twirling his water glass slowly, by its stem. His composed expression was gone. He looked exhausted, like someone who had been experiencing great pain for a long time.

And then she looked at James. He sat erect, almost aggressively tall in his seat, but he was staring at Nicholas with an embarrassing intensity, devouring the face of his son. When he began to speak, she had to strain to hear him. "I

256

called them all at school." Tears began to pour from his eyes, but he let them wash down his face. He did not seem to know he was crying. Jane looked away. "I asked them all to come tonight. You're the only one—" He cleared his throat, but it did not help. In an almost voiceless rasp he added, "C'est la vie."

This couldn't be stage fright. It was far more awful than he could have guessed. No friendly, familiar symptoms: no pounding heart, sweats, shakes, stomachache.

Nicholas was suspended between two worlds, a time-space traveler who'd pushed the wrong button and doomed himself to eternal isolation, a cosmic Match Girl looking onto warm scenes behind impenetrable cold glass. He was caught between the play and the audience, unable to enter either.

"Mr. Claybourne! It's so kind of you . . ." As he had at least fifty times during rehearsals, he heard Gina Hollander's voice quiver, then fade, as he made his entrance. She brought the tips of her fingers to her lips and delicately cleared her throat, giving precisely the impression she was supposed to: a wealthy, well-bred, middle-aged widow suddenly awakened and confounded by desire. She patted her stiff coiffeur and tried to hide behind cordiality, but the quivering of her lips twisted her smile into a grimace. "It's so good of you to come. I'm afraid—I was—I just couldn't face a visit to a law office."

He'd done it fifty times before. He set down the attaché case he was carrying and, with the calculated insouciance of a call girl, slowly unbuttoned his topcoat and eased it off. Exactly as they rehearsed it, she ran behind him and grabbed it just before it would have dropped to the floor. "Forgive my bad manners, Mr. Claybourne," she trilled. "Let me take your coat." She was doing everything she had done before. She folded his coat over her arm and, with seeming unconsciousness, began to stroke it. The second actress, who played the daughter, entered, crossed the stage, and stood, as she was supposed to, audaciously close to him, flaunting her young beauty. But her mascara had smeared horribly, making one of her eyes appear lost in its socket. "Julie, dear, this is Mr. Claybourne. The executor of Daddy's will."

He was not part of the play. He was a critic. The mother was very good. The daughter—her eye facing the audience so she must look more like the Phantom of the Opera than a love-starved teenager—spoke in the southern accent the director had been trying to stifle for three weeks. "It's Harding Claybourne, isn't it?" she drawled. He could write the review: *Jennifer Bowman, who plays Julie Donaldson, sounded like a refugee from a Tennessee Williams first draft instead of the Upper East Side adolescent she was portraying.*

As he was supposed to do, Nicholas nodded. He knew he had to. He knew she would speak again, and then it would be his turn. Maybe he would remember the words, but he would not be able to say them. He didn't belong with these two women. He looked past the young actress and, in the third row, saw Jane, his mother, his grandmother. "I saw your name on your legal stationery, Mr. Claybourne, and I thought, that name *must* mean white hair and a homburg." Her breath blew hot on his face; it had the harsh cinnamon reek of mouthwash.

His brother Thomas was beside his grandmother. Maisie was clasping his hand between hers as if they were watching something momentous: an inauguration or an execution. And beside Thomas, his Uncle Jeremiah, whom he hadn't seen in three or four years, was sitting at the edge of his seat, his tongue hanging out so far it looked like a third lip. Nicholas's eyes scanned the small theater. He did not see his father.

He didn't belong in front of the lights. He should be down there in the third row, waiting for someone to do something interesting on the stage. He'd made such a terrible, wrong decision, wanting to be an actor. Crazy. All at once he understood why his parents had been so appalled. Shame suffused him. Even after he became a lawyer none of them would ever forget his trying to act.

Simultaneously, the actresses touched him and then stiffened, realizing what the other had done. Just as they stiffened, he was supposed to say something. Something to make them competitive. He had no idea what it should be. He was of no use. The actresses might as well be vying over an invisible rabbit. He couldn't help them. He wasn't an actor. Even if he could remember his line, he couldn't say it. Something had happened to his tongue. It had swelled up so that it filled his entire mouth. He tried to move it, but there was no room. It was pushing backward like a finger down his throat. He couldn't help it. He was going to gag. His mouth flew open to relieve the nauseating pressure.

"I'd appreciate a glass of water." The words poured out of him. An instant later, precisely as they'd rehearsed it, the women lifted their hands from him and rushed downstage toward a bar cart and, as also rehearsed, collided with each other. Automatically, the small, well-practiced grin crossed his face as he watched them, and a rustle told him the audience had seen it. He inhaled deeply and let the breath out slowly. Then he spoke again, his voice strong and cold. "Julie, why don't you get it while I have a few words with your mother." The actress playing the mother scurried back to him, took his arm possessively, and led him across the stage toward a couch. As they walked past the younger actress, her hands, holding the water carafe, began to shake. The ice cubes in the carafe rattled. As they did, he put his arm around the shoulder of the older actress and drew her closer. But at the same moment, he peered over her head at the younger and gave her a slight, knowing nod.

"I'm afraid I find the details of the trust a little confusing," the older actress said as she drew him down beside her on the couch.

"I'll be glad to do anything I can to help—" he paused for the exact fraction of a second—"the two of you." He could feel the damp grip of her hand on his wrist as she tried to hold him. Across the stage, he could sense the other one straining to get close to him. He had them both. And he had the audience. "Whatever I can do to make things easier."

"Not again, Jane. You've already read it a hundred times," Nicholas said.

"I needed the practice. The hundred and one-th time is always the best. Ready?" She picked up the newspaper.

"Not the whole review."

"Only the important part." She held the *Times* on her palms, as though giving a dramatic reading. "'The character of Harding Claybourne, the smooth-talking lawyer who comes between the two women, is superficially written. However, Nicholas Cobleigh makes the most of the role and is convincing as the handsome, cold-blooded troublemaker.' That's a rave!"

"Read it again. No, not out loud."

"It *is* a rave, Nick. They just made a little typographical error and put in 'convincing' instead of 'brilliant.' Let me read it the way it should be written."

The heavy chain and padlock did not stop them. Every night at five, the men and boys would climb the eight-foot-high chain link fence that enclosed the playground of St. Catherine's School on West Forty-eighth Street and play basketball by streetlight. Except for Nicholas, all of them had grown up in Hell's Kitchen and many of them had gone to St. Catherine's; they were the ones who made the sign of the cross before taking a foul shot.

Nicholas hadn't played basketball since he was sixteen, when, overnight, half his class at Trowbridge grew taller than he, but after eight hours cramped in a cab or an afternoon in acting class assuming fifteen different postures of grief, he scrambled up the wire fence faster than any of the others.

"Here, Nicky, over here!"

He passed the ball to one of his team mates for the evening. He was the floater. The teams were divided along ethnic lines, the Irish on one side, the Italians—and one Puerto Rican—on the other. He filled in, since in their eyes he had no real identity. "What *are* you?" they'd asked him over and over, the evening they'd seen him standing outside the fence watching their game and asked if he wanted to play. "What *kind* of American?"

Off to the side, a teammate took a bank shot. It ricocheted off the backboard. "It's still ours," he yelled.

"It's out, you dumb fuck!" one of the opposition screamed.

"You got your head up your ass, Parisi."

259

"You got your head up your mother's—"

"You better shut the fuck up, asshole."

"Nicky!"

He caught the ball. He ran and dodged, and as he hooked it into the basket two of the men slammed into him. The smaller one brought his foot down hard on Nicholas's instep. Nicholas elbowed him in the side, but not quickly enough to prevent the ball from falling into the larger one's hands. "Cocksucker," Nicholas said.

He loved the game. Inside the playground, even in January, they'd throw off their jackets and play in T-shirts or sweatshirts cut off above the elbow. The icy wind from the Hudson cut over the brownstones, across Eleventh Avenue, and slashed up Forty-eighth Street, where it was blocked by St. Catherine's; vindictively, it would swirl around the playground, gathering dirt and gum wrappers and bits of glass and hurling them into the faces of the players. They ignored it, just as they ignored the padlock, the no trespassing sign, and the traditional rules and etiquette of half-court basketball. Nicholas loved playing with them because there were no pretenses. It wasn't the way the game was played, it was winning that counted. He'd stay an hour until, filthy and sweaty and nearly numb, he'd grab his jacket and climb over the fence again, his raw hands clawing at the metal links. Two hours after that, he'd be glowingly clean, standing stage right in a three-piece gray pin-striped suit while a twenty-five-year-old actress playing a seventeen-year-old girl ran to him and flung her arms around his neck.

One of his teammates, a stocky man with a neck so thick it seemed to grow out of his jaw, was about to shoot when someone whistled and called, "Time out." They stopped, and Nicholas's head turned with the others as they looked at the figure outside the fence. "Yeah, lady?" one of them demanded.

"It's all right," Nicholas said. "It's my wife."

"Oh. Didn't know you were married."

"Yes." He walked to the pile of jackets, put his on, and climbed up the fence. "See you tomorrow."

"'Bye, Nicky."

"Sorry to bother you." Jane clutched the broad collar of her winter coat in front of her so it masked her mouth and chin. The tops of her ears were purple with cold.

"Hi." The minute they were out of sight of the playground, he kissed the bright tip of her nose. "Is everything all right?"

"Well, I guess so."

"You guess so? What does that mean?"

Jane shrugged.

"The play closed and they forgot to tell me?"

"Nick, no. That would be awful."

260

"Something not so awful."

"Something—maybe—a little good."

"Your stepmother died. Just kidding. Tell me."

"Well—"

"Jane, you got me out of a good basketball game."

"I'm pregnant."

Rhodes Heissenhuber opened the door of his hotel suite. "Happy birthday, idiot," he said. He hugged his sister, accepted her kiss, and waved her into the sitting room.

"You look absolutely gorgeous! Even better than yesterday," Jane said. "Let me look at you." She pulled him toward a window. "I knew there was something. Either you lost weight or you matured. Your face looks a little less round."

"It was never round."

"A little round."

"No, moron, it wasn't. I just let my hair grow a little fuller. Speaking of round, take off your coat. You were wearing that sack yesterday." For this lunch, she'd put on her best dress. It was a white wool turtleneck with a flared skirt that she'd bought for Christmas. Nicholas had loved it. It still fit her, although she didn't like to wear it. It had gotten so tight in the waist she could imagine it choking the baby. He studied her for a minute. "You don't look pregnant."

"Well, I am. The beginning of my fourth month." She sat in a club chair so deep she might have trouble getting up. Although she had only gained a few pounds, her center of gravity had shifted, making nearly every move ungainly.

"On the other hand, you don't look *not* pregnant. But that's not news, is it? You've looked four months gone since you were ten."

"That's not funny, Rhodes. You think just because you're in New York you have to make wise remarks—"

"Eleven then. You had the biggest bazooms. You *did*. And just wait. When you're nine months gone you'll have to wear a sling to keep them off the floor."

"Rhodes, I'm not going to sit here and listen to you being a big baby when I could be having a nice, quiet sandwich with civilized people from work."

"Stow it, ugly. I ordered champagne and caviar from room service."

"Really?"

"Yes, really." Rhodes sat on the arm of a couch across from Jane. He drew one leg up, resting his ankle over his knee. He sat straight and elegantly, as if

261

expecting to be photographed. "And poached salmon for lunch, which is something *you've* never had."

"How do you know?"

"Because it would show on your face."

"Well, I've had champagne."

"Where?"

"Nick's father took us out to a French restaurant."

"Was that *after?* After she booted him out?"

"Where did you hear that?"

"Clarissa Gray's her cousin, remember? And apparently *everyone* is saying that she should have done it years ago, that he's been having affairs all these years and that's what gave her those nervous breakdowns. I mean, really public things with all *sorts*—"

"Did Mrs. Gray tell you that?"

"Calm down."

"Tell me!"

"No. She wouldn't talk to me about something like that."

"Then where did you hear it?"

"Guess."

"Oh."

"Well, since he's about to pay for your caviar, you could at least not make faces."

"I'm not making faces."

Rhodes answered a knock at the door, and a waiter rolled in a cart spread with a white cloth. "I'll set it up," he told the waiter and scribbled something on the bill. The waiter left, and Rhodes busied himself bringing chairs, opening the cart into a table, and lifting covers off dishes. He opened the champagne with a subdued pop.

"Does Mr. Gray know you're doing this?"

As she struggled out of the club chair, he offered his hand and hoisted her out of it. Then he pulled out a chair by the table and held it for her. "Doing what?"

"Charging this lunch to his bill."

"Are you serious? Boy, you don't know anything, do you? I work for him, dumbo. I have an expense account."

"You're not even nineteen."

"So what?" He spooned a small mound of caviar on a triangle of toast and popped it into his mouth. "Don't you want to try some?"

"No, thanks." She looked away from him.

"Jane, please don't start again. Okay?"

"Where are you going from here?" she asked softly.

"Switzerland for a couple of days. Then he wants to go to Italy to ski."

"In Italy?"

"It's very chic." He poured her some champagne. "Of course, it would be chic-er if I could ski. And I don't know what *he's* going to do. With that awful, gimpy leg. He limps all the time. Can you imagine him going downhill dragging his leg behind him?"

"Rhodes, stop it!"

"You stop it. Maybe they have an extra-wide single ski for gimps. Anyway, speaking of gimps, he'd like to see you and Nick tomorrow night. We're leaving the next day."

"We're on the fifth floor. Do you think he could climb that far?"

"Are you serious? Of course he could, but he won't. He wants to take us all to some very expensive restaurant after Nick's show. I mean, what would you do to entertain him, have supper for four around the tub in your kitchen? Hand out blankets if the heat goes off? It's not exactly La Place Charmante. I know I only had a quick peek yesterday, but I don't think Philip Gray's idea of fine taste is decorating the floor with little round ant traps. Of course, I could be wrong." He paused. "Why aren't you eating the salmon?"

"I don't care for fish."

"You don't *care* for fish? You certainly did marry up, didn't you, Lady Jane? Come on, try it. It's not like Mom's fish and potato croquettes. A fate worse than death."

"This isn't bad."

"This is good, you dope. And speaking of dopishness—how could you get yourself . . . didn't you ever hear of birth control?"

"If it's any of your business, yes. It so happens nothing's foolproof."

"You're certainly not. I love your timing. It's going to be wonderful bringing up a baby in that lovely neighborhood. In such a nice apartment. Get him a pet roach named Spot. Or wake up and the heat's been off all night and go kootchy-koo to a frozen blue baby. Oh, Jane, don't start crying. *Please.*"

"I'm not going to cry." She covered her face with her hands, rubbing her cold fingers over her eyelids. She felt so weary she could have spent the afternoon in that position. Exhaustion was the only symptom of her pregnancy, but it permeated her life. She awoke after ten hours' sleep longing for a nap.

Rhodes came to her side and led her across the room to a couch. He put his arm around her, something he had never done before, and patted her shoulder, and they sat together silently for a long time.

"It's that bad?" he asked finally. She drew back and nodded. "How broke are you?"

"We have enough in the bank to pay for the obstetrician and the hospital. And that's it. They told me I'll have to stop work when I start getting too big. They don't think it looks right." She paused. "It's a teenage magazine."

"That's dumb. How could you go to work at such a dumb place?"

"I didn't plan all this, Rhodes."

"Okay, I'm sorry. Anyway, what about Nick? What is he doing?"

"He stopped his acting lessons. I begged him not to, but he said he didn't need them. But I don't want him to stop. The people he meets might be important contacts, but he won't listen. He's driving a cab days again, except when he has an audition. His play is closing in two weeks, so then he's going to try and work nights. We have to move. We can't stay there with a baby."

"I know."

"We have no furniture. We have to have money for security for a new apartment, plus a month's rent. We owe two months on the telephone bill and I have to go to the dentist and we need a crib. It's just endless, Rhodes."

"What about his hotshot family? Or is poverty in such bad taste they won't talk about it?"

Jane sniffled and sat straighter. "You don't understand. *Acting* is in bad taste. For them. Not for everyone else. I mean, it's okay if I'm an actress, because who am I? But Nicholas Perfect Tuttle Cobleigh an actor? Standing up in *public* and showing emotion? Deliberately spending time with people from the Bronx?"

"He won't go to them for help?"

"He did. God, it was awful for him. They're so—I hate them. No, I don't know. I don't hate them, but they're so smug. His father said he wouldn't be a party to Nick's wasting his life. Isn't that something? He's spent his whole career doing what he hated doing—practicing law in that big firm—and all he wants is that his sons do the same thing. Oh, and he gave Nick a piece of paper. Do you know what was on it? The name of a doctor who does abortions."

"His mother's not at the funny farm any more, is she?"

"No. But she doesn't have control of the money her father left her because of all her problems. His grandmother has loads of money and she adores him, but she's over eighty."

"Did he try her?"

"Well, yes, in his way, which is so indirect you can hardly tell what's happening. But she's out of touch. She has no conception of money. She's never paid a bill in her life. After her husband died she had people to do everything for her. We spent an afternoon with her and Nick let it come out that—well, things were tight. She gave us this sweet, genuine smile and told us not to worry; she was buying the layette. We'll have the best-dressed baby in Hell's Kitchen. She's really a wonderful lady, but even though she talks all the time about how she was a poor girl from the wrong side of the tracks, she's spent sixty years insulated from reality. She did take Nick aside, though, and told him she had put something nice for him in her will."

"Maybe he could help her along."

"Oh, Rhodes." She rested her head on her brother's shoulder. "It's really crummy. He's driving two shifts on Sundays and he's so worn out. I'm just afraid when I really start looking pregnant he's going to feel pressure and just cave in and do what his family wants. Or what he thinks is best for me. But I don't want a lawyer. I want an actor. He's so good. Wait till you see him. I don't want him to waste it. I don't want to ruin his whole life." She breathed deeply and exhaled slowly through her mouth. "I did think about having an abortion," she added. "I thought about it a lot."

"Could you?"

"No. But I'm scared. It's too much for him."

"Why?"

"You've seen him. He's always been the best person in the world. He walks outdoors and the sun comes from behind a cloud. People push each other aside to be the first in line to do something for him. Until now. Until me. His family's angry with him for not going to law school and probably disappointed because he threw over this wonderfully right girl with the right looks and the right parents for me. It's not funny. Nick's always been the family treasure; you don't know how hard it must be for him. *And* he's living in a tenement and he detests it, I know he does; *and* he's twenty-one and stuck with a pregnant wife and all his old friends are flying to the Bahamas and going to nightclubs and dating rich girls and—"

"And what? Do you think he's going to walk out on you?"

"No. Of course not."

"Then what's the problem?"

"Nothing, just that I would understand if he wanted his freedom. He never thought it would be this rough."

"You're a real prize, Jane." Rhodes pulled his arm from around her and turned to face her. "Is that all you think of him? Ditch the pregnant wife and go nightclubbing with an heiress on each arm?"

"No. But Rhodes, you know what kind of a background he comes from and what he's like. He's not used to adversity."

"A few more months with you and your inferiority complex, dogface, and he'll know the true meaning of the word. Why don't you give your husband a little credit for knowing what's right? It just so happens he's going to be the father of my niece or nephew, and I'm relying on his genes a lot more than I am on yours. Half of you is cheap floozy actress, and the other half isn't anything to write home about. I should know."

"Rhodes—"

"Do you trust him?"

"Yes."

"You'd better."

*　　*　　*

The note arrived two days after Rhodes and Mr. Gray left for Switzerland. It said:

Dear Jane,

Happy birthday, and, in case business doesn't take me to New York for a while, happy birth-day. It was a pleasure seeing you and Nick again. Clarissa and I hope you will use the enclosed to buy something nice for our new baby cousin.

Sincerely,
Philip Gray

With the note was a check for two thousand dollars.

MAN'S VOICE: I have with me Professor Ritter of Brown's English department. Years ago, Professor Ritter directed the production of *Hamlet* where Jane and Nicholas met while undergraduates. Professor, do you happen to remember that first meeting between the two of them?

PROFESSOR RITTER: I do indeed. It was, if memory serves me, the 1960–1961 academic year and . . .

—WPRO Radio News, Providence

Cradling her in his arms, Nicholas brought his daughter close to his face and brushed his cheek over hers. "Little baby," he said into her ear. Her head turned to his voice. They were nearly eye to eye when her mouth discovered his nose. She clamped her lips over the tip of it and began to suck furiously. "Jane, look!" He could not believe that such a tiny mouth could have such power.

Jane, who for five minutes had been trying to control her trembling hands long enough to open the row of tiny buttons on her nightgown, finally succeeded. She reached for the baby. Reluctantly, because he found it soothing to hold her, Nicholas handed her over. Then, although it was against regulations, he slid from the plastic chair and sat next to Jane. The white curtain around her bed was drawn, giving the illusion of a private room.

The baby seemed to find Jane's nipple without any help; she emitted a small squeak and began to suck. "Isn't it amazing?" Jane demanded. "It really works!" Her face clouded. "But do you think she's getting anything?" He nodded. "I hope I'm doing the right thing." She glanced down at her opened gown. "It would be nice if I had those little marks for ounces." Nicholas reached out, putting his hand underneath her breast to support it as she nursed. It was warm and damp. She drew away, taking the baby with her. "Nick, please." She added quickly, "It's too distracting."

The baby was less than a day old, but already he wanted them out of the hospital. He was allowed into the maternity ward for only an hour, and already fifteen minutes had been wasted being introduced to her five roommates and helping her back and forth to the bathroom. She said she was fine, but she kept blinking to keep her eyes open, and when she walked beside him her knees had buckled and he'd had to grab her; he suspected the anesthesia had not worn off entirely.

As the baby nursed, Jane's lids lowered until they closed. Her lashes cast feathery shadows on her cheeks. If they were home in the new apartment, he'd get into bed with them and lie close to her, maybe open a few more buttons and fondle her other breast. What he really wanted to do—he kissed her forehead—what he really wanted to do was suck on her breast. But he knew better than to suggest it; she was easily upset by nearly any proposition beyond conventional intercourse, and he wanted her transition to motherhood to be smooth and happy.

In their second month of marriage, up at Guilderland, he'd tried to get her to try oral sex on a night where she'd tried to beg off intercourse, explaining she had menstrual cramps. In bed, he'd taken her head between his hands and guided it down. In a voice Nanny Stewart had used to persuade the twins to eat mashed turnips—at the same time cajoling and firm—he'd pressed. "Just try it. It's all right. Come on. Just put it in your mouth." Jane had torn herself from him with a "No!" surely loud enough to penetrate the flimsy boardinghouse walls. "Quiet!" he'd hissed, but then softened his tone, explaining that there was nothing wrong; it was done all the time.

In truth, only two girls had done it to him. A Pembroker named Rachel Cadman whom he'd dated right before Diana, who'd wanted to preserve her virginity, had ended every date stretched along the front seat of his car with her head in his lap; at least twice a night she'd accidentally crack her head against the steering wheel. Diana hadn't been that amenable when he'd first brought up the idea, but she'd gone along and obviously knew enough to direct him how to do it to her at the same time.

Persuading Jane became a cause, although he didn't succeed until months later, and then only because, after pleading, wheedling, and pouting, he'd lost his temper. She was a worthy antagonist only until he raised his voice to her; then she folded. He felt a little ashamed that he manipulated her so callously. He felt more ashamed that, when he held her head between his hands, the feeling of smug triumph was nearly as strong as his arousal, and that in the beginning, when she'd gagged, it had actually fueled his excitement. Still, he didn't really feel that bad. He didn't propose it often and with each succeeding time she grew, if not enthusiastic, at least more willing.

During her ninth month, when intercourse was proscribed, he felt she was merely tolerating his caresses. Her hand had sought his penis. He knew she was thinking that the faster she could induce his orgasm, the faster she could get to sleep. When she told him the doctor had forbidden intercourse for six weeks after birth, he sensed she thought of it as a vacation.

She wasn't frigid. Even though she was so modest, he knew she loved watching him walk around the apartment naked. And he could tell by her breathing, by the hardening of her nipples, by her wetness that he could excite her. But her orgasms were poorly acted. She'd obviously never experienced one, or her performance would have been better. He knew what it felt like; she didn't have the spasms Diana had, the ones that had gripped him tight and made him come. Afterward, when Jane clung to him, it was not with limp satisfaction but with lack of confidence.

Sometimes her prudishness made him angry. Sometimes he felt selfish making such frequent demands on her. But he loved her and desired her, and he loved being married, loved the combination of dear friend and available woman.

Right now, he'd be glad just to get close to her. The night before had been surprisingly unhappy. The baby had been born at ten, and he'd spent the next half hour in a phone booth calling family. Once he'd seen the baby, though, the nurse shooed him home. The new apartment seemed dead. He'd walked into the nursery and looked at the curlicue designs Jane had stenciled around the door and the perimeter of the floor, at the eyelet-draped Cobleigh bassinette he'd slept in. The secondhand dresser he'd refinished still stood on newspapers. The baby had come two weeks early. The room looked like a stage set.

The rest of the apartment seemed unreal too. If he had thought about it before their marriage—which he hadn't—he'd have guessed Jane would be a careless housekeeper. He would have been wrong. The kitchen could have passed military inspection. All cup handles pointed to the right. Aluminum-foil-covered dishes were lined up in the refrigerator labeled with small rectangles of masking tape on which she'd written *Amer. Cheese 7/22* or *Mixed Veg. 7/29*. Although she'd been in labor, she'd made the bed. The pillows aligned perfectly and were plumped to the same size and smoothness.

He needed Jane to make it homey. He tried to sleep but missed the giant mound of stomach he'd been bumping into for the past few months. He switched on the light. The room was too still, as if he weren't there. He wanted Jane. Her mumbling him to sleep had become his lullaby. "Night," she'd say, and a few minutes later "Sleep tight," and finally a nearly inarticulate "Did you turn off the gas after you made the tea?" It made him feel peaceful.

He touched the back of her hand. "Jane."

"Oh. Sorry. I wasn't sleeping. It's so relaxing, though. You begin to understand why cows are content." She peered at the baby. "She's still at it. Do you remember when I'm supposed to switch her to the other one?"

"I forget what they told you. You can ask the nurse later. Now don't close your eyes again. We have to think of a name for this kid."

"John won't do?"

"I don't think so."

"We were going to spend all this week deciding on a girl's name."

"Well, we have a half hour. I promised my grandmother I'd call her at nine and tell her the name. She probably wants to get something monogrammed."

"Probably the baby. If it's under fifty pounds, she initials it." Jane stroked the pale brown down on the baby's head. "What does she look like to you? She looks like a Miranda to me."

"No."

"Samantha? Christiana?"

"No exotic names."

"Those aren't exotic. How about Gwendolyn?"

"How about Mary?"

"Are you serious, Nick? Just think of it. Mary Cobleigh. It sounds like a barmaid. ''Alf a pint of yer best, Mary Cobleigh.' But Maria might not be bad. Maria Cobleigh."

"Too Catholic."

"Are you afraid she'll run away from home and become a nun? I think Maria's nice."

The baby had fallen asleep. Her mouth was slack. Nicholas leaned over and touched her lips with his finger.

"How about Tuttle?" Jane offered. "Then we can send her right off to your sisters' school and she'll fit right in."

"I hate that," Nicholas said. "I kept meeting all these girls named Heywood and Lockhart and they always had dumb-bunny nicknames. Although—"

"Although *what?*"

"I sort of like Heissenhuber Cobleigh. It has a distinguished ring to it. A fine old name. A noble—"

"If you don't stop I'll put Tammy on the birth certificate."

"I've got it, Jane!"

"This should be terrific."

"Dorothy."

"Even John would be better than that." Jane glanced from the baby to Nicholas. "Are you disappointed it's not a boy? Really and truly."

"Really and truly, no. I told you it didn't matter. Come on now. We need a nice, plain, pretty name. Caroline."

"It sounds like we're copying the Kennedys."

"All right. Ann."

"Ann Cobleigh. A little too simple. Even with an *e*."

"Elizabeth."

"I like that," Jane said. "But I don't know. She doesn't look like an Elizabeth."

"If you name her Zelda then she'll look like a Zelda."

"No, she won't. Let's see. You like nice, plain English names."

Nicholas nodded. "Too bad Jane is taken," he said. "Now *that's* a real name."

"Let me think," she said. "Olivia and Abigail are out. And Winifred."
Nicholas stared at the baby. Her nose, which had been squashed flat the night
before, had started to take shape, a perfect little button nose. She had the
round Tuttle face, the Cobleigh fair skin, and Jane's wide, full mouth. "I
know," Jane said. "Victoria."

"Victoria?"

"Victoria Cobleigh. It's a little regal, but that's okay. She comes from
very good stock. What do you think?"

"You're not going to call her Tory, are you?"

"No! Maybe Vicky, if she's athletic and energetic like you. But otherwise
just beautiful, elegant, gorgeous, adorable, sweet, cuddly—"

"Victoria."

The early morning thunderstorm had done little to dissipate the heat. By
eleven on the Saturday of Labor Day weekend, the sun was shimmering
behind thick, melted air. The sidewalk was so hot her feet and calves felt weak
and aching, as if they'd come down with a high fever. Central Park offered no
relief. The trees were heavy from the rain. Their dark green leaves hung
flaccid under the water's weight, and the whole park seemed in the grip of a
miasma. Still, Jane trudged down the path, pushing the carriage toward the
playground. The pediatrician had been explicit: the baby goes out unless
there's a blizzard or a hurricane. Victoria, a month old, lay asleep, her legs
bare: twigs against the ballooning, diaper-stuffed bottom of her pink sunsuit.

A lone toddler was in the sandbox, poking holes with his finger into the
muddy sand. A few other children sat under the lean-to created by the slide,
looking dopey from the weather, waiting listlessly to be taken home.

The benches where the British nannies sat were occupied by three whose
employers were unfortunate enough not to have planned for the heat wave.
They sat, white-bloused, flush-faced, hands resting on the giant perambula-
tors their charges slept in. Nicholas had probably been pushed in one of those
infant limousines. Jane thought it funny that, in a year, these servants would
deem his own daughter socially unacceptable as a playmate and would, as
she'd seen them do, usher their charges to the far right corner of the sandbox
and forbid them rides on the seesaw with the low-status children who arrived
accompanied by Negro nurses or—even more déclassé—their own mothers.

She tried to recall the lyrics to "Mad Dogs and Englishmen," but it was
too hot. The top of her head throbbed. At least the Negro nurses and the
middle-class mothers had the sense to stay out of the heat. She sat alone on
her usual shaded bench. The slats felt unpleasantly damp and slick, as if some
fungus were thriving on them. Every few seconds a drop of water would fall
from a leaf and trickle down the back of her neck or her arms. Her cotton dress
must have absorbed the humidity; it clung, sodden, to her thighs. A month

after the baby, she was still wearing maternity clothes. She'd lost most of the weight she'd gained, but her figure had not gone back to its old shape. She knew she looked ugly and solid, a human rectangle. Because she was nursing, all her old blouses were too tight. She worried that none of her winter clothes would fit and, because they could not afford new ones, she'd be doomed to wear maternity clothes until her next pregnancy. Strangers might smile at her belly for years.

She missed the other mothers. Having been newcomers recently themselves, they'd welcomed her and by her second day in the park were offering her their accumulated wisdom on diaper services and postpartum moodiness. By the end of the first week, she had singled out two women she liked and who she sensed liked her, and she looked forward to her time with them.

But out of the park, the people she saw were Nicholas's: his family, his friends from the schools he'd attended, one or two people he'd met since he'd started acting. She sighed and searched for the tissues she'd wedged between the mattress and the side of the carriage. Her neck and forehead were slick with sweat.

Nicholas was more at home with law students and stockbrokers than with actors, she'd begun to realize. Although he analyzed his own roles nearly endlessly, he was interested neither in discussions about acting as a craft nor in theater gossip, both of which she found fascinating. Sitting with a group of men talking sports or politics, he sounded like someone else's husband.

He preferred her company and rarely went out by himself, but when he did it was hardly ever to hang around Downey's or Sardi's drinking with other young actors. He sought out the sort of men who'd been in his fraternity at Brown: well-bred and athletic. They all carried their sporting equipment with dash. Jane didn't find them particularly interesting. Nor were their wives. When the men went off to play tennis or soccer in the park, the wives would talk about summer homes or shoe stores. Even the brighter ones left Jane cold. They consumed novels, plays, and concerts like gumdrops, chewing them for a minute before popping in the next. They all seemed to have spent their entire lives cushioned by money. Not one of them had ever thought twice before making a long-distance phone call.

She glanced down at herself. Her dress was limp with sweat. Her milk had leaked and a dark splotch appeared. Even though the baby was peacefully asleep, Jane wanted to get up, go home, and sit in front of the electric fan, but she was too enervated to stand.

At least Nicholas was no longer driving a taxi. With some of the money Philip Gray had given them, they'd taken a rent-controlled apartment on East Ninety-second Street between Madison and Park Avenues. It had been called a two-bedroom, although the baby's room was little more than an ambitious alcove. The building itself had a depressed, musty air, as though aware it would never be a good New York address. (Less than ten years later, the neighborhood would become more modish, but the building, long resigned to being unfashionable, never lost its gloomy atmosphere.)

For the last five months, Nicholas actually had been making a living as an actor. He'd been in two Off Broadway plays, one of which closed two nights after it opened. The other, in which he played a young Irish priest, had run two months. He'd appeared in a television commercial for an antacid: he and another actor spent a day cantering over a landfill in Brooklyn wearing chaps and cowboy hats. Again and again they'd reined in their horses. Nicholas had tossed a roll of antacids to the other actor and the actor had drawled, "Soothz? Much obliged."

It wasn't a great living. They still had no bedroom furniture other than their mattress and frame. They had no money for new clothes or for a couch or to go to a restaurant. But the rent was paid and they could afford to go to the movies. Nicholas had bought medical and life insurance. And when she'd come home from the hospital he presented her with a radio and a twenty-dollar gift certificate at a bookstore. "I don't want you to be bored," he said.

"I won't be," she'd assured him, smiling, watching him rock Victoria in his arms.

She wasn't bored. But just the day before, as she folded the baby's laundry, the tiny flowered nighties and the miniature pinafores, she'd been thinking about Nicholas's upcoming audition for a Broadway play. The part was an army captain from Alabama, and he'd gone to the Forty-second Street Library to listen to records of southern writers reading from their work, just to immerse himself in their accents. She imagined him sitting there, eyes closed in concentration, hands holding the earphones close to his head. She'd picked up a shirt, smoothed it—and stood stock still. The shirt fell to the floor. She'd picked it up, folded it swiftly, but the realization was too powerful to put aside.

She would never be an actress. Not ever. Now, sitting in the park, the knowledge was still as fresh and shattering as the day before. Jane felt dizzy. She leaned forward, rested her elbows on her legs, and lowered her head into her hands. All along she'd put it off. It was she who'd done it. She'd given up her apprenticeship at Westport to be with Nicholas and gladly worked in the Guilderland publicity office. She'd insisted on working at *Deb,* insisted that Nicholas take acting lessons, that he not burden his first crucial months in New York driving taxis or waiting tables. Once she became pregnant, he'd been determined to stop the acting lessons and go back to driving a taxi and she'd been angry. She'd counseled him: focus on your career; audition for everything; pound the pavement; talk to actors, to stage managers, to ticket takers, anyone with theater connections.

Well, he drove the taxi, but he'd succeeded anyway. He was earning a living as an actor, as she'd always known he would.

And she'd lost her chance without knowing it. She'd given up the dream, tossed aside without thinking the goal that had motivated her whole life—to follow in her mother's footsteps, to act. Nicholas knew what she had done, though. He'd never actually brought it up—what was there to discuss?—but as she thought about it, she knew he'd realized it from the moment the results of the pregnancy test came back. He'd stopped pointing out auditions for actresses in *Backstage*. When they saw a movie or a play, he no longer whispered that some actress had taken her part. There were no more parts for her. She had only two roles: mother, wife.

She couldn't take this weather. Cincinnati could be hot and humid, but it could be borne. Nothing matched the oppressiveness of a Manhattan summer. It was unnatural. Against nature. The buildings were giant fingers grasping and holding the heat instead of letting it rise as it was supposed to. Putrid vapors rose from the sewers.

Her whole head ached. Not a regular headache: her brain felt as though it were pushing against her entire skull. She pressed her hands tight against her head. It was too hot. She put her hands on the handle of the carriage and lifted herself up. She was dizzier than before. Much. Then her heart began smashing hard against her chest. Not *boom, boom*, in rhythm, but *boom, boom . . . boom . . . boomboom. . . .* It was so strong and it wouldn't stop. It must be an attack. The dizziness was so bad she was afraid she'd fall over and bring the carriage crashing sideways. She swayed and let go of the handle. She was going to fall. She squatted on the pavement to keep from cracking her head on the cement. She put her weight on her palms and stayed down on her haunches, so dizzy she couldn't distinguish the sky from the ground. Her heartbeat grew more insistent, battering against her neck as well as her chest. She whimpered with fear and humiliation. The nannies must be watching her. Talking about her. She needed help. If she fainted, would a policeman take the baby, would a stranger pass and see a carriage unattended and walk off with it, would it take so long to be found that the baby would die of the heat? Her legs gave out. Her dress billowed and she fell backward, flat on her behind. Something scraped the back of her leg. It was a sickening stab of pain. She felt under her thigh. When she brought her hand up, it had a thick smear of blood.

One of the nannies was walking over. Jane reached out, clutched the bench, and pulled herself up. What could she say? She grabbed the carriage and, as the dizziness subsided for an instant, she ran, away from the nanny, out to the path, out of the park. Her bleeding thigh stiffened, then slowed her down. When she reached Fifth Avenue, she was gasping for breath. People were turning to look at her. There must be blood on the back of her dress. She made herself breathe slower.

Her heart still pounded, but not quite so hard. Her head. She put her hand on top of her skull. It was just throbbing now, a dull throb against her sore head.

Slowly, afraid the attack would begin again, she limped back to the apartment. Inside, she left the baby in her carriage, opened all the windows, switched on the fan, and took off her dress. It was soaked with sweat. A broad red line streaked the back of the skirt. Everyone along Fifth Avenue must have thought she had her period. Her underwear felt horrible, clammy. She took off her bra and eased off her pants. They too were drenched.

She lay down on her stomach and shut her eyes. Just then, the baby began to whimper. Almost immediately the cry grew to a screeching demand. Jane got up and limped to the carriage. Seconds later, she was sitting naked on the edge of a kitchen chair on a wad of paper towels, shivering, nursing Victoria. Her thigh hurt so much she felt nauseated. She did not hear Nicholas come into the apartment. She looked up and there he was, staring at her nakedness. "Fantastic," he said.

There were only two things wrong with being in *Goodbye Cousin Willy*. One was that he'd had to get a crew cut. The other was that it was a boring play.

Actually, the crew cut wasn't that bad, even though he was startled in the morning when he looked in the mirror; it was like shaving a stranger. Jane kept bursting into laughter every time she looked at him, even after he'd told her to cut it out. They'd gone for dinner at his mother's the night before he was to leave for out-of-town tryouts. Winifred had patted the tiny spikes of hair and declared she thought it made him look very young and sweet. Earlier that evening he'd met his father for a drink and James had said "Oh, Christ" and shaken his head.

Goodbye Cousin Willy was another matter. It was like every third play on Broadway: a family gathers from near and far for some reason—in this case, the funeral of a young alcoholic poet. They dissect the past, fireworks follow, and, in the end, ugly or ennobling truths emerge.

His role wasn't big, but it was crucial. He played Bryce Thompson, a career army officer who was the same age as his cousin Willy and who, it came out, had so taunted Willy about being a sissy that Willy hadn't had the courage to declare his love to another cousin, Jenny-Sue Rawls, the one girl who might have saved him from his demons. Bryce was a bully who, naturally, had doubts about his own manhood. The part was no challenge. Nicholas modeled it on the lacrosse coach at Trowbridge, a bitter man who resented his students because of their privileged backgrounds, calling them rich sons of bitches; who routinely terrorized any boy who allowed an injury to slow him down. He added a southern accent to the coach's sneering manner. He copied the way the coach moved in too close to the person he was talking to, forcing the person to keep backing up.

"You're a grand Bryce," the show's star confided in him after their opening in Philadelphia. They'd run into each other the following morning in the coffee shop of their hotel, and she'd asked him to join her for breakfast. Beatrice Drew, whom Nicholas had admired long before he'd ever thought of being an actor, played Willy's mother.

"Thank you."

"Really, I could feel your rage under that military bearing." Beatrice was a big woman and a huge eater. She nearly inhaled all the rolls in the wicker basket on the table and even ate the parsley sprig that garnished her Spanish omelet. "Very, very fine." She seemed excited about the play, as did everyone else. Her character's big secret was that she wasn't the sweet, faithful southern homebody she appeared. Beneath her apron beat a wanton heart. In fact, it emerged that Willy was not her husband's son; he was the result of an affair with her brother-in-law, Bryce's father. Big deal, Nicholas had thought. "It's relatively easy to become enraged," Beatrice continued. "Seething silently is quite another matter. You're a splendid seether. Do you normally seethe a great deal?"

"No," he said. He wasn't sure if she was trying to be funny or just making conversation or if she was flirting with him. He was astounded how many women could look straight at his wedding ring and without batting an eyelash start trying to play games. In fact, Beatrice Drew was at that moment eyeing his wedding ring.

"Will your wife be coming down here?" she asked.

"No. We have a two-month-old baby."

"How marvelous!" He couldn't tell if she thought it was marvelous or not. Like many theater people he'd met, she had a great deal of charm but no distinct personality. "Boy or girl?"

"A girl. Her name's Victoria."

"A lovely name. I must say, though, you look very young yourself. May I ask how old you are?"

"Twenty-two."

"My goodness! You are a baby. Well, you're certainly going places fast. Twenty-two and heading for Broadway."

"I've been lucky."

"Yes. And you've been good. Are you going to finish that toast? Thank you. Now listen to me. My mother had a saying: cream rises to the top. It's really true. You're a good actor and you've got marvelous looks and a lovely manner. People like you and *that's* ninety-five percent of it. A producer will say, Well, let's see, clean-cut, can play eighteen and age to forty . . . I've got it! That nice Nicholas Cobleigh. A real pro. No tantrums. Takes direction. Talented, of course."

"Thank you. Would you like some more coffee?"

"Please." Nicholas signaled the waitress. "Let me tell you something, Nicholas. Many actors who succeed over the long run would have succeeded in any other field: journalism, dentistry, what have you. Why? Because they have good judgment. Good judgment about their roles, good judgment about curbing their own egos when it's in their best interests, good judgment about who represents them. I've been acting for thirty years, and except for the first two years when I sold stockings at Macy's, I've always made a living at it. Do you know why?"

"You're a great actress." The waitress who was refilling their coffee cups stared at Beatrice, then visibly shrugged and walked off.

"I'm a very good actress and I'm smart as well. I don't think I've ever made an enemy. Well, aroused a little animosity, perhaps, but nothing that's lasted longer than the run of the play. I have a good agent. And I know a good play when I read one."

"Do you think this is a good play?" Nicholas asked.

"Do you? Oh, please. I'm not trying to trap you. I promise it will be our secret."

"I don't know. It's . . ."

"It's what?"

"It's boring. It's like a hundred other plays."

"Like a hundred other plays you've *seen*, Nicholas. It's the sort of thing that will play for one and a half nice, pleasant seasons. It has enough histrionics and southern gothic lust that everyone feels they're getting their money's worth. I happen to agree with you. It isn't a very good play. But it isn't a bad play either. And it's exposure. And it's a living. There is Victoria to think about. And your wife. What is her name?"

"Jane."

"Well, tell Jane that I said she's a lucky girl. When we get to New York— oh, who's your agent?"

"I don't have one yet. A couple of them have introduced themselves and called me a few times, but I'm not exactly sure how to go about it, how to judge whether someone's right for me."

"When we get to New York, I want you to meet Murray King. He's my agent."

"Of course, I've heard of him. Thank you. I really don't know what to say, Beatrice."

"You needn't say anything at all, Nicholas. Save it all for Murray."

Murray King told his secretary to hold his calls, but every time the telephone whirred in the anteroom beyond the closed door of his office his torso twitched, as if each unanswered call were a mild electric shock. Still, he seemed to be concentrating. "For a little more than a year, not bad," he said. As his finger drifted down the page of Nicholas's résumé, he mumbled the name of each credit: "Mmm. *Last Will*, uh-huh; *Stu—*" He peered over the glasses that rested halfway down his nose. "They give a play a name like *Stupor*, and then they act surprised when the critics use it to beat them over the head with. How long did it run?"

"Two days," Nicholas responded. He sat in a matching chair to Murray's. The office was disconcerting because it had no desk. It looked like the living room of a shut-in who did a lot of reading. Floor-to-ceiling shelves were so crammed with rubber-banded piles of papers, bound plays, and books that if they tipped over—which they looked on the brink of doing—the authorities could sift for days before recovering the bodies. Wooden venetian blinds were drawn to defeat the most determined ray of sunlight. The grapes in the bowl beside the two telephones on the table near Murray's right hand were either very dusty or waxed.

Murray himself looked a little waxed. He reminded Nicholas of the tailors in Brooks Brothers, men with chalky fingers who wore tape measures dangling around their necks like unknotted ties, permanently hunched from marking cuffs on boys' trousers. He looked neither happy nor sad. Nicholas wished he could say something to cheer him. He couldn't think of anything, but when Murray glanced up from the résumé, Nicholas smiled at him. Murray looked a little surprised and responded with a fast, furtive smile, as if committing a misdemeanor. "Beatrice said you were a very nice person," he muttered.

"Thank you."

Murray studied the résumé again. His finger moved slowly, as if it had a tiny eye that was reading each word. "Soothz?" he asked.

"I'm sorry," Nicholas said. His instinct was to feel sorry for this man, to pat him on the shoulder and tell him things would be better soon. He had to make a conscious effort to remember Murray King was one of the most successful, respected theatrical agents in New York. Nevertheless, Nicholas thought, he wished he could do something nice for him, take him for a long walk in the country. "I didn't hear you."

"I mumble. They all say I sometimes mumble. But not on the phone. On the phone I have my best moments. Soothz. Which one?"

"The Western one. We shot it in Brooklyn. We rode up to the camera and I tossed a roll to the other actor."

"You ride horses?"

"Yes."

"How good?" Murray had an old man's complexion; all the color in his skin had exuded. Still, Nicholas thought, he couldn't be much older than his father. "Brilliant? Lousy?"

"All right. No tricky stuff."

"I'm not talking standing on your head. I'm talking English country gentleman. With the boots. Over bushes."

"I'm out of practice, but I probably could do it."

"Because I got an aftershave commercial at J. Walter Thompson. They're casting next something—Monday, Tuesday, someplace in Westchester. They want to see everyone on a horse first. You interested?" Nicholas nodded. He didn't know what to say. "What else do you do?" Murray asked.

"I don't sing or dance."

"It's all right. The whole world took tap lessons. You'll live without it. You fence?"

"No. But I'm a decent athlete. I can—"

"You got muscles?"

"Not like a bodybuilder."

"They want Hercules, they'll call his agent. Listen, you want the horse thing? My girl—her name is Toni—she'll give you a piece of paper where to go." Murray put his hands on the arms of his chair and pushed himself up with the slowness of a man arthritic or charley-horsed. "Let me know how it turns out."

Nicholas stood. Although he and Jane had rehearsed a series of proper, businesslike questions, he was disconcerted by Murray's casualness. "Is there any sort of a contract you want me—" He broke off, embarrassed, worried he'd violated one of the theater's elementary decencies.

"Oh, right. No, no. It's a good thing you said something, otherwise I'd have to go chasing after you to the elevator. No contract. Strictly handshake. I get ten percent of what you get. When I hear about something that sounds good, I'll call you. Relax. Look, I've seen *Cousin Willy*—what, three, four times? I know you're not just some pretty face. A good play comes up, you don't think I'll call you?"

Nicholas extended his hand. "I wish I could think of something original to say. Thank you."

"That's good enough. Oh, listen, Nicky, wear a hat or something up to Westchester. They don't have to see that haircut first thing. And give Toni your phone number and your address. I'll be in touch. You want to call me, call me."

"Thank you."

"Thank you. Listen, I hope you make both of us very rich."

16

. . . although the actor's sister Olivia Cobleigh-Gold, of Chevy Chase,
said she had spoken long-distance with her brother and "he assured
me the doctors had in no way given up hope." Ms. Cobleigh-Gold, a
weaver, is the wife of Mitchell Gold, Assistant Secretary of State for Latin
America . . .

—*Washington Post*

Whenever she came to visit, and she came at least once a week, Winifred
Cobleigh wore a different suit. This time it was camel with chocolate-brown
braided trim and small gold chains looping between the double buttons of the
jacket. The wool was thick and richly nubby, as if it had been lifted directly
from a flawless, camel-colored sheep. She always wore the same shoes—
alligator pumps in fall and winter, spectators in spring and summer—although Jane suspected she had as many pairs of them as she had suits, since
the shoes always looked too pristine to have had any significant contact with
Manhattan pavement.

"I don't dare move," Winifred whispered. Her granddaughter had spent
a frantic half hour racing around the living room pulling a squawking wooden
duck until, lured into Winifred's lap for a minute, she had promptly fallen
asleep. Breathing through a badly stuffed nose, Victoria made nearly as much
noise as the duck. "Could you get my handbag, Jane? Thanks. Just rifle
through it. I made a list on either blue or lilac paper. That's it. Oh, pink. I
can't seem to remember a thing. They may have to lock me up again. Throw
away the key this time."

"I don't think so, Winifred."

"The last time I was there I told someone in the dayroom I was scheduled
for shock treatments and she said, 'My, my, that should curl your hair.' And
then of course she looked at my hair and started crying. Not that my hair was
quite that dreadful. Everything made her cry, poor thing."

"You're fine, Winifred."

"Do I seem fine to you? Really?"

"Yes, and you look wonderful." Of course, wonderful was a relative word.
From photographs, Jane knew Winifred had always been poised on the brink
of homeliness. Her wedding picture was sad: a skinny, buck-toothed girl
whose neck bones gawked out from the exquisite lace bodice of her gown.
Jane marveled that with all the money the Tuttles spent on clothes and
jewelry, travel, houses—even on dogs and horses—no one had thought to get

braces for Winifred's teeth. Still, she was in much better shape than when Jane had first seen her. Finally she seemed able to smile and mean it. And for a woman who had depended on other women to raise her six children, Winifred was uncommonly patient and affectionate with her grandchild. Victoria, curled in her lap, was breathing mucus bubbles onto the sleeve of her expensive suit, and Winifred was peering down at the child as if she were depositing emeralds.

In the two years since she'd been separated from James, Winifred had had only one bout of depression, and that not a disabling one. When Jane had first met her, in June 1961, at graduation, Winifred had been so white her freckles looked like a brown rash and she'd had deep circles under her eyes. Now, her color was better, the circles had vanished, and though her eyes often had the lusterless look of someone heavily medicated, a casual observer would have guessed her to be a normal Manhattan matron in her late forties or early fifties.

Of course, normal was a relative adjective too. Normal matrons, thought Jane, do not take long walks on seventeen-degree January days without wearing gloves and stockings. Winifred's big hands were raw, as if her life had been spent picking potatoes, and her legs, as usual, were covered with the white scales of badly chapped skin. For Christmas, Jane and Nicholas had presented her with perfume, spray cologne, dusting powder, and a huge jar of scented dry-skin lotion. She'd obviously never used the last, and Jane suspected that she'd passed the entire collection on to Olivia or Abby.

"Would you read the list to me?" Winifred asked. "I can't get to my glasses." Her fingers toyed with a lock of Victoria's brown hair.

"'Pem,'" Jane read.

"Oh, yes. Cully Daniels called and asked if you'd written to Pembroke. That letter of recommendation for her daughter."

"About a month ago. I sent a copy to the girl up at school."

"Good. Thank you. You know how—well, vague these girls can be. I suppose she didn't say anything to her mother. Sorry to bother you with that again."

"That's okay."

"You don't even know the girl. She's very sweet actually. A Botticelli face with a Rubens figure. Big, gorgeous girl. I'm sure she'll be a sensation with the boys. I think Edward has a crush on her, but of course she won't give him the time of day."

"'Tickets.' To *Key to the City*?"

"Yes. Some of James's clients are coming in from Paris. He wants six. Do you think that's odd?"

"Do they understand English?"

"No, I mean don't you think it's odd that he can't lift the phone and call

281

you or Nicholas or ask you when he sees you? He has his secretary call and she says 'James Cobleigh calling' in this tinny voice. 'Is Mrs. Cobleigh at home?' Of course, she knows perfectly well it's I she's speaking with, and then I get all flustered. I suppose I shouldn't be saying this, but I think, Oh, dear, he's going to ask for a divorce so he can marry that glamour girl he's taken up with, that model, and I stand there holding the receiver and saying to myself, 'If he wants a divorce, he can have a divorce,' but all the time I'm . . . I shouldn't be talking like this at all. And then he gets on the line and says, 'Win, the frogs are coming to town. I need six tickets to Nick's play.' And then he gives me the dates and says, 'I want them sent to the *office*. Make sure it's the office.' And then he says goodbye. Isn't that odd?"

"Well, maybe he's just trying . . . I don't know. But I'm sure he'd feel awkward saying 'Can't we be friends?' or even 'Can't we talk things over?' if that's what's on his mind."

"Oh, no. James is never awkward about anything."

"He's lonely—"

"Jane, really, he's got a twenty-one-year-old Swedish model for company. He's been seen with her publicly."

"Winifred, I can't imagine he's got an awful lot to say to a twenty-one-year-old Swedish model. I think he misses being part of the family."

"But he was so seldom there. And when he was—oh, dear, just look at me." Winifred's face was flushed and she seemed agitated. "Every time he calls I'm eighteen again. If he were to ask me to take him back, I'm not sure. . . . I understand things, you know. Really I do. About self-destructive relationships. That's all the doctor ever wants me to talk about."

Winifred yanked at the bow at the neck of her silk blouse. It opened and she retied it, then pulled at it so it opened again. She did it over and over, each time drawing the bow tighter around her neck. She seemed unaware of what she was doing and gave no indication she knew Jane was in the room. She seemed unaware that her granddaughter was in her lap; when she tied the bow, she rested an elbow on Victoria's shoulder as if the child were a ledge.

Jane tried to stay calm. She wanted to feel sorry for Winifred. Instead, she felt afraid. What would happen if Winifred were having another breakdown and, instead of weeping or sleeping as Nicholas had described, she started shrieking. Smashing Victoria onto the floor. Hurling herself across the room and putting her big hands around Jane's neck, throttling her until her tongue hung out and her head rocked back and forth.

Winifred was trying to make the bow fan out, as if it were made of stiff taffeta instead of silk; each time it drooped, she grew more frustrated. Jane wanted to go and scoop Victoria from her lap, but she was afraid to startle Winifred.

"Destructive relationships. Every time I try to talk about something else the doctor won't let me," Winifred said suddenly, as though she hadn't stopped talking. "And my mother. He calls her Maisie. He doesn't seem to care about my father." She put her hands in her lap and suddenly noticed Victoria; she put her arms around the child. "Oh, well, it's not important. Forgive me. I forgot what I was talking about."

"The tickets for the play."

"Oh, yes. Could you get six?"

"Do you have the date?" Jane asked quietly.

"It's not on the list? I must have it at home. Would you call me tonight? I'm so forgetful."

"Yes. Sure. Uh, 'Moth' is next."

"Moth? Oh, *Moth*er." Winifred raised her hand so it covered the bow on her blouse, but she did not attempt to adjust it again. She sat straighter and crossed her legs at the ankles, the proper lady posture Jane had observed her assuming whenever she was entertaining guests. The posture evoked her training; Winifred's mouth curved upward into pleasantness and her voice dropped into a gracious social register. "Would you mind terribly going to my mother's house and reading aloud to her again? It's such a treat for her. She says no one reads the way you do."

"I'd love to." Jane feared she sounded falsely enthusiastic. "Really I would," she added in a more restrained voice.

"We impose on you. All of us."

"It's not an imposition."

"It is. Michael and Abby having you practically write the essays on their college applications and me with my endless lists and talking on and on, forgetting you're still a girl."

"It's fine. Really."

"And my mother calling you nearly every morning to read the editorials and the social news."

"I enjoy it. It's nice to be part of a big family."

"I suppose we must . . . you must forgive me." Winifred's head swiveled toward the hallway, as though someone had snatched her thought and was absconding with it. When she turned back toward Jane, she tried to smile. "I hope Nicholas doesn't impose on you. I mean, make too much work for you."

"He's fine," Jane said, trying to sound properly sincere, appropriately enthusiastic, and not nervous. "You did a wonderful job. He's a wonderful husband."

"I hope so."

"He is, Winifred."

"I worried at the beginning, you know." Winifred began to pull hairpins from her hair, as she spoke, and tried to retwist it into a neater chignon. Crazy wisps of hair corkscrewed around her face, making her look like a clown in a fright wig. "He wasn't even twenty-one when you were married. I worried if he'd be a good—he looks so much like his father, and all the girls were always calling the house, even when he was fourteen, and running after him, and I was afraid he'd—"

"He's fine." Jane's heart began to pound.

"I know. I'm sure he is. It's just that he's so handsome. His eyes are like James's. Girls wait for him at the stage door."

"I know. He's *fine*, Winifred. He's an actor. It happens a lot. Believe me, he takes it in stride."

"James was fine at first," she said.

"Winifred—"

"Attentive. So attentive. He would call and say he really ought to work late but he'd be damned if he was going to because he wanted . . . Until the war."

"Oh."

"When he came back from France—you mustn't let Nicholas go on that tour with the show. You're too young to understand these things. It's not only the girls at the stage door. You know what he does with that actress. Face it, Jane. It's true. Every single night."

"Winifred, it's a role he's playing. It's his job."

"What sort of a job is that! She sits on his lap and puts her hands all over him."

"It's okay!"

"Please, think of the baby. Please."

"Jessica's a friend of ours. It's her job. I know it sounds funny, but she's paid to touch Nick like that. It doesn't mean a thing to either of them. And she happens to be happily married."

"She's so young and beautiful."

"She's thirty, Winifred." Jane forced herself to speak in a placid voice. Her heart beat so hard the left side of her chest hurt. "And I know Nicholas, and I know he would never—"

"Jane, please listen to me!" Winifred suddenly moved forward. The jerking motion wakened Victoria, who began to cry.

"Excuse me," Jane said. "I'll just change her." She jumped up and grabbed the child from Winifred's lap. "I'll only be a minute." Victoria's diaper was soaked through; the ammoniac stench of urine surrounded her like an aura. Winifred's skirt had a dark wet spot where Victoria had been sitting. Jane rushed into the child's room. The clunk of Winifred's heels on the bare wood floor followed her.

Winifred stood at the dressing table uncomfortably close to Jane, pressing against her side as if they were passengers on a rush-hour subway. Neither the child's wails nor the odor from her soiled diaper seemed to penetrate

Winifred's consciousness. "The two of them were always so tight. James and Nicholas. Thick as thieves. They look so much alike and Nicholas sits the exact same way and holds his cup the same way, with two hands, and—"

"Winifred!" Jane's hands were wet from the dripping rubber pants. Her fingers seemed to have no strength. She could not open the diaper pin. Victoria's crying was interrupted by her deep, liquid cough. Jane turned to her mother-in-law. "Please, could you try this pin?"

Winifred's big, raw, red hands covered her face, muffling the noise she was making, so it took Jane a minute to comprehend that she was sobbing.

Nicholas hated to go to bars during the day. The stale, smoky darkness was tolerable at night, but since he never drank enough to relax in them, the gloom reminded him he was squandering his time. This bar was worse than most. It was out of the theater district, so there was no one to say hello to while he waited. The room was dotted with silent, lonely, out-of-town men in cheap suits. They reminded Nicholas of Willy Loman in *Death of a Salesman*, or of his father-in-law.

The waiter brought Nicholas's Bloody Mary. A tiny paper umbrella was stuck into the glass. The place was called Terry's Tiki Bar, and every mixed drink seemed to be served with an umbrella. Coconuts, or objects made to look like coconuts, were suspended from the ceiling on different lengths of wire.

Murray King threaded his way toward the table, giving the bartender and one of the patrons his customary greeting: an almost military salute with his index finger. Nicholas knew Murray had a bar or restaurant in nearly every neighborhood in Manhattan where he could always be assured of a table and good service; thus, he was never more than five minutes away from a potential deal. Why Murray had asked him to come to Terry's Tiki was another matter; it was located on an obscure block near Penn Station.

Murray approached the table carrying a bowl of pretzels he'd picked up at the bar. "You got a drink, Nicky?" he asked, looking directly at the Bloody Mary. "You want something else?"

"This is fine." Nicholas stood, took the pretzels, put them on the table, and shook Murray's hand.

They sat and Murray immediately put both elbows on the small, round pedestal table and leaned toward Nicholas. "I wanted someplace where I don't see fifteen familiar ears pointed at me when I talk. So that's why this place. Now, the truth, Nicky. Okay? Tell me straight out. Are you happy in *Key to the City?*"

"Yes."

"Oh."

"Is that the end of the conversation, Murray?"

"Of course it's not the end of the conversation. You think I had you schlep all the way down here so I could hear you were happy? I know you're happy. I just want to know how happy."

Key to the City had opened ten months before on Broadway to excellent reviews. The play was about two young reporters competing with each other for a story, the chance at a column, and the same girl. The reporter who triumphed in two of the three categories was a rough-spoken, tough, amoral New York City slum kid. He and the girl were the leading roles. Nicholas played his adversary, a boy straight out of the cornfields and Iowa State, a relaxed, good-humored young man, something of an idealist. His character won the girl at the end of the play, but even that was a Pyrrhic victory, since in the preceding scene the New Yorker had boasted to him, in the coarsest detail, of his successful seduction of the girl.

"It's a good part for me," Nicholas said. "I like playing a nice guy. For a while I thought it would be just one bastard after another. And the character has a lot of depth. He's no pushover. It's that he can't believe that someone would be that cutthroat, that evil, really."

"Interesting," Murray murmured.

Nicholas smiled at him. "What's the alternative?"

"A lot less money."

"How much less? Would it make my landlord worry?"

"Worry? Landlords don't worry. They evict. Don't give it a second thought. I'll take in Jane and Vicky. You I'm not so sure about."

"Murray, before you get started, you know what my responsibilities are. I can't afford art for art's sake. That's what you're offering, isn't it?"

"'Romeo, Romeo! wherefore art thou Romeo?' Sound familiar?"

"*Romeo and Juliet*? What do they want me for?"

"What do you think, Bugs Bunny? Romeo, of course, and guess which certain director who did *Measure for Measure* last season called—and I'll bet you a hundred bucks he didn't call anyone else first—and asked for you?"

"Lester Green? Are you serious?"

"Are you kidding? Nicky, listen. He thinks you've got it, and he thinks maybe two, three actors in the whole city have got it. You'll have to read for it because you've only done contemporary stuff, but if you don't fall flat on your face over the iambic pentameter you're in like Flynn. The only thing is it's Off Broadway, so you'll be making less than half what you're making now."

"I don't see how I can."

"Come on. So you don't eat for a couple of months. I bet Jane would want you to."

"Murray, if I spent the rest of my life doing Chekhov for the experience Jane would be happy. Part of her thinks that if you're not living in a garret you can't be a serious actor. Fortunately, I'm the breadwinner of the family."

"You think I want you to do this because I think making money is crass or something? What's ten percent of *bupkes*, of almost nothing? You think I'm an agent because of my love for the drama as an art form?"

"Yes."

"You know me better than that, Nicky. I'm a businessman. And this is a good investment."

Nicholas sipped his Bloody Mary. The ice had melted, and the drink tasted like tomato-flavored water. "I don't know."

"I do know. You're going to spend a few months working with a guy who's probably the most prestigious director in the country and, I guarantee you, Juliet and all the other people running around there are going to be first class. This is an important decision. I'm not saying it's not. You say no to a guy like this because the money's not so hot, and he's not going to come around knocking on your door again. Something wrong with that drink?"

"It's fine. I'm not in the mood."

"Take some pretzels. They haven't put *Romeo and Juliet* on in I don't know how many years, so there'll be an almost assured decent-length run and listen, the most important thing, critical attention like you wouldn't believe."

"What if I'm no good?"

"You sound like the rest of them now. What do you mean, if you're no good? If you're no good Lester Green will give you a good, swift kick in the behind and that's it."

"I mean, I may be all right, but what if I'm not really good?"

"If you're not really good you'll get stinky reviews and you'll feel like hell for two weeks and then something else'll turn up. But let me tell you something. This is important. You've made a very nice name for yourself in a very short time. Look at you, a kid, and you know what? You can spend the rest of your life as an actor. Theater, commercials, TV if you want it. You'll probably always make a living. How many people can say that? How many kids your age? The point is, you're thinking like a conservative businessman. You want to think like that, you should have made your family happy and been a lawyer, although the world needs another lawyer like it needs a hole in the head. Nicky, you're an actor. An artist."

"I am not an *artist*. Acting is a job, like being a lawyer or like being an agent."

"Nicky, why are you trying to make it into a business? So people will take you seriously? People do take you seriously. I know you come from a family where—"

"I know talent—if you want to call it a gift, fine—talent has a lot to do with it, but talent is important in any business. My particular talent happens to be for acting. I'm a much better actor than I would be a lawyer. But you know better than almost anyone else that's only the half of it. It's hard work. It's a job, Murray."

"Fine. Let's look at it as a job if that'll make you happy. Don't you want to get to be president of the company? You got a shot here at having people look at you like a leading man. Okay, this may not be your only chance. Something could happen tomorrow. Or in ten years. Maybe never."

"You wear kid gloves, Murray."

"If you can't pay your rent, I'll help you out."

"Thanks. I'm sure if I decide to take it, we'll get by."

"If?"

"I want to think about it overnight."

"You got a three-week cancellation clause in this contract, Nicky. And Lester Green isn't going to take a cruise while you make up your mind."

"It's just overnight, Murray."

"Think about how excited Jane's going to be when she hears about it. You doing Shakespeare. I'd love to see her face when you tell her."

"Can I call you tomorrow morning?"

"Why not? I'll just tell Green your phone was out of order and I sent you a telegram but you weren't home to get it because you were out looking at your bank account."

"Murray . . ."

"Nicky . . ."

"All right. I'll do it."

The Cobleighs' second child was conceived on March 13, 1964, three days after Jane's twenty-fourth birthday.

Weeks before that night, Jane realized there would be no easing into Nicholas's newest role. After two readings, he had his interpretation set; by the first rehearsal, he and his character began to meld.

He had barely started to kiss her, forcing his tongue into her mouth, when he changed his mind and tore at her nightgown. This was Nicholas's Romeo. She couldn't believe that she'd actually looked forward to it. She assumed he'd be so imbued with being a young Veronese nobleman that he'd make love gallantly, with tenderness, possibly whispering some of his lines that brought not Juliet to his mind, but her: ". . . her eyes in heaven/Would through the airy region stream so bright/That birds would sing and think it were not night." Well, he always told her how beautiful her eyes were.

He yanked the nightgown over her head and left it to her to untangle her arms from the sleeves. He was too busy grabbing her breasts. His hot breathing misted her neck. A minute into the act and already close to losing control.

She should have known. Character was more important to him than language. He squeezed her nipples hard, knowing that would arouse her. Too hard, but she was aroused anyway. His Romeo was an oversexed teenager. Romantic, but led, as Nicholas had put it, by his dick instead of his head.

He'd begun talking dirty; when he and Jeff, the actor who played Mercutio, got together, everything they said was an innuendo or a disgusting double entendre. They'd spent an entire morning in the apartment tediously explaining the play's sexual puns; "'for I was come to the whole depth of my tale.' You *know* what that means, don't you?" Yes, she'd said. She knew. There was no way a person could get through four years of college English and not know. "It means," Nicholas explained unnecessarily, "sticking it in deep, all the way." Jeff, sprawled on the living room floor, puffed his pipe and smirked. She couldn't believe Nicholas was talking to her like that in front of someone else. She told him that night, "You two behave like a couple of immature sixteen-year-olds," and his laugh had a nasty edge, just like an immature sixteen-year-old. He lowered his head and started to suck on one breast, then switched to the other, then back and forth, greedy, easily distracted.

He climbed on top of her and started to kiss her again, juicy, heated kisses all over her face. She averted her head, putting her tongue in his ear to explain her action. She ran her hands over his behind and down the back of his thighs. That, at least, she wanted to do.

He had never been in such extraordinary shape. For two months, ever since he'd taken the part, he'd been working out for hours nearly every morning in the gym and going for fencing lessons three afternoons a week. His muscles were beautifully formed rocks: he'd become Michelangelo's David zipped into skin. A few nights earlier, before he'd left for the theater, he'd been on his hands and knees playing horsie with Victoria. His upper arms bulged out of his undershirt sleeves. Before she could turn away to hide the flush that rose to her face, he saw her staring at him. A few minutes later, he put Victoria in her playpen and came into the kitchen and cornered her between the refrigerator and the wall.

But she hadn't felt comfortable with him in weeks. He offered all his sweetness to Juliet and returned to the apartment a swaggering, muscle-bound teenage hood.

Nicholas cried out, "I love you." Maybe not a hood, but a wise guy, sneaking up as she made the bed and striking her behind with his fingertips as if she were one of the boys in the locker room at school.

When the play had opened the week before, the critics had marveled at the interpretation. The youth! The passion! The vigor! Romeo, Mercutio, and Benvolio leaped and wrestled like high-spirited adolescents! Romeo and Juliet were no simpering lovers: their romance was swollen with lust! At last! A Juliet without rouged cheeks! A Romeo in the first flush of magnificent manhood! When they took off each other's shirts, he was as beautiful as she! Nicholas grabbed Jane's hand and put it around his penis.

She hated the production. She'd gone to a rehearsal and watched the director—a squat, fat man with dried streaks of food on his shirtfront—studying Nicholas and the actress who played Juliet, practically slobbering as they undressed each other. She was sure he'd insisted on modern dress only because unlacing a Renaissance bodice would have taken too long. Because it was Off Broadway, the director had taken advantage of the freedom and had Nicholas caress the actress's bare breasts. The opening night audience had almost gasped. Nicholas's roommate, Charlie Harrison, in from Boston, who'd been sitting next to her, turned to see how she was reacting and she'd given him a reassuring nod. The play could have been written by a chimpanzee for all anyone cared about language; Nicholas—leaping, jumping, turning somersaults—threw away a third of his lines. There was no poetry, no beauty. She had been ashamed; it was an ugly production. The critics would destroy him. Near the end of the last scene, she'd tried to think of something comforting she could say. Her thoughts were drowned out by the noise of the audience getting to its feet for a standing ovation, by the screams of Bravo. The critics had been unstinting in their admiration. Nicholas put his hand over hers, squeezing it tighter around his penis.

His last character, in *Key to the City*, had been so gentle and courteous. He'd touched her as if it were a privilege. He'd always asked if she was ready.

Sometimes she couldn't see the character. When he'd been preparing for *Stupor*, which had closed in two days, she'd been a little concerned; he was playing a psychopathic killer. But he'd been fine. Basic Nicholas. He would not believe her that he changed with his other roles. She'd given him examples of how he behaved, and he said it was her imagination. He sounded annoyed.

He put his hand between her legs and massaged her with two fingers. Her hips rose, presenting more of herself to him. He climbed between her legs and grasped his penis, using it to rub her with. She let out a high cry and sought his lips. He took her kiss as an invitation. He plunged right into her.

He thrust hard and deep: up to Mercutio's standards. Faster and faster, like a boy who had never had it before and was desperate not to lose his chance. Harder still, banging against her, until a minute later, he signaled the end with a yell so loud she covered his mouth with hers to stifle the sound. His entire body went rigid. Then he collapsed on top of her with a deep sigh. He drew out his penis, kissed her cheek, and moved to his side of the bed where, almost immediately, he fell asleep.

Often she drifted off easily. But this time she was still too heated up. Her breasts remained sensitive and engorged, as if he'd just stopped fondling them for a second. It had happened too fast. When he took forever, as he had with

Last Will and Testament, she'd tire, and it would be easy to unwind. She turned onto her stomach and rubbed herself against the bed; the stimulation was unconscious and unsatisfactory.

She had not had an orgasm, not that night or any other night in their nearly three years of marriage. Sometimes she thought it was about to happen. Sometimes she thought the women who claimed they had them were liars. She wanted one. Sometimes she told Nicholas she'd had one: it was wonderful, fabulous; she gave him rave reviews. Four or five times a week she waited, always hoping that particular time would be the one. But she never could. Not even Romeo could make her come.

17

EYES CLOSED in deep coma . . . wires from pressure monitor imbedded in skull . . . Jane Cobleigh in hospital today.
—Front page photo caption, *The Standard*

Maybe it had something to do with Sally's sudden death. One minute the person you love most is calling, "Have a good nap! Happy dreams!" and then you wake up and she is gone forever. Whatever the reason, Jane was no good at goodbyes.

Each morning she'd be the last mother left at the iron fence, waving long after Victoria was lost in the river of blue tartan flowing through the front door of the Burnham-Arnold School.

With Elizabeth, it was Nicholas and the babysitter who propelled Jane out of the apartment when the child's bottom lip quivered and she began the refrain every three-and-a-half-year-old wails: "Mommy, Mommy, *please*, Mommy, don't go." Halfway through a party, Jane could not rid herself of the picture of Elizabeth heartlessly abandoned in her crib, her back heaving with sobs, although the babysitter and Victoria swore that once she heard the elevator door close, forgetfulness could be bought for a cookie.

Saying goodbye to Nicholas was even worse. As he began rehearsals for each new play, Jane began steeling herself for his out-of-town tryouts by making elaborate plans for her time. She did not allow herself a moment to miss him, because the moments were too painful. Her imagination was too rich for leisure. She saw train derailments, car crashes, falling scenery. Going meant he might never return.

So, hating leavetaking, it was understandable when Maisie Tuttle died of heart failure in early February 1968 that Jane took that final goodbye very hard. While she had never gotten far enough beyond Maisie's famous charm to get really close to her, the older woman's acceptance had made her feel she'd been tapped for the best club.

"Nicholas," Maisie would say, "you *know* you've got the better part of the bargain. You don't really deserve Jane." Nicholas would smile and say he knew he didn't, but Maisie would interrupt. "No, no. You say you know, but you've been spoiled by everyone fussing over you all your life. All those children looking up to their big brother and all those simpering girls who called you Nicky. Jane doesn't call you Nicky. Do you, Jane?" Not any more, Jane remarked. "Do you hear that, Nicholas? Intelligent. Has a lovely voice, and her looks will outlast yours. When you're forty and pasty—all fair men get pasty, you know—she'll just be coming into her beauty. Men will fall at her feet, whimpering for her favors, so you'd better be good to her now if you know what's good for you later."

Since 1963, when Maisie's cataracts had made it impossible for her to see clearly, Jane had gone to her house twice a week to read to her. They shared the same favorite novels, and for nearly five years Jane had alternated *Pride and Prejudice* with *Jane Eyre;* they'd decided if they ever were bored they would begin *Anna Karenina,* but they never were bored.

Maisie tutored her. It was Maisie who finally put her at ease with Nicholas's friends from school, Maisie who dictated dinner invitations to their wives, planned menus, told her what to wear and what to say. "Say anything you please. Do you hear me, Jane? The worst that can happen is that they won't have anything to do with you again. That is also the best that can happen, but I suppose you can't say that to Nicholas. For heaven's sake don't try to be like those girls! That would be like taking a vow: 'I will be dull for the rest of my life.' I am not being fair. One or two of them may surprise you and be perfectly nice. But if Nicholas had wanted someone dull, he would have married that excessively pleasant girl—what was her name? Men like ours marry women like ourselves for a reason."

It was Maisie who dissuaded Jane from cutting her waist-length hair. "Short hair is for boys, my dear. Besides, a man wants to see a woman take down her hair."

It was Maisie who persuaded Jane to use the farm for their vacations. "Don't worry about the furniture. Antique simply means old. It's mostly good, sturdy Connecticut maple and white pine. It's lasted a hundred and fifty years or more, and it will survive Elizabeth. Please. I know what good times you and Nicholas have there."

So it was not surprising that, two weeks after the funeral, Nicholas came home late one afternoon after a long lunch with two of his uncles, Winifred's brothers, and found Jane whipping egg whites and crying. He took a dish-towel that was draped over the handle of the refrigerator and wiped her eyes. "Still miss her?"

"Yes," Jane said. "She was like my own grandmother." She put the bowl and wire whip on the counter.

"I know."

"Better. My grandmother wasn't very nice. When she died I found a pornographic picture in a hatbox on top of her closet."

"Did you save it?"

"No. Oh, Nick. I miss reading to her. I miss her telling me what the right thing is. When I was getting ready for the funeral, I kept thinking, she's the only one who could tell me black or navy and put me at ease." Nicholas put his arms around her and she put hers around him. "You're going to be a comfort to me in my old age," Jane said into his ear.

"Am I a comfort now?"

"Yes." They pulled apart suddenly when they heard giggling. Victoria and Elizabeth were standing in the kitchen door watching them. "All right, girls," Jane said. "Um, how were your uncles? Are they taking it well?"

"They're fine. The will's been probated."

Jane picked up the bowl of half-beaten egg whites. In Nicholas's family, references to money were always oblique. She compromised. "Did they discuss it at all?"

"Yes. That's why they asked me to lunch."

"Oh." She took the whisk and whipped the egg whites until her shoulder grew stiff. Nicholas watched her. "Is this something you as a Tuttle Cobleigh don't discuss with me as a Heissenhuber Cobleigh?" she asked.

"What are the egg whites for?"

"A cheese soufflé. I guess you answered my question."

"No. I just want you to finish. Vicky, Liz, would you please? This is a grown-up conversation. Go play Candyland. Go on. I'll be with you in five minutes."

She rested the bowl on the counter. "I'm finished."

"So is the soufflé. You can't just leave it like that, can you?"

"Nick, tell me what it is. Come on. You really look—not yourself."

"All my brothers and sisters and the seven cousins got very nice bequests. She didn't leave me any money."

"Nick, you're kidding! I can't believe she would do something like that. *Why?*"

"Are you ready?" Jane nodded. Nicholas reached into his back pocket and pulled out a sheaf of papers. "It's a copy of the will. 'To my beloved grandson, Nicholas Tuttle Cobleigh . . .'"

"I thought you said—"

"Listen: '. . . I bequeath and devise all my right, title, and interest in a certain property known as Tuttle Farm . . .'"

Jane began to cry.

"It goes on and on describing the boundaries. Wait: '. . . including buildings, livestock, implements, fixtures, and machinery and all other personalty and furnishings appurtenant thereto at the time of my death.' Do you know what it's worth? A seventy-five-acre farm in Fairfield County? It's only an hour and fifteen minutes from midtown. We can live there, Jane. The whole thing is ours. The house. The stables. I can ride every morning. It's going to be fine."

"It's too much."

"No it's not."

"Nick, please listen to me. It's not right. We didn't earn it. I know what you're going to say, but please—"

"Shhh. You're going to love it. Listen to me, Jane. I know it's overwhelming. I know how hard it is for you, once you've made a nest, to move out of it. If it were up to you, we'd still be in that cold-water flat with the bathtub in the kitchen."

"We don't deserve—"

"Jane, they screwed you up to a fare-thee-well and you haven't the foggiest notion what you deserve. I'm sorry, but it's true. Let me be the one who decides what you deserve. All right? Just leave it to me. We're going to be so happy there. You'll see. Instead of standing sideways in this tight little kitchen, we'll be sitting back and having our coffee at the breakfast table with a big fire blazing away in the hearth. And in the summer we'll be swimming in the pond and taking the girls for picnics on the hill overlooking that field of wildflowers. Won't that be something? It's going to be fine. Trust me. I know what's good for us."

Three months later, after the final performance of *House on Fire,* Iris Betts, the actress who had spent the entire six-month run of the play trying to lure Nicholas into her dressing room grabbed his arm and moved in so close her breast rubbed against his bicep. "Stop pulling away. I'm not going to bite you," she said. "Really, Nicky, you're impossible. You're the most incorrigibly uxurious man I've ever met. What does she have, hmmm? A little something she dabs behind the ears? The thing of it is, you *look* like such a runaround. A born heartbreaker. Sexy and ice cold and here you are, Husband of the Year. Of the Century."

"Jane," Nicholas said. Her back was toward him. She was at the front door, polishing the brass knocker for the third time. The knocker was in the shape of an eagle, and she was rubbing between the talons with a soft rag. Her work shirt, an old pink oxford cloth of his, was streaked with gray tarnish.

She turned to him. A stripe of gray crossed her nose. "If seven years ago, when we graduated, you'd have told me I'd be spending my day cleaning between the toes of a brass Federalist eagle somewhere in Connecticut, I'd have told you you were totally deranged."

"Take a break for a minute. Come here." He was stretched out on his back on the lawn in front of the house in a torn undershirt and old jeans. He and his clothes were smeared with the dark green paint he'd been using to paint the window trim and the shutters. She walked toward him. He reached out and grabbed her ankle. "A little love in the afternoon?"

"No."

"Give me one good reason."

"I have to finish the knocker. You have half the second floor to do. The hardware store is delivering the steamer to take off the wallpaper, and the girls are due home any second. Good enough?"

"No."

"You reek of turpentine and the front of your hair is green."

"Don't you like green hair?"

"Oh, I love it. But not on you. Sorry, but you just don't have the flair to carry it off." She plunked down beside him and crossed her legs. She was wearing shorts. It was late June, but already her legs were dark brown. "You're more the boring type. Bland. Blond. Dull. You know what I mean." She bent down and kissed his forehead. "Eminently forgettable."

"Thanks. Oh. I know what I was going to ask you. Do you think I'm cold-looking?"

"No. Why?"

"Iris Betts said I looked ice cold."

"Iris Betts isn't happy unless she sees steam rising from every man she talks to."

"I forgot how objective you are about her."

"Well, what kind of woman comes over to someone's wife and says, 'That's *some* man you have there'? And all those tight knit dresses and five-inch heels, so she looks like a 1958 prostitute."

"How would you know what a 1958 prostitute looks like? Hmm?" He reached out and rubbed her calf. "Was all that Cincinnati virgin business an act? I'll bet it was. I'll bet you were walking around Woodward High School in five-inch heels. A real entrepreneur, keeping up the football team's spirit and making a living at the same time. All the boys would say, 'Wow, here comes Heissenhuber,' and take out their wallets. And take out their—"

"Nick."

"I heard about you. On your back on the fifty-yard line."

"I was hoping you wouldn't find out."

"You can't hide anything from me. I know a cheap tramp when I marry one."

"Nick, be serious for a second. At that party, she behaved like I didn't matter, that all she had to do was wiggle her finger and you'd run right over me to get to her."

"She's not worth worrying about."

"Yes, she is. You're my husband."

"If you let her get you that upset, then you need your head examined. I mean it, Jane. She's a real pig. They call her the Grand Canyon."

"Nick!"

"But she can act."

"She can't act. She can wiggle."

296

"She was very good."

"She's good at playing strumpets. If she had to play a nun the audience would stampede for the exits, screaming with laughter. It's true. Why did she tell you you looked ice cold?"

"Why do you think? It wasn't her so much. It was being turned down for that deodorant commercial because the casting guy said I looked like a Nazi. That on top of the screen test."

A movie studio had flown Nicholas to California for a screen test. Afterward, the vice-president in charge of production had told Murray King that Nicholas would not be believable as a Texas rancher. His accent was good, and he could ride, but he looked, in the executive's words, namby-pamby English. His face photographed too long and the bridge of his nose was much too prominent, although that could be corrected with plastic surgery. As he was, he'd only be suited for character roles.

"The screen test! I can't understand why you even bothered. I mean it. It was a dopey cowboy movie."

"Money."

"You're making a lot of money in the theater."

"No I'm not."

"Compared to any other about-to-be-twenty-eight-year-old man—"

"Jane, that's not the standard I use when I think of how I want to support my family. Look, you're the artistic arbiter. Let me be the financial genius. All right? It would be nice to have a few more dollars and a couple of movie credits under my belt. I'd like to know that if a good play didn't come along for six months or a year, I could be busy. That's all."

"Well, go get your nose bobbed or whatever."

"Can you believe that? The bridge of my nose is unacceptable, so I'm unacceptable." He rubbed his nose. "Oh, and my bottom teeth are crooked and my eyes are a fraction of an inch too close together. Did you know that?"

"Yes, but I didn't want to hurt your feelings."

"Jane, if my eyes were a twentieth of an inch farther apart we could have Victoria's freshman and sophomore years paid for."

"Stop worrying about how you look. You look fine. I mean, we can't walk into Sardi's without some lady poking her husband and saying 'Oooh, that's him! *Him!* Isn't he *gaw*-geous?'"

"I'm not gaw-geous. You're gaw-geous."

"You're gaw-geouser," she said. "You know you are."

"Lie down. Come on. I just want to hug you. We can hear cars driving up five minutes before they can see us. Oh, that's nice."

"I don't think you're ice cold."

"I know. I'm not."

"If you want to know the truth, I think you're pretty hot stuff."

297

"I think you're hot stuff," Nicholas responded. She edged closer, so their noses touched. He took her hands in his. "Isn't this wonderful?" he demanded. "Our own grass. Our own house. Our own perfectly polished brass knocker." Her hands were rough from weeks of refurbishing. Her nails were short and jagged. He kissed the tips of her fingers. "This is paradise."

"Almost," she said. "It'll be paradise when all the bathrooms are papered."

Maybe he was uxorious. He'd looked it up: foolishly fond of one's wife. He wasn't foolish about her. He loved her. Foolish would be getting involved with Iris Betts. Or any of them.

What did they want from him, a fast roll in the hay? And did they think the best way to get him was sneaking up behind him when he was waiting in the wings for his cue—like the producer's wife of *Romeo and Juliet*—and sticking her tongue in his ear? With three or four people standing around. Didn't she care? What did she think she was going to accomplish? Or that other one, coming up to him after an Actors Against the War rally and instead of saying "Hi, I'm Mary Smith" or whatever it was, saying "I want to suck you out"? He'd never seen her before. She wore flat shoes and a cardigan sweater with pockets and looked like a social worker. He was positive he'd heard her wrong until she added, "I want to swallow every drop." Was that what he was supposed to risk his marriage for? Or for some jiggling pig like Iris Betts who walked into his dressing room, turned her back to him, slipped off her robe, and said, "Hook my bra for me, Nicky," and then got all hot and huffy when he blew up and told her to get the hell out?

Or did they expect him to have an affair with them, the way that costume designer did, after she'd asked him all about Vicky and Liz, asked to see pictures, asked all about living in Connecticut, asked him about Jane, for Christ's sake? Did they think that was the key to his heart, making him talk about his family during out-of-town tryouts and then putting a hand on his and saying, "I'll bet it's lonesome for you, hon"?

Objectively, he knew that all the majority of women would do was say Hello, how are you, hasn't the weather been awful? But almost every day now he felt assaulted by the minority. In school and college, girls had flirted but if he didn't respond they'd go and flirt with someone else. Now if he didn't respond, they tried again, harder. And they no longer began by fluttering their eyelashes. They began by offering their hand to shake and then scratching his palm with a fingernail.

Some of them were all right. Bitsy Kagan, who'd been two years behind Jane at Pembroke, who'd been in Sock and Buskin, had moved to New York and was trying to make it as a lighting designer. She never did anything overt, but she managed to be backstage at whatever play he was in, visiting a friend, at least one night a week. Or she'd call Jane at home and cry that she was down in the dumps and Jane would pressure him to take Bitsy out for a drink and cheer her up. Bitsy never came on to him, but she'd stand beside him at Joe Allen's, her face so eager he felt sick for her.

They all wanted so much. He could see it in their eyes. They all seemed to know precisely what he did not: exactly what he should do for them.

Sometimes he could read between the lines. He'd gotten a letter at the theater. The notepaper had been engraved *Mrs. Floyd Childers III* with an asterisk inked next to the name; at the bottom was *alias Diana Howard*. She'd written about how "gloriously right" he'd been in *The Importance of Being Earnest* and how much she and Floyd would love to see him and Jane if they had a free night—*We're in Darien, barely the blink of an eyelash away from you good folk*—but if their social calendar was filled, she—*inveterate theatergoer that I am*—would love to meet him one Wednesday before or after his matinee *so we might reminisce about our warm, wonderful, ancient days together*. He couldn't believe he'd come close to marrying someone who could write such a jerky letter. He wanted to show it to Jane because it was so funny and so awful, but he realized the humor might elude her. He'd dropped Diana a note saying he was busy with rehearsals, but he and Jane looked forward to seeing her and Floyd in the near future. A lie.

And what did the strangers want? They wrote to him at the theater saying how much they loved his performance and asked, *Remember me? The one in the fourth row you were looking at (I think!?!) Thursday night. I have shoulder-length frosted hair and was wearing a lilac mandarin collar shirtdress*. Or their letters said they'd love to discuss his interpretation of Algernon Moncrieff with him—*perhaps you played it a tad too tongue-in-cheek, Mr. Cobleigh, but then again, perhaps not*. Did they expect him to call and say, Hi. It's Nicholas Cobleigh. Let's meet for a drink and discuss my interpretation of Algernon Moncrieff?

Did the women who waited at the stage door want anything more than a smile and his autograph? What did the one with the camera want? She was there almost every night, with a camera and flash, and she snapped her one picture and disappeared toward Ninth Avenue. Her hair was so sparse, patches of scalp showed. She only looked at him through the camera. He never saw her eyes. Once he'd tried leaving a half hour late, but she'd been there, alone, waiting, and snapped his picture.

Did his being an actor bring it out? He hadn't wanted to belabor the subject of other women with Jane, but the couple of times he'd talked about it with her she'd ventured it might have something to do with the actor as role player. Just as actors became the characters the playwrights delineated, so they were chosen to flesh out roles in people's imaginations. Also, Jane had said, you're safe. You're not real to them. You're on the stage.

But she'd been thinking about fans. He was real enough to Iris Betts. If he were a lawyer, he couldn't imagine a woman lawyer or a secretary coming into his office and closing the door and saying "Hook my bra." It wasn't that lawyers weren't interested in sex; look at his father. His father had been better-looking than he, but he couldn't believe his father was pursued in the way he was. Picked at. As though the women were hungry birds wanting to peck out pieces of him.

He didn't know what any of them wanted really, and he suspected if he did try and satisfy them it wouldn't be enough. Early, during rehearsals, Iris Betts had taken his face in her hands and said, "Now what would it be like to see this face with this magnificent hair on a black satin pillowcase in a candlelit room? Hundreds of flickering candles." He'd pulled away, thinking it sounded awful, like some weird black mass. But later he realized Iris Betts wasn't worrying about what he thought. He really didn't matter. Her image of him was better than he could ever be. She'd imagined him so clearly that if he actually took her to bed she'd be disappointed. Probably angry too, because he'd failed her.

He rejected them all, gently or brusquely. Usually they were out of his mind before they were out of the room. Now and then one made an impression. He remembered the *Washington Star* reporter who came to interview him during tryouts for *House on Fire;* she'd worn a pink minidress and had sat across from him in a club chair in his hotel room. Her dress inched up and he could see the top of her white lace tights. She had spectacular legs, and every few minutes she'd cross or uncross them. He could hear lace against lace. He'd gotten a hard-on and had crossed his legs and clasped his hands in his lap and then realized she knew exactly what he was doing. She spread her legs apart so he could see the crotch of her tights. What did she want from him, to grab her and throw her onto the bed? When the interview was over she dropped her pen, and when she bent over to pick it up he could see her whole ass, the tights stuck in the crack between the cheeks. She wasn't wearing underpants; he could see pink flesh gleaming under the white fabric. Did she want to get laid? Was she just teasing him, trying to see how worked up she could get him? He'd walked her to the door and as he was saying goodbye she'd put her ballpoint pen up to her mouth and flicked the little button up and down with her tongue. He'd closed the door behind her, gone into the bathroom, and jerked off into a washcloth. He came in about thirty seconds, but it had taken nearly a half hour for him to feel steady enough to call Jane.

He had a right to be uxorious. She was a wonderful wife. She was a good mother. He'd been a little worried, because the only one she'd had to learn from had been Dorothy Heissenhuber, but Jane the mother was like Jane the person: loving, funny, eager to please, and painfully insecure. He had to reassure her all the time that she was doing a good job. Of course you had to yell at Vicky, he'd say. She was being a royal pain. Come on, Jane. She'll get over it.

She'd been such a terrible cook that one Valentine's Day he'd given her a French cookbook, hoping she'd take the hint. She did. Within a few months she could have gotten a job in a three-star restaurant in Paris. If he didn't stop her, she'd spend an entire day making a sauce. Until they'd moved from the city, his father had taken to dropping in once or twice a week around dinner-time, ostensibly to see the children but actually because he liked Jane's cooking—and Jane.

Everyone liked her. Murray King never addressed her by her name but with Yiddish endearments. Murray submitted plays to her before he showed them to Nick, because he trusted Jane's judgment more. "Nicky," he said, "she's got a nose. When everyone thinks it's a flower and she says it's a skunk, you know what? It's black with a white stripe down its back."

His brother Tom had spent his first year as a Congregational minister in Syracuse mailing his sermons to Jane for editing.

The actors he'd become friendly with would call Jane not only to discuss their roles but to chat. They loved her straightforwardness, thought her the epitome of normality.

His friends from college sometimes blanched at the straightforwardness the theater people adored. Instead, they thought her arty and daring. But scintillating.

Even Charlie Harrison, whose women were invariably so exquisitely bred that a hearty laugh might induce serious internal bleeding, was drawn to Jane. On his visits from Boston, he'd deposit his date with Nicholas and spend hours in the kitchen talking to Jane, while Nicholas agonized trying to find something to say to Sarah, whose skin was so white it took on the blue hue of the veins beneath it, or to Katherine, whose clothes were so tatty and whose hair so stringy that Nicholas assumed she must come from one of the best families in Boston—which she did.

Nicholas put his arm around Jane and drew her tight against him. Charlie knew what was good. She was lovely. She had a secret beauty only a few could discern. Her incredible pansy-blue eyes lit up her dark face. He kissed her and caressed her breasts. After nursing the babies, they had lost their re-silience. They were heavier, sagging a little in his hands, and the areolas had darkened from perfect rose to a reddish brown. But that made them more appealing, more his. He didn't want her to be too desirable. He didn't want her head turned. He opened the top button on her shirt.

"Hey!" Jane said, and pulled away from him. She jumped up and picked the grass off her skirt.

"What's the matter?"

"A car. Car. Nick, you're foggy. C-a-r. Hear it? It's either the hardware man bringing the wallpaper steamer or your children, but in either case it is not appropriate for us to be seen in a major clinch on the front lawn."

"Jane."

"What?"

"Do you love me?"

"Are you still feeling insecure about the bridge of your nose?"

"No. I just want to know."

"Of course I love you. How could I not love you?"

"Why?"

"Why do I love you? I don't know. Whim, I guess. It's either you or the hardware man. Don't think I haven't been tempted. I don't dare tell you what goes on in the annex where they keep the lawnmowers. Lewdness and lust."

"Jane—"

"Hey, doesn't that sound like a law firm?" She squinted at the car coming up the gravel drive. "Oh, God! I don't believe it! Nick, look who it is!"

She finished the dishes at nine, but it took nearly an hour more to get the girls into bed. They were overstimulated by their Uncle Rhodes's visit. Victoria refused to change into pajamas, insisting on wearing to bed the tiny yellow bikini Rhodes had brought her from the Riviera. It was little more than a few minuscule triangles held together with string. "Perfect for a six-year-old Connecticut child," she'd remarked to her brother, and Rhodes had responded, "Are you kidding? You know I'm her only hope." Elizabeth—usually cuddly and compliant—had jumped up and down on her bed, waving to Jane and repeating "Bon soir, ma douce" mimicking Rhodes's accent and snide manner. Jane came close to marching out and slamming the door to her room.

Rhodes grinned at her as she entered the parlor. He was lounging in an easy chair whose back, wings, and arms were so broad that merely to sit in it was to be embraced. The chair, a late eighteenth-century piece probably of Hepplewhite design, was covered in heavy silk printed with large, full-blooming flowers. Rhodes was a modern rebuke to its venerable solidity. He was so sleek, Jane thought, and so flawlessly beautiful he seemed created by machine. He hoisted the brandy snifter he was holding.

"Cheers," Jane said.

"Now I know I'm back in the States," Rhodes said. "'Cheers.' I suppose that's the official invocation at your PTA lunches. A little Bloody Mary. A little celery with cream cheese." He'd dressed for dinner like a European: white linen slacks, a tissue-thin white silk shirt—open nearly to the waist—white straw shoes. A long red scarf was knotted around his neck like a tie.

302

"In ten minutes you could be standing on Route Seven hitching a ride into New York," Jane said. "If anyone would have you."

"Everyone would have me, as you very well know. As opposed to you. How much longer do you think the toast of Broadway is going to drag you around?"

Nicholas smiled. He was sprawled along the couch, looking hopelessly provincial in madras slacks and a blue golf shirt. But, Jane suspected, half the Frenchmen in the south of France doubtlessly looked hopelessly provincial beside her brother. She walked to the couch, lifted Nicholas's legs, sat, then lowered them onto her lap. "Did I miss any good conversation?"

"We were talking investments," Nicholas said.

"Southwestern real estate," Rhodes said. "Here he is, a Tony nomination, a 'People Are Talking About' in *Vogue*, and the thing that makes him pant with delight is that they're refinancing his shopping center and he has the thrilling choice of putting his money in an apartment complex in Houston or another shopping center in Tucson. Did you know you married a capitalist?"

"I do now," Jane said. Her brother swished the brandy in his glass. Rhodes was the only person who realized what had finally dawned on her: Nicholas was a businessman. He spent more time on the phone with his Uncle Caleb, a banker, his father, and his stockbroker than he did with his agent. Nicholas skimmed *Variety,* but he devoured *Barron's*. The realization had stunned Jane: Nicholas was dedicated to carrying on his family's tradition— being rich.

"Jane isn't interested in money. She thinks there's someone like the tooth fairy who comes at night and puts money into checking accounts," Nicholas said.

"Oh, investments are my favorite subject in the world," Rhodes said. "Especially real estate. *So* stimulating. Well, my favorite subject except for commodities futures. Now *that's* thrilling. It's all I hear about. Philip's found himself a new commodities genius in Chicago and he only talks to him eight hours a day. And then for the next eight hours he wants to relive the entire conversation, so he can savor every golden syllable."

Jane massaged Nicholas's bare feet. "At least Nick keeps it to himself," she said. "Every once in a while he'll burst out with something about oil depletion allowances, but most of the time he pretends to be the strong silent type."

"Do you always do that disgusting thing to his feet?" Rhodes demanded.

"He loves it."

"It feels great," Nicholas said.

"You two make marriage seem so enticing. Oh, speaking of filthy lucre, Philip's taken to financing movies. I asked him to put in a good word about

Nick with this cross-eyed shoe-fetishist producer he's backing. The one who made *Blackwell* and *Close to Rome*."

"Thank you," Nicholas said.

"How is he?" Jane asked. "Philip, not the shoe fetishist."

"Philip? Oh, wonderfully scintillating. Out of two weeks in Cap d'Antibes, he spent thirteen days on the phone with Mr. Commodities and with some greaser in Berne who does things with precious metals. He's paler now than when we left Cincinnati."

"Well, you look wonderful," Jane said.

"What did you expect? Quasimodo?"

"I mean, you have a good tan."

"A great tan. Not dark like you, of course. But then, I don't have your checkered racial pedigree."

"My mother's mother was Spanish."

"That's what they all say."

"Just stop it, Rhodes." She looked down at Nicholas. He was watching them as if he were observing two actors doing a first reading of an amusing play. His hair, which he'd grown long for the role he'd just finished, had fallen across his forehead and was hanging into his eyes. She leaned over and brushed it back for him.

"You know," Rhodes said to her, "you could look semi-decent if you put on a little makeup instead of going around playing country squirette. I mean, no one would call your complexion peaches and cream. Why don't you leave the pristine face to the Anglo-Saxons?"

"My mother's father happened to have been English."

"Your mother's father was probably a renegade Indian."

"How was the Hôtel du Cap?" Nicholas asked.

"Fabulous. Almost worth working for Philip Gray for. But you're trying to change the subject."

"I know," Nicholas answered, "because if I don't she's going to get up and hit you."

"She won't hit me. She adores me. I mean, *really* adores me. All these years she's harbored a wild incestuous desire for me. Too bad my taste doesn't run to Amazons in pastel-flowered shirtwaists. Cute. Do you wear little flowered hats to church?"

"Hardly anyone wears hats to church any more, and if you'd come with us tomorrow—"

"Are you going to put Vicky and Liz in little white gloves with little patent leather shoes and anklets?"

"Cut it out, Rhodes."

"Did you ever go to church when you were a kid?" Nicholas asked.

"No." Rhodes shrugged his shoulders.

304

Jane looked at her brother. "Do you remember them ever talking about anything having to do with religion? Did Dorothy ever teach you to say your prayers or anything?"

"She's Dorothy now?"

"Yes."

"Did Dorothy ever teach me to say my prayers? No. Nothing. Come to think of it, I don't think I ever heard the word God in the house. Did you?"

"No. I have a vague memory of going to church with Grandma Anna and Grandpa Carl and I know I was baptized, but I guess that was my mother's influence."

"Do you go every Sunday?"

"Yes."

"Do you like it?"

Jane looked at Nicholas. "It's nice. He likes it a lot. He's used to it, and Tom went to the seminary with our minister, so it would look funny if we didn't go."

"Come on," Nicholas said. "You like to go."

"Well, I don't *love* it."

"No one *loves* church," Nicholas said.

"I don't know. Some people do."

"It's a place to go to think about things you don't usually have time for," Nicholas explained. "And it's nice to see the same people week after week. You keep expecting a profound religious experience. An epiphany. The roof will open and light will pour down on you and suddenly you'll comprehend the universe. It's not like that."

"I'll say!" Jane breathed. "Oh, come on. Don't look so annoyed. If I really had a religious bent, I'd probably have become a Catholic. Or would have, when they had the mass in Latin. All that chanting and the candles and the genuflecting. I used to go to Catholic church with my roommate Amelia freshman year. Didn't I ever tell you that? *That's* religion. Going to confession. 'Bless me, Father, for I have sinned.' Kneeling down and all that. It's kind of neat."

"What would you confess to?" Nicholas demanded.

Rhodes finished his brandy and set his glass on the rug. "What do you think she's doing when you're driving down to New York and going onstage and pouring your heart out to hundreds of patrons of the arts?" he demanded. "Do you think she's reading or making another needlepoint pillow?"

"That's what she tells me."

"She's probably out in the stable performing unnatural acts with your horse."

Nicholas laughed. "The horse is a mare."

"You don't know your wife, do you?"

305

"Rhodes, you're really disgusting," Jane said.

"How are your parents?" Nicholas broke in.

Rhodes reached out for the bottle of brandy on the table beside him and bent and retrieved his glass. He poured himself a large drink. "They're okay."

Nicholas lifted his legs from Jane's lap and sat up, facing Rhodes. "You know, I called them after Vicky was born and after Liz was born. They never called Jane in the hospital. They never indicated any interest in seeing the girls. They never sent a gift or a card. I don't understand them. Jane's their daughter. Vicky and Liz are their granddaughters. How do you think they make Jane feel?"

"I don't want to be put in the position of explaining them," Rhodes said. "I can't. My mother and Jane . . . well, the chemistry was always bad, but at least it's somewhat understandable. She's a stepmother, even though she was nowhere near as bad as Jane likes to think she was. Jane carries on like she held matches to the soles of her feet every morning before breakfast. She's really blown everything out of proportion. My mother happened to have been pretty decent to her."

"You don't know what you're talking about!" Jane shouted. Nicholas and Rhodes sat back, nonplussed at her vehemence.

"All right," Nicholas said softly. "Let's drop the subject."

"You drop the subject, damn it! You were so insulated with nannies and maids you hardly even saw your parents. Your parents were never home. You said—"

"Jane, calm down."

"You calm down! Do you have any idea what it was like living in a house where one parent hated you and the other one was completely indifferent? Do you?"

The room seemed to reject her emotion. It was old and secure and silent. The gleaming russet-brown wood paneling around the fireplace and the silvered brass dial on the cherrywood tall clock were rebukes to her raised voice. The reds, blues, and greens of the Persian rug were all in low tones.

"Dad wasn't indifferent," Rhodes said. It was his usual voice, but more mellow: controlled, calm, soothing, like the parlor. "You shouldn't minimize what he did. He was awful. I remember when he used to take you upstairs and hit—"

"Shut up!"

"It's true. Jesus Christ, Jane, it was horrible. I used to have to stay downstairs, and I could hear you screaming and screaming. I'll never ever forget it. I hated him so much."

"He *hit* you?" Nicholas asked. "You never said anything about it. Why didn't you—"

"It was nothing," Jane snapped.

306

"Are you crazy?" Rhodes demanded. Suddenly his voice was like hers: midwestern, loud, not cowed by the gentility of the New England parlor. "It must have been every damn week. For years. Until I was nine or ten. How the hell can you say it was nothing? How can you stand there and say terrible things about her after all he did to you? Don't you have any memory? Come on, Jane! You know damn well how sick—"

Jane stalked across the room, stood before her brother, and screamed at him. "Leave me alone, damn it! You leave me alone or you get out of this house. Do you hear me, Rhodes? Do you? Every time you come in you pick on me and pick on me and I'm sick of it!"

Nicholas walked to her and put his arms around her. "Jane, come on. He wasn't picking on you."

"I'm on your side," Rhodes said. His voice wobbled. "Jane, you know what he was. This boring man with his opera records and his accounting magazines was a sadistic—"

Jane's hand whipped out and cracked her brother across the side of his face. "Stop it!" she howled. "Stop it! Stop it! Stop it!"

18

WOMAN'S VOICE: Listen, we're not . . . this isn't going to be a discussion about—you know, like she's in the hospital and is she or isn't she going to have brain surgery and all that. What we're going to try to do is—uh, sit around and try and figure out what the—I'm trying to think of the right word—what the essence of superstardom is. I mean, we wouldn't have ever heard about her if it wasn't for him. And what is there about *him* that's kept him a symbol of . . . what? Of ultimate WASP masculinity? It's not as simple as that. And what is there about them as a couple that gets to us? And her? Last night, I was on line at the Regency. They're showing *Wyoming*, which happens to be his only Western, and someone said, With him everyone either wants to hump him or have him for President.
                                        —S. W. Zises, WBAI Radio, New York

Nearly everyone in California had asked him, "Do you play tennis?" And when he'd said yes, they'd responded, "Fabulous! We *must* get a game in." After a few days, he realized it was the West Coast equivalent of "Let's have lunch," so at a time when running along public thoroughfares was rare enough to be considered mildly eccentric, after each day's shooting he put on his tennis sneakers and ran through the streets of Los Angeles. He had to. He ached from the still life at the studio. Twice he'd been stopped by patrol cars and had to produce his hotel key to prove he was no psychopath or rapist on a scouting expedition. (The producer had arranged for him to stay in the Los Reyes, a small place filled with marginal moguls. His room smelled of floral Air-Wick and long-dead cigars.)

He lived in a section of Los Angeles that had no name. His hotel was a cube of yellow with tiny terraces offering the only relief from the flat facade; the outsides of the terraces were also yellow, so they looked like pustules rising from the skin of the building. From his terrace he could see the stores across the street: a take-out sandwich shop, an optician, a dry cleaner, and a pharmacy. The last had a huge cutout of a busty blonde in a two-piece bathing suit on display, an advertisement for a suntan oil, but it had been in the window so long her skin had faded to a light green. A white cube, a one-story stucco office building on the next block, was the only other sign of commerce; the sign in the front suggested a podiatrist and an electrologist were busy within, but Nicholas thought only the most desperate bunion sufferers, the homeliest human chimpanzees, would walk through the smeary glass door of 5527 North Pacific Boulevard.

All around were miles of tract houses. They looked cramped and uninviting, the sort of houses shoe salesmen would live in. Actually, when he thought about it, they reminded him of the Heissenhubers' house in Cincinnati, inhabited but unembellished, as though their owners hated them. They were ranch houses with a Spanish flavor: white with wavy red roofs that approximated tile. Some had a small rectangle of grass on either side of the front walk, but many had covered the space over with flat rocks the size of fifty-cent pieces. In the middle of one there was a statue of a liveried servant holding a lantern. Its head had been knocked off its body; the motive could be seen in the jagged remains of a black neck. Nicholas smiled whenever he passed. It was a satisfying piece of vandalism, more so because the owner was too stubborn or too stupid to remove the smashed statue; it pleased Nicholas that such a man lived in such a mean little house.

But he didn't hate Los Angeles, even though he knew it was the fashionable thing to do. He loved the climate, waking up in October and having coffee outside on the terrace. He was impressed with the aggressive informality of the city, where everyone said "hi" and no one said "hello." People exposed as much of themselves as they could. Men, if they wore jackets at all, took them off and rolled up their sleeves, opened their shirts to let you know exactly what they were: crosses, crucifixes, and stars of David dangled from chains on tanned or hairy chests. Women wore dresses of eyelet or with cutouts, to offer little peeks of what was available. Not a single person had called him "Mister" since his arrival. He couldn't imagine joining them, but he liked to watch their promiscuous kissing of acquaintances, their openly expressed glee over anything new. "*Love* the shirt!" "*Where* did you get that pen? Where in New York? God, I love it!" Many of them, he knew, were phony. But some were simply more natural than Easterners; they had an uncomplicated delight in good weather and bright objects.

Still, he couldn't be part of it. Maybe it was being dislocated, just being there for a month, knowing he was missing his first autumn in Connecticut, missing his family, missing Murray. It wasn't like an out-of-town tryout, where he knew people, where he had colleagues to have breakfast or go for a drink with. Here, he was a New York actor with a small part. Other than two not wildly enthusiastic propositions, one from an assistant director—male—and another from a publicist—female—no one showed any interest in where he went at the end of the day. He acted, read a biography of Theodore Roosevelt and several John Dickson Carr mysteries, and called Jane.

The only physical pleasure he got was from running, and that was not really fun. There was no game to it, no real skill; it was just work. But at least it knocked him out, although he had to force himself farther and farther to achieve the same effect.

Rhodes's prodding of Philip Gray—and Philip Gray's call to the producer he was backing—had obviously been effective. Within days of Rhodes's visit,

Nicholas was invited to California for a screen test. Before the film from the test was even developed, it seemed, he was offered a small but interesting role in the producer's upcoming film. The producer himself had even taken him to the Polo Lounge of the Beverly Hills Hotel and told him over drinks how he'd seen Nicholas on Broadway and was just on the verge of calling him himself when Philip Gray had telephoned. "He's your brother-in-law?" the producer asked.

"No." Many of the women milling about were so flawlessly beautiful they seemed supernatural. A brunette passed a redhead and they quickly examined each other, then turned away. The brunette wore a sarong that exposed her navel. On top she wore what looked like a brassiere made of gold chains attached to a wide gold ring in her cleavage. The redhead wore silver sandals that laced up her legs and a white minidress that bared one shoulder. They might be goddesses at a convention, but no one seemed stunned by them except Nicholas, who wondered if they were starlets or prostitutes. They didn't look real. They looked as if they never spoke. A few of them wore small, anticipatory smiles, as if momentarily expecting good news. "My brother-in-law works for Philip Gray," Nicholas added, wondering if the producer had noticed he hadn't been paying attention. The producer, glugging down his fourth gin and orange juice, apparently had not.

"Oh. I wasn't sure what the connection was." The producer looked past him and signaled for the check.

"Well, it's sort of a double connection. Philip's married to my cousin."

"Let me order you a refill."

Most theater people Nicholas had spoken with had one comment about making movies: take the money and run. The work was so fragmented as to be almost meaningless. You rarely had more than three or four lines at a time. Then you'd wait. And wait. People took up hobbies to kill the time. Jeff Barault, who'd played Mercutio to his Romeo Off Broadway, had spent two months on location in the Philippines building furniture. It had cost him five hundred dollars to ship home three ornately carved wood armchairs, and one of them arrived looking more like a pile of kindling than something to sit on. An actress he knew, a sweet-tempered woman typecast as a sour old maid— she could contract her lips into a particularly hateful line—knit mufflers whenever she made a film. Nearly everyone she'd ever worked with had six feet of intricately worked wool. In winter, an actor might pass a stage manager spitting out the purple and white fringes the sharp wind on Forty-fifth Street had blown into his mouth and say, "Is that a *Come Summer* muffler?" The stage manager, lifting a hair-thin purple squiggle from his tongue, would respond, "No. *The Twelve Months of Judith Lane*. *Come Summer* is beige and brown."

Of course, the two biggest time killers were hustling for the next job—

reading scripts, phoning agents, making friends with people at the studio who might prove valuable—and having love affairs.

Still, Nicholas mused, it really wasn't all that boring. He had spent his first day repeating the same few gestures and two lines, but it was far less wearing than acting in commercials. Once he'd spent two days filming a commercial for the California Artichoke Cooperative, walking through a door, dropping an attaché case, and having the actress who played his wife leap into his arms and demand, "Guess what I have that's green and new and absolutely yummy?" as he carried her across the suburban living room set. He'd sprained his back and spent a week lying flat on the floor with pillows under his neck and knees, with Jane having to help him up whenever he had to go to the bathroom. In the end, the cooperative had fired the agency and the commercial was never aired.

But here he had a character. True, it was another coldblooded-bastard character, but it didn't bother him. If someone was willing to give him ten thousand dollars for a month's work, he'd play the biggest bastard in the world.

The last quarter mile back to the hotel was uphill, and by the time he got to the entrance he was gasping, his throat sore as it tried to open wider and accommodate more air. In the elevator, a man in a red and pink checked sport jacket eyed him with disgust, staring at the shirt that clung to him like a membrane.

After he showered—he loved showers and they only had tubs at the house—he called Jane. She said he sounded bored.

"I'm not bored," he said, trying to chew silently the ham and cheese sandwich room service had brought a moment earlier. "A little tired. I got to the studio before six and we spent the whole day on one scene, the one where I meet them. Remember?"

"Of course I remember. I was right. You have to be bored. You know how you need to be challenged. I mean, honestly, what is this: three or four lines and then you look meaningfully at them. Isn't that the scene?"

"Yes. But it's not that bad."

"Oh, Nick, come on."

He realized, after they'd said goodbye, how annoyed he was getting with her. Every single damned night she made some remark about how terrible acting in movies was. If she wasn't telling him it must be boring or depressing that he wasn't utilizing his talents, she was giving him a negative review of the latest rerun she'd seen on TV. He hoped he never came up against such a harsh critic; every actor was prostituting himself, every screenplay was either insipid or inept.

This screenplay wasn't brilliant, but he'd appeared in much worse both on and off Broadway. The leads weren't bad. The actress, Julie Spahr, looked

311

too glossy for the antipoverty worker she was playing, but her performance rang true enough; her character was emotional, dedicated, and naive as hell. And the star, David Whitman, was first rate.

But two weeks later, he realized Jane hadn't been entirely unjust about the screenplay. His own character had less depth than the paper it was written on; he was a stereotype, a corrupt public official, a perfect villain for the antiestablishment theme of the movie: a slick bad guy helping to destroy a couple of pure, high-minded lives. He played the mayor of a medium-sized New England city, the man the two main characters, an architect and his social-worker wife, approach to get help for an abandoned neighborhood of beautiful but shabby Victorian row houses they are trying to save from the wrecker's ball and renovate as an artists' community.

The director wanted Nicholas to be charming and sincere, a shirt-sleeved, rumpled-haired Kennedy type who engages the architect's trust and the social worker's interest. The main characters have no idea that the character Nicholas is playing has been bought, bribed by businessmen who want the neighborhood destroyed so they can build an industrial park. The final scene had no dialogue. It was a series of intercuts: the wreckers, like military tanks, inching along the shady streets of the deserted old neighborhood; the architect driving off to the state capital, his face bright with the false hope the mayor has instilled in him; the social worker, at the mayor's office for a working lunch, being seduced by him; all the dilapidated but still graceful houses—one after another—being reduced to rubble by wrecker's balls and dynamite.

"I think I should show a little suspicion," Julie Spahr said to the director. "Just a little. To give a little more texture."

"Julie, you don't have any idea of what's on Nick's mind. All you know is that you're very—let's see, uptight. You're hot for him, but you haven't admitted that to yourself yet because your husband is such a terrific, perfect guy. But you're also almost giddy with relief because you think the neighborhood's been saved. So you're a mass or a mess or a lot of emotions. Okay?" She nodded portentously, as if she'd just learned the location of the Holy Grail.

Hank Giordano, the director, held Nicholas's arm and paced his walk along the curved blue line—Nicholas's color; Julie's was red—taped on the floor, around the desk to the chair Julie was seated in. "Easy," he said, as if Nicholas were a toddler who might run too fast, fall, and hurt himself. "Good. Now stand right up against the back of her chair. That's it. Press up hard against it like it was her. You're supposed to be a sexy guy. Good. Okay. Nick, get back to your desk and we'll try the whole thing. You ready, Julie?"

"Hank, I just think my hair's too messy."

Nicholas returned to the big chrome and leather chair behind what was the mayor's desk and swallowed his sigh. It was twelve thirty, and they hadn't

312

shot an inch of film. Julie Spahr had spent half the morning trying to sort out her character's emotions, even though she, Nicholas, and Giordano had had a long conference on the scene the day before. She'd spent the other half of the morning debating whether she would wear blue eyeshadow, another subject that had been discussed nearly *ad nauseam* at the conference. She thought she shouldn't wear eyeshadow. The director disagreed, saying it was her unconscious way of primping for the mayor.

"Julie, you're a social worker. You wear jeans and flannel shirts and your hair shouldn't look like you just stepped out of Madame Fifi's."

"Then why the eyeshadow?"

"Because you're not a fashion plate. You want to doll yourself up a little for this guy."

"But you just said I don't know yet that I'm hot for him."

She said this without looking in Nicholas's direction, but then she hadn't looked in his direction for the three weeks since he'd come to California. She responded to his hellos grudgingly, as if the energy expended on them was being deducted from her life force; he was, after all, merely a New York actor in a supporting role in his first film.

"You're hot for him subconsciously, Julie."

"I think it will cheapen the scene."

"Julie—"

"Hank, I wouldn't be making a stand if I didn't think it involved the integrity of the film."

Hank Giordano clasped his hands in front of his chest. He looked like a barrel with arms and legs. "I'll tell you what. We'll shoot with eyeshadow and without eyeshadow. If it doesn't work I swear to God I'll use without."

"And my hair this way and then combed out."

"No."

"Hank—"

"Let's just do eyeshadow, then we'll talk hair."

Spahr thrust out her lip in a little-girl pout. "I hate to say it, Hank, but I can't keep it in. I'm afraid you'll very conveniently forget about my hair." She was in her mid-thirties and looked it, yet she had a repertoire of childish gestures: staring directly at people with wide, awed eyes; sucking the tip of her thumb when she was, presumably, deep in thought.

"Julie, you know, you really hurt me."

Nicholas glanced away. The cinematographer caught his eye and mouthed Bullshit.

"I didn't mean—all right, we'll do it your way, Hank. But I'm putting my faith in you."

"You won't be sorry, Julie." She put the tips of her fingers to her lips and threw the director a kiss. "All right. Let's get started. Nick, you ready? When you walk, slow yourself down. You've got nothing but time. You've got to keep her busy all afternoon so she can't get back until the place is leveled. Okay."

"Quiet on the set," a voice called. "This is a take."

After three walks to the back of Julie Spahr's chair, the director was satisfied. Nicholas repeated the walk another five times while they shot Julie's reaction—which might be cut in when the film was edited.

A half hour later he did what he was supposed to. He stood behind her, pressed against the chair. As she was supposed to, Julie stiffened. Nicholas looked down at the top of her head. Her scalp was bright pink, sore looking, he supposed from hair dye. He let the corners of his mouth move upward. He needn't smile with contempt. This was film. The camera picked up the smallest gesture. Accustomed to the broader gestures of the stage, he felt constricted, ineffective. Every day on the set, his whole body ached with unexpressed motion.

He took the Styrofoam cup of coffee from her hand, leaned forward, and placed it on the desk. He allowed two seconds for her to register panic with an opened mouth and darting eyes. Then he cupped her under the chin with his right hand and pulled her head back so she was forced to look into his eyes. He peered into her eyes for four seconds, counting one-banana, two-banana . . . He brought his left hand around and massaged her throat, letting his fingers drift under the neckline of her peasant blouse. Her skin was greasy with makeup and sweat. The lights were exceptionally hot. His ears must be bright red. They were using "in limbo" lighting; only the actors and the chair were lit; the background was nearly blacked out.

He stared into her eyes. She tried to turn away but he drew her head even farther back, letting his lips part into a more open expression of amusement and contempt. He could tell her neck hurt, but he didn't ease up. He really didn't give a damn. Julie's chin quivered, as rehearsed, in his hand; he tightened his grip on it. With what little maneuverability she had, she shook her head no. Her eyes were frightened. His were cool and intent, as if observing a butterfly that he'd trapped beating its wings against a glass jar. Then he lowered his left hand deeper under her blouse, holding her chin at such an angle that she couldn't pull away. Still looking into her eyes, he gave her a cold smile of triumph.

"Cut! Print it!"

"Jesus Christ!" the cinematographer exploded a moment later. "You were incredible!"

"Thank you," Julie Spahr said.

The cinematographer nodded, then looked over her head and, almost imperceptibly, doffed an invisible hat to Nicholas.

"What time is it in California, Vicky?" Elizabeth demanded.

Jane looked across the kitchen table to Victoria. "It's a little after six now. Come on. Six minus three."

"Three, Liz," Victoria said. "Three in the afternoon."

"What's Daddy doing?"

"Same thing he's always doing, stupid. Making a movie."

"Don't call your sister stupid," Jane said. Victoria looked down at her plate, but not before Jane saw her sullen mouth, its upper lip curled like a hostile teenager's. "Come on, Vicky. We agreed to have a nice pleasant supper together."

"A real movie," Elizabeth said. "Not a cartoon movie. Not like *Heckle and Jeckle*."

"That's right," Jane said. They'd had this discussion every night for the three and a half weeks Nicholas had been in California. "Daddy's a real person, not a drawing. So he'll look real in the movie."

"But flat," Elizabeth said.

"Yes. Flat, because it's . . ." She tried to think of a way to explain dimensionality to a child not quite four.

"Because it's a *picture* of Daddy," Victoria said. "A *picture*. Did you ever see a fat picture? Pictures are flat, not fat. Don't you remember when we saw Daddy's soap commercial on TV where he said, 'You really work up a sweat playing basketball'? Remember? He had a number fifteen on his shirt."

"No," Elizabeth said. "Was that a movie?"

"Oh, God!" Victoria breathed.

Jane put her hand up. "If there's one piece of chicken left on anybody's plate there won't be dessert tonight."

"What's for dessert?" Victoria demanded.

"A surprise."

"Probably fresh fruit with brown mush spots."

"It's not. It's something very special, and that's the last thing I have to say until I see two empty plates."

"Do you want us to eat the bones?"

"Quiet! No more talking."

The girls picked up their forks. Jane watched them. In a way it was too bad. Between Nicholas and Rhodes, the potential for beauty was obviously swimming around in the genetic pool in both families, but Victoria and Elizabeth were merely ordinary, nice-looking girls.

Victoria's brown hair was so straight that, when worn short, it could only be styled in a Dutch-boy cut. With her hooded blue eyes and pale, solemn face, Victoria did look the type who would stick her finger in a dike and keep it there, saving humanity while all the other six-year-old girls were off giggling and skating. She ate mechanically, piercing bits of food and bringing them to her mouth while keeping her eyes on her sister's progress. Suddenly she cleared her throat.

"What is it?" Jane asked.

"Liz is doing it again."

"Don't be a tattletale."

"I'm not. I'm just telling you where to look."

Elizabeth, nearly four, was dexterous enough with her fork to flip any vegetable onto the floor without calling attention to her action. The wood-planked floor around her chair was dotted with broccoli flowerets.

"Liz," Jane said, "eat your vegetables. Come on. I don't want to see any more broccoli on the floor. Do you hear me?"

"They fell."

Jane exhaled slowly. "Make sure it doesn't happen again."

"I'll try, but sometimes—"

"Elizabeth!" Elizabeth looked like Victoria with a permanent. Her hair was a frizzy aureole. On damp days, it retracted into tight corkscrew curls. Her eyes were rounder than her sister's, so round that if she'd been blond, she'd have been a ringer for the flapper who squeaked, "Boop, boop, be-doop." But she didn't squeak. Her voice was low and slightly husky like Nicholas's, and adults were always telling her to speak up.

"They didn't fall, Liz," Victoria suddenly interjected. "You did that thing with your fork."

"No I didn't."

"Yes you did. You think broccoli can fall off a plate? A plate goes up on the end, stupid baby."

"Stupid dummy!"

"Stupid dork doody-head!"

"Girls!"

"Stupid—"

"Okay. That's it. I was going to take you to Winkie's for an ice-cream cone, but—"

"*Please*, Mommy."

"Mommy, we'll be good."

"We'll apologize. Sorry, Liz. Now you say it to me."

"Sorry, Vicky."

"Can we go?"

The October night's chill was cutting enough to remind her of the near-ness of winter. Jane turned on the heat in the station wagon. A spring and summer's worth of stale air blew into her face. "Warm enough?" she asked. The girls, seat-belted behind her, silent in fear of jeopardizing their ice-cream cones, nodded in the rearview mirror.

A minute later, Jane lowered the heater. She thought, he'll be home in a week. He's been away for three weeks at a time for out-of-town tryouts. She'd managed. But this wasn't New Haven or Philadelphia. This was California. So far away that when he called her it was warm and bright—I'm sitting out on the little terrace; just came back from a quick dip in the pool—and in Connecticut it was a starless night. A north wind had replaced the Indian summer breeze; your Irish fisherman's sweater is on permanent loan to the Jane Cobleigh collection. The air was still pungent from the day's burnt leaves from the farm across the road.

She could manage. She was managing. Just that morning there were glugging noises in the pipes and she'd phoned and they came and pumped out the septic tank. She'd kept up with his family. She'd entertained Tom and his wife, Nan—Miss Christian Forbearance—for a weekend; she'd driven to New York to shop for flower-girl dresses with her mother-in-law and Olivia for a cousin's wedding; she'd fought with Abby until she'd won, convincing Abby that being maid of honor for her sister did not necessarily mean condoning organized religion or accepting monogamy as a viable life-style; she'd even talked with her father-in-law each week at his office. (Twice when she'd called his apartment, women had answered. One of them sounded so young that, had she not known better, she would have thought he was babysitting.)

Nicholas could do this again, she told herself. If the movie is good—although she didn't think it was—he might accept another role. He might be away for three or four months in some foreign country. Not likely. But he got itchy if he didn't have a new play lined up long before the old one closed. What if he had to go to Europe, to Africa? Her life was strictly a holding action. She kept the children and the house, read, cooked, sewed, but primarily waited for Nicholas to come home.

They ate their cones at a tiny round marble table at Winkie's. The ice-cream parlor had been on Main Street in the little town of Farcroft for generations. It was jammed after Friday and Saturday night movies, after Fourth of July fireworks, after the annual school band concert. In Farcroft and the surrounding countryside, it was the parents' ultimate weapon: "You can—or cannot—go to Winkie's" gave them power beyond whatever natural authority they wielded. Jane hated the place. The owner sat near the door hunched over the old brass cash register, a scrawny old Connecticut Yankee glaring at her through watery slit-eyes each time she walked in, as if she had designs on his rolls of pennies. And the smell of sour milk was as old as the stained glass and etched mirrors, milk someone must have spilled making butter pecan in 1904.

"Let's go," she said.

"We're not finished."

"I want to be home in time for Daddy's call."

"Mommy—"

"You can finish in the car."

"What's the matter, Mommy?"

"Nothing."

There was no moon. The sky hung low. She drove south from Farcroft, then east toward the farm. Her headlights were the only light, although now and then they'd reflect the bright dots of some rodent's eyes on the side of the road. She drove faster. She hated the walk from the garage to the house. It wasn't a real garage. It was an old toolshed in the back, just wide enough for the station wagon, and she'd have to inch along, her back against the wall, her stomach grazing the handle of the door as she got out. She was sure she'd turned the outside light on. She thought she had. Once she'd forgotten, and it wasn't until her ankle turned in the soft dirt of the herb garden that she realized she'd lost her bearings and had walked away from the house instead of toward it.

The darkness was terrible in the country. She kept candles in every room. She was in dread of a power failure. Being alone in a black house. Not being able to see the walls.

"Mommy, are you okay?"

"Yes."

She'd been out that afternoon bringing in the last of the thyme and basil. She should have worn a jacket. Her neck ached. She pressed the metal knob with her foot to check that her bright lights were on. It seemed too dark. They had been on bright. Her throat hurt. Maybe one of the children had brought home strep. Her throat seemed to be closing up. She didn't feel well at all.

Rounding a curve, the car skidded slightly on a sheet of wet leaves, then corrected itself. She clung to the wheel, eased the pressure on the accelerator until they were barely moving.

"Mommy?"

She hissed them quiet, leaning forward, staring into the darkness the better to see the road. She started to get hot. The odor of wet wool permeated the car. She tugged at the choking turtleneck collar. Her neck was burning. She had a fever. She didn't know what to do. Should she go home? What if she needed help during the night? Should she drive to a neighbor's? Her throat was closing up. So tight.

Suddenly she was dizzy. Oh, God, she thought, I'm having an attack. Like that day in Central Park. She was dizzy and her heart was pounding as it had that time, pounding because her throat was closing and she couldn't get enough oxygen, trying to get the blood to her brain so she wouldn't faint. The air passage was needle-thin now, and she was forced to swallow huge amounts of air just to keep alive. She had to stop the car, but giant trees crowded together on the edge of the road, fencing her in. She had to pull over before they went crashing into one of them. Oh, God, her heart was going too fast.

It would give out. She would die and the two girls would be left in the car with her body, screaming sick, wild shrieks, terrified of the blackness. Shaking her harder and harder—*Mommy!*—until she fell forward against the wheel, setting the horn off in an endless helpless honk. But then Victoria, dragging the clinging Elizabeth out finally, not seeing the car coming the other way—

"Mommy! Mommy! You passed our turn."

Somehow she backed up and got the car up the long gravel drive. She stopped in front of the house.

"Aren't you going into the garage?"

"Mommy?"

Her whole left side was battered by the crazy booming of her heart: her neck, her chest, under her arm. She leaned over and opened the car door with her right hand and nearly fell onto the ground. She stumbled to the house, leaving Victoria to unlatch Elizabeth's seat belt and take her inside. "I feel a little sick," she whispered.

She leaned against the wall of the long hall of the house. She'd left the light on. The glow from the brass chandelier filled the hall and staircase with yellow warmth.

"Mommy?"

"Mommy?"

The door to the parlor was open, and the wood paneling around the fireplace glowed from the captured light of the hall.

Victoria came up beside her and tapped her arm. "Mommy? Mommy, listen. Should I dial O?" Jane looked down at her. For the first time, she saw the girl's brown hair was giving off glints of red. "Should I?"

"No. No, I feel better now."

"Are you sure?"

"Yes. Thank you. All better now."

19

MAN'S VOICE: . . . although his agent, Murray King, said, and I quote: "I don't care what anyone at the studio said, they can stand on their heads and spit wooden nickels but Nicholas Cobleigh is not going back to the set of *William the Conqueror* until he knows what's what with his wife and that's that." End quote. I don't think you can get a more definitive statement than that. This is Bob Morvillo, and now back to *Today* in New York.
—NBC *Today* Show

"Listen, Nicky," Murray King said. "It's been—what?—eight, nine months since you finished the movie, and for almost seven months you've been sitting right on top of a Broadway hit. You hardly had time to unpack. Eight shows a week and no end in sight. Do I have to count the eyeteeth other actors would give to be in your shoes? I know you don't want to hear this, but you should get down on your hands and knees and thank God. This play is a blessing. . . . Where'd you learn to eat with chopsticks like that?"

"Jane. She's taken up Chinese cooking."

"It's my second favorite after Italian. It could possibly be my first, except they don't have desserts. You know? You can't call a kumquat dessert. So it's vanilla, chocolate, or pistachio and it's not even real pistachio any more. They took out the nuts and put in cherries."

They were seated at a table in a fashionable midtown restaurant, its decor more Bauhaus than Chinese. The light was so dim, reflecting off smoky mirrors, that all the food appeared to be different tones of beige. The place had become a hangout for publishing and theater people; the food wasn't bad and they liked the sophisticated thrill—after their pupils dilated sufficiently to see, which might take up to a half hour—of discovering whether anyone at the next table had greater celebrity than they.

"Why is *A Second Opinion* a blessing?"

"Oh, that."

"Murray, I can't tell you how much I dislike it. I'm tired of running around in a towel. Half the time I enter some jerk whistles. And I'm tired of spouting 'But I thought . . . didn't you say you loved me, Lois?' and having the audience scream with laughter. It's a dopey line."

"Nicky—"

"It's a dopey play."

"It's a hit."

"That doesn't make it less dopey."

"Yes it does. Wait. Listen to me, Nicky." Murray took his glasses off and put them beside his water goblet. He massaged the indentations from where the nosepiece had rested with his thumb and index finger. At the beginning, Nicholas had felt sorry for Murray. He'd never met a person who suffered so much from eyeglasses: the bridge of Murray's nose had two permanent red ovals; the bony area behind his ears required frequent rubbing; the eyes themselves often had to be shielded by the palms of Murray's hands. But observing Murray as often and as closely as he had, Nicholas came to recognize the glasses for what they were: a prop. He waited for Murray to complete his eyeglass ritual.

"Nicky," he said at last, "I'd be a liar if I told you this was a solid gold piece of theater. It's not. It's two steps above crap, but—I say *but*—everybody likes it. It's light, like a forty-watt bulb. No big deal, but everybody laughs, ha-ha, and everybody goes home happy *and*—the big and—you're a comedy star. A big, handsome guy who loses his pants and who gets walked all over by girls because he's got such a soft heart. You've got everybody rooting for you, and when you go to the lady psychiatrist—"

"But it's so obvious what will happen."

"That's beside the point. *A Second Opinion* is beside the point. The point is that right now people are starting to talk about what a sensation you are in the movie, and they're going to start screenings in a couple of months."

"But if I get out of *A Second Opinion* now I can be opening in *Lear* when the movie comes out."

"That's just what I don't want."

Nicholas sat back. "Why?" He only realized he was drumming his fingers on the table when he noticed Murray staring at his hand.

"You got a train to catch, Nicky?"

"Sorry."

"You open in *Lear* and what happens? If everything goes perfectly, and there's a two percent chance it will, you'll open mid-September, right around when the movie does, and get great notices. But as what? You're not playing Lear. You're playing Edmund."

"It's a good role."

"For someone else. Ask yourself: Who's Edmund? Who's Edmund, Nicky? I'll tell you. Edmund's another prick. This time a Shakespearean prick, but a rose by any other name . . . Listen to me. You play a prick in the movie—they're changing the title again, by the way—and you've played enough pricks on stage so that if I didn't know you, I'd wonder whether you're really such a sweet guy. So here he is, Nicholas Cobleigh, making a big— underline big—impression in whatever the name of the movie is, playing a Triple A prick, and here he is again in *Lear* playing the same thing in pantyhose. You get my drift? You want them to think you're Johnny One Note, fine. But you know and I know that your range is very broad, and I think you'd be a dope to paint yourself into some little corner."

"But what if the movie flops?"

"It'll flop. It's not a thing that hasn't happened before. All I know is that the word on you is sensational. I could put in another line just to take California calls from the word-of-mouth on you—speaking of which, you need somebody out there."

"No, I don't."

"I'm a New York theatrical agent, Nicky. I can't—"

"Murray—"

"I can't do you justice. Come on. It's not like you to get sentimental over a business deal. Listen, I've more than made my money on you. I hope I'll continue to represent you for another hundred and twenty years in New York, but—"

"We can discuss it some other time, Murray."

Nicholas drank his tea. It was lukewarm and sour. Murray had been after him to get a movie agent, and he'd found one excuse after another not to: he probably wouldn't make another movie for a few years, Murray had negotiated a perfectly satisfactory contract for this movie, he'd met a few agents in Los Angeles and hadn't liked any of them. Murray brought up the subject frequently, and each time he did Nicholas found himself getting more and more annoyed. "You're hurt," Jane had said when he'd tried to talk to her about it. "You really see him as a father figure and you feel rejected." That was right after a visit from her college roommate, Amelia, the world's tritest psychologist. Before walking out of the room, he'd told Jane she'd be better off if she'd stop coming up with such know-it-all friends like Amelia in her search for a mother figure. They hadn't made up until bedtime that night.

"Listen, you get ninety percent, I get ten. I'm just saying you can get a bigger ninety with someone who operates out there. Nicky, don't look at me like I'm saying something terrible. You are. You're giving me one of your prick looks."

"I'm not giving you a prick look."

"All right. You want to drop it, we'll drop it. Now, are you with me on the *Lear* business? My advice—for which you're giving me ten percent of your gross income, as you well know—is that you should stay in *A Second Opinion* because it's money in the bank, and once the movie comes out in September everyone will see you being funny and vulnerable and running around half naked with your muscles bulging out and they'll say, 'Hoo-ha! Leading man.' Okay? You with me, Nicky?"

"I'm with you, Murray."

"You want to go someplace else for dessert?"

Cecily Van Doorn was Jane's first real friend in Connecticut, but it had been a long time since she had been to Cecily's house. Two or three months, Jane thought. The huge floor pillows were new. Covered with the same chintz as the couch and two of the chairs, they looked like scattered beds. The shiny white background of the fabric looked crisp and friendly enough, but the flowers and stems of the design curved sensuously around each other, defiantly tropical in such a temperate room.

She hadn't minded coming to Cecily's. She'd agreed to it. "I'd love to," she'd said directly to Cecily's questioning eyebrows. She was all right so far. But she didn't like being left alone on the screened porch while Cecily took a telephone call upstairs in her bedroom. She felt fine, though. Here she was, having lunch at her friend's, on a brilliant blue day.

It was June 1969, a year since they'd moved to the house. Jane had gotten to know it well. Extremely well, since she did not like to leave it, at least not when she was by herself.

Before Nicholas came home from California, she'd had three attacks: two while driving the car, one while waiting on the checkout line in the supermarket. That third time, she'd been waiting with a full cart behind two other women. She'd picked a magazine from the rack and to pass the time was flipping to "Fifty Fast Halloween Treats for Young Tricksters." She was looking at an ad for salad dressing. She remembered that: the celadon of iceberg lettuce, the purple slivers of red cabbage, the slimy red-orange sheen of the dressing. Suddenly a wave of dizziness slammed her so hard she was knocked sideways. The magazine fell out of her hand. She grabbed the handle of the shopping cart.

This was brutal. A blitz. Nothing gradual like the other attacks. It hit her like an ax crashing down on her skull. Terrible disabling dizziness. The floor would not stay under her. The supermarket was a giant cube, tumbling, like a child's block hurled into space. And an instant later the most horrible nausea. She stopped leaning over her shopping cart. People were looking. She might throw up all over her groceries, a cascade of vomit over the yogurt and the Clorox and the acorn squash.

The dizziness got worse, blocking out everything, even the awful sickness. She was going to faint right there with everyone already staring at her because she hadn't been able to stop: she'd moaned when the nausea hit, capturing everyone's attention; even the checkout girl had stopped punching the cash register in the middle of a giant stack of someone's Hawaiian Punch.

Jane couldn't help herself. She dropped to the floor to keep from fainting and cracking open her head. People surrounded her, a barricade of legs. Through the dizziness, all those knobs of knees at eye level, all those people knew exactly who she was, where she lived, and they'd never forget her losing control like this. Never. And they'd tell their friends, and when they met her at church or at the library they'd pretend they'd never heard about it. They wouldn't be sure whether to let their children come to the house to play with her children. She wasn't in control. Such terrible dizziness. She lowered her head, but that only made the nausea come back, rise up her chest to her throat. So sick.

The embarrassment was sickening, the helping hands extended down, the "What happened?" "Can you hear me?" "Are you all right?" The low chorus of speculation.

"Attacks?" the doctor had demanded. He'd sent her for tests. Heart. Blood. Brain. "Nerves," he told her.

"I'm not nervous," she said. "Really."

"Take time out every day. Read a book, take a nap in the afternoon. You can arrange it if you really want to."

"It was *physical*."

"The mind can do that. Just try to relax. And while you're relaxing"—he closed her folder—"it wouldn't be a bad idea to take off ten pounds."

It wasn't nerves, she'd told herself. Even if it was, which it wasn't, Nicholas's being home would make it better. But less than three weeks after he'd come home, when he was in the city rehearsing A *Second Opinion*, she'd taken the girls to the library for story hour and, as she was browsing through the mystery stacks looking for a book for Nicholas, it came again. Dizziness, nausea, and her heart too this time, banging arrhythmically, smashing against her chest as if trying to beat its way out of her body.

What is happening to me? she'd asked herself. Just what is this? By the time story hour ended the attack was over, but she was so weak she was trembling. She drove the girls home, amazed and thankful she had the control, the strength, to get them home. And then she did not drive again.

Cecily came back to the porch. "Sorry, but this one's too good to rush off the phone. They're lining up for him."

"Is this the surgeon?"

"No. The editor. Six foot two. Congenitally tweedy."

"What's he like?"

"Socially impeccable. Rich. Tall."

"Is he nice?"

"I don't know. I've only gone out with him a couple of times. Probably not."

At first glance, Cecily Van Doorn did not look like the sort of woman a socially impeccable, rich, tall man would call. Her round face might be called pretty, especially with her bright, wide-spaced brown eyes, but the fan of laugh lines at the outer edges was not merely sketched in, but etched deep. She looked—and was—ten years older than Jane. Cecily's thin, straight hair, brown also, was quite short; she usually kept it off her forehead with a tortoiseshell headband. Often tufts of hair would pop out, and she was continually removing the headband, flattening her hairline with a forearm, and slipping it back with her other hand. The best that could be said for her figure was that it was average. It hadn't changed in the twenty-one years since she'd first been a bride.

Still, she had a way with men. Whatever prettiness she had was mixed with intelligence, humor, impudence, and self-reliance, and the combination was, Jane realized, effective. Cecily sparkled, and an astounding number of men were drawn to her brightness.

"If he's not nice," Jane asked, "why are you going out with him?"

"Well, he's nice in that he's certainly polite. Opens car doors and doesn't scratch his privates. And he's good company. I just can't believe that anyone who's such a great catch can remain uncaught as long as he has—he's been divorced nearly ten years—without something being wrong. Ten years of dating can't be fun. How many times can you ask 'Where did you go to college?' I think he probably doesn't have a kind heart."

Cecily—she had been Cecily Stettin—had first been a bride at eighteen, when she quit the University of Connecticut after half a semester and married Chip Van Doorn, the twenty-three-year-old son of the president of Connecticut Sand and Stone and Farcroft's richest citizen. It was a move up. Cecily's father drove the local taxi. Everyone in town, including her own parents, assumed she was pregnant and couldn't understand why Chip's father hadn't bought her off. A year later, when Cecily and Chip threw themselves a first anniversary party, everyone eyed Cecily's flat stomach. Many people assumed she had miscarried, although the president of the Farcroft school board confided in the town's leading dentist, "You wouldn't believe it to look at her, but I hear she goes in for some far-out stuff. That's why he married her." Like what? The dentist's face grew damp and pink. The school board president shrugged his shoulders. It was 1949, and he was at a loss for words.

The marriage lasted longer than anyone predicted. It lasted nine years, until 1957, when Chip was killed when his car went out of control on the Merritt Parkway.

Cecily Stettin Van Doorn, then, was a childless widow at twenty-seven, and a relatively wealthy one, since—besides the money Chip had saved from his handsome salary as vice-president of Connecticut Sand and Stone—several of Chip's college friends were insurance brokers, and Chip had been an obliging fellow.

After Chip's funeral, everyone in Farcroft, including Cecily's own parents, sat back and with the farsighted, unembarrassed eyes of small-town citizens waited to see what she would do: take a world cruise, take a lover, take a college degree, take to drink. Cecily had always been a great girl, great fun, but after this—well, she was always driving into New York to go to museums and concerts with Chip and who knew, with all Chip's money now it could go to her head and she could just up and move to Greenwich Village and marry a beatnik and have him go through her inheritance in a year or two and then she'd have to come back to Farcroft and face the music.

For a year and a half she did nothing. She stayed the same old Cecily, maybe a little quieter now, but still—her bouncy walk gave her away—the same happy-go-lucky girl. Being a widow didn't make her act like one.

And contrary to all speculation, Cecily stayed right where she was. She remained in her jewel of a cottage on Old Mill Road just off Main Street, took walks with her golden retriever and bought five books a week from the local bookshop, a store that sold three gardening books for every novel. Now and then she'd get real wise, like asking Mr. Krinski at the delicatessen if he charged extra for the mold on the liverwurst, but that was hardly news, especially where Cecily was concerned. She replaced her old washing machine with a Maytag. Her parents came every Sunday afternoon for dinner. Her life was too boring even for Farcroft. People stopped watching her.

And when they did, near the second anniversary of Chip's death, she married her widowed father-in-law.

She was twenty-nine and Chuck Van Doorn was nearly forty years older. He sold his company to a conglomerate, retired, and stayed home with Cecily. Once a week he left their stately hilltop house for an afternoon and played golf, and the men at the club whispered about the bloom in his face and the spring in his step. For the first time, he broke eighty. There was only one question on Farcroft's collective tongue: What does Cecily have? Two questions, actually: What do they do all day in that big house? Mrs. Greer, the lady who cleaned for them, could not be persuaded to discuss the Van Doorns, leading to talk that she'd been bribed into silence. The theories about what went on were diverse and imaginative. In 1967, when Chuck died in his sleep of a stroke, the answer died with him.

Cecily wasn't talking. She bought herself a collie puppy—the golden retriever had died several months before Chuck—and continued living in the huge house on the hill. The only change was noted by the grocer: she no longer purchased Ovaltine. That was hardly satisfying, but it had to suffice. Until Jane moved to Connecticut in 1968, Cecily had no close friends in or around Farcroft.

"Where did you meet this editor?" Jane asked.

"Actually, he played golf with Chuck a few times. His uncle belongs to the club. After Chuck died he wrote a nice note and I wrote a nice note back, and then all of a sudden, about two weeks ago, he called and said he was at the club and could he drop over and say hello. And one thing led to another and that was that."

"Cecily," Jane said. Then she looked at her friend. "That's why people never stop talking about you. You're so vague you leave everything to people's imaginations. 'One thing led to another'! It sounds like you shook hands, said hello, and began rolling around on the rug."

"We had a few drinks first."

"Oh. I didn't mean—"

"That's all right. Do you think that's why people talk about me? If I was very specific would they keep quiet? Come on, Jane. I've lived here all my life."

"I don't know. Anyway, what's the editor's name?"

"Ted Treadwell. He has a very deep voice and whenever he calls he says 'Hi! Ted Treadwell here.' I think he gets great pleasure from hearing himself speak. He's always throwing in extra words. 'Thank you *very much.*' 'You look *really* nice tonight.'"

"Cecily, you're being picky."

"Probably. I don't think this one is a match made in heaven." Cecily drew her legs up under her. She was wearing jeans, a white cotton sweater, and her usual smear of pink lipstick. "Speaking of matches made in heaven," she added, "how is yours?"

"Fine."

Outside the house, hidden by one of the undulations in the hill, the gardener was working; the lawnmower's voice went from a hum to a whine as it neared the house, then back to a hum as it rolled farther away. The clean smell of the grass mixed with a trace of gasoline fumes from the mower's engine permeated the porch. Being with Cecily was almost as good as being with Nicholas: she felt free, certain no attack would come in their company. She wasn't sure how she was certain, but she was. With Cecily, it would have been better to have been at the farm, but she'd been evading Cecily's invitations for too long.

"Fine?" Cecily asked.

The porch was Jane's favorite room in Cecily's house. It was all white— painted wood floor, wicker furniture—and flowery. There were flowers on the fabric covering the cushions and pillows; flowering plants in mid-sized pots were suspended from the ceiling and overflowed giant white cachepots and baskets on the floor. Whenever a breeze blew through the screen walls of the room, one of the plants would respond by emitting a spray of perfume.

"Yes, fine. Well, Nick's not too happy with the play, but I told you about that. His agent says he should stick with it until the movie opens, and that's what he's doing."

"And that's it?"

"Well, he doesn't like running around stage half-naked eight times a week and he'd prefer doing *Lear*, but he says—"

"Jane, come on." Cecily took a cigarette from a pack she'd placed on the floor beside her. She lit it with one hand, by holding the matchbook on her palm and striking the match with her thumb. She blew out an impatient stream of smoke. "You're no longer driving. You're no longer going into town. Nick comes home after a month in California and finds a wife who's going from doctor to doctor—"

"He doesn't mind."

"—and then who stops going because she can't drive and she doesn't like traveling on parkways. Come on, Jane! Don't tell me he doesn't mind."

"I stopped going because they all told me the same thing. And Nick doesn't mind. He's been very . . . " She really wished she could ask Cecily to drive her home right away.

"He's been very *what?*"

"Very understanding. Marvelous."

"He doesn't mind chauffeuring you around?"

"Cecily, he always drives when we go someplace. I don't think I've ever driven when he's been with me. I mean it."

"He doesn't mind chauffeuring the girls?"

"No."

"No? He doesn't think it's peculiar that you can't drive and you can't go to the library and—"

"I *can*. I just don't feel like it."

"Jane—"

"He understands. He says I should lean on him a little, that's what he's there for."

"Does he understand?"

"What do you mean?" Jane's hands were moist. She wasn't going to have an attack. She didn't think she was. Still, she was no longer comfortable. Cecily snuffed out her cigarette and the tip smoldered in the ashtray, giving off an acrid odor. Jane rubbed her hands together.

"Am I upsetting you?" Cecily asked. "I'm sorry."

"I'm fine."

"Jane, does he know you won't go into town?"

"I *do*, Cecily. We went to a movie last night."

"You go with him. Does he know you won't go anyplace by yourself?"

Jane stood. "That's not true!" she said. "Not true!"

"Where do you go? Come on, Jane. I've been at your house enough times and seen enough deliveries. Groceries. The stores. United Parcel could get up your drive blindfolded. You're ordering everything by phone because you can't go—"

"I can. I'm just not in the mood."

"Oh, Jane!"

"Really, I've been feeling much better the last few weeks. I'm just taking it easy."

"And Nicholas approves."

"He understands that it's easier to call a department store and have something sent instead of making the trip and wasting a lot of time. He doesn't mind."

"I wish you'd talk to somebody about this."

"Cecily, I've been to four different doctors. They all say it's nerves or stress. I have a prescription for tranquilizers if I need them, but I'm telling you, that's not the problem. I'm fine. I'm happy."

"Jane—"

"I'm just the compleat homebody. That's all there is to it. I'm happy when I'm making a dinner party or curled up on the window seat reading. That's what I like best. I'm home so much because that's where I really want to be."

The studio's New York screening room was a small, narrow theater on the nineteenth floor of an office building. The seats were uncommonly comfortable, except that they were covered in a material that felt like a blend of suede and human skin.

"No popcorn?" Winifred murmured to Nicholas. The man seated in front of her turned and gave her the glance awarded by insiders to those outsiders naive enough to condemn themselves by their own words: ennui enlivened by a slight sneer.

"It won't seem like a real movie," Nicholas remarked.

The man in front of his mother probably worked for the studio. He wore a business shirt and tie without a jacket, and his lounging sprawl indicated he was in possession of his customary seat. The man glanced toward Nicholas, ready to sneer more broadly, but when he saw Nicholas's face his mouth puckered for an instant into a circle of recognition, the silent "oh" of the urbane fan. But something about the way the man continued to stare at him gave Nicholas the sense that the man knew his face from the movie, not from having seen him on stage; the man obviously felt no compunctions about staring because, to his mind, Nicholas wasn't quite real. Nicholas fought the urge to avert his head. He peered directly into the man's eyes, as if he were nine years old and having a staring contest with Thomas. It took less than five seconds for the man to give up; he raised his eyes above Nicholas's head as if all along he had been searching out the location of the projection booth.

People were still coming in, searching along the rows for familiar faces, waving, mimicking a swoon of amazement at seeing someone they probably hadn't seen in a week and a half. This was the first New York screening. Most of the people in the small theater had something to do with *Urban Affairs,* the final title of the movie. He and the man who'd played a hippie artist were the only two actors present, but he'd recognized one of the screenwriters and a few other people he'd met out in California. The head of the publicity department, a man with a satanic goatee, had waved at him wildly and thrown a loud, chirpy kiss to him from the front row. But he'd never seen the man in front of his mother.

"Oh, dear, I'm all fluttery," Winifred said. She hadn't noticed the man at all. "It all seems so strange."

"Well, you've seen me in every play I've ever been in. Even the clinkers."

"But this is different, Nicholas. This is the movies."

Jane, seated on his other side, was beyond the flutters. She was staring ahead, mesmerized by the darkened screen. She looked stunned or in shock, as though she'd just learned for the first time that he'd made a movie and she was about to see it.

His father sat on the other side of Jane, thus well insulated from Winifred. There had been an awkward moment when the four of them had met outside the screening room. James and Winifred had greeted each other with the restraint of strangers meeting at a funeral and then had looked to Nicholas for guidance as to what to do next. Nicholas motioned his father into the row of seats and, after a split second's indecision, propelled Jane in after him.

His father looked like what he was: a handsome, aging corporate lawyer. His gray hair was clipped short and combed neatly; his three-piece gray pinstripe suit fit perfectly. But James Cobleigh was behaving like a nervous corporate lawyer. He kept swiveling his head, looking at the walls and ceiling of the screening room as if they were superb examples of baroque architecture instead of plain flat walls and ceilings. Nicholas couldn't decide if the cause was his son's impending screen debut or his wife's presence. (James and Winifred had lived apart nearly eight years. They'd seen each other only at Thomas's and Olivia's weddings and at the christenings of their grandchildren. Neither had ever bothered to seek a divorce.)

The screening room darkened. It was weird, not like watching a commercial he'd made on TV at home with Jane. This was going to be a real performance. The coffee he'd had a couple of hours before sloshed in his stomach; he felt slightly queasy. This was so distant, so public, so awesome. The camera moved lovingly over a long street of Victorian houses, and the credits rolled. His mother grabbed his forearm as his name came on the screen. NICHOLAS COBLEIGH. All capitals. It was weird to be sitting in an audience waiting for his own entrance.

And then it began. A tracking shot following Julie Spahr and David Whitman, running down the street, laughing, bending to grab handfuls of

330

dandelion puffs from between the cracks in the sidewalk, blowing fine sprays of fluff at each other; then a closeup of them kissing, the sun catching the fluff twinkling against Julie Spahr's auburn hair. A scene with a group of artists. Then Spahr asleep, curled up on a furry rug, Whitman, his eyes filled with love, looking at her from his drafting table. The movie could have been in Swedish for all he comprehended of the dialogue. It was weird. None of it fit together. He tapped Jane's shoulder. "Shhh," she whispered.

Then there he was. In a blue oxford shirt, top button opened, tie loose, his hair hanging down onto his forehead. He stood, walked around his desk, and greeted Whitman and Spahr. "Glad you could make it," he said. He sat on the edge of his desk and the camera cut to Whitman, then moved back to get Spahr. Suddenly he was on the screen again. A reaction shot. He was nodding as Whitman spoke. Nicholas stared at himself. He couldn't believe it. He was so handsome.

After the big fund-raising banquet scene there he was again, in black tie, in a men's room accepting the surreptitiously handed envelope—his bribe—slipping it into his inside pocket. The audience gasped. They were actually surprised.

Later with Whitman in the mayor's office on a weekend, both of them dressed casually: Whitman in rough corduroys and a scratchy-looking red shirt, himself in jeans so well cut they looked custom-made and a white turtleneck; the camera caught the contrast between textures, the rough red wool and the soft, rich white cashmere. They leaned over blueprints and sipped cans of beer. Whitman looked intense and genuine. Nicholas watched himself closely; he was a real prick, covering his boredom with a mechanical smile. He rested his can of beer on the blueprint. His contempt of the beverage and the project came through in that one gesture. There had been over twenty takes on that scene. Whitman had insisted on real beer for authenticity, and they'd drunk can after can. Nicholas had staggered back to his dressing room; Whitman had to be guided off the set.

The movie continued. He looked at Jane. Her eyes darted, following the action, but her breathing was deep and slow, the way it was in the middle of the night.

And at last, the end. There he was, standing behind Julie Spahr, pulling back her head. There was so much power in that scene. Really. Maybe not. Maybe blown up larger than life anything seemed momentous. But he could actually feel the power of his own performance: the cruelty, the triumph, the evil, and, finally, the deadness in that handsome face that, incredibly, was his.

And then it was over. People stood, stretched their arms. The lights were raised. His mother was speaking. Jane squeezed his hand. Her grip was strong, but when the lights came on full her face was as close to pale as he'd ever seen it. His father had a silly, sideways smile and patted his shoulder over and over.

It was as if he were still in the movie. The three of them were talking but he couldn't fathom the dialogue. He couldn't read their expressions. He couldn't tell if it was pride or embarrassment or politeness. He wished he were by himself.

For a second he was. Jane and his parents were pushed aside. He was alone. Then the audience seemed to implode against him. "Brilliant!" "Holy shit, baby! Bravura performance!" "Nick! First rate!" "Excuse me, I'm Mindy, Mr. Rosenthal's assistant, and—" "A dream! A veritable dream!" "Mr. Cobleigh! Mr. Cobleigh!"

Maybe this was traditional. Hugs, handshakes, backslaps. Then they'd leave the building and say to each other, "Not bad," "So-so," "C-plus."

He finally got away, although taking the head of publicity with him; the man's arm was too tight around his shoulder to shake off. He found his parents and Jane at the reception desk outside the screening room. They stared at him, all three of them. He introduced them to the publicist, who beamed at them and boomed, "Wasn't that TNT? Wasn't it? You must be dying!" Then he turned to Nicholas. "First thing tomorrow. Nine A.M. Major meeting, Nick. I mean, big guns. A-bombs. Is nine okay for you?" Nicholas nodded. "Not nine. Don't kill yourself getting here. Ten. How about ten?" The man finally let go of his shoulder and hurried toward the elevator.

The four of them stood where they were, wooden. Finally Jane moved forward. Tentatively, as though afraid he might make a cutting remark, she came up to him.

"Well?" he said.

"Extraordinary." Her clear, straight voice had a knot in it.

"Really?"

"Really." Her eyes were misty. He put his arms around her.

"Nick," his father said. James seemed flustered. He kept smoothing the side of his hair with his hand. Finally he said, "Well done."

Nicholas turned to his mother.

"I hated you!" Winifred burst out. She was clutching her handbag against her chest. "Him, I mean. I hated him! I kept telling myself, that terrible man is really a *nice* man and he's Nicholas. But what a cad! And so handsome! Nicholas, all I could think about was when you were born. I woke up and they handed me this sweet, tiny thing all wrapped up in a little blue blanket and you opened your eyes and they were the same eyes as on that screen. Nicholas—"

"What is it?"

"You're a very good actor."

332

"Thank you." He was still holding Jane. Her head was resting against his. He couldn't tell if she was still so wrought up.

"Only—" his mother continued.

"Only what?" he asked.

"Nicholas, how in the world could you have let them force you to kiss that dreadful, cheap girl?"

Giving added weight to the seriousness of her condition was the arrival in London of her brother, Rhodes Heissenhuber, an investment consultant from Cincinnati. Mr. Heissenhuber, who had been vacationing in the Greek islands, conceded to reporters that he had been told by his brother-in-law, Nicholas Cobleigh, that his sister's condition was "quite serious."
—*Cleveland Plain Dealer*

"It must feel a little like being the pope," Jane said. She attacked a giant block of chocolate with a large knife, and small chunks of it dropped off onto the wooden chopping table.

"What do you mean?" Nicholas asked.

"Everyone wants an audience with you. Probably better than the pope, because what can he do? Give a blessing?"

"That's more than I can do."

He watched her scrape the knife along the table, gathering pieces of chocolate into a mound. Then she went back to the block. Here she was, making chocolate ice cream for fifty people. He'd offered to have the party catered. Jane, he'd said, don't knock yourself out. Do you have any idea what that would cost? she'd demanded. We can afford it, he'd told her. His last two films had done so well they could do pretty much anything they wanted. She could sit back and watch a kitchen full of cooks prepare a party for five hundred. Five thousand. But she really didn't want to hear that.

"The world is divided into two kinds of people," she said.

"The good and the bad."

"No."

"Chocolate people and vanilla people."

"No. Nick, listen to me and while you're listening get me the big double boiler from the bottom pull-out drawer. There are two kinds of people. Not today. Today is all good people. But the others. The ones who want to talk to you so they can tell their friends, 'Well, just the other day I was up at Nick Cobleigh's farm and he said he really wants to do a science-fiction film and play an android who falls in love with a beautiful scientist.'"

"Don't make fun of that script. Some poor writer spent months—years— working on that thing."

"They should shoot him and put him out of his misery. And then there's the other half who don't want to talk to you. Who only want to look at you with their mouths hanging open and then go upstairs and try to sneak into our

334

bathroom to see what's in the medicine cabinet. Why do they want to know? That's what bothers me. Why in the great scheme of things is it important if Nicholas Cobleigh uses a roll-on or a stick deodorant or if your shaving brush looks mangy? It looks mangy, by the way. I ordered you two new ones, one for here and one for your travel kit."

Nicholas put the pot on the table beside the block of chocolate, took the knife from Jane's hand and put it down, and put his arms around her.

"You owe me a kiss," he said. She looked fabulous. He loved her casual like this, in bleached-out jeans and a red T-shirt that buttoned up the front with tiny red buttons. Every time she stabbed the chocolate her breasts quivered. She kissed him softly on the lips. He put a hand behind her neck and pulled her close. He put the other hand under her shirt and rubbed her back. Her skin was still perfect. Velvet. He kissed her harder, until she opened her mouth, then ran his tongue over hers. He tasted chocolate. She'd been cheating. She was supposed to be on another of her diets, losing the same few pounds she'd been putting on and taking off for the last few years. He could never tell the difference and told her so, which annoyed her. What do you mean, you can't tell? she'd said. I'm at my rock-bottom weight. Look at my waist. It looked like the same waist she'd always had, a little bigger since the two children.

She took his lower lip between her teeth and bit down gently. She'd obviously been reading one of those how-to sex books. The last time he'd come home—he'd been on location for three and a half months making a Western in Wyoming—they'd gotten into bed the first night and he'd gone for her, a little roughly after those months of celibacy. (During the filming, he'd flown home every other weekend, but the combination of saddle sores, jet lag, and exhaustion from making amends to the girls for his absence had taken its toll; he'd been able to make love only a few perfunctory times.) That first night had been so awkward. He ripped her nightgown and was apologizing at the same time he was grabbing at her. Nick, she'd said. Nick! He tried to cool down. Is there anything special you'd like? she'd asked. He must have looked at her as if she were crazy because she'd quickly explained: any special sex thing? If you'd rather do it some other way. I mean, oral sex, or if there's anything else. . . . She tried to distract him to cover her embarrassment, climbing on top and straddling him, her hair falling forward, spilling over his shoulders. She ran her hands up his arms and over his shoulders, kneading his muscles with the pads of her thumbs.

The gesture caught him off guard, a blow all the more stunning because it was unanticipated. And so false. This wasn't Jane. Worse, the gesture was the one his co-star in *Jenny and Joe* had used in their big, steamy sex scene; the director had showed her what to do, kneeling beside her near the edge of a swimming pool while Nicholas lay belly-up in the grass, the two of them leaning over him, four thumbs rubbing away at his muscles until his arms were streaked with red and they'd had to send him back to makeup. You know you can ask me to do anything, she'd said.

He'd had to blink, otherwise tears would have come to his eyes. She was afraid of losing him. So afraid that she'd probably ordered a stack of books and studied them: How to Keep Your Man or some stupid thing like that; Behind the Bedroom Door; Feel Free; Do It the New Way. He held her tight. I love you, he'd told her. You don't need tricks. But Nick, please, if you want something. Then I'll let you know, Jane. Still, he couldn't blame her. He guessed he'd be reading sex manuals if their positions were reversed.

The year before, 1970, after *Jenny and Joe,* his second film, was released, when she would still leave the farm, go places with him, they'd driven into New York. It had been a disaster. Two girls in a convertible had spotted him and followed them all the way from Connecticut down to the Bronx, driving alongside them, sideswiping them several times, once nearly driving him off the road, all the time waving, throwing kisses at him. When they finally turned off, he looked at Jane. Her eyes were shut. Her hands were clasped tight in her lap, but not so tight he could not see they were shaking.

They'd gone to a cocktail party given by the chairman of the board of one of the major studios. It was in a spectacular penthouse, all white with minimalist furniture and what looked like a brilliant collection of abstract expressionist art. He'd had one minute to savor it. Then people started to surround him, asking him the same questions over and over: How does it feel to be nominated as best actor? What are you doing next? How do you feel about being a male sex idol? An overnight sensation? A waiter came around with a tray of little meat balls and he'd taken one, but then he'd had to answer somebody with his mouth full. The minute he answered one person's question, it was someone else's turn. There even seemed to be an etiquette to talking to him. Two minutes and then the person would back off, giving someone else a chance. They would not leave him alone. People elbowed other people aside to stand next to him. They stood closer than was necessary, examining whatever part of him was at their eye level. For what? To check the quality of his suit? To look for blemishes? To see if his teeth were capped?

Jane had been pushed away after thirty seconds. Unfortunately, she had been pushed into a corner near where two women were discussing him. "You slept with Nicholas Cobleigh?" one asked the other. "What do you think?" "How was he?" "What do you think?" "God, that body! That swimming scene! I almost died. Are you still seeing him?" "Of course."

Listen, he'd said when they'd left, wiping her eyes with his hand, I don't do that. You *know* I don't, and if you're going to believe that shit—it *is* shit, damn it—then we're in trouble. Believe me. Trust me. You have to because it's not going to get better.

336

From the party they went to his father's apartment. What should have been a five-minute crosstown walk took more than half an hour. People stopped him for autographs, to deliver critiques of *Urban Affairs* and *Jenny and Joe*. This was Manhattan, where people were supposed to be born unimpressible. Oooh! girls shrieked. It's *him!* The more subtle poked each other with elbows, pointed him out with their heads.

In his father's building a woman had gotten onto the elevator with them, a nearly middle-aged woman wearing the kind of baggy camp shorts and cotton blouse that Vicky would wear. But these were obviously meant to be fashionable; she tugged at the hem of her shorts, trying to get a little more flare. She glanced quickly at Jane's clothes—a black cotton dress and pearls— and even more quickly looked away, bored. Then she happened to look at Nicholas. "It's not. It can't be!" she announced. The elevator door closed. "I don't believe it! It's you! I'm here with you alone on the elevator." He glanced up. The floor indicator showed they were at the ninth floor. His father lived on the twenty-third. "Oh, I don't believe it, your eyes really are that color! What is it, aqua? Turquoise? It's just beyond comprehension, being here with you! If it wasn't you, you'd tell me, wouldn't you?" He held onto Jane's hand and didn't say a word. "Wouldn't you? Well, you could at least answer me, for chrissake!"

A delicious morning breeze blew through the kitchen, chilly, a little moist, absolutely fresh, a New England June breeze. Everyone trying to get him to move to California kept telling him, Once you get spoiled by the climate, you'll never be able to live back East again. But they'd made themselves forget this sweet breeze. You couldn't remember it and not long for it.

Nicholas kissed the lobe of Jane's ear, then her neck. "You smell like lemons right here," he said.

"Lemonade. Seventy-five lemons. I hope it's enough." She sighed and breathed, "Oh, God."

"What's wrong?"

"Maybe I should have made a cold buffet. Pâtés, chicken, ham. A barbecue isn't right . . . it's too self-consciously simple."

"You're crazy."

"Maybe we should call St. Lambert's and have them send up—"

"This is perfect. Besides, what are we going to do with the twenty buckets of coleslaw and those huge things of mustard?"

"I hope it will be okay."

"It will be wonderful. When have you ever served a bad meal?"

"How about the first year we were married?"

"I forgot about that. I hate to say it, but it was pretty awful. You made some strange salads."

"I cringe every time I think of it."

337

"Everything had marshmallows in it."

"Not everything," Jane said. "Not my Velveeta paprika egg froth. Remember that? True culinary excellence. Even you couldn't fake your way through that one. Remember? Your mouth got all puckered up and your face was absolutely ashen. You couldn't swallow it."

"Sorry."

"*You're* sorry? I'm sorry. A year of torture. You bore up nobly." She pulled back from him and picked up the knife. "If I don't get going, fifty people won't have a choice of what to put on their pie à la mode. They'll think I'm only capable of vanilla, and I can't afford to have my reputation sullied. Could you get the cream? It's in quart containers in the fridge."

"Jane."

"What?" She stabbed the block of chocolate.

From beside the refrigerator, he lifted a quart of cream in a toast. "Happy anniversary." She smiled at him. "Here's to ten more and ten more after that."

"Only thirty?"

"And another ten and another and . . ."

"I'm only here to advise you," Murray King said. He exhaled a cloud of moist breath onto the lenses of his glasses, then polished them with his tie. He held the glasses up to the light of the gooseneck floor lamp beside his chair. The lamp was the only new object he'd bought for his office in the years he'd made hundreds and hundreds of thousands of dollars as Nicholas's agent. He was obviously proud of it, giving demonstrations of how the neck of the lamp could be bent down for reading, up to bounce light off the ceiling, and no doubt he believed that was sufficient redecoration. He'd demanded of Nicholas, Doesn't it give the place a whole new look? It's very modern.

"That's what I want, Murray. Advice."

Nicholas scratched the mustache he had grown for his new film. It was supposed to make him look rakish. Jane said it made him look like the portrait of a Confederate general. "You should be hanging in the courthouse in Biloxi, Mississippi," she'd remarked.

"My advice to you is this. You're two people. You're Nicholas Cobleigh the actor and Nicholas Cobleigh the movie star. The first one can do comedy. He can be a villain, a pervert, a nebbish. He can go wherever your talent takes you. Okay? Agreed? But the movie star is variations on one theme: the cold prick who inside has a warm heart but you have to break through the ice to get there, and the only ones who can break through the ice are a good pal or a kid or a girl. Preferably a girl, so you get more chances to take your shirt off. You know that as well as I do."

"I don't think that's true."

"Listen to me. It's true. You want to do FDR before he got polio, a real deep complex psychohistory where in the end you see his heart's a bigger block of ice than his outside, you do it on the stage."

"It could be a tour de force, Murray."

"On *stage*, Nicky. On film, unless he winds up rolling off into the sunset in a wheelchair with Eleanor on his lap because he finally realizes he's crazy for her, it's going to be Snore City. You want to do it as a play, wonderful, I'm with you a hundred and one percent. Take six, eight months off. A year off. Stay home. It'll do all of you good."

"I can't afford to."

"Who are you talking to, some *schmegegge* who's never seen one of your contracts? Come on, Nicky."

"I can't afford a year without a film. I'm thirty-one years old. It's not going to last forever."

"What? You think you'll look like Dorian Gray's picture when you're forty?"

"No, but I can't afford to lose my momentum."

"Nicky, you've got the world by the balls. You can do whatever you want. Write your own ticket."

"I can't do a play. Do you have any idea how complicated it would be? Just security alone. And every critic would be gunning for me."

"You're gunning for yourself. Hey, where are you going?"

Nicholas stood. "I'm writing my own ticket to the men's room. Can I have the key?"

Murray's building wasn't seedy, but, as he'd conceded, it was not the place to look for *Fortune*'s Five Hundred. The corridor to the men's room was tiled with small hexagons of black and white, like somebody's bathroom, while the men's room itself, recently remodeled, had the cheery primary colors of a pediatrician's waiting room. Only the white urinal gave it away. The toilet booth, which was occupied, was bright red. The walls were yellow.

Nicholas unzipped his fly. The door of the men's room opened and, from the mirror to his right, he saw a man entering, a small, weak-faced, middle-aged man in a cheap suit, the sort who pushes papers in someone else's office. Nicholas started to urinate. The man stood off to his left and reached for his zipper tab. Nicholas noticed the man's cuffs ended at his ankle, leaving a couple of inches of white ribbed cotton socks showing.

"Oh, God!" The man gasped. "I know who you are!" Suddenly he was right beside Nicholas, staring up at his profile. Nicholas turned away abruptly; a spray of his urine hit the wall beside him. The man bent forward, sticking his face between Nicholas's face and the urinal. "Nicholas Cobleigh!" He breathed his lunch into Nicholas's face. The man in the booth began shuffling, picking up his pants, opening the lock. "When I tell my wife—" the man continued. Nicholas stepped back too quickly. Urine splashed on his and the man's shoes. The man didn't notice. "Can you beat this!" he went on. Nicholas managed to aim the rest into the urinal. Hurriedly, he tucked himself back in and zipped his fly. "Oh, Nick!" the man called. Nicholas was out fast, nearly colliding with the second man, who came rushing from the booth to see him. "Nick!" the first one cried. "That false mustache didn't fool me!"

Murray took a bottle of scotch from a shelf and poured some into a coffee mug. "Here, Nicky, take a belt." He put the mug between Nicholas's hands. "Come on. Down the hatch." Nicholas took a sip, closed his eyes, and shuddered. He'd always hated scotch. Then he took another sip. "Listen, Nicky, I'm sorry."

"It's not your fault."

"I'll have a bathroom put in for you."

"Murray, it's all right." He finished the scotch, took the bottle from Murray's desk, and poured another three fingers. "I don't know why this should get to me more than anything else."

"Are you kidding? You were brought up in a classy situation, Nicky. Everybody was a gentleman."

"No, they weren't."

"But I bet you they acted like it. They have a sense of limits, not like this *farshtinkener* bastard. A guy taking a leak is a sacred thing."

"Come on, Murray." Nicholas started to laugh.

"I mean it. At least with theater fans, they go up to you and what's the worst they can say? Your Julius Caesar left me cold, or Gee, you look older in real life. Big deal. You live. Here, with this movie thing . . . Nicky, listen, I wasn't born yesterday, but every goddamn cockroach in the country comes crawling out for you. It kills me."

"It's not so bad."

"Stop talking Protestant. Of course it's bad. It's terrible, such craziness."

In the room outside Murray's office, a secretary hired solely to work on Nicholas's affairs sat behind piles of fan mail. Nicholas no longer read any of it.

Dear Cobleigh Shitass,

When your not looking I'm gonna get you and lock you up in the basement and shove turds down your throat and kill you SLOW. I cant wait to hear you choke you stinking shit you. . . .

> There is another, I know,
> Who fills your night with
> Eager lips and fingertips.
> Another who sleeps beside you
> In pale, silent dawn streaked by passion's red.
> And I, wakening to solitary gray . . .

Dear Nicholas,

Let me tell you what gets my pussy wet. I bet it will get you hot too! What I want is you to tie me up to a bed. Real tight so the ropes cut into my wrists until they bleed and I scream please don't, but you just laugh and smack my face till its all black and blue and swollen. Then you go out and come back with a red hot branding iron with NC on it, and I . . .

What disturbed Nicholas most was that many of the letters were signed and had return addresses. Somewhere, there were people impatient to hear from him.

Exactly one month after her father's thirty-second birthday, on August 2, 1972, Victoria Cobleigh had her tenth birthday. Although Nicholas had tried, he had another three weeks of shooting in Yugoslavia and could not get back to Connecticut in time for her party.

"Let me look at you," Jane said to Victoria.

"I look okay." The girl was built like her grandmother Winifred: tall, lean, sinewy. Unlike Winifred, however, whose essential expression was a bemused half smile, Victoria's was somber and concentrated, as though she had been assigned to write a report on a book a year above her reading level.

Victoria wore tennis shorts and a sleeveless shirt that emphasized her gangly limbs. Her room, furnished to her taste, was as spare as she was. A faded needlepoint rug lay before the unadorned maple tester bed. A white popcorn spread matched the white-painted walls, and a white crocheted runner covered the top of her plain maple chest of drawers. Her tennis and lacrosse trophies were so densely packed they nearly hid the runner.

Standing beside the stark Victoria, Jane, in a flowered peasant dress, looked puffy and soft, like an overdecorated cake. She smoothed her daughter's hair. "Stop it!" the girl said. "I brushed it."

"Vicky—"

"They'll be here any second." She marched to a large closet. It was fitted with special compartments and filled with sporting goods: hockey and lacrosse sticks, baseball bats and mitts, ice skates. She grabbed one of her three tennis racquets.

"Mrs. Platt can get the door, Vicky. I just want to—"

"Mom, come on."

"I just want to go over the plans."

"Why are you making such a big fuss? First we'll play tennis, then we'll swim, then we'll have dinner, then we'll see a movie in the screening room, then we'll tell ghost stories, and then we'll go to sleep. And *please* don't come in while we're eating and ask if everything's okay like you did last year."

"I have no intention of embarrassing you in front of your friends, but considering the time and effort I—"

341

"Who asked for this? I didn't want another stupid slumber party! I told you a million times!"

"And I told you if your attitude doesn't change there won't be any party."

Victoria slammed her racquet against the bedpost. It made an ugly cracking sound. "I don't care! Go ahead. Go downstairs. Tell them you've called it off and I don't even want the presents. All I wanted was to take over Winkie's and have all the kids—"

"That's not the kind of party Daddy and I had in mind."

"It's just because *you* wouldn't come."

"Vicky!"

"You wouldn't!"

"Vicky, I would if I could. You know that."

"It's so awful. We're the only kids in any of the car pools who have to be driven by a chauffeur. We have a chauffeur, and they have mothers. And if Daddy's on location we might as well be orphans. You didn't come to the Thanksgiving play, you didn't come to Track and Field Day."

"But we had all the children come here! We hired a bus and we brought them all and we had the band and the big tent. You know, a lot of people would think that you're spoiled—"

"A lot of people would think that you're crazy!"

"Vicky, I'm warning you!"

The girl's fair skin was such an angry red it obscured her pale brows, making her look odd, sinister. "You won't even go outside any more! You won't even try! Don't you think we know? You wouldn't even walk down to the courts to watch Liz's lesson. It's a two-minute walk and you won't even try! I saw! Daddy came back to the house and you wouldn't even go with him. He was holding your hand and—"

"I want you out of this room right now."

"You sent Mrs. Platt outside to grill the hot dogs last night. You won't even go out the back door any more, for God's sake. Not out the back door. What are you afraid of? There's nothing wrong with you! Everybody says—"

"Get out, Vicky!"

"Why didn't you let me go to Yugoslavia to be with Daddy? I could have gone there and had fun instead of having to tell all my friends, 'Oh, my mother has hay fever so she can't come down to the pond to watch us swim and that's why we had to have a lifeguard.' Don't you think they know it's a lie? I hate it! I could have been with Daddy!"

"Ten-year-old girls don't pick up and go to Yugoslavia for their birthdays."

"They do *too* if their father's a famous star and he wants them. He wanted me and Liz to come, and you said no because you were afraid he'd make you come with us. Murray would have taken us, or Uncle Ed, and you could just stay here reading eight million books. Why do I have to be stuck here in stupid Connecticut in this stupid house for my tenth birthday with you?"

For this picture, he'd gotten everything he wanted, and it had been so easy. They'd balked at making his brother Edward associate producer—he's only twenty-three fucking years old! they'd screamed—so Murray had begun shoveling papers back into his briefcase and they'd agreed to it. They'd also agreed to his cinematographer and wardrobe assistant, the former the man who had photographed him so brilliantly in *Urban Affairs*, the latter a kid he'd met doing *Wyoming* who was a first-rate tennis player. When he re-peated Jane's criticism, that his character—a world-weary playboy who in the course of the film realizes he is in love with his glamorous wife—was so controlled he seemed more pathological than intriguing, they'd sent the direc-tor and the writer up to Connecticut and then had agreed that Nicholas could direct his next film. They'd hired his bodyguard-driver, Ernie, and paid Nicholas for his services at a rate greater than Ernie's annual salary.

They'd rented a villa for him. It overlooked the Adriatic and had a tennis court; every morning at dawn Ernie would drive to the local hotel, pick up the kid, and he and Nicholas could get in two sets before six thirty. They'd outfitted one of the rooms with his trapeze and rings, so he could work out late every afternoon with a full view of the sea. At night he flipped a switch and light flooded the private beach below. A few times a week Edward and the girl he was seeing, the powder girl, would come over and the three of them would swim and have a picnic on the sand, in bathing suits and sweatshirts, served on china by a Serbian butler who sounded as if he'd trained with the Royal Shakespeare Company.

What burned him, what really burned him, was that it was August. Summer. Jane and the girls could have spent the summer with him. He tried to understand. He knew how miserable it made her. Once they'd been read-ing in bed, and all of a sudden she turned to him and said, with such profound sadness in her voice, "Why can't I be like everybody else? Why can't I go to a bookstore?" You *can*, he'd said, but it had come to nothing. He'd even gotten the name of a psychiatrist, but the psychiatrist told him he would not come to the house. Jane would have to come to his office for treatment. She has to be willing to take the first step, the psychiatrist said. She wasn't willing. *Please*, she'd beg him, whenever he suggested she try, *please* don't make me.

She was fine at home. Your wife is some charmer! Nick, where have you been keeping her? She was superb. Gracious hostess. Delightful conversa-tionalist. Informed. Witty. Well-read, naturally. Reporters loved her. "Warm." "Real." "The rarest of rare creatures: the contented spouse of a star."

"'Nicholas is the elegant taper. Jane is the soft, sure flame that casts a

343

warm glow.' They paid her for writing that," Jane commented, looking up from the magazine article she was reading to him. "Someone gave that woman money to write that sentence."

He'd pleaded with her to come. It will be just a seven-hour flight. We can use the studio's corporate jet. *Please*. You can take a pill and knock yourself out, and when you wake up you'll be there. I'm sorry, she said over and over. I'm sorry.

How many sets of tennis could he play? How many murders in English vicarages could he read about? How many evenings could he spend with Edward and his nineteen-year-old girl friend?

Everything had been done to make him happy. Their shameless eagerness to please him occasionally made him want to say, "I know. I'm being unreasonable." And they would have said, "Hey, Nick, you *should* have five thou a week spending money. Who wants to get caught short in Yugoslavia? Right?"

They'd fixed up his trailer the way he'd told them he wanted it done. The first time he entered it he was stunned; it looked very much like his grandfather Samuel's study. Each day there were copies of the *New York Times*, the *International Herald Tribune*, and the *Wall Street Journal* on the table. They'd even filled the bookshelves with leatherbound copies of British whodunits and histories of World War II; he did not know how they discovered his taste in books. It was a spartan room, except for the bed they brought in. It was too big for the space and had an ugly padded leather headboard. He hadn't used it until the last few days, when he'd finally succumbed to inertia.

There were some things they could not do for him. Shooting had come to a standstill. It poured, and when it didn't pour, a greasy fog blew over the beach. They only had two scenes left: one from the middle of the film, when he had to pull his wife out of the water at night, where the drug traffickers had left her, wounded, to drown; and the penultimate scene, where he had to stalk a densely packed beach, around supine bronzing bodies, just another blasé stroller shouldering past standard Riviera types—bikinied exhibitionists, musclemen, fat men with fat cigars—trying to find the man who'd kidnapped his wife, before the man found him.

Nicholas was sprawled across the bed, a blanket over his legs. It was cold in the trailer. He was wearing his costume, formal dress. A white dinner jacket hung beside him on a straight-backed chair. They were waiting for the weather to clear so he could drag Laurel Blake out of the water. He yawned. It was after ten. The night was black. Sheets of rain slashed against the trailer. He'd agreed to stay until midnight to get the damned thing over with. The weather reports had been favorable, the director optimistic. His brother had said good night an hour earlier.

344

He'd been worried about Edward, but it had turned out well. With his scrawny build, straggly red beard, and his clothes, bib overalls and no shirt, he looked like a migrant laborer, but he was personable and, to Nicholas's surprise, relatively hard-working. For someone who had flunked out of three colleges and nearly gotten a dishonorable discharge from the army—he was caught selling hashish to undercover military police in Vietnam—Edward was behaving like a solid citizen.

The noise of the rain was loud enough to drown out the knock on his trailer door, and he didn't realize someone was outside until the knock became a wild pounding. He opened the door. For an instant he did not recognize who it was. But when he looked closer, he saw it was Laurel Blake, his co-star, in a soaked trench coat, a green plastic trash bag covering her hair. Her high-heeled gold slippers were dotted with mud. "I hate to bother you," she said.

"That's okay. Come in."

Actually, she really hadn't bothered him too much. In the first of the twelve weeks of shooting, she'd come on to him, hinting she'd like to see his villa, half teasing about rehearsing their love scenes. But whatever desire she had for him had been counterbalanced by her awe of him, and she was nervous enough in his presence not to pursue him.

She was young and beautiful and missed being dull-witted by a hair's breadth. But when the actress who'd been chosen to play his wife changed her mind the day before she was supposed to sign, he'd agreed to see Laurel's first film. She'd had a small role playing what, in fact, she was: a high-fashion model. She looked lovely on film—he'd heard many models did not. Her diction was clear, her voice well-pitched, and she seemed to be able to act convincingly.

Gingerly, Laurel took the trash bag from her head. Her hair, a chestnut brown, was pulled back tight into an elaborate topknot of curls that was held in place by jeweled clips. The curls were not hers and the jewels were fake. Laurel would be flailing in the water until he pulled her out, and after each take they'd stick on a dry hairpiece.

"How is everything going?" he asked. She was looking around his trailer. He assumed she was comparing it with her own.

"What?"

"How is everything?"

"I'm bored."

"It can get boring. Would you like to borrow a book?"

"No, thanks." She was an unusual beauty. Her eyes were large and dark, and they slanted up, giving her face an exotic Eurasian cast. Her skin, though, was fair, her lower lip unusually full. Her nose was too small, too cutely upturned for the sophistication of her face, but instead of detracting, it added to the sum of her appeal. "What do you do when you get bored?" she asked.

"I'm working on my next film. . . . I'm directing. And I read. Make business calls. Speak to my wife and children."

"Do you think we'll be able to shoot tonight?"

"No, but I think he'll want to keep us here until twelve, just in case."

"In case what?"

He didn't think she was faking it. She seemed genuinely dumb. "In case it clears."

"Oh." She put a hand on the belt of her trench coat. "Could I take it off? It's all wet."

"Sorry. Sure. Let me help you with it."

"That's okay." She slipped out of the coat. She was wearing nothing under it.

"Oh, Christ!"

She had a magnificent body. He'd never seen anything remotely resembling it, not even in men's magazines. Magnificent, slender, soft. Her breasts were small but full, with the same upturned curve as her nose. Her waist was tiny, as though pieces of her had been artfully chiseled away. Her pubic hair was a triangle of rich fur.

"Put on your coat and get out," he said.

She dropped the coat to the floor and walked to him, her legs long and sleek in the high gold shoes. She stood before him, hands at her sides, motionless. The clips in her hair threw off blue and green sparks. He waited for her to make her move, to put her arms around him and draw him against her, kiss him, go for his pants. Then he could push her away and say "Out!" She did nothing. Her shoulders were creamy, with a pale pink gleam, like the inside of a seashell. If she took half a step forward, she'd be pressing against him. She stayed still.

I don't want this, he thought. I don't want any of this.

He lifted his hand and cupped her breast. Firm. The skin so hot. Her arms remained at her sides. He held her other breast, rolled the small nipple between his fingers, then let his hand graze down her belly, to the soft triangle. She was just standing there, letting him do anything he wanted. Just standing there.

Enough was enough. Things were going too far. He could feel himself at the edge, wanting to tear off his shirt and feel her hard little nipples against his chest. He had to get her out. Out.

He plunged his hand deep into the patch of fur. The heat rose from between her legs and warmed the tips of his fingers.

"Kiss me," he said. "Come on. Do it." She turned her mouth up toward his. That was her only movement. "Kiss me, goddamn it." Her mouth waited for his. "Did you hear what I said? Kiss me."

Then he grabbed her. He held the back of her neck as tightly as he could and brought her forward, slamming her mouth against his. He held her body tight, crushing her breasts against his starched formal shirt. Suddenly she gave in. Her arms reached around his neck. Her hips thrust forward. Her mouth opened, pulled in his tongue, and sucked on it. He grabbed her behind and squeezed hard. She let out a squeak of pleasure. "Now," he said, as he threw her onto the bed, "now I'm going to give you what you came for, you goddamn stupid bitch."

21

. . . although a spokesman for the hospital said a decision as to whether neurosurgery is indicated would be made within the hour.
—WTOP Radio, Washington, D.C.

"You always do this," Jane said, putting the old gym bag Rhodes had brought as a suitcase on a footstool in one of the guest bedrooms. "You never call. You just drop in." She peered at the bag with its fraying handles. "Is this chic?"

"For me, yes. For you, no." Rhodes unzipped the bag and handed her a package. It was wrapped in burgundy paper and tied with a long, thin ribbon that spiraled like Shirley Temple's curls. "Why should I call? You're always home."

"Stop that."

"I merely made a statement of fact."

"But what if I'm having other guests? I mean it, Rhodes. People are coming here all the time to work with Nick between films."

"A, Nick is away. B, if push ever comes to shove, blood relatives come before the hired help. You'd just roll the little old Italian director out of the bed and say 'Ciao, Mario darling. My brother is here.'" Rhodes reached down to unpack. His socks, folded rather than rolled, were in a flat plastic case, his undershorts in another, and his undershirts, the sort with straps Jane assumed had become fashionable in Europe again, in still another. Each shirt and sweater was wrapped in its own cellophane package. "Would you open the present? Once you see what it is you'll be a little nicer to me .·. . if you have an ounce of taste."

"It's gorgeous!" It was a shawl of antique lace. "Just magnificent! You shouldn't have. It must be terribly expensive."

"It was, but I had to. I may be enjoying your hospitality for a while." His voice was wrong; she could feel prickles under his smooth delivery. His appearance, however, was aggressively relaxed. He'd arrived from the airport in shorts—actually cut-off, overbleached jeans—and a faded black T-shirt. He unzipped a plastic case and put his socks in a drawer, smoothing them down in neat lines, each pair equidistant from the next.

"Oh," Jane said. "Glad you're staying." Rhodes slid the drawer closed but continued to face the dresser. "Does Philip have a lot of meetings in New York? Or are you meeting him . . . Rhodes, what's the matter?" He stepped out of his sandals, stretched his toes with the lazy ease of a cat, and flexed his

348

legs, movements so at odds with his tight voice she knew he was putting on one of his cool acts. "What's wrong?"

"I left him."

"You *what?*"

"I said, I left him." There was a catch in his throat. He did not turn to face her. He rested his arms on top of the tall chest of drawers and laid his head on them.

"Oh, Rhodes." Jane stood. She was about to walk to him and put her arms around him, but then, through the thin cotton of his shirt, she saw his back stiffen. "What happened?" she asked, remaining by the gym bag.

"Nothing."

"Rhodes, please."

Her brother straightened and turned toward her. He had not been crying as she'd thought, but his face was slack. His eyes looked more inward than outward, as though he were terminally ill. "I'm almost thirty years old. Do you know what that's like?"

"Yes. I've been through it. But I didn't leave Nick."

"Oh, cut it out. You couldn't leave Nick. I hear you can't even get past the front door any more."

"Rhodes—"

"I know all about it, okay? Vicky told me before I had a chance to get out of the car. What's wrong with you? What are you afraid of?"

"You're managing to get off the subject, aren't you?"

"I asked you a question, Jane. What are you afraid of? Or are you afraid to answer?"

"I'm not afraid."

"Are you afraid of bees?" His voice was sharp, honing itself for attack. "Are you afraid you're allergic like your mother? Is that it?"

"No. Now stop it!"

"One little zap and it's checkout time. Bye-bye Sally, hello Dorothy." Jane grabbed a package of undershirts and hurled them at Rhodes's face. She missed. The package landed on top of the dresser. "Thanks," Rhodes said, and opened another drawer.

"Speaking of checkout time, Rhodesie," she hissed, "are you still paying rent on seven rooms overlooking Eden Park? Sorry, does Philip Gray pay the rent? Or did he stop paying the rent and . . . "

"And what?"

"Fire you." His eyes widened. He seemed to be surprised not only at her words but by her anger. Surprised, then wounded. He took a step back. "How can you make fun of my mother's death?" she asked, softening her tone, realizing he was far more hurt than she. "What's wrong, Rhodes?" He held onto the edge of the opened drawer as if he needed it for support. "Come

349

here," Jane said. She sat on the bed. Rhodes hung back for a few seconds, then came and sat beside her. He tucked his right foot under his left thigh. When they were children, he'd sat that way in their gentlest moments, when he sneaked into her room with a storybook. "Tell me about it, Rhodes."

"You know how long it's been for us. Eleven years."

"I know. It was just before Nick and I—"

"I've seen him every single day since that first day. Every day. Even when they went away together, without me—and that was only a couple of times—I'd go and stay in another hotel. And he's been completely . . . Listen, Jane, I have to talk. You know what the score is, don't you? About Philip and me."

"You mean that you're lovers."

"Yes. I mean, Mom thinks I work for him, and I knew you knew, or I thought you knew, but it wasn't something I thought we had to talk about."

"Do you honestly think she believes it's an employer-employee relationship?"

"Jane, please get off her. This isn't about her, okay?"

His pleading tone unnerved her. In the past few years, she had grown so dependent on the services of others that she'd forgotten what it was like to be depended on. People were hired to drive for her, clean and shop for her, mother her children when they left the house. Sometimes she forgot there had been a time when she was strong. "I'm sorry. Please, go on."

"Eleven years. When we're off together, just the two of us, it's perfect. Even if he's on the phone half the day. We never get bored with each other. I'm not just talking about sex."

"I know."

"Books, movies, people, art, music, you name it. Even when I was a kid, eighteen, we were turned on to each other in every way. And it's only gotten better."

One of his eyebrows was ruffled. Jane stroked it back into place. "Then why did you leave him?"

"Because—" He broke off, unable to speak, and shook his head.

"Do you want to be alone for a few minutes?"

He shook his head. "No. I'm okay. Let me finish what I was saying." He took a deep breath. "When we're away, it's heaven. And we get away a lot. You know we're always off someplace. But in Cincinnati . . . we have to be careful. We used to go out together, but then people started talking so we stopped. *He* goes out. He goes with her."

"He still lives with her?"

"He lives with her. They're Mr. and Mrs. Philip Gray, and they're invited *everywhere*. And when they finish going everywhere, he drives to my place. Some of the time. Sometimes he stays with her."

350

"Do you think they still . . . "

"Yes. Most nights, weekends, they go their own separate ways and we're together. But we're together in my place or at one or two friends' houses. And that's it. This is your life, Rhodes Heissenhuber."

"What about work?"

"Come on."

"What do you mean?"

"Do you really think he'd ever let me into that part of his life? Do you think I have any real understanding about what he does? Do you think I care?"

"Oh."

"I go in a couple of days a week, sit in my office, make a few phone calls. I do things for us. Hotel reservations. Keep up with friends in Europe. Call the shirtmaker. I'm twenty-nine years old, and that's all I can do. I never went to college. I never had a job. I never got a paycheck. He pays for everything. All I've done is . . . been with Philip. That's some résumé, isn't it?"

"Rhodes, did he ask you to leave?"

Rhodes snorted a laugh. "Of course not. He won't even know I'm gone until late tonight. He and Clarissa are having twenty pillars of the opera in for trout in aspic, and he won't come . . . Forget it. Fuck it."

"You didn't tell him you were going?"

"I left him a letter."

"Why did you leave?"

"Oh, Jane!" he demanded. "Don't you understand? He's never going to leave her. *Never*. For the rest of my life I'm stuck in Cincinnati, spending nine months of the year waiting to go on vacation. I can't make my own friends because we have to be very, very sure our friends are oh, so discreet, so there are five people, *five*, I can see. He checks up on me. He knows where I am every minute. Once he had me followed."

"By detectives?" Rhodes nodded. "Why?"

"Three guesses. Then he laid down the law: no bars, no drugs, no anything else. Like he was my father, you know, and I was a kid hanging out with a bad crowd." He rubbed his temples with the heels of his hands. "Oh, shit. I'm nothing. I don't even have a checkbook. He's set up charge accounts. I drive around in a forty-thousand-dollar Lamborghini wearing custom-made two-hundred-dollar loafers, and I have two bucks in my pocket."

Jane put her arms around him, stretched up, and kissed the top of his head. "Rhodes, he's terrified you'll leave him."

"I wouldn't. He should know I wouldn't. He should trust me."

"He's frightened. He knows you could . . . he knows you have choices."

"Choices? Jane, he *owns* me. Do you know how I got the money to come here and buy you that lace thing? Last night I took three hundred dollars from

351

his wallet. Isn't that nice? Made me feel real fucking proud of myself." Rhodes began to cry. Tears poured from his eyes as though someone else were weeping. He neither sobbed nor shook, but sat utterly still on the bed.

"It's all right," she said, kissing him again.

"No. It's *not* all right. What am I going to do? Find someone else to keep me? And then another and another until I'm so old all I'll be able to do is—"

"Speak to him. Tell him what you're telling me."

"Don't you think I have? He passes it off. 'Oh, come on, darling, do you really want to learn to read an annual report? If you want to I'll be glad to teach you, but you know how boring it's going to be.' And he's right. I have zero interest in it. Oh, and then he says, 'You don't need money. Don't you know I'll always take care of you?'"

"Tell him you don't know he'll always take care of you. That you don't want him to. Tell him you're an adult. Take a cue from the women's movement. I mean it, Rhodes. You're a person. Tell him you want to be treated like one. You want a salary. You want to pay your own way."

"Let's not go overboard."

"Rhodes, you're not going to gain his respect, his trust, until he sees you can stand on your own two feet and not leave him. He has to see you're staying with him out of choice, not because you have to. You're with him because you care about him." She swallowed. "Because you love him." Rhodes shrugged his shoulders. "If he knows you can't function without him, it's never going to be an equal relationship. You'll always have to do things his way, because you've surrendered control."

Rhodes took her hand in his. She gazed down. Their hands were so alike in size and shape, with the same long, slightly flattened fingers, that they might have been part of the same body. "Listen to yourself," Rhodes said. Some of the sharpness had returned to his voice. Jane tried to inch away, but her brother held tight to her hand. "You give very wise advice, Jane. Now, the question is: what about you?"

"What do you mean, me? Don't pull your old trick. We happen to be talking about you. I'm fine. My marriage—"

"We did very well, considering where we started. Married up, didn't we? And to two of a kind. Oh, yes, we did. Rich, social, smart, dynamic, powerful. Definitely powerful. Always running the show. God, talk about father figures. It's so blatant it's not even worth thinking about."

"I don't think you can compare—"

"Minus ten."

"I mean it, Rhodes."

"Minus twenty. Jane, look where they are and then look where we are. Look!" She yanked her hand away from his. "Look, idiot," he snapped. "We do precisely what they want us to do. They have us just where they want us, unable to live without them. Do you see now? It's not that they're gods, above it all, deigning to throw a little gold dust on us by recognizing our existence. They need our love desperately and they take everything we have to give. But they're shrewd enough and powerful enough to use our love for them—our weakness—to control us. They're two of a kind, Nick and Philip. And so are we."

He was a pig, rutting in the mud. But each time he wanted to get out, to stop being a pig, he slipped and fell right back in. Every day Nicholas made up his mind to end it. Every night Laurel was back in his bed.

Everybody knew. The third day, the wardrobe mistress came into her trailer. "Oh!" she'd squeaked. She'd dropped Laurel's costume. He'd been in a chair, fully clothed. Almost. Laurel had unzipped him and climbed onto his lap. They were going at it hard, rocking back and forth. She'd been bare-assed, wearing only knee socks and a little pink T-shirt. "Sorry. I'm really sorry," the woman whimpered. Then she bolted.

Minutes later, when he emerged from the trailer, everybody knew.

People had always kidded him on location, calling him Naughty Nick because he was so straight; teasing him, sending him messages that the hookers he'd sent for had called and were waiting for him back at the hotel; hanging pornographic postcards on the mirror in makeup every morning autographed *To Nicky. Thanks for everything*. No one teased him any more. Everyone was polite, pretending not to watch when Laurel climbed into the limousine with him each afternoon.

Murray, who'd been scheduled to fly in from New York, called and cancelled. "I'm really pressed here, Nicky. Do you mind?" Murray's voice was thick with artificial cheer, and his words rushed over the transatlantic wire, as though he wanted to get them out as fast as he could. "Pressure, pressure. Pure craziness here, Nicky." Murray had heard. Nicholas hung up the phone numb with shame.

She was so stupid. He tried to talk to her, but it wasn't part of her repertoire. Only sex was. Whenever she did anything different, and she had no end of tricks, he'd think how many times she'd done it before. One night she was licking him all over and he thought about all the photographers, magazine editors, garment center executives, producers, directors, and journalists she'd licked before. Her rough, dry tongue was expert and impersonal. But the knowledge did not help him. He could not extricate himself. Whenever he tried to stop being an animal, she'd haul him back into the mud with a new trick.

He behaved so badly to her. He tried to be pleasant a couple of times, to kid around with her, but he could have been performing to an empty room. She didn't seem to care how he behaved. Her indifference only made him go

353

at her harder, but nothing got a rise out of her. "Did anyone ever tell you you were a dumb cunt?" He'd actually asked her that. He'd never spoken to anyone like that before. And she'd giggled. The whole thing made him sick.

The worst of it was, after all the propositions from women—hundreds, thousands for all he knew—after all the years of knowing he could have anyone he wanted and nine tenths of the time not even being tempted, here he was, getting done by a cheap, stupid tramp. That was what she said. "Let me do you again, honey."

Everyone knew. The president of the studio called and Nicholas could hear the man's silky pleasure, his knowledge that he'd located a potential weak spot. "How's Laurel Blake working out?" the man asked.

His brother knew. Edward never said a word. He'd just tell Nicholas his plans each afternoon—"Rosie and I are going to a restaurant that's about an hour away. Mind if I run?"—so Nicholas wouldn't have to offer any embarrassing explanations for not wanting to spend his evenings with them.

He couldn't believe he was doing something like this with a member of his family as witness. Making Edward a silent co-conspirator, the way all of them had been for years when his father came home drunk, stinking from other women.

No one, not Murray, not even his brother, said, "Stop. Are you *crazy?* What's gotten into you? She's slime. She's turning you into slime." He'd become exempt. Everyone wanted him to do whatever pleased him. Nicholas Cobleigh must, at all costs, be kept happy.

The journalists knew. There were blind and not-so-blind items in gossip columns; photographs, innocent enough, in English and Italian papers. The captions were not so innocent.

He called Jane one afternoon. "Hi!" she'd said. "You're early."

"How are you?"

"What's wrong, Nick?"

"Nothing."

"Come on. You don't sound right."

"I don't know. I'm upset."

"Why?"

"There are a lot of rumors going around about me and Laurel Blake."

"Oh, that. There are always rumors. When have you made a rumorless movie?" He could just see her, almost reflexively turning on a smile. Some nights, lying awake while Laurel slept, he wondered if Jane knew, if she had, in fact, taken the conspiracy to its limit, to the point where she'd become his most willing accomplice. Cheery, unquestioning, loving. Keeper of the best-documented hearth in America. He wondered if she had believed in his faithfulness all the years he had been worthy of her trust. "Do you think I'm going to start believing that sort of thing at this late date?" she asked.

"Jane . . . "

"What?"

"It's worse than usual this time. It's ugly."

"Stop worrying. Oh, Nick, sweetheart, you know it happens every time you go away. No one with any intelligence believes it. And you know I don't."

"I feel terrible."

"Don't. But tell me about her. Is she gorgeous? Built like a brick you-know-what? Should I abandon all hope and call a divorce lawyer?"

"She's stupid."

"Oh, good! Now come on, I want you to stop sounding so down in the dumps. Please. Oh, hold on a second. I've got to read you Liz's letter. But don't have a heart attack."

"Why?"

"I think she's in love. The letter is hilarious. His name is Chris and he lives down the street from Tom and Nan and he's quote 'completely icky' unquote, and then she goes on about his complete ickiness for a page and a half. If that isn't love, I don't know what is."

"Jane, I love you," he'd said. "You know I do."

"Of course I know. I love you too."

There was no Indian summer. A week after Labor Day and it was autumn. The Manhattan store that three times a week trucked their premium fruits and vegetables to the Cobleigh house at exorbitant rates had included two gallons of the season's first fresh-pressed apple cider with their last delivery. The cider came in brown crocks and, Jane finally admitted, cost ten dollars a gallon.

"If she waited one more week, she could have it for less than a dollar at Gil's farm stand up the road," Cecily Van Doorn said to Rhodes Heissenhuber. "In plastic bottles." They were seated across from each other at the dining room table.

Jane buttered a small piece of homemade bread. Her dinners, small and large, were celebrated. Her recipes had been circulated around the world: "Jane and Nicholas Cobleigh Give a Clambake!" "Signora Cobleigh Prepara Spiedini di Gamberi." "American Excellence: Easter Sunday Breakfast at the Cobleighs'." She was wrapped in Nicholas's renown, and no one cared or dared ask why she was always the hostess, never a guest.

"But if she got her cider from Gil, she wouldn't have these adorable little jugs," Rhodes remarked. "The epitome of country cute. And if dear old Gil—he is a dear old Connecticut farmer, isn't he?"

"No," Cecily said, "he's in his early twenties and he looks like he sprung from the Jukes and the Kallikaks. Extra-long arms and the eyes a little too far apart."

"Well, anyway, even if she could arrange for him to deliver the cider, he might ring the bell and if it were Mrs. Platt's day off there Jane would be, face to face with the Great Outdoors and *Gil*. And what if Gil said, 'Gee, ma'am, these plastic bottles sure are heavy. Could you come out to the car and help me with them?' Then what would she do? Go out? *Jane?*"

"Enough, Rhodes," Jane said. She pushed up the sleeves of her dress, which was actually an ambitious sweater: a slim tube of red cashmere that stopped at her ankles.

"Walk out the front door?" Rhodes continued, as though she hadn't spoken. "Our Jane? Never."

Jane set down her fork. "I said enough."

"Oh, sorry," her brother said, but he continued to look at and talk to Cecily. "We all know she could go out if she wanted to. That's what she says, and if she says so it must be true. But she just hasn't had a chance to go outside because she's such a busy little housewife. That's her *job*. She's very, very busy being a feminist housewife. Totally liberated, of course, but she doesn't have a second to go outside. She probably gave away her coat, so she certainly can't go out and risk pneumonia for a person with dubious chromosomes and cheap cider. It's just not worth it."

They all thought it was so easy. Just walk out the door. Jump in the car and pick up some cider and a jar of apple butter at the farm stand. Come *on*. *Do* it. All that was standing in her way was a little neurosis. A little self-indulgence. A little fear. How many people had taken her aside and said in such satisfied tones, as if they'd discovered a brilliant therapeutic technique, "'There is nothing to fear but fear itself'"? How many? Fifteen? Twenty? All of them, even all those relentlessly Republican Cobleighs, quoting Roosevelt as if that were all she needed: a good, bracing, Democratic cliché. It had galvanized the masses once before and she was, after all, one of them. Shape up! Show us what you're made of! You can do it! Snap out of it! Stiff upper lip!

They all thought she wasn't really trying, she, who had a husband who—nods of approval all around—did absolutely everything he could for her. Hadn't he persisted, calling expert after expert until he finally found a psychiatrist who made house calls? Paying five times the man's normal rate, providing a car and driver to bring him to the house four mornings a week for analysis. They'd worked in the parlor, she lying on a couch, the psychiatrist sitting in an easy chair behind her. All she could see of him was the white of his leg between his pants and his droopy socks. She'd been afraid she'd get emotionally involved with him and slip and say something terribly revealing—tell him she wanted to see what his penis looked like or even that she wished he wore over-the-calf socks—but that never happened. She talked to him about her mother and Dorothy, but she knew he was waiting for her to talk about her father, as if he knew precisely what she was withholding. He had lasted a year and a half. When he left, she was no closer to being able to leave the house than when he'd first arrived. And then there were two others. The woman who kept at her: "Let go of your anger, Jane." The man who said, again and again, "You have too many 'shoulds.'" All that help, all that money, all that hope, and nothing to show for it. Come on, Jane, people said. If not for yourself, do it for that husband of yours. That loving, devoted, patient man. Come on! Make him proud of you.

Did they think it was fun not making him proud? I can't go to the Academy Awards with you. Standing there in the living room, head hanging, while he shouted Goddamn it! Goddamn it! slamming his fist down on the bass keys of the piano. I can't, Nick, I can't, I can't. Watching him leave for Los Angeles, once with Vicky, another time with Liz, accepting his weary kiss. Take care of yourself, Jane. I'll call. Watching on television when the camera panned the audience and focused on four other actors and their wives or girl friends and then on Nicholas, holding the hand of a little girl.

And did they think it was fun those times, being late for her period? Waking up every day nearly deranged with anguish? Go through a pregnancy? Be dragged from the house—shrieking, held on a stretcher with restraining straps—into an ambulance at the very last minute? Or planning how to avoid it, how to kill it? To half poison herself, to murder a fetus with pills, or to risk a coat hanger because she couldn't go out the door? Did they think it amused her? Did they think she enjoyed breaking down, sobbing with relief until she was faint, when her period finally came? Did they think it was laughs, that she felt every act of intercourse put her life and her sanity on the line?

Did they think she didn't mind what she had become? A mother whose children were daily disappointed in her. A wife who could not sit on the front steps and watch a sunset with her husband. The co-owner of a beach house on the Pacific and an eight-room Manhattan cooperative she would never see. I can't stay in hotels, Nicholas had explained. People find the room. They bang on the door in the middle of the night. Buy a place, she'd pleaded with him. You have to be there so often. It makes sense. Not without you, Jane. *Please,* she'd begged him. It's all right.

Did they know her loneliness? Did they know how often she imagined Nicholas's loneliness and all the ways all the women sought to comfort him? Did they know what it felt like not to be able to do the things that no one else thought about? Did they know what she would give to have dinner in a restaurant? To take her daughters to the movies?

Did they know what it was like to have Nicholas plead with her? I love you. Trust me. I'll hold your hand. Just take the first step with me. Please, Jane. *Please.* Did they know what it was like to have to say, I can't. I can't. I truly can't. Did they know?

Cecily finished her cider and glanced at Jane. "That dress is absolutely magnificent on you. Really, I've never seen you looking so gorgeous. You really ought to save it for when Nick—"

"You're changing the subject, Cecily," Rhodes interrupted.

"—for when Nick comes home tomorrow. Don't be a pain, Rhodes. I know exactly what I'm saying."

"Nick called just before you came. He won't be in until the day after," Jane said. "Or until the weekend. He's stuck in Paris."

"Pity him," Rhodes said.

"He and the screenwriter have to scout locations for his next film in a farm region someplace south of Paris, and he says he'd rather get it over now, on the way home from Yugoslavia, than to have to go back a month from now."

"She could be in Paris," Rhodes said, "checking off numbers at Saint Laurent instead of walking around in that sweater thing that makes her look like an ad for the Playtex Cross-Your-Heart bra."

"She looks beautiful," Cecily said.

"She looks tolerable. And only because Nick's makeup man came up to Connecticut before Nick left and threw her onto the floor and wouldn't let her up until she agreed to look like an adult."

"That didn't happen," Jane said to Cecily.

"Of course not," Cecily agreed. "I know Rhodes by now."

"You know," Rhodes said, "it's one thing for *Newsweek* to call them the golden couple, but it's another for her to have skin that's literally golden. Yellow, actually. The sun hasn't seen her face for months. She has to wear makeup or people will think she has hepatitis."

"Rhodes, I'm not going to allow you to get me angry," Jane said. She smoothed her napkin across her lap over and over.

"You can't get angry any more," he said. "You're taking so much Valium the most you can get is mildly pissed."

"That's not true. I'm only taking—"

"Maybe the yellow dye in the Valium is what's doing it."

"Maybe you should just stop," Jane said. She left her chair and walked to the fireplace. She opened the screen, knelt, and pushed open the flue. "Do you think it's nippy enough for a fire, Cecily?" she asked.

"Not yet. By next week." Cecily turned to Rhodes. "I hear you're leaving us soon. Tired of Connecticut?"

"I was tired of Connecticut the minute after I crossed the state line. It makes Ohio seem exciting. No, the man I work for has been calling ten times a day ever since I got here, and it's either pull the phone out of the wall or go back to Cincinnati, so I'm going back. I really wanted a longer vacation, but the office is falling apart without me. Anyway, it's been a little less than amusing hanging around here celebrating Be Kind to Shut-Ins Week for nearly a month."

"Don't, Rhodes," Cecily said.

"It wasn't as much fun as I thought. She's only had one attack, and it was no big thing. All she did was sweat a little and run up to her room."

"Shut up!" Cecily snapped. "She's too good to you for you to treat her like that. I mean it. Have a little compassion."

"I have."

"Then show it."

Jane stayed still, kneeling by the fireside. Finally, she closed the flue and stood, brushing the soot from her hands. Suddenly, Rhodes was beside her. "Please, Rhodes," she said, "I've really had enough for one night." He rested his elbow on the mantel. Jane looked at him. He should be the star, she thought. His face had gotten stronger, the planes of his cheeks and jaw squarer and more manly, but that merely deepened his beauty. He grinned at her. Even his teeth were flawless. "Let's de-escalate, Rhodes." She smiled at him, trying—in vain, she knew—to flash a grin to match his.

But his expression turned somber. "You need help," he said quietly.

"I've had it."

"Jane, please, just listen to me. Before I leave I want to know you're—"

"We're being rude to Cecily." She nearly chirped. Hurriedly, she moved away from him, returning to her seat at the table.

Rhodes followed her but stood behind his chair, watching her. "Sorry, Cec," she said. "The two of us have been horrendous. It's just that we have this need to let loose, to test whether the old sibling rivalry is still in working order."

"Jane," Rhodes said, "you can't go on living like this. It's not living."

"Rhodes, this little exercise really isn't necessary."

"For God's sake, Jane, it's the most necessary thing in the world. You're dying and this house is your fucking tomb! Don't you see that? Don't you—"

"I have a guest, Rhodes." She looked at Cecily. "I apologize. I thought it would be fun for all of us to have one final dinner together before he goes back home."

"*Jane*," Rhodes began.

"Not now."

"You can't keep—"

"Not now!"

Cecily looked from Jane to Rhodes and back to Jane, then lowered her head. When she spoke she could barely be heard. "Listen to him, Jane."

"I thought we'd agreed this wasn't a subject for discussion, Cecily."

"No. *You* told me it wasn't a subject for discussion," Cecily replied, her voice strong now. "And so I played along, because I figured that was the price of the friendship. Well, do you want to know something? It's too damn high a price."

"Why can't both of you believe me? I've told you over and over I'm *fine*. I'm happy. I have everything I want in the world right here in this house, and there's no reason for me to leave. But you just can't let up, can you, Rhodes, you—"

Cecily reached across the table and put her hand over Jane's. "Your brother loves you." Rhodes looked away. "You know he does." Jane shrugged. "And it hurts him to see you like this. Jane, don't get up and walk off in a huff. Listen to us. You need professional help."

"No! No more psychiatrists. They don't help."

"You know what's so ironic?" Rhodes said. "Ninety-nine percent of the women in the world would change places with you in a minute. You have everything they want."

"I do! That's right. I have everything a woman could ask for, so why don't you leave me alone?"

"Because you're sick!"

"*I'm* sick? What about—"

Rhodes banged his fist on the table. The glasses shivered. "You listen to me, damn it. I can choose what I want to do with my life. You can't. You need help. Your world is getting smaller and smaller. You're going to wind up living on the head of a pin!"

"Rhodes, you really don't know what you're talking about."

"Jane, listen to him," Cecily said. "Listen to *me*. Life is too short. I know. Please, don't throw it away."

Laurel Blake lay on her back on the canopied bed in a pair of lavender bikini underpants. She brought one foot close to her face to examine the polish on her toenails and to give her the opportunity to spread her legs. The underpants were so tight and so sheer all they did was emphasize her vulva and tint it lavender. There was one tiny, wet purple stain. "The French really do a nice job," she said, examining her toes.

The telephone rang. "If it's my wife, you get the hell out of here," Nicholas said.

"Can't you take the call inside?"

"Christ!" he said, and stalked off, slamming the door, into the living room of the hotel suite. He picked up the phone on the third ring.

"Bonjour, Nick! How's Paris?"

He stepped away from the floor-to-ceiling windows. "Fine," he said. He was naked. When he leaned against the wall, the plaster felt cold and damp on his back. He stood straight. "Jack?"

"Of course it's Jack! Who were you expecting, Louis B. Mayer maybe?" Jack Crowley had a particularly irritating manner with Nicholas, starting conversations by putting on what he obviously assumed was the voice of a Hollywood insider, hyped up, with a whine that was supposed to be a Yiddish inflection. He was the senior tax partner in his father's law firm and with everybody else sounded like what he was: a boring Wall Street lawyer. "Boy, you must be tear-assing around the City of Dreams. I've been leaving messages for *days*. Anyway, this is the reason for my call. You there, Nick?"

"Yes."

Laurel Blake opened the door and waited. Then, not receiving any gesture of dismissal, she sauntered into the room. She had removed the lavender underpants. He stared at her. The half-drawn drapes subdued the daylight, but he thought she'd rouged the tips of her breasts.

"We have a syndication you might be interested in, Nick. Just among some of the partners and preferred clients. One of the oil deals. There's an exciting exploratory play in the Anadarko Basin. A lot of major companies are purchasing leases in that area."

"Where is it?"

Laurel edged behind him and put her hands on his haunches. He reached back and pushed her away.

"Oklahoma. There's been a really successful wildcat discovery. And when I say successful, Nick, I mean it. This is pretty impressive. Pretty damned impressive."

Laurel slid around front. She knelt before him and took his penis in her mouth. He lifted his hand to push her away, then let his hand drop. Within seconds he had an erection so powerful it was almost painful. She ran her tongue lightly and rapidly around the top.

"Which isn't to say it isn't speculative," Crowley said. "You know that as well as I do."

"Right," Nicholas said.

Laurel's arms went around him. Jack droned on. With her hands on his behind, Laurel coaxed him forward, driving him deeper into her mouth. She dug her fingers into the muscles of his behind.

"But it can be written off totally in the first year."

"That's an advantage," Nicholas said.

"Of course it's an advantage. Also, and this is the thing, the payback should be pretty quick."

"Good."

Laurel eased a finger into his anus. Nicholas gasped. Quickly, he cupped his hand over the telephone speaker. Laurel's finger moved around and around, in and out, slowly.

" . . . but that's if it goes," Crowley was saying.

"Good," Nicholas managed to say.

"Sounds pretty good to me too, Nick. That's why I kept calling. I figured you'd want to be in on it."

"I appreciate it."

Each time Laurel sucked, she sucked a little harder.

"They're being sold in minimum units of a hundred and fifty thousand dollars."

Nicholas reached in back of him and grabbed her wrist, forcing her finger higher inside him. She took his cue, thrusting her finger in a faster rhythm. Her mouth took up the same beat. He closed his eyes and leaned his head back. He couldn't take any more.

"Do you want me to put you down, Nick?"

"Please."

"How many units? . . . Hello, Nick? You there?"

"Just thinking."

"Bad habit."

"Give me a minute."

It was happening too fast. He was ready. The top of his head felt as if it were coming off. He began to ejaculate and clamped his hand over the phone again. His breath came in fast, deep pants until, with a final jolting spurt, it was over.

"Some people are saying oil is to the seventies what real estate was to the sixties. Let's hope so. Right, Nick?"

Laurel withdrew her finger. Nicholas opened his eyes and looked down at her. She was spitting out his semen; she'd told him it was two hundred calories a shot and she'd rather use it up on white wine. She wiped her chin on his stomach.

"I think two units should do it, Jack. But do me a favor. Check with my father, and if he thinks I should take three, that will be fine."

"Sure. By the way, I saw your two girls yesterday."

"My daughters?"

Laurel lay down on the rug. She grabbed his foot so unexpectedly he nearly fell over. He braced himself against the wall. She brought it between her legs and put his big toe against her clitoris.

"Yes. They came down to New York to spend the day with your father. There he was, Grandfather of the Year. He gave them each a legal pad and a bunch of pencils and they sat there in his office while he made his calls. Cute as buttons."

Nicholas pulled his foot away and stood straight. "Thank you."

"There he was, Grandpa Jim. Putty in their hands. Can you beat that? I think he said he was going to take them to lunch and then to some magic show. Two swell girls, Nick."

After he hung up the phone, Nicholas felt chilled. He looked toward the ceiling, to see if he was under an air-conditioning duct. Gooseflesh rose on his

362

upper arms and thighs. His teeth were almost chattering. Laurel grabbed for his ankle. He rushed for the bedroom. He was so cold.

He didn't even shower. "I really have to hurry," he told her. "I have to get back." He put on underwear. Laurel grabbed one of his socks and drew it slowly between her legs. He pulled it away from her, then threw it aside and put on another pair. Then he opened the door of his closet. Laurel sidled in between his suits. "Come on, Laurel," he said.

"You're not really going. I know it." She pushed the suits on either side of her to the ends of the closet. "Come on in here. Come on. Close the door. I want to do you in the dark." He took out a dark gray suit. "Standing up," she said softly. "In the pitch dark."

"I told you, something's come up. I have to get back to the States."

"Just like that?"

"Just like that," he said. He selected a tie. Ernie would pack for him, then take a later plane. He'd buy two seats, so no one could sit beside him. Murray would arrange for someone to meet him in New York and take him through Customs.

Laurel stepped out of the closet. When he glanced at her, he was stunned. Her face was dark with anger. "Just goodbye, fuck off, Laurel?" Her pleasant voice had turned raw. He stepped back. She had never displayed any emotion before; now, her forehead was so dark he thought she might have a stroke.

"I'm sorry," he offered.

"No warning. Just eat it, sweetie, I'm going back to the wife and kids."

"Laurel, come on. You knew all along—"

She stuck her hands on her hips. The bright red tips of her breasts stared like angry eyes. "You going to stick me with the hotel bill?"

"Of course not. Come on, now. We've had a good time—"

"You had a good time, big stud, shooting your wad two, three times a day."

"I didn't say I didn't, Laurel."

"Big stud. Had yourself one big party, didn't you? Did you ever ask me if I was having fun? Did you? No. You were too busy fucking your brains out, having a good time."

"Listen to me—"

"Maybe I'll call little Janie up and tell her what a good time you had. *You* had. Not me. Let me tell you, I can name a hundred who can do it better than you, big stud. Your stomach's harder than your prick. It's true. You're starting to get old, you're—"

He knew what he had to say. He forced himself to. "What do you want, Laurel?"

"What do you mean? Do you think you can buy me off, just because you're hot shit? Big star. Big society man. Do you think I'm some cheap trick you can just throw over? I'm an actress."

"Of course you are." He had never been so terrified in his life. He willed himself to smile at her. A small smile. Sincere, a little hurt. "You know, I feel like a heel, Laurel, but I have to get back fast." He was trembling inside and was afraid it would break out and he'd begin shaking. He contracted every muscle he could, trying to get control. "You know I wouldn't go if it wasn't urgent." His voice needed more warmth; he added some. "Please, you stay on. Stay through next week. You know I'll take care of everything."

"What am I supposed to do in Paris by myself?" Her hands were still planted on her hips. "Go to restaurants alone while you're home sticking it up little Janie?"

"You must know people from your modeling days," he said. "Maybe—"

She did not hear him. "Finger-fuck myself? You're lapping her cunt and I'm here playing diddly with myself?"

He breathed in deeply and stepped closer to her. Gently, taking pains to make sure his grip wasn't too tight, he took her by her wrists and put her arms around him. "Do some more shopping," he said softly. He pulled her even closer. "You know you didn't get everything you want. Laurel, honey, I want you to buy yourself a present from me. Something nice. I wish I had the time to do it myself. I was planning to surprise you with something nice, and now I have to rush off like this." He rubbed his cheek against hers. For an instant he imagined putting his hands around her throat, his thumbs on her larynx, squeezing, squeezing, listening to the crunch of the bones breaking in her neck, watching her tongue hang out and turn black. "You know how special you are, Laurel. You know my reputation. I don't go with just anybody. You're Laurel Blake. You're going to be a big star."

"You're just saying that."

"You know it's true. You're special. You can make history. You know it, don't you? I know you do. Now listen, honey, I want you to buy yourself a very special present. Something you'll have to remember our special times."

She didn't say a word, but she stayed, leaning against him. "How much should I spend?" she finally asked.

"I think," he said slowly, "I think you should be able to find something you'd like for about ten thousand."

"Ten?"

"Twenty-five," he said quickly. "I think that should do it, don't you?"

"Oh, honey," she said and gave him three tiny pecks on his cheek. "That's nice." She gave him two more. "Thank you."

"You're welcome."

22

The hospital's administrator has given over his office to Cobleigh, so he is
further isolated from the press. However, reporters who spotted him
leaving the Intensive Care Unit said he was pale and appeared angry at
them when they . . .

—WPIX *Action News*, New York

Nicholas had come home the night before with two more Oscars, one for Best
Actor, the other for Best Director. He put them on top of his chest of drawers
beside his others, casually, along with his hairbrush and the leather box where
he kept his cufflinks and shirt studs. He dropped the shirt he was wearing—
his old Alpha Delta Phi sweatshirt—onto the floor and scratched his stomach.
Jane watched him from bed. He brought his arms together high above his
head, stretched and yawned, then took off his jeans and undershorts, tossing
them beside the sweatshirt.

He could afford to be casual. He was thirty-six and a half years old and—
after the world's heavyweight boxing champion—had the most famous face in
the world. He was recognized by more people than the pope and the President of the United States.

He was rich. Fifteen minutes earlier, Jane had signed their joint tax
return. "Do you know what?" she called out.

He mumbled something from the bathroom, his words obscured by
toothpaste. A few seconds later he appeared in the frame of the door to the
bathroom. "What?" He wiped his mouth with a hand towel, then tossed the
towel overhand back into the bathroom, as if he were passing a basketball.

"You're the richest person I know."

"You're rich too." He sauntered back into the bedroom. "You co-own
most of the real estate, and there's a lot of stuff in your name. If I kick off,
you'll be a very merry widow." The new curtains she had ordered were to be
delivered the next day. The windows were bare, and the cold light from the
outdoor mercury vapor lamps that had been installed with the security system
shone on him, deathly blue-white.

"Nick, don't say things like that. It's bad luck."

"It is?"

"Well, if it isn't it should be."

He pulled down the covers. "Even if you decided to run off with someone
tonight, you'd be in solid financial shape."

"If I ran off with someone, the farthest I could get would be the kitchen,

365

and I don't think I could carry on a passionate affair with the girls sitting around the table making snide remarks about my performance." She smiled, he chuckled. She had not left the house in more than six years.

"You could have someone sent in. Have the deliverymen bring him right up to the bedroom," he said, and climbed into bed. "You have everything else delivered. Just pick the kind of man you want. Six, eight, ten inches. Check the appropriate box. High school, college, graduate school."

"You're not funny."

"I didn't say I was funny." He left the covers bunched at the foot of the bed. "Maybe Bergdorf's has some kind of shop-at-home service. Think about it. I'll be away for two months. It might pay to look into it." Jane turned onto her side so her back was toward Nicholas. He tapped her shoulder. "Listen, you spend enough money there. I'm sure they'd accommodate you."

"Leave me alone."

"Speaking of Bergdorf's, it's interesting. For someone who doesn't go anywhere, you have one hell of a wardrobe. All those little cubbyholes you had built just for your shoes."

"If you think I'm spending too much money, why don't you just say it."

"I don't care. Spend whatever you want."

She could feel his breath on her shoulder. He was only an inch or two away from her. "Whenever you're home you have people coming up three or four nights a week," she said. "If you want me to wear tacky little house-dresses and look like Mrs. American Gothic—"

"You're starting to sound like your brother."

"What's wrong with that?"

"Because I don't like getting into bed with a Cincinnati faggot."

She turned and glared at him. "You can go to hell, Nicholas." She started to turn back, but he threw his leg over her. "Let me go," she said.

"Let's not fight," he said.

"I didn't start this. Ever since you came home from Los Angeles you've been in a disgusting mood. Being absolutely rotten to me, snapping at the girls. You didn't even say hello to the new housekeeper. You didn't even nod."

"She had her mouth hanging open and her tongue hanging out. Where did you come up with her? She looks like a retard."

"Nick, just cut it out. She was a little nervous, seeing you in person for the first time. What's gotten into you?"

"Nothing."

"Nothing? You're acting like the whole world should stop what it's doing and genuflect every time you walk by. You're acting just like every actor you've ever criticized. Calling and speaking to Murray like that, as if he were your errand boy."

366

"He screwed up on a reversion clause."

"Is that any reason to start shouting into the phone?"

"Enough, Jane." His leg was still over her. Using his knee, he began manipulating her nightgown higher. She pushed it back down. "Why are you doing that?" he demanded. He reached over and pulled it up to her waist.

"Do you really think I'm in the mood? You come home and play Nicholas Cobleigh, Superstar, and I'm supposed to swoon? Do you think when you act so tough it puts me in the mood—"

"Do you think I was in the mood two nights ago?" he snapped. "Do you, Jane? Sitting there with my mother. Going up and accepting two awards and both times giving the same old smile and saying 'Jane, this is yours too' or whatever the hell I said. The fifth goddamn time I've been there without my wife. Don't you think people talk? Or don't you give a damn any more? Are you so wrapped up in your own problems you can't see what anyone else feels? Oh, shit! Don't start that crying on me."

She couldn't help it. Like a child who's fallen and injured herself, she couldn't even catch her breath. And when she finally could, the first rush of oxygen built up so much pressure that, as an involuntary reflex, tears sprang forth. Her breath came in little hiccups, and it took her some time before she could speak. "I thought you meant it."

His head was raised. He was staring at the headboard. "Meant what?" He sounded bored, and annoyed at being bored.

"Meant what you said at the Academy Awards."

"Oh, Christ. I meant it. All right?" He raised his voice. "I said I meant it. Come on. Stop crying. Stop it. There's nothing to cry about." She swallowed and took a deep breath. He waited. She knew he knew her so well. He knew just when she was calm. And at that precise minute he began to roll up her nightgown again.

She knew him too. As he pulled it over her head and dropped it onto the floor, he leaned over and kissed her. He would kiss her for less than a minute. Then he would fondle her breasts and, seconds later, ease down the bed and begin to kiss them. That would take a few minutes and then, once his erection was established, he'd move up and kiss her once more—again for less than a minute—and then climb on top of her, where he would rub against her and caress her for ten to fifteen minutes, until he determined she was ready for intercourse. Once in a while he'd pull her on top of him. Now and then he'd push her down the mattress, his signal that he wanted oral sex, or rise on his knees to indicate he wanted to straddle her and ejaculate between her breasts. But most nights were predictable, like this one.

Here it was, right on top of her: the body everyone wanted. A magnificent body. Powerful but graceful. Fabulously muscular without the grotesque excess of the bodybuilder. The ideal body.

367

It was not the body she wanted; it was not the body she had married. Nicholas's beautiful, natural form had disappeared. He'd become an Adonis. His body was a creation, just as a statue was.

He worked at it tirelessly, every day. Since his second film, he'd appeared semi-nude in every movie he'd made. His face was his first fortune. His manner, steam under ice, made him his second fortune; his ability to act his third. His professionalism, his shrewdness, his reputation as an aristocrat, his cool charm made him even richer.

But his body set him up for life. It had become an international standard of excellence: French wine, Southern hospitality, Nicholas Cobleigh's physique. At thirty, he'd begun doing a half hour of exercise each day. Now, with his gymnastics trainer, he was doing two hours on the rings, rope, horse, and trapeze. He spent another half hour working with weights. For most of their marriage, his first act each day had been to curl up against her and deny it was morning. Now it was slipping out of bed to do two hundred sit-ups.

Nicholas Cobleigh's famous chest, perfectly formed, solid, pressed against hers. How many women dreamed of this?

Sometimes she dreamed of Charlie Harrison. He'd spent a weekend with them the previous summer and one afternoon came into the house after a swim in the pond. He was wearing baggy plaid bathing trunks. His shoulders were still the massive ones of a college football player, although his stomach had become a gut, pushing against the waistband of his trunks, threatening to overhang it in a year or two. But his chest had a thick covering of brown hair, and it sparkled with the droplets of water that adhered to it. He'd stood by the stairs and chatted with her for a few minutes before going up to change, resting his elbow on the newel post. The hair under his arm had hung in wet, dark strings.

She imagined rubbing him dry with a towel, having him reach for her and take her into his arms. Feeling Charlie's messy, hairy, damp masculinity, sensing how he would let himself go in a way sleek, shining, perfectly molded Nicholas never could. She thought of going to bed with him, having an orgasm. "Charlie, Charlie, I'm coming," she'd cry out. He'd have to clap his hand over her mouth to keep her quiet. But he'd want her to cry out. He'd want to hear it.

"Ready?" Nicholas asked.

"Yes."

Smooth, muscular, hairless Nicholas. No excess anywhere. He could be photographed from any angle. Perfect. Cut, print. In such splendid shape sex was no exertion. His respiration did not alter. He did not perspire. His thrusts were so rapid and regular they felt automated.

Charlie would want her to writhe under him. To scream. He would want to hear her losing control. It would make him willing to surrender the last bit of control he had. His sounds would be low and rumbling, a tremor in the earth.

She didn't cry out for Nicholas. She no longer pretended to have orgasms. One night she'd kept silent and he'd merely continued until he was finished, just as he always had, just as he was doing now. He didn't seem to notice. He didn't seem to care.

Jane finally fell asleep. He wished he could get her to keep the curtains off the windows. She was so beautiful in the light.

The month before, she had turned thirty-seven. She hated the four months when she was a year older than he. "I make old hags look young," she'd said.

"You're more beautiful than when I married you."

"No, I'm not. You're more myopic."

She was more beautiful, although he knew she didn't believe him. Her features were still strong enough to suggest her personality, but the hard edges of her jaw had softened. Her wide mouth, which had sometimes looked too big, was now—he looked at it, slightly slack—luscious. And her coloring: the black hair, those deep blue eyes, along with her velvet skin. She said her glow was makeup, but he thought it was something more, an aura that had descended over her. It was a terrible thing to think, but being a prisoner became her: pressure from interior turmoil and exterior walls creating a perfect balance.

Charlie had hinted at it the summer before. "Jane looks well," he'd remarked. Nicholas had nodded, and Charlie had added, "She's like a hot-house flower." Then, sensing he'd said the wrong thing, Charlie dropped the subject. But he'd been right. For the first time in her life, after nearly seventeen years of marriage, Jane was in full bloom.

But the more desirable she became, the less she seemed to desire. The more desirable he became, the less she wanted him.

Everyone else wanted him. Women might start out flirtatious, aloof, maternal, friendly, or even hostile, but he knew they all wanted to end in the same place, and after the disaster of Laurel Blake, he didn't want to be there with anyone else. A few times, worn out by loneliness and tempted by the need just to bury himself inside someone, he'd given off a signal: a hand that rested seconds too long on an actress's shoulder, a soft thank-you kiss to a hostess that landed on lips instead of cheek. But the signals emitted in response had been too strong; they'd nearly knocked him senseless. So here he was, where he belonged, with his own wife, the one who knew him best, the only one who didn't want him.

The moment they had finished intercourse, she'd leaned over, groped on the floor, found her nightgown, and hurriedly put it back on, as if to preclude

369

skin from brushing skin during the night. In her sleep, Jane drew up her arm to shield her eyes from the unaccustomed brightness of the room.

She didn't seem to care that in a week he'd be leaving to spend two months on location in Alaska. Beyond reading and commenting on each draft of the screenplay, she hadn't said a word about his film. She didn't seem interested. He'd had to bring up all the details about the writer, the supporting actors, the political coups he'd pulled off against the studio. He'd had to show her the sketches for costumes and set design; she'd never even asked. He'd had to remind her to call the bookstore to order his books, and she hadn't said a word about having his family and Murray for dinner, a traditional event before he left for location. The way she was behaving, he could have been a car salesman about to go off for a half-hour demonstration drive.

She didn't seem to want him. Not in the way she had all through the years, ever since college. Her need had always been strong, sometimes bottomless, so blatant and desperate he'd actually pitied her. Now, half the time she didn't even try to pretend. Half the time she acted as though she didn't even care.

The year before, the gardener had put in hundreds of bulbs, and now from the kitchen Jane could see the hyacinths—pink, purple, and white— stretching down the slope in the back toward the pond, lying like a giant elongated Easter egg in a grassy basket. Their scent was powerful and inordinately sensual, far too blatant for Connecticut. She waited, holding the telephone receiver in one hand and the newspaper clipping Cecily had given her the morning before in the other. Both hands trembled.

"Hello." A voice finally came onto the line. "This is Dr. Fullerton."

His name was right there in the article: "Dr. Judson Fullerton, the psychiatrist who founded—" The name had a false, pretentious sound, as though chosen as a stage name by a young actor who was foolishly patterning his career after Nicholas Cobleigh's: yeah, man, Judson Fullerton just oozes class.

Maybe Judson Fullerton was an anglicization of Jack Fleigenbaum or something like that. Even though she knew better, she still imagined psychiatrists as Jewish and bearded: tweedy, middle-aged Freuds. She wasn't sure she wanted to trust someone who had to become a Judson. Her heart fluttered. She thought of hanging up.

"My name is Jane Cobleigh." She said her last name fast, so it came out like Coe-bee. That way, if he didn't sound right, she could just hang up and he'd never muse whether the Cobleigh who'd called was related. He'd never be able to tell all the other psychiatrists, I got a call—highly neurotic woman, hung up—but I had the distinct impression it was Nicholas Cobleigh's wife.

"Sorry. I didn't catch your last name."

"Cobleigh," she said. "C-o-b-l-e-i-g-h."

"What can I do for you?"

She waited for him to say Mrs. Cobleigh. Ms. Cobleigh. She didn't think she sounded like a Miss any more. He didn't say anything. They waited for you to say it. "I read about your phobia clinic."

"Yes."

They waited for you to make a fool of yourself. She'd probably make some terrible Freudian slip, say "my father" instead of "my husband" and then he'd say, Would you like to talk about that? No, she'd say. I wouldn't. But he already had her last name. He'd probably talk about it that weekend at a cocktail party in Westport: Well, ethically you know I can't mention names, but just the other day I got a call from a very famous actor's wife. . . . "I read about how you work with women," Jane said. "With people who can't—" She couldn't think of the right way to say it. He was absolutely silent. He didn't even breathe into the phone. "People who can't leave the house."

"Yes, we do."

"That you've had success even after regular analysis or—what do you call it?—therapy failed."

"Yes."

"It says if they can't come to you, you send someone to them."

"That's right. Are you having difficulty leaving your house?"

"In a way."

"I see."

She could tell; he was just waiting for her to break down and spill everything. This probably happened ten times a day. His motto was probably *Give them enough rope and they'll hang themselves*. His wife probably had needle-pointed it onto a pillow: the motto and *Judson Fullerton, M.D.*, in a herringbone stitch. "I haven't been out of my house in six years."

"That's a long time," he said.

"I've never seen my daughters' school."

"And you'd like to."

"Yes," she said.

"Would you like to have someone come to your house and talk to you?"

"What if I don't want to? What if I decide—"

"No one will force you to do anything you don't want to do. Now, what would be a good time for you?"

"Any time."

"This afternoon?" he asked.

"Please."

Nicholas stood before her in gray sweat pants, a towel around his neck. An hour had passed. She had not left the kitchen table. "I'm not saying there's

371

anything *wrong* with it," he said. "I'm just saying you should be careful. Do you have any idea who these people are?"

"He's a psychiatrist. You read the article."

"But what's his reputation?"

"I'm sure it's good. He was written up in the paper. It's the first phobia clinic in this part of Connecticut."

"But who is he? Where does he come from?"

"I don't know."

Nicholas wiped his hands on the back of his pants. "Don't you think we ought to check into this first?"

"Cecily's looking him up in the library. She's going to be calling any minute."

"And Cecily Van Doorn is an expert on psychiatry. Is that what you're telling me? She marries a father-and-son combination, and now she's going to marry a town maintenance man who drives the goddamn snowplow—"

"He's a poet."

"A poet. Twenty goddamn years younger than she is and *she's* going to evaluate a psychiatrist for you? Are you serious?" He pulled out a chair and sat. His body had the sour smell of dried sweat. "Jane, I can't tell you how happy I am that you want to try again. But this is a problem you've had for years, and all I'm doing is suggesting you wait another day or two and let me have him and this clinic checked."

"I can tell when I meet whoever they're sending over. I have judgment."

"Jane, I'm not saying you don't. I just think you're in a vulnerable position, and you don't want some slick—"

"He's *not*."

"How do you know?"

"Read the article again." She pushed it at him. "Read all the quotes from people he's helped."

"Jane, there are people who are helped by witch doctors. Come on. I just want to protect you. You're not the average American housewife, you know." She took the article, folded it, and eased it into her skirt pocket. "You're my wife. I can't afford having people I don't know anything about probing into my life."

"It's my life!"

"It's our life. You know it is. He hears the last name and a light bulb goes off in his head. If he's not on the up and up, do you realize the damage he can do? Do you?"

"Nick, please."

"I've done everything I can in the last couple of years to keep my name out of the paper. I haven't given an interview in over eighteen months. That's all for a reason. We both agreed that privacy—"

"He's a psychiatrist!"

"Listen to me. They're all voyeurs. If they weren't they wouldn't be sitting there all day, getting their thrills by listening to other people's secrets. Don't you think it would be a thrill for some third-rate local psychiatrist to know all about Nicholas Cobleigh, the inside scoop? It would make great cocktail party conversation."

She stood, rested her palms on the table, and leaned forward toward Nicholas. "That's all you can think about, isn't it? Me, me, me."

"That's not true."

"Me, me, me," she crooned. He rose and faced her. "Me—"

"Shut up!"

"Me, me, me. Let me stay here *another* six years, let me rot, as long as you aren't embarrassed. Keep bringing in psychiatrists who report back to you, telling you I'm being resistive."

"It was just that one, and he said he had your permission."

"Do you want to know the real reason you don't want me to see him? You're going to Alaska the day after tomorrow, and you want me to pack for you and listen to your lines and play sweet, little wifey-poo. 'Oooh, Nick, you are just one big, beautiful hunk of brilliance and this is going to be your greatest film, an American classic, and I'm honored to have the most infinitesimal role in making it happen. Deeply and profoundly honored.' That's what you want."

"Jesus. Jesus. How can you say that?"

"How? Easily. Because it's the truth."

Ice was going to be Nicholas's triumph. He'd known it from the minute he read a review of a biography of Sheldon Jackson, a missionary who'd gone to Alaska in the late 1870s and dedicated himself to helping the Eskimos survive. Jackson had fallen in love with the real Alaska, not the Alaska being plundered by trappers and miners. Shocked by the near-starvation of the Eskimos—the basis of their livelihood, the fur seal, had been wantonly butchered by whites—Jackson had fought the establishment he was part of for the Eskimos. Displaying enormous ingenuity, he had introduced reindeer as a replacement for the nearly decimated seal population. The final scene had come to Nicholas in a bright flash: Jackson and his Eskimo friends stand desolate on an endless stretch of glaring white, when suddenly hundreds of reindeer surround them, and they laugh, cry, hug the animals, and whoop with glee.

Nicholas had planned everything. He'd bought the rights to the biography even though Jackson was an actual personage. He wanted no lawsuits, no controversy, to tarnish the reputation of *Ice*. He'd spent half a year working with three different writers to see that the screenplay was flawless.

373

As executive producer, he signed the best craftsmen in the business, chose the finest actors, designers, and cameramen. He'd gathered together meteorologists, Eskimo guides, survival experts. He'd engaged a company that designed scientific equipment for research in Antarctica to come up with casings for cameras, lights, and sound equipment. He'd allowed a generous two months on location and had arranged for the rest of the film to be shot at the studio in Astoria, in Queens, so he could be driven home nights and be with Jane for the second two months of the project, something he'd never been able to do before.

And, as star, this was going to be his finest hour. Every critic who ever claimed he "held back," or was "too WASP," would see emotion enough for five films: rage, terror, lust, grief, aching gentleness. *Ice* would prove his seriousness to Jane too, because he knew she thought films second rate, even though she claimed that wasn't "necessarily true." It was true. He knew she wanted him back in the theater. For eight years, she'd never stopped working on him—"Don't you miss an audience?" "Don't you want to do something different?" "Wouldn't it be nice to test yourself again?"—never realizing that he had moved into a whole different league. He'd give her a performance that would make anything done in the last ten years on the New York stage look sick. A hundred, two hundred years in the future they'd still be studying *Ice*.

But nothing about *Ice* was what Nicholas had forecast. The meteorologists had fed everything into their computers and agreed that April and May were still wintery enough to look awesomely Alaskan, though not so wintery that the weather would hold up shooting. But nearly every day it snowed, and the wind drove the snow so hard it whipped horizontally. They could not leave their hotel for five days. When they did, they discovered the reflectors on the spotlights had shattered and two of the microphone booms were irreparably cracked. They called for replacements, but then the snow began again, and even the most daredevil Alaskan pilots stayed on the ground.

The inactivity affected the company. Nicholas realized that nearly everyone in the cast and crew was taking drugs. He began drinking six or seven bourbons a day—the hotel bar had run out of everything else and deliveries were suspended indefinitely. Snowed into the ugly, plastic-modern hotel, the company fought with each other, had fast sexual liaisons, then wandered through the halls looking for other partners or another fight.

Nicholas drank even more but couldn't get drunk. He thought of his father's ability to lose control and for the first time envied him. All he felt was numbness in his arms and legs, as if the only thing the alcohol affected was some mechanism in his circulatory system. He stayed in his room, the Presidential Suite. All red, white, and blue laminated plastic from the last year's bicentennial, with a fake white fur spread on the bed. He was always cold. He had no place to go, no one to talk to. Murray had offered to come, but bringing

374

Murray to Alaska made as much sense as bringing a polar bear to Sardi's. Still, he'd always talked to Murray every day when he was on location and now, with phone service erratic, all they could do was shout a few frustrated words at each other. "Stay well, Murray." "Love ya, Nicky! Don't freeze your whatsies off."

Shouting was all he could do with Jane. "How are things?" "Fine!" she'd shout back, although he knew the volume was not a reflection of their enthusiasm. He felt truly out of touch. Even later, when phone service improved, their conversations seemed lifeless, as if affected by the climate. "Have you met that psychiatrist?" he finally asked. "Not yet. But someone's been to the house a few times," was all she said. "How are things going, Jane?" "Okay," she replied. "I'll tell you all about it when you get home." Their phone conversations had always lasted for an hour. Now they were brisk and efficient, as though they were partners in some well-organized business that almost ran itself.

He called the girls at their school in New Hampshire, the same school his sisters had attended. Neither of them sounded right either. Victoria was only concerned that he might not be home in time for Father-Daughter Weekend in early June. "If Kippy's father can come, and he's Majority Whip, I don't see why you can't. Really, Daddy. I mean, you *know* where I was on Mother-Daughter Day. In the stacks, doing my term paper." She sounded like a petulant girl friend. The older she became, the less satisfied she was with what she got from him.

Elizabeth was bubbly and diffident at the same time, trying, as always, to win him over, but never confident she could succeed. "Daddy, want to hear a joke? Only if you want to. Okay? What's green and sings?"

"I give up."

"Oh." She had failed to interest him. He could hear her unhappiness. She was so easily bruised.

"Lizzy," he said, brightening his voice, "you know how terrible I am at riddles. Now tell me the answer, so I can tell everyone what's green and sings. We need some laughs up here."

"Elvis Parsley!"

"Elvis Parsley," he repeated slowly.

"Don't you get it? Green and sings, Daddy."

Nicholas closed his eyes. "That's a great joke, honey. I'll tell it to everyone."

"Want to hear another one?"

Ice was so over budget it made him sick. Literally. He had sharp, violent stomach pain at night, like jagged rocks being jammed into his intestines. Each drink seemed to ease the pain at first, and then to make it hurt more. The only way he'd finally gotten some sleep was to take the codeine and

375

aspirin pills the assistant director offered him. The third night, having dinner sent up by room service—cold poached eggs served on an orange cafeteria-style tray—he began anticipating his pain so he could take the pills. Frightened, he flushed the pills down the toilet and lay under the heavy fake fur cover doubled over, hugging his stomach, imagining—quite accurately, it turned out—the terrible concessions the studio would now demand of him.

When they were finally able to begin shooting, he knew just how bad *Ice* was going to be. The pivotal emotional scenes seemed merely hysterical. The scenes of subtle feeling were heavy-handed, preachy, and boring. His acting was false and he couldn't even figure out a way to fake it. The dialogue—"I won't let you down, my friend. Not for anything"—which in Connecticut had been so right, so true, came out like lines from a rusty Western.

The stomach pains grew worse. Nearly every night he threw up what little food he'd been able to get down during the day. Too sick even to hold up his head, he'd sit on the bathroom floor, his chin resting on the freezing rim of the toilet, and retch until nothing came up but small amounts of bitter liquid that he could not get out of his throat. The icy tile floor permeated the bath mat he sat on. He could not control his shivering. After another week, he stopped drinking, but still the retching did not stop. His cheeks became hollow and took on a gray cast his makeup man could not entirely obscure. He looked old.

He felt old. The project was fatally flawed. The studio flew in their man to "assist," to wrest control of the film from him. The daily rushes drove him, daily, into deeper despair. Everything, from camera work to costumes, looked cheap, like a quickie TV movie.

Nicholas looked around, hoping he was the only one who was troubled. He wasn't. The truth was written on everyone's face. *Ice* wasn't even half filmed, but the whole company knew exactly what he knew: Nicholas Cobleigh had failed.

23

Inside this house are the two people who molded Jane Cobleigh: her parents, Dorothy and Richard Heissenhuber. Inside this house, right behind me. And what, we wonder, is inside the hearts of these two people tonight as the daughter they nurtured . . .
          —Lou Unterman, WLW-TV News, Cincinnati

Ellie Matteo looked as though she belonged in a spaghetti-sauce commercial. Her dark Italian prettiness was tempered by a skeptical expression, as if she had to be convinced that all the ingredients were fresh and no preservatives were added. Her black eyebrows were tweezed into thin, challenging arches, adding to her somewhat daunting demeanor. She did not look like a woman who had spent twenty years on a single block in Stamford, Connecticut, unable to cross a street.

She stood beside Jane in the center hall, under the chandelier. "Okay," she said, "today we're going to try standing in the open doorway. If you can."

"What if I can't?" Jane asked.

"I'll put a gun to your head. No, seriously, if you can't we'll go into the kitchen and have another cup of coffee and I'll come back in a couple of days. Now, here we are, right?" Jane nodded. The front door was closed. Sunshine streamed through the narrow windows on either side of the door, forming two bright parallel lines on the floor. She and Ellie were perpendicular, forming a capital H. "Okay. Imagine the door open and you standing right smack in the middle looking outside."

"You're not going to open it?"

"Not unless you tell me to. Now just imagine it."

Jane shut her eyes for an instant, then opened them. No clear picture formed in her mind, but she imagined the shiver of cool morning air on her arms. She was wearing a short-sleeved blouse, and when she rubbed her upper arms she could feel gooseflesh. A shudder crossed her shoulders, as if she'd been standing outside, inappropriately dressed, far too long.

"Now," Ellie said, "what do you feel? On the one-to-ten scale. One, you're relaxed; ten, you're having a severe panic attack."

"Three."

"Okay. How would you feel about my opening the door?"

"Can we wait a minute?"

"Sure. Now, we're just going to stand in the doorway today, okay? You

377

may feel, whoopee, this is a piece of cake, let's take a stroll down to the main road—"

"I won't feel that."

"Okay. But just in case, remember we take one step at a time. That's all. You spent—what, six years in the house?"

"Yes. And another couple not being able to do things—go into town, drive. For a while I'd go with my husband or with a friend, but—are you going to open the door?"

"Do you want me to open it?"

"Not yet," Jane said. Her lips were so dry they kept sticking together. "The first time you tried. What did you do?"

"You mean with my phobia? Oh. I stood on the corner of my street for three quarters of an hour with the woman from the clinic who was helping me—she'd had an elevator phobia—and then I went home. The next time I put one foot into the street."

"And then?"

"And then, one step at a time. Just like today. You're not going to New York. You're not going to any big parties where people are going to surround your husband and separate him from you. You're not going to the Academy Awards. You're going to stand in the doorway of your own house. If you want to."

"Could you open the door?" Ellie did, then came and stood beside her again. The day was warmer than Jane had thought. She remembered a day that had felt like this—warm spring so sweet the air was almost syrupy—soon after they'd inherited the house. She and the girls had planted annuals to the left of the house. She even remembered what they were: petunias and larkspur, clouds of purple and white brightened by green foliage. She could recall turning a clod of earth with her spade and hearing Elizabeth's oooh of delight when two worms crawled out.

"One to ten?" Ellie asked.

"Oh. Still three. Four. Four because I know I have to—"

"You don't have to."

Jane took a step toward the door. Ellie stayed beside her. "Still four," Jane said. She turned to Ellie. "What if all of a sudden I run upstairs screaming?"

"You'll run upstairs screaming."

"Is that what you're trained to say?"

"Pretty much."

"Oh. You're very honest."

"I have to be. You have to have confidence in me."

"What did your husband say when you told him you put your foot into the street?"

378

"Something like 'Hey, Ellie, way to go.' He gets that from the kids. He's a math teacher, but he coaches the girls' swimming team."

"'Way to go,'" Jane said softly. She walked toward the door briskly, as if it were a thing she did several times a day, but stopped abruptly when she was a foot away.

"One to ten?"

"Five." Her heart was starting to thud. She was so close to fresh air. She should raise her head and sniff. Along the drive that led up to the house, she saw a huge bed of white geraniums. She hadn't known the gardener had put them in; to have seen them would have meant looking straight down from an upstairs window, something she did not like to do. Hundreds of geraniums. A profusion, a dazzling excess, an indulgence of rich people. "Four."

"Want to try another step?"

She was about to say Not yet when her body moved for her. Her feet stepped onto the molding, her arms flew up, and her hands grabbed the doorframe. "Seven!" she shouted. "I can't catch my breath. My heart—eight. I can't."

"Do you want to step back?" Ellie asked, standing right behind her.

"Seven."

"Good."

"I can breathe now." Jane swallowed. "But my heart—" It was pounding and with frightening irregularity would skip a beat. The metal weather stripping on the doorframe cut into her palms, but she could not lower her hands. She might fall if she did, tumble outside. "Eight again. Going up. Eight."

"Eight," Ellie repeated.

"Oh, God. It's a beautiful day and I can't even appreciate it. I should be feeling the warmth and—"

"One step at a time."

"Smelling flowers."

"One to ten?"

"What? Six. But I can't. I can't do it. Oh, God. Seven."

"Jane, you're standing in the doorway."

"What?" Dizzy. She was afraid to look back at Ellie, afraid to lose her balance.

"You've been standing there for over two minutes. You did it."

"I did?"

Murray King leaned against the paddock fence. He wore his country clothes: a brown suit, a white business shirt unbuttoned at the neck, and a pair of cracked leather ankle-high boots he told Nicholas he'd bought in 1957 or '58, in anticipation of a blizzard that never occurred. "Who cleans up the horses' business?" he asked.

"We have a girl groom," Nicholas said. "She takes care of everything."

"You know, when I was a kid in the Bronx, there were still some horses. The milkman and the knife-sharpener man had them. I'd see these big things of horse manure in the street. You know? With all that straw sticking out of it. Feh. I used to think there was some guy who came along at night and sprinkled straw all over the stuff so it wouldn't stick to people's shoes, and I couldn't figure out why he never did it for the dog poop. Another half cent's worth of straw, big deal." Nicholas glanced down at the fence. Murray's hands were getting old-looking, the veins knobby, the skin blotched with liver spots and irregular red patches. "I can't believe Janie," Murray said.

Nicholas banged one boot against the other, knocking off some dried mud. "She's making progress."

"All these years. And now, all of a sudden, two, three months . . . I couldn't believe it, Nicky. She came out to the car and gave me a kiss. My mouth dropped three feet. This is some doctor she's got."

"It's a clinic. Most of it's done by former phobics. It's a kind of behavioral psychology. They're not interested in getting to the root of the problem."

"Who needs roots? She goes outside. She goes in a car."

"Just to the clinic twice a week, for therapy."

"Still. It's like a miracle." Nicholas nodded. He scraped the bottom of his boot on the lowest slat of the fence. "Something wrong, Nicky?"

"No."

"Is that no, nothing's wrong, or no, this isn't the kind of thing we talk about in good company?"

"Murray, please."

"All right. I'm only saying she looks happier than I've seen her since . . . You're looking better, Nicky."

"It's only temporary. We start cutting *Ice* Monday. Mary Rooney, the editor—"

"Yeah?"

"She said it's going to be a smash."

"She did?"

"With white fetishists. She said there's so much glare from the snow she'll have to wear sunglasses."

"She's not too optimistic?"

"She says we can play with it. You know what that means."

"At least she didn't take cyanide. Listen, Nicky, don't let it get to you so much. Everybody comes up with a stinker now and then. You're not God. You're not even his second cousin, rumors to the contrary."

"It's going to affect every deal I make. You know that."

"Nicky, they'll put the screws on a little, but that's all. It's not like you died. You just made one slightly drecky film. Nothing personal."

"Thank you," Nicholas said curtly.

Murray stood straight. "Did you read that Steve Greenlick screenplay?"

"Yes."

"You're allowed more than yes or no answers, Nicky."

"Yes, I read it, Murray. I don't want it."

"Why not? It's good."

"He wants to direct."

"So? Come on. You can't direct every film you make. And right now, you'd make a lot of studio people fall madly in love with you again and send you chocolate creams and Valentines if you agreed to do the Greenlick film. It's a winner. You know it's a winner."

"He'll have final cut?"

"He's the director, Nicky."

"I'm the star."

"Nicky, all I'm saying is to be realistic. Take things a little easy. You're entitled. You're not some kid from the slums who's suddenly made his first million and is crazy afraid of losing it. Let go. It's the perfect role. Enjoy just acting. You can afford to. You're established. This is an ideal setup. Three months' shooting. On location in New York. How can you beat that?"

"What if I don't take it?"

"I think you would make them happy if you would. Listen, Nicky, one lousy film is one lousy film. Fine. Finished. But now you need a winner."

"I *need* a winner?"

"Let's put it this way. You had the world by the balls. You still do, but one of the balls has slipped a little. It's up to you. If you want to get both balls back, you have to jiggle things their way. You get me?"

"And if I don't?"

"Then you'll be taking a risk. You want to take a risk, that's fine with me. You're the conservative one. But using your conservative standards—okay?— I'm telling you, if you take a risk, there are a lot of people who are going to be watching. And if you fall flat on your face, Nicky, they'll be applauding. And if you fall on your face one more time after that, they'll start kicking you while you're down. Real hard. You know them. They'll make sure you'll never be able to stand up straight again."

Jane admitted that she wouldn't call it a hill. The house was on a rise in the terrain. The land sloped downward in the back and then continued flat. The house—a block of white against the sky—could be seen from almost any point in the back: from the pond and the woods beyond on the right, or from the stables, barn, and farmland on the left.

The land dropped in a sharper angle in the front, so that, a thousand feet down the gravel drive that curved through the trees, all that could be seen through the gray-brown grid of intersecting branches were the two giant stone chimneys.

By the time she reached the mailbox, nearly a half mile from the house, the drive had curved so far to the left that the house might have dematerialized. There was only a gray, battered mailbox with BENSON painted on in black block letters. On close inspection, there was a gray undercoat beneath the "Benson," a slash of paint that obscured the "Tuttle" they had never had a chance—Nicholas's fame came too fast—to change to "Cobleigh."

They'd left the name "Tuttle" on the mailbox until they realized there were fans who had as great a knowledge of Nicholas's genealogy as he himself had, sometimes a greater knowledge, for he'd stopped reading the articles that connected him with every Tuttle who'd ever passed through New York.

One woman had driven right up to the house and leaned on her car horn for fifteen minutes. When she finally drove off, she left behind an offering, a cage with two live chickens. There was no note to explain their significance. Jane gave them to the man whose farm bordered on theirs and who worked their land. He'd dropped back the next day and told her he'd killed and buried them since the woman was obviously some nut case with Nicholas Cobleigh on her brain and the chickens might be poisoned. "Wouldn't even feed 'em to the pigs," he'd told her.

Less than a month after that, a man had walked up from the road, waving, as he approached the house, calling "Nick! Nick!" Nicholas had been in California making a film. The man had worn an orange wool hat somewhat askew; an earlap hung over his eye. "Nick! I'm here!" The police had finally come and taken him away.

Jane had suggested Austen or Brontë for the mailbox, but Nicholas had said they were a dead giveaway and chose Benson, the name of a character in a screenplay he was reading.

The red flag was down, rusted into position. For a short time, before they'd realized things were missing, mail was stolen from their box. Birthday cards, magazines, bank statements, letters: anything with Nicholas's name printed on it seemed to have value. Now, the housekeeper's husband—who worked as a handyman and runner of errands—drove into town each morning and picked up their mail at the post office.

Still, Jane stood by the empty box, peering down the road as if expecting the most important letter of her life. This was her task. Walk down the drive. Stand by the mailbox for a full five minutes. Walk back up the drive. She'd worn an old watch of Nicholas's, one with a second hand. Thirty-five seconds had elapsed.

Her legs trembled. Not nerves, she said to herself. Not nerves. Out of shape. Her right knee buckled and she grabbed the mailbox, hugging it to her waist as if it were an adored child. Six years of inertia, and a half-mile walk on a gravelly road where the rocks were ball bearings, sliding under the slick soles of her flats.

Pretty flats. Yellow outlined with a thin line of bright blue. Frivolous, but she'd done it anyway. And the other pairs on the same page of Bonwit's catalog, a red accented with purple, a pink with kelly green. For two years she'd bought and bought, studying department store catalogs as she once had Restoration comedy. Buying everything. Cowl-neck cashmere sweaters in six colors, so she would not realize, too late, that she'd forgotten the most important shade; leather pants, leather tunics, leather vests, a leather dress as pliable as cotton; three pairs of cowboy boots; five fringed silk scarves; fourteen leotards and matching tights still in cellophane.

You never wear the same thing twice any more, Nicholas had said. That's not true, she replied. She'd been wearing a new black terrycloth jumpsuit, which she'd also ordered in forest green and terra-cotta. You were never a clothes horse, he'd continued, as if she hadn't spoken. She'd demanded, Do you see all those women from Manhattan who come up here? Do you want me to dress like the headmistress of some third-rate school? How would you know what a headmistress looks like? he'd countered. Thanks, Nick. Let's keep the class lines clear. I didn't mean it that way, damn it. I just meant you never get out, so how— Forget it, okay? It just bothers me that you're throwing money away. I am not! I need to look decent. You need something to kill the boredom. That's why you're doing it. Spending fifteen minutes on the phone with some salesgirl talking about belts. You never gave a damn about belts. You just—

The shoes pinched her feet. One minute and forty-five seconds. A little dizziness. All right. She was going to get dizzy. Fine. Her heart too. No one ever died from a panic attack, Dr. Fullerton had told her. She believed him. Face what is happening. Give it a number. It was a five.

Five was high, but she was tired. The walk down the drive had tired her. She held on to the mailbox. The rusty seams were probably staining her sweater. A huge fluffy angora sweater. Hand-knitted. French. Beige and white. The week before, the wife of the president of the conglomerate that owned the country's biggest chain of theaters had worn one. A woman taller even than she, and about twenty pounds thinner, who had looked at Jane's suede pants as if trying to come up with a compliment but unable to. A cold, chic bitch in a five-hundred-dollar sweater.

At dinner the woman told Nicholas about her job. She took wives of foreign tourists and diplomats shopping in Manhattan. It paid, she declared, not well but enough to keep her in stockings. Even Jimmy—she nodded at her short, blubbery, rich husband—can't afford my stockings. I *adore* really good hosiery, the woman went on. Pantyhose are the scourge of civilization. Jane waited, looking for Nicholas's look, the one he often flashed to her that no one else could see: Pretentious. The look never came. Nicholas chuckled. He gazed at the woman over his third glass of burgundy, amused, impressed with her job, charmed. Tiny fluffs of the woman's angora sweater were still in the air the next day.

Everyone was working. Cecily had bought and expanded the town's bookstore. She worked six days a week now. Everyone Jane knew worked. Her sister-in-law Abby was an assistant U.S. Attorney in New York. Her roommate from Pembroke, Amelia, had gotten her doctorate and was teaching psychology at Northeastern. Her friend from high school, Lynn, who for years had appeared to be the world's happiest housewife, had opened a store in Cincinnati called the Elegant Table; it sold cloths, placemats, and napkin rings. Even her sister-in-law Olivia worked. She had a loom in her living room and wove afghans that actually sold for six hundred to a thousand dollars each. *Naturally, I dye my own wool,* Olivia had written. *Believe it or not, there's a lot of interest in quality down here in Washington, and not just in Georgetown.*

Two minutes, twenty seconds. Her mother-in-law worked as a volunteer four days a week, taking around the library cart at Sloan-Kettering, the cancer hospital. "I view it as a job," Winifred had told her. "I'm there at nine on the dot, work until four. Rain or shine. It's my work. No more dashing from meeting to meeting for me."

No one was home any more. Everybody had a niche. When she called Cecily at night, she often spoke to Cecily's new husband. Cecily, exhausted after a day's work—and, Jane assumed, love with a man twenty years younger who'd dedicated a book of poems to her—flopped into bed early. Do you want me to poke her? the new husband had asked. She still seems to be breathing. No, Jane said. Let her sleep. I'll call her in the store tomorrow. Half the time when she did, Cecily said I'll call you back and then didn't.

What if this treatment worked? What if she finally got beyond the mailbox, got beyond the next task? One step at a time. One step at a time and she'd be forty and what could she do then? Go to stores and shop? Meet her friends on their lunch hours? Make batches of black raspberry preserves and embarrass herself and everyone else by trying to sell it? "Jane's Homemade Jams." They would talk about her behind her back, or someone would get botulism. Of all the people who passed through her dining room, few asked, What do you do? It was obvious. Her house was perfect. Every soap dish, every picture frame, every candle was the best there could be. They didn't have to ask, they all saw what she did. She did nothing; she bought.

Three minutes, fifteen seconds.

She had been locked out of the world. And now? If she managed to get back in? There was no place for her. She could bake unnecessary tarts or trail

Nicholas from location to location and fulfill the two traditional roles women everywhere were abandoning: homemaker and camp follower.

Her legs quivered. Her knee buckled and then, suddenly, it gave out. Her leg shot back. She fell sideways onto the ground, half pulling the mailbox off its post. She sat there staring at her leg. Her stocking was shredded by the gravel, her blue-trimmed yellow shoe plastered with the mud it had unearthed. She picked off the gravel. Her leg was covered with polka dots of blood. A spasm of nausea hit her. Red dots surrounded by black bits of grit. She lowered her head. She was so dizzy. Terribly dizzy. Give it a number. She couldn't give it a number. Her heart was going *smack, smack*—and then it stopped. Oh, God! *Smack, smack!* She dragged herself up. Her heart was stopping more than it was beating. She heard herself whimper, a far-off terrified sound. Then she rushed back up the drive, limping, crying, bleating, I can't! I can't! I can't!

"You've had setbacks before," Judson Fullerton said. "Remember that first time, at your mailbox? This is just one more."

"I guess," Jane said. Her hands rested lightly on the chrome arms of the chair. She fought her instinct, which was to clutch them as tightly as she could. She hated his office. The chairs were all chrome and leather. Instead of a desk, he had a rectangle of glass on a chrome base that looked like a model of a DNA molecule. The desk was bare except for a telephone, a rosewood pen and pencil holder, her folder, and a chrome picture frame placed so that the photograph was facing him. To get a look at it, she would have had to walk right up to his desk and lean over. Most of the time she thought the photograph was of his wife, if he had one—he did not wear a wedding ring—and children, if he had any, but now and then she wondered if it was a young, gorgeous, curvaceous, bikinied blond cookie, her lips parted enough to show the edges of her sharp little teeth.

"Well, it's not the first setback and it won't be the last. You know that. Do you want to talk about what happened?" he asked.

"Well, I went into town. My assignment was to walk from one end of Main Street to the other and to stop and look in at least four store windows. Ellie Matteo dropped me off, then drove down to wait for me at the other end. And it was all right at first. I stopped at a shoe store. And they have a gourmet cookware store right in town now. All these beautiful cheesecake pans, and I—"

"What happened?"

He interrupted. This was not like regular therapy, her old shop-at-home psychoanalysis. They would let her go on about cheesecake pans. They might talk about cheesecake in her past, or cheesecake's symbolic value, or what pans meant to her. "What happened was that I started feeling very uncomfortable. People were staring at me. I know you think I'm being paranoid, but they were."

"I don't think you're being paranoid. You've been photographed with your husband a good deal. Most people must know you live in the area. It's not surprising you'd be stared at."

"And I haven't been there in years."

"Do they know why you haven't been there?"

"No. Most people don't know. My friend Cecily said they think I do all my shopping in New York. I guess I do. All I have to do is call and say 'This is Mrs. Nicholas Cobleigh,' and someone in every department store and Madison Avenue boutique and fancy food shop leaps to attention. Whenever I call Saks for Nick's underwear—"

"How did you react to feeling you were being observed?"

"The usual." Judson Fullerton waited. "My heart," she elaborated. "Not being able to get enough air. The dizziness. I had to grab on to a lamppost."

"How did you try to deal with these feelings?"

"Oh, just tossed back my head and laughed them off." He did not smile. She still didn't know if he lacked humor or if this was part of his therapeutic technique. In the four months she'd been seeing him, he'd given no hint of being charmed or amused by her, or of even considering her pleasant. "I didn't try to deal with the feelings. That was the problem. I forgot every single technique I've learned and just gave in to the panic."

He was looking straight at her. She lowered her head. Not that he had a face to make her blush. He was Mr. Average. Dr. Average. When he'd come home from Alaska, Nicholas had demanded, "What does he look like?" Average, she'd answered. Average height, average weight, average face, fiftyish. Hair thinning in front. Or not thinning. Maybe it's already thinned. He wears wire-rimmed glasses that are too small for his face.

"You didn't allow the feelings to come?" he asked.

"No, I fought them. I ran from them. All my old routines. And as soon as I could I ran down Main Street to the car. People must have thought I was crazy."

"Maybe they thought you were in a hurry."

"I don't think so."

"I think you're being a little hard on yourself, Jane." What was she supposed to do? Call him Judson? Jud? "Haven't you ever seen anyone running down a street?"

"Dr. Fullerton, before I ran I was gripping the lamppost for dear life."

"For dear life?"

"Well, my fingerprints aren't embedded in the metal, but I was holding very tight."

386

"With one hand or two?"

"One."

"I'll concede it's possible people were staring at you and thinking your behavior by the lamppost odd. Now, will you concede that it's equally possible that they merely thought you had stopped and were resting your hand on a lamppost?"

She breathed out slowly. "I guess so."

He always stared straight at her. Although his windows were covered with vertical venetian blinds, some sunlight came into the office and reflected off his glasses, so he appeared to be studying her with one eye and one beam of light. She lowered her eyes so as not to meet his glance. He was wearing a flowered summer tie. English. Nicholas had several. The only thing not average about Judson Fullerton was his clothes. He dressed conservatively but elegantly, very much like Nicholas. The suit he was wearing, a beige linen, looked just like the one Nicholas had, although she supposed Judson Fullerton's wasn't custom-made.

"You're doing very well," he said. "But setbacks occur. It happens to everyone. You shouldn't let it throw you." He never moved. He never picked up a pen or shuffled the papers in her folder. "Were you premenstrual that day?"

"About three weeks." She gave him a small smile he did not return.

"Were you under any particular tension?"

"That was—let's see—Tuesday. Oh. The night before my husband and I had a little fight. Nothing serious."

"Do you want to talk about it?"

"It was about sex." She'd never mentioned sex before. Neither had he. She assumed he must want to hear about it, being a psychiatrist. He kept looking at her and gave no indication that his interest was aroused—her third psychiatrist wiggled deeper into his chair when anticipating a juicy revelation—but she wondered if he really wasn't dying to hear about Nicholas Cobleigh's sex life. Which happened to be her sex life also. "He said I don't seem interested any more."

"Are you?"

Jane shrugged. "I don't know how much I'm supposed to tell you," she said. She'd talked about sex, but she'd never been able to tell the other psychiatrists that she couldn't have an orgasm. That, and about her father. She hardly ever thought about him at all, but being with a psychiatrist made her remember. She looked away from Dr. Fullerton to the wall of diplomas behind him, too far away to read. Then she remembered how, when her father had lifted the covers to get into her bed, he'd hold them up for a minute before getting in beside her, watching her turn away from him, draw her legs up defensively, cover her breasts with crossed arms.

387

She looked down at her lap. The doctor was watching her reaction. Her dress was blue linen. She felt flustered. She nearly broke into a nervous giggle. When she'd walked into the office she'd wanted to say, Hey, we're twins. We're both wearing linen today. She hadn't.

"This is not the sort of therapy you've had in the past. If the fight with your husband has a bearing on the treatment of your phobia, then it should be brought up. My function is simply to deal with your phobia in its context. You may want or require additional therapy at some time, and if you like I can recommend another psychiatrist."

Jane made herself look right into the center of his eyeglasses. Her arms were as cold as the chrome arms of the chair. "I don't get all that much out of sex," she said. "Well, sometimes. Not that much lately." She waited for him to ask, What do you mean by lately? He didn't. He didn't even move. "I've never had an orgasm," she finally said.

"Never?" She might have announced that her favorite color was red. Neither his voice nor his glance altered.

"No."

"Have you ever masturbated to orgasm?"

"No."

Judson Fullerton made no note in her folder. He didn't even reach for his pen. "You might want to consider additional therapy" was all he said.

He couldn't believe how she was dressed. "Are you sure you want to wear that?" Nicholas asked.

"What's wrong with it?" Jane snapped. She turned from the mirror where she was putting on an earring. Diamond and ruby drops. He'd bought them for her a month before, to celebrate her first trip into Manhattan.

"Nothing. Forget it."

Her dress, a cocktail wrap of red silk, looked entirely proper from the back. The front plunged halfway to her waist.

She gazed at herself in the mirror. "It really doesn't show that much," she said. She held the pads of her thumbs under her ears, pushing the lobes forward to see that her earrings were properly placed.

"I said forget it," Nicholas said. It showed all the cleavage she had and at least a third of her breasts. "What are you doing for a bra?"

"Does it look like I'm wearing one?"

"To anyone who knows what's under there."

Jane spun around. "If you don't want to go, fine. Just say so. But you don't have to insult me."

"Stop it. I was kidding." He walked across the long bedroom of their Manhattan apartment and stood behind her. He put his hand into the deep slit of her dress. "You know how I love them." He cupped his hand under her

388

breast and held it even higher than the sewn-in bra. It felt pendulous in his hand, and he let it drop back into the bra.

"You don't think they're too saggy?" she asked.

"No. Of course not."

They were. She was in terrible shape. Her body could look good, especially in a dress like the one she was wearing, but it had as much muscle tone as an overripe piece of fruit. That's what she was like, something past its peak. For years he'd thought her quintessentially feminine, utterly desirable, but now he was beginning to feel as if he had brainwashed himself. Now that she'd gotten out of the gentle, flattering light of the house, now that she was so involved with herself that she barely had time for him, he could study her and see her with great clarity. He peered down into her dress. She was like a melon gone soft. Still sweet, but the flesh was far too yielding. When he made love to her, he avoided touching her belly; it rose up, as if to meet his hand, but it was mushy.

She pulled her hair behind her left ear, pinned it into place, then covered the pins with an antique diamond clip. He hated her hair now. She'd cut it the week before without even warning him. She'd just said, "Could you have Ernie pick me up at Kenneth's?" and he thought she'd gone to get a trim or have her nails done. When she'd gotten back to Connecticut and climbed out of the car, her beautiful hair that had hung to her waist was gone, chopped off to shoulder length: black, straight, ordinary hair. And she'd come at him grinning, saying, "I know it's a shock, but I just had to do it. You'll get used to it."

"Is my makeup okay?" she asked.

He looked into the mirror rather than at her. "Fine."

"Ready to rock and roll?"

"Don't you want to take something? A shawl or some kind of sweater?"

"Nick." She exhaled. He could hear her impatience, as though she were dealing with a difficult child. "You asked me what I wanted to do and I told you. If you don't—"

"Let's go."

How do you want to celebrate? he'd asked. Five months and you're a new woman. Do you want to go to Europe? Oh, Nick, I can't fly. I'll probably never be able to fly. One step at a time. That's all I can do. He'd suppressed his sigh. All right, what then, Jane? A big party? A cruise? Should I charter a boat? Do you know what I want? she said. I want to walk into the best restaurant in Manhattan on your arm, right past the chic-est people in the world, in a low-cut dress and great jewelry, and I want everyone to say, Who is that man with that gorgeous woman? Listen, he'd said, it would be easier if we slip in through the kitchen. They arrange it so I sit with my back toward the rest of the restaurant and no one bothers me or stares, no one comes up asking for autographs or— All right, Jane. If that's what you want. That's what I want, she'd said. The new earrings and your grandmother's diamond necklace and a dress that goes down to my belly button. It will be the first dress I shop for myself, Nick. I'm going to go to Bendel's and get in the elevator and do it. Alone. And if I can't find what I want I'll have it made. Good, he'd said. Wonderful.

"I'm so excited," Jane said. "A little nervous, but mostly good, wonderful excitement."

"Good." He handed her her evening bag. "Let's go."

"Nick?"

"What?" he asked. She looked so flashy. People would stare, then see him. It would be awful. He dreaded the entire evening. He took her arm and led her toward the door.

"I feel like my life is just beginning."

24

Nearly everyone is willing to discuss the Cobleighs, and, apart from the knife-in-the-back remarks that are endemic to show business, most people interviewed speak of the couple in glowing terms. Phrases recur: "Top drawer," "The best and the brightest," "A perfect match." However, few will speak for attribution, as if the price of their friendship . . .

—*Boston Globe*

"Would you be more comfortable over there?" Judson Fullerton asked. She had not seen him in several months. For the first minute she'd thought he'd grown, but then realized she'd never seen him standing except for the first time she came to his office, when he'd risen and extended his hand. "On the couch."

"Thank you." Jane moved from the patient chair, where she'd automatically sat, to a chrome and leather couch that looked like someone had found two more chairs exactly like the one she'd just been in and glued them all together. She was not more comfortable.

Dr. Fullerton lifted the chair she'd been sitting in and brought it opposite her, close, about three feet away. He sat. She felt more than uncomfortable. She looked past him, across the room. On his desk was a pile of papers and folders under a large paperweight. The paperweight was a chunk of crystal, and a sword-shaped letter opener, like Excalibur, was embedded in it. He must have seen her looking at his desk. "I was just getting caught up on some paperwork," he said. "The only solid block of time I can get is on weekends." It was late Saturday afternoon. He was dressed casually, in slacks and an argyle sweater. He'd opened the door of the clinic himself, and she'd been as startled by his sports clothes as if he'd been naked. "I hope you're not uncomfortable," he said. "About putting aside the doctor-patient roles."

"Not at all," Jane replied. "I mean, I wasn't in analysis or anything. And a lot of the volunteers were patients. Like Ellie. Weren't they?"

"Yes." His glasses were off, and he looked like another person. Younger, less serious, less trustworthy. His eyes, which she'd finally decided were light brown, were actually hazel, although the left one had a thick line of brown from the pupil to the bottom of the iris.

"No. I mean, I'm glad to be here."

"Good. First, I want to thank you personally for your donation to the clinic. It was very generous."

He had written a "Dear Mr. and Mrs. Cobleigh" note thanking them for

391

their five thousand dollars. She had wanted to give ten. *Ten?* Nicholas demanded. Are you kidding? Five's overly generous. He doesn't need more. Come on, stop being so touchy. You know what I mean. He has a minimal overhead and fifty suburban ladies in tennis dresses doing all the work for him. Who do you think really helped you? Him? Or that Italian woman who was here almost every day?

"You're welcome," she said. "I'd like to do more. That's why I want to get into the next volunteer training program. Not only for altruistic reasons. I mean, here it is 1978, and every other woman my age has had a chance to become a person in her own right. I mean, the women's movement marched right by my door, and I was locked in the house. Here I am, thirty-eight years old. Practically the only housewife left in America." He crossed his legs, resting his right ankle on his left knee. She looked directly at his face to keep her eyes from being drawn to the apex of the triangle created by his legs. "And I'm a housewife whose children go away to school and who has people to clean the house and do the laundry and drive and do the errands. I'm not what would be diagnosed as overtaxed."

"I'd be happy to have you in the program."

"Oh," she said. "Thank you. I didn't expect it would be that easy." He didn't say anything. "I mean, I thought you'd require sixteen credits of psych and five thousand miles of solo driving. I still can't drive to Manhattan," she added.

"One step at a time."

"But then, I don't have to drive. That's part of the problem. My husband's . . ." She searched for the right word. "My husband's position really helped me avoid a lot of the confrontations I would have had to face years earlier. I didn't have to drive the children. I could have a hairdresser come to the house to trim my hair." She realized she was talking like a patient. A boring patient. She felt her face flush. "Anyway, thank you for letting me into the program. I mean, I appreciate your confidence."

"I'd like more from you than that," Dr. Fullerton said.

"What?" She couldn't look at his face. She studied the navy and maroon diamond shapes on his sweater.

"I'd like more from you than just being a volunteer. Let me be frank with you. The most important thing we can do is get the word out to phobics that they can be helped. That they're not doomed to being locked in their houses or out of their cars or away from any place that has cats or escalators or what-have-you for the rest of their lives. They can be helped in a relatively simple, nonthreatening manner. Nonthreatening in the sense that they don't feel they have to delve down and come up with their childhood traumas and hand them over to a psychiatrist for microscopic observation in order to overcome their problem."

She nodded. She had never heard him talk so much. He had a trace of a New England accent, more like Amelia's than a Boston one, as if he'd come from New Hampshire or Maine.

"Now, how can we best reach them?"

It wasn't a prep school accent. He'd gone to public high school. A self-made man. She didn't know how she knew, but she knew. He lacked the loose-limbed ease of Nicholas and his friends; they were graceful men, self-controlled, but their arms and legs took up a little more space than they were perhaps entitled to. Dr. Fullerton's arms stayed close to his body. Even his casually crossed legs did not extend beyond the limits of his chair. And his clothing, while surprisingly elegant for a psychiatrist—so much like Nicholas's—was too perfect. They were the same cordovan loafers, but Nicholas's were a little scuffed, as if scheduled to be shined the following day; Dr. Fullerton's gleamed dark, flawless red.

"I suppose the best way would be to get as much publicity as possible. Newspapers, TV."

"That's right."

He seemed to be waiting for her. She didn't know what to say. "Well, I guess that is the best way," she repeated. She couldn't breathe deeply enough. She had been on a diet and had finally gotten into size ten pants, but the waist was very tight and the top of the front button was gouging into her stomach. There might be a roll of flab hanging over her pants. She shouldn't have tucked her sweater in; it was a gesture only the naturally thin should make. She yearned to touch herself to see if she was bulging, but she was afraid he'd realize exactly what she was doing. They were always aware of how women patients felt, how self-conscious they were. Now he knew she was thinking about him and was waiting for her to come to her senses and say something. "That's how I found out about the clinic. In the *Record*."

"Yes. But that's just one small local paper. We want to reach out to all of Fairfield County and northern Westchester. To the whole metropolitan area, for that matter. There are other clinics in the city and on Long Island. It comes down to this, Jane. Newsworthiness. Are we newsworthy?"

"Yes. Of course. Look at the work you're doing. Look how my whole life has been turned around." He was giving her his steady psychiatrist look, more unnerving without his glasses. She kept wanting to stare into the eye with the brown streak and so deliberately made herself look into his other. "Oh," she said. "You want me to—you want me to go public. To get publicity."

"I'd like you to consider it. I know it's asking a great deal and that it's an imposition." He uncrossed his legs and leaned forward. "And believe me when I say I'll understand if you say no."

"Can I think about it?"

"Of course. Jane, I know there must be enormous pressures living in

393

your situation, and the need for privacy must be very, very strong." He seemed to have more color, as though infused with compassion. He had never looked so human. His face was close enough that she could see the tops of his cheeks were pitted with acne scars. "I don't want you to feel used."

"I appreciate that."

"That's the last thing I would want. It's just that there are so many people out there who are suffering, and you could help us to reach out to them. Just think about it. That's all I ask."

"I really do want to help," she said.

"I know you do, Jane."

"Let go of my arm!" Jane cried.

"How could you do it?" Nicholas shouted. "How could you?"

It was only nine in the morning, and already he was wiped out. They'd been going at each other since seven thirty, an out-of-control fight where shrieks plummeted into growls, roars into groans. "How could you?" he kept wanting to know. Fifteen minutes into the fight, he'd dashed up the stairs, chasing her. His ankle had turned and he'd fallen hard on his ass, had bumped down step after step on the base of his spine, until near the bottom of the stairs he was finally able to grab the railing and stop himself. He sat there, his robe gaping open, cradling his twisted ankle, trying to overcome the agony in his back and catch his breath. When it came, he began to cry. It was too much, that Jane could betray him. He'd remained there, his face in his hands, heaving with silent sobs. His unshaven cheeks scratched against his hands; a man should not cry like this. But he could not stop until he heard the house-keeper sliding open the parlor door, checking to see—now that the shouting had stopped—if the coast was clear. He'd hauled himself up and limped upstairs.

"How could you?" His voice was steady now. It had been for nearly an hour. But he was worn out. His hand was shaking so much his grip on her arm weakened. Jane pulled out of his grasp and leaned against the bathroom sink. Four finger marks splotched her upper arm. She stared at them, then rotated her arm to observe the tender inside part, inspecting the red circle from his thumb. She probed it delicately with her finger. "For Christ's sake," he said, "stop carrying on. I didn't hurt you."

"You did. Look."

The newspaper was still rolled in his pocket. He pulled it out and shook it at her. "You look!" He unrolled it. It was folded to the offending page. "Look, I said!" She turned her back to him and opened the door of the medicine chest. He slammed the paper against her nose. "Read it, goddamn it! The goddamn *New York Times*. No? All right, I'll read it. 'In 1969, Nicholas Cobleigh began his film career and his ascent to stardom. In that same year,

Jane Cobleigh, his goddamn wife, began her descent into what she calls her "private hell."''"

Jane tried to pull the paper from his hand. She succeeded in ripping off two thirds of it. "Stop it! Please, Nick. Listen to me. It's nothing. It's—"

"Eighteen years of marriage," he said. "And it's nothing to you. Piss it away for the women's page of the *New York Times*."

"No!"

He threw the shreds of the newspaper he was still holding to the floor. "You promised me we'd talk about it before you spoke to any reporter. You *promised*. You knew how I felt about that prick doctor exploiting you."

"He wasn't exploiting me. He wasn't." She tried to slide past him. "He's a dedicated psychiatrist and he's helping people, and *I'm* helping people by going public with this." She was wearing a black slip; with it and the bright red lipstick she was wearing she looked like an over-age 1950s starlet. "Nick, please. Let's both of us calm down. Please. Read the article *calmly* and you'll see there's nothing bad about you in it. Everything it says about you is *good*, how you cared and worried about me and were supportive and tried everything—"

"Shut up!"

"Stop yelling at me!"

"Shut up, damn you!" He was screeching, out of control again.

"Listen to yourself!" she screeched back. "Just listen!"

"You lied to me, goddamn it. You said you wouldn't do anything—"

"They were planning a whole big piece on agoraphobia."

"Then they didn't need you. Did they? Did they? Answer me, goddamn it."

"They *did*," she said. "I was the hook."

He wanted to slap her, throwing around bullshit PR talk. He balled his right hand into a fist and punched his left palm. She recoiled. "Why didn't you ask me?" he demanded.

"You were in California."

"Aren't there phones? You call me two, three times a day. 'Nick'—he used a falsetto—'do you think I should get tassel pulls for the shades in the apartment? Nick, Lizzy says all her friends are going to camp in Scotland and she wants to go too. What do you think, Nick? What should I do? Should I go to the bathroom, Nick? I have to pee.'"

She slapped him so hard across his face his teeth clamped down on the inside of his cheek. Then she ran out of the bathroom. Before he could follow her, he had to spit a mouthful of blood into the sink.

"I don't have to justify what I do!" she shouted as he entered the bedroom. She stood on the far side of the bed, using it as a barrier. "I'm a person too, damn it! I have a right to say whatever I want to say."

395

He held onto the low post of the bed as if it alone could support him. His mouth was filled with the salty taste of blood. "Even when you're destroying me?" Bloody saliva dribbled down his chin. He wiped it on the shoulder of his robe.

"I'm not destroying you." She edged backward, watching him all the time.

"What the hell do you think I'm going to do?" he shouted. "Spring at you?" She stepped into her closet and came out with a dark dress. She held it up against her. The coyness, the false modesty made him sick. "Where are you going?"

"I have a lunch date in the city."

"With whom, if I'm allowed to ask."

"With Dr. Fullerton and someone—" she paused for an instant—"with someone from *Newsweek*." She turned her back to him, slipped the dress over her head, and then faced him again. "You don't have to worry. You'll come out just like you did in the *Times* piece, smelling like a rose. Better than you deserve."

"What do you mean?" She didn't answer. She began to fasten the long row of buttons that ran up the left side of her dress like a military tunic. She buttoned with rapid precision. "I said, what do you mean, better than I deserve?"

She did not look at him. "I mean, you never really wanted me to get better."

"What?"

She lifted her chin to fasten the buttons on the tunic collar. She spoke to the ceiling. "I know that now. You had me just where you wanted me. Your devoted, adoring prisoner. You had my undivided attention. Nothing to distract me from being the perfect little wife for you."

The knot in his stomach pulled tighter. "You know that's not true."

"Isn't it? If I'd been able to go out, to be my own person—"

"Jesus Christ—"

"If I had a job, do you think I'd have had time to be the perfect mother, spending hours and hours with them, reading, critiquing their homework like it was *Ulysses*, baking five million gingerbread men? All so you could go away for four or five months with a clear conscience, knowing they wouldn't shrivel up from missing Daddy. And would I have had the time to make dinner for your thousands of business people or keep your family together because your mother gets rattled when she has to serve more than three cups of coffee, much less Thanksgiving dinner? Oh, and entertaining your father's endless parade of girl friends. 'Dad, how nice of you to drop in.' 'Jane, I want you to meet Prissy. Oh, sorry, Missy. I'm just teasing. I know it's Sissy.' And I'd say, 'Oh, *do* stay the weekend, Dad.' And if I'd had a life to call my own—just

396

listen to me, damn it—would I have been able to read every screenplay that came into the house? To go over and over your characterizations with you? To—"

"You *wanted* to!"

"It was the only thing I had."

"And you think . . . you think, Jane, that all those nights I held you and you cried and I begged you, *Please* let me help you, let me find someone else to help you, I love you, I want to help . . ."

She walked back to her closet. "Maybe you weren't aware of what you were feeling. It's possible. I'm not saying you *consciously* subverted me."

"What are you talking about?"

She came out with a pair of black and red high-heeled sandals, the sort of shoes an expensive call girl would wear. "Dr. Fullerton said—are you going to listen or not?—he said sometimes the spouses of agoraphobics have a vested interest in maintaining that kind of abject dependency."

"You're crazy! You've gotten things twisted. What has he done to you? I mean it! What has he done to you?"

"He's gotten me better, that's what. He's gotten me out of the house and you can't tolerate it, can you? I'm not forced to live vicariously any more. I'm not forced to wait three, four, five months while you're off on location, waiting for you to come home so I can help you prepare for your next film. So I can give you the summaries of all the novels I read and then have you toss them aside and say, 'Oh, thanks. I'll get to them in a couple of weeks.' *Thousands* of terrible books, just to find the perfect vehicle for you. Reading screenplays twenty, thirty times, making sure they were perfect for you." She sat on the bed and fastened the strap of the shoe around her ankle.

"No one forced you to do a goddamn thing."

"No? How else was I supposed to express my talents?"

"I don't get you."

"That is painfully obvious. You can't see beyond yourself any more, can you? Let me refresh your recollection. It so happens I was involved in the theater long before you were."

"What does that have to do with anything?"

"Are you serious?" She fastened her other shoe and stood. "Have you become so totally egocentric that you can't see anyone else any more?"

He stared at her. She had thick red combs holding back her hair. Huge black button earrings. All black and red, with that shiny red slash of a mouth. "I don't know what you're talking about," he said. He didn't. She looked hard, dramatic: an expensive tramp. Men would notice her.

"I'm saying," she droned, with exaggerated patience, "that if it weren't for me, you'd be some drudge in a law firm today. I coached you. I guided you every step of the way."

397

He couldn't move from his place at the bed. He couldn't speak. She strolled to her dresser, opened a bottle of perfume, and dabbed it onto her neck, her arms, behind her knees.

"I gave up my career for you," she said.

"Jane!"

"I did."

"You were the one who—"

"I'm not saying I begrudge it. I did it freely. But the point is I did it, and if I had it to do all over again, I don't know if I would. I mean, it was a different era. And I was so in awe of you and wanted you to be happy and—"

"Jane, I begged you not to give it up. I was driving a taxi, remember? Don't you remember? I pleaded with you to keep at it."

"But it was better that I did give it up. Wasn't it, Nick? That's what you really wanted me to do. That gave me all the time in the world to work with you, to nurture your talent. You got the actor's dream: a live-in coach. And she did the dishes too, and anything else you wanted. Not bad for the price."

He wasn't going to cry again. He wouldn't give her that.

"Just once," she said, "after we had Vicky, if you had just come and said, 'Okay, I'm making some money now, why don't you try and audition? We can get a babysitter.'"

He wasn't going to cry. "Do you want to know why I didn't?" he asked. She leaned against her dresser and looked at him. "Really. Do you?"

"Yes," she said. "I do."

"I didn't want you to audition because I didn't want you to get hurt." Her big, made-up eyes opened wide. "You're making me say this, Jane; I didn't want to. You just never had the talent."

Jane delved through the blueberries in the colander, taking off stems and leaves. "Do you know how they say that if you cook with love the food will come out tasting wonderful?"

"And?" Cecily asked.

"It's not true. I'm filled with hostility and I made the sauce for the *vitello tonnato* and it's perfect. Exquisite. And the pasta salad will be perfect and the blueberry tart will be perfect too. He'll have an absolutely exquisite birthday dinner."

"Maybe you're not as hostile as you think." Cecily sat at Jane's kitchen table tracing her initials in the wet frosting of a glass of iced coffee. "Maybe subconsciously you're still madly in love with him."

"Well," Jane said, "he's my husband." She picked out two undeveloped green berries and put them in the pile of stems and leaves. "I don't *not* love him."

She could no longer say that she did. She felt empty. She avoided looking

398

at him. When she did, she saw the familiar face of an actor she'd seen in many, many films. She knew he felt something close to what she did. His manner was polite and distant, as if they were two strangers in a foreign country who, by some fluke, had been forced to share a hotel room. In bed, they slept so close to the edges of the mattress that it was only a matter of time before one of them would fall off during the night. He'd reached for her only twice in six weeks. The first time he didn't kiss her. The second, his erection disappeared and he'd said, "Never mind."

They exchanged information. "Vicky's guidance counselor says she should apply for early admission to Brown." "Murray asked if we could make an appearance at the American Film Institute dinner."

Tension pervaded their lives. In their Manhattan apartment, she'd walked in on him as he was drying off from a shower, his leg up on the toilet seat, and he'd glared at her as if she were a crazy fan who had invaded his dressing room. She'd turned and walked out, not saying a word. When the *Newsweek* article became a cover story about behavioral psychology—with her picture on the cover—he did not speak to her for an entire week. Instead, he gave her the ripped-out pages of the article, with his underlinings in red ink.

"I felt utterly hopeless," Jane Cobleigh said. "There was no place for me to turn. My husband was gone for three, four months at a time. . . ." She had her first panic attack in 1968, when Nicholas was in California making his first film. . . . And in her case, there were pressures that far exceeded those of the average housewife-victim. Her husband is one of the most sought-after men in the world, an object of almost universal desire. His reputation is that of a cool, sometimes unapproachable aristocrat. He is also a busy, highly successful businessman whose economic savvy puts him in a league with the shrewdest money-men in the country. Associates say he spends as much time on his holdings as he does on his films.

Cecily went to the freezer, took a handful of ice cubes, and dropped them into the already iced coffee. "Jane, you can't sustain a level of tension like this."

"Want to bet?"

"Stop quipping, okay? I've been married three times. I've had fights all three times. Bad ones. I'm an expert. Chip was always insecure and could never make a decision, and Chuck was terribly domineering and every time I said no to something he'd take it personally and go fuming off, slamming doors. And Steve is moody. And not just if a poem gets rejected. If something happens to the fan belt on his car he'll be nasty for the next three days. But there's always an end to it. With all three of them. Eventually you kiss and make up. But there's no end with you and Nick. It keeps escalating, and that makes it dangerous."

Jane wiped her hands on a paper towel and sat at the table with Cecily.

With her thumbnail, she pared bits of blueberry out from under her other nails. "What am I supposed to do, clam up?"

"I don't know."

"All our lives, it's been Nicholas first, last, middle. Aren't I entitled to something?"

"Of course you are. But your something is in complete contradiction to his something, his mania for privacy."

"But I'm not talking about *him*. I've had chances to invade his privacy, and I never, ever would. Four different publishers have contacted me, wanting me to write a book about being agoraphobic, but I know what they really want is some juicy stuff about the marriage. I'm not naive. They want my story, but they also want some goodies about Nick. I wouldn't do anything like that. I *told* him that."

"What did he say?"

Jane chewed her lower lip for a minute. "He said the only reason I'm getting attention is that I'm his wife, that if I were Mrs. Joe Blow no one would care. And that's partly true, but it's not all true. I have something to say, and I say it well."

"I know you do."

"But Nick says it's all a smokescreen. All they really want to know is what he's like, and since he won't talk they'll get what they can from me. He says the only reason *People* did that piece was because their reporters have been trying to get up here for five years, and this was the only way they could do it. He twists everything so he gets all the credit. Nicholas Cobleigh is the center of the universe; everything revolves around him. And I've betrayed him. I've humiliated him. I'm an ingrate. I have no class. I'm the walking wounded. That's what he called me. He said I was a sick woman, and that it was in Judson's interest that I don't get well."

"*Judson's* interest?"

"Stop looking at me like that. We've been working together on the publicity and the phobia conference, and he said it would be easier if we were on a first-name basis." Cecily was peering into her glass as if it were holding a fascinating liquid she'd never seen before. "Cecily!"

"I think you're getting emotionally involved."

"I'm not!"

"Is he married?"

"Yes."

"How do you know?"

"He told me."

"He *told* you?"

"God, Cecily. He happened to mention he and his wife were going off to the Cape in August."

"All I know is that for the last few months, it was Dr. Fullerton this, Dr. Fullerton that, Dr. Fullerton walks on water."

"Oh, come on."

"And now it's Judson. I think you're putting your energies in the wrong place. I think you should forget about Judson. Concentrate on your marriage and work things out."

"I appreciate your interest."

"Yours very truly. Jane, don't shut down on me. Listen to me. It's normal to get a crush on a shrink, but—"

"I don't have a crush on him! We have a good working relationship. I have a great deal of respect for him, and that's that."

"Okay, he's your colleague. Fine. Great. But what about your husband?"

"My husband screamed at me last night because I dared to invite his family up for his birthday without telling him. As if it were a huge surprise. I only do it every single year."

Cecily sipped her drink. The ice had melted, and the coffee looked like brown-tinged water. She made a face and set it aside. "Did you ever consider that your husband is in a bad emotional state? His entire life has changed. You've come out of the closet, so to speak. You're challenging him for the first time in your relationship. The whole political balance of your marriage is changing. He needs time to adjust."

"Cecily, he won't even try. He won't talk to me. If I accidentally brush him when I walk past, he recoils. I said to him *Please*, let's talk and he said, Why? You do all the talking you need to the media."

"He's hurt."

"He's self-involved. I can't begin to tell you what it's like. The whole world wants to please him. I'm the only one who doesn't, and therefore I'm sick."

"Did he actually say that?"

"Yes. And if I'm not sick . . . when we went to that Retarded Infant Services Ball, and I was wearing that ice-blue gown with the low back, he told me I looked like a hooker. Excuse me. An over-age hooker. I'm over-age. He's so busy running to dermatologists getting different face creams because he has a wrinkle in his forehead that he doesn't have time to breathe. Did you ever have that? Get into bed with a man and the moisturizer smell is coming from him? It's a real turn-on."

Cecily reached across the table and put her hand on top of Jane's. "Jane—" Jane yanked her hand away.

"And he's so wonderfully sensitive. My husband cannot meet a woman any more without turning on that famous understated smile. You know, where he barely shows his teeth. Oh, they love it. I can see how much they love it. Do you know how? Because he keeps showing me. We're standing right next to each other and he's lighting fires under every woman who walks by. He puts his arm around them, takes their chin in his hand, and holds it to look at them better. Looks right into their eyes. He won't touch me. And do you know what? When I tell my beloved husband that his flirting bothers me, it humiliates me, do you know what he says, Cecily? He says, 'Why don't you discuss your anxieties with Dr. Fullerton?'"

25

. . . that Nicholas Cobleigh has Long Island roots as well. In fact, Tuttle Pond, just west of Locust Valley, is named for his . . .

—*Newsday,* Long Island

Judson Fullerton sat in a pink padded chair that looked as if it came from a 1950s beauty salon. "I feel uncomfortable," he said. A paper towel, tucked in at the neck, covered the front of his shirt.

"Doc," the makeup man said, "normally I don't pressure men into makeup if they don't want to, but you'll be sitting next to Mrs. Cobleigh." He turned and smiled at Jane. Jane smiled back and the man smiled even more broadly, no doubt hoping he could someday smile his way into Nicholas Cobleigh's dressing room. He turned back to the psychiatrist and blended pancake makeup over his nose with a damp sponge. "You see, she's got this very intense color and you'll be sitting between her and Gary, and Gary's *ultra* tan plus wears makeup, so you'll look like a cadaver without anything on." The makeup man whirled the chair around so Jane could see him. "What do you think?"

"Maybe a little blue eyeshadow," she said.

Judson flushed and took off the paper towel. The makeup man looked quizzical for an instant and then laughed, a deep Santa Claus ho-ho-ho, much heartier than necessary. "You're a real kidder!" he observed. Then, lowering his voice to espionage level, he asked, "Do you kid around with your husband?"

"Sometimes," she said very softly. She noticed that Judson cracked a smile.

"Speaking of blue eyeshadow," the makeup man said, "don't let *anyone* talk you into it. Ever, ever. A little highlighter under the eyes and *gobs* of mascara. Just goop it on. All you have to do is frame those *gorgeous* eyes. Now tell me, who talked you into that eyeliner? Some ditz at Bloomingdale's?"

"My husband's makeup man."

"Jane—can I call you Jane?" She nodded. "A lit-tle eyeliner is okay on blondies. It *defines.* Separates their pale skin from the whites of their eyes. If you had your husband's coloring, I'd be screaming 'Bring on the medium brown pencil this *second!*' But with your skin color and *especially* with those magnificent eyes, it's adding coals to Newcastle. You know what I'm saying?" She nodded. "Is this your first TV show?" the makeup man asked.

"Yes."

"You'll be fabulous. The camera is going to fall in love with you." He reached over and patted her cheek. "You're not nervous, are you? Oh, come on! You've got it made."

A short girl with a clipboard and two pencils sticking out from her frizzled hair led them to the area behind the set. "Just stand back here," she whispered. "I'll come back and seat you during the break."

"How are you doing?" Judson asked.

It made her nervous to be standing so close to him. "A little nervous." Her whisper sounded weak to her. "What if I get an attack when I'm sitting there?"

"You tell me. What if you get an attack?"

"Face it," she said. "Get right into it."

He nodded. He looked very distinguished. Not in the stereotypical psychiatrist mode—a pipe and elbow patches—but in a light gray suit, red raw silk tie, and a white handkerchief arranged into many little peaks in his breast pocket. He could be a diplomat or a quiet titan of industry.

She had never really stood beside him. He was taller than she, about six feet. The makeup and the dim backstage light smoothed out his face, making him look ten years younger. It did not make him good-looking. Without exception, his features were bland and too small for his large face. His jaw was soft and ill defined, so his face seemed to flow into his neck.

"Are you nervous?" she asked. Immediately she felt embarrassed. She had never asked him a personal question.

"A little."

Instead of letting it go, she dug herself in deeper. "What's your biggest fear?"

"Are you the psychiatrist now?" he asked.

She flushed. "You're being evasive," she said. Bold. That's what her stepmother would have said: You're such a bold girl.

She didn't feel bold. She felt frightened. He must be aware of her attempts to sound relaxed and lighthearted with him and—if he was capable of pity, which she couldn't tell—feel sorry for her. This must happen all the time: women trying too hard to appear easy. She wondered if it meant anything to him. Psychiatrists weren't supposed to take it personally, but she wondered if somewhere in their minds they kept a list and checked off, with a little internal smile, each woman patient as she inevitably succumbed.

He patted her arm. It took all her control not to flinch from the shock of his touching her. "I am being evasive," he said. "Let me see. I've been on radio several times and done fairly well, but this is much more intimidating." He looked at the lighting and the booms beyond the flats, hanging over the

404

set. "I suppose I'm afraid my voice will crack. That's it. That I'll be appearing on *Talk*, on national television, and squeaking like a prepubescent boy."

"And the whole world will hear you squeak, and until the end of time people are going to come up to you and say 'Hi, Dr. Fullerton.'" She squeaked the greeting. "Is that it?"

He patted her arm again. "I'm sure we'll both be fine."

She wondered what his wife was like. She had two possibilities. One was a middle-aged woman, very thin, with hollows under her high cheekbones and short gray hair brushed away from her face. She had originally imagined someone dumpier, in tie-dyed Indian cotton skirts and a great deal of ethnic jewelry, but then decided such a woman would not match Judson Fullerton. The other possibility disturbed her more. Someone in her late twenties. Small, but a superb athlete, always in tennis clothes. A second wife who made him feel young again.

"Let's go," the girl with the clipboard suddenly said. Jane jumped. "As quickly as possible, and don't trip over the cables."

"Thank you, Dr. Fullerton," Gary Clifford said. His voice was such a rich baritone that all during the time he was questioning Judson, Jane half expected him to burst into song. He gazed into the camera. "Now *that's* dedication," he said. He looked like an Italian singer. His features were Mediterranean and powerful, his skin was bronzed to brilliance, and his teeth were flawless white chiclets. His black curls shone in the light. They were the sort of curls women would want to stick their fingers into. He was perfect show business. Any moment he could break into "Arrivederci Roma." Instead, he turned to her. "All right, Jane Cobleigh. It's your turn now on *Talk*. Are you ready to talk about phobias?"

"Unless I have a panic attack and go screeching off the set," she said. She gazed straight into his eyes.

"Ha-ha-ha!" Gary Clifford chortled. People on *Talk* laughed too hard.

"But then they could replay it on the six o'clock news."

"Ha-ha-ha!"

"Good publicity, I guess."

She smiled at him. The only thing Nicholas would tell her about how to behave on television was to look directly at the person speaking to you and never look at the cameras or any of the equipment. When she'd asked him to pretend to be the interviewer, he'd simply breathed "Jesus Christ" and walked out, leaving his dinner unfinished on the kitchen table.

"Are you nervous now, Jane?" Gary Clifford asked.

"Yes. Of course I am. But it has nothing to do with being phobic, at least I don't think so. Right now I'm nervous because I'm on television. Housewives

405

don't normally sit around in the afternoon being interviewed by Gary Clifford."

Gary Clifford beamed at her. She forced herself not to look at the monitor. She smiled back at him. Out of the corner of her eye, she saw the gray sleeve of Judson Fullerton's jacket.

"Phobias are different from normal, reasonable fears," she continued. "I mean, I guess it's normal for me to be nervous being here today."

Gary Clifford reached across the set's coffee table and patted her hand. Everyone was patting her today. Except for Nicholas. He had left the day before on a fishing trip to Canada with his father and his brother Michael, saying pointedly that he wanted quiet: no radios or television up there, he'd said.

"But phobias aren't a normal response to anything," she went on. "There was no rational reason why I spent two years barely able to get into a car, avoiding going to town—we live near a tiny town in Connecticut. It's not as if it were Manhattan, big and noisy and overwhelming. It's underwhelming. And after that I spent another six years unable to leave the house. Literally. I could not stand in an open doorway. I couldn't take even one step into my back yard."

"Would you call it a mental illness?" Gary Clifford asked gently.

"Absolutely not. But I would have called it that, if you'd asked me eighteen months ago. I'd have said, Yes, I'm a sick woman. I can't function. I can't perform the simplest tasks of normal life. I can't go outside and cut roses. I can't visit a friend. I can't take a walk with my husband." Her eyes began to brim with tears. She couldn't believe she was being so emotional on television. It was awful. She blinked. Partly awful. The housewife was humiliated. The actress lifted her finger, wiped away a tear from beneath her eye which had not even fallen, and said, "When my daughter played Pocahontas in the fourth grade, I had to tell her I couldn't go." She sniffled twice, half shaken, half amazed at her audacity. "She said, 'Please, Mommy, just try. For me.' And I *couldn't*." Jane covered her face with her hands for an instant, then took them away. "I'm sorry," she said. "I'm fine now."

Gary Clifford's big brown eyes were misted over. "Jane," he said tenderly, "tell us more."

"Really," Jane said, "it was just show business hyperbole. When they say superb it means tolerable. Brilliant means pretty good. At least they didn't say, 'I'm speechless.' That means you were so bad you should have been exposed on a mountaintop at birth. Nick was once in this terrible Off Broadway turkey, something called *Stupor*, and at the cast party someone came up and put his hand on Nick's shoulder and said, 'Nick, what is there to say about your performance? There just aren't any words.'"

406

She and Judson Fullerton were in a small marble oasis between four elevator doors. On either side, narrow trails of brown tweed carpet rolled along the network corridors toward infinity.

"But you were good," Judson said. His face was so bright it looked sore. Immediately after the show, he'd gone into the men's room and scrubbed off his makeup, but he'd missed his upper lip, so he appeared to have an apricot-colored mustache.

"So were you," Jane said. She pushed the button to summon the elevator even though she'd done it a moment before. "It's taking a long time to get up here. If it doesn't come in a minute, I'll probably work myself up into a major elevator phobia." She glanced at him. His expression rarely changed. He seemed to be concentrating so intently on what was being said that he could not express his reaction to it: to laugh or raise his eyebrows might mean to miss the crucial nuance. "At least it would be convenient. I mean, to get elevatoraphobia with you right here. I could be cured by the time we got to the ground floor."

He obviously felt he did not have to respond. They waited. A high-pitched *ding* signaled the elevator's arrival. There were enough people in it so she would not be tempted to talk again. She relaxed; her shoulders actually slumped with relief. Once she started talking to him, she got nervous and babbled. She was sure he didn't like it; he was too economical.

Maybe that was why he'd stopped being a Freudian or whatever he'd been and become a behaviorist; ten or fifteen years, forty-eight weeks a year, forty-eight hours a week of babbling free association was simply too much for his nature to bear. She sneaked a fast glance at him. He was peering up at the floor indicator. His gold collar pin grasped the two rounded ends of his collar in perfect symmetry. He liked things crisp and controlled. He didn't like babblers.

Outside, the early evening air was unusually dry and cool for late July, as if, as a final courtesy, NBC had arranged for the streets around Rockefeller Center to be air conditioned. The last of the office workers leaving their buildings sensed the specialness of the evening, and instead of hurtling themselves eastward and westward toward the subways, they strolled, swinging attaché cases and handbags. Still, Judson ran his finger under the high collar of his shirt, as though it were a scorcher. They had not spoken since they'd gotten on the elevator. She couldn't decide whether just to say goodbye or to shake his hand and say something like Thanks for everything, or a lower-key Nice seeing you again.

"Where are you going from here?" he asked.

"You mean tonight?"

"Yes."

"I couldn't tell whether you were asking a regular question or a cosmic question, like where is my entire life going." She was babbling again. He wasn't even looking at her; he was looking down, adjusting one of the peaks in his pocket handkerchief. "Tonight. Well, we have a place uptown. On Fifth and Seventy-fifth." She was giving too much information. "I guess I'll just walk home, kick off my shoes, and have a minor breakdown. I mean, from nerves from the show. I wasn't nervous when I was on, but I was before and after."

"Was your husband watching?"

"No. He's in Canada on a fishing trip." She shifted her shoulder bag higher and stuck her hands into the big pockets of her flared skirt. "He didn't want to see me on TV."

"He's still upset that you're talking about your agoraphobia."

"It's in direct proportion. Every time I open my mouth, he gets more furious. He thinks what I'm doing is absolutely tasteless, like one of those third-rate actresses going on the Johnny Carson show to promote their auto-biographies, discussing all their sleazy love affairs and how terrible their parents were to them."

"How do you feel about it?"

"I think he's wrong."

Without discussion, they began walking together, eastward toward Fifth Avenue, then uptown. He looked straight ahead as he walked, as if walking took as much concentration as talking, and it gave her a chance to study him. Although he was fair-skinned, with graying, light brown hair, he had a heavy beard. Dark prickles were sticking out around his short sideburns down to his chin. It was an excess she was sure he didn't like. Every once in a while, she'd get a whiff of pine fragrance. She wasn't sure if it was his aftershave or the scent of trees in Central Park. She wished he would say something to indicate if he was being polite and walking her back to her apartment or if he had an appointment uptown.

"Would you like to go for a drink?" he asked suddenly.

Jane made herself keep walking at the same pace, although she was certain she was going to trip on a crack in the pavement, *splat*, right on the sidewalk; her skirt would fly up. "Yes," she said. "Fine." The "fine" was unnecessary. If she didn't watch it, she'd say: Terrific. I'd love it. Isn't that nice of you to ask me. Thank you so much. Wow. Gee.

The irony was, she really could handle herself with people. Eighteen years of rubbing up against Nicholas's smoothness had had its effect. Also, as his fame grew, she'd been charmed by the best. The whole world wanted to sit at her dinner table. And so she'd learned, a little, how to charm back. But all that seemed to count for nothing. She'd felt more socially adept in her senior year at Woodward High School than she felt with Judson Fullerton.

"I have a place on East End."

"Oh," Jane said. She had to think of something to say. She couldn't just say oh. "I assumed you lived in Connecticut."

"I do. In Westport. But I teach at Cornell Medical School one day a week, so I have a studio."

"What do you teach?"

He looked at her as if she were crazy. "Psychiatry," he said.

"White wine," she called. He'd disappeared into his slot of a kitchen. "If you have it."

It didn't look as though he had very much. The studio seemed to have been rented furnished, or at least decorated by someone with even less imagination than the person who had fixed up his chrome and leather office. The couch, two small armchairs, and an ottoman were from no particular period, and their inconsequentiality was underscored by their upholstery; they were all covered in the same nubby mud-gold fabric. The room's two tables, a long rectangle and a small end table with a lamp, were laminated with something too shiny to be wood, although it was dark brown and had a distinct grain. The only other objects in the room were medical and psychiatric journals, which were scattered about with surprising randomness. She leafed through one on the table beside her chair. An advertisement showed a man with a window in his torso, his intestines on view. "'What do you see, Doctor?'" the ad began. She went on until she came to a page that said "Fracture of the Month" and then put it aside.

"I have a Montrachet," he announced from the kitchen.

"That will be fine."

There was a psychiatric journal on the table, but she didn't want to look at it. There could be an article about agoraphobia that might say something about phobics she didn't want to know.

Somewhere he'd taken off his jacket and unfastened his collar pin. He came out of the kitchen with two glasses of wine and handed her one. "You've stayed off the tranquilizers?" he asked. He sat on the other chair and put his feet up on the ottoman.

"Oh, yes."

"Cheers." He lifted his glass. "Well, it went very well. It's too bad it was a live show."

"I'm taping it. I have one of those—" Babbling again. She would go on and describe every button of the video cassette recorder. She sipped her wine to camouflage her silence.

He hooked his finger around the knot of his tie, loosened it, pulled it off, and opened the top button of his shirt. He tossed the tie onto the coffee table. She waited for him to get up and fold it flat. He didn't. "I think after today you're going to be in great demand. Every talk show is going to want you."

409

"You too," she said. "You were very good."

"We could tour, like a vaudeville act." She stared at him. He had said something amusing. At least she thought he'd meant it to be amusing. She smiled. He didn't. "What are you going to do if you get more invitations to go on TV?" he asked.

"I don't know." She took a second sip of wine. He had finished his. She was so used to being the hostess she wanted to ask him if he wanted more. "There's the problem with my husband."

"How bad is it?"

"Pretty bad." She wanted to tell him about Nicholas, about how bad it really was. She wanted to ask, What did I do to make it this bad? How did it get so that he never undresses before me any more, that he always wears a bathrobe—even to walk from the bathroom to his chest of drawers—as if depriving me of the last bit of access I have to his body? His renowned body. She wanted to talk, but he wasn't being a psychiatrist. His wing tips were off, his feet were up, and she was sitting sipping his wine. And calling him Judson. Instead she said, "I don't know what to do about the publicity. I want to help, but how much? Do I become a vaudeville act?"

"I didn't mean that in a derogatory manner," he said.

"I know. But that's what I can become. For you, this is just another small item on a very long résumé. But for me—" She sighed. "I don't want to be a professional basket case."

"You're not a basket case."

"Well, a professional ex-basket case. You know, when Nick made his first couple of films, he'd go on these promotional tours. It's not just the *Tonight* show. Every city has something: *Good Morning Detroit, A.M. Boston, Hello Saratoga Springs*. I know that being Mrs. Nicholas Cobleigh I could get onto any show I want. And I know it would help people. I know that in every city there are people who can't leave their houses, who have nothing to do *but* listen to these shows. But is that what I want to do?"

"Well, do you have anything you're really burning to do?" She shrugged. "Do you still want to be part of the training program? To go and work with phobics the way Ellie Matteo worked with you?"

"I don't know," she said. And then it slipped out. "I don't think so. I don't know why. I just think of Ellie's patience, standing there with me until I was able to get into a car. Just to get into it, not even drive. I don't think I'd have that patience, even though I've been through it myself. I'd probably want to shove the person into the car and say, 'Oh, come on. Stop being stupid.' Isn't that terrible?"

"No." He ran his finger over the rim of his glass. She drank the rest of her wine so quickly she felt a little lightheaded. "Let me get some more wine," he said.

410

He returned from the kitchen carrying the bottle and refilled their glasses, placing the bottle on the psychiatric journal she hadn't wanted to see. She leaned forward to pick up her glass. He sat on the arm of her chair.

She didn't dare lift the glass. She'd shake. She'd spill it. His thigh pressed against her arm. It was really nothing. She was misinterpreting it. He was just being informal. His shoes were off. She leaned back. His arm was there to receive her. His hand felt so warm on her arm. He bent down and kissed her.

A light kiss. A long one. His lips brushing back and forth over hers, getting the feel of them. She should say something, she thought for a second. Now was the time.

Instead she strained her neck, pushing up her head to increase the pressure between their lips. Judson pulled back, keeping the pressure soft, a slow extended exploration of her lips, the lightest brushing. She parted her lips to receive his tongue, but he kept his mouth closed, rubbing his closed lips first against the top and then the bottom of her opened ones.

Her hands, prim and awkward in her lap, floated up as in slow motion ballet, reaching for him. He pushed them back into her lap. "Slow," he whispered. He continued his light, torturous kissing.

He kept kissing her. She was too excited. It was so humiliating. She couldn't sit still. Her hips made crazy, irregular circles in the chair. He took her bottom lip between his teeth and gnawed on it. Then he sucked it. It was too much. She tried to pull back. He kept toying with her lip. She put her hand on his thigh.

He pushed it off. "Easy," he said, and went back to her lip.

"Please, let me get undressed." She couldn't believe she'd said that. He stood, took her wrist, and pulled her up from the chair. Standing up seemed to cool her down, enough to feel the rise of unease, but that only lasted an instant, because he began kissing her again, still lightly, keeping a distance between everything but their mouths. She yanked the cotton sweater out of the waistband of her skirt.

"Do you have a curfew?" Judson asked.

"What?"

"Do you have to be home at any special time?"

"No," she whispered.

"Then what's your hurry?"

The kissing seemed to go on forever. Finally, when he pulled her hard against him, she let out such a scream of pleasure she immediately tried to wrench away in embarrassment.

He didn't seem to notice. He held her tight and moved his lips from hers to the side of her face and then down, to her neck. He remained still. She couldn't. She ground herself against him.

"Jane," he said at last, "this feels so good."

411

She was so inflamed she was beyond thought. She tried to tear off her clothes, but he held her hands behind her and said "No." He undressed her slowly, spending so much time kissing and caressing her neck, her shoulders, even under her arms that by the time he unhooked her bra she nearly cried out with gratitude, as though he were relieving her of a terrible burden. "Touch me," she pleaded, grabbing for his hands, trying to crush them against her breasts. "Judson, touch me." He would not. He caressed her back, then knelt and kissed her midriff and stomach. "Touch me! How can you not touch me?" He drew her down onto the floor. The carpet was dry and scratchy, tiny hangnails clawing against her back.

He stopped her from pulling off her underpants. "Don't." When he finally eased them off for her, he worked them slowly down her legs, teasing, the way a stripper would.

He lay beside her, kissing her, stroking her. When he ran his tongue over her stomach, her muscles contracted so violently they hurt. "Do you like that?" he demanded. "Do you?"

His beard abraded her skin wherever he kissed her. His slacks itched her leg. "I can't stand this," she said. He would not touch her breasts or her genitals. She tugged at his hands.

"Stop it," he said.

She was soaked. He rubbed his fingers in the wetness that had dripped onto the inside of her thighs. He rubbed the wet fingers over his lips until they were shiny. Then he kissed her.

Tears poured down her face. She reached out, half blinded, feeling for the bulge in front of his slacks. He arched away from her.

"Not tonight."

She opened her legs wide and thrust her hips toward him. He ignored the invitation.

"Why not? Oh, please, why not?"

"Because," he said slowly, "tonight we're just beginning."

26

WOMAN'S VOICE: . . . and we're fortunate enough to have Beatrice Drew with us. Miss Drew is one of the *grandes dames* of the American stage and is here in Houston re-creating her role in the celebrated Broadway drama *Starry Night*. Miss Drew, before we talk about the play, I understand you are a close personal friend of Nicholas and Jane Cobleigh and actually appeared with Nicholas years ago. Can you tell our viewers, have you had any late word on her condition?
—Patricia Obermaier, KTRK-TV News, Houston

Nicholas had seen the girl before at New York University. That spring, the night before commencement where he was awarded an honorary degree, she'd been hovering in a corner in the President's Lounge, sipping what must have been a soft drink through a straw. She looked tiny, and the only reason he'd noticed her was that, coming from a family of redheads, he'd been wowed by her hair. This was a red no Tuttle had ever had: sleek, unfrazzled, a dazzling red with golden glints. She wore it straight down her back, and because she was so young and delicate—built on a much smaller scale than either of his daughters—she'd reminded him of a redheaded Alice in Wonderland. Whenever he'd glanced at her, she'd hung her head, obviously ashamed she'd been caught staring at him. He mused that she must be the teen-aged daughter of one of the professors and then she'd passed from his mind; he had encounters like that every day.

He'd agreed to a visiting professorship at NYU for that July only because he was at loose ends, between films. Although Jane could leave the house, he realized he did not want to spend a month alone with her, either traveling or in Connecticut. They needed time apart. At least he did. Her tongue, always pointed, had become knife-sharp. She'd held up a screenplay he'd admired, saying, "You *like* this? It's a parody of every film you've ever made. I mean, I could see this as a sketch on television, with some comedian in a blond wig with his shirt off doing a take-off of you." She'd opened the screenplay and read, "'I've given you all I can, Jeannie. I have nothing more to give.' Please, Nick, it's an embarrassment. Think of the children. All the girls at school will point their fingers and mock them." He'd grabbed the screenplay from her hand, gotten in the car, driven to Manhattan, and spent the night alone at the apartment. He loved having the king-sized bed all to himself and slept better than he had in weeks.

The next morning he'd called the chairman of the department and agreed

413

to teach two hours a week during July. Not an onerous schedule, but enough to give him some time away. He needed time to think, although when he was alone he couldn't think except to acknowledge that he was angry, she was angry, they were having problems. And he was very unhappy.

When he was a boy, whenever his mother had lost anything—a bracelet, a book, a favorite watering can—she'd sigh. "I feel as if I've lost my best friend." He and Tom used to make fun of her. "What?" Tom would say. "You can't find your jock strap? You must feel—" And Nicholas would break in, "I feel as if I've lost my best friend." Now the sentence would not stay out of his mind.

But there was that girl again, in his seminar, with that glorious cascade of hair. He'd been surprised when he saw her in class, because he'd been told the seminar was composed of five doctoral candidates. She didn't look over sixteen or seventeen. She was very quiet and usually kept her head down, scribbling notes as if she were responsible for a complete transcript of the seminar.

At the third session, he'd told them he wanted to get their names straight and called off their cards. She was P. MacLean.

"Mr. Cobleigh," one of the men called out. Nicholas wasn't sure if this was B. Nussbaum or L. Drutman. He was even darker skinned than Jane. His posture was unnaturally rigid and he wore mirrored sunglasses all the time, so he resembled a blind jazz musician.

"Yes."

"How do you compare your oeuvre with that of Orson Welles?"

"I don't—"

"Forget *Citizen Kane*," the man said. "Think of *The Magnificent Ambersons*."

"Well, it's hard to judge Welles on the basis of that film, because whichever studio it was—"

"RKO," the man said wearily.

"RKO cut about an hour out of the film and eliminated what Welles thought were some of the most important scenes."

"Do you see any resemblance between your work and Welles's?" B. Nussbaum or L. Drutman demanded.

"Not really."

"None at all?" He sounded astounded at Nicholas's obtuseness.

"No. Do you?"

"To answer that," Nussbaum/Drutman said, "would take ten hours." He seemed to be waiting for an invitation.

Nicholas turned to the other four students. "Any other questions before we get started?"

P. MacLean's head stayed down. She looked more like Alice in Wonder-

414

land than ever. She was wearing a blue dress that looked like the old-fashioned pinafores his sisters used to wear, without the white apron but with the
same puffy little sleeves that only emphasized her scrawny arms. He couldn't
believe they made dresses like that for adults, although she was so small she
could probably wear a child's size. Why she would want to was another
question entirely. He wondered what the P was for: Patty, Penny, Polly. He
hoped she wasn't saddled with something too large for her, like Phoebe.

Fifteen minutes later, when he was discussing how he, as director, had
worked with the different art directors, he caught her staring at him. Not at
his face. At his crotch. Little Alice in Wonderland. He wanted to laugh, but
then he realized she knew he was aware of where her interest had been
directed. Before she lowered her head he could see her face turn almost
purple with mortification. She began writing furiously, but her note-taking
hand must have quivered because she dropped her pen. When she bent down
to retrieve it, her seat tilted and nearly fell over. He wished he could give her
a look to reassure her. She was so young. He felt sorry for her. But she would
not raise her head for the rest of the class.

Nicholas looked ahead, into the long mirror that covered an entire wall of
the bathroom in the Manhattan apartment. He looked like hell. Three days
fishing in Canada and he had such a bad sunburn the lids of his eyes had
puffed, so he appeared to be squinting. The skin over his nose and his cheeks
was blistered and so dry it pulled tight. Even worse, there had been a plague
of blackflies at the lake, and his neck and the back of his hands were dotted
with bites that itched so badly they hurt. The only advantage, he thought, was
that his appearance was so distorted he could probably walk the eighty blocks
from the apartment to NYU and not be recognized.

He would never eat trout again. They had caught so many. It seemed all
they had to do was drop their lines into the water, and fifteen trout fought
each other for the honor of getting hooked. After the first few heady hours, the
fishing had ceased to be fun.

It was even less fun because Michael, who was thirty years old, behaved
so stuffily he seemed older than James. He was a banker, but so humorless, so
conservative and stodgy, he seemed a caricature of one. He looked old,
stringy, with a milky aura around his eyes and the pursed, tight mouth of a
man who'd known decades of bitterness. The only subject that animated him
was the Federal Reserve System. His red hair was clipped so close his head
looked like a rusty scouring pad.

Nicholas and James stayed up drinking that night. In the dark haze just
before dawn, James had said, "It's been sixteen and a half years."

"What?" Nicholas asked.

415

"Sixteen and a half years. Your mother threw me out December 1, 1961. Threw me out. It was the psychiatrist who made her do it."

"Dad—" Nicholas said.

"It's all right. Just watch yourself. That one who's getting interviewed with Jane all the time."

"Everything's fine."

"Good." James poured another drink. They were drinking vodka in paper cups. "Listen, it's going to be all right."

"I know," Nicholas said. His stomach hurt. "Everything will be fine."

"I mean with Win."

"Oh. Yes, she's been fine. In good spirits," Nicholas said. "She has a volunteer job at Sloan-Kettering she's involved with. And she looks well."

"I *know* she looks well."

"You've seen her?"

"I went up there. The maid wouldn't let me in. Didn't know me. New maid. New wallpaper. But then Win—your mother—came to the door."

"Did she seem surprised to see you?" Nicholas couldn't think of anything else to ask. He couldn't say, Did she throw you out? He couldn't ask, After sixteen and a half years' separation, after all your women, how did you have the nerve, the courage, to go and see her?

"She was surprised," James said slowly. Nicholas had felt embarrassed, as if he were about to hear something about his parents that a son should not know. "But it turned out all right."

"Good," Nicholas said, relieved. He supported himself against the rough wall of the cabin and stood. "Well, I'm going to try and get a couple hours' sleep. How about you, Dad?"

"She's taking me back," James said.

"*What?*"

"Don't say *what*. You're not in the movies now. You don't have to give a dramatic performance."

"Dad—"

"You heard me. We're going to France for August, and then I'm moving back into the apartment. Sixteen and a half years, even though she never stopped loving me, all because of that psychiatrist."

"Don't you think—" Nicholas began.

"You better not let that bastard get his hooks into Jane," his father had said.

In his bathroom, Nicholas wet a washcloth with cold water, leaned his head back, and put it over his face to cool his sunburn. He didn't feel like meeting Murray for lunch in the Village and then going to teach. His lips were dried and cracked, and it hurt when he had to smile.

He wasn't smiling that much. "How's my Janie, my celebrity?" Murray would ask. Nicholas threw the cloth into the sink and walked into the bedroom. The chairs and the chaise longue were piled with boxes. Before he'd left for Canada he'd ordered an entire small wardrobe, enough clothes to keep in the apartment so he wouldn't be forced back to Connecticut just because he wanted a fresh suit. He needed a checked sports shirt. He opened a likely looking box from Saks, but it was cotton pajamas. He got a paper cut on the next box. It wasn't sports shirts either.

It was underwear for Jane. Not the usual white, beige, and the couple of black things she usually wore. This was lacy, sexy stuff in wild colors: gray, wine red, bottle green. One yellow bra had such dainty straps and low-cut cups that it would probably break under the strain the first time she wore it. Nicholas hurled it across the room. It landed in a little mound on the rug, like a dead daffodil. He was so angry at her. Every time he thought he'd reached his limit, she'd do something else to get him even angrier.

What did she think, that new underwear would make everything all right? That she could be as sarcastic and hostile as she pleased, that she could make a public spectacle of him by playing crazy lady on TV and then trot around the bedroom in dark green panties and he'd lunge for her? It was such a stupid, simplistic solution, like a women's-magazine piece: How to Rekindle Your Husband's Ardor. Jiggle up to him in brand new sexy underwear. He won't be able to resist. It was the sort of trick the old Jane would laugh at, the new one would embrace: cheap, quick, and meaningless.

He strode across the room, took the bra, and shoved it back into the box. She was in Connecticut, at a planning meeting with that creep psychiatrist for some phobia conference. He'd love to call her at the guy's office, break into the meeting, and say, "Guess what, Jane? You wasted your money. My money. The underwear isn't going to work."

Nicholas spotted her hair almost immediately, but she was halfway across Washington Square Park before he was sure it was she. From the back, in shorts, sneakers, and a T-shirt, she didn't even look like a teenager; she looked like a ten-year-old. Her arms were laden with a huge watermelon and so burdened it looked as if the melon weighed as much as she did. She took tiny irregular steps. He knew it was she when she stopped at a bench, put the melon down, and turned slightly. She was too far away for him to see her face. The front of her shirt had a face he couldn't distinguish either. But the name Alice Guy-Blaché—the first woman film director—was emblazoned across her shirt. It had to be P. MacLean.

He was across the park before she had time to pick up the melon. "P. MacLean," he said to her. "Right?" Her face, pale, with a few freckles across a long nose, turned so white he thought she'd faint onto the bench, over the watermelon. "What's the P for?" he asked.

417

"Pamela."

He picked up the melon. It was heavy, even for him. "Do you usually eat this much?" he asked.

She shook her head, then realized she had to speak. "It's for a watermelon basket. For a birthday party."

"Yours?" She shook her head again. "Let me carry it for you. Are you going home?" She nodded. "Do you live around here?"

She swallowed. "Bank Street," she said. Her voice was as tiny as she. "You don't have to bother."

"That's all right."

They walked through the park. When they reached the street, a taxi swerved, nearly running them down at the curb as the driver spotted Nicholas. Pamela looked terrified. "It's all right," he said. "It happens all the time. I haven't been killed yet."

Words finally broke from her. "I feel terrible about your doing this. A friend got it for me for six cents a pound and it's fourteen at the Key Food near my apartment, so that's why I have to carry it. From her place to—" She glanced up at him. "I'm very nervous, talking to you."

"I know," he said. "Don't be."

"Could I be quiet for a few minutes?" she asked. "Just till I get used to the fact that you're carrying my watermelon?"

"Sure," he said. She walked like a child, slightly pigeon-toed. He was touched by the combination of her shyness and candor.

She wasn't pretty at all. Her nose was too long and her lips were too thin and the chin of her heart-shaped face came to a sharp point. Still, there was something appealing about a girl who knew she had only one good feature and, with sweet desperation, did the most she could with it. Her hair, held up on either side by a blue barrette, fell halfway down her back. Her hair was it. Her figure was like a boy's who would never make a team: delicate, with knobby freckled knees and elbows. Under her Alice Guy-Blaché T-shirt, she wasn't wearing a bra, but she didn't really need one: the only indication of breasts were two small dark swellings under the *l* and the *h*.

"Where did you get that T-shirt?" he asked. "Oh, can we talk or are you still observing your few minutes of silence?"

"My mother had it made for me. I'm doing my dissertation on Guy-Blaché's work in America. Are you familiar with it?"

"No. As a matter of fact, all I know is her name and that she was the first woman director."

"You mean you haven't heard of *The Monster and the Girl* and *The Girl with the Green Eyes*? Or *Tarnished Reputation*?" She was smiling. She had small spaces between her teeth. "Everyone asks me what's my topic and I tell them and they say 'Alice *who?*'"

"Alice *who?*" Nicholas said. "Just kidding. Did she make any sound films?"

"No. Her last was *Vampire* in 1920." She lifted her hair for a minute, as if to cool the nape of her neck. The sleeve of her T-shirt gaped. She had a fluff of red hair under her arm.

"Just out of curiosity," Nicholas asked, "how come you're in my seminar? I don't begin until 1969."

"No," Pamela said.

"No?"

"You began in 1940."

"That's right," he said. "How did you know?"

Pamela looked away from him and focused on the watermelon. "Because," she said, "I've had a crush on you for eight years."

"Do you have a telephone?" Nicholas asked. The apartment was so bare, he was afraid she couldn't afford one. There were two chairs in the living room, but all her books were spread on the gray carpet, and he realized she used the floor for a desk. The carpet was worn so thin patches of brown backing showed through in spots.

"In the kitchen," Pamela said.

"Why not here?"

"Because it's so small in there I have to stand, so I can't get comfortable and talk and talk. That's how I keep my phone bills low."

"You're very smart."

He felt so relaxed, stretched out on her narrow bed with its sheets printed with tiny nosegays tied with pink and yellow ribbons. Her cheek rested on his chest. He stroked her hair and leaned down to kiss the top of her head. Pamela put her arms around him and kissed him. "Not very smart. Just plain smart," she said.

He ran his hand down her naked back. She was so slender and small. He was enchanted by her daintiness. It was as if he were playing with a doll. A doll with perfect breasts that protruded no more than two joints of his finger. "Even if you're just plain smart, you know that if you kiss me like that you're only going to get me started again and I'll never make my phone call. I need two minutes. I was supposed to meet my agent for lunch an hour ago and he's probably still waiting at the restaurant. Wait here. Don't move anything."

"I have to move something because we only have a half hour before class. Twenty minutes, because it takes ten to get there."

Nicholas massaged the delicate vertebrae that protruded down her back. "Forget the phone," he said. "You and I have more important business to discuss."

Nicholas watched Jane from the bedroom. She stood before her wall-long

419

bathroom mirror, fanning her lashes with her hand. As soon as the mascara was dry, she applied still another layer.

"Could you stop for a second?" Nicholas called.

"I can't. I don't have time. You can talk."

She was dressed in white linen slacks with red and white high heels and a sheer white bra. A white blouse hung on a hanger over the bathroom door.

She didn't look real any more. He knew part of it was the comparison to Pamela; Jane looked grotesque, a swollen human female. But there was her artificiality too. She couldn't leave herself alone. Every time she got dressed she behaved as if she were dressing for a *Vogue* shooting; everything—belts, jewelry, stockings—was part of an intricate plan. And her makeup: along the marble counter in the bathroom were enough jars, bottles, sponges, and brushes to service the entire cast of a De Mille epic.

"I only have another five minutes," she said. She emerged, putting on the white silk blouse. He realized, objectively, that she looked good. Even beautiful. She had finally grown into her big, strong looks. When they went out together, men's eyes turned to her. Not the way women's did to him, but she was noticed. But her appeal, her beauty, was external. It wasn't real; it looked as if it could be peeled off. It had nothing to do with what was inside her. The old plain Jane was the one who had been beautiful.

She held her chin aloft so as not to get makeup on the front of the blouse while she buttoned it. She couldn't do anything naturally any more.

"Where are you going?" he asked.

"Lunch with an editor from *Redbook*. They want me to do a column."

"On what?"

"That's why we're having lunch. And you don't have to sound so sarcastic. It would be a general interest column. A new topic every month, so you don't have to worry that I'd be writing about our marriage and violating your privacy." She went to her closet and came out with two red handbags and held them before her, as if making a momentous artistic decision. She chose a flat rectangle of red straw. "This may not have occurred to you," she said, "but people are interested in what *I* have to say."

"If your name were Jane Heissenhuber, do you think anyone from *Redbook* would give a good goddamn about you?"

"I've made a name for myself."

"As the big-mouthed, neurotic wife of a famous actor." He waited for a slap. He was ready to slap her back. Instead, she marched to her dresser, upended a white handbag, and picked over the contents, transferring some of them into the red. "Did you hear me?" he boomed at her. Her back stiffened, but she did not respond. She opened a drawer, took out a jewelry box, and put on a pair of pearl button earrings. "Don't you realize people are laughing at you?"

"Leave me alone."

"Give her a microphone and she'll do anything. Don't you realize how pathetic it is? Listen to me. I'm trying to save you from becoming even more of a public laughingstock. You go on TV and—"

"You're the one who's sick," she said. Her voice was oily and false. "It so happens that after I was on *Talk*, NBC got over five hundred letters, and they want me back on in a few weeks to talk about how I plan dinner parties."

"You're pathetic," he said. "You really are. That jerk will say, 'Well, Jane, what's it like to have all the biggest and most glamorous stars gathered around your table?' and you'll say—"

She hurled the white handbag onto the bed. "Don't you have anything better to do? Just leave me alone."

"I won't leave you alone!" The blood was rushing to his head. She did it all the time, made him so furious he lost control. His head felt ready to explode. "You're a goddamn parasite, that's what you are. That's all you've been. You're using me—"

"I am not!"

"You're using me the way you always used me. You know goddamn well why you married me. And you got just what you wanted."

"What are you talking about?" Her mouth hung open. She looked stupid.

"You married me for my money."

"Money? Are you serious? We had nothing. I had to go out to work and—"

"You knew damned well it wouldn't last forever. You liked the idea of my money and my social position. Don't bother to deny it. You were very ambitious, but you didn't have five cents to your name and you had no place to go. That lovely, charming family of yours didn't want anything to do with you. So you grabbed onto the golden ring. What the hell did I know? I was twenty goddamn years old."

"It so happened I loved you," she said. Her voice was so mild he knew she had to be putting it on. "I loved you very much."

"Oh," he trilled, "thank you so much, my dear. And I, of course, loved you too."

"Nick, please, I can't take any more."

"I remember how my heart beat, pitter-patter, when I first saw you. It was so deeply and profoundly moving. You the brilliant, gifted actress and me, a dumb fraternity jock. And how you deigned—"

"Nick, *stop*. We have to stop! What kind of a marriage is this? At least we can—"

"At least we can admit you were a gold digger. A nice, bright, pleasant gold digger, but still and all, you loved that smell of New York money, didn't you?"

"I married you because I loved you, Nick."

"You know, I'd at least respect you if you were honest with yourself."

She picked up her handbag and held it in front of her chest as if it would protect her. "Do you want honesty?" she demanded. "Then be honest about why *you* married me. You wanted a doormat. You married me because you wanted—no, you needed—someone who was so blindly in love with you, so grateful for whatever attention you could spare, that she'd lie down and let you walk all over her. And I did. Anything you wanted, I was only too happy to give you."

"You're wrong, Jane. You never had the foggiest idea of what I really wanted."

There was silence. They faced each other for what seemed endless minutes, staring into each other's eyes, waiting to see who'd break first. He wasn't going to let her off. Her eyes, huge, dark blue, surrounded by the thickened lashes, looked like eyes in a bad painting. Cheap waif eyes. He stared into them. Jane broke first. He knew she would; she had no real class, no courage. She turned her back to him, took a string of pearls from her jewelry box, stuffed it into her handbag, and rushed out of the bedroom.

Nicholas followed her into the hallway. Her heels clacked on the curved stairway that led to the first floor of their duplex. "My parents want to meet us tonight for drinks and dinner. Seven at my mother's." She continued to clack downstairs. "Did you hear me, goddamn it?"

She stopped on the second to the last step and looked up. "I won't be able to make it," she said.

"Listen, I don't ask very much of you any more. All you have time for is being your own person, and I say fine, go ahead, be your own person, whatever that is. But you know damn well you're not doing anything that's so important it can't wait."

"It so happens," she said, "that I'm taping *The David Susskind Show*. But please give your parents my best. Tell them I'm glad . . ." She paused. "Tell them I'm glad things worked out for them."

"It's all terribly one-sided," Pamela said. "I know so much about you. It's not that I tried. I just have a retentive memory."

"What do you know about me?" Nicholas asked.

They had been lovers for a week. It wasn't just sex, although that was a big part of it. Nicholas loved how affectionate she was. She did not just carry on a conversation. She carried on a conversation curled into a small ball in his lap, snuggling beside him or holding his hand and tracing the veins in his arm with her finger. He was sitting on her threadbare gray rug, his back against the wall, his knees bent to form a cradle for Pamela's head. She, in turn, was tracing the shape of his hand as it rested on her stomach; the span of his outstretched fingers was nearly as wide as her pelvis.

422

"I probably remember everything I've ever read about you. Isn't that awful? That you played lacrosse in college and you like symphonic music but don't like opera that much. And you hate oregano. Is that true?"

Nicholas laughed. "Yes. But I can't believe it was ever written up. Where was it?"

"Let me think." She closed her eyes and put her hands over his, pressing it harder onto her stomach.

"Does that help you think?" he asked. He was getting aroused but trying to hide it. Pamela had to be wooed out of her shyness. He couldn't just grab her; he'd tried that the first time and she'd gotten horribly upset, saying *Please, no,* shivering even in the heat of her un-air-conditioned apartment. He had to approach her gently, kissing her hair, her cheeks, cuddling her, almost like a child, until slowly she began to open up, curling herself around him, running her hands over him until they were like two wild, eager little animals racing over his body. Each time, at the start, he had to reassure her: It's all right. Easy, Pam. Shhh, don't be afraid. But when she opened up, she wanted to hear him let go. To talk dirty. Tell me, she'd insisted that first time. Tell me what it feels like. He'd felt embarrassed, barely able to say what he realized she wanted to hear; it was like scribbling dirty words on a church wall. But as he spoke she grew more abandoned, and so did he, and now he could barely contain himself until she got worked up enough for him to turn from sweet talk to smut. He loved it; each filthy sentence raised them higher.

But she was being softly girlish. "Your hand feels so nice," she said. "Oh, I know where I read about the oregano."

"Where?"

He felt something was wrong. Pamela lay absolutely still but then pushed away his hand and sat up, curving her legs to the side. "It was in some woman's magazine. An article about you and your wife." She put her head down, then lifted it to look at him. "Nicholas, I don't feel right about this."

"I told you," he said, "the marriage hasn't been good for a long time."

"But it's still a marriage. Nicholas, I'm not cut out for this. I don't want to be a one-week or a one-month stand or—"

"Pam, stop it."

"It's going to end, it's got to end, and I won't be able to stand it. Okay? I wish I could be sophisticated about this, but I can't. I'm twenty-two years old and I've spent twenty-one years of my life in New Jersey and that doesn't equip me for casual liaisons with worldly men. I'm sorry the whole thing ever got started. It was like a dream, and I guess I was the sleepwalker. But I have to wake up. It's the wrong kind of dream. I don't belong in it."

He reached out, pulled her against him, and would not let her get away. "In all the things you read about me, did anything ever imply that I was a ladies' man?" For a moment she stayed pressed against him, motionless. Then he felt her shake her head. "All right. This is not a casual liaison. Do we understand each other?"

"Yes," she said against his chest, then peered up at him. "But I don't want to be a kept woman." Her lower lip was thrust out.

"Pam, there's no reason why you have to eat tuna fish five nights a week."

"There is a reason. I have very little money. It's no shame. Someday I'll have my doctorate. I'll be working. And I won't ever eat tuna again." She paused. "That sounds like *Gone With the Wind*: 'I'll never be hungry again.'"

"Pamela, indulge me. Let me be selfish. *I* don't like floors. *I* don't like narrow, lumpy beds. *I* happen to hate tuna fish almost as much as I hate oregano. So please, let me find us a place."

"Nicholas, I'm so confused."

"There's nothing to be confused about," he said. He took her face between his hands and brought it close to his. She flushed. He couldn't wait to make love to her again and began kissing her cheeks, her forehead. "I want to be happy with you. That's all. Please let me."

27

Cobleigh Coma?
NBC Quakes
—*Variety* headline

Sexual heat takes six months to dissipate. At least that's what an article Jane read said. Lovers can endure only six months of the hell-heaven of lust, of seething with unceasing desire. A half year of obsession and swollen genitalia is all any two people are permitted. Then the ego saves itself from incineration; after those six months comes peace. The flesh cools and the lovers part. Or passion chills into mere proficient sex and the mindless pawing, screaming need for each other becomes companionship.

Jane read the article when her affair was eight months old and knew it was wrong. Her appetite for her lover was not merely insatiable; it grew after each encounter, so that there came a time when nothing in her life besides Judson Fullerton could satisfy her. Not only satisfy her but interest her.

On March 10, 1979, on her thirty-ninth birthday, she sat at her in-laws' dining room table between her daughters and tried not to hear them. She, the celebrated housewife and mother, wished her children gone. Brilliant, intense Victoria—tall, large-boned, somber—at sixteen and a half a freshman at Brown. Adoring Elizabeth—big-eyed, fluffy-haired, short, and voluptuous (an anglicized version of her grandmother Sally)—in her third year at prep school, a little more than fourteen and eager to try to enumerate the innumerable virtues of her sixteen-year-old boyfriend. The girls kept at her: Mom, did you read my Congreve paper? Mommy, were you surprised to see us? Mom, did you know Congreve had a daughter by the Duchess of Marlborough? Mommy, David's Bernese mountain dog—her name is Snickerdoodle—she's pregnant and not by a Bernese mountain dog. They think by a Labrador.

The role of mother was being thrust upon her. She did not wish to play it, it was tired and trite, but she forced herself to go through the motions. Smile, nod, speak of Congreve to Victoria, smile even more broadly and ruffle Elizabeth's hair. There had been a time when she relished reading Victoria's spelling test, when she knew the names of all Elizabeth's friends' dogs and cats.

Jane stared into the small, upright flames of the slow-burning creamy tapers in the silver candlesticks, barely even seeing Nicholas, who sat in dimness across the table. She only wanted to be alone and think of Judson.

They met two or three times a week. On Wednesday nights in his Manhattan studio and early evenings in his office in Connecticut. She commuted when Judson did, regardless of where Nicholas was. I'll be in New York today, she'd lie. I have research to do for the Op-Ed piece for the *Times*. I guess I'll sleep in the apartment. Nicholas was either in Manhattan or out on the eastern end of Long Island, working on the film he'd be shooting that summer, and was so embroiled he barely listened to her lies. Several Wednesday nights he'd left messages saying he was staying out on the Island overnight, so she'd spent the night at Judson's, the two of them on that narrow sofa-bed, getting up sore the next morning from too little room and too much sex. We're too old for this, she'd said, but they couldn't seem to get enough. She'd been with Judson the previous evening in Connecticut.

"Mom, have you ever seen a production of *The Way of the World?*"

Jane started. "What? Oh. No, Vicky. Just *Love for Love.*"

The night before, Judson had set her, naked, on the cold glass top of his office desk and he'd lain on the floor beneath, directing her into different postures. Flat on your stomach. Come on. Now sit up with your legs over the edge. Every time she became self-conscious and tried to cover some part of herself from view, Judson would knock on the glass and say, Stop that.

"Nicholas," James said. "A toast to Jane."

She recalled how her face had flushed. She'd sat on the desk with her legs as far apart as she could get them. Jane closed her eyes. She wanted to remember exactly how Judson had gazed up, studying her, how he'd traced her labia on his side of the glass.

Nicholas's chair shuffled against the rug. She opened her eyes and saw him rising. "To Jane," Nicholas began. He paused for a moment, trying to think of something to say.

Later, she'd lain back flat on the glass. So cold on her back. Hard on her head. Judson had stood by the desk, wrapped her legs high around his waist, and entered her slowly.

"This isn't the big one yet," Nicholas said, "but thirty-nine does deserve attention." It was his Academy Awards voice, strong and falsely pleased to be present on such a grand occasion.

Judson was so big, and he penetrated deep into her. She'd had nothing to grab on to. She'd clawed at the glass.

"From all of us, Jane—" Past the bright light of the candles, she saw Nicholas's shirtfront. He was holding his wineglass directly in front of him. "All the best."

Judson had stayed inside her for nearly a half hour, moving in and out. She'd watched the red root of his penis slide into her over and over.

There was silence at the table. Nicholas had finished and was sitting down.

She lifted her glass and tilted it slightly toward Nicholas. "Thank you," she said. "All of you." But Nicholas was no longer looking at her. He'd begun talking again with his sister Abby, the only Cobleigh offspring who had done what James had expected from his four sons: become a lawyer. Abby's boyfriend, another lawyer, sat on the other side of Nicholas; he was so unnerved by Nicholas's presence, the apartment, the maids, or perhaps by everything that three times his food had fallen from his fork to the rug on the way to his mouth. That had happened once to her in the beginning, but Jane didn't care about him or his discomfort. She wished he, all of them, would just go away. She looked back into the candle flame, skimming through the previous night, trying to find her place.

Judson. During intercourse he'd rubbed her clitoris with his finger, so she had orgasm after orgasm, each set of contractions drawing him farther into her.

Kiss me goodbye, Judson, she'd said. He'd given her a perfunctory kiss, the sort a man gives to his wife as he leaves for the office. See you Wednesday at five thirty, he'd said.

He'd been rushed. They'd stayed even longer than usual. His wife had invited her parents for dinner.

Judson had been married for twenty-five years. All she knew about his wife was that her name was Virginia, she was called Ginny, and she was a strong swimmer. She swam two miles every day. What does she do? Jane had asked, and he answered, She swims. He'd also answered that she was forty-seven and she'd never been able to conceive. How come you never adopted? Jane asked. He'd shrugged. That was before Jane realized Judson had given her all the information she was going to get. He talked to her about business: They want you to address the Middle Atlantic Phobia Conference. Business and sex. He'd walked her to her car and said, Next time, no intercourse. We'll just go down on each other the whole night. All right? He didn't want to talk about anything else.

"David's mother speaks Russian," Elizabeth was saying.

"Really," Jane breathed.

"Does she read it?" Victoria demanded, leaning across Jane.

"I don't know," Elizabeth said.

"Don't you *ask*?" Victoria's tone was brittle.

"I'll ask if you want me to."

"Oh, forget it, Liz. It's not for me. It's for you."

"For me?" Elizabeth asked.

"You really don't have an ounce of intellectual curiosity, do you?"

"Girls," Jane said. "Please."

427

Judson wouldn't talk about Ginny. Was he happy with her, she'd asked, and he'd said, Jane, what's the point of this? The point is, I want to know where I fit into your life. You know how much I care about you, he'd replied, giving her one of his voluptuous kisses. But neither of us is ready to make any changes yet, are we? God, you have a wonderful mouth.

But they never really talked. And they never did anything together besides have sex. Can't we go out for a drink? she'd pleaded. Jane, you're too public. People will recognize you. But they won't know we're—she'd begun. Jane, he sighed, stop that. Don't you think it's hard on me too? I should have followed my instincts, she'd told him. Gone to a Jewish psychiatrist. At least if I'd taken up with one, I'd get some conversation and a corned beef sandwich. If you feel I'm not giving you what you need, Jane . . . No, she said, I just wish we could go someplace besides your apartment and your office. He hadn't responded.

He wasn't that cautious with his wife. He would tell Jane he'd have to be home by seven, then stay with her in his office until eight thirty or nine, letting his answering machine respond to the ringing phone. She couldn't tell whether Ginny knew or not. Once Ginny had called when she and Judson were in Manhattan and he'd said, Ginny, is this an emergency? He waited, tapping his fingers on the hard surface of the table. I told you, this is my time to be alone. Please don't call me here. Does Ginny know? she'd asked him once. He told her he didn't think that sort of discussion was appropriate. This is between you and me, Jane. Let's leave her out of this. She doesn't belong.

He was willing to speak about Nicholas, although it was always in a sexual context. Did he ever do this to you? Judson would ask. Did he ever go like this? Did he ever try this? Is he as big as I am? Judson, please, she'd said. *Is* he? No. No, he isn't. What's the longest he's ever fucked you for? You *never* came with him? No. The world's great sex god never made you come? Judson . . . Did he? No, I told you. He never made me come. Only you.

Judson said little about himself. He was born in Maine, near the Quebec border, and put himself through college and medical school. His father had owned a liquor store. Was he nice? Not particularly, Judson said. Why are you so closed-mouthed about your past? That's just the way I am. Jane, maybe I'm wrong for you. Maybe you need someone who's more forthcoming. No, no. I was just wondering, that's all.

"James." Winifred beamed at her husband across the table. "Isn't Jane's new bracelet dazzling?"

"Very nice," James said.

Winifred turned to Jane. "Did Nicholas surprise you with it today?"

"Yes." She smiled. Two days before, Nicholas had told her to go to Cartier and pick out something for her birthday. She hadn't even been hurt. She'd selected a thin gold bangle thick with diamonds and sapphires, something he'd dismiss as too garish. "Doesn't Nick have wonderful taste?" Jane asked, holding up her wrist. For a moment, Nicholas stopped talking to his sister and stared across the table at her. She picked up her wine and drank deeply, concentrating on the convoluted crystal stem of the goblet.

Judson. After the first night, they'd never even had a glass of wine together. Once she'd brought a bottle to his studio. He'd put it on ice, and then they'd forgotten it.

If you don't want to talk about your father, she'd asked, can we talk about my father? She'd been thinking of Richard a great deal lately. Could a man sire a child, watch her grow up in his house, and not care about her? Not care a thing? Have a child and not call her or write to her in over seventeen years? Was it because of what she'd let him do to her?

The psychiatrists were wrong; some things should not be thought of. Maybe her father had loved her. Maybe he had loved her too much.

Then how could he have let Dorothy hammer her into the ground? Every sour thought prefaced with an endearment: Jane, dear . . . Her father must have known. He must have felt the hate. Of course he had. He and Dorothy were collaborators. Richard, this girl has been so bad. You must do something. Upstairs.

Judson, please listen. My father. He did all kinds of things. When I was in high school he used to get into my bed—

Jane—

Please. And before that, when I was younger, he'd take me up to his room and pull down my pants—

Jane, stop it. I'm not your psychiatrist any more.

Judson, I *know*, but I want to tell you—

I gave you the names of some good men who—

Judson, please, *please*. I have no one to talk to, to tell this to. I've never told anyone and I keep thinking about it and wondering—

Jane, you're making it very difficult for me.

I just want to talk to you. Person to person. Not patient to psychiatrist. Don't you understand? Who else can I talk to?

You know who you can talk to. Jane, stop it. You're being highly manipulative. You know that. I'm the last person you should be talking to—

Judson!

—unless this is an attempt to drag your father into bed with us.

No! I swear it!

Okay, then let's drop it. Come here. Let me hold you. Easy.

Don't you care about me?

Of course I care. Slow breaths now. Not too deep. That's right. Are you feeling better?

I'm sorry.

That's all right. Come on now, calm down. Calm down. Go get a tissue. Did he force you to have intercourse with him?

No.

Did he make you perform fellatio?

No. Nothing like that. But he—

These things happen more frequently than you would imagine. Are you calmer now? Then let's put the matter aside.

"Mommy?"

"What, Liz?"

"Are you having a mid-life crisis?"

"Elizabeth!" Winifred said. "Where did you hear such nonsense?"

"Mommy's so quiet," Elizabeth said. "Quiet and flaky. And it's her birthday. It happens all the time. Thirty-five to forty. Ask any psychiatrist. David's mother had one. She took too many diet pills and had to go to the hospital to get off them. Then she got better and had a face lift, but you can't tell anyone about it."

Jane looked down the table to her mother-in-law and smiled. "Who knows? Maybe I am having a small crisis," she said. "I can probably get by with a nose job and mild catatonia."

"Not you, Jane," Winifred said, beaming back. "Your bad times are behind you. Aren't they, Nicholas?"

Barbara Hayes, the producer of *Talk*, looked intimidating. She was nearly as tall as Jane but much larger-boned, although she had absolutely no fat. Her body and face were entirely angular, as if she'd been assembled from an assortment of geometric pieces; her cheekbones were so high and pronounced they could be columnar implants of silicone, her nose an acute triangle. She was black, and her dark skin had a red underglow. The four times Jane had seen her she'd worn man-tailored shirts with black ribbon ties, pin-striped suits, and a large, expensive man's gold watch. Her hair was cropped close to her head. Her only feminine attributes were high-heeled shoes and a slit in her straight skirt, halfway up her thigh, although the bulging, spherical muscle of her calf diminished the slit's effect; even Nicholas didn't have a muscle like that.

But even though intimidating, she was engaging, Jane thought, one of those behind-the-scenes people in television and films so incorrigibly charming and well-bred she made everyone believe the talk of the entertainment industry's being crass was just vicious gossip. "Look at them look at us," she said to Jane as they entered the restaurant. The businessmen were looking at them. "We *are* tall, but they're staring as if we're the first wave of the Invasion of the Amazons." She'd smiled. She seemed to use her smile as she did her charm: when it was necessary. Jane felt relieved that Barbara thought it necessary to charm her.

Barbara was obviously well known in the midtown restaurant where they were having lunch. Finger signals brought waiters in tight bolero jackets scurrying to provide a second round of drinks, the menus. She smiled again at Jane. "I suppose you're wondering why I asked you to lunch."

Jane tried to think of a quick comeback. She couldn't. "Yes," she said.

"Every time you've been on the show you've been a hit. You're a natural. You were born to be on television."

"I always wondered why I was born."

"Now you know. Is your fish all right? Good. Let me get to the point. Gary Clifford is going on vacation for two weeks. We'd like you to guest-host the show for one week."

Jane stared at her. Barbara Hayes was making small sandwiches of smoked Scottish salmon, sprinkling onions and capers over the top, behaving as if they were having a perfectly normal conversation.

"Me for a week?" It was the only thing Jane could think to say.

"Yes. We're having Jerry Gallagher from the *Today* show for the other week. You must have seen him. The one with the freckles." Jane recalled the man. He looked like a ventriloquist's dummy. "Very truthfully," Barbara Hayes went on, "we're testing the waters." Jane nodded. "We don't know if a woman would go in that time slot." Jane couldn't think of any adult-sounding questions to ask. But Barbara continued as if she was talking to a mature woman instead of a housewife with too much jewelry who could only think of escaping the conversation and going to the bathroom. Jane had rushed out of the apartment; she wished she'd made time to go. She shifted in her seat. Her bladder was so distended it rubbed against the top of her legs. "Four to six is an iffy time slot. We have housewives, working women just coming home, and men, although they're only twenty-two percent. The thinking on the host has always been: male, friendly, slightly sexy, but an authority figure."

"And Gary Clifford's . . ."

Fortunately, she did not have to finish her sentence. Barbara pointed a finger at her and said, "Exactly."

"I see," Jane murmured. She did not.

"Too sexy, not authoritative enough. And not smart. You see, it's all changing. Audiences are getting bored with the same old format: another cookbook author dragging in her pots and making linguine with clam sauce; another novelist who wrote a bestseller while she was nursing triplets. *Talk*— the show—needs good talk."

"So Gary's two-week vacation—"

"You've got it." Jane wondered what it was she had gotten. "It may be

431

two weeks, it may be forever. He has five more months on his contract, so we can easily buy him out."

She understood. She thought about Gary Clifford. Barbara was right. He wasn't smart. But he was nice. Jane felt sorry for him. She wondered if he knew NBC was planning his execution. "Are you using me as a female acid test or—"

"Jane, you're tough. You're pinning me to the wall." Barbara smiled. Jane smiled back. She still wasn't sure what Barbara was talking about, and whether she was being condescending or admiring: one savvy lady to another. "We're using you, yes. But first we're testing you for *you*. Obviously we're impressed. Every time you're on—well, you know. You're warm, you're sincere, you're vulnerable. And bright. Educated. Articulate."

"Thank you." She hoped she could remember all the adjectives so she could repeat them to Cecily. Vulnerable. Educated.

"You're welcome."

Bright. She had to sound bright. Incisive. "How much does this offer have to do with my husband?" Jane took another piece of fish and for the first time actually tasted it. It was underdone in the trendy, nouvelle cuisine manner; she didn't like it. It felt slimy in her mouth, as if it weren't completely dead. She swallowed it whole and anticipated Barbara's answer: Your husband? He has nothing at all to do with it.

"It has a lot to do with your husband," Barbara said. "There's a certain glamour, class, what-have-you, attached to the name Cobleigh. There's the built-in recognition factor. The automatic curiosity about what you're like, or, more precisely, about what sort of a woman Nicholas Cobleigh likes."

"I see."

"But surely, Jane, you also know there are hundreds of wives of famous men running around town. Do you see them on *Talk?* Of course not. Your husband may be the springboard, but you're the one who's going to be doing the dive."

"Or taking the dive."

"If we thought that would happen, I wouldn't have asked you. But from our point of view, even if it doesn't work out . . ." Barbara let her voice get lost in another bite of toast and salmon.

"You can still get some idea if audiences will accept a woman as host."

"Exactly."

"Do you want more about my agoraphobia?"

"Oh, no. Phobias are finished, overdone." Jane watched Barbara's face. She didn't show any sign she was discussing anything but a question of programming. "We want you because you can talk about a broad range of subjects. And because you ask the questions that every woman sitting home wants to ask. You're not afraid of putting yourself on the line, of looking foolish in front of the experts. We saw that when you were on with that professor of women's studies. You plunged right in and got the answers and showed her for what she was."

"A pretentious pain in the neck who looked down on housewives."

"That's right," Barbara said. "Well, what's your reaction? Are you interested?"

"I'm flattered. And of course I'm interested, but . . ." She couldn't think of how to say she really wasn't up to the job. It was a fluke. She'd been a guest. Not host of a network talk show. Look at her now, at a complete loss for words.

Barbara Hayes leaned forward. For a flickering instant, she looked unsure of herself. "But what?" she inquired. She set her fork in the middle of her plate. She was actually concerned. "Please, if you have any questions at all, ask them."

Jane rested her elbow on the arm of her chair. They liked her. Barbara Hayes and NBC thought she was warm and sincere. Articulate. Her entire body relaxed so quickly her elbow nearly slipped off the chair. She sat straight and smiled at Barbara. "No. No questions at all. The only 'but' is you'll have to talk with Murray King about the details. He's my agent."

Barbara gave Jane an even wider smile, bright with pleasure and relief. "Jane, of *course*," she said. "That goes without saying."

NBC gave Jane a five-year contract, cancellable after each thirteen-week segment. She was to be paid $2,500 a week. At the end of four weeks, Murray King called Barbara Hayes, and two days later NBC agreed to pay Jane $3,000 a week for the second thirteen-week segment.

"Hi." She spoke to Camera One. "This is Jane Cobleigh on *Talk*. Let me ask you a question. Have you gone out recently and spent eleven or twelve dollars on a hardcover book, or two ninety-five for a paperback, something that looked like it was going to be terrific? You know, with all these wonderful quotes on the back: 'Wise and witty, warm and wonderful.' 'A breath-taking, gut-grabbing, page-turner of a thriller.' 'An exquisite evocation of time past, rich and resonant.' And then you started reading this rich and resonant book and it was"—she placed her hand on a foot-high stack of books on the table before her—"*boring*. This brilliant, highly acclaimed, widely touted book was badly written, shoddily edited, and the binding came apart so pages 247 to 318 fell out. Today on *Talk* we're going to try to find out what's happened to publishing, and why so many good books"—she shrugged and gave a small, sad smile—"are so bad. We'll be back after three scintillating commercials."

Sometime after his third film, Nicholas had told her, "When you become famous, when you're a highly marketable commodity, people expect you to behave so outrageously that if you're just ordinarily decent they're stunned.

They're so stunned that you end up getting as much as if you made all sorts of outrageous demands, just so long as you're low-key and polite and ask how their children are."

After five weeks, NBC told Jane they wanted to redecorate her office. How would she like it? She had gray and peach in mind, and Deco furniture, but she stayed low-key. Something nice and feminine, she'd said. Easy on the eye.

Instead of Deco, she got Louis XVI, with pale pink walls, chairs covered in rose silk, and soft green silk drapes tied back with huge silk bows. It even had a chaise. With all its ormolu, the office looked like the sitting room of the king's new favorite at Versailles.

"Wonderful show," Barbara Hayes said. "And you saw the latest ratings?" Jane nodded. "Now they think I'm a genius because I suggested you. They're giving *me* a new office."

"Didn't you just get a new one around the time I came on as a guest?" Jane asked.

"Yes, but that had windows only on one wall."

"And this? Two?"

"Windows on two walls and five flights higher. It's like being assumed bodily into heaven. *And* they asked how I felt about sea green."

"I hope you laughed at them, Barbara."

"No. I'd never make a joke about something as serious as this. Decoration is an expression of power. I told them I'd like something spare and off-white. Isn't that a good word? Spare. A very cool, ascetic, chief-executive-officer word."

"You may wind up with a rug, a telephone, and no desk."

"Probably. And I can't wait to see how they interpret off-white for me." Barbara took a marking pen from the inside breast pocket of her jacket and lifted the clipboard. "All right. Tomorrow and Friday we're doing the prejudices and antagonisms of housewives and career women toward each other. I hope it's good, because it cost us a fortune to airlift and put up four members of your Woodward High School Class of '57 in New York."

"It will be good."

"We could have done Abraham Lincoln High School in Brooklyn for cab fare and lunch."

"But to anyone out of town, they're still New Yorkers. These women are going to be a hundred times more effective because they're *not* fast-talking and funny. For these kinds of things, I want to stay away from New Yorkers. And Californians. I don't want anyone saying, 'Jane, I have something I want to share with you.' Okay?"

"It's your show."

"It's your show."

434

"It's both our shows, and we can airlift Ohio if the ratings stay at this level." Barbara lifted some papers from her clipboard. "Here are summaries of the interviews with these four. And here's next week's schedule. We switched weight obsession with why only three hundred people in the country really care about foreign policy because we wanted that stiff from the State Department and he could only make it Tuesday." Barbara put the papers on Jane's desk. "Anything else?" she asked.

"No. That's it."

"Going back to Connecticut tonight?"

"No. I'm really tired. I'll stay in the city."

"See you tomorrow," Barbara said. "Get a good night's rest."

Jane put her elbows on her desk and buried her face in her upturned palms. She wasn't going to get a good rest. It was Wednesday, her night to be at Judson's apartment.

Five shows a week. Lunches, dinners, dictating memos, having meetings, giving interviews. A photographer sent by *TV Guide* taking two hours of pictures in her office. She was exhausted. Her legs and arms ached and she felt she might burst into tears any minute, like an overstimulated child. For the first time, she didn't ache for Judson. It was fatigue, she thought. Total and complete fatigue. She just wanted to go back to the apartment, have a bowl of corn flakes, and go to sleep.

Her intercom buzzed. "Dr. Fullerton on the line," her secretary said. Her secretary.

"Thanks," Jane said, and lifted the phone. "Hi."

"You're late."

"I had a meeting with my producer."

"Okay. Get over here now."

"Judson—"

"Come *on,* Jane."

Nicholas looked as tired as Jane felt, so perhaps that was why, the following morning, too exhausted to preserve the territorial integrity of their own halves of the mattress, they awakened in the center of the bed in each other's arms. Her cheek lay on the warm ledge made by his shoulder and neck, and when she opened her eyes, the first thing she saw was a cross, her black hair falling across a lock of his gold.

In that moment of wakening before consciousness, Nicholas breathed deeply and pulled her closer to him and Jane eased her arm farther around him and tucked her hand under his back.

Then, like a photograph being ripped in half, they tore away from each other. Jane cleared her throat, sat up, and stretched. Nicholas put the crook of his arm over his eyes as if to shield them from the light.

Still, without even seeing his eyes, she could tell he was tired. Despite his days walking the Long Island beaches with his cinematographer, preparing for his film, which was to begin shooting in two weeks, he was uncommonly pale. Not merely his usual fair color, but white with the gray cast of extraordinary weariness. His lips were almost the color of his face.

"What time did you get in last night?" she asked. Fortunately she'd been at the apartment; it was her closest call yet. She'd left Judson's after one, too drained and too stiff to spend the night in his narrow bed, and he hadn't tried to dissuade her. She'd thought Nicholas was spending the night on Long Island; his secretary had left the message with her secretary. But sometime after she'd fallen asleep, he'd slid under the blanket, murmuring, It's me. After an hour, still drenched with the panic sweat of near-calamity, she'd put herself back to sleep with a double brandy. What if she had stayed at Judson's?

"I don't know. One or two. I was at Ken's working on the screenplay."

"I thought you were staying out on the Island."

He drew back his arm from over his eyes and put it behind his head, on the pillow. There were gray shadows under his eyes. "No. I had to get back."

"You look tired." He nodded. He was looking up at the ceiling, not at her. "Is there a problem with the screenplay?"

"The dialogue was stilted in a couple of scenes."

"Do you want me to have a look at it?"

"What?" His *what* jumped from him, too loud.

"I said, do you want me to look at the screenplay? I don't have to be in the office until ten thirty."

"That's all right."

"You worked it out last night?" He stared at her. "You and Ken. Did you fix it up last night?"

"Jane," Nicholas said. He edged up the bed and put his back against the headboard. He reached behind him, drew out the pillow, and put it over his stomach. With both arms, he held it against him like a giant hot-water bottle. "Jane," he said, "we have to stop this charade."

"What?" she asked. But her voice barely worked. He knew. Somehow he'd found out. He wasn't even angry; his words were quiet and pained and came from a distance. She might have overheard someone else's sad conversation in a corner at a cocktail party. "What charade?" Oh, God, she didn't want any part of what was coming. It was going to be so awful. She could see in him how awful it would be. He was strangling the pillow, squeezing it so tightly to his body that the entire border of the case, the part with their monogram, was crumpled in his hand.

"The charade of the marriage. Jane, I can't take it any more." She knew it was too soon to cry. Tears should be held in reserve. They flooded out

436

anyway. "Please don't cry," he pleaded. "Jane, I'm so sorry it's turned out like this."

"Nick." What was she going to say? It was just sex. Just sex. I'll give him up. A thunderclap of a sob broke from her, a shattering burst of protest: I don't know if I *can* give him up. Through her tears she saw his fright at her noise. He was pale, terribly pale.

"Please listen to me," he said. "This is the hardest thing I've ever had to say." She drew up her legs and hugged them to her, hiding her face against her knees. "Jane, you know what's been going on. You know about all the lies." Another sob, this one coming out like an inverted scream. "I'm sorry. The last thing I want to do is hurt you like this, but I can't go on living this way. Jane, it's killing me, lying and lying and lying to you."

"Lying to me," she breathed. She lifted her head. His eyes were on her, red, ready too for tears. "Oh, God, Nick."

"Jane—"

"You weren't with Ken last night."

"You *know* I wasn't. I haven't been anyplace where I said I was. You know that. Deep in your heart, you've known all along. Night after night, months and months. Jesus Christ, going through this charade. Both of us, like a couple of two-bit—"

"You have someone?"

"Jane, don't do this. You've known—"

"No!"

"We haven't slept together in a *year*, Jane. A year. I haven't been in Connecticut in months. Most of the time—"

"You were out in Montauk."

"I was in the city. We have an apartment."

"Who? What apartment?" Her eyes darted back and forth around their apartment bedroom.

"Pamela and I."

"Pamela." Her heart hurt. Her head hurt. This wasn't an attack. This was worse. This had a reason. "Who is she?"

"Someone I met last summer when I was teaching at NYU."

Jane threw aside the blanket and scrambled out of bed. She ran to her closet and tore a robe from a hook. The sleeve was inside out and she couldn't get into it. She kept punching at the fabric, trying to fit in her arm. Nicholas came and took it from her. He put it back on the hook. "Give it to me!" she shouted. "I'm going to get some coffee. I have to get to the office." He put his hands on her bare shoulders; they felt clammy and hot. "Get your hands off me!"

"Jane—" She pulled out of his grasp but could not move farther. "Jane, I still love you."

"Stop that!"

"Listen to me. But I love her too. If it had just been a fling . . . but she's brought something into my life."

"I don't want to hear this!"

"I want to be with her. I have to be. I can't spend a couple of nights with her and then have to say goodbye, so I can sneak home at three in the morning. It's not fair to her. And it's not fair to you. Jane, I have to tell you this. I'm going to move in with her."

"Oh, *no!*"

"Jane, you have the apartment. And the house. You think now it will be hard, but really, it won't be that big a difference."

She stared at him. The whites of his eyes were entirely red. "You just said you're going to live with her."

"But you and I haven't really been *living* together. And it will only be for a while."

"For a while? Two weeks? A year? Should I block it off on my calendar?"

"I need time to make sure."

"Make sure of *what?* Of whether you love her more than me? Of whether she's suitable to be the second Mrs. Nicholas Cobleigh? Or whether it's still better for your image to be half of the Golden Couple?" She turned, walked away from him, and sat on the edge of the bed. She was panting. Her mouth was dry and coated with last night's brandy. Her breath must smell foul. She tried to remember what he'd told her, but she could not. "Where did you meet her?" She began to breathe a little more slowly.

Nicholas came and sat, leaving a foot of space between them. "At NYU. Last July."

"Who is she?"

"She was in my class. She's a doctoral candidate. History of the cinema."

"The cinema." It took her a minute before she could speak again. "The cinema. Of *course*. All the better to know how exalted Nicholas Cobleigh's position will be. How perfect. Has she compared you with Eisenstein yet?" She glanced at him. His neck was starting to flush. "How old is she?"

She could hardly hear him. "Twenty-two."

"Nick!"

"She'll be twenty-three August seventh."

"I'll send her a card."

"Jane, stop it. She happens to be—"

"You're going to be thirty-nine in a few weeks—don't you dare stop me. You're going to be thirty-nine and then forty and you're like a woman, your whole life is tied up with your looks and you're so afraid of getting older you

438

take up with some young thing to hold back the tide." He put his hand over hers. "Don't touch me!"

"She's not some young thing."

"Then what is she? She's twenty-two, hovering on the brink of twenty-three. But you didn't fall in love with her just because she's young and she helps you delude yourself into thinking you're never going to be forty. *No.* She's a wonderful human being. So intelligent. You love her mind."

The flush spread to his face and ears. "She happens to be brilliant. She was *summa* at Princeton—"

"Shut up, you ass!"

"Jane, I know you're hurt, but please—"

"Please what? Please let's be civilized. Please let's sit down and discuss Pamela. Oh, good. Let's. Tell me all about her. Tell me about your little love nest." Nicholas rubbed his forehead. "Please, I want to hear about it. Does she have her diploma up on the wall? A poster of Charlie Chaplin in *Modern Times?* Do you and your twenty-two-year-old *summa* sit on the floor and smoke grass and discuss the art of the cinema?" She swallowed, a too-loud gulp. "Where is your apartment? I asked you a question." Nicholas looked straight ahead. She put her mouth to his ear. Before he could jerk away she shrieked, "Where is it?"

"Don't do that!" He massaged his ear.

"Where is it? I want to know."

"Lower Fifth."

"Nice. Nice address. How many rooms?"

"Five."

"Nice. Modest. Is little Miss Summa paying half the rent?"

"No. She comes from a poor family. She's been on full scholarship all along."

"You could at least do something different the second time around. Or is that part of the Cobleigh package deal? Instant upward mobility in return for—"

"Jane, please don't. Listen to me. We have to talk some more. I need time."

"And you're trying to buy it with a twenty-two-year-old."

"I need time with her. She's going to be my assistant when I'm shooting *Land's End.*"

"How is she going to assist you? On her back?"

"Jane, please don't!" Without realizing it, she had stopped crying. Now, just as she felt the burning dryness in her eyes, the tears began to flow again. "I'm sorry," he said. "But I want to be with her. I have to. I owe it to her. She's been so completely understanding, so patient."

"A saint. Pamela is a saint. You can't beat a twenty-two-year-old saint."

"Jane, I know how this must sound, but you'd like her if you met her."

"Like her? I'm sure I'd love her. And so will the girls. They can go out to Montauk and spend some time with you and Pamela. Just remember to put your pants back on before you open the door for them. It'll be fun. Especially for Vicky. Great fun, having a friend so near her age."

"Pamela's six years older," he said wearily. "Jane, age has nothing to do with it. It's Pamela. And it's us. The marriage has gone bad. You know it as well as I do. In all those years, until Pamela, I never . . . I'm not saying I want a divorce. I don't know what I want."

"Do you want to know what I want? I want you to drop dead."

Nicholas continued as if she hadn't spoken. "I know you're beginning a career, and I don't want to embarrass you. I'll be discreet. I promise you that. No one has to know. If you and I have to make some appearances together, we will, until this is settled. There's no reason for anything to become public, because *I* don't know what's going to happen."

"I do. You're going to spend the summer at Montauk fucking Pamela."

"Don't talk like that."

"Why not?"

"Because it isn't you."

"You have no idea what I am."

"Jane, we've been married for eighteen years. I know you better than I know anyone else in the world. And that's why it's so terrible for me."

"Poor Nicky."

"Jane, I can't throw away eighteen years. I love her. I love her very much, but you're such a part of my life I can't just say goodbye."

"You are saying it."

"No. Not yet."

She ran her cold, bare feet over the rug. "And you want me to wait until you make up your mind. How long should I wait, Nick?"

"I don't know." He began to cry. "For two weeks all I've been thinking about is you being alone all summer, knowing—"

"Knowing that you're fucking Pamela."

"Jane, I still love you."

She stood, strode halfway across the room, but then turned and came back. She stood before him. His head was lowered and she could only see his bright hair. "Nick."

"What?"

"At least this will give me more time with Judson."

"What?"

"Oh, we've done lots of other things together. Lots. Do you want me to tell you about some of them?"

"No! I don't believe you!"

440

"Since last July. The same as you and Pamela. Isn't that a lovely coincidence? Maybe we can celebrate our anniversaries together."

"Jane!"

"Maybe not. Judson and I celebrate alone. He's a wonderful celebrator, Nick. Wonderful. Wonderful in bed. You should see what we do. Things you never even thought about."

"No!"

"Oh, yes. He's so good. I come with him. Over and over. It's called multiple orgasm, Nick. It's what women are capable of if they're made love to properly. And Judson knows how to make love properly. And not so properly. When he lets loose, he's unbelievable."

"Stop!"

"He loves to eat me." Nicholas clapped his hands over his ears. Jane grabbed his wrists and dragged his hands away. "We're being honest with each other. You told me about Pamela, and now I'm telling you about Judson. She's twenty-two. He's fifty-one. She went to Princeton. He went to Bates. I don't think he was *summa*, but—"

"Don't do this."

"There's one thing about him that's *summa*. He's so big, Nick. I don't think you've ever seen one like it. Big and thick—don't cry. I'm just trying to tell you how I've been keeping busy while you've been so busy with Pamela."

She thought she was laughing, but then she realized she was choking on her tears. Her chest heaved, expanding for the air it wasn't getting.

"Jane," she heard him say.

At last, gasping through her mouth, she caught her breath. Her throat felt swollen with the effort. "I'm fine," she whispered. "Fine." She wiped the tears from her face. "See?"

441

28

FEMALE VOICE: Hello? Hello?
ANNOUNCER: Yes. This is Reverend Joe and you're on the air.
FEMALE VOICE: Reverend Joe, I'm wondering about that Jane Cobleigh. I was reading Ephesians 5:24, where it says—
ANNOUNCER: "Therefore as the church is subject unto Christ, so let the wives be to their own husbands in every thing."
FEMALE VOICE: Yes, well now, maybe if she was a proper Christian wife 'stead of acting smart-alecky on the television, if she was standing by his side, the Lord might not have smote her down. If she was a good wife—
ANNOUNCER: "House and riches are the inheritance of fathers: and a prudent wife is from the Lord." Any of you out there can cite chapter and verse on *that* one, you call Reverend Joe at . . .
—*Calling for Christ,* KMT Radio, Arkadelphia, Arkansas

Nicholas had never been sensitive to noise. He had grown up in Manhattan, and the constant hum, clatter, and klaxon of Park Avenue traffic had simply been part of his environment, as had the din of five younger brothers and sisters. In Connecticut, the 5 A.M. blare of birds hardly ever wakened him, and when it did, the simple act of pulling the blanket over his ears was sufficient to send him back to sleep.

But in his new house in Santa Barbara, the ceaseless crash of the Pacific against the cliffs below bothered him. The roar, the wild splash of spray, was unnecessarily dramatic, the sound of inexorable doom in a low-budget film. This was the spot he and Pamela had picked, the perfect place to relax. But after a week of constant meetings in Los Angeles, he could not relax with the clamor fifty feet below. The wet surge of sound made him anxious; it was a *Watch out, something is about to happen!* noise.

One entire wall of the master bedroom was glass. When he peered straight down, he could see neither the entrance to the house nor the road, only the cliffs and the ocean with its crazed white foam belying its deceptive blue calm. Pamela could stretch out on her stomach and watch it for hours. He found himself avoiding the window. It almost made him understand what terror Jane had felt in her bad years; when he looked down, he imagined some typically eccentric California natural disaster—a rockslide, a typhoon—and the house heaving forward and crashing down onto the spiked rocks. He saw himself impaled. A horrible, helpless feeling. Thursday night, in the hotel suite in Los Angeles, he'd said to Pamela, Let's spend the weekend here.

442

Why? she'd asked. We have Santa Barbara. And you have to unwind after all those meetings.

Endless meetings about *William the Conqueror*. The bankers were even more high-strung than the studio executives, and the executives' corporate palpitations made the film's mercurial English director appear calm to the point of somnambulance. Thirty-five million dollars on the line for an epic about an eleventh-century political and military genius whom Nicholas Cobleigh and an eccentric screenwriter who shaved his head found fascinating. When the money men shook Nicholas's hand, they held it too long. They were frightened. How are things? they'd ask in high-pitched voices. Fine, he'd say, keeping his voice low. Aren't things fine, Arthur? he'd ask the director. Fine, the director squeaked. It was April 1980. Shooting was to begin in less than three months in England. It was too late to stop. Was everything fine? He didn't know.

Nicholas stood at the rear door. He preferred the back of the house. A series of landscaped terraces led to a long grassy knoll and, at the end, a bright blue swimming pool. The back too was excessively dramatic, but in a reassuring way; he'd bought the house from the owner of a newspaper whose wife was an amateur decorator. Nothing immobile escaped her designing eye; even the pool tiles had a geometric Greek pattern. Just as she was ripping out all the English ivy on her trellises on the side of the house and getting ready to replace it with Comtesse de Bouchard clematis—her husband related this at the house closing to Nicholas with tears in his eyes—she'd dropped dead of a cerebral hemorrhage.

Nicholas could not see Pamela from the house, although he could hear her rock music. From a distance, most of the music itself was lost and all he could hear was the percussion and the sound of the group's voices. The lyrics were unintelligible to him even at close range, although Pamela, with her spongelike memory, could recite every single word; from far away, half the lyrics were blown out to sea and the other half resembled the wild barking of seals on the rocks.

Pamela would swim laps in the pool, then go into the gazebo at the far end to hide from the sun. Her skin was so fair that even for her half-hour's swim she wore a T-shirt to protect her back and shoulders.

He stared at the gazebo. It looked like a doll's house made of white latticework. After the swim, Pamela would strip off her T-shirt and bikini bottom, wrap herself in a terry bath sheet to keep warm, and curl up on a wrought-iron bench and listen to the music she knew he couldn't tolerate. He wanted to go down to her but Murray was due any minute, and if he went into the gazebo he wouldn't get out so fast; he'd probably wind up trying to coax her out of her towel. He knew much of Pamela's shyness, her awe of him, after almost two years, had to be a game, but it was a game he did not want to stop playing.

Her rubber thongs were two dots of yellow before the entrance to the gazebo. It was a warm day. Maybe she had taken off the towel. It was too bad she couldn't sunbathe nude in one of the big chaises by the pool so he could watch her. When her clothes finally came off, she was wonderfully unself-conscious. For her twenty-fourth birthday, he'd given her a five-carat emerald ring. He'd slipped it on her finger one day when she was in the bathroom naked, her foot raised up on the rim of the tub. She'd been rubbing some sort of lotion onto her heels and soles. Here, he'd told her. You shouldn't go around without anything on. You could catch cold. Her skin was milk white.

Nicholas turned his glance from the gazebo and looked at the sky. It was royal blue, with no clouds. For some reason, he thought about Jane. Their first summer in Connecticut, she'd spend entire days in the sun. Now and then she'd grab for the bottle of suntan lotion, but only to rub another coating onto the girls' fairer skin. By the end of the summer, he'd become pale gold; Jane's skin was rich and dark, as if she'd been cast in bronze. One morning he'd placed his forearm against hers; the contrast was striking. Do you think I'm terribly exotic? she'd demanded. Or just dark? Terribly exotic, he'd told her. And beautiful.

On March 10, her fortieth birthday, he'd left the meeting he was in, went into somebody's office, and turned on *Talk*. There she was with a Broadway chorus dancer who had just turned thirty, a fifty-year-old housewife whose husband had just left her, and an eighty-year-old poet, talking about getting old. She'd been wearing a white blouse with puffy sleeves, and its scooped-out neckline showed off her dark neck and shoulders. She had looked exotic. Her hair was pulled back to one side and she wore giant hoop earrings. The poet had asked her what sounded like a put-up question: How does your husband feel about your turning forty? He'd gotten angry, because while they'd agreed not to make their separation public for the time being, they would not do anything to play upon the old Golden Couple image. But Jane hadn't done that. She'd just shrugged and said, It doesn't seem to bother him at all. Very smooth, with a nice smile. He'd turned off the TV and gone back to the meeting.

The week before that, he'd spent hours wondering if he should send her a gift. Something simple, like a book. A grand impersonal gesture, like an Italian sports car. Finally he'd just called her and said Happy birthday. He'd half expected her to break down and cry. When she didn't, he asked, Is there anything you'd like for your birthday? No. No, thanks, Nick. But I appreciate your calling.

For the time being they were husband and wife, although months passed without his seeing her. Often he turned on her show thinking she'd look

444

different; have a gray streak in her hair or be grotesquely fat. But there she was: Jane.

They hadn't even gone to lawyers, although he knew that was coming. Just around Jane's birthday, Pamela had said, You know, I'm going to be twenty-five next August. She'd been leaning back in a chair, and her hands rested on her stomach. He'd realized she was thinking about having a baby.

Pamela had been so understanding. You're a good, faithful, honorable man, Nicholas, she'd told him. You can't toss aside—what is it?—nineteen years of marriage. And even though it doesn't create an ideal universe for me, it's the thing I admire most about you. Your essential goodness.

He'd finally said, Let me finish *William* and we'll go back to New York and I'll set my house in order. Do you understand, Pamela? She'd nodded, so sweet, small, quiet, not demanding any more assurance than that, and he'd added, We'll make the separation public, and then the minute the divorce becomes final, we'll get married. She'd thrown her arms around him and cried. I don't want to pressure you, Nicholas. You know that. But I want to have your children, and—her voice broke. He said, I know. I know.

The doorbell chimed, and by the time he got to the front of the house the maid had let Murray in. Murray's only concession to California was a Panama hat with a plaid band. When he'd first bought it, on a trip several years earlier, he'd asked, Hey, Nicky, doesn't it make me look like a real sport? Nicholas looked at him: a sport in a dark blue suit and a maroon tie.

"Hey, Nicky," Murray said, "it's done. They're renting you some house on a hoo-ha square in London. Two servants plus driver, plus bodyguard, plus gymnastics trainer, and they'll set up a whole gym for you."

"A secretary?" Nicholas asked.

Murray twirled the hat by the brim. "You've got it. You want to take Florrie, or should she stay in New York and they get you someone in London?"

"Let Florrie stay in New York. I need her there." The maid managed to pry Murray's Panama from his grip. She left the front hall with it. "Do you want a drink?" Nicholas asked. Murray seemed content to carry on their conversation in the hall.

"Club soda."

Nicholas led him over rugs, tiled floors, planked floors, and marble floors, through the house into a small barroom that overlooked the back. The bar was an elaborate system of mirrored shelves set on mirrored walls, so the pouring of a single drink had enormous reverberations. "Lime?"

"No, thanks. This is fine. Hey, Nicky, this house is really something."

Nicholas, pouring himself a glass of wine, caught Murray's eye in the mirror. Murray looked down and made himself busy, rotating his glass to reduce the carbonation. Since he'd flown in the week before, Murray had been a mass of nervous mannerisms. They could barely spend time together without Murray shredding a napkin or mutilating a paper clip.

"You don't like the house, do you, Murray?"

"Nicky, what kind of a question is that?" They talked to each other in the mirror.

"It's a straightforward question."

Murray drained his glass. Then he tapped Nicholas on the shoulder. "Can you turn around, so I can figure out which is your right and which is your left? It's not normal to talk to mirrors." Nicholas faced him. "Now you're not reversed. Good." Murray paused. "Do I like this house? Why not? It's a gorgeous house. Ninety-nine point nine percent of the human race would clutch their chest and fall on the floor with a major coronary if someone offered them this house." Murray smiled. Nicholas watched him. "Nicky, why are we going through this?"

"I just asked you a question. You're avoiding answering it."

"You're in a mood again."

"I'm not in a mood." Nicholas put his glass of wine on the lowest shelf, threw some cracked ice into a large glass, and poured vodka over it. "You're the one who's been having moods lately. Ever since you got here."

"So if I'm in a mood, why are you drinking vodka?"

"Because I feel like drinking vodka."

This was happening more and more. He and Murray were becoming like an old married couple, bickering over nothing. He wasn't sure why. Tension over a thirty-five-million-dollar movie. Maybe just to distract them from a harsher battle. They bickered on and on. I want the right of first negotiation and last refusal on any sequel. Nicky, it's a trivial point. What kind of sequel would there be on this: William the Conqueror Goes Hawaiian? I want it. You win on a dumb point like this, you lose on a biggie. Murray, I told you . . . Nicky, you're losing the forest in the trees if you . . .

"So go ahead. Drink vodka."

Nicholas took a long drink. The bottle had been in the freezer, and the vodka was syrupy and smooth. "I asked you a question. Do you like this house?"

"For me, yes. I'd live in this house if I was the kind of person who would live in California. The neighborhood I'm not so sure about. I mean, they wouldn't burn a cross on my lawn, but they wouldn't throw a Hello Murray party either. But for someone else, it's beautiful."

"For me?"

"For you, it's obviously fine."

Nicholas banged his glass onto a shelf. Drops of vodka flew up and landed in clear beads, reflecting themselves in the mirror. "Let's have it out, Murray."

446

"Have what out?"

"Whatever's been bothering you the last six months."

"Nothing's been bothering me for the last six months."

"Bullshit."

"Don't tell me bullshit, Nicky. I don't speak to you like that." Nicholas looked across the room, out the glass doors. The trees and flowers on the terraces blocked his view of the pool. Only a white line, the top of the gazebo's roof, was visible.

"For Christ's sake, Murray—"

"You want to talk to someone like that, you get another agent. I mean it, Nicky. You say bullshit, I say shit. I've taken a lot of shit from you, and not just the past six months. FYI, it's been the last couple of years."

"Murray—"

Murray's suit and tie were so dark. He was dressed more for a New York funeral than for a California cocktail hour. His expression was somber, the ends of his mouth drawn down. "Nicky, I love you like a son. You know that. But enough is enough. I'm too old for this. All my life I've worked with actors. All my life I've seen them screwing up their lives. Okay, fine, it's a sad thing to watch, but it goes with the territory. They're artistic, emotional. People kiss their ass and say 'Go ahead, do whatever you want to do,' so they do . . . it happens. And it happens that sometimes I have to take a certain amount of crap. People under tension behave—I don't know—pretty crappily. But you were always different, Nicky."

"Murray, this isn't necessary."

"Then I'll take my hat, please."

Murray's New York voice suddenly went cold. It hit Nicholas hard and fast, knocking his breath out of him, as if he were a kid tackled by someone twice his size. "Murray," he said at last, "all right. I apologize. I'm sorry. I didn't mean to cut you off."

"All I want to do is have my say, Nicky. Let me tell you something about you. You were always a man before you were an actor. A real man. With a wife and—let me finish—kids and a house in the country. A good person. Even coming from where you came from, you were for real. Not a snob. Not a the-whole-world-owes-me type. And you weren't some little two-bit *plosher* hanging around waiting to be famous so you could treat people like dreck. You were a good man."

"What am I now?"

"A good man still. But an unhappy man."

"Murray, I knew that's what you were getting to. But it's not true."

"You're happy?"

"Yes. I know it doesn't suit your hopes for me, but I'm very happy."

"This is happiness, living in some too-fancy *House Beautiful* house with a girl almost young enough to be your daughter? Ha-ha. Go ahead and say, '*Sure,* why shouldn't it be happiness, a house with bathrooms the size of Yankee Stadium and a little sweetie with long red hair who could fit on the top of a wedding cake?' But you're not happy. I know you're not."

"If I'm not happy, it's because I'm sad about what happened with the marriage. I'm sad it went bad."

"It didn't go bad. You hit a rocky stretch—"

"Murray, it went bad. We married too young, for the wrong reasons. The flaws were built into the marriage. She needed someone strong, and I needed someone who could light a fire under me, get me off the path my family had laid out. At twenty, twenty-one we suited each other's needs. At forty—"

"Nicky, *that's* bullshit. You loved each other."

"I'm not saying we didn't. But the problems were always there. She grew up and didn't need anyone strong any more. I need peace now. I don't want any more fires lit under me."

"So? What marriage doesn't have problems?"

"Murray, it just didn't work out. And I am sad about it. I'm sad about Jane and sad that the girls feel so strongly about Pamela that they won't— Forget it. They'll come around in time."

"Maybe." Murray walked away from him, toward a modular couch shaped like a fat U. He sat in the middle, at the bottom of the U, sinking low and deep. Nicholas came over and sat at an end. "And maybe they won't come around. Did you ever think that, Nicky? Did you ever think this little sweetie—"

"Don't call her a sweetie. She's a kind, sensitive human being."

"Pardon me. Did you ever think that this kind, sensitive human being may poison your relationship with your daughters for good?"

"I think they'll come around."

"And if they don't? What'll you do? Write them off and have a couple more kids with little Pammy?"

"Murray, I won't have this!"

"This little brilliant sweetie who wants to talk all the time about dead French directors and lap dissolves is worth throwing away a beautiful wife and two fine daughters for? Is she? This sensitive little scholar who only wants to get her Ph.D. is schlepping around the world with you wearing emeralds and teeny-weeny custom-made sable coats and she hasn't seen the inside of a college since— Nicky! I'm not going to stop. You want to know something? When I got out of that car here today, I got out thinking there's a good shot that when I get back in, I'll have lost my best client and my dearest friend. You want to know something else? Knowing that isn't going to stop me."

"Murray, it wasn't only me. You know damn well Jane was having herself a high old time."

"What? With that *oysvorf* psychiatrist? So what?"

"So what? I wouldn't cast her as the wronged wife."

Murray struggled to sit straight. "Nicky, she was wrong. She was stupid. She was all sorts of things. But what did it mean? She'd been so unhappy all those years and then this guy comes along like Prince Charming and abra-cadabra! The spell is broken and she's grateful and so on and so forth. It wasn't right. I'm on your side. It was sneaky and dumb. But she's not Adolf Hitler, Nicky."

"I know she isn't. But it wasn't a flash in the pan either. I'll bet she's still seeing him."

"Because you're not there. Because she's in limbo."

"Murray, it's gone too far. There's nothing left to save."

"Nicky, the two of you together. Visiting you at that house was like getting an invitation to the Garden of Eden. When she used to—"

Both men jumped. Pamela stood outside the sliding glass doors, knock-ing. Nicholas rushed across the room and let her in. She stood on tiptoes to kiss him. "Hi, Murray," she said.

"Hi," Murray said from the couch.

"How do you like the house?"

"It's really something."

Nicholas looked away from him and down at Pamela. She had wrapped the blue and green striped towel around her. It was so long it hung to the floor, and she looked like a child dressed in her mother's strapless evening gown. Her collarbones seemed incredibly fragile, like parts from the frailest sparrow. Nicholas put his arm around her shoulder. Her hair was still damp and looked deep orange-red in the dim light. He could smell the flowery fragrance of her shampoo. Everything about Pamela was feminine and deli-cate. Unlike Jane, Pamela never smelled of mere soap or perfume or sweat. The light scent she wore became part of her essence. When he held her, he was holding an armful of flowers.

Pamela nestled against him. She'd once told him she did not feel com-plete unless she was being held by him. I don't mean that in an antifeminist sense, she'd said. I know, he'd answered, holding her tight. His body could feel her words true: she was always that way with him. Never clingy, always a natural adjunct. After a party, she would cuddle against him in the car and emit a sigh of genuine pleasure and relief: finally, she was a part of him, at peace.

"Did you see the composite print of *Land's End* yet, Murray?" Pamela asked. Murray just shook his head. Nicholas let out a muted sigh. She tried so hard with Murray even though she knew how close he was to Jane, both as agent and as friend. "It's his greatest work as a director. I envy you the experience. It has all the warmth you associate with Wyler, but with Nich-

449

olas's special directorial stamp: very American, very human, but with an overriding urbanity."

"That'll be nice," Murray said.

"And his acting is superb."

"Who does it remind you of?"

Nicholas stiffened. Murray was baiting Pamela.

"It doesn't remind me of anyone. Nicholas is *sui generis*. One of a kind."

"I know what *sui generis* means, Pamela."

Nicholas closed his eyes. All he wanted to do was get out of the house, get moving. Run for miles.

"Oh, Murray. I hope you didn't think I was being condescending. Honestly, I have this obnoxious tendency to behave as if I'm teaching a freshman—"

"That's okay, Pamela. Nicky, I'll be in LA till Monday. If you decide you want me, you know where to find me. Pamela . . ." He paused.

"Yes, Murray?"

"Take care."

"I will, Murray. Thanks for dropping by. Oh, would you like to stay for dinner? It's no problem. The maid can just throw on another salmon steak."

Murray stared at her. "No, thank you. I don't want to put your maid to any trouble." Then he turned to Nicholas. He looked old and, suddenly, so listless he seemed almost feeble. He could not get up from the couch. Nicholas went to him and helped him up. The moment he was standing, Murray dropped Nicholas's hand. "I have a lot of paperwork back at the hotel," Murray said. "Besides, I'm sure the two of you want some time alone."

"Murray," Nicholas said, "please stay."

"I can't, Nicky. I'm tired."

On July 2, the night of his fortieth birthday, Nicholas came home from the suburban London studio where he had been toasted with champagne, drank half a bottle of vodka and about as much wine, and found himself about to pass out at the dining room table. He was unable to keep his head from rolling to the side and was vaguely thankful when it came to rest on his shoulder. His arms drooped over the sides of the chair. Just before his eyes closed, he looked down and saw his fingers curled up, apelike. He knew he was drunk. It didn't bother him. That was good. He was very tired. He only hoped his face hadn't gone slack and stupid, the way his father's had when he was really in the bag. He tried lifting his lower lip to close his mouth, but it wasn't worth the effort.

He heard the butler—who had just brought in whatever was to come after the awful pink chilled soup Pamela had ordered—suggest to her that he might help Mr. Cobleigh upstairs. Pamela, obviously not relishing a candlelit dinner for one, agreed. "He's been working so hard," he heard her explain.

Nicholas knew he was about to be taken up to bed, but was still startled when the butler bent over him, wiggled his head under Nicholas's arm, grabbed onto his wrist, and hoisted him out of the chair. Nicholas didn't want to be manhandled. He fought for his wrist and tried to swing around his other arm so he could punch the butler in the gut. But the butler made a soothing English humming sound—not so different from a nanny's—and Nicholas allowed himself to be walked and dragged from the dining room, hauled up the stairs of the London townhouse, and put in a narrow tester bed in a small back bedroom that smelled of camphor.

He liked the butler. The man took off not only his shoes but his socks and covered him with a light quilt. Nicholas fell right into a deep sleep. He needed it. It had been a rough day.

It had been a rough month. At the last moment, the studio fired his relatively unknown co-star and hired another actress to play William the Conqueror's wife, Matilda. The actress they hired was Laurel Blake. His lawyers agreed Nicholas's contract allowed him to approve his co-star and he could challenge the casting of Laurel Blake, but they suggested the litigation would take longer than the filming and, while not quite so costly, it would be, as they put it, "complex."

Pamela came to the studio every day, and Laurel had her lover—whom she called her manager—with her, a man in his mid-twenties who had appeared in several pornographic films; still, their presence only mildly discouraged Laurel. She sent Nicholas unsealed notes, using the script girl as a messenger. They began with a relatively innocuous *Remember Yugoslavia?* *Remember Paris?* but when he did not respond she wrote, *Remember the good times? Want some more?* and finally, *Remember how you loved my finger up your ass?*

He took her aside after a script conference. "I want those notes to stop," he said.

Laurel smiled. "You know how to stop them."

Late one afternoon, when they were resting a few minutes after nearly twenty takes on a scene between them, Pamela came over to him and put a cool, wet cloth on the back of his neck. Laurel had stared, taking in Pamela's diminutiveness, her jeans, sneakered feet, and T-shirt. Then, in a voice so loud the entire crew heard, Laurel said, "I see you have what you've always wanted, Nick. A boy."

Everyone had felt sorry for Pamela that day and went out of their way to be kind, but most of the time they avoided her. Nicholas realized she did not fit in. As much as she knew about film, she knew nothing about film people.

451

She was shy, and when she finally found the courage to speak, she'd try to discuss craft. "Are you familiar with Gianni Di Venanzo's work?" she'd ask the cinematographer. She'd meant it as a social gambit; he'd taken it as a criticism of his technique. "Who do you consider your major influences?" she'd asked the director. "My mum and my dad," he answered. "No, really, Arthur," she'd persisted. "My brother George."

They avoided her, and because she was nearly always pressed against him, they avoided Nicholas. In the kindest way. As star, anything he demanded he got. As he walked through the studio, smiles wreathed faces, hands waved, cheery hellos bellowed forth. But although his habit was to keep pretty much to himself, he found himself with too much time on his hands. He and Pamela stayed alone in his suite of rooms in the studio. He made love to her more often than he would have liked. He called his brokers and lawyers more often than necessary. He was the star, the reason why *William the Conqueror* was being made, but he was not part of the company. He missed the camaraderie. Pamela's shyness was so intense it drew him into its shadow.

The formal dinners, routine entertainment for visiting celebrities, were painful for her. No one, she told him, wanted to talk seriously: not novelists, not statesmen, not university professors. She'd gone over to one of the world's most gifted playwrights just to tell him how much she'd admired his work, and he'd spent an hour talking about his shoemaker. An hour on different lasts, grades of leather, and who the shoemaker's most renowned customers were; he'd mentioned the Prince of Wales and Nicholas Cobleigh. They all wanted to gossip, she told Nicholas. She tried to have intelligent conversations and no one was interested. When they tried to pry information from her about him, or gossiped about people she'd never met, she just clammed up. She couldn't help it. She was not cut out for cocktail parties, for superficial chatter or hypocritical intimacy.

He watched the men seated beside her attempt light conversation. Her responses were either painfully terse or agonizingly long-winded. He watched the Englishmen; their eyes, rarely the mirrors of their souls, almost danced with relief as they turned to the women on their other side. The women seated next to him darted fast glances at her and back to him, hardly disguising their wonder at Pamela. Their silent inquiry—what does she have?—was so obvious it might have been shouted.

It wasn't that he was embarrassed to be linked with her. It was just that he wished she could enjoy herself.

At one party, the men rose after the second course and changed dinner partners. A man, Lord Something-or-other, was seated beside Pamela. To Nicholas, down the table, the man didn't look very aristocratic in his badly tailored shiny blue suit. Still, he was a lord. Someone, as Jane would say, to write Rhodes about. Pamela did not say a word. She sat rigid, spooning up tiny dots of summer pudding and cream. She answered his questions with staccato responses, which Nicholas—far down the table—heard as peeps. *Peep*. Like a tiny bird.

Jane would have turned to the man and said, "I never met a lord before. We didn't have any in Ohio." Or asked him if *noblesse* really did *oblige* these days; or whether he was able to recognize another aristocrat on sight; or if he'd please explain what the Liberal party was. Jane would have gotten him talking. Smiling. Looking down her dress. And after the party, she'd carry on as they'd be getting ready for bed. He could almost hear her: "God, a lord! Did you see? I sat there and carried on a whole conversation with a titled Englishman. Except he looked like a Mafia capo. Didn't he? With that suit and that weasel face. But he called me 'My dear.' Nick, admit it, you're jealous. Lord Whatever calling me his dear. But what a mean face. Thank goodness there's no *droit de seigneur* any more."

In the limousine going back to the house on Berkeley Square, Pamela said, "I'm glad *that's* over."

He hated the house. It was a double townhouse, big, gray, cold. There was a car showroom across the green and a smelly Arab restaurant down the street. It was like living on a bad block on the West Side.

He'd never liked the West Side. Jane thought it romantic, bohemian. New Yorkish. He remembered. It was her and her brother's highest accolade.

Jane popped into his mind more often in England than she had when they were both in the States. It was an intrusive kind of popping; he often resented her for it.

Sometimes he thought about her and Judson Fullerton. His imagination wouldn't let go of her description of Fullerton's penis, how she'd spoken of it. Nicholas saw it as a battering ram. He pictured them in bed, Fullerton ramming into Jane, Jane shuddering with orgasm after orgasm as she'd never done with him. He heard her screaming: Judson! Judson! It made him sick to his stomach. Then angry.

But sometimes her intrusions were more gentle. Pamela had said, "Nicholas, I can't believe that in a year or two I'll be carrying your child." He'd looked down at Pamela, lying naked, gazing up at him, the tiny points of her pelvic bones protruding, the concavity of her stomach. He'd tried to imagine her pregnant. But the only pregnant woman who came to his mind was Jane.

Jane, belly swollen big by her sixth month with Victoria, climbing up the flights of stairs to their cold-water flat. Was it on Forty-fifth or Forty-sixth? He couldn't remember. She would know. Climbing up those steps with him after dinner at his mother's. Take it easy, he'd told her. Every few steps he'd pat her behind in encouragement.

The brown line that crept up the center of her belly. The way the tips of her breasts turned brown too. I can't stand it, she'd said. I'm such a cow. No, you're beautiful. Pregnancy was natural to her: broad-hipped, big-breasted, born to be a mother. The bigger she got, the prouder he'd become. He knew it was foolish, but nonetheless, Jane was a walking advertisement to his prowess: Nicholas Cobleigh did this to me! her belly proclaimed.

He could not imagine Pamela pregnant. She wasn't made for it. It would look wrong. Like a tumor.

Two nights before his birthday, about 3:00 A.M., he'd woken up thinking about Jane. He'd slipped out of bed, glanced down at Pamela, who was sleeping curled like a child in the middle of the bed, and tiptoed down into the library. He'd looked around, a little confused, then picked up the phone. He called the apartment, then Connecticut.

Nick! Jane had said. How are you? This is so weird. I was just thinking about you. Just this second! About the time you were rehearsing Romeo and—never mind. Tell me, how is *William* coming along?

Their old ESP. It used to work all the time. Jane swore she *knew* when his plane touched down at JFK because her whole body suddenly relaxed; he was safe. And he'd had an extra-sense of Jane. When she was nursing Elizabeth he woke and, still dopey from sleep, grabbed one of his sweaters and brought it into the baby's room. He'd wrapped it around Jane and she said, I can't believe it! It's the weirdest thing. Just three seconds before you came in I started shivering.

Most of the time, he wished he could get her out of his mind, even though thinking of her was comforting. Like in the old days. When things were rough on location, he'd think about her and the girls.

He missed the girls, but most of the time he pushed them out of his mind. He could hardly bear to summon up their faces and see how they saw him. He had flown back to New York on Christmas Eve, and they refused to come to the hotel to be with him and Pamela. Just spend some time with her, he'd pleaded. Get to know her. Victoria had been nasty, Jane to the third power: Can I call her Mommy? she'd demanded. Elizabeth had broken down and sobbed. Don't you want to be with us and Mommy tonight? The next day, he'd left Pamela in the room for a couple of hours and had gone to his parents' apartment. Looking into their eyes, too bright, sparkling determinedly to show what a happy family holiday it was. Jane and the girls were there too, of course. Family. Merry Christmas, Nick, Jane said. She'd even kissed his cheek. Then she'd turned to the girls, hanging back, sullen. Say Merry Christmas to your father. Say it!

He felt disloyal, as if he were cheating on Pamela by letting Jane in his mind so often.

He tried to think about bad things. All the years Jane had made their lives so miserable. Making them all share her prison. That she had made it a beautiful prison he granted her, but still . . .

454

Her using him.

Her snide remarks. Her nasty wit. Her resentment. Her anger.

Her adultery. It wasn't the same for her. She wasn't tempted, titillated, worked on every damned day of her life. He lay beside Pamela. More bad things. Jane's physical inertia. Her big body gone soft. Loose, saggy breasts. Heavy thighs that shook as she crossed the room. Broad, flabby behind. The complete lack of muscle tone no diet could change.

He didn't want to think about her. He was only thinking about her because he wasn't havng a good time in England. Laurel Blake. Isolation on the set. Hysterical calls from Los Angeles. Exhausting sessions—it was getting harder and harder—with a new gymnastics coach. Do you want to keep in shape or don't you? the man had demanded. When you get older, you have to work harder. Use it or lose it. Don't abuse it.

England wasn't fun.

One thing he realized on his birthday. England was a foreign country. He couldn't turn on a television set and see *Talk*. He hadn't looked at Jane in over a month.

When Nicholas realized that, he realized just how badly he missed her.

MAN'S VOICE: Today's *Talk* was taped last week just before Jane Cobleigh left for London. We hope . . .

—Voice-over as credits roll, *Talk*, NBC-TV

Cecily had asked the question a month before. Why hasn't Nicholas asked for a divorce?

Jane didn't know, and she'd asked herself the question months before that.

She'd told Cecily, Maybe he can't admit that he failed in something; maybe he doesn't want to do any more damage to his relationship with Vicky and Liz; maybe he's not ready to marry Pamela, and if he got a divorce he'd feel obligated to; maybe seeing his parents back together and so happy makes him feel—I don't know—queasy about anything as final as divorce; maybe it's inertia; maybe he's so busy that he can't put his mind to all the emotional and financial complications a divorce settlement would bring.

Maybe he still loves you, Cecily said.

One thing she knew wasn't love was what she felt for Judson Fullerton. It was barely even passion any more. In the last year, their sexual encounters had changed. There was no arcing spark, no hot sizzle of two bodies coming into contact. What remained was two minds. Sex had become a creative challenge, having little to do with lust and a great deal to do with making up the elaborate scenarios they required to stimulate desire.

"There are three of them holding you prisoner," Judson said. "Three big black men."

"Could you make one a Puerto Rican?"

"A Puerto Rican?"

"Never mind."

"They've been holding you for two days. They've only let you have a little water. You're starving. Okay? And terrified. They haven't done anything yet, but the tension is growing and growing." He was lying on her elbow. She shifted to the left and her elbow came free. "Now where are you?" he asked.

"Here." They were in the guest room of her apartment. She had never taken him into the master bedroom she'd shared with Nicholas.

"Where *are* you? With the three black men."

She couldn't think for a minute. Finally she said, "Swaziland."

456

"Come on. *Here*. In the United States."

"South Avondale," she said quickly.

"What?"

"South Avondale. It's in Cincinnati."

Judson propped himself up. Jane did not look at his face. He had a circle of hair around his navel, like a wreath. "Are you playing games with me?" His erection was deflating; his penis turned from bright red to the palest pink.

"Of course we're playing games," she said.

"You know what I mean."

Their games had less and less to do with sex. They reminded Jane of the elaborate stories she had told her friend Charlene Moffett when they were six or seven years old. Dark dungeons with creaking doors, wicked stepmothers who got boiled in oil, castles with clouds floating atop their towers, handsome princes with golden hair. Elaborate stories to deliver them out of late-afternoon lethargy, fantasies for everyone, no need unmet.

"Maybe this isn't my game," she said.

Judson lay back down, head on the pillow. The bedding was a bright yellow. Too bright. It did not flatter him. "All right," he said, exhaling as he spoke. "We'll start from the beginning." She glanced at his penis; they would have to. "Do you want to do blacks?"

"How about Filipinos?" she asked.

"Filipinos?"

"Bosnian-Herzegovinians."

He leaned forward and pulled the sheet up to his waist. "All right, Jane. It's clear this isn't our day."

"I guess not."

"I just wish you could have called. I had the chance to have drinks with the head of the department, and I turned him down to be here by seven."

She lifted her watch from the nightstand beside the bed. "It's seven twenty. If you rush, you could still squeeze in a gimlet."

"Okay," he said. He sat up and put his feet on the floor, his back toward Jane. A line of hair grew out of the crack between his buttocks, pointing slightly to the right of his spine. He lifted an inside-out sock and stuck his hand into it. Then he turned to face her, his dark blue fist resting on his thigh. "You're hostile. That's obvious. Would you like to talk about it?"

"We've been seeing each other a long time."

He nodded and pulled the sock right-side out. "I see."

"No you don't."

"Yes I do. We had this discussion last year, right before the July fourth weekend."

"No we didn't."

"Yes we did, Jane. You were very direct then. You asked me if I had any

457

plans to leave Ginny, and I was equally direct. I told you no. And I told you why."

"You told me she was fragile emotionally."

"She is."

"That's not why you stay with her."

"I see. You're going to explain me to me. You've become a lay analyst. Go ahead. I'm all for enlightenment."

"No you're not, but I'll tell you anyway. You stay married because you need someone you can cheat on. Someone who's guaranteed to eat her heart out every Wednesday night because she knows you're in New York spending the night with someone else."

Judson's nostrils flared. "This isn't worthy of your intelligence."

"You stay married because you need someone to torture."

"This is ridiculous."

"Someone who'll be totally miserable every time you say you'll be home at six and you show up at nine with your hair mussed and your shirt not tucked in properly." Judson compressed his mouth into a slash. "I see the way you leave me to go back to her. You stuff your tie into your jacket pocket and leave an end hanging out."

"You've concocted quite a story, haven't you?"

"No. I just know you. I know that you're the neatest man on earth, and the only reason you go home looking like you just got out of bed is because you want to stick it to her. 'See, Ginny? Look! I just got out of bed.' That's half the excitement, isn't it, Judson? Does she cry each time? Does she? Does she beg you to give me up? Do you wind up in bed together afterward?"

"Stop it." He put on both socks, then stood. He picked up his undershorts and held them by the waistband like a bullfighter's cape. He watched her. "Well?" he finally said.

"Well what?"

"Are you finished with your little scene? Or should I get dressed and leave?"

"Get dressed and leave," she said. Her voice was so deep, self-assured. Her best voice. Hello, this is Jane Cobleigh speaking for the American Cancer Society. Hi. Today on *Talk* we're going to be discussing adultery. Why do people do it? Before you laugh, stay tuned and listen.

She should be shaking, her voice coming out in weak, high bleats.

After Judson put on his jacket, he took a comb from his pocket and ostentatiously ran it through his hair. He walked to the big round mirror over the dresser and readjusted the already tight perfect knot on his tie. Then he walked back to the bed. "I don't think we should see each other for the rest of the week," he said. She said nothing. "Perhaps not even next week," he

458

added. If she waited long enough, he'd say, Not even the week after that. Not until Labor Day. Veterans' Day. Thanksgiving.

"Judson, I think it's over."

"What?" he said. He looked so perfect: white linen suit, blue shirt, blue, white, and orange silk tie. Completely in control, from his perfect polished shoes to his perfect combed hair. But he couldn't stop blinking. He blinked over and over, a terrible tic, as if he could not believe what he was seeing.

Jane lay on the sheet. She did not bother to cover herself. "It's over, Judson."

"Just like that?"

"I don't know any other way to end it."

"Do you have someone else?"

"No."

His blinking slowed but did not stop. "No? What do you plan to do for sex then?"

"I don't think I want to discuss that with you."

All that time. Two or three times a week. She should at least manage a few delicate sobs. But her eyes were dry and unblinking. It was a completely, astoundingly neutral moment. Years. She felt she owed a tear for all that time, but she could not squeeze one out. The only thing she felt was relief. He would be gone within minutes. She could get dressed and drive up to Connecticut before dark. Maybe the wild ducks that stopped by the pond early every summer would be there—one brown, one black with a blue-green iridescent head—gliding across the dark, still water in back of the house. A wild-duck couple who flew everywhere together.

"Jane."

"I'm sorry it didn't work out, Judson. But it wasn't really designed to work out, was it?" He blinked. She thought he might be getting ready to cry, but no, not Judson. He didn't even look sad. Stunned. Annoyed. He'd missed cocktails with the head of the Department of Psychiatry and three black men holding her captive. He'd probably go back to Connecticut too.

"You don't love me?" he asked. A cool, clinical query.

"No. I don't love you."

"I see." He picked up his change, keys, and watch from the other night-stand. "Goodbye, then," he said, as he walked out the door.

She didn't even like him.

"Well," Rhodes said, "what are you going to do?"

"I don't know."

He sat across from Jane, but the table was so small she could see him perfectly. Still so incredibly lovely, but random lines were etched under his

459

eyes—some nearly obscured by the thick fringe of lower lashes—and a few pearly gray strands lightened his brown hair. At first she'd been surprised he allowed the gray to show, but then she realized Rhodes knew it would detract from his beauty to counterattack nature. Besides, there was no need; nature loved him and would always treat him tenderly.

The table was round, with a pink cloth that hung to the floor and a yellow flower that looked like a constellation of tiny stars in a vase in the center. Their espresso cups and brandy glasses were in front of them. The restaurant was one of the most elegant in New York. It was where she took her most important guests. "Madame Cobleigh! Bon soir!" The maître d' was always thrilled to see her. He always trilled her name loud enough so the patrons closest to the front turned, saw her, and whispered, "That's her!" When she'd come in with Rhodes, the maître d' gave him a slower than usual once-over and his mouth had formed a quick Gallic pucker of surprise: this one was no ordinary *Talk* guest; this one was incredible, special, a . . . "This is my brother, Louis," she said quickly. "Ah," the maître d' said. "A pleasure, monsieur." This time he'd meant it.

"So you've gotten rid of the shrink for good?" Rhodes asked. She nodded. "Well, good riddance to bad rubbish."

"Rhodes—"

"He had a face like a potato. When I saw the two of you on *Talk* that first time, I thought, God, to have to look at Mr. Potato Head for forty-five minutes two times a week. Little potato eyes. And then you went and—"

"He was fantastic in the kip."

"Oh, cut it out, turkey. 'In the kip.' Little Miss New York Trendy. Do you know how pathetically clichéd that affair was? Do you know how many stupid douche bags wind up in bed with their shrinks? At least sixty percent."

"Shut up, Rhodes."

"You invited me to New York to talk. Remember?"

"You were coming in anyway in a few days with Philip on your way to Europe, and I thought I'd like to spend some time alone with my brother. My brother who cares for me, who's sensitive to my feelings. I guess I was wrong."

"Shut up, Jane." He lit a cigarette, blew a slender column of smoke toward the ceiling, then reached over and patted her hand. "Okay. Truce. Now, what do you want? I mean, for the rest of your life." She shrugged. She couldn't say it. "Tell me. I know what it is anyway."

He rested his hand on top of hers, finely shaped, with long, strong fingers. She had always loved Rhodes, but this was one of the rare times the love blazed through her, brightening her entire being.

"I love you," she whispered.

"I know," he answered. "I love you too." His hand stayed over hers for another moment; then he drew it away. "Okay, Big J," he said, in his familiar wise-guy voice, "tell me what you want."

"I want to be married to Nick for the rest of my life."

"No divorce?" She shook her head. "No more love in the afternoon ⸳ ⸳th dip-shits?"

"No. Just Nick." She had chosen the wrong place for their discussion. They should have stayed in the apartment where she could have come apart, put her arms around Rhodes, and wailed. She took a deep but shaky breath. "But of course," she said quietly, "that's only what I want. It's not what he wants."

"Have you asked him?"

"No!" She softened her voice. "Sorry. No. Rhodes, he's been living with her for two years. It's not a quickie affair with some little chippy. They're inseparable. Literally. I hear she can't keep her hands off him."

The Cobleighs' separation wasn't public, but it wasn't private either. People in the know knew, and they loved telling Jane about it. We saw Nick the other night. With *her*. Really? she'd say. And then they insisted on sharing their knowledge: She's tiny. Prepubescent, but no nymphet. *Boring*. Won't let go of him. Literally. They observed Jane carefully as they spoke. She let them see nothing.

"And can Nick keep his hands off her?" Rhodes asked.

"I guess not." She ran her finger around the small rim of her espresso cup. "In the last month or so . . ." Her voice faded into silence.

"What? Tell me. Are you breaking for a commercial?"

"Rhodes, just give me a minute. Okay?" She exhaled slowly. "In the last couple of months, he's been calling more. Mostly about the girls at the beginning, trying to get me to get them to spend some time with him and Pamela. At the beginning all he wanted to do was fight. You know, 'Do you think it's fair? Don't you think that if they knew about you and that unethical so-and-so—'"

"He called him a so-and-so?"

"He called him a son of a bitch. Anyway, he's been calling a lot lately. Late at night. Three, four in the morning London time. He always starts with some legitimate topic. Did the accountant send the check for Liz's tuition? How are his horses? He hasn't been to Connecticut for two years and he's still paying someone to take care of his horses every day. But then he starts talking."

"What does he talk about?"

"The film. *William the Conqueror*. He reads me a page or two of the script and asks what I think of it. Or he asks me about *Talk*, what shows I'm planning, what this or that guest was like. Or he'll remind me about Olivia's

461

anniversary or ask me who was the set designer in some Off Broadway play he was in in 1963."

Rhodes held his brandy snifter but did not drink. He peered into the liquid, as if it could be read like tea leaves. "It sounds like husband and wife talk," he said.

"A little. But there are definitely no I-love-yous. There isn't even warmth. It's very oddly casual."

"Does he talk about her?"

"No."

Rhodes looked at Jane. "What's that funny expression on your face? Did you ask him about her? You are *such* a nit, Jane. I mean it."

"No. I said 'How is Pamela?' one time. And he said 'Fine.' But I guess he was annoyed, because that was essentially the end of that conversation. I don't know. I called him last night, for his birthday. She answered the phone and said he'd had a hard day and had gone to bed early." She looked at her brother. He was staring into his glass again. "I hate her," she said. "She has a little teeny voice, like a Walt Disney mouse. 'I'll tell Nicholas you called,'" Jane squeaked. "How he can stand to listen to it I'll never know."

"Maybe he can't any more." Rhodes looked up. His eyes were so beautiful. Like hers: everyone who saw them together said that. But his eyes had changed. They were no longer merely big, deep, dark blue, and always sparkling: eyes to evoke oohs. They had become the eyes of a man of interesting character. She supposed hers had changed too. Rhodes gazed straight at her. "I think he may be sending you a signal. Do you?"

"I don't know."

"Does he know you ditched Dr. Potato?"

"No. But that's not something we ever really discussed other than when it first came out."

"Okay. Let's get back to where we started. What are you going to do? Are you going to try and get him back?"

"I'm afraid to."

"Why?"

"He has Pamela. She's twenty-four, twenty-five years old."

"Oh, stop it! She's a wimp. You're coast-to-coast hot shit. For a reason. You're alive, you're real. People respond to you."

"But maybe he doesn't want someone so alive. Maybe he wants a wimp."

"Maybe. Maybe he wants a wife."

"He could have her."

Rhodes leaned forward and put his elbows on the table. The tiny bud vase shuddered. "Jane, Nick could have anyone. The point is, he's had every opportunity to get you off his back and marry her and he hasn't done it. Why? And why, all of a sudden, is he up at three in the morning making overseas calls? Insomnia? He doesn't want to wake the wimp? He could call anyone. A hundred million people would be glad to hear from Nicholas Cobleigh at three in the morning or any other time, and believe me, he knows it. So why does he call you? That's a rhetorical question. Don't bother answering."

"What should I do?"

"Confront him."

"What should I say?"

"Say 'Nick, I still love you. Do you still love me?'"

"Do you think that's how men and women talk to each other?"

"It's how people who want to cut the bullshit talk to each other, and stop acting like a snotty New York bitch."

A waiter approaching their table with a pot of espresso heard Rhodes and backed off. He took cautious little backward steps, as if he were in a film being rewound.

"What if he says he loves Pamela?"

"Then say okay, sorry to have bothered you. Have your lawyer call my lawyer and get on with your life. But do you think that's what he'll say?"

She truly did not know. Some of the time she had an image—admittedly an adolescent one—of meeting. She'd be in Connecticut, just getting ready to go into the city, putting her notes for the show and her shoulder bag on the passenger seat of her car. Suddenly another car would come crunching up the gravel drive. It would be Nicholas's old gray Porsche. Silly. He'd sold it years before. He'd leap out, run to her: Jane, Jane. Other times, she saw Nicholas in a gloomy parlor filled with dark Victorian furniture. A single beam of light broke through the heavy brocade drapes, but its power was diffused by thousands of specks of antique dust suspended in the air. He held the telephone receiver away from his ear. It hurt him to hear her. He was filled with discomfort at her declaration of love, embarrassed, and, finally, sad for her.

"Rhodes, I don't want to be one of those desperate women who read a thousand meanings into every How-are-you. Look at the objective evidence. He's living with her. They bought a house out in Santa Barbara together, and they were looking at co-ops in the city last December."

"That's real estate. Real estate isn't love."

"What if he says no, I don't want you. I don't love you. I stopped loving you years ago. What if he says that the phone calls weren't signals. They were just friendly calls. He can afford to be friendly. He doesn't care any more. Don't you see, I could make an absolute ass of myself. He'd pity me! He'd get off the phone and tell Pamela everything and—"

Rhodes raised his hand like a policeman stopping traffic. "Wait a second."

"What?"

"A phone call? This isn't chitchat. Think about it. Didn't you want me here, face to face, for this talk? It seems to me that if you see each other . . ."

"How am I supposed to see him? They're in London, and then they're going on location through the fall. He'll be tied up for months."

"Go there, stupid."

"Go where, London? How can I go to London? I don't fly. Rhodes, really, I've never been on a plane. It's one of my last big fears. Every time I think of being on a plane that's taking off, my heart starts—forget it."

"Okay. Forget it."

"Even if I could get there by ship—and I wouldn't want to be in the middle of the ocean either—what could I do? Go and ring his doorbell? Go drop in at the studio?"

"Yes."

"And say what? Excuse me, Pamela. I'd like a few minutes with my husband. And then say to Nick, I love you. I want you back. Get rid of her. I'm your wife. We can make it work because we've always loved each other. We've always loved each other more than anything else in the world."

"Yes," Rhodes said. "That sounds right."

"Oh, Rhodes, what if he says no?"

"Isn't it worth the risk? What if he says yes?"

An eight. Eight points of terror. No. Nine. There wasn't enough air in the cabin. The stewardess kept smiling. Smile, smile. A thousand miles across the Atlantic Ocean, faster than the speed of sound, and she had a smile on, even though soon she and all the passengers would be gasping in a vacuum. We regret to say there is no oxygen available on this flight. Huge, symmetrical, too-white teeth, as though she'd borrowed a friend's. She came down the aisle, and the smile stayed put.

"Is everything all right, Mrs. Cobleigh?" The smile grew wider. Even the back teeth showed now. She'd obviously seen *Talk*. Knew a phobic when she saw one.

"Fine." A crinkle sound the smiler didn't hear: the airsick bag in readiness, tucked under Jane's left thigh.

"Good!" The stewardess smiled for them both. Encouragement. Or perhaps auditioning, hoping for a *Talk* show on the problems of flight attendants or cosmetic dentistry. Didn't understand the *Talk* format. "We had Mr. Cobleigh a month or two ago."

Hardly any air, and what there was was too cold. "Oh." The smile quavered, upset by the neutral response. Jane added a hurried, "That's nice."

The quavering stopped. Lips, teeth, gums went back into business. "He ordered the exact same wine you did!"

"Well—" Face the fear. An eight. No air. Some air. A seven. Six or seven. She looked right up into the smile. It was secure now, as big and

464

dazzling as it could get, shining just for her. "That's what happens after nineteen years of marriage," Jane said.

London is hotter than New York was yesterday, but inside the limousine it is cool; the rich are rendered immune to climate. Jane gazes out the window, but the blue-tinted glass makes everything back projection. Only she and the driver and the car in the foreground are real.

The manly odor of the leather seats mingles with the perfume of a red rose in a crystal vial attached near the window. She takes a mirror from her handbag even though there is a lighted mirror in a cabinet beside the bar. She looks tired, but she is wearing only a little blush, a little mascara, a little lip gloss. Nicholas never liked her in makeup. She thinks of wiping off the lip gloss. It will feel greasy if he kisses her. But without it she will look too sallow. Too old.

Ridiculous. He will either want her or not want her and will neither leap forward nor recoil because of anything that coats her lips. She thinks he will want her.

Two nights before, he phoned. Their longest call yet. For the first time since they parted, he spoke of the past.

He said, Do you remember when we first moved to the house and I painted it? I had all that green paint from the shutters in my hair, and you were doing something—you had a smudge on your nose.

Polishing the brass knocker, she said. That stupid-looking eagle.

That's right. I was thinking about it. Do you know, that was the last time I had an obligation to do something. I'm not talking about contractual obligations or my obligations to the girls . . . or you. I mean, that was the last time I had a job I couldn't delegate. Ever since then, there have been people I can hire or who volunteer to do—to do almost everything. Well, I am busy. I mean, I *need* to have things done.

What's the matter, Nick?

Nothing. I was just thinking about that day. Lying there in the grass. Remember?

Yes. I remember.

It was fun, wasn't it?

She puts back her mirror. If he were only reminiscing about a pure, perfect moment in what became a dead marriage, he wouldn't have bothered to call her at three thirty in the morning, Greenwich Mean Time. The marriage is not dead.

Her hands lie on her lap, the nails trimmed, unpolished. Natural, as he likes them. Through the two years they have been separated, she has worn a wedding band. She has many: entwined white and yellow gold; platinum;

465

jade; diamonds and sapphires; diamonds and rubies. Thin ones and thick. This one is thin, plain gold, the one they bought in Maryland a half hour before they got married. It has lain in the bottom of her handkerchief box for several years. She has been wearing it for less than twenty-four hours.

When she saw him last, Christmas Day, he was not wearing his. But she is sure he still has it. He will not even have to search for it.

Jane prays, Don't let me be wrong. But she believes Nicholas loves her.

The limousine slows. They are far from central London, somewhere in the suburbs. Trees keep their branches raised, defying the heat. Across the street are two granite columns. On one there is a large brass plaque: BLACK-HEATH STUDIOS.

The limousine stops. The driver turns. This is it, Madam. Shall I drive in?

Yes, she says. But then— Wait! She sees another limousine, a twin to hers, pulling out of the driveway between the two columns. She strains to see inside the car. Suddenly she is sure she sees a fair head.

I'll get out here.

She jumps from the car and waves to the other limousine. It turns left, slowly, into the street.

Nick! she calls. Nick!

The limousine starts to pick up speed. She runs across the street.

Nick! It's me!

The saying is true. She does not know what hits her. She never sees that other car. All she knows is sudden horrible pain. And then she is flying above England, and then she crashes onto the street.

Hear my prayer, O Lord, and give ear unto my cry; hold not thy peace at my tears: for I am a stranger with thee, and a sojourner, as all my fathers were.

O spare me, that I may recover strength, before I go hence, and be no more.

—Psalm 39

Laurel Blake, playing his wife, Matilda, was saying, "What is England to us, William? Stay with me here." Emotion muted her voice. Her dark lashes had beads of tears. The camera moved in on him for a reaction shot, and Nicholas, the warrior-politician-nobleman William, gazed into Laurel's brimming eyes with a grief so profound it nearly matched her own.

"Cut," the director called. "Print."

Nicholas turned his back to Laurel and yawned. His hand was halfway up to cover his mouth when he saw Murray King shouldering his way past the boom man. Nicholas's hand, palm facing inward, froze at chest level.

He knew Murray was in London, of course. Murray had arrived two weeks before with a suitcase full of screenplays and two blue suits. But Murray, ever the theatrical agent—happy, buoyant, secure backstage in a theater—did not like movie sets. He was distinctly uncomfortable in the midst of cameras and cables. He had visited Nicholas only once during a shooting, years before, and had glared at the sound men, gaffers, grips, and cameramen with rancor foreign to his decent nature, as if the only job these technicians were hired to accomplish was the submersion of his client's career. Murray never even visited a studio if he could avoid it. Intricate negotiations with film company executives and financiers were held over lunches that blended into cocktail hours and slipped into dinners. Yet here was Murray, nearly tripping over a curled edge of tape on the floor, hurrying toward him.

"Murray?" Nicholas said.

Something was really wrong. Murray's complexion was horrible, pale, with a phosphorescence nearly green. His glasses, shoved on at a crazed angle, were about to slip down the side of his face. "Nicky," was all he said.

Nicholas swallowed, then cleared his throat. He was too tired, drinking too much, his nerves rubbed raw. It was embarrassing, actually, the way he kept overreacting. He was so worn out a simple good morning seemed a cataclysmic announcement.

"Nicky." Murray slipped his arm around him. Nicholas let himself be led off the set. He didn't even ask what was wrong. It was something very bad: Murray shepherding him up the stairs, never letting him go. "Where's your dressing room?" he asked. Nicholas walked down a hall and tried to open the door. His sweat-drenched hand slipped off the knob. "Here, let me, Nicky."

It was very bad, but let it be the least terrible of possibilities. His father . . . something with his liver. Probably bad. In the hospital. His mother. She had seemed fine before he left, but maybe her old illness, her consuming sadness . . .

"It's Jane, Nicky."

No.

"An accident. She was hit by a car and thrown. Nicky, listen to me. She's in the hospital."

The silence was so strong it became physical, like air. "Bad?" Nicholas asked.

"Yes. Very bad. A head injury. They have her in intensive care. . . ."

"Where?" Let it be New York, not Connecticut. Thousands of doctors, bright white modern equipment.

"Nicky—"

Nicholas bolted. He ran from Murray into the bathroom, slamming the door behind him. He sat on the toilet and leaned his cheek on the porcelain sink.

Murray knocked on the door. "Are you okay?"

"Yes."

"Nicky." Nicholas pulled himself up, turned on the cold-water faucet, and put his wrists under the cool flow. That's what Jane had always done when the girls came in from playing, agitated, sweating. Nice cool water. Let it run over your wrists. You'll feel like a whole new person. "Nicky, please."

Nicholas opened the door. "Get the first plane out," he said.

"Listen to me, she's—"

"If there's not one leaving within the next hour, charter something."

"She's *here*. In London."

"In *London?*"

"It happened less than an hour ago, outside the studio."

"No. How could that happen? There's some mistake. Some other Cobleigh."

"There's no mistake."

"Jesus, it has to be. How could she be in London?"

"Nicky—"

"Murray, listen to me. She's never been on a goddamn plane in her life. How could she get here? She probably couldn't even take a boat. Come on, Murray. It's not her."

"It is, Nicky. It's Jane."

468

"No."
"Yes."
"No!"

They were waiting for him outside the corridor of the emergency room:
the hospital triumvirate—the administrator, the neurologist, the neurosurgeon—more nurses than were necessary, the press.

"Out!" the administrator called to the photographers. He put his hand in
front of a lens that was pointed at Nicholas. "You are not to—"

"Mr. Cobleigh, I'm Alfred Sadgrove, the neurologist, and this is—"

"Where is she?" Nicholas bellowed.

"Nicky." Murray tried to soothe him.

"Where the hell did you take her?"

"Look at him!" one nurse said.

"Shorter than I expected," said another.

"—the neurosurgeon, Sir Anthony Bradley. He will tell you—"

"Where is she, for Christ's sake?" It was so hot in that corridor. All those
damp red foreheads shining at him.

"You see, Mr. Cobleigh—"

The rumbling of wheels, the slap of fast-moving feet cut the doctor off.
Murray grasped Nicholas's arm and pulled him to the wall so a patient on a
hospital cart could be wheeled in. Not Jane. A man with a fat belly, his hand
and forearm wrapped in a blood-drenched towel. "Coming through!" an atten-
dant pushing the gurney shouted. The man's wife rushed along, running to
remain at her husband's bedside. "Stanley," she whimpered. "Stanley." Suddenly she slowed, stiffened, and stopped. She stood before Nicholas, eyes
expanding. Her hand, an upside-down pendulum, patted her hair again and
again. She was so close. He turned and squeezed his eyes shut. He opened
them a moment later, when he felt her go. She was running toward the
emergency-room doors closing behind her husband, shouting "Stanley!"

One of the three was beside him. The Sir. Very tall. Nicholas looked up.
"She's been taken to intensive care, Mr. Cobleigh. You may see her shortly. I
ordered a CAT scan of her brain as soon as she was brought in."

"Her brain," he said. Her head, Murray had said. "Not her skull?"

"Oh, yes. She has a basilar skull fracture on the right side. Compound to
the right ear."

"Her brain?"

"Yes. You see, it is rather a serious injury. Apparently, she was hit,
thrown into the air, and crashed to the ground. Her head hit the pavement.
When she was brought in, she was not communicating coherently at all."

"Well, she was hit by a car." What did they expect her to do, hold a
conversation with them? "The accident was a shock," Nicholas tried to explain

469

to the man. "And if she had a skull fracture, then . . ." Nicholas stopped talking. The neurosurgeon was looking down at him over his hump of a nose.

"Mr. Cobleigh, I'm afraid it is not that simple. Your wife has contusions on both sides of the brain. The CAT scan shows no focal clot at the moment, but we must monitor her carefully."

Nicholas tried to nod his understanding. He didn't understand. "Why?" he asked softly.

"We must be concerned about a delayed intercranial hematoma."

"What?"

"A blood clot. Right now, she's slipped into a somewhat somnolent state. We are inserting an intercranial pressure monitor to make certain—"

"If the pressure builds?"

"We might well have to operate."

"Then she'll be all right?"

The surgeon peered at Nicholas, searching his face, as if he were a fan looking for a signal that a request for an autograph would be granted. "Mr. Cobleigh," he said tentatively.

"Yes," Nicholas breathed.

"We simply don't know."

They waited for the elevator: the Englishmen in a tight knot, Nicholas and Murray behind them.

"Listen, Nicky," Murray said, "maybe it's not so bad. Maybe we'll get up there and she'll have a big smile on her face and say 'Hey, get me out of this place.'"

"Murray, please. I don't feel like talking." Nicholas was watching the neurosurgeon. He had a noble head, one that would be more appropriate on a pedestal than on a human neck. Nicholas decided to check if his title was inherited or conferred; if it was inherited, he would not let him near Jane.

"Nicky, just one thing. This could be one big zero. I mean, you hear about people having fractured skulls all the time. I remember, this wasn't a fractured skull, but still . . . I was representing—years ago—Harry Bluestone, the comedian. Remember him? The one with the monologue about his brother Irving? A Mack truck drove over his foot and you know what happened? Nothing!"

Jesus, dear Jesus, she looks like a puppet. A small circle of shaved scalp. A piece of implanted metal.

"The pressure monitor," one of the Englishmen said.

A puppet. Wires snaking out from the metal in her skull. Intravenous tube from her arm. Ugly yellowish tube coming out of her mouth.

Jesus, let her not be dead. So still. So white. Never like that before. Her

470

golden color gone. She nearly blended with the sheet. But she breathed, she breathed.

The other arm bandaged against her chest. At an odd angle, like a chicken wing.

"Simple fracture of the humerus," one of them said. "Nothing to be concerned about." They all sounded alike, those English voices.

She was so straight, as though laid out, which was awful, even if she was breathing. Unnatural, because even in the deepest sleep she would fling an arm across the pillow or lie on her side and draw up her knees. Never flat like this, so stiff, fingers rigid, as though they'd been glued onto her hands. Her fingers always had curled in sleep, like a baby's. When he'd slip his finger into that loose fist she always made in sleep, her hand would close tight upon it. "Jane."

She did not move.

"Jane."

He stared at the white hand. Such a wrong color for her. And there was her wedding ring. Real gold! the jeweler in Maryland had assured them. Real! His was in the box with his cufflinks. He'd slipped it under the velvet lining, so he wouldn't have to see it every day.

He looked around. Murray was right beside him. "My wedding ring's in my cufflink box," Nicholas said.

"Fortunately, there's no cervical spinal injury," one of the three declared.

"However," another declared, "you do understand, Mr. Cobleigh, that the prognosis is . . . guarded."

Her feet were sticking out from the sheet that covered her stomach and legs. He sidestepped to the end of the bed and put his hand around her ankle. Not warm, but not cold.

"Naturally, if you wish to call in other . . ."

"Although you're fortunate, you know. We have excellent facilities for dealing with this sort of injury. Not all hospitals do. And of course, Sir Anthony's reputation is . . ."

Nicholas rubbed his thumb back and forth. Velvet. Her skin was still pure velvet. Then he pulled down the sheet and tucked it under her feet.

"Mr. Cobleigh, I have arranged for you to use my office while you are here. We certainly don't want you disturbed further by photographers."

"Murray," Nicholas said, "I want my ring."

Nicholas sat in the desk chair. It seemed to be adjusted for someone with a back condition, because it thrust him forward, forcing him to lean on the desk. Murray stood behind him.

"Nicky," he muttered, "you're very appreciative, blah, blah, blah."

Nicholas glanced across the room to the administrator of the hospital. "I appreciate your letting me use your office."

"It's nothing, nothing at all, Mr. Cobleigh."

"It's after nine," Murray said. "We'll be leaving for the night. Naturally, if there's any change in Mrs. Cobleigh's condition—"

"Of *course*," the administrator said. "We'll call immediately."

Nicholas allowed Murray to lead him again, this time through another corridor and out a side entrance, where a taxi waited. Nicholas's limousine, parked in front of the hospital, was being watched by reporters. "You want to go back to the house, Nicky?"

"What?" Nicholas asked. He wasn't absorbing things. Between visits to the intensive care unit, he'd spent the afternoon in the administrator's office, a palace-sized room with dark hunting prints blotching the yellow walls. Horses and hounds leaped over hedges; foxes were blood-red streaks. Despite its high ceiling and the massive desk, the room felt insubstantial, a set for some Grade C film he was doomed to make. He'd sat, numbed, patient, waiting for a director to come along and tell him what to do. He pressed his fingers against his eyes. They felt too big for their sockets, the way they did after too many takes under high-key lighting.

"Do you want to go back to the house, Nicky? You can come back to the hotel with me."

He couldn't think straight. He covered his face with his hands and was taken aback by the mass of hair; he'd forgotten the beard he'd had for three months, that he'd grown for *William*. He put his hands in his lap.

"The house," he said finally. "The girls are going to call when they get to the airport in New York." The taxi crept through the empty streets as if there were a massive traffic jam. "Did you get Rhodes?"

"Finally. First you get the Mykonos operator and explain you want to speak with someone named Rhodes Heissenhuber. That took three quarters of an hour. Then they had to find him. Anyhow, they'll get the first plane off the island to Athens and then come straight to London. Rhodes and his friend—who's married to your cousin."

"Philip Gray."

For several minutes, about an hour after he first saw Jane, a fit of activity had seized Nicholas. He'd issued commands: get one—no, two—of the best American neurosurgeons and fly them over; check on this Sir Anthony Bradley; charter a plane to get the girls from camp in Maine to JFK and book them on the first plane to London; find Rhodes; arrange with Arthur for them to shoot around me. Then, as if he'd run ten miles or played four sets of tennis, he slipped into weak-limbed lethargy. He could barely lift the endless cups of tea people kept placing before him.

472

"Philip Gray," Murray repeated. "You know he's into cable TV, don't you?"

"Yes."

"But they say most of his money's in things like Japanese steel and rare metals." Murray had burst into tears after they'd left the intensive care unit, but once he'd regained his composure, he'd begun talking double-time, as if an assault of ceaseless, easy patter could topple reality and reinstate a life where everything was normal. "Anyway, Rhodes said they'll come right to the hospital. Rhodes'll call from the airport but just in case there's a mix-up, here's the phone number of Gray's apartment. He keeps an apartment here. Pardon me, a flat." He tucked a folded rectangle of paper into Nicholas's hand. "What else?" Murray asked himself. "Oh, the two American neurosurgeons are due to land any minute. They'll go from Heathrow right to the hospital, then call you. I put them up at the Connaught, but if you want, they'll come to the house to report to you."

The taxi stopped at a red light. The driver turned around and gazed directly at Nicholas. The light changed. The driver continued to stare, a bright expression of triumph in his eyes: a trapper who'd set out expecting rabbit and found ermine instead. Nicholas averted his head. Murray's relaxed, conversational pose vanished. Suddenly, he sat upright—a martinet—clenched his fist, and banged on the partition between them and the driver with a fury that startled Nicholas nearly as much as it did the driver. The taxi raced toward Berkeley Square.

When Murray dropped Nicholas at the house, the door opened before he had climbed the first step. He walked into the dim hall, half expecting the butler to take his coat. He sighed. It was summer. He wasn't wearing a coat. He was still in costume—cotton trousers and a tissue-thin leather vest—with the white doctor's smock someone had gotten for him when he started to shiver. He glanced around but did not see the butler.

"Oh, Nicholas!"

He looked down. There, arms wide open, was Pamela.

"Nicholas, I'm so terribly sorry." Her arms went around his waist. "Such an awful, awful shock." Her head leaned against his chest. "Even after all this time. You must still feel so—"

He pulled away from her. It was not easy. Her thin arms were strong. "Nicholas!" She followed as he walked to the library. "Let me get you a drink." She scurried past him and, the moment he sat, pressed a large straight vodka into his hand. "There," she said. "Finish that and I'll pour you another."

She stood before him, waiting for him to drink. He looked straight ahead, so all he could see was the print of her silk pajamas, crescents, silvery slivers

473

of moon on darkness, but with her so close he saw only the space between her narrow hips, and the pattern didn't look celestial at all, but resembled giant fingernail parings. He put the drink down onto the rug.

Pamela knelt and picked it up. "Here. Take it. You're in a state of shock." She held the glass out to him. He did not take it. "Nicholas, please." She put the glass back on the rug and took his hand. "I wish I could wish it away," she said. "So you wouldn't have to go through this pain." He looked at her hands holding his. She wore the emerald he had given her on her left finger, like an engagement ring. It covered the area between her two knuckles. "Oh, Nicholas," she murmured. "It's so awful. Did you call the girls?"

He nodded, now looking at the crescents on her sleeve. She put her hands under his chin, lifted up his face, and gazed into his eyes. She bent down and softly kissed his forehead, then his mouth. Her loose hair fell like blinders on either side of his face.

"Pamela," he said.

"Yes."

"I'm sorry."

"Please. I understand. If you weren't moved, I'd wonder what kind of a person you were. It just shows—"

"I think you'll have to leave."

"Leave?"

"I'm sorry. I don't know how to say this any better, and I'm too shaken up to—"

"The girls will resent my being here. I know you're probably right, and if you want, I'll go to a hotel, but Nicholas, in the long run, I think it's much better for them to deal with the realities of the situation."

"The realities," he said.

"I honestly think so, Nicholas." Again, she lifted the drink. This time he accepted it. "You know I won't be intrusive. But I think I should be a presence. And also, from a purely practical point of view, I can be here to help. You need someone to lean on."

"Pamela, I would like you to leave London."

"No." She knelt and rested her arms on his knees. "Nicholas, no." He eased her arms off, so she looked like a supplicant before him. "Don't give in to appearances, Nicholas. Please. I promise you I won't do anything or say anything—"

"It's not that."

"Then why can't I stay here? I'll go to a hotel, okay? But I have to tell you. I'm completely aware that you're under enormous stress, but I think you're treating me very shabbily."

"I know I am. And I'm sorry about it, but it can't be helped."

"Will you have Murray or your secretary take care of reservations?"

474

"Pamela, listen to me. The reservations will be plane reservations. You'll go back to New York, to NYU, and resume your life. I know how long you've wanted to go back to your doctoral work and—"

"*No.*"

"Please. I know it's awkward and abrupt, but there's no other way I can handle it."

"When can I come back?"

For the first time he looked into her face. "Pamela," Nicholas said. "I'm sorry. I don't want you to come back. It's over. I'll take responsibility for getting you settled in New York and for your tuition and—"

"*No.*"

"Yes. Listen to me. Try to understand. Ever since we've been in London—even before—all I've been thinking about is Jane. She's my wife. I want to be with her. I belong with her."

"It's because she's been hurt. You're in shock. You feel guilty, responsible, but you're not. Nicholas, I'm telling you, the minute she gets better—"

"I belong with her."

Pamela rose. He looked up, and she seemed to have swollen to normal adult size. "You belong with her? She doesn't even know you're there. I heard the radio. Her condition is grave. She's unconscious. There's possible brain damage. Didn't they tell you that?"

"Yes."

"And?"

"It doesn't matter."

"It *does*. You're sending me away. I know this sounds brutal, but what if she dies or becomes a vegetable? Did you ever think of that? Did you, Nicholas? You're very emotional now, but try to project into the future. Don't let some medieval notion of gallantry cloud your thinking. Be at her sickbed. Fine. Good. I admire you for it. Everyone will. I understand completely that there's a certain public stance you have to maintain for the time being."

"Pamela, I'm sorry. I really am."

"Nicholas, *think* before you talk. *Please*. Who would you have if something happens to her?" Pamela's hair looked dry and stood out from her head, like a child's drawing of hair made with a red crayon. "Think. You know you need me."

"I'm sorry. I need Jane."

"All right, then. All right. I'll go. I'm hurt, deeply hurt, but I understand. And when you want me— Nicholas, listen to me. If something happens to her—"

"No, Pamela."

"Listen, *please*. I'll come back."

"No!"

She clutched her left hand to her chest. "Do you want the ring back?"

"No. It's yours."

Once more she knelt before him. "Nicholas, try to understand. You think I'm being selfish, not wanting to leave. But I'm thinking of you. In all seriousness, if she—if something happens, who would you have?"

"I'd have no one," he said.

"Daddy."

"Dad."

Nicholas could not get enough of his daughters. He had not held them for two years. He stood outside the door of Jane's tiny room in the intensive care unit and held them against him. Through their light summer dresses, he felt their warmth, just as he had when they were infants, holding them in diapers and their undershirts with the tiny snaps. Elizabeth's bare arm was the same texture as Jane's, as soft as anything could be: velvet, talc, new moss, baby skin.

"Can we go in?" Victoria asked.

"Yes. But remember what I told you about the way she looks. And she's still unconscious." Victoria stepped away from him. Her glance was of surprise and anger, as though he'd failed her by not planning anything better.

"You've seen her this morning?"

"No. I spoke with the English neurosurgeon and the Americans I told you about. They're doing everything that can be done."

Elizabeth stayed with him, and he put his empty arm around her and stroked her brown, fuzzy hair. She was the affectionate child, still cuddling with Jane at an age when most teenage girls could only bare their teeth at their mothers. "I'm scared," she whispered.

"I know. Come on." He reached out and brought Victoria back to him. "We'll all go in together."

When Victoria saw her mother, she gasped and went rigid. Elizabeth began to sob, "Mommy, Mommy."

Jane remained absolutely still, wires and tubes reaching out of her, searching tentacles. Nicholas stood holding his daughters for several minutes. After two years he should be saying something properly paternal to them, but he couldn't think of a single thing. He felt almost as young as they, surely as frightened. He thought, I am forty years old, but that neither consoled nor energized him. The best he could do was act.

He inched away from the girls, closer to Jane. She looked old enough to take charge. Strong enough too. Her nose and jaw asserted themselves even in repose. If she would just open her eyes, the family could fall into place again. He would revive, feel like the man he was supposed to be. He lifted her hand and kissed it, but it was a completely unself-conscious hand, unaware it

476

was being kissed, heavy to lift. Her skin had taken on a medicinal smell, as if someone had sterilized her during the night. He laid her hand back on the bed. He remembered the French soap she loved, a shelf full of it in the linen closet in Connecticut, all wrapped in crinkly paper and sealed with red wax. My not-Cincinnati soap, she'd called it. He'd love to wash her hand with that creamy pink soap and warm water.

"Dad," Victoria asked, "is it very bad?"

"Yes. That's why I had you come."

He reached out to his daughters, a correct, fatherly gesture. Victoria stayed back. Elizabeth came to him. Her shoulders shook with the heaves of her silent sobbing. "My baby," he whispered. He almost said, It's going to be all right.

Then he glanced around at Victoria. She turned her head away from him, staring at an intravenous bottle that dripped into the tube in Jane's arm. Victoria's cheeks were burned and slightly puffy from her first week as a tennis counselor in the girls' camp she'd attended since she was seven. Her arms, with the athlete's bulge of bi- and triceps, seemed too competent for her pale blue dress with its scalloped cap sleeves.

"Come back here, Vicky." He put his arm out.

"What about *her?*" Victoria asked. Her eyes, blue-green like his, looked from under their heavy, hooded lids into his eyes and held them.

"She can't hear us," he said.

"Not Mom. *Her.* Your little friend."

"Don't use that tone with me." His voice was thin. His words sounded more like a plea than a command. He hadn't acted like a father for two years. Now he didn't sound like one.

But Victoria's voice softened slightly. "What about her? I mean, she wasn't at the house and—"

"She's gone."

"For good?"

"Yes."

Grudgingly, Victoria took a step back into his arm's reach and allowed him to envelop her too. "You're positive?"

"Yes, Vicky. No more questions."

"Does Mom know?"

"I said—no. Not yet."

Elizabeth leaned forward and looked at them both. "Daddy, maybe if you tell her . . ."

"Liz, honey, she's unconscious. She can't hear us."

"Christ, Liz. Look at her! What do you want him to do, tap her on the shoulder and—"

"Enough, Vicky!" he snapped.

477

Elizabeth broke from his arm. She ran to the edge of Jane's bed and grabbed the low iron railing, crib bars for adults. "Mommy!" she cried.

Jane's eyes should blink open. But there was no change, not a flutter of movement.

"Mommy! Mommy!" Her words, chopped by sobs, rang through the tiny room.

"Liz." Nicholas tried to pull her back. "Please, baby, she—"

"*Mommy!*"

Her shriek ripped through him, from his throat to his gut.

"Make her stop!" Victoria began to cry. "Oh, Daddy, make her—"

"*Mommy!*"

The door crashed open. The three neurosurgeons stood before them. "If you don't mind—" Sir Anthony began. The girls folded against Nicholas, forming a tight triangle. "If you don't mind, please wait outside. We'd like to get on with it."

Nicholas stood. The neurosurgeons entered the administrator's office in a tight pack, but then the two Americans stayed back. Sir Anthony had been elected. He offered no reassuring smile. Not even a nod. He did not say, Shall we sit? He said, "Mr. Cobleigh."

"Yes," Nicholas said. Victoria and Elizabeth edged away, willing to wait and hear a softer version of the news filtered through their father. He stood alone.

"There is cause for concern."

"Yes."

"We've repeated the CAT scan."

"I see." He wanted to say, Why couldn't you have told me? Why did you let us sit here the whole damn morning? Do you have any idea what we were imagining? "What did it show?" he asked instead.

"There is a clot in the left temporal lobe. We'd had indications. Mrs. Cobleigh was rapidly developing a weakness in her right side. Her blood pressure was rising, her heart rate slowing. Her left pupil was beginning to dilate."

He should ask an intelligent question. He'd thought of many all morning in that awful yellow office, making meaningless conversation with the girls, taking calls from his parents, brothers, and sisters, rubbing his sweating palms together, waiting for the surgeons to get back to him. He'd tried to hide his rising panic at the doctors' absence. But Nicholas couldn't ask even an unintelligent question. He was overcome by the overwhelming nausea of terror.

"The dilation is a sign of increasing intercranial pressure," Sir Anthony went on. "And indeed, the monitor did register an acute increase."

"I see." He just wanted to sit down.

478

"Do you have any questions, Mr. Cobleigh?"

"What can you do?"

"Ah. I would like to perform a craniotomy. That is a procedure for the evacuation of a large blood clot."

"An operation?"

"Yes. An operation."

Nicholas looked to the two Americans. They'd been staring at him the whole time. They nodded their concurrence. He felt even sicker. "What are her chances?" he managed to say.

"Fair, Mr. Cobleigh. Only fair."

Nicholas had expected Rhodes to burst into the administrator's office like a matinee idol making his first entrance: all dash and drama. So he jumped when Rhodes sat beside him on the small couch and murmured, "Nick."

"Oh, Rhodes. Good to—glad to see you."

Nicholas reached out to shake his hand, but Rhodes put his arm around Nicholas and drew him into an embrace. They held each other for so long that at any other time Nicholas would have drawn back, queasy, but now he held onto his brother-in-law's strong comfort for as long as Rhodes would allow it.

"How is she?" Rhodes asked finally, letting go of Nicholas.

"They took her to surgery about a half hour ago. He said the chances were fair."

"Oh, shit."

"Uncle Rhodes."

Victoria and Elizabeth stood before Rhodes. He got up and hugged them, separately and then together. Nicholas wished he could stand and join them. He hadn't realized how much he'd missed his brother-in-law in the last two years. He looked up at him, recalling the pleasure he used to get watching Rhodes and Jane. They'd called their sparring The Heissenhuber Hour, pronouncing the H in hour with immature, dopey glee. They had so much fun.

That's what he was aching for. In two years with Pamela he had not had any real fun.

Rhodes gave the girls a final squeeze, then let them go. He sat down again beside Nicholas. "I'm sorry," he said softly, as they crossed the large room back to their chairs.

Nicholas glanced at him. The whites of Rhodes's eyes were spidered with red, and under his tan his cheeks were flushed. Nicholas suspected he had been drinking ever since he'd gotten Murray's telephone call, eighteen hours earlier. He certainly hadn't looked in a mirror. Rhodes's long hair flopped over his ears and down, into his eyes, and it was dotted with grains of sand. Unshaven, he did not look rakish, merely messy. "How long do they think the operation will take?" he asked.

479

"Three, three and a half hours," Nicholas answered. "Do you want anything? A drink?"

"No. I've had enough. It doesn't do anything anyway."

They sat in silence. Rhodes's shirt sleeves were rolled up, and there was sand on the thin gold chain he wore on his wrist, and on the hair on his arm.

"Where is Philip?"

"At the flat. He'll come later. He thought it would be better for us to be alone for a while. Nick . . ."

"What is it?"

"I made her come here. I really pressured her into it. She wanted to talk to you, to try and—you know—try again, and she was going to call you and I talked her out of it. I gave her a lot of shit, told her this was something that had to be done face to face. She was so afraid of getting on a plane, but she did it because I made her feel that if she didn't, she'd never get you back." Rhodes rubbed his fingers back and forth across his mouth so hard Nicholas could hear the abrasive hiss.

"Easy," Nicholas said. He put his hand on Rhodes's arm. "What did she say? Please tell me."

"She still loved you. She wanted to try and get you back from the wimp." Rhodes's head jerked up. "Sorry. I suppose I'm sorry. I don't know."

"It's all right. She's gone back to New York."

"Is she history?"

"What? Oh, yes. She's history. Not my most shining hour."

"Nick, it wasn't Jane's shining hour either. She knew it."

"Did she say anything to you about him?" Nicholas asked.

"The Great Healer? Sure. She told him to take a walk about a month ago, but it was basically over before that. It's just that she was alone and at least he provided some friction. She said she'd met more amusing turds."

Nicholas smiled. "She didn't say that. You did."

"She said he was boring. Same thing."

Nicholas glanced across the room. The girls had moved from their chairs to the floor. Victoria was leaning against a wall, her long legs stretched out straight in front of her. Elizabeth lay perpendicular, her head on her sister's lap. Victoria, usually the least affectionate of creatures, who'd fondle the handle of her tennis racket before she'd stroke a horse or a dog, who found books far more intriguing than people, sat with her hand on her sister's cheek, patting it gently as the younger girl's eyes closed.

Nicholas turned to his brother-in-law. "I can't believe I pissed away two years of my life," he said quietly.

"You both did," Rhodes said.

"I only hope . . ."

"I know."

480

"A stupid waste. We were supposed to be so damn smart, and look what we did to ourselves."

"You know," Rhodes said, "I was up in Connecticut one time. You were off on location somewhere and we sat around, Jane, me, and Cecily Van Doorn. Jane was in her worst sicko stage, and I was trying to get her to get some more help and she wasn't having any part of it. And then, all of a sudden Cecily looked up and you know what she said? 'Life is too short.' I remember, I looked at her and thought, Well, she should know. She's had two husbands crap out on her. But I didn't get her point then. I mean, yes, she was telling Jane how pathetic it was to be wasting all those good years locked in her own jail. But she was talking about vulnerability too. We're all so goddamned fragile."

"Last night," Nicholas said, "I stayed up with the girls until about two. I finally got them to sleep and I was so wiped out I could hardly make it back to my room. But then all of a sudden I was wide awake. I had this shock of realization—a real shock, an electric shock. I realized that some part of me always believed Jane and I would get back together. We had to. We're made for each other. You can laugh, but I truly believe that."

"I'm not going to laugh," Rhodes said. "Look, Nick, if the two of you weren't made for each other, you would have married Miss Perfect Person, the one you were going with first. The only way someone like you and some-one like my sister could have gotten together is if it were meant to be. The old match-made-in-heaven number. A gift from the gods. It happens. I know."

"I know you know," Nicholas said. "But I threw the gift away."

"You put it aside for a little while. So did she. And look what both of you got: Dr. Dirty and the wimp. The gods' way of saying 'You stupid fuck-ups.'"

"Pamela was—I don't know—a diversion. She was never real to me. Remember what I was telling you about, that I always knew I'd go back to Jane? I guess I thought, What the hell, at our fiftieth anniversary party who's going to remember a few years when it wasn't so great? What are two or three lousy years in a whole lifetime? How can they matter?"

"Just for a moment," the neurosurgeon said.

Her head swathed in bandages. Her silky dark hair gone, recollected only by her brows, two black accent marks.

He'd once taken her braid, put it across his upper lip, and demanded, Well, do I look like Clark Gable?

Her skin was still so wrongfully white.

"Jane. Jane!"

He expected nothing, but her eyes opened. His filled with tears. She saw him. She knew him.

"I love you," he said. "Jane, I love you more than anything."

481

"Nick." He could hardly hear her. "Love you."

"I know," he said. "I know."

She closed her eyes.

The neurosurgeon called him at home at midnight. "There's been an obliteration of consciousness."

"What?"

"I'm afraid Mrs. Cobleigh is comatose. We did another CAT scan. There is no clot, but the intercranial pressure is increasing again. The contusions are quite severe. There is a great deal of swelling."

He made himself ask, "Will she live?"

"It looks grim. Of course, we are doing everything possible and there is a chance that we can turn things about."

"How big a chance?" Nicholas whispered.

"Not very, I'm afraid."

Dear God, please. Don't take her.

They return to the yellow office that night and do not leave. On the second day after surgery, in the late afternoon, Sir Anthony Bradley comes and stands in the threshold. "Mr. Cobleigh."

They all rise.

"Both pupils have dilated. She is no longer triggering respiration on her own."

"What does that mean?" Nicholas asks.

But he knows. He does not have to hear Sir Anthony's answer. He stands alone with his children and his brother-in-law and knows in his heart that what Cecily said was true.

Life is too short.

AUTHOR'S NOTE

I sought advice and information from the people listed below. All of them gave it freely and cheerfully. I want to thank them—and to apologize if I twisted the facts to fit my fiction.

Arnold C. Abramowitz, Eric Bregman, Robert Carras, Teresa Cavanaugh, John B. Comerford, Jr., Frederick T. Davis, Mary M. Davis, Jonathan Dolger, David Dukes, Robert F. Ebin, Janet Fiske, Robert B. Fiske, Jr., Mary FitzPatrick, Michael J. Frank, Phyllis Freeman, Lawrence Iason, Helen Isaacs, Morton Isaacs, Leonard S. Klein, Edward M. Lane, Susan Lawton, Josephine McGowan, Bonnie Mitchell, Catherine Morvillo, Otto G. Obermaier, Estelle Parsons, Frank Perry, Paul K. Rooney, James Rubin, Jeffrey M. Siger, Paul Tolins, Alfred F. Uhry, Herbert Weber, Stephen Wilson, Brian Winston, Jay Zises.

Members of the staffs of the following institutions were very helpful: The Cincinnati Historical Society, the Cincinnati Public Library, the New York Public Library, and, especially, the Port Washington (New York) Public Library.

My friends Consuelo Baehr, Mary Rooney, Hilma Wolitzer, and Susan Zises encouraged me and gave me valuable criticism and lots of attention.

Gloria Safier, my agent, and Larry Ashmead, my editor, were—as usual—wise, patient, and completely wonderful.

And Elkan Abramowitz is still the best person in the world.